LOS NEFILIM

Also by T. Frohock

LOS NEFILIM

T. FROHOCK

HARPER
VOYAGER
IMPULSE

An Imprint of HarperCollinsPublishers

EPub Edition APRIL 2016 ISBN: 9780062428967

Print Edition ISBN: 9780062429001

10 9 8 7 6 5 4 3

For my daughter, Rhiannon Hopkins.
I will always fight for you.

CONTENTS

Part One: In Midnight's Silence
1

Part Two: Without Light or Guide
139

Part Three: The Second Death
295

Acknowledgments
453

PART ONE:
IN MIDNIGHT'S SILENCE

you show me again?" He smiled, but the child was too immature to camouflage the spite in his eyes. He'd already tried to slam the fallboard on Diago's fingers at the start of their session. This was almost certainly another ill-disguised attempt at a maiming.

Not that Diago hadn't experienced his share of hostilities through the centuries. He had survived Torquemada, an encounter with a Borgia, and numerous altercations against both daimons and angels. *At least I had a fighting chance against them.* He considered Enrique's wicked grin, and decided he would gladly revisit them all to avoid sitting beside this child again.

Unfortunately, he had little choice. The bourgeoisie had tightened their purse strings of late. Jobs of any kind were hard to find, harder to hold, and he needed the work. Miquel already bore the brunt of their expenses as Diago tried to establish himself in Barcelona, and while Miquel never begrudged Diago a *peseta,* Diago was determined to generate his own income. His pride demanded it. The Ferrer family was his key into the Casa Milà's residents and their deep pockets. And so, ironically, he swallowed his pride and found himself Enrique's teacher for the next six weeks.

Diago took a deep breath and steeled himself to sit beside the boy. He glanced at the clock just as the second hand swept over the number twelve. "Six o'clock, Enrique. We are done for today." He wasted no time in rescuing his sheet music from the stand.

"But I'm not finished." The boy's cheeks turned blotchy with rage.

Diago foresaw a hellish tantrum rising. He hoped to make it out of the apartment before the squall arrived.

"Enrique!" Señora Ferrer stood between the living room and the foyer with a glass of sherry in her hand. A beautiful woman with dark eyes and high cheekbones, she was given to dressing with all the flair of the Casa Milà's *nouveau riche*. Today's ensemble included a narrow skirt and silk blouse, both of which were just tight enough to leave nothing to a man's imagination. "We are paying Maestro Alvarez for his time. Your lesson is over for today. Go with Elena."

Enrique slammed the fallboard hard enough to vibrate the piano's strings before he stomped out of the room. Another premonition told Diago the instrument would have to be tuned if the child continued to abuse it; although he had to admit, having Enrique vent his rage on the piano was preferable to another of the boy's vicious kicks. Diago exhaled slowly as Enrique's malice followed him out of the room like a dark cloud.

Episodes like this always made him grateful he was childless. Neither he, nor Miquel, had the necessary patience to deal with ill-tempered children. Whenever it came to a battle of wills with a youngster, Diago resorted to negotiations and Miquel bribed them with sweets or toys. Miquel had observed on more than one occasion that while they made wonderful uncles, they would be terrible parents. Diago had to agree.

Señora Ferrer turned and spoke to her maid. "See to Enrique, Elena. I will escort Maestro Alvarez out."

Oh, God, no, not again. Diago's heart pounded

harder as he picked up his metronome and stored it in this briefcase. The last thing he needed was a moment alone with Señora Ferrer. In the few seconds it took him to arrange the sheet music beside the metronome and latch his briefcase, he felt as if she'd stripped him naked with her eyes. As he walked toward her, his face warmed with blush.

She mistook his embarrassment for pleasure and smiled. For such a petite woman, she possessed a remarkable ability to block a doorway with her presence. "Has anyone ever told you what beautiful eyes you have, Señor Alvarez? They are a most lovely shade of green and seem to change color depending on the light. I think it is because your lashes are so black."

Odd that she spoke of his eyes when her gaze remained fixated on his crotch. Diago moved his briefcase in front of his hips like a shield as he halted in front of her. "So I have been told, Señora."

She raised her glass. "Do you have time for a glass of sherry?"

Navigating a daimon's lair was less treacherous than this apartment. Diago knew that Enrique's violent temper had descended directly from his father. He could just imagine Ferrer's displeasure should he return home to find his young wife entertaining his son's music teacher over sherry. Christ. Was the woman trying to get him killed?

"I'm afraid not, Señora." Diago moved to step around her, and she slithered to block his path again.

"I've been trying to convince my husband to trim his beard as neatly as yours, but he insists on keeping those outdated muttonchops. Of course, his hair isn't fine and black like yours." She lifted the glass to her mouth and tongued a drop of sherry from the lip. "He's more wooly. Like a sheep."

"Perhaps if you spoke to his barber." He took a step closer and when she didn't move, he said, "I hope you will forgive me, Señora, but I would like to catch my roommate before he leaves for the evening."

Señora Ferrer pursed her lips, disappointed that he wasn't rising to her seductions. "I see." She turned sideways but made sure to press her breasts against his arm as he passed. "This roommate of yours must be someone very special, since you're always hurrying off to catch him."

More than you know. Diago grabbed his coat and hat. He offered her a genuine smile at the thought of spending some time with Miquel. "Good evening, Señora." Without waiting for her reply, he slipped out the door and closed it behind him with a relieved sigh.

No sooner had the latch clicked into place than Diago fled down the stairs. He didn't slow his pace until he reached the lobby, and paused there only long enough to put on his hat and coat.

Outside, an October fog, heavy with the smell of the sea, inched through the streets. Diago turned up his collar against the northern chill. He missed Sevilla's warmth more with every passing day, but Miquel had needed to come to Barcelona—Guillermo had ordered it.

As a member of Los Nefilim, the group that monitored daimonic activity for the angels, Miquel was bound by his oath to go wherever he was assigned. So when Guillermo had called him north in August, Miquel insisted that Diago come, too. Alone, Miquel noted, he was easy prey for either angel or daimon, both groups that were seeking to press Diago into their ser-vice.

And it was that point, which Miquel had hammered into Diago over and over, that had led him to endure the three most miserable weeks of his life. Unlike Miquel, Diago had made no oath to either side and could live wherever he chose.

Unless your lover is an officer of Los Nefilim, Diago mused as he maneuvered through the crowd of pedestrians. In that case, his choices narrowed to following Miquel, or living alone. Although he had initially resisted the move, in the end he knew he'd made the right choice. Being without Miquel was akin to living without love, and that was an existence he never wanted to endure again.

Picking up his pace, he left the main avenue and took a shortcut. He crossed a narrow street, barely avoiding a truck carrying several men and women in the bed. As they passed, he paused to watch them. They shouted slogans and waved signs advocating membership in CNT, the workers' union responsible for violent strikes throughout Spain. Cans of petrol rocked heavily between the legs of the riders.

With vivid clarity, Diago recalled the smell of churches burning in the south. The summer had been a vicious one for Spain. Now it appeared the flames would reach Barcelona once more. Like the angels and the daimons, the mortals never seemed to tire of war.

Well, I'm tired, he thought as the truck and its dangerous cargo disappeared around the next corner.

"Anarchists." A man halted beside Diago and spat in the gutter. "They should be shot." Then, without further ado, he launched into a fierce tirade about the Bolsheviks, Masons, and Jews being the architects of Spain's ruin.

As the man's words washed over Diago, the weight of the centuries bowed his shoulders. Exhausted by mortals and their perpetual hatred for one another, he turned his back on the man and resumed his journey. More than ever, he needed some time with Miquel. Just a word or a touch from his lover always lifted Diago from these black moods.

The afternoon's tension rode the cords in his neck all the way to the Carrer de Montsio in the Gothic Quarter. There, he and Miquel rented a room from Doña Rosa Iniguez in her once grand home. The noblewoman had fallen on hard times—primarily due to her son's gambling—so she rented rooms in order to make ends meet. Diago and Miquel had been fortunate enough to secure the attic's loft.

Diago glanced upward out of habit. The loft's window was dark. Had he missed Miquel? Disappointment slowed his steps.

He debated dropping off his briefcase and going downtown to the Villa Rosa where Miquel played guitar, but after today he wasn't sure if he was up to fighting his way through the noise and press of mortal bodies on the Paralelo. No. If Miquel had already left, Diago would simply wait up for him. Right now, he wanted nothing more than silence and a glass of wine.

He let himself inside the house and closed the door as quietly as possible . . . but any hopes he'd entertained of simply heading straight to the loft were immediately thwarted by his landlady. No matter how he tried, Diago found he could never avoid her, and there were times Miquel joked that she had a bit of daimon blood in her. But Diago knew better. She was just a lonely nosy woman. And tonight was no exception. He stepped through the door to be immediately accosted by the scent of Doña Rosa's talcum, which she used to cover the odor of urine that followed her like a stray dog. Dressed from head to foot in black, her pale doughy face floated out of the hall's dimness like a benevolent ghost.

She stood in her doorway and offered him a coquettish smile. "Good evening, Señor Alvarez."

Diago tried not to flinch. He dreaded these tête-à-têtes almost as much as Enrique's playing. However, Miquel emphasized it was best to remain in the doña's good graces. The rent was relatively cheap, and the room relatively spacious. Perhaps more important, her home had one of the few telephones on the street, and the doña was generous enough to place it in the hall so that her tenants could make use of it as well. Diago couldn't help but agree that they would be hard put finding another house with so gracious a proprietor.

Besides, the words cost him nothing. A few minutes of his time in the morning and evening were a small price to pay to maintain the peace with Miquel. Still, he hoped to keep tonight's chitchat to a minimum. He removed his fedora. "Good evening, Doña Rosa."

"I'm glad I caught you."

Caught him, indeed. She had been lying in wait with her ear pressed to the door. He forced a smile and feigned what he hoped was a look of polite inquiry. "Oh?"

"You had visitors today. They left something for you." She turned to the occasional table by her door, where she retrieved a small rectangular package wrapped in plain brown paper. She presented it to him as if it was a personal gift.

Diago took the box, surprised by its weight. No address or name. "Are you sure it's for me? I am expecting nothing."

"The gentleman who left it said that it was a belated birthday gift." She brightened. "I didn't know you had a birthday recently."

Neither did Diago. He'd never considered birthdays until Guillermo had insisted they all acquire passports. When pressed for a date, Diago had chosen April

eighth, simply because it happened to be the first date
he noticed on the calendar in Guillermo's kitchen.

Doña Rosa leaned forward expectedly.

"I, um, haven't," Diago said. He cleared his throat.
"My birthday is in the spring. That is what makes this
so odd." He seized the excuse. "And disconcerting. Did
the gentleman say who was?"

"He said he was your father."

Diago's fingers tightened around the box. As far as
he was concerned, his father was a nonentity, a figure as
ephemeral as God, and with a presence just as opaque.

A thin line of anger wormed its way beneath his uneasiness. If this was a joke, he wasn't amused. Someone
played a very dangerous game tonight. "My father?"

"Yes. Your father." Doña Rosa tilted her head and
scrutinized Diago's features. "You look very much like
him."

Diago felt his cheeks warm beneath her gaze.

"And he had a young man with him."

"I see," Diago said, not that he did.

A shadow moved behind Doña Rosa, and Diago
made out the hulking shape of her twenty-eight-year-
old son, José. He and Diago had developed a visceral
dislike of one another within minutes of being introduced. Even Miquel had not managed to warm José
with his charm.

Now José paused and narrowed his eyes at Diago.
He rubbed the knuckles over the large signet ring he
wore on his right hand and regarded Diago warily.

Doña Rosa continued. "The younger man claimed to be your brother."

Diago chose his words carefully. "I had many *brothers*. I was raised in an orphanage." It was a convenient lie, one he had used often enough. In truth, the woman who had called herself his aunt had sold him to slavers sometime early in the twelfth century, because she hadn't wanted another mouth to feed. He'd been five years old when she abandoned him. She had promised that if he did what he was told, he would be fed. In his ignorance, he thought she planned to come back for him at the end of the day. He never saw her again, and his hard-won meals soured in his stomach. Sometimes it was better to starve.

José smirked. "I hope it's a nice gift to make up for leaving you there."

Doña Rosa tossed José a nasty glare before she turned back to Diago. The pity in her eyes was not insincere, and Diago felt somewhat chastised for his earlier thoughts about her. She was not a bad woman.

"I am so sorry," she said. "I had no idea."

No, not a bad woman. And yet he found her compassion harder to bear than José's insults. More than ever, he wanted to be with Miquel. "If you will excuse me, Doña Rosa."

"Of course. If you need anything—"

"I'm fine. Thank you."

She hesitated, and for one frightening moment, Diago was certain that she intended to hug him.

"I'm fine," he insisted, hoping to neutralize any maternal urges she might act upon.

"Very well then, Señor," she murmured, and bowed her head to him. "Good night." She stepped back into her apartment and shut the door.

The low staccato of her rebuke burst like machine-gun fire and reached through the walls into the hallway. José's protests were barely audible. He wouldn't raise his voice to his mother, but later in the evening, he would drink himself into enough courage to beat a prostitute.

It disgusted Diago, knowing that José would somehow blame him even as he abused a young woman. Yet there was nothing he could do about it. He had more pressing concerns. Someone had found him, knew his name, and the apartment he called home. The fact that the individual came in the guise of a father Diago had never known did nothing to ease his nerves—if anything, it only increased them. As much as they distrusted him, none of Guillermo's Nefilim dared ridicule him with such a charade.

Diago hurried up the stairs and forced his key into the lock with a shaking hand. Inside, he shut the door and bolted it. The heavy shadows of the furniture loomed in the pale gray light leaking through the windows.

The easy chair Diago had claimed as his own sat in the corner that faced the door. A low table squatted before the chair and was strewn with musical scores. Diago's guitar leaned against the wall, stored neatly in its case. Miquel's guitar rested on the short sofa beside the chair.

"Miquel?" Diago called softly, not really expecting an answer. When Miquel was home, the rooms overflowed with his presence. This silence was heavy enough to be felt.

A low hum of panic seeded itself in Diago's heart. He closed the curtains in each of the windows, his movements slow and deliberate. He paused before the glass and looked down into the fog. Nothing moved, and even if it did, he would be hard put to see it. As he walked through the rooms, he noted the wrongness of the scene.

Miquel's empty guitar case was still on the bed beside the clothes he had selected for the evening. His hat and coat hung by the door. Wherever he'd gone, he had not intended to be gone long.

Had he seen the visitors? Diago castigated himself for not asking Doña Rosa when the alleged father and brother had arrived. It was possible they'd left minutes ago and that Miquel had gone out to follow them. Yes, that was plausible. In the fog, Diago might not have seen them. Miquel could be back any moment.

Diago clutched the package against his stomach and told himself these comfortable lies, hoping they were true. A half-empty cup of coffee sat on the dining table next to the day's newspaper. Diago touched the cup. It was cold. His hope tumbled into a pit of black thoughts he didn't want to indulge.

Of course, maybe the cold cup meant nothing.

Miquel was often distracted and sometimes left his plates behind for Diago to wash and put away. It was one of his more irritating habits: a forgotten sandwich left to draw flies, coffee grounds littered around the pot, a half-empty mug turned cold by neglect, because he had left in a hurry, had not even taken the time to write a note, because he had not intended to be gone long . . .

Keep telling yourself that, Diago.

"Where are you, Miquel?"

In answer, the package grew heavy in Diago's hand. He carefully placed the box on the scarred tabletop beside Miquel's mug and sat. His mouth was dry as he peeled away the paper to reveal a mirrored box.

A richly engraved calling card had been carefully placed on the lid. The raised script said "Beltran Prieto." The name meant nothing to Diago. He turned the card over and examined every ridge. The paper carried the faintest odor of rosewater, but there was nothing distinctive about the scent. It could have just as easily come from Doña Rosa. Diago set the card aside and turned his attention to the box.

The casket was made of mirrored panels, and on the lid, a triptych had been etched in the glass. Diago went to the table in front of his easy chair and rummaged through the sheet music until he found a brass medallion that fit comfortably in the palm of his hand. It had been a gift from Miquel sometime in the late seventeenth century. He'd thought the magnifying glass concealed within the brass case to be most cunning.

Diago returned to the table. He pivoted the glass free of the cover in order to enlarge the tiny scenes. The detail of the relief was amazing, and executed with the skill that only a supernatural creature could possess.

The first panel showed the silhouette of a woman poised to dance, her arms raised over her head, her face turned upward as if looking at the sky. She was dressed in rags that rose behind her, which gave her the illusion of having wings. The ethereal figure seemed to twist and turn in the light. Around her throat was a small serpent with golden scales.

Chills rippled down Diago's back. He had known only one Nefil who could evoke such a pose while dancing, a Gitana named Candela.

She had owned a little yellow snake with eyes the color of blood.

Diago had blocked the memory of her from his mind, partly from shame and partly from guilt. They had met in the slums of Triana where the music was deep and wild, like a cry in the night, and had known one another as Nefilim the moment their eyes met.

Beneath the open stars, she had whispered to him that she alone possessed the secret to a song that would end the conflict between the daimons and angels. She promised to teach him, and he, in his lust for peace, had believed her.

He had gone there to search for a song, and instead he found her.

Acutely aware of the sound of his breathing, Diago steadied the magnifying glass and moved to the next panel. The second scene showed two figures dancing together. The couple's features were indistinct. They were shadow-people who embraced one another beneath a frosted moon. The golden snake encircled their throats like a lemniscate, the symbol for eternity, and bound them together face-to-face. Diago recalled the supple scales against his skin. Once more, he tasted Candela's mouth on his and thought of anisette and honey and almonds.

She had wanted to take him to her bed. She needed his dreams, she said, the whisper of his darkness. His father had been a Nefil, the son of a daimon, and his mother had been an angel, who had taken her mortal form to give birth to him. He was the only Nefil who carried the power of both angel and daimon in his magic. Candela insisted that his unique heritage gave him the ability to understand the song, and no other Nefil would do.

He had objected that he belonged to another, yet his protests had sounded feeble even to his own ears. The lure of the song proved too hard to resist. If peace came to the angels and the daimons, then Los Nefilim would be free like the mortals, who lived their lives as they chose. No longer would they be forced to exist in shadow-armies, always looking over their shoulders, distrusting all whom they met. Infidelity to Miquel seemed a small price to pay for such a song.

Throughout their lovemaking, the little yellow snake had wound itself into her hair, then curled around her throat and mesmerized Diago with its ruby eyes. Candela's assurances had been low and gentle, like the sweep of the desert wind, or perhaps a snake, burnished by the sun. She had seduced Diago into her bed with a tongue filled with lies.

Humiliation flushed his cheeks. He clenched the brass case in a white-knuckled grip. For days he had submitted to her attentions, and done all that she asked without question. He recalled the smell of the carnations she kept by her bed, the odor of rotten wood, and the sharp hard scent of tin.

And then, one morning, she was gone. The little yellow snake lay dead on the windowsill, and Candela had disappeared as if she had never lived. Too late, Diago realized the serpent had been an enchantment. When Candela had achieved all that she desired, the spell broke, and the snake had died.

She had made a fool of him. Ashamed of his culpability, he had never spoken of the tryst, not with Guillermo, and especially not to Miquel. Such a betrayal would have broken his heart. How did one explain an allure such as Candela's, one that made Diago go against his very nature? The truth was complicated, and he had no faith in his ability to convey the misery he'd felt when he realized what he'd done. So he had hidden his sin behind lies of omission, because lies were easier.

Unless the truth drove them into the light.

Diago wiped his sweaty palm across his thigh before he continued. The third panel showed a child around the age of five. A heavy mane of hair framed a face just beginning to lose its baby fat, to take the angular form of a youth. He stood with his arms raised over his head in the male form of Candela's pose—a boy pretending to be a man. Like Candela, his clothes weren't much more than rags, and around his throat was a little yellow snake with eyes the color of carmine.

Diago frowned. He didn't remember a child.

I will give you a song, Candela had said. She'd held Diago's face between her palms and pressed her mouth against his. *With your dreams and the whisper of your darkness.* She had kissed him again and took him down beneath a velvet moon.

Diago put his hand over his mouth and stared at the boy etched in glass. The child's features were as indistinct as the other figures on the triptych. Yet no lack of detail could hide the bold thrust of his chin, the tilt of his hips. He exhibited an unconscious grace of form . . . which Diago recognized as his own.

"A son?" He dropped the magnifying glass. It clattered to the tabletop, the glass pivoting halfway back into the case like an eye that wanted to close against the truth. Diago's heart rapped staccato beats as his gaze wandered again to the snake around the boy's neck.

"This can't be." Maybe he was mistaken. It was possible that he read far more into this triptych than was true. Surely if he had fathered a child, Candela would have found him before now.

He picked up the magnifying glass again. In the first panel, etched within a miniature scroll beneath Candela's feet were the years 1895-1929.

"Jesus Christ." If the dates meant anything at all, Candela was dead. "And if Candela is dead, where is my son?"

Diago glared at the calling card that bore Beltran Prieto's name. The ink bled into the fibers of the paper, and the lines eddied like ripples across a pond. Prieto's name disappeared as the ink took the shape of an hourglass, the sand rapidly running out. In a series of seemingly random swirls, the lines formed new words: *He needs you. Come alone or not at all.*

Diago reached for the card, but before he touched it, the words dissolved and spelled out the name Beltran Prieto. He withdrew his hand.

What did that mean? An hourglass? And who needed him? His son, or Miquel? Or both?

The answer lay within the box. He knew that now like he knew with a terrible certainty that Miquel had not left to follow the two strangers who had brought this tainted gift. Miquel was not coming back.

The room felt cold in spite of the radiator ticking against the wall. Diago's gaze fell to the casket's latch. He hummed a low and deadly note, and parted the air with waves of sound. The timbre of his voice took the form of silver light and hung suspended over the box. Diago used his finger to manipulate the waves into a sigil of protection. Moving with confidence, he quickly traced four vertical and horizontal stripes in the air. He surrounded the lines with a circle that ended in an elaborate tail.

The glyph spun lazily and covered his hands as he lifted the lid. Inside, settled atop a bed of white silk, was a ring that Diago had given Miquel. The wedding band was an exact match to the one that Diago wore on a chain next to his heart.

A cold wash of fear flooded his stomach and spread down into his thighs. Did Miquel know about Candela? Had Beltran Prieto told him? Suddenly, Diago saw nothing but the hurt on Miquel's face. The image settled against his mind like a blow.

Diago took the ring from the box and slid it onto his index finger. *Calm down and think.* He couldn't imagine Miquel taking off his ring and placing it in the mirrored box, no matter how angry he might be about Diago's adultery. That simply wasn't his way. Miquel was too emotional for such a cold good-bye.

Diago examined the silk within the box. In one corner was splash of blood. Diago licked his finger and touched the blood. He lifted his finger to his tongue and tasted silk and parchment and the bitterness of rosemary. Diago knew the taste of his lover's blood. Miquel was hurt.

He pressed the ring to his mouth. The metal was

cold against his lips. Miquel had not left him, not voluntarily. Perhaps even now he was with Diago's son, but where?

The faint sound of chimes interrupted Diago's thoughts. From the downstairs hall, in its niche beside the phone, Doña Rosa's great clock tolled seven times.

CHAPTER TWO

Diago switched on every light in the loft. Nothing appeared to have been disturbed, and there were no signs of a struggle. Miquel's gun was still in his suitcase, along with his bowie knife, gifts from Guillermo. Diago closed the suitcase and shoved it back under the bed.

In the front pocket of Miquel's pants he found a crumpled theater bill. The heavily creased paper advertised a new bar not far from the Villa Rosa, where Miquel usually played. A large black scorpion had been drawn to dominate the top of the page. The tail formed the "S" within the club's name and swirled to encircle the words: Club d'Escorpí. The bill proclaimed an unparalleled show filled with *cante jondo*—deep song. *Miquel's specialty,* Diago thought as his gaze moved down the page.

The bill announced Beltran Prieto as the singer.

The dancer was unnamed. Miquel de Torrellas was listed as the guitarist. That couldn't be right. Miquel had made no mention of working in a new club, and the artwork indicated the handbill had been weeks in the making.

Diago refolded the advertisement and pushed it into his back pocket. He would begin his search at the Villa Rosa before moving to the Club d'Escorpí. Perhaps one of the other performers had seen or heard something about this new club. Any information might help him circumvent more of Prieto's surprises.

Diago switched from his shirt and tie to a worn sweater with frayed sleeves, so he would blend in with the mortals that frequented the area. From beneath the bed he yanked out his suitcase and opened it. Inside, concealed beneath a false bottom, were his Luger and a long wicked knife.

His hands no longer shook. Initiating a course of action steadied him. He checked his magazines. One was full, the other half full. Diago emptied a box of silver-tipped bullets onto the bed and added rounds to the second magazine.

Yet, even though he had a plan, it didn't change the fact that he had no idea what was going on. He considered the clues he had so far, but he could find no way to connect them. As far as he could remember, Candela had never mentioned anyone named Beltran Prieto— -but to be fair, they hadn't spoken beyond murmurs of passion and her whispered lies.

Another spasm of guilt twisted his stomach before

he shut Candela from his mind. *Think, God damn it.* The etched triptych indicated supernatural skill. That was a start, but Diago had no idea whether Prieto was angel or daimon. His motivations were just as veiled as his character.

What can he possibly want?

"He needs me," Diago murmured. Specifically, Prieto needed skills that only Diago possessed. *But what?* The answer to that question required a meeting. One that Beltran Prieto was about to regret.

What else have I got? Diago pressed bullets into the magazine and thought of the hourglass. They used to mark time with hourglasses. There was a clock ticking somewhere. Whatever Prieto needed, time was of the essence. "Okay." Diago inserted the fresh magazine into the Luger, then tucked the gun into his holster. "Let's not keep him waiting." He pulled the long sweater down over his hips to hide the weapon, then pocketed the second magazine. The knife he secured to his calf, using the wide pant-leg to conceal the blade.

As long he was able to avoid the police, he'd be fine. He wasn't all that worried; the section of the Paralelo closest to the wharfs operated under its own laws, which would make Diago's fact-finding mission somewhat easier.

He returned to the kitchen, where he wrapped the glass box loosely in the paper and tucked it, along with the card, into his coat pocket. From the tabletop, the brass of the magnifying glass winked in the light. Diago snapped the glass into the case, then jammed the medallion into his front pocket with his change, thinking the thing might be useful if he needed to examine the triptych again.

He left the apartment and descended to the first floor, pausing by the phone. Instinct told him to hurry, yet he hesitated. Although he had sworn no oaths to Los Nefilim, Guillermo was his friend, and had asked Diago to let him know if anything ever happened to Miquel. The call would only take a moment, and Diago decided he would feel better if someone knew where he was going.

The sound of a radio soap opera blared through Doña Rosa's closed door. If he wanted privacy, now was the time to call.

Before he could change his mind, he gritted his teeth and lifted the receiver, relieved that no one else was using the line. Even though they were only mortals, the sound of disembodied voices nattering away disturbed him more than he wanted to admit.

He gave the operator Guillermo's number, and she put the call through. The phone rang, a tinny sound made thin by the distance. Diago's heart pounded three times between each of the five rings. *Ten rings. I'll give it ten rings, and then hang up.*

As he waited, he noticed a deep scuff in the wainscoting to the left of the telephone table. The pale wood stood naked against the richer shades of brown and black. The gouge was fresh. Someone had obviously knocked the table against the wall, probably José coming home after a night of drinking. Maybe. Diago ran his thumb along the groove and frowned. But the direction of the scar indicated it had been made by someone approaching from the stairwell opposite the front door.

Before he could examine it further, a man answered the phone. "Hello, you have reached the residen—"

"Suero, it's Diago. I need to talk to Guillermo."

There was a pause. The line crackled between them. Suero said, "He's not here. He won't be back until late."

"What about Juanita?" Guillermo's wife handled any problems with Los Nefilim in Guillermo's absence.

"She is with Guillermo."

"Damn it." Diago breathed the words and glanced at Doña Rosa's door.

An announcer's smooth baritone purred an advertisement for Myrurgia's face powder. The noise from the radio might cover his conversation, but it also set Diago's rigid nerves on fire. He clamped his fingers around the receiver and calmed himself. "All right, give Guillermo a message for me. Tell him that I have lost the key. I am going to look for it."

Suero was silent. Diago imagined the cogs clicking in the younger Nefil's mind upon hearing that news. The key was their code for Miquel, and Suero loved him like a brother.

A note of wariness touched Suero's voice. "Do you need me to come, Diago?"

"No. It could be nothing." The calling card's warning flashed through his mind: *Come alone or not at all.*

He hastened to reassure Suero. "I'm going to the Villa Rosa and the Club d'Escorpí. Everything is under control."

"Until it isn't."

Argumentative little fuck. Diago gripped the phone and glared at the scuff along the wainscoting. While his lack of an oath allowed Diago to move freely between the ranks of daimon and angel, it also created a certain amount of resentment with Guillermo's Nefilim. They treated him like he might betray them on a moment's notice, and Suero was the most suspicious of the lot.

Diago knew one harsh look would intimidate the younger Nefil to his proper place, but the telephone robbed him of the finesse he enjoyed in a face-to-face encounter. This gave him a whole new reason to detest the device.

Suero must have sensed that he overstepped his bounds, though. He broke the long silence and attempted a more conciliatory tone. "How long, Diago?"

That was better. Not good enough to make Diago forget Suero's transgression, but better. "Four hours."

After another brief pause, Suero said, "The clock is ticking."

Of that, Diago had no doubt.

CHAPTER THREE

The train rolled into the station just as he reached the platform. Maybe his luck was changing. He joined the other travelers and squeezed into a car. Too restless to sit, he stood and clung to the cold steel bar, watching the passengers with a hunter's eye.

They were all mortals. Whoever Beltran Prieto was, he wasn't following Diago, or having him followed. The fact that Prieto trusted Diago to come to him alone bespoke excellent planning and knowledge of his prey. It was just another detail that increased Diago's anxiety.

When the train finally lumbered to his stop, Diago was the first one off. The trip from the Gothic Quarter to the Paralelo cost him almost forty minutes. How long did he have to keep this rendezvous? Diago had no answer to that question, but thought it best not to waste a second. He climbed the stairs two at a time and found the fog heavier here by the sea.

The street was clogged with the usual evening crowd of pedestrians, cars, and a few horses and carts, all vying to be first along the roadway. Diago shoved his way past the -people and managed to catch a tram for the final leg of his journey. The tram's bell sent out one discordant clang after another as the fog slowed everything to a crawl.

The traffic was no less congested on the Avenue of the Paralelo, but the width of the street eased some of bottleneck. Diago leapt from the car before the tram had rolled to a complete stop. With three quick steps, he caught his balance and pushed his way toward the opposite street corner in the direction of the wharfs.

Here, Barcelona sang a thousand different melodies, from the refined theaters that catered to the nobles and the bourgeoisie down to the lowest bars near the docks. The Villa Rosa lay in an area that teetered between the extremes.

Mumbled lyrics and songs half sung trickled into the street as some of the club performers practiced their routines. A door opened, and Diago caught the first fragile notes of a tune. The hesitant chords were followed by more confident strumming, punctuated by rhythmic finger taps against the body of a guitar.

Someone clapped rapid beats while a woman coached a dancer through her steps: *"Gólpe, gólpe, vuelta . . ."*

Strike, strike, turn. . .

Just as the dancer's footwork and the guitarist's melody began to move in tandem, the door slowly descended on the woman's voice and swallowed her words. The next bar offered a different refrain of the same song, and from one establishment to another, the music rolled on.

Within another hour, the tributaries of side streets and alleys that streamed off the main avenue would be packed with jostling men and women, all of whom would be looking to make their troubles disappear for an evening. The songs would be wild and sad, but that was all right; the misfortunes of others never bit as hard as one's own troubles.

And tonight Diago understood the mortals and their desire to forget, especially with his own dread nipping at his heels. In a past incarnation he might have walked away, rather than try to save his lover and son, but Miquel had changed him. Slowly, inexorably, he had taught Diago that love was worth fighting for. *And I will fight for them,* he vowed as he shouldered his way through the crowd.

The fog clung to everything like a second skin, obscuring faces and buildings. People passed Diago as shadows made indistinct by the mist, their conversations subdued by the encroaching darkness.

It was as if the world echoed his mood.

Diago stepped off the main avenue and followed a circuitous alley. From there, he passed the tobacco shop, which signaled his next turn. Two streets deeper into the maze, and he found the Villa Rosa with her doors open, spilling golden light onto the cobblestones.

A woman stood just within the tavern's rim of light. She glanced his way, and Diago recognized her. She called herself Estrella, though he doubted that was her real name. Like every other performer along the Paralelo, she cast herself a new persona made of half-truths and wishes.

Diago didn't blame her. Although she was mortal, she was a kindred spirit to him and Miquel. Their duplicity consisted of passing themselves off as humans and just good friends. Pretenses surrounded their lives, both among the mortals and Los Nefilim. Sometimes the truth was a hard thing best kept close and private against the heart.

Tonight, Estrella's carriage was tense, and her foot rapped the cobblestones with her impatience.

Out of nowhere, the invisible tutor's voice returned to Diago's head.

Gólpe, gólpe, vuelta . . .

Strike, strike, turn. . .

He shook the words from his ears and focused on Estrella.

She pinched a cigarette between her fingers and nipped a vicious toke as she speared Diago with her glare. "Where is Miquel?"

Diago opened his mouth, but she lifted her hand and cut him off. "He'd better be dead. We were supposed to rehearse this afternoon and he never showed. No one stands me up." She sucked on the tip of her cigarette, then spat a malicious cloud of smoke into the fog. "I hope you're here to tell me he's dead. Then I won't have to kill—"

Diago's face must have given away more than he intended, because as he neared her, she suddenly stopped talking and stared at him. Her lower lip trembled. "He's not with you?"

He shook his head and stepped next to her.

"He's . . . not dead, is he?" All traces of anger had left her, and it was clear she regretted her harsh words. The ashes from her cigarette were dangerously close to cascading down her bodice and scorching her dress. Her hand trembled. Diago caught the ashes and flicked them into the darkness. He wiped his palm against his coat. "No—not dead. But I need to find him, Estrella."

She swallowed hard and nodded.

"You might be able to help me. Tell me, did he speak with anyone last night?"

Estrella tossed her cigarette to the gutter. "He speaks with a lot of -people. Everyone wants a minute with him." She picked at one of the ruffles on her skirt. "He listens to them all, and they love him for it."

A tear slipped over her lashes, and Diago evinced a level of patience he didn't feel. He brushed away her tear before the moisture could smear her makeup. "Don't cry. You've got to dance tonight."

She sniffled. "Not without Miquel."

He sighed and shook his head. Miquel had remained with her for too long; Diago saw it in her longing for him. His lover was still young enough to think himself more human than angel, and he forgot the effect he had on mortals. Estrella, for all her street smarts and toughness, was just as susceptible to Miquel's allure as anyone else. He had played for her, and she, in turn, had absorbed some of his magic into the art of her dance. She was connected to it now, and felt his absence more keenly than any of the others at the club.

Diago had seen mortals who had become too intimate with Nefilim commit suicide when they were deprived of the being's company. He feared Estrella might be too far gone, and an ache filled his chest. She deserved better.

He sidled closer until his lips brushed against her ear. "Think for me, Estrella: was there anyone in the audience last night that was new? Anyone who stood out for any reason?" He cupped her chin and caught her gaze with his. No. She remembered nothing, at least not consciously.

He rarely used his power on mortals, and he never opened their minds against their will. As far as he was concerned, such a violation was an act of rape. "I need to know," he murmured gently, easing her into a dreamlike state with tender reassurances. *Exactly like Candela did to me,* he thought bitterly, then quickly absolved himself. *Estrella leaves me no choice. Besides, if she knew it was for Miquel, she would offer herself to me.* Sometimes the worst lies were the ones he told himself.

In spite of being acutely aware of the time, he didn't rush, using every ounce of willpower not to crack open her mind like a gourd. As badly as he wanted to see her thoughts, he forced himself to be patient, and take only what she offered him through her words.

Anyone passing by might think them lovers, snatching a kiss before the show. A moment slipped between them as Diago deepened her trance, willing her to remember. "Close your eyes for me and think very hard. It's for Miquel." He leaned forward until his lips almost touched hers. "Was there anyone new at the club last night?"

Her heavy lashes fluttered. She murmured, "He came during our final set when Miquel played for me." She bit her lower lip and smiled. "He always plays special for me."

"Shh, who did you see?"

"A new customer sat near the stage."

"Was his name Beltran Prieto?"

She considered his question. "I heard no name."

Damn. "What did he look like?"

"He had . . . long silver hair. He was old, very graceful, very beautiful. He was angelic."

"What do you mean?"

"You'll think me mad, but I thought I glimpsed three sets of wings descending down his back. One moment they were there, then the next, he was a man again. I was drunk with the music. Sometimes I see things that are not there."

Diago wasn't sure whether to be relieved or disturbed by the information. Either way, he didn't think her mad. At least one question was answered: Prieto was an angel. And while he surely hadn't intended for Estrella to see him—he had probably dropped his disguise in order to show himself to Miquel—she had been caught up in the song, and thus was exposed to it, too. "Did he speak to you, or Miquel?"

"I turned." Estrella's tongue flickered between her lips and grazed his mouth. He tasted nicotine and the salt of the sea. "And I turned and he was gone."

Of course Prieto disappeared. Whatever business he conducted with Miquel would have happened after the performance. Miquel hadn't mentioned the meeting, but that wasn't unusual. He never discussed Los Nefilim business with Diago. Something must have gone wrong.

Clearly something went wrong! he said to himself in silent rebuke. His frustration was seeping into his own musings, and he felt his hold on Estrella's mind slip. He renewed his grip on the spell and asked, "One more thing: the Club d'Escorpí, have you heard of it?"

She frowned and shook her head. "No."

God damn. That wasn't good at all. The performers always kept a close eye on competing establishments. Did the club even exist?

Estrella stirred. "Did I help?"

"Yes." *And no.* Either way, she had no other memories to offer him. It was time for him to go. In the way of an amends, he kissed her and warmed her soul with a shield of light that would protect her from feeling Miquel's loss too deeply. In doing so, he opened himself to her and allowed her to see his true nature—that he was daimon, a creature borne of the darkness, his soul made of dreams earthy-sweet and whispers in the night. Yet he was also angel, filled with fire and stardust and eternal light. He was a thousand contradictions, bound to the clay and water of the flesh, but that was his magic, the spell that was his to weave.

Better she see the true me than lose herself to the lie Miquel's power has over her.

He held Estrella's head steady between his palms and touched his forehead to hers. "Miquel is not coming back to the Villa Rosa, Estrella."

She moaned, and her sorrow rose between them as soft and blue as smoke. He inhaled and took her pain for his own.

"But that is all right. You don't need him. You have all that you need right here." He touched her breast, just over her heart, and poured a little more of his magic into her soul. *Let her be all right. If there are angels and daimons, surely there might be a god somewhere, and if there is, let her be happy.*

She leaned against the wall and looked upward, her eyes glassy with her trance.

Diago released her and stepped back. "When you hear my song, you will wake and go inside. Forget that you saw me. I am no more." He walked until the fog almost hid her from sight. At the street corner, he hummed a mellow tune.

Estrella jerked awake and glanced up and down the street. Her sadness dissipated. She wore her anger loosely as a shawl. Her gaze passed directly over him as if he was invisible. She went inside the Villa Rosa.

Tonight she would be angry, and tomorrow she would be melancholy. In the end, she would go on with her life and that was what mattered. Diago wished his worries could be erased so easily.

The time. What was the time? There were no clocks nearby. Exasperated, he withdrew the playbill and read the address for the Club d'Escorpí. The bar was located three blocks deeper into the Paralelo's tangled backstreets. *At least I'm close.* He crammed the playbill into his coat pocket and hurried down an alleyway. The noise of the main avenue fell behind him. Here, the fog thickened until Diago could barely see a metre ahead.

The quiet was too heavy to be anything other than supernatural. The hair on his arms rose in response to the power around him. Barcelona was behind him, along with the mortals and their everyday worries. Diago had stepped into a different realm. No matter how many times he moved between the spheres of mortal and angel, he never got used to the insidious slide from one reality to another. He paused to get his bearings.

In the same way that earth was an echo of other realms, this new place was a mere reflection of the Paralelo. On a superficial level, everything seemed the same: the walls were brick, the fog was blue, yet this new place was smaller, paler, less complete than the original. The handbills and advertisements were faded, nearly illegible. The scent of the sea became a memory embedded in the fibers of Diago's clothes. Sounds of the Paralelo's revelers diminished until the clamor vanished. Time stood still and soft, like the moments embedded in midnight's silence.

Diago drew his Luger and held the gun close to his thigh. Not even silver tips would stop an angel, but holding the weapon comforted him with the illusion of protection. The skin on his exposed hands tingled. He paused, his palm damp against the grip of the gun.

The distant strains of a guitar drifted out of the fog. In those notes, Diago recognized one of Miquel's favorite *falsetas*. This one began *por arriba*, high along the frets, shifting rapidly through the notes. A wedge of hope pushed back his fear. If it was Miquel, then he might be all right.

The tune picked up speed. The player missed a chord. The song halted.

Diago froze.

The music began again—louder, closer—although Diago had not moved. Whatever approached was coming to him. The fog became electric. Drops of moisture sizzled against the black windows and shadow doors that lined the alley.

The strings hummed when the player missed his next chord. It *was* Miquel. Any doubt was erased by that error. When he grew tired, he always failed to make a smooth transition between F and E. Judging from the screech of his fingers along the strings, he was exhausted.

But he's alive. He's alive, and that's what matt—

The song ended abruptly.

Diago thought he heard voices. He cocked his head.

A man spoke a command.

Miquel answered. "I can't."

The man spoke again. His tone mocked Miquel's pain. "You will."

Miquel began to play.

Rage flared through Diago's chest and into his head, almost blinding him. He clenched his jaw and pushed down his anger. He needed his mind clear.

The sounds drew closer still. Miquel's ring was warm on Diago's finger. Diago searched the gloom. *Come on. Stop tormenting us and show yourself.* As if in answer, a door appeared in the wall on his left. Cold blue light spilled across the threshold and shouldered the fog aside. Over the open door, an electric scorpion writhed and blinked in neon splendor.

Diago crept toward the entrance and peered inside. The room was gray, like the walls and the floor had been sculpted from the mist. The same lack of color that diluted the details of the bar enhanced the three figures within.

Miquel played a worn guitar, his fingertips dark with his own blood. Sweat dampened his black curls. Other than a bruise that spread across his left eye like a poison sunset, and his worn fingertips, he seemed to be all right.

Even so, Diago's heart hammered at the sight of him. Adrenaline flooded his body with an intoxicating mixture of relief and rage.

The loud click of marbles striking wooden trays re-directed his attention to the table where an angel in his mortal form sat across from a child. Diago focused on the angel first. He was the same one Estrella had described. To any human who happened to glance at him, he appeared as a beautiful man with long silver hair pulled into ponytail that cascaded down his back. A closer look revealed that he had only four fingers on each hand.

Safe within his lair, he made no attempt to hide his feet, which resembled the clawed talons of a raptor. Thick fur covered his ankles and disappeared beneath the seams of his pants. The eyes were the worst. Great crimson orbs shot through with streams of silver. He possessed no pupils, no whites.

An hourglass stood on the table. Yellow sand trickled from the top bulb into the bottom. The thin line of sand in the top half left no doubt that Diago had arrived just in time.

A mancala board was placed between the angel and the child. They used brightly colored marbles for their game pieces. The boy was fixated on a large marble that rested in the angel's mancala pit. Diago recognized the marble as a Blood Alley. Guillermo's daughter Ysabel had a similar one, but hers contained swirls of milky white quartz. Unlike Ysabel's marble, this one was as dark as carmine.

Like the eyes of a golden snake. The thought came from nowhere and gave Diago a jolt.

His heart picked up speed as he finally looked to the child.

My son, he corrected himself in wonder. *This isn't*

just any child. He is my son. No amount of abstract reasoning had prepared Diago for the emotions that assaulted him as he examined the boy. It was one thing to realize he had a child. It was something entirely different to see that child in the flesh for the first time.

A flat cap pushed the boy's thick bangs into his eyes. His hair was as blue-black as Diago's, but the waves that curled the ends belonged to Candela. The child's magic was as wild as his hair, and tangled around his small body in hues of amber and jade. Another Nefil would easily recognize him as Nefil. To mortals, in spite of the filth, he was simply a beautiful child.

A forest-green jacket threaded with yellow hung on his thin body; the sleeves were rolled back to his wrists. He clutched a worn rag-horse with button eyes. The toy had obviously been salvaged from someone's trash. His scabby knees showed more bone than flesh. One sock was rumpled around his ankle, the other clung to his calf, ready to let go its precarious hold and join its mate. The boy was filthy, as if he'd been living on the streets. For all Diago knew, he had been. He had no idea who, if anyone, had cared for him since Candela's death.

Why didn't she tell me? Did she think me so evil that I'd desert him? He might not have wanted a child, but he certainly wouldn't have run from the responsibility. Not like his father had.

The boy chose a tray and scooped up the marbles. He counted them out and frowned at the board, tapping his fingers against the table in a slow rhythm, like a cat twitching its tail. The familiarity of the motion stunned Diago. He often did the same thing when distracted.

He is mine. And on the heels of that thought came the obvious: *I have to get him out of here.* He glanced at Miquel again. *I have to get both of them out of here.*

"Come in, Diago," said the angel. "We have been waiting for you."

Miquel stopped playing and looked up. His dark bangs fell over his forehead, but not before Diago saw the pain that cut crystal tears into his eyes. The last note hung blue and lonely in the air.

Advancing slowly, Diago surveyed the room one last time. When he was sure they were the only occupants, he holstered the gun—the weapon was useless here. Halfway to the table, he hesitated, torn between going to Miquel and snatching his son away from the angel.

He gauged the distance between him and Miquel, who was less than a metre away. Miquel gave a single shake of his head, discouraging Diago from coming closer.

The last grain of sand fell through the hourglass. The door slammed shut. Diago whirled, reaching for his gun again. He expected to see the two men Doña Rosa had mentioned, but the short hall was empty. His fingers slid from the gun's grip as he turned back to the angel. "Who are you?"

"Beltran Prieto." The angel tipped his head and spread his hands. "At your service."

"That's not your name."

"It's the only name you'll have from my lips." He leaned back in his chair and looked toward the door. "Expecting someone?"

"Two men delivered your gift. Where are they?"

"Ah," Prieto murmured. The marbles clicked together as he placed each one in a pit. He won himself a second turn. "There were no men. Doña Rosa lied to you. Oh, don't look so shocked. José is in a great deal of debt to some rather unscrupulous characters. She was praying for his immortal soul, and I went to her. I promised to remove José's desire to gamble if Doña Rosa told a little white lie and delivered a gift for me."

The boy offered helpfully, "He appeared to Doña Rosa in church and made her believe she had a vision from God." When Diago shifted his attention to the child, the boy's cheeks reddened. "He let me watch," he whispered, his fledgling confidence disappearing beneath Diago's gaze.

"I see." Diago nodded in what he hoped was a reassuring manner, as he edged closer to his son.

A tremulous smile returned to the boy's mouth.

He wants to be loved so badly. Diago saw the need in his son's eyes and something tore inside his chest. *If I can just get to him.* He managed to take one more step closer before Miquel warned him with another shake of his head. Diago halted in his tracks.

"A lesson to him." Prieto pretended to ignore them and considered his next move. "He needs to understand the power of a true angel, one who is not sullied by mortal flesh." He chose stones from his side of the board. "A lesson Miquel should heed since he refused to arrange a meeting between you and me." Prieto spared Miquel a quick glare. "He wanted to check with Guillermo first. In the old days, a Nefil would have obeyed me without question, then informed Guillermo. Los Nefilim are becoming arrogant, it seems. What do you know about that, Diago?"

"Nothing. I stay out of their business."

"Hmm. No pillow talk. That's a shame." Prieto dropped the marbles into their respective pits. "It's a good thing most mortals still respect us. Those that don't can be bought. I had to pay José for his help, but the expense was worth it. He proved quite clever for a mortal. He waited until his mother left to visit a friend. Then he just announced a phone call from you, and of course, Miquel, knowing how you hate the phone, assumed it was an emergency. José took him down quite skillfully. One punch to the face. Miquel never saw it coming."

The gouge in the wall by the phone. . .

Miquel looked away, but not before Diago saw his shame. He had been caught off guard by a mortal. The error might have been forgivable in a younger Nefil, but for Miquel, the lapse in judgment was inexcusable.

Prieto said, "He should have done as I asked." He gestured at Miquel, who took a sharp short breath.

A flash of silver light coursed beneath his skin and through his veins. A sigil spun just over his heart. It was an ugly creation made of jagged lines and serrated edges, like a circular saw blade. Diago recognized it immediately. It was a binding sigil. He knew from experience the agony of such a glyph. Disobedience caused the ward to clench a Nefil's heart, and send electric shocks through the limbs.

Diago took three steps toward Miquel before Prieto's voice stopped him.

"Leave him, Diago. I can make it worse." Prieto clenched his fist. The sigil burned brighter. Miquel cried out.

"All right!" He halted and snapped the words like bullets. "Stop hurting him!"

Prieto opened his hand. He'd made his point. The sigil disappeared.

Diago's apprehension receded marginally as Miquel took a deep breath. *And what about my son?* He backed up and examined the boy. No silver streaked his veins, nor had Prieto bound him with a sigil. The boy clenched the toy pony's mane and regarded Diago with naked curiosity.

Prieto missed nothing. His tone turned parental as he coaxed the youngster. "Greet your father, Rafael."

Rafael. The name went through Diago like a shock. Suddenly, he smelled the hard scent of tin—*and carnations, she kept carnations by the bed*—and recalled Candela lazily tracing the scars on his chest. The golden snake had slid from her hair to coil over his heart, cool like water, soft like silk. The serpent had watched him with ruby eyes, but Diago had barely been aware of anything other than Candela's voice, murmuring the name she would call her song.

"Rafael," he said, echoing his memory.

Rafael parted his lips as if he meant to speak. Whatever question poised on his tongue was drowned by the dissonant note of the guitar when it hit the floor.

Miquel stood and shoved the instrument aside with his foot. "Your what?"

Prieto's eerie gaze sparkled with delight. "You never told him?"

Diago's mouth went dry. He willed his brain to think. Fear swallowed his thoughts and gave him nothing in return. *I will lose him over this.*

"Told me what?" Miquel's tone grew fierce as he circled the table, moving toward Diago.

Prieto grinned and did nothing to stop Miquel's advance. "That he took a lover. In Triana. What did she call herself there, Diago?"

"Candela," Diago whispered.

Miquel's voice lowered a notch. "Candela?"

Diago licked his lips. "I knew her in Triana."

"I heard that part." Miquel pretended to ignore Prieto's chuckles, but Diago saw each laugh cut Miquel to the heart. He was a proud one, his Miquel. "How could you?"

"She claimed to have a song that would help us."

"And did she?" Miquel stopped right in front of Diago, his dark eyes ablaze with his fury and pain. "Did she give you your song?"

They were almost nose to nose, but Diago didn't

back away from him. *I brought him this pain and, though it will kill me, if he wants to go, I will not stop him.* "She said it would come to me."

"And so it did." Prieto snatched the carmine marble from his tray. He held it between finger and thumb, pretending to examine Rafael through the glass. "Forgive him, Miquel. She was an angel. He couldn't have resisted her if he'd wanted to. She enchanted him. Only the angel-born Nefilim can know the pure of heart, and Diago's daimon nature clouds his eyes. That is his weakness. Our Candela deceived the deceiver."

Diago locked his knees so he didn't fall. The dance had shifted beneath his feet. Candela was angel? But that couldn't be. Surely he would have recognized her as such . . . or would he? How had she fooled him so thoroughly?

By telling me what I wanted to hear. She had beguiled him with his own wishes and he had followed her like a lamb.

The feathery brush of fingers against his palm caused Diago to start. He looked down to find Rafael peering up at him.

"Is that true?" he asked. "Are you my papa?"

Diago brushed a curl from the child's eyelashes. The hope in Rafael's eyes tore Diago's heart. He knew what it was to be abandoned and alone. And on the heels of that thought came another: what about his own father, the man he'd hated for so long? Had he even known about Diago? Or had he been clueless about his son's birth, the same as Diago hadn't known about Rafael? Diago tucked those questions away. He would examine them later in the light, but not now. In this moment, he needed to acknowledge his own son. "It's true. You're mine."

Rafael twined his fingers with Diago's. "May I live with you?"

Diago touched Miquel's wrist in order to get his attention. Miquel didn't pull away, but he didn't acknowledge Diago's touch either.

Diago wished for the privacy Prieto wouldn't give them. He lowered his voice. "I won't leave him like my father left me. If you don't want to stay—" *I will sorrow for ten thousand years.* Diago swallowed hard. "I'll understand."

Miquel made no sign he heard. He glared at Prieto, his fists working at his sides. Afraid that he might forget himself and attack the angel, Diago eased in front of him, although it meant putting his back to Prieto. He waited until Miquel met his gaze before he mouthed: *Please. I need you.*

Rafael wiped the corner of his eye with the sleeve of his coat. "I don't want to go back to Sister Benita."

"You won't," Miquel snapped.

Diago released the breath he'd been unaware of holding. He clutched Rafael's hand and maneuvered the child between them.

"That's so sweet." Prieto rolled the red marble beneath his palm in small circular motions. "But you won't get to keep him, Diago. He's ours. Candela hid him from us. We were looking in Sevilla, but here he was in Barcelona, tucked behind the black skirts of the nuns. Such a waste." He ran his tongue over his upper lip. "Sister Benita was more than happy to turn him over to me. She thinks he is the devil's son. I made sure she knew he was merely a daimon." Prieto chucked at his own joke.

"You think this is funny?" Miquel turned his rage on Prieto. "If what you're saying is true, Candela took her mortal form and raped him."

Diago felt like he'd been punched. "What?" He instinctively put his hand over Rafael's ear. The child didn't need to hear this. Diago wasn't sure *he* wanted to hear it. How had a tryst turned into rape?

The soul of reason, Miquel asked, "Would you have done it if she had not enchanted you?"

"Of course not." Or was that true? Diago wasn't sure of anything anymore. At the time, he had thought himself perfectly in control of the situation with Candela, but that could have easily been part of her spell. And even if he wouldn't have had sex with her without an enchantment, what were the ramifications of such an admission in front of Rafael? The child was only six; how much did he understand? Diago pointedly looked down at the boy, and when he met Miquel's gaze again, he saw most of the anger had bled from Miquel's face and was replaced by ruthless cunning.

Damn him. Miquel had provoked that response on purpose. "Why did you do that?"

"I had to know the truth."

"Am I such a liar that you have to test me?"

Miquel didn't answer. Diago knuckled down on the hard knot of hurt that settled in his gut, because he knew the answer. This was a conversation they would have in private. Later.

If there was a later.

Diago noticed that Prieto seemed to be enjoying the exchange and was in no hurry to move them along. What was he waiting for? He allowed them to be distracted with a quarrel—for what? To test their allegiance to one another? Diago looked back to the table for some clue. While he and Miquel had been engaged in their argument, Prieto had flipped the hourglass again. The time. Prieto was in no hurry, because he awaited the proper hour. *But to do what?*

So Diago asked. "What do you want, Prieto? You didn't stage this little drama for your own amusement. You need something from me, or we wouldn't be here."

Prieto's eyes swirled with malice. "What do I want? Only that which you alone can give, Diago. I want your firstborn son."

"*What?*"

Miquel took a step toward the table. "This is sadistic."

"No," Prieto said. "I am many things, but I am not a sadist. This task gives me no pleasure whatsoever. The daimons are using their Nefilim to incite the mortals into a second world war. The daimons don't care who wins, they simply want to feed on more mortal hate. We cannot stop the humans from savaging one another again, but we can mitigate the damage and bring the war to a stop within a reasonable period. My orders are to bring back the weapon that will end the conflict at the right time."

"What is a reasonable amount of time?" Miquel asked as he sidled between Diago and Prieto.

Prieto took up the red marble. "Four, maybe five mortal years. Less than a minute to the angels. An hour to Los Nefilim." He rolled the marble across his fingers in a balancing game.

Rafael peeked at Prieto. "That is mine," he said, indicating the marble.

Diago rested his hand on the boy's head in order to acknowledge his words, but he didn't answer him. He directed his question to Prieto. "What do you need me to do?"

"It's very simple, Diago. Moloch has a coin, a very special coin, one that we require."

"Moloch." Diago murmured the name through numb lips. Guillermo had faced the daimon Moloch on the battlefield once and still carried the scars of that fight. A daimon of war, Moloch's renown for engineering new ways for mortals to murder one another reached greater pinnacles with each technological advancement. "Moloch doesn't hoard money."

"Moloch hoards death." Prieto tossed the marble into the air and caught it while fixing his horrific eyes on Rafael. "The coin you're going to bring me represents an idea, a concept, one that we need to implant in a mortal's mind so that he might develop the weapon."

"This idea is about murder," Diago said.

"But not as an act of evil," said the angel.

"Not if you do it," Diago retorted.

"I detect sarcasm, Diago." Prieto touched his chest where his heart might have been if he was human. "I'm hurt."

Diago scoffed. "And what is the price for this coin? This idea? What does it have to do with Rafael?"

"Moloch is hungry."

Diago's stomach lurched in a slow somersault. Now it all fell together. In the days of Solomon, the -people had sacrificed their children to Moloch in order to buy peace. Diago's fingers unconsciously tightened on Rafael's shoulder. "No."

"He demands a sacrifice," said Prieto. "He wants the child of a Nefil."

Diago shook his head. "I have done terrible things, but not this. This I will not do."

Prieto pursed his lips and dropped the marble into the tray. "We have exhausted every option in our negotiations. This world war can last for four years or four decades. You remember the Inquisition, Diago. How long do you want them to suffer? For every year the mortal war drags on, the daimons feed on misery, and that simply whets their appetite for more. The daimons' power will grow. We must give Moloch what he wants."

"No. *You* have to give him what he wants. I don't owe Moloch a God damn thing."

"The parent must give the child. No one else has the right. Those have always been Moloch's terms. He is as intractable as he is ancient. It's a small sacrifice. One life for the good of the many. You are the one who is always crying for peace, Diago. Are you willing to pay the price?"

Diago barked an incredulous laugh at the audacity of the question. "No. I refuse."

Prieto's humor vanished. He utilized all three sets of his vocal chords. "I won't be disobeyed."

The sound plummeted through Diago and into his bones. Rafael clamped his hands over his ears. The stuffed horse flopped in the crook of his arm. Miquel flinched from the sound. He placed his hand over Diago's and linked their fingers together, giving Diago a gentle squeeze. It was a conciliatory gesture, an old signal between them, one that asked for forgiveness for his earlier harsh words.

Relieved, Diago returned the gesture. Together they shielded Rafael from the angel.

The silver threads in Prieto's eyes swirled. He was furious. "Candela lied. There is no song, Diago. Not in that child, or any other. He is a *sacrifice*. Candela was supposed to give him to Moloch, but she wore her mortal body too long. Her emotions interfered with her ability to complete the act. She hid the boy and destroyed herself before we could find him."

Rafael buried his face in Diago's coat. A low whine escaped his throat in a melody of grief and fear and anger.

Diago hugged the child against his leg. Hoping to mitigate Rafael's sorrow, he said, "You're lying."

"Everything dies, Diago, even the angels."

Diago barely heard him. Movement within the hourglass caught his attention. A low rumble pulsed through the floorboards. The base of the hourglass rattled against the tabletop. Yellow sand swirled in miniature tornados, gusts and twirls made to dance to a hidden rhythm. The reverberations beneath Diago's soles grew stronger. The table shook. The mancala board rattled to the edge and tipped over, spilling the marbles to the floor.

The carmine marble rolled toward them. Miquel knelt and scooped it into his hand. Rafael didn't notice. The child's terror held him rigid at Diago's side. Miquel passed the marble to Diago. He dropped it into his pocket without taking his gaze off the hourglass.

The sand danced, coalescing into a single funnel that spun toward the upper chamber. Prieto stood and unfurled three sets of silver wings that descended down his back. The colors in his eyes whirled like the dangerous clouds before a storm. A great wind filled the room and drove Prieto's illusions into the mists.

Diago hummed a chord. He thrust it into his throat like a vicious cry. Miquel joined Diago's voice with his own. Their souls mingled as one, and Diago took courage from Miquel's presence. He traced a glyph of protection into the air. The sigil glowed with silver radiance to spin like a top. The lines merged to form a shield of light between them and Prieto.

Prieto spoke a word and the sigil over Miquel's heart blazed. Miquel choked on his song and staggered. Diago caught his arm but couldn't prevent Miquel from falling to one knee. The protective sigil faded on the strength of Diago's voice alone, breaking apart and falling like shimmering flakes of snow.

Enraged by his inability to protect them, Diago shouted his frustration at the angel. "Let them go and I will give myself to Moloch!"

"You? What do you have to offer Moloch? Your innocence?" The angel sneered. "Your innocence died in the days of Solomon when you betrayed your king. You have nothing to give Moloch but your son. And that you *will* do."

Before Diago could retort, Prieto reverted to the language of the angels, and the ethereal vibrations shattered the realm in which they stood. Diago's teeth ached from the pressure in his head. His flesh flattened against muscle and bone. All around them, the images of walls and wood bent against time and space, as if they had been thrown into a surrealist painting where the colors bled hot upon the canvas.

Rafael screamed. Diago went to his knees beside the boy and pulled him close, but he didn't let go of Miquel. To Diago's relief, Miquel's strong fingers grasped his wrist. Rafael's arms encircled Diago's neck. The little stuffed horse was squashed between them. In spite of the gale threatening to tear the three of them apart, they held onto one another.

The wind sculpted the walls into a tunnel made of steel and concrete. Girders shrieked and the stone groaned. The tempest gradually died. Diago opened his eyes. They were on a subway platform. There were no exits. A train waited on the tracks, hissing as if it was a great silver dragon seething in pain.

Prieto held up the hourglass. The sand had collected in the upper chamber, suspended there by Prieto's will. "I can go no farther into the daimons' realm without violating our treaties. The train will deliver you to Moloch. Get on."

Diago managed to get one shaking leg beneath him. He had no idea what he intended to do, but right now, he wanted nothing more than to be away from Prieto.

Rafael clung to him, forcing Diago to let go of Miquel, or risk falling on them both. He rose slowly. The boy's heart beat quick and hard.

Diago tightened his arms around Rafael and whispered against his ear, "Trust me."

The boy shuddered.

Miquel stood and placed himself between them and Prieto. "You can't ask him to do this."

Prieto's smiles were gone. "That's where you're wrong—I'm not asking. You have two hours." He pointed at Miquel. "Or the sigil explodes, and with it, his heart. And should Miquel decide to be noble and sacrifice himself for the child, know this, Diago: if you fail, I will take Rafael from you and keep the boy with me. You can't hide him. I found him once, I'll find him again. And we will play this game over and over until I win." He scraped one long nail against the hourglass. The sand began to run. "The clock is ticking," he said.

Horrified by the angel's game, Diago snagged

Miquel's sleeve with his fingertips. The brief contact was enough to get Miquel on the move. The train's doors shut behind them when they boarded. Diago glimpsed the platform through the window. Prieto was gone.

The train rolled forward. Diago would have fallen with Rafael in his arms if Miquel hadn't caught him and pushed them into a nearby seat. Still in shock from the encounter with Prieto, Rafael clung to Diago's neck and made no sound. Diago rubbed his back gently as he used to do for Ysabel when she was afraid.

Miquel dropped onto the seat beside them. He hooked his arm around the pole and stared at the opposite side of the car with glassy eyes. Diago watched his reflection in the window. A long jagged cut severed the bruise where José's signet ring had caught the side of Miquel's face. He hadn't noticed it before . . . and he felt guilt for that failure, too.

Diago groped for the self-confidence that he'd possessed back at the apartment and found it gone. Prieto had slammed them through the realms with no preparation at all, and their bodies bore the shock of the transition. Worse, he didn't have the slightest idea how to circumvent Prieto or Moloch. When the train stopped, they would be at the daimon's door.

He and Miquel didn't speak. The only sound was the wheels clicking beneath them. Diago watched the lights fade, until everything outside the train was in darkness. Another rumble announced a second train passing in the opposite direction. Ghostly figures wandered the aisles of the other train. The creatures stared blankly out the windows, their faces circles of white, their mouths full of black. The images blinked by and were gone.

"Did you see that?" Diago asked Miquel's reflection.

Miquel didn't answer. He turned his head to the left and examined the car following theirs. He allowed his head to rest against the window behind them so he could look into the car in front of theirs. "They're on our train, too," he said. "Where's your gun?"

Mention of the gun restored some of Diago's equilibrium. He scooted far enough forward for Miquel to lift his sweater and retrieve the Luger.

"Silver tips?" Miquel asked as he slid the weapon from Diago's holster.

"You know they're all I use."

Rafael stirred as Diago slid back again. The boy pulled away from Diago and looked to the car behind them. With slow careful movements, he worked himself down to sit between Diago and Miquel. He made himself as small as he could, and hugged his ragged horse against his chest in a defensive posture that Diago recalled using when he was a child himself. Smaller targets passed unseen.

Rafael's wide eyes followed Miquel's hands as he checked the gun's magazine. "What are they?"

"Nefilim that have been turned," said Miquel.

"Into what?" Rafael asked.

Diago tilted his head until he could see into the adjoining car. Three of the creatures stood at the window.

They were naked, two males and a female, their flesh pale from their days underground. Their heads were unnaturally long, with pointed chins and ears. Dry cracked lips spread around their enormous canines. Eyes like saucers shined with the Nefilim's preternatural glow. The female's right arm ended at her elbow. The tallest male bore thick ropy scars across his chest, as if burned with acid. The other male showed no overt injuries, but Diago was sure that he, too, suffered the scars of a daimon attack.

Diago opted for discretion. No use terrifying the child even more, and while he wouldn't lie, he saw no point in being direct. "They are *'aulaq*," he said. "They were once Nefilim. Rather than face another incarnation, they choose to serve the daimon that turned them."

Rafael plucked his pony's mane. "I don't understand."

"If a daimon scars a Nefilim, we regain those wounds in our next life. It is like they scar our souls so that our bodies will remember. We cannot escape the curse of their damage, and some would rather remain dead than endure such agony with each rebirth."

"How do they stay alive?"

Miquel checked the round in the chamber. "They're vampires."

Rafael's eyes widened and he clutched his horse. He crossed himself three times in rapid succession and mumbled his way through several Hail Marys.

So much for discretion. Diago slipped his arm around

his son's shoulders and spoke to Miquel. "The bullets won't stop them."

"Their memories of pain will. And the silver *will* burn them." Miquel raised the gun and pointed it at one of the males. "It's something, at least."

All three of the 'aulaq ducked out of sight.

That wouldn't last long. "Why do they shadow us?"

"They're making sure you take Rafael to Moloch."

"I'm not giving him to Moloch."

"I don't expect you to."

"You're not angry about Candela?"

"No, but you should be. She r—"

"Miquel." He inclined his head at Rafael. He switched to Old Castilian—a medieval form of Spanish that bore the same relationship to modern Spanish as Old English did to English—so that Rafael couldn't understand him. "Not in front of the boy. There is nothing worse than to hear you're not wanted."

Miquel closed his eyes and exhaled slowly. "All right. Later then. We'll talk. Right now, we need to figure a way out of this."

Relieved, Diago switched back to Catalan. "I'm open to ideas."

"It's simple. We replace Rafael."

Diago knew Miquel too well to think he meant another child. "But how?"

"A golem."

"A golem?"

"Exactly. We can make Moloch think it's a real child by using Rafael's hair and blood."

Rafael narrowed his eyes at Miquel and tightened his jaw. Diago knew the incredulous look well because it belonged to him. It was just the first time he'd ever seen it on someone else's face.

He hurried to reassure the boy. "It will be a small cut and will only hurt for a little while."

"Mamá said I wasn't to do magic, that the mortals wouldn't understand."

Miquel pointed out the obvious. "There are no mortals here."

"Sister Benita says that magic belongs to the devil."

Miquel lifted Rafael's hat. "Is Sister Benita here?"

"She says that even if she doesn't see my sins, God will know."

Diago remembered hearing a similar conversation between Guillermo and Ysabel. "Of course, God will know," he parroted Guillermo's explanation. "God gave you that power, and if it came from God, it must be good? Yes?"

Rafael considered this. "I hadn't thought of that."

"Obviously, neither has Sister Benita," said Miquel. "It's settled. We'll use a golem."

"Except I can't create a golem. Only the angel-born Nefilim can breathe life into a golem."

Miquel leaned over Rafael and blew a soft gust of air against Diago's cheek.

Diago closed his eyes. "You would do this for him?"

"Is he yours?"

"Yes."

"Do you love him?"

"I want to try."

"Then how can I not?"

"I don't deserve you."

Miquel slid his wedding band off Diago's finger and put it back on his hand. "No. You deserve better. You just won't let yourself believe it."

A loud scraping noise drew Diago's attention back to the window. The three *'aulaq* had risen. The tall scarred vampire tapped the glass with a long ragged nail. Miquel raised the gun again. They flinched but did not hide.

Diago turned his face away from the *'aulaq* and said, "Moloch will expect a trick such as that."

Miquel shrugged and lowered his voice. "How is he going to know? He cannot touch the boy without destroying the child's innocence. Such an act would render the sacrifice impure. He must rely on the parent to validate the gift." Miquel rested his hand on Diago's shoulder. "He is so hungry he is bartering with angels. You are half daimon. You can convince him the sacrifice is real." He gave Diago's shoulder a reassuring squeeze then released him.

Rafael tugged at his pony's mane. "Am I angel or daimon?"

Diago ignored him and spoke to Miquel. "I'm not sure I can."

"Of course you can. Our lives depend on it."

The train slowed and, in counterpoint, Diago's pulse picked up speed.

"Papa?" A low whine crept into Rafael's voice.

Diago closed his eyes and made a conscious effort not to snap at the boy. "What?"

"Am I angel or daimon?"

"You are like me." Diago stood and tugged Rafael's hand. "You are both."

Rafael refused to budge. Diago couldn't help but wonder how so small a child could gain such weight on a moment's notice. He tugged harder, but Rafael resisted him. "Are we going to hell?"

Diago opened his mouth, then immediately shut it again. The fear in his child's eyes sapped him of any reassurances. *I have nothing to offer him but lies that even I don't believe anymore.*

Miquel stood as the train slowed to a stop. He took Rafael's elbow and slid him off the seat. "We're here."

That seemed to answer more than one question.

CHAPTER FOUR

Diago followed Miquel onto the platform. The tall scarred *'aulaq* stuck his head outside the door. Miquel raised the gun and took three steps forward. The *'aulaq* ducked back onto the train. No others emerged. Moments passed before the doors shut. The train rumbled away.

"Why didn't they get off?" Diago watched the lights disappear around a bend.

"They didn't need to. We are exactly where they want us to be. Where are we going to go?" Miquel asked, looking around.

Diago's eyes took in the wide platform, and he realized Miquel was right. A set of stairs descended into a dim hall. The only other exit was the tracks themselves, and Diago had no doubt that the *'aulaqs* were waiting for them in the darkness.

Rafael hugged his horse and craned his neck to look

down the stairs. "Is this hell? Sister Benita said hell was made of fire. I'm cold."

"I'm starting to wish Sister Benita was here." Miquel fingered the gun's trigger.

A note of warning crept into Diago's voice. "Miquel."

"*Ya, ya, ya.*" Miquel waved Diago's concern away. "But still."

Rafael linked his fingers with Diago's. "I lost Mamá's tear. Señor Prieto took it from me." His nose reddened.

Diago recognized the signs of distress. A full-blown crying jag would soon follow if he didn't figure out what Rafael was talking about. "Calm down and tell me, what tear?"

"It looks like a marble."

"Ah." Diago reached into his pocket and produced the carmine marble. Rafael brightened as if he'd been given the sun.

Warmth spread through Diago's chest, and he couldn't deny the pleasure he felt at mitigating the crisis with so simple a move. He glanced up at Miquel, who didn't appear half as pleased, but at least he wasn't frowning anymore.

Rafael clenched the marble in his fist. "Thank you! Mamá said as long as I held her teardrop, she would be with me." He shivered from the cold.

Now Rafael's attachment to the marble made sense. It wasn't a marble at all, but an angel's teardrop. Diago recalled that Candela's eyes had been that color, gold and carmine with streaks of black. An angel's tear was as precious as gold to a Nefil. No wonder the boy had been so frightened about its loss. "Put it in a safe place."

Rafael tucked the teardrop into his shirt pocket over his heart.

Diago's gaze quickly swept the barren station. "There is nothing here to make a golem with."

Miquel went to the steps and looked down. "Maybe down there."

Diago joined him. "How far to Moloch, I wonder?"

"Prieto gave us two hours. How long was the train ride?"

"Too long," Diago said. Every moment wasted on that train worked against them, but that was what Prieto wanted. Any advantage he gave to Diago and Miquel would be seen by the daimons as an attempt to cheat Moloch of his prize.

Miquel sniffed the air. Diago did the same and wrinkled his nose. Rafael mimicked them. Beneath the oily scent of industrial smoke and sewage was the distinct odor of decay and death.

"I'll go down first." Miquel lifted the pistol.

Diago shook his head and retrieved his knife. "No." He lowered his voice. "If there is anything down there, I will deal with it."

Rafael was pale beneath the dirty florescent light. He stared at the concrete steps, his lips pressed together.

Diago squatted in front of him and finally managed

a believable lie. "It's going to be okay. Will you trust me on that?"

Rafael touched the pocket that held Candela's teardrop. He nodded.

"Not much choice, huh?" The jibe won Diago a weak smile. "Stay with Miquel and do exactly as he says." He took off his coat and wrapped it around the boy like a cloak.

Rafael clenched the collar at his throat and gave Diago another nod.

Diago kissed his cheeks and rose. As he moved to the stairwell, he paused in front of Miquel. "If I call out, take your chances on the tracks. Watch out for him."

"You know I will." Miquel linked his pinky with Diago's.

They were close enough to kiss, and Diago considered it. They never knew when the last time might come, but he was also acutely aware of Rafael's presence. In all probability, Sister Benita had rendered her opinions on homosexuals, too, and Diago had no doubt those judgments encompassed the proverbial trinity of hell, fire, and damnation.

So with regret, he slipped away from Miquel and stepped onto the concrete steps, watching the shadows for any movement. Water dripped nearby and the hiss of steam curled through the air. He held the knife close to his body and out of sight. From this point forward, he intended to be the one giving out surprises.

He reached the base of the stairs without incident. A single bulb sputtered weakly and illuminated a door no taller than Diago's hips. Graffiti covered the door and the surrounding wall. A crude drawing of a red-lipped mouth with oversized canines opened around the words "TENGO HAMBRE." *I AM HUNGRY.* Someone else had scratched profanities into the paint with a rock or knife.

With his hand on the latch, Diago listened for any movement on the other side. He detected nothing. *Time to take a chance.*

The metal door groaned in protest as he forced it open. He hunched over and stepped across the threshold, quickly turning first left, then right. He was alone.

Feeble light revealed that he was in a sewer. The entire tunnel was no more than two metres wide. A trough ran between two narrow walkways. Judging from the amount of debris—newspapers, random pieces of clothing, stuffed animals, and abandoned toys—this sewer hadn't been flushed in decades. A heavy coating of sludge had accumulated in the gutter, probably the combination of a recent rain and seepage from a storm drain farther away.

The brickwork indicated this section had been around since the Romans had occupied the city. Like all of the old Nefilim, Diago knew the tunnels and tombs beneath Barcelona. They had used them to hide from the Church during the Middle Ages, and well into the eighteenth century. Even so, there were por-tions of the city where Los Nefilim dared not go, and this, like other sections, was one such place.

Diago quickly took stock of his surroundings. A square sign hung from one rusting bolt on the opposite wall. The street name had been scratched out, and someone *(or something)*, had written: "THE WAY TO PEACE."

If you find peace through death, he thought as he looked to his right. There, the tunnel disappeared into blackness so thick it could be felt. He couldn't navigate in such darkness. Although his night vision was far superior to that of mortals, he still needed a small measure of light to see.

He shifted his attention to his left, where the passageway continued for several metres before it branched into two separate tunnels. A narrow concrete footbridge linked the walkways across the troughs. The passage on the left disappeared into complete darkness. Within the right-hand tunnel, a few scattered ceiling lights blinked and flickered.

The slow steady throb of industrial machinery mimicked the pounding of drums. The sounds were disorienting, seemingly pouring from all directions at once, and Diago didn't discount that possibility. The sewer was most likely a labyrinth of side passages that amplified and distorted the acoustics.

Hypnotized by the beat, he stared down the tunnel and remembered. *They pounded the drums to cover the cries of the children as they burned. Those horrors had come during Solomon's last days, when his mind had succumbed*

to the terrors of the night, and I lived in banishment from the
palace and all that I knew.

Diago shuddered and forced the memory away.
The past was done, and lingering over ancient incarnations was the route to insanity. Besides, it was the
future that needed saving.

Keeping Rafael's face in his mind, Diago sheathed
his knife in his belt and got busy. Within moments, he
had scavenged through the muck to find a few sticks
of wood, an armful of clothing, and a -couple of shoes.

Back upstairs, he motioned for Miquel and Rafael
to move as far away from the stairwell as they could.
Diago deposited the items he'd collected against the
far wall. Miquel wasted no time sorting through the
refuse for the parts he needed. He used the wood to as-
semble a makeshift body for their golem. While Miquel
worked, Diago made another trip down into the sewer
and found an abandoned coat. He filled it with sludge
that he hoped was mud, and several newspapers and
handbills. When he passed the door on the way back
upstairs, he pushed it shut behind him. Hopefully, it
would be enough to block their conversations from
anything that might be listening below.

By the time Diago reached them the second time,
Miquel had already lashed together the sticks, using
one of the old shirts. He took the mud and paper that
Diago brought and shaped a crude head.

Rafael cast furtive glances at the stairwell and
chewed his lower lip as he handed the mismatched
shoes—one black, the other brown—to Miquel.

Miquel tied the shoes to the sticks and inspected his work.

Diago's heart sank. "No one is going to believe that's a child."

"Oh, ye of little faith," Miquel muttered as he concentrated on his work. "Give me a few locks of his hair."

Diago exhaled slowly and gestured for Rafael to come to his side. He took out his knife and cut three locks from Rafael's curls. The boy watched with interest as Diago handed the hair to Miquel, who sprinkled the shorn tresses over the golem's head.

"Now his blood. Not too much. Feed them too much and they take on a will of their own."

"Give me your hand," Diago whispered.

Rafael clenched his fingers into fists and backed up two steps.

Diago couldn't blame him. The knife must seem huge to him. "Please trust me, Rafael. It will only sting. Just a little." He held out his hand and was surprised when Rafael returned to him with no further coaxing. Diago took the stuffed horse away and set it aside. He opened Rafael's hand and hummed a short spell against his palm to numb the nerves. The song was too quiet to relieve all of Rafael's pain, but it would keep him from feeling the worst of the cut. "I'm going to prick your hand, and it might hurt. Don't cry out." He held Rafael's palm over the golem's head.

The child's face was white, but he gave Diago a tight nod nonetheless. As quickly as he could, Diago sliced a shallow gash across Rafael's palm. Tears leaked from the boy's eyes, but he made no sound.

"You are my brave child," Diago said as he moved the boy's hand back and forth over the golem's head. Rafael's blood dribbled over the misshapen brow.

Miquel used a sliver of wood to carve the symbols for life in the golem's forehead. The strands of hair took root, and grew until they were an exact replica of Rafael's thick hair.

Rafael was so intent on the changes within the golem, he barely noticed Diago binding his hand.

Miquel put his mouth on the golem's and hummed a low note. The pearlescent hues of his aura divided the air and flowed between the golem's mud lips. The golem lifted its eyelids and blinked slow and heavy.

Rafael gasped and took a step backward.

The hair on Diago's arms went up and he fell back with Rafael. "Jesus, that's creepy." He could have sworn the creature looked hurt by the pronouncement. The lopsided mouth merely amplified the eerie expression.

Miquel examined it critically and kept his voice low. "It's missing something."

"It's missing a lot."

Miquel took Rafael's hat and carefully adjusted it on the golem's head. "There. That's better."

Only because it shadowed the eyes, but Diago didn't say that. The sand was slipping through the hourglass. He had to hurry. "I have to carry it, don't I?" he asked, dreading the answer.

Miquel sat back on his heels and studied his handi-work. "Of course you do. He doesn't have knees."

"Jesus."

"Will you stop whining?"

"All right, all right." Diago stuck the knife in his belt and knelt before the golem.

The golem turned its bulbous head and looked from Miquel back to Diago. It whimpered.

Diago gritted his teeth. "What's wrong with it?"

"He senses you don't like him."

"Jesus."

Rafael glanced at the stairwell. "Sister Benita says we shouldn't take the Lord's name in vain."

Miquel made a face. "I hate Sister Benita."

"Everyone else does, too." Rafael came to stand beside Diago and held out his stuffed horse to the golem. "I'm sorry you're ugly and have to die for me. This is Aurelius. He is my friend. Hold him and he will comfort you." He tucked the stuffed horse into the crook of the golem's arm.

The golem snuffled at the horse's mane and re-warded Rafael with a grimace that Diago assumed was supposed to be a smile.

Rafael reached into his pocket and withdrew Candela's teardrop. He clenched it in his fist and glanced at the stairwell. "Did you mean it when you said I could live with you?"

Diago didn't have to think about his answer. "Yes. I promise."

Rafael nodded and twisted Diago's finger until Diago got the hint. Rafael pressed the tear in the center of Diago's palm. "Hold still," he said.

Miquel craned his neck to see what was happening. "Mamá said, '*Gólpe, gólpe, vuelta.*'"

. . . *strike, strike, turn.* . .

Rafael tapped the teardrop twice with his index finger before turning it clockwise. At first, nothing happened. Keenly aware of the time, Diago almost pulled away. Then the teardrop pulsed against his skin. Any thoughts of withdrawing from Rafael's touch left him. Golden light swirled up from the depths of the stone and became the veins of color within an angel's eye.

The teardrop split neatly in half, like a pair of carmine eyes. Diago half expected them to magically twinkle with Candela's mischief. Rafael hummed a mellow note. His aura passed through his lips in shades of green and amber. The breath of his magic swirled around the ruby eyes and became a small golden snake.

Rafael kissed his finger and pressed it to the snake's head. "Watch over my papa."

The snake slithered up Diago's arm to encircle his throat before it tickled his neck and coiled behind his ear. He felt the soft scales against his skin and realized this tiny spell didn't have the sophistication of Candela's magic, but Rafael's enchantment didn't need that level of refinement. He wasn't trying to deceive or lure Diago into acting against his will. This was a friend to carry, much like he had given up Aurelius to comfort the golem.

Impulsively, Rafael threw his arms around Diago's neck and kissed his cheek. Diago felt the warmth of a child he barely knew touch his soul, and that gave him the courage he needed to pick up the golem and stand.

Rafael hugged Diago's coat around him and returned to the far wall where he squatted with his back to the cold concrete. He gave Diago a small hesitant wave.

If we survive this, I'll do the best I can by you. I swear it. Diago returned Rafael's shy wave with one of his own, before he and Miquel descended back down to the sewer.

The thin slats that formed the golem's legs bounced limply against Diago's thigh. One of the shoes fell off. Miquel quickly reattached it and made sure the laces were knotted more firmly.

The golem was heavier than the sticks and clothes made it appear. Miquel had given it weight in order to fool Moloch, but it also meant the thing would be a burden to carry.

At the door, Miquel held the golem while Diago slipped through first. Miquel passed the creature back to Diago, who stood and gazed down the lit passageway again.

Miquel joined him on the walkway. He scanned the filth and discarded toys with contempt. "Moloch must lure them somehow. Look." He nudged a porcelain doll's head with his foot; the painted face wept tears of mud. "I haven't seen one of those since the sixteenth century." He glared down the tunnel. "How long has he been down here?"

"Want me to ask him?"

"Don't be an asshole." Miquel turned back to Diago and caressed his ear where Rafael's snake curled around his earlobe. "I'm not worried, you know."

"I'm glad one of us isn't."

"We've been through much worse than this."

"You always say that, and I'm always hard-pressed to remember just when."

Miquel slipped his hand behind Diago's head and kissed him hard and fast. Just as their lips parted, he whispered, "I love you."

Diago nodded, because for a moment, he didn't have the breath for anything more. "I'll be back for you."

"I know you will." He offered the gun.

Diago shook his head. "The knife will do. There's another magazine." He nodded at his left hip and Miquel liberated the silver tips from Diago's pocket. They didn't say good-bye. They never did. It always seemed so final, and Miquel feared "good-bye" might jinx them, so Diago said, "Watch for me."

"I will."

Without another word, he settled the golem firmly on his hip, and set off toward the lights. The golem leaned its head on Diago's shoulder. The stink of the thing roiled his stomach.

Where the tunnels branched, Diago used the narrow footbridge to cross. He didn't want to risk stepping across and losing his footing. If he stumbled and shattered the golem, there wasn't time to make another.

Several minutes later, he reached a bend in the tunnel. He glanced back. Miquel was gone. Diago licked dry lips and started walking again.

The passage seemed to go on forever. Overhead, the lights sputtered and left thick pools of darkness where the footing was treacherous. Diago lost all track of time—other than to know it was passing for Miquel—as he negotiated the narrow walkway and followed the lights. The pounding drums began to sound like the second hand of a clock, ticking away in the night.

Eventually, the scent of smoke tickled his nostrils as he drew close to Moloch's lair. The tunnel developed into a gradual incline and grew wider. The trough became shallow and soon disappeared, leaving a smooth floor beneath Diago's feet. All around him, hues of orange and yellow supplemented the harsh electric light. The air grew warmer until it became as hot as a summer day. The stench of rotting corpses gagged him. Diago found it hard to pull a clean breath into his body.

The golem squirmed in his arms. "I love you," it mumbled with a hoarse voice.

"Oh, sweet Jesus." Diago put his palm over the golem's face, not so much to shield it from what was to come, but to prevent Moloch from seeing it clearly. Regardless of his intentions, the motion seemed to soothe the golem. It clutched the stuffed horse and shivered less. If Diago merely glanced at the creature, he almost believed that he held Rafael. Maybe it would fool Moloch after all.

Diago held onto that hope as he rounded another bend. The passage opened into a cavernous room. Fire and electric light joined together to cast hellish shadows against the walls. Narrow stairs led up to a catwalk over seven metres off the ground. The catwalk spanned the greater part of the room and ended at an iron stage on the far side of the chamber.

Mounted in the center of the stage was a bronze statue with a bull's head and a man's torso. Twin tanks took the place of lions at either arm of the figure's throne. The wings of biplanes curved upward from the effigy's back. A string of hollowed bombs formed a necklace, and machine-gun turrets fashioned the crown. In the center of the statue's chest was an open door. Flames burned inside the cavity. The arms were held out, palms up, ready to accept the offering.

Through the metal latticework of the stairs and platform, Diago saw two 'aulaqs near the statue. He recognized the shorter male and the one-armed female from the train. The male's flesh had been burned from his back and thighs, leaving puckered scar tissue instead of skin. He pushed a coal cart filled with the severed limbs of corpses, which had probably been scavenged from Barcelona's tombs and graveyards. The male stopped next to the statue's massive hands. The female helped him load the body parts onto the upturned palms. When the hands were full, the two 'aulaqs pulled the chains that lifted the sacrifice into the open furnace.

Moloch needed to feed, and while the dead did not give him the same energy as a living sacrifice, the corpses prevented him from starving to death. The daimon was out of sight, but Diago had no doubt he was somewhere near the effigy, where he could inhale the smoke from the burning corpses.

The tall scarred 'aulaq that had almost followed them off the train was absent. Diago looked around the room. The missing vampire bothered Diago. The 'aulaqs traveled in packs, so the third one should be somewhere close. *But where?* Diago stared into the darkness. Nothing moved but shadows. If the third 'aulaq had backtracked to Miquel and Rafael, Miquel would deal with him; of that, Diago had little doubt.

As it was, he couldn't linger any longer. Not with time ticking against him. The metal walkway shuddered beneath his feet as he climbed the steel steps and mounted the catwalk. Far ahead, the female 'aulaq stepped away from the effigy, and Diago finally saw Moloch. Unmindful of the heat, the daimon stroked the statue's knee and cooed in a language so ancient that even Diago didn't recognize the syntax.

Halting halfway between the stairs and the statue, Diago waited for the daimon to recognize his presence. Moloch took his time. When he finally turned around, he trailed his fingers over the effigy's knee as if they were lovers interrupted.

Made with thin legs and thin arms, Moloch was a

brittle stickman who was no man at all. His elongated skull and pointed chin were more pronounced than those of his 'aulaqs, which were merely pale reflections of their master. The daimon's eyes were the color of smoke and nickel, white eyes, as if he had no eyes at all.

Dressed in a ragged robe, his only ornament was a leather pouch that hung around his neck. Moloch grinned around sharp teeth. "You came. Prieto said you wouldn't, but I knew you would." He extended one clawed hand, as if he could reach across the distance between them. "And you brought him."

Diago glanced at the golem. Rafael looked up at him. Diago's heart stuttered. Had he gone mad?

Then the golem blinked, its countenance listless, nothing like Rafael's expressive features. Diago's pulse slowed. Miquel's magic had finally taken hold. From the top of his head down to his mismatched shoes, the golem looked exactly like Rafael. As disconcerting as the resemblance was, Diago felt a small measure of relief. This might work, after all.

Moloch tapped his long claws together and licked his lips with a pale tongue. "Oh, Diago, I've always known you were one of us."

CHAPTER FIVE

Rafael sniffed the collar of his papa's coat and smelled the spicy odor of his sweat. Excitement tickled his belly. How many nights had he gone to sleep dreaming of being rescued from the nuns and their harsh voices full of fear? More than he could count. More than one hundred and one nights, or a thousand nights, or ten thousand nights, and more than he thought he could bear. His mamá had promised him that when he found his papa, he would finally be safe. Now they were together, and Rafael would never have to face Sister Benita or the other sisters again.

He tugged the coat around him. Something heavy caused the garment to hang to the left. Rafael reached inside the pocket and allowed his fingers to travel over the rectangular shape. The sensation of his father's warm magic bled through the paper. Rafael peeked into the pocket to find a thin ray of silver, gleaming in the pallid light. Was his papa rich?

A quick glance at the stairwell assured him that Miquel had not returned, so Rafael enlarged the opening to reveal the box Señor Prieto had given to Doña Rosa. A drop of blood from the cut on his hand smeared across the glass. Rafael tried to wipe away the smudge, but he merely succeeded in dirtying the glass even more. He smoothed the paper over the box, then took his hand from the pocket. Maybe Papa wouldn't notice the dirt, or if he did, maybe he wouldn't think that Rafael had made the mess. He didn't want to make Papa angry, so he formulated the lie he would tell about how the box got dirty. Sister Benita had taught him—indirectly—to always have a lie prepared in advance, because any hesitation on his part meant an extra whack from her ruler.

The sound of Miquel's footsteps startled Rafael. The top of Miquel's head came into view. He paused on the stairs and looked down as if he was examining something at his feet.

Curious to know what Miquel might be looking at, Rafael stood quietly. He was very good at being quiet, because Sister Benita could hear pins drop on angels' heads, or something like that. Rafael could never remember exactly how the saying went, because Sister Benita usually delivered her speeches while waving a ruler in his face, and the ruler always distracted him.

Miquel's breathing was labored like when Señor Prieto had placed the sigil over his heart, and that wasn't good. Rafael had worried that Miquel might die, but Señor Prieto had promised that as long as Papa did the right thing, Miquel would be fine.

Miquel certainly didn't look fine. Rafael's heart kicked up a notch when the older Nefil stumbled over the top step. He righted himself and pressed his palm against the wall. Color returned to his cheeks and the episode seemed to pass. Rafael remembered the hourglass, and Señor Prieto telling them they had two hours. Had it been two hours? Miquel offered Rafael a wan smile that did nothing to reassure the youngster. He came to Rafael's side without further incident and sat with his back against the wall.

A gentle tug on Rafael's coat sleeve was all it took for Rafael to sit and lean against Miquel. He jammed his hand back into the coat pocket and fingered the mirrored casket, not caring if he tore the paper. He needed something to hold.

Miquel put his arm around Rafael and pulled him close. "Now we wait. Be very still and quiet."

The gun rested in Miquel's lap, alongside a magazine that held more bullets. Entranced by the blue metal and the lingering remnants of his father's aura around the grip, Rafael tentatively touched the gun. Miquel moved the weapon out of Rafael's reach, but not before Rafael noticed the beat of Miquel's pulse against his wrist. His heart pounded very fast, like Rafael's did when he knew he was in trouble with Sister Benita, only Miquel wasn't frightened. Nothing seemed to scare him. He had fought Señor Prieto, and although Miquel lost, he had caused Señor Prieto to be afraid for just a moment. The thin lines of silver in Señor Prieto's eyes had constricted until they were almost nonexistent, just like Mamá's eyes changed when she was afraid.

Rafael was sure that Miquel's fast heart had nothing to do with fear. Something else was wrong, and Rafael suspected it had to do with the sigil. He touched Miquel's wrist.

Instead of pulling away, Miquel hugged Rafael a little tighter. "I'm all right."

That was a grownup lie, like when Sister Benita said that she would forgive Rafael as long as he told the truth, but then punished him anyway. The only difference was that Rafael knew Miquel wasn't trying to trick him, so he nodded even though he could see that Miquel wasn't all right.

Gently, so as not to disturb Miquel, Rafael pulled the box from his pocket and peeled it free from the paper. He ran his thumb over the figure of his mother and tried to remember her face, but her features were lost in the mists of his memories. His stomach ached with grief.

He hugged the box to his chest and snuggled closer to Miquel's warmth, his gaze locked on the stairwell. He recalled summer evenings when the heat faded from the day. He and Mamá had danced to a phonograph record made more of scratches than music. Mamá taught Rafael to listen past the record's defects to find the strains of the guitars.

Listen to the music, Rafael. The guitarist tells you what you must do. Let him move you. Trust your body.

He could almost hear the record now, a distant rhythm that pulsed quick and hard. Rafael tightened his grip on the box and closed his eyes. He dozed and dreamed that the golden serpents on the mirrored box came to life. The three snakes slithered from their places and coiled together to become one mighty serpent. The magical snake crawled off the glass and onto the back of Rafael's hand. From there, it climbed through the folds of his ragged clothes to reach his mouth.

As the snake slipped through Rafael's parted lips, a different music chimed through his dreams. The notes were more ethereal, like the sound of rain, or of stars sighing in the night. Rafael inhaled and, in doing so, he took the magic into his soul.

Listen, Mamá had said. *Trust your body.*

CHAPTER SIX

"**O**h, Diago, I've always known you were one of us," Moloch crooned again. His gaze was locked on the golem. A string of drool hung from his lower lip.

"I am nothing like you," Diago said.

"Oh, but you are." Moloch tilted his head and squinted at the golem. "And for that reason, I do not trust you."

Fortunately, the golem chose that moment to move. It murmured against Diago's shoulder. "I am your brave child. I love you."

Diago shushed the golem and attempted to summon an expression of parental concern. Instead, he feared he showed nothing but disgust. He covered his bad acting with chatter. "Look at the child. He is suffering. Let's make this deal and be done."

The daimon only smiled.

What is he waiting for? "Do you really believe I would

try to trick you? Do you think I'm suicidal?" Diago gestured to the *'aulaqs*. "I'm outnumbered. They're faster than me. I'd never make it back to Miquel." He shook his head and managed a conciliatory tone. "Stop playing games, Moloch. Give me Prieto's coin and take your place. I will see to the rest."

Moloch touched the small leather sack he wore around his neck on a thin piece of leather. "You'll hand this death machine over to Prieto?"

"He holds Miquel hostage."

"You'll trade your son for your lover?" Moloch rubbed his palms. His long nails scraped together. The sound reminded Diago of roaches clicking across a floor. "Betray one to keep the other? No. This is too easy. I don't trust you, Diago."

The feeling was mutual. Something was wrong. Moloch was too confident.

Where is that missing 'aulaq? Concerned that Moloch might mistake vigilance for fear, Diago didn't survey the floor. He held Moloch's glare with his own.

Centuries of hiding his homosexuality from others helped him knuckle down on his emotions. Diago knew the rules: *Never let them taste your fear. Never let them know you're different.* People saw what they wanted to see and heard what they wanted hear. They made assumptions based on their personal beliefs, which often blinded them to the truth. Daimons were not unlike mortals in this respect. All Diago had to do was give Moloch the ritual words, and then let the daimon's mind do the rest.

"I am the father of Rafael Díaz de Triana," Diago said. "And as his parent, I vouch for this sacrifice in order to gain peace for our -people. The parent guarantees the child, Moloch. Those are your rules."

"Any blood relative can give the child."

"I have no blood relatives in this life."

"Yes, you do." The daimon exuded triumph.

Beneath Diago's feet, the walkway quivered as someone mounted the platform behind him. His heart hammered. He tightened his grip on the golem and felt something brittle puncture his palm. *The sticks.* Jesus, he had to be careful or he would break the thing apart. He loosened his hold on the creature and affected a calmness he didn't feel.

Diago turned to face whatever horror Moloch had summoned. He wasn't surprised when the third *'aulaq* finally arrived. But he still didn't know what the daimon had in mind.

The vampire crept forward until only a -couple of meters separated them. He narrowed his eyes at Diago, but his words were directed at Moloch. "You promised me, Moloch. You swore he'd never know what happened to me."

"No, Alvaro." There was no mistaking the glee in Moloch's voice. "That is what you *wanted* to hear. I only swore that he would never seek you out."

Alvaro. His surname of Alvarez was the only clue Diago ever possessed about his father's name. Alvarez meant the son of Alvaro.

His son. . .

"No," Diago said. The smoke crawled into his throat and threatened to choke him. "I'll not be the butt of your jokes, Moloch. This is a lie."

"Look closely, Diago," said Moloch. "Look very closely, and tell me it's a lie."

The vampire didn't flinch away from Diago's examination. They bore no resemblance to one another, or none that Diago could see. Moloch had twisted the *'aulaq's* flesh into a parody of humanity. Only the dark green eyes retained the slightest hint of mortality . . . and something more. In those irises, Diago thought he glimpsed the same strange lights that illuminated his own gaze. His blood turned to ice.

Jesus, his eyes—they are like mine.

"This is the truth, Diago." Moloch cackled, high and thin, like nails on glass.

Alvaro took a step forward, and Diago backed away before he caught himself and stopped. He glanced over his shoulder and gauged the distance between him and Moloch. They were less than fifteen paces apart. Flight was impossible. Diago had nowhere to go. He faced Alvaro again and he saw the truth in the *'aulaq's* face. Alvaro was his father.

Stunned, he almost strangled on the questions he wanted to ask. There were too many. *Why did you do this yourself?* was one he kept coming back to. And deep inside his heart, the child within him cried, *Why did you leave me?* But Diago locked those words behind his teeth. He wouldn't show either Alvaro or Moloch his vulnerability. Not here. Not now. All he could push through his lips was, "Why?"

Alvaro gripped the railings on either side of the walkway, his knuckles white and hard. "Because I couldn't stand to watch you suffer anymore."

Diago scoffed. "Me?"

"Yes. You. I know what they did to you in your first-born life."

Diago shook his head. "No. The past is dead. Leave it in its grave."

Alvaro had no intention of doing so. He advanced slowly, as if he approached a dangerous animal. "You can deny the truth all you like, but the angels, the daimons, Solomon—they all destroyed the good inside of you. They cursed you, Diago! Every incarnation after your firstborn life was a misery." He spoke halt-ingly at first, but as he articulated his grief, his words grew like a terrible flower and bloomed with his wrath. "You fought the world, and you fought alone, full of helpless rage. You forgot how to love. I stayed by your side as long as I could. Call me a coward if you like, but the day came when I knew I couldn't bear to watch you go through another life in such sorrow."

"So you just walked away." Diago flung the words like a blow.

Shame flushed Alvaro's cheeks until they were as ruddy as the effigy's flames. "Why should I continue to suffer when you refused to change?"

Diago couldn't believe what he was hearing. "You abandoned me, and that is *my* fault?"

Alvaro stopped in front of Diago. His gaze flickered from the golem back to Diago. "How dare you judge me!" He spat on the ground. "Look at yourself, Diago. Nothing's changed. You're going sacrifice your child. And for what? Your lover? Your happiness?" Alvaro snorted in derision. "We are the same. Look at me and see your future."

"I will never be like you." He wanted to wipe Alvaro's smugness into Moloch's fires, but he knew he couldn't say a word without destroying both Miquel and Rafael.

Alvaro held his arms out. "Give me the child. You're not worthy of him."

Diago hesitated. What would Alvaro do when he discovered the golem wasn't Rafael? If he really reviled Diago for offering his son as a sacrifice, he might play along with the deception. Maybe. Could he even disobey the daimon? Diago couldn't take the chance.

"The boy is mine," he said as he whirled on Moloch. "Trust me or not, Moloch."

"I choose not. Give him to Alvaro. If Alvaro says the child is true, I'll give you the pouch. Then you can go. Alvaro can make the offering in your stead. At least he is a true child of the daimons, unsullied by angel."

The golem whined. Diago shushed the creature and turned back to his father. He had no choice. If he lingered here much longer, he would never make it back in time to Rafael and Miquel.

As he passed the golem into Alvaro's arms, he met his father's gaze and said, "I learned to love." It was the only defense he had.

Alvaro sneered. He cuddled the golem and muttered reassurances to it as he measured its dull gaze. Alvaro's motions slowed. Comprehension slowly morphed over his features. He ducked his head so Moloch couldn't see and whispered to Diago, "I misjudged you. And I am glad."

Relief washed over Diago. He might save Rafael, after all. He gave no indication that Alvaro had spoken, had no idea what he would say if he could've answered without Moloch hearing his words.

Moloch's voice shattered the moment. "Is the child true, Alvaro?"

Alvaro nestled the golem into the crook of his arm. "The child is genuine." Fury returned to sparkle in his eyes as he glared at Diago. "You are dead to me."

Diago made no sign the words meant anything to him one way or another. His father's curse was meant for Moloch, not him. Alvaro had chosen to shield his family over servitude to the daimon. They both knew that Alvaro wouldn't live to see another nightfall. Whatever else his faults, Alvaro had just attempted to save his grandson's life. Whether they actually made it out of the tunnels alive was now up to Diago.

He held out his hand. "The coin, Moloch."

Moloch lifted the pouch over his head and threw it to Diago. He caught it neatly and opened the bag. Inside, a silver medallion rested at the bottom of the pouch. White light spun and flashed brilliantly in the center of the coin before it dimmed. Diago closed the pouch and clenched the prize in his hand.

"Run, coward," said Alvaro as Diago passed him. "Run fast."

Diago took his father's warning to heart. When Moloch discovered he'd been cheated, they would come for Diago next. He wouldn't let his father's martyrdom be in vain.

The golem reached out for Diago as he passed. "I love you." It sounded so much like Rafael, Diago almost went back. "I am your brave child," cried the golem. "I am brave, Papa."

Diago ran.

The golem's shouts grew panicked as it called after him. "Papa! I love you! Kiss me! Papa! Can I live with you? Do you promise? Do you promise? *Kiss-me-I-love-you!*"

Diago clattered down the stairs and almost fell when his foot hit the concrete. *Too much blood. We used too much blood, and now it has taken a will of its own and doesn't want to die.*

"*IloveyouIloveyouIloveyouIlove . . .*" Moloch took up the golem's cries, and the horrible duet echoed off the walls of the daimon's chamber.

Diago fled from that sound, across the massive

room and back into the passageway. After he was around the first bend and well away from Moloch's lair, he ducked into an alcove and opened the pouch with a shaking hand. He spilled Prieto's coin into his palm and thought the angel's designation of "coin" was highly inappropriate. The medallion was far too heavy to be a modern coin. Another bright flash radiated from its center before dimming back to a dull silver color. Diago closed his hand over the coin and searched his pockets.

All he had were two *pesetas* and a few *centimos,* each of which were too small. Sick with despair, he reached deeper until his fingers touched the magnifying glass. The circumference of the brass case was a little large, but the weight of it was close to Prieto's coin. It would have to do. He had nothing else. Diago transferred the coin to his pocket and placed the magnifying glass in the pouch.

He clenched the pouch in his right hand and resumed his flight. The walls blurred as the tunnel narrowed again. He summoned the Nefilim's speed, alert to the sounds behind him. The daimon's mimicry had stopped, and silence pervaded the darkness.

The smooth floor gave way to the sewer's trough. Diago found the concrete walkway that led back to the subway station. Overhead, the lights winked out one by one as he passed beneath them. A hitch formed in his side. He ignored the pain and didn't slow.

Over the pounding of the machinery, Moloch's enraged howl suddenly filled the tunnels. The sound ricocheted off the walls and seemed to envelope Diago in its wrath.

Moloch had discovered their deception. He yowled at the remaining 'aulaqs, and while the distance obscured his words, the intent was clear: they were coming, and they were furious.

Diago drew his knife. Terror lent him speed. If he could make it to the door, he could slam it shut and bolt it—if there was a bolt, that is. He desperately tried to remember if there was one. He glanced over his shoulder. Nothing but darkness bled behind him.

The lights overhead flickered and dimmed.

And if they go out, I will drown in the dark. A sob crawled into his throat. He swallowed it and rushed onward. The time for self-pity was long gone.

The passage curved hard to the left. Diago slowed and took the turn at half speed. Meters away, the two tunnels joined together. The little footbridge was just beyond the juncture. Past the footbridge, Diago saw the door that led to the station. With sanctuary in sight, his hope surged. He summoned the last of his energy and sprinted for the door.

At the junction of the two tunnels, the scarred male emerged from the second passage. He slammed against Diago and caught him midstride. Diago was still moving when they hit the wall together in a tangled mass of limbs.

Searing pain lanced Diago's hip and shoulder. Tumbling into the sewage, they slid through the muck, neither of them able to gain an advantage. Diago clutched the pouch in one hand. With his left, he slashed wildly with his knife and caught the *'aulaq's* eye with the tip. The vampire screeched and fell backward.

Diago kicked the *'aulaq* in the face. His heel caught the vampire in the mouth. The move won him a brief respite. Diago didn't waste it.

The lights flickered overhead, but they didn't go out. Not yet. Moloch wanted him to see his death coming, of that Diago was certain.

Unable to get his feet under him, he crawled to the footbridge. He grabbed the slab and pulled himself up. Before he got to his knees, the female *'aulaq* appeared from the shadows. The ball of her foot caught his chin. He spun and dropped the knife, but the pouch remained tight in his hand.

The male *'aulaq* grabbed Diago's fist. "Let it go. I'll tear your fucking fingers off." He pried at Diago's pinky and wormed his thumb into the space between Diago's palm and finger.

The female grabbed Diago's other wrist and jerked his arm high against his back.

Overhead, the ceiling vibrated gently. The train. The train was coming, but Diago knew he was going to miss it. He tried to twist away from the vampires, but they held him immobile.

Down the passageway, two eyes shined like lamps as Moloch strolled out of the darkness. He grinned and held Alvaro's severed head before him like an offering.

Diago's throat burned. *I will watch for you, Alvaro. I*

will watch for you, and when you come in your next incarnation, we will begin anew.

Moloch's voice interrupted Diago's grief. "Did you really believe you could win, Diago?"

The male *'aulaq* succeeded in forcing Diago's pinky open. He leaned down and bit Diago's finger off.

The pain was terrible. It was as if acid flowed through his veins. Diago screamed. He bucked so violently that the female almost lost her grip on him.

Hot with nausea, Diago looked down. The wound smoked, cauterized by vampire's poison.

Moloch positioned Alvaro's head in the trough in front of Diago. "He didn't resist. He knew he was dead the moment the lie fell out of his mouth. Do you see the destruction you leave in your wake, Diago? *You* killed him." The daimon stepped back and admired his handiwork. "Now I need a new *'aulaq*." He considered Diago as if seeing him for the first time. "You can take your father's place. Come to me willingly or I will force you. Your choice, Diago. Say the words. Swear your oath to me and keep your spirit whole. Otherwise, I will make you my slave." The daimon shoved his signet ring beneath Diago's nose.

Diago spat on the ring.

"Break his arm," said Moloch. "He'll let the pouch go."

The male grinned and snapped Diago's arm like twig. Diago heard it before he felt it. Both times he was almost sick.

Excited by the violence, the female snapped at Diago's face. He turned his head. Her fangs dug furrows into his cheek. The male leaned down and licked the blood away.

Overhead, the lights went out.

The darkness came down in one ugly rush.

"Soon, you will like the dark," Moloch whispered.

The male *'aulaq's* teeth touched Diago's throat.

Rafael's golden snake struck.

Rafael sat up straight when he heard the strange voice howl. His father's scream followed soon afterward.

Rafael's heart pounded. "Papa?"

Miquel jerked upright and fumbled for the gun.

Somewhere in the distance, a train rumbled. Rafael couldn't tell if it was coming their way or not. He stood and threw off his father's coat, clutching the mirrored box. He stared at the stairwell and willed his papa to come up the stairs. Nothing but blackness yawned from the depths.

"Stay here," Miquel commanded. "He needs help. I'll be back."

But he was moving too slowly. The sounds of a fight echoed up the stairs. There wasn't time to wait for Miquel. Rafael bolted for the door.

"Rafael! Stop!"

Rafael ran down the stairs as fast as he could. Just as he reached the bottom landing, Miquel appeared at the top of the stairway. The sigil writhed around his heart, twisting like snakes in a nest until the lines joined and formed an hourglass. Their time was running out.

Rafael ignored Miquel's order to return upstairs. He had waited so long for his papa. He wasn't going to lose him now.

He pulled the little door open and squeezed through. Light pushed back the tunnel's blackness. The scene froze him in place.

To his left, he saw his papa on his knees. Blood tangled his hair and dripped from his chin. His face was so bruised, Rafael almost didn't recognize him. One arm hung limply at his side, the bone jutting through his flesh.

One of the vampires staggered away from Papa. Rafael's golden snake was wrapped around his head, blinding his eyes. The 'aulaq clawed his face and made little grunting noises.

The female 'aulaq used her stump to hook the cord of a small sack off the ground. She draped the string over her head, and the pouch swung between her flabby breasts. She narrowed her eyes at Rafael and the light behind him. Unconcerned about his presence, she did little more than growl while tightening her fingers on Papa's wrist.

The creature in front of his papa was the worst. He could only be Moloch, the daimon that Señor Prieto wanted to appease.

Moloch smiled with the same kind of gotcha smile that Sister Benita used whenever she caught Rafael doing something bad. "There you are, my pretty child."

The daimon's mellifluous tones surprised Rafael.

He had imagined Moloch's voice as being both loud and hard. Instead, the daimon's timbre made Rafael think of the sea. He imagined waves gently lapping at the beach. Lulled by the serene beats, Rafael lowered the box and took a step toward Moloch.

"That's right, sweetness," the daimon cooed. "Come to me. I will give you peace."

Papa twisted hard in the vampire's grip. The motion broke Rafael's paralysis.

"Run, Rafael!" Papa shouted. "The train! Get to the train!"

The female vampire slapped him, but she was too late. Moloch's illusion fell away, ruptured by his papa's fear. The hair on Rafael's arms rose. He lifted the mirrored box and sang like his mamá had taught him.

A loud boom shook the air. Sparks flew when the bullet nicked the tunnel wall just over the male vampire's head. Rafael lost his song and looked over his shoulder.

Miquel had finally come. He lowered the gun and sang a chord of his own. His magic brought forth a white sigil borne of rage. The lines sawed the air and left blades of light in its wake. Miquel channeled the glyph at the male 'aulaq. The sigil struck the vampire's chest, and he shrieked like he was on fire.

Deafened by the reports in the enclosed space, Rafael panicked. His mother had told him to listen and now he couldn't hear! He shook his head but sound eluded him.

Two more shots thundered through the tunnel. The female yowled like a burning hound and clutched her eyes. Cordite filled the air and tickled Rafael's throat.

Listen to your body, his mother had said.

Moloch shoved Papa aside with his foot. Rafael raised the mirrored box a second time and focused on the daimon. Buried within the tinnitus caused by the shots, he found his mother's ethereal tones once more. The stars sang their lonesome song, and Rafael caught the notes one by one with his boyish soprano. He exhaled, and in doing so, released his mother's magic from his soul. Mist traveled through his lips and turned into a mighty golden serpent, ten times larger than the little magic he had sent with his papa. The snake from his dreams. It touched the mirrored panels of the box and transformed into a million golden snakes. They struck Moloch as one.

The serpents wrapped the daimon in their shimmering scales. Moloch twisted and tried to bat them aside. One snake slithered into the daimon's mouth. His flesh smoldered and smoked. He tore at the serpents, but they bit him and ripped his thin flesh from his hooked black bones.

Rafael felt his father's tenor lend strength to his fledgling song. Together they sang their spell to life.

The rumble of the train provided the bass.

The female 'aulaq fled back toward Moloch's lair, clutching the pouch as she ran.

The decoy had worked, but Diago felt no triumph at the deception. His only concern was for Rafael. Darkness feathered his peripheral vision. He fought to remain conscious.

Suddenly, hands were on his collar—it was Miquel. He dragged Diago away from Moloch, jerking him to his feet. Miquel shoved him toward the door. "Go!"

To Diago's horror, though, he saw Rafael standing in the center of the trough. The boy faced Moloch, who was merely meters away. Rafael sang with his angel's voice, and his spell rose straight from his heart.

Shards of glass and golden light flew out of Rafael's hands. Diago barely had time to sing a chord of his own. He lent his fading strength to his child's magic, pushing his own sigil behind his son's spell. Splinters of light pierced Moloch's flesh.

The daimon's shrieks cracked the walls.

Stunned by effect of his magic, Rafael staggered back and looked at his empty hands in wonder.

Diago started toward his son—*my brave, magnificent son*—but Miquel caught his arm. "Go!" he repeated. "I'll get him!"

Diago cradled his injured hand and didn't argue. He was in no condition to carry Rafael. He lurched toward the door.

Overhead, the train was slowing.

Miquel grabbed Rafael around the waist and lifted him. "Hurry!"

They got through the door and slammed it shut as Rafael's spell died. They half fell, half staggered up the stairs where the train awaited them. No *'aulaqs* peered from the windows. The train's doors whooshed open.

Miquel pushed them inside. They had barely entered the car when the doors closed and the train rolled away. Moloch's howls followed them down the tracks.

Diago hooked his good arm around a pole and spun into a seat. He reached into his pocket and withdrew Prieto's coin. He expected relief, only to be confounded with sorrow. He'd won, but the price had been dear . . . and he wasn't thinking about his arm.

Miquel collapsed beside him. Rafael worked his way between them. Diago barely noticed when the small golden snake slithered down his arm and into Rafael's waiting palm where it once more became a perfectly round angel's tear.

Rafael closed his fist over the teardrop. "My ears hurt."

Miquel made a sound that was lost somewhere between a sob and a laugh. He covered his mouth with a shaking hand.

Diago glanced down at his arm. Bone glimmered wetly beneath the torn skin. He closed his eyes and took several deep breaths until his nausea subsided. He promised himself he wouldn't look again. "Hold on, Miquel. We're almost there." He reached over and touched Miquel's thigh.

Rafael looked at the sigil on Miquel's chest. He lifted Candela's tear to the angel's glyph, and hummed a song that was almost inaudible beneath Diago's tinnitus and the rumble of the train. To Diago's surprise, Prieto's sigil weakened beneath Rafael's magic.

Color slowly returned to Miquel's face. He opened his eyes and regarded Rafael with wide eyes. "Diago?"

"I see it." No other Nefil could untangle a sigil created by an angel, not this easily, and Rafael was just a child.

What would he become when he learned his song?

The train slowed, and another question leapt to his mind:

What would Prieto do when he saw I cheated Moloch? Diago's heart quickened. He remembered Prieto's threat: *You can't hide him. I found him once, I'll find him again.*

We'll see about that, you son of a bitch. "Rafael, hide."

"I'm not done."

"I'm better, Rafael." Miquel took the boy's wrist. "Do as your father says. Now!"

Rafael ran down the car and scooted under a row of seats. He curled up in the shadows. Prieto's sigil slowly gained strength again, but not so much as to prevent Miquel from standing. He helped Diago rise, and together they moved away from Rafael's hiding place.

The train stopped and the doors opened. Prieto waited on the platform. He glanced at Diago's hand. "What happened?"

Diago threw the coin at him.

Prieto caught it and flipped it once before making it disappear within the folds of his clothes. Without taking his eyes off Diago, he gestured for Miquel to step forward. When Miquel was before the angel, Prieto placed his hand on Miquel's chest and, after several moments, the sigil disappeared. Only then did Diago breathe somewhat easier.

Prieto repeated his question. "What happened?"

Diago had his lie prepared. "Moloch tried to cheat me. He wanted my son, then refused to give me the coin. I fought him for it and won."

"You're lying."

"I am the deceiver."

"I can force you to answer."

"You got what you wanted. Leave me to my pain."

Prieto considered Diago, and for a terrible minute, Diago thought that Prieto would push his advantage. Instead, the angel surprised him and said, "Get off at the next stop. I summoned Guillermo. He'll be waiting for you with a car."

"Does he know what happened?" Miquel asked.

Prieto stepped back, away from the train. "He knows what I told him, and I told him less than I told you."

Which meant he had informed Guillermo there was trouble that involved Diago and Miquel, but little else. Prieto waved his hand and the doors closed. The train eased away from the station.

Diago remained standing until Prieto was out of sight. He watched his own reflection in the glass and tried to see his father's face in his own. All they shared were the same haunted eyes.

Miquel stroked the back of Diago's neck. "Come. Sit and rest."

Diago obeyed him. He didn't have the strength for anything more. Suddenly, he wanted Rafael's warmth near him. "Rafael? You can come out now."

The boy scrambled from beneath the seat and settled in between them. Diago put his arm around his son and hugged him close. While Rafael dozed, Diago told Miquel about Alvaro. Twice his grief choked him so hard, he couldn't go on. But he didn't cry. Diago's tears had abandoned him long ago, and left nothing but a desert in his soul.

They emerged from the train into an empty station. Diago had no idea where they were. On the far wall, a clock moved its hands toward the hour of three.

Diago leaned heavily on Miquel as they followed the stairs up to the surface. Between his injuries and his trauma, he could barely lift his feet to navigate the endless steps. Every footfall sent bolts of agony through his body. The 'aulaq's poison had settled in his veins. He clenched his teeth together so hard, his head hurt. He was cold, and couldn't remember what he did with coat or his hat, or even why he was out so late.

For some reason, he kept thinking they had left Rafael behind, but whenever he called his son, Rafael answered him. He sounded far away, and Diago began to fear that Prieto had made good his promise, and stole the boy away again.

Then they were outside. The fog had cleared, blown

away by a breeze borne by the sea, and the stars shined overhead, brilliant in the black sky. The pungent smell of cigar smoke wafted over them.

Diago heard Guillermo's voice before he saw him. The big man easily took Diago from Miquel's arms. "Hurry. The car is over here. I've had to pay the police off twice already. No one is supposed to be here this time of night."

Diago laughed before he could stop himself. *He's worried about the police . . .* Unnerved by his own hysteria, he covered the sound with a cough. Were it not for Guillermo, he would have fallen to the pavement.

With Miquel's help, Guillermo maneuvered Diago into the backseat.

Suero was in the driver's seat. He watched them in the rearview mirror. "Do you need help?"

"No," Guillermo and Miquel answered simultaneously.

Diago tried to see beyond Miquel. "Rafael. Where is he?"

"Who's Rafael?" Guillermo asked as he squeezed in beside Diago.

"I'm here, Papa."

"Come quickly." He held out his hand and Rafael approached the car as if it might bite him.

"Is this your car?" Rafael climbed into Diago's lap and curled up against him.

Guillermo's mouth dropped open. "You want to explain this, Diago?"

"I'll explain." Miquel leaned inside and gathered Rafael into his arms. "Ride up front with us, Rafael. It's a bumpy trip, and Papa's hurt."

Guillermo took off his coat and spread the heavy garment over Diago. Careful of Diago's arm, he shifted his bulk sideways in the seat, and placed his palm over Diago's forehead.

As they pulled away from the curb, Guillermo growled. "Talk to me, Miquel."

So Miquel talked, and while he spun their tale, Diago passed into fever-dreams. He dreamt of a fire that burned white-hot, and a city reduced to ashes. He dreamt of people running through the streets, their bodies blackened by the flash that incinerated their homes. The dream-fires morphed into sigils, wards that spun and guarded the lanes leading into the town of Santuari, where Guillermo's Nefilim lived.

Diago felt the magic of Los Nefilim wash over him and cool the fire in his veins. He dozed fitfully and awoke when gentle fingers brushed against his forehead.

Juanita spoke to him, but her voice was distant, like Rafael's had been at the train station. He wanted to ask her if she ever regretted taking her mortal form. Did she ever wish she was angel again, and could she find Candela?

Before he could form the questions, Juanita spoke to someone behind her. "Bring him to my examining room. I'm going to go wash up." Then she left them, her black hair flying behind her as she ran toward the house, her bare feet skimming the ground as if she weighed no more than air. Maybe she still had her wings. Maybe they just couldn't see them anymore.

Guillermo picked Diago up as if he was a child and carried him to the side entrance that led to Juanita's small clinic. Miquel opened the door. Guillermo managed to get Diago inside without bumping his arm. He placed him on a cold white table.

Juanita had already scrubbed up and was filling one of her vicious needles.

Diago found his voice. "No morphine."

Juanita ignored him. "Cut off his sweater for me." She capped the needle and set it aside.

Miquel grabbed a pair of scissors and went to work.

Guillermo kept his hand on Diago's forehead. "He's burning up."

"One thing at a time, *corazon*. First the arm. He is healing too fast and I'm going to have to break it again before I can set it." She opened a bottle. "The fever is coming from an infection. I'll deal with that next."

Miquel peeled away the sweater and breathed a curse. Diago didn't bother looking at the bruises that covered his torso. He winced at the smell of alcohol. "Where's Rafael?"

"I'm here, Papa," he said from the doorway.

Lucia nudged the boy aside with her hip as she came into the room, carrying a pot of steaming water. "Where did he come from?"

"He's Diago's son," said Miquel.

Lucia did a double take and set the water on the

counter. "You see, Miquel? You can't trust daimon." She fixed her vicious glare on Diago. "Are your lies catching up to you, Diago?"

"Shut up, Lucia." Miquel shot her a murderous look.

"All of you shut up." Juanita didn't spare Rafael a glance. "Take the boy out of here, Lucia. He doesn't need to see this."

Lucia shrugged and started to go.

Diago grabbed Guillermo's wrist. Not Lucia with her caustic mouth and jealous eyes. She made no secret of her dislike of Diago, or her love for Miquel, and she would gladly sacrifice the one for the other. She would torment Rafael with questions and twist his answers to suit her gossip. All these thoughts crystalized in Diago's mind in a flash, but he couldn't push the sentiments past his dry tongue. All he managed to say was: "Not her."

Guillermo nodded. "I'll take care of him, Lucia. You see to Ysabel and make sure she doesn't wander down here. Come on, Rafael."

Rafael looked up at Guillermo and held his ground. "I want to be with my papa."

"We'll come back when the doctor has set his arm."

"But—"

Diago caught Rafael's eye with a small wave of his hand. "Do as you're told."

And Guillermo, intuitive to others as he always was, reached down and picked up Rafael as easily as if he was a puppy. He brought the child to Diago. "Say good night. My wife is the best doctor in the world and she'll have him up and about in no time. Your papa will see you when he wakes up."

Rafael leaned down and pushed Candela's tear against Diago's palm. "Do you remember how to do it? *Gólpe, gólpe*—"

"*Vuelta*," Diago whispered. "I remember."

White gauze hid Rafael's worried face as Juanita draped the loose bandage over Diago's cheek. She gave Miquel a mask and instructed him to hold it over Diago's mouth. She asked, "Are you sure you don't want the morphine?"

He nodded. The sickness that accompanied the drug brought him worse agonies than the pain of a broken arm.

"Breathe deep." She turned a dial on a small tank and he smelled ether flow into the mask. "Count backwards for Miquel. Diago?" Her palm rested against his face. "Count for Miquel. Ten . . ."

" . . . nine . . ."

"That's it," Miquel murmured.

And at seven, the pain receded beneath the veil of sleep.

Diago awoke to moonlight creeping across the bedroom's floor. He wore someone else's pajamas. Judging from the size alone, the shirt belonged to Guillermo, which was just as well, since it easily fit over the plaster cast that hugged his arm. His cheek was swollen and stiff. He probed the gauze and felt the stitches beneath.

Thousands of aches assailed his body, and he would have remained perfectly still, except a wave of nausea cramped his stomach. He tried to sit up.

Guillermo's large hand came out of the darkness to grip Diago's bicep. He helped him sit on the edge of the mattress and held a bucket while Diago vomited. With nothing in his stomach, Diago suffered through a few minutes of dry heaves before the sickness passed.

Guillermo handed him a handkerchief and set the bucket aside. "You've got a nasty infection. Here." He poured a glass of water and added a white powder. "Juanita said to drink this. It will settle your stomach."

He took the glass and tossed back the mixture like a shot. He didn't even ask what it was. The soapy after-taste made him wince.

"That's one of her nastier potions." Guillermo took a flask from his pocket. "Chase it with this."

Diago took a long pull from the flask and tasted sweet red wine. "You have a bottle of this somewhere?"

"Trust me. You're not ready for the bottle." He fixed the pillows and helped Diago sit up before he took a second glass and poured water in it. "Sip. If you hold all of that down, I'll give you some aspirin; although I recommend the morphine."

"Aspirin will be fine."

"Tough guy."

"How long have I been out?"

"Three days in and out of consciousness. It's not the break but the infection. It looks like the fever has passed, though, and that's a good sign."

"Where's Rafael?"

Guillermo sat back in the chair and pulled a cigar from his pocket. "We put him in with Ysabel for now. He was exhausted the first night. Fell asleep standing up while I bathed him. But he was in top form today and full of himself. He asks about you all the time. You can see him in the morning. Miquel wanted to stay with you, but he wasn't in much better shape than Rafael, so I pulled rank. He takes the days and I take the nights." He offered Diago a cigar. "Want one?"

Diago shook his head and pressed the cool glass against his chest, quietly absorbing all that Guillermo told him. Rafael was safe for now and that was all that mattered.

"Congratulations, by the way. I have to admit I'm a little jealous. I wish I could have skipped the diapers and the teething and the tantrums, and just had a five-year-old deposited on my doorstep."

"He's six."

"Really?" Guillermo snipped the end off his cigar. "He's what the Scottish would call a wee one." The flare of his match sent spirals of light through the stone in the large signet ring that he wore. "Want to talk to me about what happened?"

"What if I don't? You'll pull rank?" He instantly regretted his tone—that was the pain biting. He leaned his head against the headboard and tried to wish the words away.

Guillermo seemed to take no offense. He tilted back his chair and opened the window. His tone remained mild, but he cut to the bone nonetheless. "Don't be angry with me. I'm not the one biting your fingers off in exchange for your oath."

"That's not how it happened."

"Don't tell me Moloch didn't try to bring you under his banner."

"He tried."

"And you said no."

"That's why I'm here and not there." Diago sighed. He didn't want to fight. "What do you want to know, Guillermo?"

"Miquel says that an angel took advantage of you in Triana."

"I'm not sure which of us took advantage of the other."

"Miquel seems certain."

"She said she had a song."

"And she gave you one. I delved his soul. This is his firstborn life, Diago. He has no past, only a future."

"Then does it matter which of us was the aggressor?"

"It matters to Miquel, because if Candela raped you of your will before she raped your body, he doesn't have to face the question of your infidelity."

Diago took a nervous sip of water. He hadn't thought of that, not in the rush of Prieto's accusations and Rafael's fears.

"Likewise, if you assert that you had a hand in your own seduction, you don't have to face the question of your vulnerability. Given the two scenarios, I'd say Miquel's is closer to the truth. Candela enchanted you."

Diago's throat was on fire, but when he tried to drink, he choked on the water. He swallowed the truth hard. Guillermo was right, but that didn't mean that Diago had to love him for it. "Sometimes I hate you."

"I'm your friend, not your dog."

"I don't have a dog."

"You should get one. They always love you and never question you."

"Call it rape if you want. It doesn't change how I feel about Rafael."

"And it shouldn't. It's not his fault." Guillermo drew on his cigar. He added softly, "Or yours."

Maybe. Maybe not. Diago tapped the glass with one restless finger. He sidestepped Guillermo's compassion by changing the subject. "Did Miquel tell you about Alvaro?"

"Your father?" Guillermo nodded. "Yes. What happened to Alvaro isn't your fault either. Whatever his reasons, he made his choices."

"I have some decisions to make, too." He stared at the opposite wall.

"What do you want, Diago?"

"I want Rafael to be safe."

"He can't be safe and be Los Nefilim. We are born to fight for one side or the other."

"Except for me."

"Except for you." Guillermo exhaled a cloud of sweet-smelling smoke into the air. "How's that working out for you?"

Diago remembered Alvaro words: *You fought the world, Diago, and you fought alone. You sustained yourself on anger, and you forgot how to love.*

Guillermo tapped the ashes from his cigar into a saucer. "This is the part where you usually say 'fine.' "

Jerked from the memory, Diago started. "What?"

"Fine. I say: 'How's that working out for you?' And you always respond with: 'Fine,' like you're biting the word in half. But now you're not saying that it's fine to be a loner."

"I'm rethinking my position."

"I see."

"Rafael changes things."

Diago glimpsed Guillermo's crooked teeth as he smiled. "You're right about that. Ysabel is why I've settled here and let the younger Nefilim be my eyes and my ears across the land. One day, she'll be old enough to take care of herself. For now she needs protection."

"So does Rafael."

Guillermo nodded. "Yes, he does, more so than you know. Miquel told me what that child can do. He's powerful, Diago, and the daimons will try to take him while he is young so they can shape his allegiance to their needs."

"I know."

Guillermo lifted the cigar to his lips and took two

puffs before he realized it was out. "Stay here at Santuari as long as you need to."

"Because of Miquel." The others wouldn't protest Miquel's place in the small town Guillermo had spent years building with his most trusted Nefilim, and they tolerated Diago for Miquel's sake.

Guillermo seemed to read his thoughts. "You know if anything ever happens between you and Miquel, I will make a way for you to stay here."

"I make my own way."

"There's that fucking pride of yours," Guillermo muttered. He found his matches and relit his cigar. Again the flame illuminated his ring. He met Diago's gaze before he shook out the match and plunged them back into semidarkness. "What do you want to do?"

On the bedside table, tucked between two bottles, was Candela's tear. Diago relinquished the glass and took the carmine teardrop in his hand. A thin line of gold flashed once from the depths of the stone, and it brought to mind Rafael holding up the mirrored box. Guillermo was right. Once Moloch spread word of the child's power, the daimons would come for his son as they had come for him.

"It's time I picked a side."

Guillermo frowned in the glow of his cigar. "Are you sure about this?"

"Yes. If I swear allegiance to you, Los Nefilim will have to watch over Rafael, too."

"You don't have to swear your fealty to me so I'll watch over your son."

"I trust you, but what about the others? What if something happens to you, or me, or Miquel? What then? The daimons and angels will treat him like they treat me: a battleground in the flesh." He raised his fist to his lips and clenched the marble so hard, he feared it would break. "They'll manipulate him and maim him because the end justifies the means." Diago wiped his mouth, uncertain how the rage that normally burned so deep within him had suddenly risen up like molten lava.

Guillermo extinguished his cigar in the saucer and leaned forward to touch Diago's shoulder. "Hey. You need to rest."

Diago got out of the bed.

"What are you doing?" Guillermo started to rise.

Diago held his hand up, staying him. "Don't move. I can do this."

"You don't have to do it tonight."

"Yes, I do." He knelt before Guillermo and almost lost his balance beneath a wave of dizziness.

Guillermo caught his arm and steadied him. "You are proud and stubborn, Diago Alvarez."

"You should know. They're your qualities, too." Diago pressed Candela's tear between his palms and waited.

Guillermo sighed in defeat and placed his hands over Diago's, so that they looked like a priest and supplicant praying together. "Pledge your magic to me. No one or nothing else."

"I pledge my body and my magic to you, Guillermo Ramírez de Luna, the one true King of the angel-born Nefilim. I swear to uphold your laws and remain true and faithful to you and the angel-born Nefilim in this life, and in all my lives to come. This I do swear." He took Guillermo's hand and pressed his lips against the signet ring that bore the multicolored stone.

Guillermo leaned down and kissed Diago's cheeks, careful of the bandage that covered his stitches. "And I accord you, and your family, all of the protections and privileges and rights of Los Nefilim." He kissed Diago's cheeks again. "Now please, for the love of Christ, get back in the bed before my wife comes in and kills us both."

"You will arrange a formal ceremony. With witnesses. They all must know."

"Yes." Guillermo helped Diago back into the bed.

"And Los Nefilim will watch over Rafael."

"Yes."

"And you and Juanita will be his godparents."

"We will be honored."

"I need Miquel."

"I'll get him. Now rest. We will talk more tomorrow." He drew up the quilts to Diago's chin. "You've done the right thing, Diago." He turned, and for such a large man, left the room without a sound.

Moments later Miquel slipped inside and shut the

door. He came straight to Diago and took his hand. "Christ, you're frozen." He went to the open window, pulled the shutters closed, and shut the window before he returned to the door.

Diago heard the lock click into place. "What are you doing?"

"Giving us some privacy." Miquel slid under the quilts and wrapped his arms around Diago.

He smelled of cigarettes and soap and beneath it all, a fragrance all his own, a scent both hard and sweet for which Diago had no name. Diago rested his head on Miquel's chest and closed his eyes, savoring the warmth of him.

Miquel murmured, "Guillermo said you swore fealty."

"Why do you sound sad? I thought you'd be happy."

Miquel arms tightened with his frustration. "I wanted so badly to prove that I could take care of you."

"You do. You give me what matters."

Miquel relaxed somewhat, but he was still upset. Diago heard it in his pounding heart. "I just wish you had talked to me first. It was a big decision. I should have been a part of it."

Diago traced the tattoo on Miquel's bicep. The intricate seal of Solomon matched the one engraved in Guillermo's signet ring. Sensation was slowly returning to his numb fingers, and he felt the power of Guillermo's binding within the tattoo's ink. "All this time together, and we still manage to hurt each other."

Miquel made no answer, but his heartbeat slowed as his anger left him.

"And I'm sorry," Diago said against his chest. "I should have told you about Candela. I just felt like a fool when it was over. And I was ashamed."

Miquel's arms tightened around him. "You have nothing to be ashamed of. The angels bewitch us into thinking that we make our own decisions so we'll do their will. She used you badly. They all have." Miquel stroked Diago's hair. "But they won't use you anymore." His voice turned hard and made him sound angry, even though his heart beat calmly. "Now you are one of us, and we watch out for our own."

"It doesn't matter. I think that is what I finally realized. Even under Guillermo's protection I would've had to submit to Candela, if that is what they wanted." He lifted his head and was surprised to see Miquel smiling.

"Oh, my bright star." Miquel gently smoothed the tape that had loosened on the bandage covering Diago's cheek. "You're not the only one who has been keeping secrets."

"What do you mean?"

"Guillermo has plans, and you were the only missing piece. No matter how much the others have pushed, he said he would never force you to take the oath because of a promise he once made to you. Now that you've joined us, we can move forward."

"Move forward into what?"

"Be still and sleep. We'll talk in the morning." Miquel hummed a tender song.

Diago fought the pull of his magic. Guillermo had insisted that Diago pledge his magic to him and no one else . . . and something clicked. What Diago couldn't do alone, they might do as a group.

"He is going to rebel."

Miquel stopped humming. "Not rebel. We can't do that without harming the mortals, but neither will we follow the angels blindly anymore. That was why I defied Prieto." Miquel whispered against Diago's hair, "And I will do it again for you. Never doubt that." He resumed his tune.

Diago closed his eyes. His pain dissipated beneath Miquel's magic and sleep crept over him. Down the hall, a grandfather clock ticked the seconds away, one majestic minute after another. Diago lost track of the beats and eventually fell into a deep dreamless sleep.

CHAPTER SEVEN

Voices murmured outside his door.

"Is he awake?" It was Rafael.

"Shh, I'll look." Ysabel answered him.

"Your mamá said don't."

Ysabel sighed with as much exasperation as a seven-year-old could muster. "I know what I'm doing. Now you be quiet and let me work."

Diago sat up and blinked against the midmorning light. Miquel had left him. The spot where he had slept was cold. Sometime during the night Miquel had placed Candela's tear back on the bedside table.

Diago ached all over, but not nearly as badly as he had last night. He was never sure which hurt worse: the actual injury, or the rapid healing that came afterward. Either way, the pain set his teeth on edge.

"I don't know, Ysa." Rafael continued. "What if Papa gets mad?"

While the children argued, Diago found the bottle of aspirin Guillermo left. He dry swallowed three. After a brief moment of consideration he tossed a fourth into the mix.

"Uncle Diago won't get mad," said Ysa. "Sometimes he gets cranky. Then he looks at you from the side of his eyes like this."

Diago knew precisely what kind of look she meant. He was making it as she spoke.

"He is really very nice once you get to know him."

"Thanks a lot, Ysa," he mumbled as he looked across the room.

Someone must have gone to Doña Rosa's house to retrieve their belongings, because his suitcase and guitar were beside the wardrobe. At the sight of the guitar, a tremor passed through his hand, but Diago didn't look to his missing pinky. *I'd do it again. I would do it all over again to keep them safe.* He curled his remaining fingers around the edge of the cast.

Rafael lowered his voice. "I'm scared, Ysa. I don't want to go back to the nuns."

Shadows moved beneath the threshold as Ysa moved closer to Rafael. With a child's innocence, she misinterpreted Rafael's angst. "You don't need to be scared of nuns. Do you know what my papa says?"

Draped over the chair Guillermo had used last night was Diago's old dressing robe. Miquel must have put it there for him. Diago managed to stand and put on the garment without too much difficulty.

"My papa says—" There was another pregnant

pause, during which Diago imagined Ysa checking both directions to make sure no grownups were near. "We are the sons and daughters of angels. We are Los Nefilim. Nobody fucks with us and wins."

Diago made a mental note to discuss that statement and its particular phrasing with Rafael. He limped toward the door.

"I don't know what that means, Ysa. What are fucks?"

"Shh! Not so loud."

Rafael whispered, "I just want my papa to love me."

Diago paused with his hand on the doorknob and breathed his son's name. *I know how now, Rafael. I know how to love, and that I can give you.* Diago exhaled past the knot in his throat and opened the door. "Good morning."

Both children jumped back from the door in surprise. Ysa's cheeks turned almost as red as her long auburn curls, which were wild around her face. She quickly read the disapproval in his eyes. "That's the face," she whispered to Rafael.

Rafael went white.

"What face would that be?" Diago raised an eyebrow at her.

Obviously, figuring the best defense was a solid offense, she filled the hall with chatter. "Are you feeling better, Uncle Diago? You look much better. Doesn't he look better, Rafael?"

Diago raised his hand, and she stopped talking. "Would you do me a favor, Ysa?"

She nodded. "Anything for you, Uncle Diago."

"Would you find Miquel and let him know I'm awake?"

Relief washed over her countenance. "Yes!"

She whirled and was halfway down the hall before Diago called her name. "Just to let you know: if your mother heard that language, she would be very angry. At both you *and* your papa."

Ysa paused and considered this. "Okay, Uncle Diago. You won't tell, will you?"

"Not this time."

She grinned at him before she turned and thundered down the hallway to find Miquel.

Diago turned his attention to Rafael, who had backed against the opposite wall. The boy was nothing like the urchin Diago had rescued from Prieto, yet he seemed even more delicate without all the dirt shadowing his face. His hair had been brushed until it gleamed. He wore a pair of Ysabel's trousers and one of her old sweaters. The clothing swallowed his small body. In his arms was one of Ysabel's rag ponies.

Before Diago could speak, Rafael blurted, "It's-one-of-Ysa's-old-toys-she-said-I-could-have-it-I-didn't-steal-it." Then he burst into tears.

The sudden onslaught of emotion took Diago off guard. "Good God, what is this? Why are you crying?" Although it was an effort, he knelt and held out his arms. "Come here, Rafael. It's all right." He coaxed the child into his arms and hugged him. "I believe you. Ysa has a good heart, and she gives a lot of her toys away."

Rafael sniffled and clutched the pony to his chest. "You're not mad?"

"No. I'm not angry, and no one is sending you away." Diago stood and offered Rafael his hand. "Come inside and let's talk."

Rafael held onto Diago as if he was afraid to let go.

Diago guided him into the room, then closed the door. As he did so, he realized the child must have been worried sick over an uncertain future these last few days.

"Come up here." Diago sat on the edge of the mattress and patted the coverlet.

Rafael climbed onto the bed as gentle as a kitten.

"Look at me." Diago drew him close. "You are so important to me, I was willing to face a daimon. And you, Rafael Díaz, saved my life. Now after all of that, do you think I'm going to send you back to an orphanage and that awful Sister Benita?"

"Are you?"

"No. Not ever."

"Am I in trouble because of the fucks?"

Diago laughed before he could stop himself.

Rafael's lips trembled with a smile. "What's funny, Papa?"

"Nothing." He shook his head. "No, you're not in trouble, but don't use that word."

"Okay," he wiped his eyes. "We weren't expecting you to be up. You just scared me when you opened the door so fast."

"Maybe." Diago conceded the point, although he

suspected Rafael's fright came from someplace deeper. "Maybe you're frightened because you're in a new place with -people you don't know?"

"I know you and Miquel. And Ysa is nice to me and lets me play with her toys. Don Guillermo is loud but he is very kind, and Doña Juanita likes it when we're quiet."

Diago smiled. It all sounded very apt. "But?"

Rafael plucked at the pony's mane and admitted, "But I don't know how to act here."

"Why don't you be yourself?"

"Because being myself makes grownups angry."

"You mean grownups like Sister Benita?"

Rafael nodded.

"Hmm, well, we are going to do things differently. I know it's frightening for you to be in another new place, and you and I, we barely know each other. This is very hard for all of us. But we're going to work at understanding one another." Diago took Candela's teardrop and placed it in his palm. "Now, I promise to be patient with you while you get used to living in Santuari." He kissed the tear, then placed it in Rafael's hand. "Can you promise to be patient with me while I learn how to be a father?"

Rafael nodded solemnly. "I promise, Papa." He kissed the teardrop and handed it back to Diago.

"No. You keep it."

Rafael wrapped his fingers around his most prized possession. "Are you sure you don't need it anymore?"

"I'm sure. You keep it safe."

A relieved smile brightened Rafael's face. "That means you're going to be okay, right?"

"For now." Diago smoothed the child's hair, glad to see him calm and smiling again. "No more staying away from each other. If you get scared, you come find me, and we will talk. All right?"

Rafael deposited the teardrop in his pocket and hugged Diago. "Okay."

"Good. Tell me what you've been doing."

"Ysa showed me the farm. Her cat had kittens, and she said I could have one. Can I have a kitten, Papa?"

"Let's think about that."

"Is that a maybe or a no?"

"Maybe."

Rafael searched Diago's face with the intensity that only a child could have. Diago had no idea what kind of internal debate the boy entertained, but he eventually decided that let's-think-about-it-maybe was the best answer he was going to receive. "Okay."

A knock came on the door and Miquel entered, cradling a tray. "Ah, you found him." He brought the tray to the bed and set it beside Diago.

Rafael said, "I know I'm not supposed to bother Papa while he's getting well, but he said I could come in."

"Well, I'm not the doctor, but—" Miquel pressed his palm against Diago's forehead and pretended to assess his temperature. "I think you've made him better. His eyes look brighter and I thought I heard him laugh a little while ago. He's not so gloomy when you're around. We'd better let you stay with him all the time."

A slow smile spread over Rafael's face at Miquel's teasing.

Miquel lifted the cloth napkin and feigned surprise. "Oh, look at me. I forgot the spoon. Can you go to the kitchen and get one from Lucia?"

Rafael scooted off the bed and paused. He returned to pat Diago's hand. "I'll be right back, Papa." Then he left them.

When Diago was sure Rafael was out of earshot, he turned to Miquel. "How is he doing?"

"If he becomes afraid in the night, he goes under the bed and sleeps there. He gave Juanita a hell of a scare the first time she went in to check on him and she found him gone."

"He probably feels safe there. Ask her not to chastise him for it. We'll teach him he doesn't have to be afraid anymore, but it'll take time."

Miquel poured Diago's coffee and added some hot milk. "I know. We're still working on you." He gave Diago a sweet roll. "Eat something for me."

Diago accepted the plate but didn't touch the food. "Are you sure you're all right with this? With Rafael?"

"Honestly?" Miquel's movements slowed as he poured himself a cup of coffee. "I don't know how to be a parent and the thought of it scares me." He met Diago's gaze evenly and lowered his voice. "But I do know this: I love you. And because I love you, I will try to be a good father to him."

Relieved, Diago squeezed Miquel's shoulder. "I couldn't ask for more."

Miquel smiled and spread a thick coat of jam across a piece of toast. He nodded at Diago's untouched sweet roll. "Eat. Guillermo said we can have the guesthouse out back. Lucia has aired it out for us. We can sleep there tonight if you like."

"I would like that."

"I'm going into town this afternoon." He wiped the crumbs from his fingers. "Juanita has taken Rafael's measurements, so I thought I'd pick him up some clothes. He needs new shoes."

Diago put down his coffee. "I don't have money for all of this. Sell my guitar. I can't play it anymore."

Miquel made a face. "I'm not selling your guitar. You'll play again. Just be patient with yourself and don't worry about money."

"Miquel—"

"Don't worry about money." He dropped the napkin over the spoon just as Rafael entered, triumphantly bearing a spoon from the kitchen. "Everything is going to be all right. Isn't it, Rafael?"

The child looked from Miquel to his father and back again before he smiled and guessed the correct answer was, "Yes?" He almost upset the tray as he climbed back onto the bed and presented Miquel with the spoon. "Is Don Guillermo rich?"

Diago fixed him a plate. "Yes."

"Are we rich, Papa?"

Diago chuckled. "Us?"

"See?" Miquel finished his coffee. "You come back and he smiles. You make us rich, Rafael." Miquel winked at Diago. "I'll be back this evening. Don't overdo it. Juanita said you took some very bad hits."

"I'm fine." Diago waved away Miquel's concern and glanced at Rafael. "Leave the tray. I'll take it in when we're done."

"Are you sure?"

He gave Rafael a sweet roll. "Yes, I'm sure."

Miquel barely made it to the door before Guillermo arrived to peek inside. "Ysa is shouting to the heavens that you've returned to us."

"He'll be back to his old surly self in no time," Miquel said as he passed him.

Guillermo laughed and slapped Miquel's back. "Rafael, I need to talk to your papa. Can you help Ysa count the kittens again and make sure they're all still there?"

Rafael brightened at the mention of the cats. "Can I, Papa?" he asked around a mouthful of food.

"Swallow, then go."

Rafael grinned. "Thank you, Papa!"

Once Rafael left, Guillermo shut the door and turned to Diago. They measured one another, and Diago instantly recognized the sly look in his friend's eye.

"What are you up to, Guillermo?"

He sat in the chair and took out a cigar, composing himself into the very picture of innocence. "Me?"

Diago wasn't having it. "Los Nefilim aren't obeying the angels blindly anymore. Prieto questioned me about it."

"Ah, that." He rolled the cigar between his finger-tips, but he didn't light it. "You're not ready for that information yet. First we have the ceremony, then you take my mark, then we talk. For now, I can't treat you any differently than I do the others. Meanwhile—" Guillermo took out an envelope and handed it to Diago.

Diago opened it to find more money than he'd made in a year while working in Sevilla. "I can't take this. I've done nothing to earn it."

"Oh, you'll earn it. I've even got your first assignment for you."

Diago closed the envelope.

"You're going back to the Casa Milà to pay a visit to the Ferrers."

"Back into the lioness's den?"

Guillermo grinned. "Tell Señora Ferrer that you cannot teach Enrique anymore."

"You have my eternal allegiance for that alone."

"Pay her back any advance that she's given you. That is what part of the money is for. Make sure she's happy."

Diago frowned. "How happy am I supposed to make her?"

"Make her happy with money. Arrange your visit while Señor Ferrer is home. See if you can get him to give you his thoughts on the political situation. I want to know where his allegiances rest. Don't try to sway him. Just find out what he thinks."

"That man hates me."

"He'll like you better—" Guillermo gestured at Diago bruised face "—like you are now."

"Beaten to a pulp?"

"He thinks himself a pugilist. A man's man. He'll ask you what the other guy looks like and you tell him."

"That I killed my father?" Diago wasn't sure which of them was more surprised by the statement. "I'm sorry." He swallowed hard, looked up at the ceiling, anywhere other than at the empathy in Guillermo's eyes. "I don't where that came from."

"Came from your heart," Guillermo said. He leaned forward and tapped Diago's knee. "Hey. Look at me."

Diago met his friend's gaze.

"Your father gave his life for you the same way you were willing to lay down your life for Miquel and Rafael. You did not kill him, Diago. He made his choice. Honor him and watch for him. That's all you can do."

Diago hardened his heart and pushed down his emotions. Guillermo was right. "Okay."

"Good. So you tell Ferrer you were in a fight with an anarchist and you kicked the son-of-a-bitch's ass. You saved a little child from a crazy man with a bomb. You're a fucking hero."

Diago nodded. "Okay, I got it. Why is Ferrer important?"

"His family has stakes in a munitions factory that might help us when the war comes."

"You're sure there is going to be one?"

"I've had dreams, powerful dreams. I saw a column

of death marching up from the south. Madrid was an open crater full of the dead. I'm afraid Spain will soon be soaked in blood." Guillermo rose and tucked his cigar between his lips. He started for the door, then paused. "That coin Prieto wanted, did you get any idea what it was about?"

"Moloch made it."

"That's bad."

That was an understatement. "It's a bomb of some kind and it's devastating. I dreamed it flattened an entire city."

"In Spain?"

Diago tried to recall faces of the -people. "Somewhere in the east. Korea? Maybe Japan? I don't know for sure." He shook his head. "But Prieto said something odd. He said that with the bomb, the war would stop after four, maybe five mortal years. He said it would be less than a minute to the angels, an hour to Los Nefilim."

Down the hall, the clock chimed one soft note after the other. Guillermo chewed the end of his cigar thoughtfully. When the music ended, he said, "I have a bad feeling this is going to be a very long hour for us, my friend."

"Even so, I'm glad to be in your ser-vice again." As Diago said the words, he knew them to be true.

"And I'm glad to have you. Now rest. We'll soon have much to do." Guillermo slipped out of the room.

Diago relished a moment of respite. Outside the children laughed as they passed by his window on

PART TWO:
WITHOUT LIGHT OR GUIDE

CHAPTER ONE

Barcelona
30 November 1931

Bright sunlight fell onto the crowded boulevard at the Liceu metro station. The clear, sharp notes of light drove back the sounds of darkness feathering beneath the trees. The city's clamor fashioned waves of sound, which sent ribbons of color over the silhouettes of people and cars.

Diago's eyesight blurred at the profusion of pigments and distorted motions. It was like the Nefilim's version of double vision.

An attack of vertigo, accompanied by mild nausea, washed over him. He swallowed his bile and forced himself to focus. *I've got to learn to manage this.*

Miquel opened his mouth, but Diago silenced him with a gesture. He narrowed his eyes and looked over Guillermo's shoulder. A curl of blue-gray waves trailed a car, dissipating as the vehicle turned the corner. Two men stood beneath a tree on the avenue. They laughed, and the golden colors of their mirth bloomed like flowers before their lips, obscuring their faces.

Another wave of dizziness washed over him. *Damn it.* It was no use. If he moved now, he'd risk falling. He clenched his teeth and waited for the episode to pass. Glancing down at the sidewalk gave him no relief. Milky spirals wavered around pebbles as a train entered the station below their feet.

"Is it the chromesthesia?" Guillermo asked.

Diago managed a quick nod. All of the Nefilim were able to see color in the sound waves around them— the ability enabled them to work their magic—but the vampire that had bitten off Diago's finger was one of the old ones known as the *'aulaq,* and the older the *'aulaq,* the more potent their venom. Likewise, Diago's advanced age had saved his life. The amount of poison he had absorbed would have killed a younger Nefil, but he hadn't escaped unscathed. Besides the obvious loss of his finger, the toxin seemed to have amplified his natural faculties to the point of disability. While Juanita—Los Nefilim's doctor, and Guillermo's wife— said it wasn't a textbook case of chromesthesia, the symptoms were close enough, so they had all added a new word to their vocabulary.

One that Diago could have happily lived without.

Miquel edged closer to Diago until their arms touched. It was a casual movement that gave them a few moments of contact without seeming intimate to others. "Do you need to sit?" he asked.

"No." Diago lied. "I can manage it." At least the episodes were becoming less frequent. The same couldn't be said for the phantom pain from his missing pinky. Diago curled his fingers into a fist around the white bandage encompassing his hand and forced himself to focus on the ground.

A trail of rose-quartz patterns followed the click of a woman's heels. The designs scattered like crumbs as the sounds gradually settled into the distant shadows Diago was used to seeing, and these were easily ignored.

Relieved, he said, "It's passed."

Guillermo frowned at Diago's discomfort. "Are you sure you're ready for this?"

I'm ready to be home in bed, but he didn't say that. "I can do the job."

Guillermo evaluated him. "I think you need another week."

"We don't have a week." It had already been three weeks since he had emerged from the metro after his battle with Moloch. This meeting with the munitions industrialist, Salvador Ferrer, was Guillermo's idea, and Diago needed a way to prove his loyalty to Los Nefilim. He touched the scar on his face, which had faded to an ugly red slash. "No mortal heals this fast. If we want to deceive Ferrer with your story, I have to go now."

Guillermo withdrew a cigar from his breast pocket and lit it as he considered the situation. "Compromise with me. We could wait two days."

A pair of nuns descended into the station. One of

them scowled at Guillermo and his cigar. He gave her a wolfish grin. She crossed herself and kept going.

Diago said, "I don't have that luxury."

"What are you talking about?"

Miquel jammed his hands in his pockets and watched the crowd with restless eyes. "You worry too much."

"I don't worry enough," Diago snapped. He lowered his voice to a whisper and leaned close to Guillermo. "Some of the other members of Los Nefilim have insinuated that because my father gave himself in service to Moloch, I will do the same." Guillermo opened his mouth, but Diago didn't give him a chance to speak. There was nothing to deny. Alvaro had sworn himself to Moloch and became a vampire, an *'aulaq,* in order to avoid reincarnation. It was the greatest shame a Nefil could bring upon his name or family.

Diago continued. "They are saying I will never betray the daimons because of him. I have to put those rumors down. If enough of them speak against me, they can persuade you to send me away."

"The hell they can. You took a vow—"

"And they won't ask me to forsake my oath, but with enough pressure, they can force you to station me far from Santuari."

Miquel lit a cigarette, a sure sign he was both bothered by the direction of the conversation, and that he knew what Diago said was true. "We've lived apart from Santuari before. We can do it again."

"It's not about you and me. It's Rafael. His mother

hid him in an orphanage, then died before she could return for him. He has been thrust into an existence he doesn't understand with a father he doesn't know. He is just beginning to adjust and needs more time. A year, maybe two, then I'll go wherever you need me. But now—at *this* moment—I need to be in Santuari. Where he feels safe. For Rafael's sake."

Diago stepped back. "Besides, this is an easy assignment. Your people have laid the groundwork for me. All I have to do is give vague references, take credit for stopping the anarchist's attack, and see what I can dig up about Ferrer's political associations. I'm in, I'm out. If I have another attack of chromesthesia, I'll go back to Santuari. I promise. But let me prove myself to them. And to you."

Guillermo evaluated Diago through the haze of cigar smoke. "All right. We'll stay on course. While you're seeing Ferrer, Miquel and I are going to look for our friend Prieto."

Beltran Prieto: the angel who had sent Diago to confront Moloch in the first place . . . and "introduced" him to his son. Diago would like to find Prieto, too. He had questions of his own for the angel. *Especially about Rafael's past.* Unfortunately, Prieto had not been seen or heard from since Diago's return from Moloch's realm.

Miquel said, "We need to find him and his bomb."

"It's not an actual bomb." Diago corrected him. "It's the *idea* for a bomb."

Guillermo noted the distinction. "I'd like to find

out more about that idea before he implants it into a mortal's brain." He pitched his voice low. "This whole thing stinks. Angels and daimons openly bartering for bombs and children? I've never heard the likes of it. I still haven't found an archangel who will accept responsibility for Prieto's alleged order to bargain with Moloch."

"And you probably won't," Diago said. "I'm worried he's rogue."

"It's possible. I'm not discounting anything until I have the facts. Miquel and I will begin with your former landlady. Maybe Doña Rosa or her son, José, remembers something important. When you're done, we'll meet you at Els 4 Gats."

The proximity of the restaurant, Els 4 Gats, had been one of the highlights of living in Doña Rosa's neighborhood. Diago knew the establishment well.

Miquel slipped his hand into Diago's coat pocket. A tin warmed by his flesh touched Diago's fingers. "Aspirin . . . and something stronger if you need it."

"I don't—" Miquel cut off his protest with a gentle squeeze before he withdrew his hand. Diago had no intention of clouding his mind with Juanita's drugs. He needed his wits about him, but for Miquel's sake, he relented and accepted the tin. "Okay."

Guillermo nodded. "Good. And remember, you won't be alone. Garcia is going with you."

Diago glanced across the street where Inspector Juan Garcia's dark wiry frame was partially hidden in the shadows. Garcia was all edges and serrations, with a temper thin as a blade. He wasn't as old as Guillermo, Diago, and Miquel, but he had a couple of centuries on the younger Nefilim. His age and loyal service had won him trusted positions from Guillermo. Now he served as a police inspector in Barcelona's Urban Guard. He touched the brim of his hat when he caught Diago looking at him.

Diago returned the gesture with a nod, but that was as far as his courtesy went. "Anybody but him."

Guillermo glanced over his shoulder at Garcia. "I know you two have had differences in the past—"

"He threatened to arrest me on deviancy charges."

Miquel popped the knuckles of his right hand. "I had a talk with him about that."

Guillermo frowned. "So I heard. You're my second-in-command, and I won't have you settling disputes with your fists."

Miquel opened his mouth to protest.

Guillermo cut him off. "Control your temper. From now on, if you have a problem you can't fix with diplomacy, you come to me."

Miquel's dark eyes slid away from Guillermo's gaze in a *maybe, maybe not* look Diago knew too well. Hoping to stave off further argument, he asked, "Why can't Miquel go with me? I trust him."

"I have a rule: two Nefilim who are"—he hesitated and looked over the crowd as he chose just the right word—"devoted to one another are never paired in any assignment. It's too easy for one partner to be used as a hostage."

Fair enough. "Fine. But why Garcia?"

"Because the others trust him. A good word from him will go a long way toward winning over the doubters."

Guillermo was obviously more worried about what the others thought than he had previously admitted. Diago took no satisfaction in being right. He had a long road ahead of him with Los Nefilim, and he knew it. "I'll work with him."

"Good. Garcia will have your back." Guillermo nodded and looked down the street, his mind already moving to his next task. "Try and meet us by five. I promised Juanita I would have you behind Santuari's wards before dark."

As Miquel passed, he touched his index finger to Diago's chest, just over his heart. "Be careful."

"I will." *I have no choice. Rafael is depending on me.* The thought of his small son waiting at home centered him. Besides, compared to the feats of espionage other members of Los Nefilim performed, the task before him was a simple one, and a small price to pay for keeping Rafael safe in Santuari.

It's merely a job, Diago assured himself, *like teaching music.* So what if he didn't like Garcia? He hadn't liked the Ferrer boy, Enrique, either, but he'd still managed to teach the child. *You do things so you—and the ones you love—can survive. This was no different.*

Diago glanced across the street. Garcia was gone.

So much for having my back. He'd probably been waiting for Miquel and Guillermo to leave so he could slip away on one pretext or another. Fine. Diago was more comfortable working alone anyway. He turned and gazed down into the stairwell.

At the bottom landing, the light turned into shadows. A stream of mist drifted across the steps. Diago thought he detected the smell of burning flesh, then a woman's cologne obliterated the scent. But the odor had been there, resurrecting the memory of corpses burning in Moloch's effigy. Diago's heart bumped up a notch.

"It never goes away does it?" said a voice right by his ear.

"What?" He turned his head so fast, he almost lost his hat.

Garcia had eased up beside him. He lit a cigarette, cupping his hand around flame. "The fear." He allowed the match to fall to the stairs below.

"I don't know what you're talking about."

"Uh-huh." He lowered his voice until he was barely audible beneath the busy sounds of the city. "You forget. I've spent time down there, drowning in the dark. I know how the nightmares eat your sleep. No matter how many times it happens, going back never gets easier. Not even for you." Garcia took a long drag on his cigarette and blew a cloud of smoke into Diago's face. "And you're one of them."

"I am angel, too." How easily they all forgot his dual nature. "And now I'm Los Nefilim. Just like you. I'm willing to forget the past if you are."

"Is that an olive branch?"

"Take it or burn it."

Garcia turned his head and spat.

Then fire it is. Diago's cheeks warmed with his fury. *What the hell made me think I could work with Garcia?* He went downstairs to purchase his ticket, aware that the inspector followed. They made no further attempts at conversation as they waited on the platform, and that was all right with Diago.

They weren't there long before the sound of an oncoming train flowed into the tunnel. Diago's heart accelerated. He wasn't ready for the sudden anxiety that peaked in his chest and descended into his thighs. For one horrible moment, he thought his knees would give way. He stiffened his back, hating Garcia for being right, because the fear never truly went away.

It's just a train. Just a normal everyday train.

He glanced upward to avoid the gloom on the tracks. The overhead lights rained crystal notes over the waiting passengers, falling like silvery snow into their hair and onto their shoulders. The sparkling sounds were the first indication of another spasm of chromesthesia. Diago clamped his eyes shut and found no safety behind the darkness of his lids. He envisioned Miquel dragging Rafael onto a different train. Both of them were spattered with Diago's blood. Rafael had twisted in Miquel's grip, the child's eyes widening when Diago stumbled.

He'd thought I wasn't going to make it. At the time, Diago had wondered himself. He remembered lurching across the platform, determined to reach the train before—

Garcia bumped his shoulder. "The doors are going to shut."

Diago opened his eyes. A vortex of sound waves rushed around him. Nauseated by the sight, he forced himself through the brilliant colors of the mortals' chatter. He spotted an empty seat by a window and fell into it.

Nearby, a mother rocked her child and hummed a lullaby.

The tune was identical to the one Rafael sang to Diago while he recovered from the 'aulaqs' attack. *Sleep, child, sleep / Mamá has gone away / she sets the stars alight all through the night / and watches while you sleep.* The memory of his son's boyish soprano relaxed him.

Garcia jostled him as he took the seat next to Diago, shattering the pleasant recollection. "You okay?"

Diago opened his eyes. The violent colors and sound waves receded. His vision returned to normal. The episode passed, along with his fear. Excellent. No need to mention the chromesthesia. *I moved through it.* That small victory heartened him. "I'm fine."

"Good," he said, although Diago sensed he really didn't care one way or another. Garcia reached into his coat and removed a small novel.

All around them, the mortals settled into their places as the car started to roll. The train picked up speed and passed into the tunnel.

Electric lights were spaced at regular intervals, illuminating the tunnel's concrete and steel girders. As they rode, Diago noticed deeper shades of purple and black that spread tentacles of darkness between the tiles. The colors indicated the outer edges of a bridge between the mortal world and the daimonic realms.

Odd. He'd ridden this route before and never noticed the bridge, so it must be newly formed. He glanced at Garcia but said nothing. Even though the angel-born Nefilim weren't as receptive to the existence of the bridges as the daimon-born, they could still perceive them. Diago's dual nature simply increased his sensitivity to such phenomena.

If he pointed out the boundaries, Garcia would have no difficulty seeing the bridge. Maybe this would be the first step toward building trust with the other Nefil. Diago lifted his hand to touch Garcia's arm, and then he froze.

Several metres away, the threads of color coalesced into a solid form as if a hole had materialized in the wall. A man stood on the mortal side of the bridge.

No. Not a man. No mortal could pass over a bridge without daimonic help. Whoever it was had to be a Nefil.

As the train approached, the Nefil turned his head. Anguished eyes looked out of a face twisted with agony. His mouth was forced open with a grayish-green band of light, which extended his chin almost to the hollow of his throat. More of the same dull radiance poured through his nostrils. Not light, Diago realized as the train slowed to take the curve. The pulsating colors were streams of magic, and Diago recognized this palette as belonging to Moloch.

Judging from the streaks of puce flowing through the gray, Diago surmised Moloch was still injured by his encounter with Rafael, a testament to the child's power. However, while the daimon's injuries might keep him close to his fires and out of the mortal realms, he obviously wasn't so incapacitated that he couldn't send an emissary.

The Nefil stepped onto the narrow walkway between the tracks and the bridge. His features bespoke a Berber lineage diluted by Visigoth blood. Black lashes encircled his dark green eyes. Cut into his forehead was a single word: LIAR.

Alvaro. Diago carefully lowered his hand back to his thigh and hoped Garcia hadn't noticed the movement. *He couldn't let Garcia see this.* A quick glance assured him the inspector was engrossed in his book.

Diago returned his attention to the figure on the bridge. He'd only seen his father's face when he'd worn the distorted features of the 'aulaq. At that time, Alvaro had looked nothing like Diago.

Now he does. There is no mistaking us for father and son because he no longer wears the flesh. I am seeing his soul, his true self. He is dead. But he lives.

Alvaro twisted his head and worked his jaw. The perverse gag of Moloch's magic writhed down his throat.

His voice. Moloch had stolen his voice.

As Diago's car neared, Alvaro frantically snatched the train's smoke and twisted the mist into words. *Diago, my son, help me . . . help . . . she hunts . . . help me . . .*

My son. The old familiar hurt rose in his chest. When had Alvaro ever called Diago son? *Never.*

Then Moloch's tether tightened around Alvaro's throat and yanked him back into the daimon's realm. Diago flinched. His father vanished within the pulsating darkness.

"Something wrong?" Garcia muttered.

Diago started. He shook his head. "No."

"You're pale."

"It's nothing." He kept his gaze straight ahead, highly conscious of Garcia's scrutiny. He couldn't tell Garcia about Alvaro. He would see a conspiracy between father and son, or make up one to suit his needs.

"What is happening, Alvarez?"

"Nothing." Diago repeated. He twisted his fingers into the fabric of his coat. Somehow Moloch had entrapped Alvaro's soul.

And? Diago deflected his pain with a hard loop of hate. *What does it matter to me?* Alvaro made his choices. He had abandoned Diago when he was a child, bartered his soul to Moloch in order to avoid reincarnation, and thrived on the blood of others as an *'aulaq.* Diago didn't have one damn reason to care what happened to Alvaro.

Except Alvaro gave his life so I could escape Moloch and save Rafael. The act won Diago's respect. *But there's a long walk between respect and forgiveness.* One selfless act didn't negate a lifetime of neglect.

Nor did it explain Alvaro's sudden reappearance.

Had he come back to warn Diago? Of what? *She hunts?*
What the hell did that mean?

And who is she?

"Alvarez?" Garcia's voice took an edge.

"I'm fine." *Say it enough times, it might come true.* He
fixed his eyes on the car in front of them. "I'm fine."

Garcia lowered his book and watched Diago for
the rest of the ride. When the train finally rolled to
a stop at the Passeig de Gràcia station, Diago rose.
The moment the doors opened he was off and moving
toward the station's exit. He took the stairs two at a
time and didn't slow until the sun drove the image of
his father's tormented face into the shadows.

CHAPTER TWO

Once above ground, Diago assumed a more causal pace. He observed the people who went about their busy lives completely unaware of the supernatural world moving beneath their feet. Before he'd joined Guillermo's group of Nefilim, Diago had enjoyed pretending to be mortal. He'd only used his magic when absolutely necessary and left the matters of angels and daimons to the clergy.

LIAR. The word carved on Alvaro's forehead jumped into Diago's mind. *I lied to myself for too long.* He'd feigned normalcy for many centuries and disregarded incidents like the one he just experienced.

It's like waking after a long sleep. He mourned his old life for only a moment. As he passed a shop window, Alvaro's face haunted him. Again Diago saw the words: *help me . . . she hunts.*

She hunts. What could it possibly mean?

Diago parsed the clues as he walked. If Alvaro knew of this mysterious female, then she was most likely a daimon, or maybe an 'aulaq. Either way, she was looking for something, and whatever that something was, Alvaro felt the need to warn Diago about her presence. Other than their relationship as father and son, the only two things linking Diago to Alvaro were Rafael, and the idea for the bomb Prieto had taken from Moloch.

Diago's mind immediately jumped to Rafael. Did the daimons hunt his son? Like Diago, Rafael carried the magic of both the angels and the daimons in his spiritual heritage. If the daimons could turn Rafael to their cause, they would acquire a powerful weapon against the angels and Los Nefilim.

Yet the analysis didn't fit. Concerning Rafael, the daimons had nothing to hunt. Moloch knew Rafael was with Diago, and no one had made any secret of Diago's presence at Santuari. No. Whoever "she" was, she couldn't be after Rafael. That left Prieto, and the idea for the bomb.

Diago's musings were cut short when a hand gripped his arm. Startled, he turned to find Garcia had caught up to him.

Diago tried to pull free without drawing attention to them but Garcia's grip tightened. "What—?"

"Just shut up and move." He steered Diago into the mouth of an alley.

Diago jerked free and put his back against the wall. "What the hell is wrong with you?"

Garcia jabbed Diago's shoulder with one sharp

finger. "I asked you a question on the train and you lied to me. I'm going to pretend it was because of the mortals. You've got one more chance to get right with me. What happened?"

Be careful. You need him. You need him to vouch for you. Diago evaded the question and kept his tone even. "I don't report to you."

Garcia coughed a humorless laugh. "You're confused, my friend."

"We're not friends."

Garcia's tone turned sly. "Then you'd better make some, Alvarez. You might have fooled Guillermo, but the rest of us see you for what you are. You're daimon and you'll wind up just like your father. You did in your firstborn life and you will here, too." Garcia punctuated his last statement with a hard jab to Diago's shoulder.

You'll wind up just like your father. The accusation sealed any doubts Diago had about telling Garcia what happened at the bridge. "Don't touch me again."

Garcia ignored the warning. "You report to whomever asks you a question. Do you understand me?" He stabbed his finger in Diago's direction.

Diago's temper overrode his reason. He caught Garcia's fist and squeezed until Garcia's knuckles popped.

Why did Garcia push him? *Does he want me to lash out?* Of course, he did. This was probably how he provoked Miquel into punching him. The whole discussion was nothing more than an attempt to rouse Diago's temper. *And it's working.* Except Diago wasn't quite as hotheaded as Miquel. This altercation didn't need to progress any further than it already had.

Striking Garcia wasn't necessary. *Let him feel my power, acknowledge it with his face.* Holding tight to the other Nefil's fist, Diago waited until Garcia's lips thinned to a single white line. Only then did he speak. "Until I know who I can trust, I report to Guillermo. No one else." He opened his fingers.

For one tense moment, Diago was sure Garcia intended to escalate the confrontation. Something in Diago's eyes stopped him.

Garcia looked away and fumbled for his cigarettes. When he struck the match, flakes of sulfur cascaded to the sidewalk. "I'm going with you to see Ferrer."

No. Not now. Not even if you begged. Diago wasn't going to be monitored by the likes of Garcia. "No."

"You're going to botch this without help."

Or you'll make sure the interview goes badly for me. Garcia would love nothing more than to report Diago's incompetence to Guillermo. *Work around him.* "How can I earn your trust if you are always looking over my shoulder? I go in alone or not at all. Then you can explain the situation to Guillermo."

The tip of Garcia's cigarette glowed like the fire in his eyes. He exhaled a cloud of smoke as caustic as his words. "Go alone. But I'm watching you."

Diago didn't flinch from the inspector's stare. "Fair enough." *So much for Guillermo's hope our working together would cement trust between us.*

He turned and walked away, acutely aware Garcia

trailed him as he approached the Casa Milà's entrance. Garcia could stalk him the entire day for all Diago cared. He had no intention of giving the inspector cause for complaint.

Except for the lie of omission about the bridge, his conscience needled him.

Yet nothing about the bridge was urgent. The numerous treaties allowed the daimons to form their own pathways between the realms under certain circumstances. No, the existence of the bridge didn't create the issue. It was Alvaro's presence which complicated the affair.

So simply tell Guillermo on the way home. The drive to Santuari would give him ample opportunity to find a good moment to mention the bridge and Alvaro. Then Los Nefilim would have the information, and Diago would be spared yet another slur about his daimonic lineage.

Satisfied with his compromise, Diago nodded to the doorman as he entered the building. The ornate metalwork of the railings directed his eye toward the stairs. He loved Antoni Gaudí's integration of stone and metal, which formed naturalistic designs in modern architecture. Taking the stairs gave Diago ample opportunity to appreciate the small details of Gaudí's work. If only he hadn't suffered two attacks of chromesthesia in such close succession.

But I did, and I can't risk an attack on the stairs. The vertigo could cause him to fall, and with only Garcia to find and help him, Diago decided to be cautious.

With a sigh of regret, he bypassed the stairs and took the elevator.

The lift attendant spent the entire ride sneaking glances at Diago's scarred face. Diago kept his gaze straight ahead and ignored the boy. He needed to focus on his assignment.

Guillermo wanted an idea of Ferrer's political leanings, which would require small talk—another thing Diago hated—but Miquel had helped him rehearse some lines last night after Rafael had gone to bed. The difficulty would be getting Ferrer to drop his guard. The industrialist made no secret of his dislike for Diago. He considered music teachers to be worse than useless. The only reason he'd financed the lessons for his son was to appease his young wife, who likewise had no interest in music, but seemed to have developed a predilection for men of Diago's particular build and coloring.

Christ, the whole family gave him a headache. Diago dry-swallowed three aspirin just as the lift finally reached the fourth floor.

"Have a good day, sir." The young man shut the gate as soon as Diago cleared the lift.

"Yes, I would like one of those," Diago muttered as he approached the Ferrers' apartment. He gave two firm knocks and waited.

Their maid, Elena, opened the door. Beneath her stiff white cap, a few silvery strands of hair comingled with her dark bob. She was barely forty. Even for a mortal, she was far too young to be going gray so soon.

Of course, working for this family, Diago was sure his hair would have been white within a year . . . if he'd had any hair left.

"Maestro Alvarez? I thought we agreed you'd use the servants' entrance."

"I never agreed to that, because I am not a servant in this house." He met her look of disdain with utter indifference. "Is Señor Ferrer at home?"

Her gaze hardened into a glare. She straightened her back and peered down her nose at him. "He is."

When she didn't invite him inside, he asked, "May I see him?"

He half expected her to close the door in his face and make him wait in the hall. She must have considered it, because she regarded him for almost ten seconds before she stepped aside and allowed him into the foyer. Nor did she offer to take his hat and coat. "Wait here."

Instead of going to Ferrer's office, she turned and went down the hall toward Enrique's room. Odd. Given the hour, Enrique should have still been at school.

Elena was gone for only a few moments before she returned and said, "Follow me."

From her quick step to her rigid frown, Diago realized she was still angry over his remark. Miquel was right. He really needed to work on his interpersonal skills.

In an attempt to make up for his brusque comment, he said, "I hope Enrique is all right."

She turned on him with military precision and threw her sentence at him like an accusation. "He's ill."

He backpedaled in the face of the verbal assault. While he didn't particularly care for the boy, he'd never wish an illness on anyone's child. "I'm sorry. I hope it's nothing serious."

She seemed to sense his earnestness and some of her animosity faded. "The doctor said the sickness should pass soon."

"That's good to hear."

She nodded and started walking again. Her pace wasn't quite as furious. Diago congratulated himself on his tact.

As they passed the sitting room, he noticed the grand piano was gone. Enrique must have finally killed it. Señora Ferrer was nowhere to be seen. If the past was any indication, she was probably lunching with friends after shopping. She spent as much time as possible away from the apartment and the stepson she loathed.

Elena paused before an open pocket door. "Señor Ferrer will be with you momentarily." She left him alone.

This was a stroke of luck. Prior to today, he'd never been allowed any deeper into the apartment than either the foyer or the parlor. Maybe he could get the information Guillermo wanted without having to chit-chat with Ferrer.

Diago waited until Elena's footsteps receded down the hallway before he sidled over to the desk. An open briefcase contained an account book. He removed the ledger and flipped through the pages, quickly calculating the numbers in his head. If the figures were accurate, Enrique hadn't murdered the piano after all. Ferrer had probably sold the instrument.

Apparently the munitions factory, Ferrer y Esperanza, was running in the red.

Diago slipped the ledger back into the case and turned his attention to the newspaper clippings littering the desk. Each article described protests orchestrated by the CNT, the anarchist worker's union responsible for rousing employees to demand fair wages through strikes. Many of the names were circled.

Thus far, the CNT hadn't been terribly successful in unifying the workers, although they had managed to strike fear in Spain's upper classes. With Russia's February Revolution firmly entrenched in their memories, the nobility throughout Spain used the police and the Civil Guard to suppress any strikes. By quashing the protests, the upper classes and clergy thought they were avoiding a Spanish version of the Russian catastrophe. Without enforcing any reforms, though, they were about to usher in the very insurgency no one wanted.

Next to the newspapers were several typewritten sheets bearing Ferrer y Esperanza's emblem of crossed rifles. Names and job titles were listed. Any workers with associations within either the CNT or the more moderate Socialist workers' union, the UGT, carried a black mark beside their name.

So Ferrer fires the union members before they can make trouble. That should give Guillermo the information he needed about the industrialist's political leanings. It was troubling but not unexpected. Having watched the landowners in Andalusia starve the farmworkers into compliance, Diago hadn't expected a man like Ferrer to be any different.

As he replaced the papers, he noticed one of the desk drawers was partially open. Inside, a heavy manila folder marked "CONFIDENTIAL" caught Diago's eye. He removed the memo. Then he carefully replaced the folder in the drawer.

The short message indicated three men were to deliver a shipment of firearm primer to a destination in El Raval. As Diago puzzled over it, he kept coming back to the address, which made no sense at all. *There aren't any factories in that area.*

What the hell was Ferrer doing?

The front door banged open. Diago jumped at the sound. He whirled toward the door and banged his bandaged hand on the corner of the desk. *Oh, shit, shit.* Pain throbbed up his arm and into his shoulder. *Can this day get any worse?* He folded the memo and quickly jammed it into his coat pocket. Maybe Guillermo could make some sense of it.

"Elena!" It was Señora Ferrer, and from the pitch of her voice, Diago knew she was irritated at some perceived affront. "Is my husband still home?"

May God help him. Cradling his injured hand, Diago looked over the briefcase and the papers. Satisfied everything seemed as it was when he'd entered the room, he went to the pocket door and leaned out.

Elena hurried into the foyer from the direction of the kitchen. "He is, Señora."

"Take these packages." Señora Ferrer clacked down the hall on her precariously high heels, wavering slightly. Knowing her fondness for sherry, it didn't take much to guess she was drunk. "Salvador!" she cried out. "Why have they canceled our account at Santa Eulalia?"

Santa Eulalia. No wonder Ferrer was going broke if his wife shopped at such high-end stores.

In the foyer, Elena juggled the packages. One thin box slid from the pile. The maid knelt to retrieve it and glanced toward the office.

Diago ducked back inside; in doing so, he jarred a picture on the wall. He caught the rosewood frame and righted it. Encased behind the glass was a manuscript fragment. Judging from the reddish color of the ink and the amber coloration of the paper, the document was ancient.

The fragment was small, no more than eight centimetres wide and ten tall. The edges were charred, as if someone had tried to push it into a fire with a poker.

A sigil was drawn in the center of the page. Scorch marks obliterated most of the details, yet Diago clearly made out an "X" superimposed over a cross. The left and right arms of the cross bore crescent moons facing away from one another. The position of the opposing moons told Diago the glyph was for a daimon.

But which one? And why would Ferrer have a dai-monic sigil hanging in his house? Very few mortals knew or cared about the Nefilim, and of those that did, none hung glyphs openly in their homes. Mortals who engaged in supernatural activities were more secretive than Los Nefilim.

Intrigued, Diago reached out with his left hand to lift the frame from the wall.

"Señor Alvarez." Ferrer's voice was loud and close.

Diago started and looked up at the industrialist. Ferrer was built like a bull, broad-shouldered and still somewhat narrow at the hips in spite of middle age thickening his paunch. He towered over Diago.

This is awkward. Think of something. He pointed at the fragment. "This is an extraordinary piece. I didn't know you collected antiquities."

Ferrer was nonplussed by the compliment. "I don't. It was a gift from one of the old families in the Gothic Quarter. Iniguez was the name."

"Don José Iniguez?"

"Why, yes. He stopped by yesterday and presented me with the fragment as a gift. He is interested in in-vesting in Ferrer y Esperanza. Do you know him?"

Clearly not as well as I thought. Diago never imagined José would be interested in investing money in any-thing other than whores and gambling. He realized Ferrer was waiting for an answer. "I rented a room from his mother Doña Rosa. I had very little contact with Don José, but Doña Rosa is an honorable woman."

Ferrer nodded. "Good to know."

"Why hang such a lovely gift in the dark?"

"Don José said to keep the fragment in the shadows in order to preserve the ink."

I'll bet he did, Diago thought. Nothing rendered a daimonic sigil impotent like too much sunlight. "It's an intriguing document. Did he say where he found it?"

"No." Ferrer's tone indicated he didn't care either. He'd probably only accepted the gift and given it a token place in his home in order to court José and his money.

Diago wondered how José had come into possession of the document. Prieto? Maybe. The angel had paid José to trick Miquel. He'd also promised Doña Rosa he would divert José from his self-destructive behavior. Maybe Prieto had made good on his agreements. But why give José a daimonic sigil? Was Prieto trying to hide it *from* the daimons or *for* the daimons? And why here?

So many questions . . . and not nearly enough answers . . .

Ferrer interrupted Diago's speculations. "Elena said you wanted to see me."

"Ah, yes." Diago reined his questions under control. There would be plenty of time to puzzle through the mystery later. "I came to repay you." He withdrew an envelope from his breast pocket. "You gave me a most generous advance, but I'm afraid I won't be able to continue as Enrique's instructor."

Ferrer took the envelope and thumbed through the banknotes. No amount of restraint could hide the pleasure in his eyes. "It's no matter. We sold the piano. Enrique showed no interest in it. I'd be happy to give you a referral."

"I appreciate the offer, but I've secured employment elsewhere."

"Really? With whom?"

"Don Guillermo Ramírez. He is a landowner just outside of Barcelona."

"I've heard of Ramírez. Isn't he something of an artisan?"

"He does ornate metalwork on commission."

"A blacksmith."

"Like Gaudí was in construction."

Ferrer grunted and didn't look impressed. He went to his desk and opened the file drawer, removing the CONFIDENTIAL folder. Diago's pulse kicked up speed. He almost didn't hear Ferrer's next words. "I understand from Inspector Garcia you stopped an anarchist from setting off a bomb near a child."

Diago nodded and barely managed to move his numb lips. "That is true."

Ferrer placed the folder in his briefcase alongside the ledger. "CNT?"

Some of the tension loosened in Diago's chest. "It all happened very fast, but Inspector Garcia assured me the anarchists were involved. He asked I not say too much, because they're still investigating."

"I understand." Ferrer snapped shut his briefcase, and Diago's heart rate returned to normal. "Thank you for coming, Alvarez."

Ferrer's abrupt dismissals used to rankle Diago to no end. Today he felt nothing but relief. He bowed his head in Ferrer's direction. "Please give my regards to your wife and son."

"Thank you." Ferrer rang for Elena.

Diago followed her to the door, trying hard not to step on her heels. He expected Ferrer to call him back into the office to explain why he'd been pawing through the man's private papers.

They had reached the foyer when Señora Ferrer's voice called from the kitchen. "Elena! Don't we have another bottle of La Gitana?"

"An excellent sherry," Diago said as he aimed himself toward the door. "I'll see myself out."

Elena's jaw tightened with irritation.

He didn't wait for her answer. Instead, he fled the apartment and headed for the elevator, quite happy to be done with the Ferrers once and for all. *Except for the fragment.* That might necessitate a return trip. He would let Guillermo decide what to do with the information.

Diago rode the elevator to the main floor and exited the building. Outside, Garcia was nowhere to be seen. Either he had hidden himself well, or he was off on another task for Guillermo.

Relieved, Diago turned toward the Gothic Quarter and decided to avoid the metro. Another encounter with Alvaro was the last thing he needed.

He had just crossed the street when a police car rolled to a stop beside the curb. Had Ferrer discovered the missing memo? Diago made a conscious effort to keep his hand away from his pocket.

The youth behind the wheel cranked down his window with ferocious speed. "Excuse me, Doctor Alvarez!"

Doctor? Oh Jesus, what now? Diago bent over and saw Garcia's terse face glowering from the passenger side of the car. This day was not getting better.

Garcia emerged from the car. The urgency in his step alarmed Diago. His concern shifted from the stolen memo to Guillermo and Miquel. Had something happened to them?

Garcia rounded the bumper.

"What's the matter?" Diago asked.

Garcia clenched Diago's bicep and propelled him to the car's back door. "You're a doctor now, do you understand?"

Diago twisted free and lowered his voice. "Don't touch me again."

"Just get in the fucking car."

"At least tell me what kind of doctor I'm supposed to be."

"An alienist."

Diago calmed somewhat. Guillermo was in no danger if he had sent for Diago to play the role of a criminal psychiatrist, and that likewise meant Miquel was safe.

Whenever mortals were involved and his friend had needed someone to read the patterns of a daimon attack, he'd called on Diago and passed him off as an alienist. Now that he was Los Nefilim, Guillermo must have decided wining and dining him was no longer a necessary component of the request. "And what kind of crime am I investigating?"

"We don't have time for questions." Garcia jerked the door open. "Get in."

No use arguing. The sooner he got inside, the sooner they'd arrive . . . *where?* There could be only one place. Guillermo had mentioned a visit to Doña Rosa Iniguez. Diago got in the car.

Garcia slammed the door hard enough to rattle the window in its frame.

Diago caught the young mortal's gaze in the rear-view mirror. "What's happened?"

The young man licked his lips. "He killed them all," he whispered. "He's insane."

Garcia rounded the right bumper.

Diago resisted the urge to lean forward. "Who?"

The officer clutched the wheel in a white-knuckled grip. Before he could answer, Garcia jerked open the door and got in the front seat.

"Drive."

CHAPTER THREE

The lump, which had settled in Diago's stomach outside the Casa Milà, grew heavier when they stopped at the corner of Carrer de les Magdalenes and Carrer de Montsio. A few doors down Montsio, two young officers guarded the entrance to Doña Rosa's home.

Don't assume the worst. Maybe Doña Rosa escaped whatever calamity befell her house. She could easily have been at church, or out with friends. Diago didn't ask. He didn't want his illusions shattered too soon.

Their driver stopped the car in front of one of the barricades. More police blocked both ends of the street and held back a crowd of spectators. Death didn't just draw the ravens anymore.

Diago got out and followed a few steps behind Garcia. They had only gone ten paces when a photographer stepped away from the crowd and aimed his camera at them.

Just what I don't need. Diago dropped his head and angled his hat to obscure his features. Judging from today's adventure, Ferrer read the papers extensively. What if he saw Diago's picture and a caption identifying him as an alienist investigating a crime scene? Christ. Garcia should have brought them in through the alley behind Doña Rosa's house. *Too late now.* Diago gritted his teeth.

The flash popped and spun back the shadows. Garcia shoved the camera into the man's nose. The crunch of cartilage was loud enough to carry over the murmurs of the crowd. A spectator cried out at the sudden violence. The man dropped his camera and clutched his bleeding face.

Garcia ripped out the film. "Arrest that man. I'll deal with him later."

Brutal but effective. Diago didn't wait for Garcia. The inspector caught up with him faster than he would have liked.

"Was that really necessary?" Diago muttered.

"Mortals are like dogs, Alvarez." Garcia straightened his sleeves. "Make an example of one"—he gestured over his shoulder at the photographer, who was being shoved into a police car—"and the rest of them stay out of our way."

Diago wasn't sure if Garcia's "our" referred to the police or Los Nefilim; although knowing Garcia's contempt for mortals, Diago guessed it was the latter. He would have argued the point, but they had reached the front door. Both of the older mortals guarding the entrance gave Garcia twin smiles of tacit approval over his handling of the photographer.

Diago had to admit Garcia knew how to manipulate their allegiance. *Maybe he does know what he's doing, but it doesn't mean I have to approve of his tactics.*

One of the officers opened the door. "It's ugly."

"I'm sure the doctor has seen worse." Garcia gestured for Diago to enter first.

Inside, the smell hit his sinuses like a club. Diago withdrew his handkerchief and used it to cover his nose. The thin cotton did little to mask the odor of feces and rotten flesh. The first analogy entering his mind was Valencia during the plague years, but that was wrong. The plague had left a definitive odor of illness in its wake. There was no smell of sickness here.

This was a charnel house. A fly dragged its bloated body along the scuffed wainscoting. The telephone stand was crushed to splinters, the telephone itself lost somewhere beneath the rubble.

When Diago had sufficiently gotten his gag reflex under control, he lowered the handkerchief. Like the touch of a ghost, he detected the faint scent of Doña Rosa's talcum. The smell hung in the foyer and left a sickly sweet taste on his tongue.

Garcia closed the door on the street sounds. Silence descended over them. Diago thought of tombs and the quiet dead.

He looked at the blood-spattered walls. Notes of a black song inched across the wallpaper. One sound wave fluttered beside the banister, buoyant as a moth.

In it, Diago heard the echo of a moan. He thought he recognized the voice of one of Doña Rosa's other tenants: Anselmo was his name. That was all Diago could remember about him—his name and his love of sour candies, the wrappers of which followed him like a trail. The echo of Anselmo's death touched a bloodied handprint on the wall, then slithered into the stain to disappear beneath the wallpaper.

Diago glanced at Garcia, who made no sign the sounds bothered him. Just like on the train, the inspector was less receptive to the resonances than Diago. So while Garcia might glimpse the vibrations from the corner of his eye, he wouldn't see them as clearly as the daimon-born. Too, in a place as old as Barcelona, the Nefilim had learned to tune out the darker sounds as a matter of self-preservation. Those who listened too long, or too deeply, sought suicide as a release from the echoes of grief.

Like the others, Diago detached himself from the darkness around him, but he didn't blind himself to the shades of death. *Blindness creates mortals like Ferrer. Or Nefilim like Garcia.* It was better to see clearly. Even the ugliness of the world had its place.

Eventually, the death-song in Doña Rosa's house would fade. Only the most sensitive mortals, perhaps those with a touch of daimon in their soul, would perceive something bad ever happened in this house. Decades from now, the dark sounds would be gone, washed away by time and the resonances of new lives.

Diago looked away from the ghostly whispers. "What happened?"

"José murdered his mother and the two tenants."

Diago felt as if he'd been punched. He hadn't realized how much he'd been hoping poor Doña Rosa wasn't dead. He recalled the sympathy in her eyes when he told her he'd never known his father. *She didn't deserve such an end.* A touch of anger filtered into his voice. "When?"

Garcia shrugged. "The coroner is working out a time frame. We know they'd been dead for several days. A neighbor called about the smell. The police found José up there this morning." He nodded at the stairwell. "Writing on the walls. Don Guillermo got here and charmed his way inside. Chief Inspector Mieras knew I had business at the Casa Milà. He sent a car to find me while I was babysitting you."

That explained Garcia's rage back at the Casa Milà. He had missed being first on the scene. Babysitting apparently kept him from his more important duties. "Where are the bodies?"

"They've already taken them to the morgue. What was left of them."

Diago winced. "José?"

"They've taken him to the hospital."

"Which one?"

"Holy Cross."

The lunatic asylum.

The creak of footsteps on the boards caused both of

them to look up. Diago recognized Miquel's footfall. His scuffed boots emerged on the threadbare carpet. He stopped at the landing and squatted. The shadows hid his features and for one terrifying instant, Diago thought his face had been erased. *Stop it. You're spooking yourself.*

Miquel shifted his position and was bathed in the electric light's harsh glow. "Our alienist has arrived."

Guillermo's voice drifted down from the top landing. "Dr. Alvarez?"

Miquel gave Diago a wan smile. "Yes."

Whatever was up there, it was bad. That much was clear from his lover's face.

Miquel rose and backed against the wall. People were coming down. Within moments, another police inspector descended, his eyes as glazed as if he walked in his sleep. Blunt-faced and stout, he made Diago think of a bear. His fierce appearance was dulled by his slack jaw and vacant stare.

Suero accompanied the man, holding his elbow and guiding him toward the first floor. Like Miquel, Suero held a coveted place in Guillermo's inner circle. When he wasn't coordinating the movements of the other Nefilim, he posed as Guillermo's driver.

His quiet song spun webs of gauze over the mortal's eyes. A thin sheen of sweat coated Suero's forehead; he had been at it for a while. Blinding mortals to the truth was a difficult task. Whatever evidence this house held, Guillermo wanted it badly.

Suero and his charge halted in front of Garcia. The mortal's mouth worked as if he chewed the words carefully before ejecting them from his tongue. "Inspector Garcia, I want you to bring Dr. Alvarez's findings back to the station when you're done."

Garcia nodded to the mortal. "Of course, Chief Inspector Mieras."

Mieras wavered slightly as if drunk before he faced Diago's general direction. His gaze finally landed somewhere just over Diago's left shoulder. "Dr. Alvarez."

"Chief Inspector. I'll examine the premises and get a written report to you. I assume photographs have been taken?"

"Yes." Mieras hesitated, looking first from Diago to Garcia, then back again. "Yes." He affirmed once more. "Yes."

"Good. I may need to see those later." Diago continued the pantomime of conversation as he glanced at Suero and wished the younger Nefil could read his mind. *Get him out of here.*

Diago wasn't sure if Suero intuited Diago's thoughts, or maybe he was simply growing weary from the energy he expended on Mieras, but he got the message. His song changed in pitch and speed, offering a note of urgency.

Mieras straightened. "I hope you will forgive me. I must return to the station. I have important matters to attend."

Diago and Garcia murmured good-byes. Diago was

certain Garcia was as relieved as he when the awkward interaction ended and the door shut on Suero and Mieras.

"We need to hurry," Miquel said from his place on the landing. "Guillermo and I have overstayed our welcome already. Mieras had come up to tell us it was time to leave."

"Let's go," Diago said.

At the top floor, they followed Miquel into the loft. The furniture was as Diago and Miquel had left it. Nostalgia for their days in the small apartment touched Diago as he followed his lover to their old bedroom, but he didn't give the feeling room to grow. He wasn't here to reminisce.

Guillermo stood by the bedroom's sole window and examined the wall. Words were written on the wallpaper in both ink and blood. In some places the force of the pen had torn through the paper to gouge the wall. Bits of plaster were scattered around the baseboards.

Miquel said, "I'm going downstairs in case the mortals get curious. Four knocks means your time is up."

Guillermo nodded. "Good idea." He turned to Diago after Miquel left. "How did it go with Ferrer?"

"Their maid had me wait for him in his office. I took advantage of the opportunity." He withdrew the memo and handed it to Guillermo. "I couldn't make sense of it."

Garcia sounded amused. "So were you playing the spy?"

Diago shrugged and waited to hear Guillermo's judgment on the document's value.

Guillermo scanned the paper, then gave it to Garcia. "He's helping the police use agents provocateurs within the CNT."

"How did you get that out of a primer shipment?" Diago asked.

"It's code." Guillermo explained. "The people he's listed will hide the 'primers,' the sparks that will set off an incident. During the next CNT protest, one of the primers will guarantee the march turns deadly. They'll attack the police."

"Or innocent bystanders." Garcia added. "When the protestors are arrested, the 'primers' are released. They're never booked. They just disappear. The protestors are sent to prison."

Diago felt as if he'd bitten into something sour. "They help the people oppressing their coworkers and get away free?"

"Your politics are showing, comrade." Garcia passed the memo back to Guillermo.

"I have no love for Lenin."

"A socialist, then." Garcia dug a cigarette out of his pack and lit it. "Doesn't matter to me. It's mortal business of no interest to us."

Guillermo pointed one blunt finger at Garcia. "*All* mortal business is of interest to us. I have a gut feeling the angels' game is bleeding into our realm, and if it is, their wars affect the mortals." He folded the memo and tucked it into his breast pocket. "Not what I wanted to hear, but at least now I know. Good work."

The compliment warmed Diago. "There's more," he said. "I found a daimonic sigil hanging on the wall in Ferrer's office. The fragment is ancient. Ferrer told me José had given it to him."

Garcia said, "I've been in Ferrer's office three times and never saw a fragment."

"According to Ferrer, José just gave it to him yesterday." *Which meant José was at Ferrer's office while the bodies remained here.* Diago stifled a shudder. "Besides, it was hidden in the shadows. I wouldn't have seen it if I hadn't bumped into it."

"You're a clumsy spy." Garcia grinned.

Diago ignored the jab. Garcia was baiting him, and trading insults would get them nowhere.

Guillermo took his lighter from his pocket and flipped the lid open and shut, a nervous habit Diago knew well. "Could you determine the sigil's purpose?"

Diago shook his head. "I didn't have enough time."

"Or you're protecting the daimon," Garcia said. "A relative of yours, perhaps?"

Diago didn't dignify the comment with a response.

Neither did Guillermo. "Let's forget the fragment for a minute and look at what we have in front of us." He checked his watch. "We're running out of time. The police said José claimed to hear voices, telling him what to do and write."

"Which indicates a possession." Garcia tapped the

ashes of his cigarette onto the floor. "And a possession
means daimons."

Diago glared at the mess. "People died here. Show
some respect."

Garcia sneered, but after a hard stare from Guillermo, he relented and stubbed out the cigarette in a
cup beside the bed. "You've been living among the
mortals too long."

Maybe he had, but at least the experience had left
him with a modicum of empathy, a quality sadly lack-
ing in Garcia. *He's trying to rattle me. The best defense is
to do my job.*

Diago turned his attention to his task and touched
the wall, hoping to pick up some vibrations left behind
by the daimon. The sounds within the magic were
almost dead now. Too much time had elapsed since the
daimon had possessed José.

Perhaps José's cramped script held an answer. The
same expressions were scrawled over and over. Bits of
Latin were superimposed atop Spanish and Catalan. It
was as if something had scrambled the language center
of José's brain.

> *Let me in OUT in Let me in tell me his name a name
> give me his name
>   the son will follow let him follow his father the son
> will follow the father*

Garcia picked out one phrase. " 'The son will follow

the father.'" He sniffed. "It's almost like José is talking about you, Alvarez."

The statement spread glacial claws of fear through Diago's limbs. Were the daimons trying to turn Los Nefilim against him so he would return to their side? Or did they mock him?

Stop it. José's ramblings have nothing to do with me. Garcia is using a random phrase to goad me.

Then what *did* José's writing concern? *Tell me a name. Give me a name.*

"'She hunts,'" Diago murmured.

Guillermo shut the lid of his lighter. "I don't see that phrase."

Because it wasn't there. Another round of uneasiness washed over Diago. The information about the bridge and Alvaro had suddenly become urgent. "I have to talk to you. Alone."

"Garcia is your partner; anything you say to me, you can say in front of him."

"Guillermo—" *Please. I've made a terrible mistake.*

Guillermo pinned his glare on Diago. "What's going on?"

Garcia raised his eyebrows.

Diago considered lying. He actually contemplated saying, "Nothing," in order to circumvent the humiliation of admitting he saw the bridge and Alvaro yet remained silent in the face of Garcia's questions.

Then he thought of Alvaro, standing on the bridge with the word LIAR carved into his forehead. *Will Los*

*Nefilim give me the same brand? Liar? Because that is what
I am.*

The room was suddenly too warm.

If the events here at Doña Rosa's house and the appearance of the bridge were linked, Diago would be
seen as hiding crucial information. Garcia would glee-
fully twist the facts and make it appear as if Diago was
protecting his father, and by extension, the daimons.
His life as one of Guillermo's Los Nefilim would be
over before it started.

No. One lie of omission was enough. He swallowed
his pride and said, "During the metro ride, I found a
new bridge, which wasn't there in October. Alvaro
stood on the mortal side."

"I knew it," Garcia said. "I knew something happened and you were holding back."

"I wasn't sure what I saw at first." The lie was a bad
one, nor did it mitigate the damage. Diago deduced
from the narrowing of Guillermo's eyes he was simply
digging himself deeper. "Alvaro sketched a few words
with the train's smoke: 'help me . . . she hunts.' I don't
know what he's trying to communicate to me."

Guillermo thumbed the lid of his lighter open and
shut, and it sounded like the banging of a gavel to
Diago. "Why didn't you tell Garcia?"

It was time for honesty. "I knew he'd make it sound
as if I was attempting to collude with Alvaro and the
daimons."

"Well?" Garcia's grin returned. "Aren't you?"

"No. I am not."

Guillermo sighed and shook his head. He was disappointed but not angry. Not yet. *He will be if I don't learn how to work with the other members of Los Nefilim.* Diago would have preferred anger. He knew how to react to rage, but Guillermo's frustration was harder to bear. *He took a chance on me and this is how I repay him.*

"I'm sorry. I should have said something."

"You're damn right you should have." Garcia snapped. "I even cornered him about it after the ride and he—"

"That's enough." Guillermo scowled at Garcia. "Stop with the insinuations about Diago working for the daimons. You make goddamned sure you've got some kind of proof to back up your allegations, or just shut up."

"And this admission isn't proof enough?"

"It's proof he can't trust you to represent the facts accurately."

Garcia's self-satisfaction vanished.

"Now"—Guillermo stabbed his finger at the wall—"you said, 'she hunts.' Tell me how Alvaro's message is linked to José's ramblings."

Relieved the momentum of the conversation moved away from him, Diago clarified his line of reasoning. "This, here." He touched the phrases: *Tell me a name. Give me a name.* "She is seeking a name, she is hunting, but as much as Garcia would like for this to be about me, I don't think it is. I believe the daimons are looking for Prieto and the idea for Moloch's bomb. The phrase 'the son will follow the father' could have come from José's mind."

"And what if it didn't?" Garcia asked.

He was a tenacious bastard, Diago had to give him that. "Or the daimons are playing on the distrust already seeded within our ranks by creating agents provocateurs from gullible Nefilim." He nodded at Garcia, whose face darkened with fury. *Good. Let him be angry for a change.* "Maybe they're hoping to keep us off-balance and fighting among ourselves while they widen the bridge." Anything was possible at this point.

Guillermo twice flipped the lighter's lid open and shut. "Let's go with the first premise. Why would a daimon be hunting Prieto?"

The answer was blatant to Diago. "If Moloch can't have Rafael, then he will seek the return of his idea. It's a matter of honor. The vibrations I saw holding Alvaro indicate Moloch is still too injured to leave his realm. But he isn't going to let a lot of time pass before he hunts what is his."

Garcia said, "So he's hired a bounty hunter to bring back the idea."

"Exactly." Diago touched the wall again.

Guillermo asked, "Can you tell who she is?"

"Her magic is almost gone. It left with the fragment." But she hadn't completely vanished. Traces of her song remained like the residue of a madman's dreams. Diago allowed his fingers to rove over the letters, especially seeking those written in blood, because that was where the daimon's magic would be the strongest. He thought of patterns.

"What did you say?" Guillermo asked.

Diago hadn't realized he'd spoken aloud. "Patterns," he said again, louder this time. "Magic, songs, stories—they all follow patterns."

"And what is the pattern here?"

That was the problem. He couldn't detect one. Her true essence eluded him, dancing just beyond his reach like a leaf blown by the wind.

He traced his finger over the word "father" again. "She wears many faces. All of them mortal. So she is entirely spirit. Without a corporeal form, she has no voice with which to open the realms and sing her way across a bridge. That explains why she needs the fragment. She uses it as an anchor to the mortal realm. The song that opens the way must be inscribed in the glyph."

Guillermo said, "Then she uses the mortals to transfer the fragment from one location to another so she can possess her next victim."

"Exactly," Diago said. "She must utilize whatever ability the mortal owns in order to communicate her will, but sometimes when you pour hot liquid into a corrupt vessel, the cup can break. When she ordered José to murder his mother, I think the slaughter unhinged him. José was a terrible person, but he was not a killer, and he adored his mother. His emotional instability would have then disrupted the daimon's ability to communicate its will."

"So the daimon left José and moved to a more viable host," Garcia mused. "If Prieto is the target, then we should summon him."

"Christ's blood, Garcia." Guillermo shot the inspector a dour look. "You know it's not that simple."

Because otherwise, Guillermo would have done it weeks ago. In order to summon Prieto against his will, they would have to know how to sing his true angelic name. From what Diago had been able to discern by listening to conversations between Guillermo and Miquel, Prieto was something of an enigma, even to the other angels. None of the members of Los Nefilim found any trace of him. Juanita had even failed to find another angel who would admit to knowing him.

Garcia persisted. "We have a duty to warn him. He is a Messenger angel. He is on our side."

Guillermo frowned at the wall as if he could divine the answers from José's script. "We really don't know whose side he's on."

"I know this," Diago said. "The fragment José delivered to Ferrer was here first, and look what happened. We've got to get it out of the Ferrer apartment."

"I've got someone who can take care of that." Garcia was quick to offer.

"So do I," Guillermo said. "Leave it to me."

Garcia tried not to show his disappointment.

Interesting. Guillermo evidently didn't trust Garcia in all things.

Guillermo pocketed his lighter and checked his watch again. "Anything else?"

Whatever this daimon was, José fought it. Maybe he could shed some light on how he came by the fragment in the first place. "I need to see José."

Garcia shook his head. "You won't get anything useful out of him."

Four loud knocks jarred them into silence.

Garcia said, "The other officers won't question my presence here. I can tell them I'm wrapping up the investigation for Mieras, but all of you must go. Where is the car?"

Guillermo answered. "Els 4 Gats. Is there a servants' entry?"

"Behind the downstairs kitchen," Diago said as they moved toward the stairs.

Wasting no time, they were at the first floor within moments. Suero had already left.

Miquel turned to them. "Two other policemen were here. I managed to get the guards to put them off but they'll be back soon."

"We're done." Guillermo turned and looked down the hall.

Garcia took Miquel's place by the door. "I'll handle them when they return. I'll need a written report from you, *Doctor*."

"Tell Mieras I have to see José before I can give him a preliminary report. Call the doctors at Holy Cross and tell them to suspend any medications. I need him in the same frame of mind as he was when he committed the murders."

Garcia pursed his lips so hard, his mustache bristled.

Probably because he doesn't like taking orders from me. Too bad. "I want to delve his mind. If we can find out where he got the fragment, we might be able to determine who or what this daimon is. From there, we can figure out how to stop her."

Guillermo pointed at Garcia. "Good idea. Get us both in there."

"I won't be able to get you inside today." Garcia protested. "Calling the doctors and circumventing Mieras takes time."

"Then schedule the visit for tomorrow morning. Call me when you have it arranged." Guillermo touched Diago's shoulder. "Let's go. We're going back to Santuari."

Diago turned to follow Guillermo and Miquel. A low moan caused him to pause and glance up the stairs. Another sound, delicate as a moth, crept down the banister. This one came in the guise of Doña Rosa's voice:

"I'm glad I caught you, Señor Alvarez. You had a visitor today. She hunts . . ."

CHAPTER FOUR

On the ride home, Diago sat in the backseat with Guillermo. He tried to distract himself with the passing scenery, but had little success. Instead, he listened as Guillermo briefed Miquel and Suero.

Miquel sat sideways in the front beside Suero, his left arm thrown casually across the seat. Although Guillermo glossed over the friction between Diago and Garcia, Miquel inferred what had happened from Guillermo's carefully chosen words. The downward curve of his lips bespoke his concern.

He knows Garcia and me too well. Diago avoided eye contact with his lover. He couldn't take back his lie of omission to Garcia. It was done. Now he would have to begin anew to win the inspector's trust. He only hoped he hadn't shaken Guillermo's faith in him.

I'll do better tomorrow. This was just like writing a

song. He had to work through the keys until he found the right melody.

Beating his self-confidence with a cudgel of guilt would get him nowhere. It was time to release the day and look forward to the evening. He consoled himself with thoughts of Rafael. His son would be covered in cat hair and straw, his fingernails stained with finger paints, or the lead from his colored pencils, because he loved to draw almost as much as he loved to dance.

"What now?" Miquel asked when Guillermo finally finished.

Guillermo lit his cigar. "We're going to move fast," he said through a cloud of smoke. "Suero, where is Amparo?"

"She is living in El Raval, near Chinatown."

"I have a job for her."

Suero nodded. "I'll find her tonight."

"What does Amparo do?" Diago asked.

"She is the best thief I've got." Guillermo rolled down his window a few centimetres. "She'll get the fragment. Then we can study it at Santuari."

The supple branches of the almond trees swayed in a light breeze. Buttery shades of sound fluttered around the limbs. Diago blinked. *Another attack of chromesthesia*. He shifted his gaze to Guillermo and pretended nothing was wrong.

Like the smoke from his cigar, Guillermo's words were soft and gray. "Can you sketch the layout to the Ferrer's apartment for Amparo?"

"Of course."

"Good." Guillermo stared at the passing orchard. "Suero, while you're there, see if Amparo has found out anything about Prieto."

Suero acknowledged the order with a nod. "She's had her ear to the ground for a month and hasn't heard anything."

"Tell her to look to the skies, then," Guillermo quipped.

Diago couldn't resist a quick jab at Garcia. "Garcia thinks Prieto is our friend."

Miquel scoffed. "Garcia is the kind of Nefil Prieto would love."

"Even Garcia knows he's to clear any angelic orders with me first." Guillermo rolled the cigar between his fingers. "Incidents like the one with Prieto have made me cautious." His words lost their colorful vibrations as the episode of chromesthesia passed.

Diago rubbed his eyes. "There have been others like Prieto?"

"Yes." Guillermo took a long draw from his cigar before tossing it out the window. "I think the angels are headed toward a civil war. The signs are there and mirror our situation in this realm."

"But why fight amongst themselves? What do they have to gain?" Diago left the most important question unspoken: and whose side will Los Nefilim take?

"I don't know," Guillermo admitted. "Juanita has lost two of her contacts among the Messengers. No one is talking. The only thing I know for certain is the angels are using Los Nefilim to carry out assaults on one another. I've lost two good Nefilim to bad orders and angels' games, and our numbers aren't so great that I can afford to throw Nefilim into battle. What Prieto did to you, Miquel, and Rafael was unconscionable."

Suero and Miquel's calm acceptance of Guillermo's suspicions told Diago Los Nefilim had suspected such a war for some time. *And because I wasn't a member of Los Nefilim, Miquel couldn't talk to me about either the situation or his fears. He'd carried his burdens alone.* Now Diago understood why Miquel spent so much time with Suero. He needed someone who understood his troubles, and Suero fulfilled a role Diago had consciously avoided. *I had purchased peace for myself, only to drive Miquel into Suero's confidence. I can do better by him now and be the kind of partner he has always been to me.*

Shamed by his selfishness, Diago glanced at Miquel as the yard came into view. The shadow of a beard darkened his cheeks. The top button of his shirt had come undone, revealing the hollow of his throat. He turned his head and said something to Suero, and as he did, his dark eyes caught Diago watching him. His mouth broadened in a smile meant for Diago and no one else, unleashing a flood of desire low and deep in Diago's stomach.

Diago touched his chest where he wore his wedding band on a chain beneath his shirt and returned his lover's smile.

Miquel winked at him, and then their moment of

intimacy ended as he returned his attention to the grounds, but the vigilance he'd exhibited in the city was tempered here. Wards and sigils protected Santuari, so most of the Nefilim's patrols were cursory at best.

But he watches anyway. What was it Miquel had said? *We watch out for our own.*

Suero stopped the car and cut the engine. The villa's doors opened to reveal Lucia, Ysabel's governess. In truth, she served double duty as the child's bodyguard during the day when Guillermo was absent from the grounds. Between her presence and Juanita's, Guillermo had surety of his daughter's safety.

He insisted on the same protection for Rafael. Diago would soon have to choose a "governess" for his son. One thing he knew for certain: he didn't want Lucia watching Rafael any longer than necessary. She made no secret of her hatred for daimons . . . or of her love for Miquel.

Lucia patted her light brown hair, which was coiffed into fashionable waves. She smiled at Miquel and stood sideways in the doorway. After making sure she had Miquel's eye, Lucia smoothed her dress. Her palm moved flat against her stomach and traveled down to fall away just before touching her crotch.

The maneuver looked like something he'd seen in one of those lurid American films Miquel loved. Diago recalled Señora Ferrer and her almost identical attempts to seduce him. Did they all watch the same movies? Lucia possessed all of the subtlety of a cat in heat.

He clamped a sharp comment behind his teeth and did well to hold his tongue as he and Miquel passed her. No need to antagonize her; not when the object of her desire was devoted to him. He positioned himself to block her view of Miquel and gave her his most charming smile.

Her glare should have turned him to stone.

"Papa!"

Diago whirled, forgetting all about Lucia.

Rafael ran down the stairs as fast as he could, and Diago held his breath, hoping the boy wouldn't fall. He was small for a six year old, and Guillermo's house was old, with tall narrow steps.

"Look at what I can do!" Sure-footed as a goat, Rafael jumped to the flagstones from the second step, lifted his arms, and twirled. He stamped one foot and simultaneously slid the other, executing the chufla, a flamenco dance step, like a professional. He brought down his arms until his hands rested by his hips, then looked up at Diago. "Are you proud?"

All of the horrors and failures of the day faded in the face of Rafael's hopeful smile. "Yes. I am very proud. Come see me." He lifted the boy in his arms.

Rafael hugged Diago. Just as he'd suspected on the ride home, his son smelled of horses and hay and sunshine. He pressed his cheek against Rafael's curls and inhaled the boy's warmth. "Did you have a good day?"

Rafael nodded against Diago's shoulder.

"Did you draw me pictures?"

Another nod.

"He's been kissing kittens." Miquel teased.

"Have not!" Rafael lifted his head, and his grin shook the last remnants of the day from Diago's heart. "Are we going home now, Papa?"

Home. Diago liked the sound of the word better every time he heard it. He nodded. "Where are your shoes?"

"Ysa's room."

As if summoned by her name, Ysa pounded down the stairs.

"Papa!" She jumped off the fourth stair from the bottom, and Guillermo caught her. She opened his coat and patted his breast pockets. "Did you bring me something?"

"You want a cigar?"

Ysa made a face. "Yuck."

"Then I have nothing for you but myself."

"You didn't bring me a sweet?" Ysa pouted as he set her down.

"You're sweet enough." Guillermo tugged her braid. "Where is your mamá?"

Juanita emerged from the small room she used for a clinic. Her long black hair was pulled back into a bun against her neck. Eyes the color of indigo and gold flashed at Guillermo. "Did I just hear you offer your daughter a cigar?"

"Absolutely not." Guillermo pointed Ysa toward the stairs. "Run before she starts to question you."

Ysabel giggled and escaped up the stairs.

Diago put Rafael down. "Go and get your things."

He ran after Ysa as Juanita turned her attention to Diago. "How is your arm?"

Diago flexed the fingers of his right hand. Although the compound fracture he had sustained in his fight with Moloch's 'aulaqs had healed in three weeks, his arm was still weak. "It's getting better. I've been resting it like you told me to do."

"Good. I had time to examine Rafael today. Come inside so we can talk."

Diago followed her into the room and gestured for Miquel to come, too. If Juanita had bad news, he didn't want to hear it alone.

Guillermo stuck his head inside and rapped the wall gently to get Diago's attention. "Listen, in spite of everything, you did well today."

Diago felt a flush of shame warm his cheeks. "No, I didn't."

Guillermo waved Diago's denial away. "You know what went wrong and you'll fix it. I know you will. Don't give up. I trust you."

Warmed by Guillermo's faith in him, Diago picked at the bandage around his right hand and said nothing.

Guillermo said, "I've got to talk to Suero for a minute. I'll send him up for the map after dinner."

"I'll have it ready."

Guillermo pointed at Diago. "Get some rest tonight."

Lucia came to the door after Guillermo departed. "I put the applications for Rafael's governess on the table by the door. Pick them up on your way out."

Diago answered her. "Thank you, Lucia."

She smiled sweetly and lowered her voice. "Thank Miquel. If it wasn't for him, I wouldn't care what happened to you or your bastard."

Miquel slammed the door in Lucia's face and whirled on Juanita. "Why don't you do something about her?"

Juanita didn't spare him a glance. "We all have promises to keep, Miquel. Guillermo made his to Diago, and I have mine to Lucia. If you can't respect her, respect my oath."

Diago stood with his back to the examining table. "What if Rafael hears her call him a bastard?"

"She says things like that to upset you, not Rafael."

"She'll move to him next."

"I will speak to her. I promise." She picked up the small handheld light she seemed to love shining in his eyes of late. "I had more time to work with Rafael today."

Miquel sat on the examining table and put his hands on Diago's shoulders.

Diago leaned against him. "He can't read or write. Did you find something wrong with him?"

She shook her head. "Wherever he was, they simply didn't bother with even the most rudimentary education. I spoke with Father Bernardo, and he gave Rafael some books. Bernardo is going to visit you later this week."

"He can't go to school if he's so far behind. The others will torment him."

"That's why Bernardo is going to visit. He'll show

you what to do. Meanwhile, read to him and encourage him to focus on letters and words. Make it fun."

"So . . . he's not . . . you know . . ."

"Mentally deficient? No. Rafael is a bright boy, Diago. He'll catch up to the others in no time." She assured him as her cool fingers touched his chin. "Wish I could say like son, like father . . ." she mused, a playful smile on her lips, which fled at the dark look Diago gave her. "Bad day?"

Diago shrugged.

Miquel chided him. "Not as bad as he thinks. He's always harder on himself than anyone else." He blew on Diago's ear. "It's part of his charm."

"Stop it." Diago swatted at Miquel, but his fingers only touched air. Any annoyance at his lover was feigned. Between his relief for Rafael's good health and Miquel's playfulness, he managed a smile.

"That's better." Juanita smiled and flicked on the light. "Look straight ahead."

"Do I have to?"

Miquel poked him in the back. "Yes."

Diago sighed and tried not to blink when Juanita shined the light in his eyes.

"Did you have more episodes of chromesthesia?" she asked.

"Nothing serious."

She snapped off the light and stepped back. "Don't lie to me, Diago. You're no longer a loner. A mistake on your part could take all of us down."

Diago instantly saw the word LIAR tattooed on

Alvaro's forehead. The memory punched him harder than it should have. *Don't lie to me.* Did they all think him a liar just like his father?

"I'm not lying, and I haven't made a mistake." *But I am lying and I did make a mistake today.* He sighed and rubbed his eyes, trying to calm himself. With a conscious effort, he softened his tone so he didn't sound so waspish. "I just wish everyone would stop questioning my loyalty."

Miquel's hands massaged his shoulders. "Easy."

Juanita said, "I'm not questioning your loyalty, Diago."

Of course she wasn't. Juanita had always spoken up for him, even when the others wouldn't.

"I know, I know. I'm sorry." He sighed again and wished he could start this day over. "It's just that all day, I've listened to Garcia second-guess my every motive."

"Ah. Now I see," Juanita murmured. "I understand your frustration, but you have to remember: the others recall you in your firstborn life. When you were Asaph, you swore an oath, and then you betrayed your king."

And not a single one of them acknowledged that Solomon and Asaph had begun as friends. *During our youth, we had loved one another like brothers.* They had rarely argued until the daimons managed to drive them apart. Pride and a desire for revenge had turned their final days to ashes. *But that was the past, and the past was as dead as Solomon and Asaph.*

"Is it asking too much to be judged on my actions

in this life? Asaph died an ugly death. Diago lives and hopes for better. I can't earn their trust if they've already decided I'm guilty." He held Juanita's gaze. "Do you see? I'm just asking for a chance."

She touched his scarred cheek. "I can only speak for Guillermo and me: we trust you. Miquel trusts you, and you seem to have won Suero's faith. Small steps will lead to great strides. Just be patient."

The children came back downstairs, their laughter pealing through the house.

Juanita glanced at the clinic door, then back to Diago. "I'm going to ask you again: did you have more episodes of chromesthesia?"

"A couple. I had two severe attacks in the city and a third mild one on the way home."

"That's three."

"Two and a half."

Miquel's hold on him eased. "None of the attacks debilitated him. He moved through them."

"I'd feel better if you rested tomorrow," Juanita said.

"I'm going with Guillermo to Holy Cross."

"I'll talk to Guillermo." She put the light away. "If you like."

"Don't. We're hunting a daimon. The others won't see the signs I can see. Not even Guillermo."

"And you think by defeating a daimon, Los Nefilim will believe in you."

He couldn't tell if she thought him noble or pathetic. Not that it mattered to him one way or another. "I took an oath."

She considered him carefully for a moment. "The others might only see your daimonic nature, but I see the angelic in your eyes." Then she turned to Miquel. "Make sure he rests."

Later that evening, Diago woke on the couch in the guesthouse a little after sunset. *Guesthouse. No. It's our house now,* he thought as he indulged in a languid stretch.

Through the parlor window, the sky retained hints of purple. The stars were gauzy points of light through the clouds. He remembered changing clothes and sitting down to sketch the map of the Ferrer apartment. Rafael had settled on the floor, pad and pencils arrayed around his latest drawing. Having finished the map, Diago had closed his eyes, meaning only to rest for a moment.

Judging from the light, he'd slept for a couple of hours. Someone, most likely Miquel, had taken off his shoes and covered him with an afghan. Diago sat up and noticed a sheet of paper on the table. Rafael had drawn a picture of their house. In front of the home, a child with dark green eyes stood between crude representations of Diago and Miquel.

No. Not entirely crude. The drawings had a primitive appeal. The shapes of the faces and stances were good likenesses. They were all smiling and holding hands. A white kitten with one blue eye and one green eye sat at Rafael's feet. Overhead, a bright yellow sun with angel's wings beamed down on them.

At the bottom of the picture, Rafael had printed "My Family" in block letters. Diago held up the paper to the light and detected the pencil marks beneath the colors. Miquel had printed the letters and Rafael had traced over them.

Warmth filled Diago's chest. *Miquel is so unsure of himself, but he's a better father than I am. He knows how to give.*

From the kitchen came the smell of roasting vegetables and the sound of a knife rhythmically hitting the wooden cutting board. Miquel was cooking dinner.

Rafael's voice wafted into the small living room. "Do you want me to wake Papa?"

"Not yet." Miquel said. "Doña Juanita said to let him rest."

"I checked him a few minutes ago and he was still breathing."

Miquel laughed. "That's always a good sign."

"It's not funny. Sometimes Papa breathes so soft I can't tell if he's alive. But if I touch his cheek, he wrinkles his nose and turns over and that's how I know he's not dead."

"That sounds very scientific."

"Sister Benita said I was silly when I did things like that. She said I was supposed to trust God. She said if I really loved God, then I would trust Him. But that doesn't feel right. Can you love someone but not trust them, Miquel?"

Miquel was silent for a moment. "Yes. I think you can love someone but not trust him, or her."

Diago wondered if Miquel was thinking of Candela. He looked down at Rafael's drawing of the winged sun. The child wasn't far from the truth. The angel's presence lingered over their every waking moment in the form of Rafael. Yet Miquel had not once complained about having the boy in their lives. Diago held the picture against his chest. Through the paper, he felt the outline of his wedding band beneath his shirt. He touched the chain of his necklace and fished the ring to his finger.

"I don't understand," said Rafael.

"Well . . ."—the knife slowed—" . . . think of it like this: love is a gift that's given. Trust is a coin that's earned." The chopping sounds stopped altogether. "Do you know how to peel garlic?"

"Yes!" The chair scraped the floor. "Then can I check on Papa again?"

"Only if you promise not to wake him."

"I promise."

They hummed a tune together as they worked.

Unbidden, the memory of Alvaro resurfaced. *Diago, my son, help me . . . help. . .*

Diago closed his eyes and tried to muster any recollection of his father—a touch, a scent, a word—but nothing came immediately to his mind. He conjured the image of Alvaro's soul wrapped in Moloch's magic, and contemplated the shape of Alvaro's face. From the farthest reaches of his first memories, Diago recalled a man with similar features. He had carried Diago into his aunt's home and left him there with a promise that he would return.

But he never did. He never came back. And Diago had shut the pain of that first betrayal deep within his soul, never to be examined . . . until today.

But why? How could he have deserted me if he truly loved me? Diago tried to imagine leaving Rafael with strangers. Although the child had been in Diago's life for only a few weeks, he couldn't bear to abandon him so heartlessly.

What reason did Alvaro have? During Diago's brief meeting with his father, Alvaro claimed he left because Diago had forgotten how to love, but was that true? If Diago lacked the ability to love, he wouldn't have cared if Alvaro abandoned him. *But I did. I loved Alvaro. His betrayal was so traumatic I buried it.*

Diago opened his eyes. Alvaro's statements didn't fit. *He claimed he'd remained by my side as long as he could, but how old was I when he left me with my aunt? Four? Five?* If a father couldn't bear to watch his son go through another life in sorrow, did he simply abandon him before he knew whether or not the child could change?

Was Alvaro so selfish and callous?

On the other hand, he *had* helped Diago deceive Moloch, had given his life so they could flee. *Why would he help me save Rafael if he didn't care?*

Diago pressed his wedding band to his lips. None of it made sense. The two aspects of his father—the cold Nefil who abandoned his son, and the repentant one who saved his grandson—didn't mesh. An integral piece was missing from the puzzle, leaving Alvaro and his motives tantalizingly out of focus.

Miquel crossed the kitchen and took from the cupboard two glasses and a bottle of homemade wine. He glanced into the front room where Diago sat. "Look who is up."

Rafael's chair scraped again.

"Don't"—Miquel pointed his finger in Rafael's direction just as a thud shook the floor— "jump." He sighed in resignation.

Diago happily released the enigma of Alvaro. The problem created by his father made his head hurt.

Rafael ran from the kitchen and into the living room. The papery garlic husks were still stuck to his fingertips. He threw his arms around Diago's neck and kissed his cheek. "Did you have a nice nap?"

"I certainly did." Diago let the ring drop to his chest. "Did you make this for me?"

Suddenly shy, Rafael climbed onto the couch beside Diago and concentrated on picking the husks from his fingers. "Do you like it?"

"I do. You are a very, very good artist."

Rafael blushed and pointed to the words. "Miquel helped me."

"I couldn't see that at all."

"You don't lie very well, Papa. It's easy to see." Rafael held it up to the light and traced the letters with his finger. "See? Miquel wrote in pencil, then I colored the words in."

"I'm still proud of you."

Rafael noticed the wedding band on Diago's necklace. He lifted the ring and turned it around. "That's like Miquel's ring, except his is gold."

Diago gave himself a mental kick. He should have tucked it back into his shirt before Rafael saw it. "Yes, it is."

"Don Guillermo and Doña Juanita have matching rings, too, but they always wear theirs. Ysa says their rings tell everybody else they're married. Is that why your ring is like Miquel's?"

Diago dodged his son's question. "It's a symbol of love." He wasn't sure if he was ready to explain to Rafael his relationship with Miquel. Thus far, the child had accepted his new home and the fact that Diago and Miquel slept together without question. The guesthouse only had two bedrooms, so Rafael most likely figured their arrangements were from necessity. Besides, he probably had no comparable experience. Diago and Miquel were careful not to display any overt affection toward one another around him. They'd agreed to tell him together when he was older and better able to understand.

And in the meantime, pray he *would* understand. Perhaps Rafael's lack of education was a blessing in disguise. The Church maintained its stranglehold on the schools and the curriculum, indoctrinating their poisonous philosophies into the children's minds. Unlike schools in other towns, the youngsters of Santuari learned the true mysteries of the universe from the old Nefil, Bernardo—*Father* Bernardo, that is. Rafael's only encounter with the Church appeared to be in the form of the rather daunting specter of Sister Benita. Diago hoped she hadn't inflicted too much damage on his son's worldview, but until he was sure, it was best he and Miquel were circumspect with their affection.

Rafael asked, "But if you love Miquel, why don't wear your ring?"

"It's . . . complicated." Diago unclasped the hook and slipped the ring from the chain.

Rafael touched the silver band. "Miquel wears his ring."

From the kitchen, Miquel sang out, "Yes, he does!"

Rafael looked up at Diago and frowned. The child was genuinely trying to understand. The situation perplexed him, but he was determined to work through it with the same tenacity he used on all his problems. "Is Miquel your wife?"

Miquel's laughter rang out in the kitchen.

"No, he is not my wife." Diago shot a glare at the door. *A little help in here would be nice.* But Diago held no hope of getting any. He looked into his son's questioning eyes and knew he couldn't lie. "Miquel and I are . . ." *What? Married? Lovers?* He groped and finally seized the word he desired. "We're partners. We made a sacred promise to each other, because we love one another."

"Like brothers?"

"Like a partner. Someone I want to spend my life with."

Rafael considered this explanation for a moment. "Then why don't you wear your ring?"

"Because he thinks our love is dark," Miquel said from the kitchen doorway. He spoke gently enough, but Diago detected the familiar bitterness edging into his words.

How many times had Miquel asked him not to hide the symbol of their love? *You murder me, Diago. Every time you deny our love, you murder a piece of my heart.*

Ashamed, Diago looked down at his ring. Miquel disappeared back into the kitchen. The sounds of plates rattling onto the table seemed to carry more force than usual.

I've upset him. Again.

"Love isn't dark, Papa." Rafael touched the ring in Diago's palm. "Love kills the dark. That's what Mamá always said. Love drives the dark away."

"I don't believe love is dark." Not anymore. Not after his years with Miquel. But still . . . "I'm afraid not everyone will understand."

"They don't understand because you don't wear your ring. If you wore your ring, they would understand."

Diago had no answer for that, and he now wondered if it was *he* who didn't understand, and Rafael got it just fine. He simply sat there with his son next to him, gazing at the wedding band he wore beneath his shirt like it was a dirty secret. Yet Los Nefilim knew. They all knew. Some didn't approve, but they didn't dare say anything to Diago or Miquel's face. What were they going to do? Kick him out? The thought of it was ludicrous. Once a Nefil swore allegiance, he never left the service of his king.

And how can I commit to Los Nefilim and not to the man who has stood by me all these years? The chain slithered between Diago's fingers and fell to the floor.

Rafael bent down and scooped up the necklace. By the time he'd risen, Diago had slipped the wedding band onto his finger. He held up his hand and admired the silver band against his skin.

Rafael examined the ring critically. "It looks very handsome on you."

"Yes," he said. "Yes, it does."

Miquel cleared his throat. He had returned to the doorway. His dark eyes shined in the half light. He was pleased. Diago fell in love with him all over again.

"Um . . ." Miquel held up his glass. "Dinner is ready if you two are hungry."

"Yes!" Rafael jumped down and scooted past Miquel.

Diago wasn't able to move past him with the same ease—especially since Miquel blocked the door. He fingered the ring on Diago's hand. "Are you sure about this?"

"As sure as the night I said, 'I do.' "

Miquel touched his cheek against Diago's and whispered in his ear. "I'm glad."

"Come on, Papa! I did the garlic." Rafael was already in his seat, spooning vegetables onto his plate. "Sister

Benita said that garlic keeps the vampires away. Since 'aulaqs are vampires, does garlic keep them away?"

"No," he and Miquel answered simultaneously.

They moved apart, suddenly self-conscious of their closeness in front of Rafael, but the child only noticed them when they joined him at the table.

Miquel cut the bread and added a slice to Rafael's plate. "Eat it at the table. Don't take it in your room. I'll leave two pieces on the counter tonight. You can come get them if you get hungry in the night. Okay?"

"Okay, Miquel."

Diago smiled behind his wineglass. All three of them knew they'd find crumbs scattered like an offering around Rafael's pillow come morning.

"Will you be home tomorrow, Papa?"

"No, I have to go into town with Don Guillermo. You'll be good for Miquel, won't you?"

"Yes. He said I can help interview the governesses. Don't worry. We'll get someone very nice."

"I'm not worried." Diago assured his son. Not about governesses anyway.

Rafael spread butter on his bread and continued. "We'll make sure she likes cats, too."

Diago glanced at Miquel, who had taken a sudden interest in his food. Then Diago recalled the kitten Rafael had drawn in his family portrait. "We don't have a cat."

"Ysa said I could have the white kitten and you said that maybe we'll think about it." Rafael folded his hands in his lap, but he wasn't completely still. His right leg swung back and forth, and his heel struck the leg of his chair with a soft rhythm. "So. Did you maybe think about it?"

Diago nudged Miquel's knee. "Help me out here."

Miquel kept his head down and shadowed his face with his hand. "I think a kitten would be nice. She could eat the rats that come into Rafael's room, looking for bread crumbs."

Aghast, Diago stared at him. "Stop helping me."

Rafael protested. "I don't have rats in my room!"

Miquel lifted his head and put his finger against his lips.

Rafael smiled and nodded. "Yes, Papa! She can keep the rats out of my room."

"You don't have rats in your room."

"But if I did, she would eat them."

Diago looked at each of them. He didn't really want a cat in the house. He had a dismal history with animals of all varieties. Unfortunately, he saw the truth. "I'm losing this fight, aren't I?"

"The battle was decided in our favor before you entered the field," Miquel said.

"I'll take care of her, Papa. You won't even know she's here." Rafael nodded enthusiastically.

"Okay, a kitten. But she's yours, and if you need help cleaning up after her"—Diago pointed at Miquel—"that is your assistant."

Miquel gave him a closed-fist salute. "We will take command of the conquered territories."

Rafael returned the salute with a grin.

"Just make sure our furniture isn't shredded and the house doesn't stink." Diago returned to his dinner and resigned himself to the inevitability of cat. "When is she coming?"

"We have a week or two." Miquel assured him. "She isn't ready to leave her mother quite yet."

Rafael ceased to kick his chair leg. "Thank you, Papa. Her name is Ghost. You'll love her, and she will love you."

Diago reached over and daubed a piece of spinach from his son's lip. "You're welcome. Now finish your dinner."

Their pleasant dinner morphed into a quiet evening, interrupted only by Suero stopping by for the map to the Ferrer apartment. He didn't stay long and refused even a drink. Left alone again, they resumed their reading, and by midnight, they were all abed.

The nightmare struck at three o'clock. Diago dreamed himself drowning in the dark. The blackness swept over him and clouded his eyes. It filled his nose and his lungs, then took him down beneath ground and left himself faceless in the dark.

He awoke with a scream on his lips and Miquel's palm over his mouth.

"Shh, don't wake Rafael."

Diago closed his eyes and tried to get his breathing under control. *I am home. In bed. Loved.* He chanted the mantra in his mind until his heart rate slowed.

"Be still now," Miquel whispered as he drew Diago

into an embrace. "You're safe. You're safe with me." He gently massaged Diago's shoulder. "Tell me what is making you so tense."

"I'm afraid," he blurted, and immediately wished he could take back the words.

When Diago didn't continue, Miquel gave him a gentle prompt. "I'm listening."

"I'm afraid the others are right, and I'll become like Alvaro."

"You're nothing like Alvaro."

"You knew him?" Diago lifted his head.

"I knew of him. They said Moloch made him his right hand. Entrusted him with secrets."

Diago rested his cheek against Miquel's shoulder. That would explain Moloch's rage at Alvaro's betrayal. To bind a soul to his realm took a great deal of effort, not a task Moloch would undertake lightly, especially with the injuries he sustained during his fight with Rafael.

Miquel pulled him closer. "They said Alvaro was ruthless and gave no quarter. You're not Alvaro."

"I lied to Garcia today. That is something Alvaro would do."

Miquel sighed. "Garcia. God, what an asshole. You've got to stop being afraid of him."

"I'm not afraid of him."

"You are if you're lying to him."

As much as he wanted to argue, Diago knew he couldn't. Miquel was right. *He knows me better than I know myself.* "I don't know how to work as a member of Los Nefilim. How do I do this, Miquel? How can I be a part of them?"

"There is your mistake." Miquel propped his elbow on his pillow and looked down at Diago. "It is not 'them.' It is 'us.' You see?"

Diago shook his head. He had no idea where Miquel was going with this train of thought.

Miquel touched Diago's temple. "Your daimonic nature leads you to think in terms of singularity. You have to get in touch with your angelic side. Los Nefilim moves as a unit. So your first step is to stop thinking of yourself as being separate from Los Nefilim. You are a part of us now. Instead of saying: 'How can I be a part of them?' you must learn that the question is: 'How can I be a better part of us? How will my information benefit all of us?' Then you proceed from there."

"I see now. I will try. I swear I will try."

"I know you will." Miquel lay down again.

Diago thought about the questions and realized it might be easiest to apply the philosophy in his relationship with Miquel first. *How can I be a better part of us?* Yes. He would begin asking himself that every day. Maybe he could help make Miquel's life easier while learning to be a member of Los Nefilim. The thought appealed to him while simultaneously making him aware of how poorly he'd acted until now.

"I can be so damn difficult." Diago stroked Miquel's wrist. "Do you ever think of leaving me?"

Miquel brushed his lips against Diago's shoulder. He reflected on the question for several moments before he said, "Once."

"When?" Diago held his breath.

"Right before we left Sevilla. You kept walking around the apartment, touching everything so you could remember it all. I was ready to leave and let you catch the next train to Barcelona by yourself."

Diago smiled and slapped Miquel's hip playfully. "I'm being serious."

"So am I." Miquel took his hand and linked fingers with him. "I don't want to leave you. Now sleep, my serious Diago. Please."

Safe in Miquel's arms, Diago stopped his questions, but he couldn't sleep. The nightmare clung to the edge of his consciousness and gave him no peace.

After Miquel's breathing deepened, Diago rose and went to Rafael's door. He looked down on his son, who was curled on his side, his arm around his stuffed horse, and his thumb plugged firmly between his lips.

. . . *she hunts.* . .

Although the daimon hunted Prieto and his bomb, her inquires might lead her to Diago's door. Better to be safe and reinforce the protective wards around his home. He checked the window to make sure it was locked. After strengthening the sigil over the latch, he paused to watch it spin lazily in the dark. If anyone, mortal or supernatural, tried to enter, the ward would awaken Diago and Miquel. Then God help whoever or whatever tried to harm Rafael.

The child stirred and turned over in his sleep. Diago paused and tucked the blankets around him. As he did, Rafael opened his eyes, saw it was Diago and smiled.

Diago smoothed his hair and kissed his cheek. "Sleep."

Rafael closed his eyes and snuggled into his bed. A few errant crumbs drifted to the floor. Diago left the bread under Rafael's pillow. He remembered his own childhood. The nights he'd lain awake on a bed of straw with hunger gnawing his belly were just as fresh as if they'd passed yesterday.

Do what they say and you will eat, his aunt had promised.

But they didn't feed him. Instead, he was forced to fight the other boys for his bread, and though he was small, he discovered viciousness trumped size. And when the strangers who visited the brothel touched him, he learned not to cry. He taught himself to smile with his mouth, and never let them see the hate he buried in his heart.

Long memories were the Nefilim's curse. Just when he thought he'd finally chained all of his phantoms into the past, they rose to haunt him again.

Like Alvaro.

. . . she hunts. . .

Restless now, he walked through the house and

checked the windows and doors, making sure his sigils protected each one. When he was done he turned and walked through a second time, and then a third. Three times he walked, and three times he touched each window and door. Three times: once for the son, once for the father, and once to drive away the ghosts.

CHAPTER FIVE

The next day, a gray bank of clouds set the backdrop for the asylum at Holy Cross. Palm trees presided over the empty courtyard, where benches were placed under the arcades and out on the lawn. In sunnier weather, the atmosphere might have been inviting. With the gloom of an early November storm hanging over them, the mood was much more subdued. Other than a few nuns intent on their nursing errands, the yard was mostly empty.

Diago had to admit, Guillermo certainly knew how to arrive in style. Suero had polished the Mercedes-Benz 770 to a high luster, and drove the vehicle like he had been born behind the wheel. He skillfully guided the long black car up to the curb. Diago considered it a pity no one was around to receive them.

Suero halted the car in front of a fountain, got out, and opened the back door. Diago emerged first and stood beside the car. Once Guillermo joined him, Suero moved the vehicle farther down the curb where he could watch the entrance and wait for them.

Guillermo's gaze drifted to Diago's wedding ring for the seventh time that morning. He'd probably been thinking of clever ripostes for the entire ride. Might as well get it over with.

Diago asked, "Is something wrong?"

"Nice ring." Guillermo gestured to Diago's hand. "It's been a while since I've seen it."

"That's it? An hour ride, and that's the best you can come up with?"

Guillermo treated Diago to a most wicked grin. "I've been biting my tongue all morning, because I promised Miquel if you ever started wearing it, I wouldn't tease you." After a brief pause, he said, "I assume he is happy?"

Diago made a contented noise in the back of his throat. "Yes. Very happy. We spent the evening—"

"No details." Guillermo's blush extended down into his collar. "I don't need details."

"—reading to Rafael." Diago allowed himself a smile, enjoying Guillermo's discomfort. "What did you think I was going to say?"

He tugged at his collar and shot Diago an amused glare. "I know what you just did."

"I didn't do anything. Your brain jumped to its own conclusions."

"Touché." Guillermo chuckled and they stood quietly for a moment, listening to the wind hiss through the fronds. "Garcia said to meet him here. I wonder where he is." He looked up at the windows overhead.

"Most likely somewhere nearby," said Diago as he strolled away from Guillermo and searched the arcades for any sign of the inspector. Garcia was far too servile to keep Guillermo waiting for long.

A cloud of cigarette smoke billowed from behind a column at the far end of the porch. *Got him.*

Diago kept to the grass and followed the scent of tobacco. He heard Garcia's voice, speaking just above a whisper.

Why the secrecy? He glided forward on cat's feet, hoping to eavesdrop on the inspector.

Without warning, Garcia stepped backward and punctuated a comment with a sharp jab of his finger.

Diago ducked behind a pillar. *Someone is going to break his hands one of these days.*

Curious as to who had Garcia in such a state of righteous indignation, he peeked around the column.

Within the shadows of the porch stood a stout muscular man with short blond hair and a reddish cast to his skin. He answered Garcia in heavily accented Spanish. Diago pegged him for a German until the sun peeked from behind a cloud, momentarily lighting the dim corner. A ray of sunshine illuminated the man's eyes, which were deep lavender and shot through with streams of gold. Diago froze. Garcia's companion wasn't German at all.

He was an angel disguised as a mortal.

Well, this is interesting. Garcia wasn't doing anything

wrong, per se. To the best of his knowledge, Guillermo hadn't forbidden the other Nefilim from speaking with the angels as long as they reported back to him.

Still. He'll want to know about this. A quick glance revealed Guillermo had wandered in the opposite direction, and now stood by the fountain, gazing into the water.

Diago checked the porch again to find Garcia alone. The angel had disappeared.

The inspector smiled and put out his cigarette. Whistling a jaunty tune, he kept to the shelter of the porch as he walked in Diago's direction.

Damn it. Diago returned to the path and hurried back to Guillermo. Had the German left the grounds, or was he somewhere inside the asylum? Diago had no way to know, and the mystery would have to wait. He reached Guillermo's side just as a young mortal emerged from the hospital. The doctor turned and called a greeting to Garcia, who appeared and shook the mortal's hand.

This must be the doctor they awaited. The youth sported a thick mustache and heavily gelled hair, which was combed back in an attempt to tame his unruly waves.

"Don Guillermo, Doctor Alvarez. I apologize for our delay," Garcia said.

Guillermo treated Garcia to a scowl—he never liked to be kept waiting—before he gave the mortal a quick once-over. He might as well have been appraising a bull for his pens.

Garcia's genial demeanor showed no sign he was perturbed by Guillermo's umbrage. "Dr. Vales, this is Don Guillermo Ramírez. He has an interest in this case."

"Don José's mother was a good friend." Guillermo touched his heart. "I promised her family I would oversee this matter."

Dr. Vales's smile grew pinched. Guillermo's scrutiny increased the likelihood Vales's superiors would hear of any mistakes regarding Don José's treatment. To his benefit, Vales didn't appear unnerved by Guillermo's statement, which spoke well to the young doctor's self-confidence. He simply seemed inconvenienced by an outsider who presumably didn't understand the medical field. "I'm sure you'll find our facilities meet with the approval of both you and Don José's family."

Garcia treated Diago to his most contemptuous smile. "And this is Dr. Diago Alvarez, an Andalusian."

Andalusian was delivered with such a sneer Diago was only mildly surprised when Garcia didn't follow "Andalusian" with dog. Whose politics were showing now?

Dr. Vales's smile warmed slightly toward Diago. Mortals were so transparent. Vales saw in Diago another professional, who might prove to be an ally should Don Guillermo misinterpret a procedure. "Inspector Garcia tells me you are staying with Don Guillermo at his estate."

Diago offered his right hand. "Yes."

Vales took Diago's injured hand gingerly, barely

shaking, probably afraid of hurting him worse. "It is good to meet you. I'm afraid I haven't had the opportunity to familiarize myself with your work."

A rare moment of honesty from a doctor. Diago waved the admission aside. "I'm not surprised. I don't write very much these days. I had all but retired when I was called back into service."

Guillermo smiled at Diago's play on the truth as Vales led them inside the hospital.

Vales fell into step beside Diago. "I'm not sure how much you will get out of Don José. We've had to keep him in restraints since his arrival yesterday." He handed Diago an envelope as he guided them to a service elevator large enough to hold a gurney. "I had my secretary copy my notes for you."

Once the elevator started to move, Diago opened the file and glanced at the contents. Guillermo feigned indifference while Garcia pressed himself against Diago's right shoulder in order to see the file. The combined odors of cigarette smoke and cologne clung to the inspector's damp clothes and hair.

The stench caused Diago to gag. He turned his head and whispered in Garcia's ear. "If you get any closer, we'll have to get married."

Garcia stiffened and immediately stepped back.

Guillermo coughed his chuckle into his fist.

Vales's cheeks grew pink at the exchange, but he pretended not to notice. He nodded at the folder. "On the second page, my secretary transcribed some of his ramblings. It was . . . disconcerting."

"How so?" Diago asked.

"It was almost as if he was speaking to someone. Then he would answer himself in a different voice. It's not uncommon in some cases of schizophrenia, but it's the first time I ever witnessed it."

It's quite common in daimonic possession, too. Diago kept the thought to himself and hurried to reassure the young mortal. "It can be downright chilling."

Relieved that Diago seemed to understand, Vales relaxed.

Diago returned his attention to the page where a series of phrases and questions were neatly typed.

*J. (as himself): tell me his name a name give me . . .
Mother? . . . I asked her and she wouldn't tell me.
J. (speaking in a woman's voice): Ask harder.
J. (as himself): She said she didn't know. Mamá?
Mamá? Help me? Answer the question, Mamá!
J. (speaking in a woman's voice): Give her to me and
I'll divine the answer.*

Diago's stomach clenched. The thought of poor Doña Rosa's terror settled in the back of his mind and left an ashen taste in his mouth.

Vales nodded at the folder. "Disturbing, isn't it?"

"It never gets easier," Diago said, uncomfortably reminded of Garcia's first words to him at the Liceu station.

Garcia raised an eyebrow, but said nothing.

The elevator churned to a halt. Vales directed them

to a door that opened onto a ward. "We're almost there."

Diago felt his skin crawl as the heavy door closed behind them. The vaulted corridors were worthy of a cathedral, but all semblance to holiness ended there. The ward was more like a prison than a hospital. The orderlies were young muscled men, who possessed hard eyes and the swagger of guards. A few nuns carried out errands involving metal trays and cups of pills, but their faces reflected little sympathy for their charges.

An old man sat in a chair outside his room. He twisted a rag doll in his fingers and mumbled to himself. From behind another door, a man sang a lewd song. One of the sisters chastised him and he cursed her to hell.

Just ahead, a nun emerged from a cell. As she passed them Diago noticed she carried a small metal tray with several syringes lying in military precision on a white towel. A speck of blood dotted the fibers beneath the needle of an empty syringe—one of the patients had fought his injection.

The nun ducked her head when she noticed them. Diago barely glimpsed her face before her wimple shielded her features. For a strange moment he thought he'd recognized Elena, the Ferrers' maid.

That's ridiculous. The Ferrers were difficult, but he'd doubted they'd ever driven anyone into a nunnery. This woman simply favored Elena.

Nevertheless, he paused and glanced over his shoulder after she passed them. Completely oblivious to him, she stepped purposefully into the room with the bawdy singer.

The syringes probably held some kind of sedative—something to chase the patients' madness into the shadows, or barring that, a medical cocktail to render the men more compliant. Diago just hoped she'd skipped José's room.

But the blood.

Any one of the patients might have struggled. It was probably nothing.

Diago returned his attention to Vales, who had stopped before the third cell. The doctor opened the door and Diago followed him into a room that held nothing more than a bed and a small table, both of which were bolted to the floor.

José had become a shadow of the man Diago remembered. The heavy leather straps binding his wrists and ankles to the bed made him seem almost childlike.

Diago might have summoned more pity for him had he not known of the prostitutes José had brutalized during his days on the Paralelo. At least those women had one less abuser prowling the streets.

Dr. Vales, on the other hand, seemed embarrassed by José's restraints. "My apologies, Don Guillermo, but we don't have these facilities in our first-class wards. In spite of appearances, I can assure you Don José has been treated with the utmost dignity."

"The boy murdered his mother and two innocent

men." Guillermo's voice was a low growl. "You do as you see fit, Doctor."

Vales exhaled with relief. Diago could only imagine the tightrope the young doctor walked between providing care for his patients and appeasing the entitled demands of the privileged.

Diago went to José's side. From his peripheral vision, he noticed Garcia halt at the foot of the bed. Guillermo remained in the doorway, fulfilling his role as observer.

Vales stood across from Diago. He spoke gently to José as if soothing a distressed animal. "Hello, Don José. How are you feeling today?"

Diago looked down at the young mortal. Don José appeared to be having a very bad day. Dark circles blackened his eyes, which darted right and left, from Vales to Diago and back again. A thin whining noise hissed through his lips.

Suddenly, José's eyes rolled upward until only the whites were visible. His muscles visibly contracted, and his body went rigid. The smell of urine filled the small room. José had wet himself.

What the hell? Diago barely finished the thought before he realized what was happening. "He's having a seizure. Grand mal." Diago glanced up at Vales.

"Grant who?" Garcia asked.

Vales enunciated. "A grand mal seizure." He withdrew a stethoscope from his pocket and pressed the chest piece against José's heart.

José wasn't prone to seizures. If he had been, Doña

Rosa would have mentioned the fact during one of her many monologues to Diago. No, something else was wrong with José.

Something was very wrong.

The nun's tray of needles. Diago tossed the folder to the table and pushed up José's sleeve. A circular indentation around his upper arm indicated a tourniquet had been recently used. The pinprick of a needle was seated on his inner arm.

Diago recalled the blood on the towel. "I asked that he not be medicated."

"He wasn't!"

"He's been given a shot within the last ten minutes."

Pink foam appeared on José's lips. Dark red spots speckled his cheeks. His lips took on a blueish tint. *Cyanosis.* He didn't have enough oxygen in his blood.

José grinned at Diago.

No. He's not grinning. "Risus sardonicus."

"What?" Garcia stepped closer to the foot of the bed. "Speak Catalan! Or Spanish! What the hell is risus sardonicus?"

"Muscle spasms in the face." Diago explained. "Risus sardonicus gives the mistaken impression that the victim is grinning."

"Heart rate is rapid." Vales jerked the earpieces away and jammed the stethoscope back into the pocket of his white coat. "I don't understand."

José's back arched, rising off the bed. His heels dug into the mattress and his body bowed. The strap across his chest barely held him down.

"Jesus Christ." Garcia crossed himself. "He's possessed."

"Don't be a fool." Diago snapped. He cataloged the symptoms and quickly arrived at a diagnosis. "It's strychnine."

"What?" Guillermo advanced into the room.

"Poison." Diago was sure of it now. "He's been poisoned with strychnine."

"No," Vales said. "That's impossible."

The seizure finally ended and José's body went limp. His head lolled on the pillow.

"You've got to get him to the infirmary." Diago motioned for Vales to go. It was a fool's errand. Nothing in the infirmary could save José's life, but he needed to confer with Guillermo without Vales's mortal ears to hear. "Get a gurney!"

The order was enough to break Vales's stupor. He ran from the room, shouting for orderlies and gurney.

Guillermo came to Diago's side. "How bad?"

Diago didn't sugarcoat the news. "If he's at this stage, he's going to die. And I can't delve his mind, not without the risk of losing part of my soul to him when he succumbs to the poison. I won't take that chance, not even for you."

"Nor would I ask you to." Guillermo turned on Garcia. "Why didn't you have guards posted?"

Garcia cheeks were florid. "Vales said there was nothing to worry about. The cell was locked at all times."

"You let a mortal make a decision for you?" Guillermo took a step toward Garcia.

Garcia fell back, his face blanched with fear. "Mieras made the decision. Not me. I counseled him to use guards. He said we couldn't spare the manpower. I had no say in it."

Liar, Diago thought. Neither of Garcia's reasons presented a sufficient explanation for the lack of guards. If ever there was a time for a Nefil to exert his influence over a mortal, Garcia should have recognized that moment and pressed either Vales or Mieras into doing his will.

Diago kept his suspicions to himself. Not that he needed to say anything. Judging by Guillermo's glower, he had arrived at the same conclusion as Diago.

"Fucking hell." Guillermo's hands opened and closed at his sides. He looked ready to strangle someone. "We're right back to square one."

Garcia flinched and backed toward the door.

Diago saw his opportunity. Now wasn't the time to criticize. He had to offer a solution while Garcia remained paralyzed. "Maybe not," Diago said as he thought of the nun and her little metal tray of death. "There was a nun, who carried a tray of syringes. If we find her, we can question her." Diago looked to Garcia. "Did you get a look at her face?"

"I'll recognize her if I see her again." Garcia fingered the grip of his gun.

Another lie. Diago detected the doubt in Garcia's

voice, but calling him on his deception would only lose them more time. "Help me find her. Question every nun on this floor if you have to."

"Move!" Guillermo bellowed at him.

From another cell, a man screamed. "Move! Move! Move! Move! Move! Movemovemovemove!"

Whether Garcia fled Guillermo's rage, or the madman's cries, Diago didn't know. He asked Guillermo, "Do you trust him?"

"No. He's up to something, but I haven't figured out what." Guillermo grabbed the folder off the table and rapped it against his thigh. "I'll stay here. Go. Keep an eye on him if you can, but finding that nun is the priority."

"Understood." Diago slipped past Guillermo and almost collided with Vales as he returned to the room. He caught the mortal's arm. "I'm going with Inspector Garcia. We need to find the nun who poisoned José."

"Should I lock down the ward?"

Diago shook his head. "Too late. We were with José long enough for her to have left this floor. She could be anywhere."

"Do you want me to send some orderlies with you?"

"No." Nor did he have time for more questions. "It would be better if you had them search independently. Enlist the sisters, too. We can cover more ground."

Vales nodded. "Meet me at my office when you're done."

Diago made no promises. He released Vales and

went to the room of the bawdy singer. The man slept peacefully. Both of the nuns were gone. Another dead end. He left the room and walked fast to catch up with Garcia, who was already halfway down the hall.

"You mentioned you were at the Ferrers' apartment," Diago said.

Garcia's lips were thin and white with his rage. "What are you implying?"

"That you would recognize the maid, Elena, if you saw her again."

"You think it was her?"

Could it have been? Diago decided to hedge his answer. "Someone who looked like her."

The corridor ended in an intersection. Four nuns walked down the hallway on the right, and two were moving in the opposite direction on the left. Garcia pointed left.

Diago couldn't question the nuns and watch Garcia. *One crisis at a time.* He nodded and followed the nuns while Garcia went right.

Word must have spread fast, because orderlies were ushering patients into their rooms, trying not to panic them. Diago kept his pace quick and marked the face of each nun he passed. None of them fit the description of the woman he'd seen.

Three winding corridors and five angry nuns later, he still hadn't found her. Of course not. If it had been him, he would have already ditched the habit for street clothes and be on the next train out of Barcelona. This was fucking futile. *But necessary,* an inner voice warned him. He didn't want to return to Guillermo without having made a thorough search of the floor.

Diago turned right. The long dim corridor was empty but for him and a single nun. "Excuse me, Sister."

She neither acknowledged him, nor stopped walking.

Diago picked up his pace. "A moment, Sister! I need to speak with you." He grabbed her shoulder. The veil came away in his hands, and the habit fluttered to the ground. Empty.

"What the hell—?"

From an adjacent corridor, a patient's shriek cascaded down the hall in streams of purple and gold. Diago had enough time to think, *No. Please. Not now.* Then the colorful sound waves exploded around him.

Diago staggered backward. Whispers fluttered down the hall in rivulets of gray and green. Streams of pale yellow oozed through the air. The wails increased in volume. Violet shades of rage and fear flooded the air.

"Chromesthesia," said a nearby voice in hues of crimson and gold. "I haven't seen a Nefil undergo such a violent attack in centuries."

Diago recognized the voice. He shielded his eyes and tried to look through his fingers, but Prieto's light was blinding. He was in his angelic form and didn't bother with the trappings of the flesh. The brilliant colors sent tears streaming down Diago's cheeks. He ducked his head and shadowed his eyes with his palm.

"How is Miquel?" The angel asked conversation-ally. "Is he happy that you're sucking Guillermo's dick alongside him?"

Prieto's irreverence enraged Diago. Did he think playing with their lives was some kind of joke? Dia-go's fury fell in sound waves as black as soot. "Fuck you."

"You're still angry."

"Jesus Christ, you almost murdered my son!"

"Don't be wearisome, Diago. If I'd wanted Rafael dead, I would have given him to Alvaro. I made your presence a part of my conditions for Rafael's surren-der. Alvaro hasn't proven himself. His allegiance has always been to the highest bidder. You, on the other hand, have always remained faithful to your morals. I knew you would fight for Rafael, and that's what he needs—a father who will fight for him. Moloch only agreed to my game because I gave him no choice."

The colors of Prieto's speech grew more urgent with shades of vermillion. "But your oath to Los Nefilim surprised me. Now that you belong, we can trade information."

Diago tried to retreat. Prieto gave him no escape. The angel surrounded him with the vibrations of his essence.

With his back against the wall, Diago asked warily, "What kind of information?"

"An answer for an answer. You have a daimon on the loose in Barcelona, and I know her name. I want to know about Los Nefilim's allegiance. You scratch my intellectual itch and I'll scratch yours. Guillermo isn't following orders like he used to . . . why?"

Diago found that if he tilted his head and gazed at the tiles just beyond Prieto, he could stand to look in the angel's general direction. "This daimon is your concern. She is hunting you. Moloch wants to take back his idea for the bomb."

Prieto exhaled, and his breath hissed across Diago's face in a wave as cold as the stars. "If all I had to worry about was Moloch, then I wouldn't be here. Moloch doesn't give a damn about the idea, but others do. Entities far more dangerous to me than the daimons." The angel's light wavered, and then grew strong again. "Again: why isn't Guillermo following orders?"

Diago felt time slipping around them. He needed the daimon's purpose, but he couldn't put Los Nefilim at risk. How much did the angels already know? *Compromise. Give him the obvious and let him draw his own conclusions.* "Guillermo has lost two Nefilim to angels and their contradicting orders. Your bargain with Moloch and the ensuing stunt with Miquel, Rafael, and me did nothing to reassure him the angels are working together. He's become cautious."

The vibrations of Prieto's essence paled as he considered Diago's information.

Diago held his breath. Had he given him enough information for an exchange?

Prieto said, "You're the one who is in danger. The daimon you're seeking is Lamashtu. She is a minion of Sitra Akhra."

Sitra Akhra, the darkest of the daimons' realms, where only the most wicked survived. "Samael's kingdom." Samael, the fallen angel, had defected from the angelic realm in order to create Sitra Akhra. There, he ruled the corrupt daimons, and they worshipped him as a god.

"None other," Prieto said. "Beware that bridge, Diago. Moloch seeks to lure you close to it."

"Me? Why me?"

"Lamashtu's power is greater when she is near the bridge. She has been sent to make sure the son follows the father."

"I won't follow Alvaro."

"Christ, Diago, stop thinking like a mortal. *Your* son will follow *his* father."

Diago went cold. Now José's mad writings made sense. The son will follow the father. It wasn't a prophecy.

It was a plan.

Lamashtu was an old and powerful possessor. If any had the ability to successful take over the mind of a Nefil, it would be her. "They mean for Lamashtu to possess me."

"Now you're thinking like a Nefil. Have you taken Guillermo's mark yet?"

Diago shook his head. "No. The *'aulaq's* poison is still in my blood. Guillermo fears the venom will taint his seal of protection."

"He's right. Pity. Without his mark, you're still fair game to the daimons. You should leave Barcelona."

Diago wanted nothing more than to flee and take his vulnerable son with him, but flight wasn't the answer. The daimons would find him no matter where he went. Better to stay on familiar ground and fight the devils he knew.

"I'm staying here. I'm daimon, too. I know their patterns." Yet Prieto's explanation missed one vital factor. "Lamashtu tortured those mortals for a name, and it isn't mine. I think she *is* looking for you, too."

"I never said she wasn't looking for me. She seeks my name," Prieto admitted. "The daimons believe I revealed the true song of my name to the mortals in order to gain their compliance. Sometimes it's necessary; this time it wasn't. Lamashtu wants to sell my song to the angel who is hunting me so he can summon me against my will."

"What angel?"

"He calls himself Engel. He is the one who seeks the idea Moloch gave me. He wants it for the Germans."

That explained the German angel Garcia had conferred with in the arcades. Except with Prieto, it seemed one answer begat eight more questions. The most important of which had to do with Garcia's involvement with Engel.

Prieto's colors merged and shifted until he took on the greenish whispers of the insane. He was like a chameleon, changing colors to camouflage himself against his surroundings. "I'm out of time."

"Wait!" Diago reached out blindly in a futile attempt to stop the angel. "Whose side are you on?"

Prieto leaned close, his breath soft against Diago's ear. "Mine." Then he was gone.

Diago sagged against the wall. The sounds settled back into their usual shadows as the chromesthesia faded. So Prieto was on the run and hiding in the asylum. But why hadn't he dispensed of the idea to the mortal destined to create the bomb? Or to an archangel? Or even another Messenger? Why the intrigue?

Unless Prieto wasn't supposed to have Moloch's idea, or the mortal destined for the idea wasn't yet in Spain. Either way, Prieto was on his own.

Diago had the more immediate concern of Lamashtu. *And the daimons. Samael working with Moloch? That was unheard of.* Somehow Ba'al, the king of daimons, had managed to focus the daimons on a common course of action.

All so Lamashtu could possess Diago. And what if she was successful? What then? Lamashtu would raise Rafael while Diago watched helplessly from some vacant corner of his mind. If the daimons intended to execute such a plan, now was the time. Rafael was at a critical crossroads. Whatever happened to him over the next few years would shape his attitudes and allegiances. The daimons wanted the child badly enough to take Diago by force if necessary.

We'll see about that. He wasn't running, though. He was done running.

Guillermo's voice echoed down the corridor and jarred Diago from his thoughts.

"There you are." Guillermo strode toward him. Anger burned in his tawny eyes.

Dear God, what now? Diago straightened.

"We have a problem." Guillermo paused and registered Diago's features.

"Oh, we have a whole host of problems," Diago said. Still shaken from his encounter with Prieto, he ran his hand through his hair.

Guillermo's frown deepened. "You don't look good."

"I had another attack of chromesthesia. And I saw Prieto. He offered to exchange information. He gave me our daimon's name. Lamashtu. She is a minion of Sitra Akhra."

"Samael's realm," Guillermo muttered. "And what did you give him in return?"

"Only the obvious: two Nefilim have died due to conflicting orders from angels. He's extremely concerned about your allegiance. I told him you were simply being cautious." Diago's tension eased with Guillermo's nod.

"Don't worry. It was bound to come out sooner or later. I wish we knew more about his intentions."

"For now I'm worried just as much about Garcia." At Guillermo's raised eyebrow, Diago told him about seeing Garcia talking to the German angel, Engel. They conversed in hushed tones and used Old Castilian to prevent any mortals, who strayed down the corridor, from understanding their discussion. By the time they finished, Guillermo had his lighter out and was furiously flipping the lid open and shut.

"Engel," Guillermo muttered. "It's German for angel. He's mocking us."

A pair of doctors ventured in their direction as they conferred over a patient's chart.

Guillermo said, "Let's get out of here."

Diago fell into step beside the taller Nefil. "You said we had a problem. What did you discover?"

"The Ferrers are dead."

"Jesus Christ." He stared at Guillermo. "When?"

"Last night. It looks like they died in their sleep."

"You said Amparo was the best. You said she'd get the fragment. What happened?"

"Strychnine." Guillermo snapped. "Sound familiar? They suspect it's the maid, Elena. They can't find her."

Horror settled like a noose around Diago's throat. He recalled Señora Ferrer's penchant for sherry and music teachers. She had been young. Too young to be married to a man twice her age and forced to mother a child that resented her.

The Ferrers were like a grotesque reflection of Diago's family. *Miquel, so much younger than me, suddenly forced into raising a child that wasn't his, and Rafael . . . did he resent us taking the place of the mother he idolized?* Worse still, was this how they would end up? Poisoned, murdered in their sleep, and left as carrion for strangers to pick over their bones?

Diago cut off the thought. This was how the mortals stroked their fears, and he had plenty of complications without imagining more.

Guillermo paused in front of the elevator and stabbed the button like he had a vendetta against it. When the car arrived, he opened the gate and Diago followed him inside. A doctor and two orderlies hurried in their direction. The doctor called out for them to hold the car.

Diago stepped forward, but Guillermo slammed the gate shut and punched the button for the ground floor.

The maneuver didn't bode well. Diago put his back against the wall and listened to the whirr of machinery. He tapped a quick rhythm against the wall, hoping he was wrong. "Please don't stop the car—"

Guillermo rapidly punched a button.

The car shuddered to a halt.

"—between floors. Jesus, Guillermo, you make me so nervous when you do this."

"Stop whining. I'm tired of looking over my shoulder to see if the mortals are listening. At least we have some privacy." Although Diago couldn't see Guillermo's hand, he heard the steady click of the lighter's lid. "What is Lamashtu protecting by killing the mortals? José was insane. No one was going to take his ravings seriously. Why leave such a murderous trail in her wake?"

Diago thought about the question for a moment. "Not 'what' is she protecting, but 'who.' Someone, mortal or Nefil, had to help her get the fragment to

José in the first place. The daimons wouldn't concern themselves with protecting a mortal. They'd simply kill him or her. But a Nefil, someone under deep cover, someone hard to replace, now *that* would be worth this trail of death. Lamashtu is killing the mortals to prevent us from finding the name of a traitor. Think about it. She has been one step ahead of us ever since the beginning." He hesitated. Guillermo wasn't going to like what he was about to imply.

"Say it."

"Someone in Los Nefilim is feeding Lamashtu information. I think it's Garcia."

Guillermo shook his head. "I can see Garcia conspiring with angels, but not the daimons. He hates them too deeply." Before Diago could object, Guillermo pointed one blunt finger at him. "I know him, Diago. He would cut his own throat before he made an oath to daimons. No." He punched the button again and the car lurched into motion.

Diago breathed a little easier. "What if he asks me about today? You said I was to share everything with him."

Guillermo pursed his lips. "Keep him in the dark for now. Let him investigate the Ferrers' murder and run interference with the Guard. I want to see if he mentions his little meeting with Engel to me. I'll give him that much of a chance. If he doesn't, then I'll deal with him tomorrow."

At the ground level, they left the elevator and walked to the exit in silence. Outside the mist had stopped but the weather remained chill and overcast.

Diago raised his hand to signal Suero. The younger Nefil waved in response and got into the car.

Guillermo withdrew a cigar from his breast pocket. "Prieto said you should leave Barcelona."

"I'm not running. Not away from them. Moloch is trying to lure me to the bridge. I should go."

Guillermo lit the cigar and blew a cloud of smoke into the damp air. "No."

"We don't have the fragment. We don't know where to look. If we can't burn the sigil on the document and sever Lamashtu's link to the mortal world, then we have to cut the life-strand that links her soul to the fragment. The only way to accomplish that is to follow her to the borders of the daimonic realm right where they're trying to entrap me.

"What if we turn the tables on them and hunt Lamashtu? What's the old saying? 'The best way to beat an ambush is to spring it.' I can entice her away from the bridge so we can take her down."

When Guillermo made no immediate answer, Diago lowered his voice. He hated to plead, but he had no choice. "I've spent my whole life running, Guillermo. I ran from my true nature; I ran from Miquel's love; I ran because I was afraid. It stops today. I'm not running anymore. I have to face them and make a stand."

Suero pulled the car up to the curb. He opened the backdoor and waited, his gaze flickering from Diago to Guillermo.

Guillermo smoked and considered a distant spire. Almost a full minute passed before he spoke. "All right. We're going to my apartment on Carrer del Carme." The street was only a seven-minute walk from the Liceu station, close to the bridge. Guillermo put out his cigar and got into the backseat. "Let's hunt a daimon."

CHAPTER SIX

Suero stopped the car in front of a shabby apartment building on Carrer del Carme. Guillermo leaned forward and gripped the back of Suero's neck. "Find Amparo and bring her to number eight. She will answer to me. I want to know what the fuck happened last night. Then you call Juanita. Be careful and use code. We don't know if anyone is listening on our lines. Tell her we've been delayed in the city, and ask her to get Miquel to bring the kitten into our house for the night."

The kitten was their code for Rafael. Any doubts Diago might have entertained about joining Los Nefilim dissipated. Guillermo would keep his word and protect his family. He put his hand on the door handle, but Guillermo wasn't done.

"I want you to put a tail on Garcia. I think he's communicating with an angel, a German. He calls himself

Engel. I want to know Garcia's every move. What he eats for dinner, who he sees, when he goes to bed—everything. Stay away from Engel right now. I don't want him to know we're on to him. Understand?"

Suero nodded. "I'll see to it myself."

"Pair up. Everyone pairs up until I've gotten to the bottom of this. If anyone fucks up, I will have that Nefil's head on my gate. Am I clear?"

"Yes, boss."

"Spread the word and make them believe."

Suero's Adam's apple bobbed twice in rapid succession. It was the first time Diago had seen the young Nefil anxious about his orders. "I will, boss."

Satisfied with Suero's response, Guillermo opened the door and stepped onto the sidewalk. Diago got out and followed him through the maze of alleys winding away from Carme. Eventually they reached a building with a narrow entrance. Inside, the stairwell reeked of cheap beer and stale cigarettes. People moved behind the doors, conjuring images of rats in a nest.

At the second floor, Guillermo went to the end of the corridor and inserted a key in the door of apartment number eight. The cheerless apartment possessed one window, which looked down into the alley. A thin layer of grime covered the furniture, as if the residue of the other tenants' lives had somehow leaked through the walls to coat the furniture.

Diago took off his coat and hung it alongside his hat on the rack by the door. A quick tour of the apartment revealed one bedroom with a wardrobe against a wall.

"Bathroom is down the hall," Guillermo said. "If the door is shut, make some noise as you walk. Someone might be in there shooting heroin. You don't want to startle them into rupturing a vein." Guillermo flung his coat over the back of the sofa and tossed his hat beside it. "That's messy."

Diago retrieved the garments and hung them properly by the door. "I don't need the bathroom." *Thank God.*

Guillermo went to a cabinet and returned to the table with glasses and a bottle of Veterano. "I hope you don't mind your brandy in juice glasses." He didn't wait for an answer and poured them each a round. "But I need a drink while we wait for dark."

Diago sat at the scarred table. "They expect us to wait for tonight. We should go soon."

"You want to walk the tracks with the trains running? Are you serious?"

"I think we should avoid the tracks, precisely because that is what they are expecting us to do. I thought about it on the ride here. I know another way in, through the sewers. We can come up behind them."

"You don't intend to cross the bridge, do you?"

"No. That would be a fool's mistake." Diago sipped his drink. Guillermo might serve his liqueur in juice glasses, but he always made sure to buy the best. "I want to get close enough to show myself, and then lead Lamashtu back to you. Together, we can take her down."

"How?"

"If Lamashtu is possessing mortals, then she has left her corporeal body someplace safe—I'm guessing in Sitra Akhra where Samael protects her."

"And she possesses the mortals with her spirit?"

Diago nodded. "She infects them like a virus and lodges herself in her host's brain. Then she manipulates the mortal by controlling the person's muscles and nerves." *Just like she intends to do with me,* he thought and quieted the shiver stealing over him. He nursed another sip of his brandy before he continued. "In doing so, she effectively becomes that person."

Diago stroked his glass with one finger. "We've got to kill the mortal she has possessed. In this case, Elena. It's the only way to force Lamashtu's spirit into the open."

"I thought you didn't like murdering mortals," Guillermo said.

"I don't," he admitted. "But Elena is already the primary suspect in the Ferrers' murders. If we manage to eject Lamashtu from her body, what does Elena have to return to in this life? Imprisonment? Execution?" He shook his head. "Knowing how involved she was with the Ferrers, she will be horrified that she had a hand, no matter how unwillingly, in their deaths. She'll become like José, a shell of person. That's not living."

Guillermo withdrew his lighter and flicked the lid open and shut just once. "All right, we kill Elena; then what happens?"

"Lamashtu will flee Elena's dying body and return to spirit form. She will have two silver threads extending from her soul. These threads are the tethers that anchor her spirit to her corporeal form. One will lead to the fragment, the other back to her body in Sitra Akhra. We have to sever those threads with a sigil that looks like this." He hummed a short note in C and used the sound waves to carve an intricate sigil in the air. The double-edged lines were thin and sharp like a knife—the perfect glyph to sever a spiritual tether. "You try it."

"I can't go that high."

"Try it in D."

Guillermo followed Diago's example and crafted a ward that, while it wasn't quite as sharp as Diago's, could certainly function as a blade.

"That's good," Diago said. "When I find her—or when she finds me—I will draw her as far from the bridge as I can. Once we've eliminated the host, we sing our glyphs to life. You sever the thread leading to the fragment—it will be the thinner of the two. I'll cut the tether that connects to her body with the sharper sigil. We hit her hard and fast before she realizes what we've done. Once we've disabled her anchors, her spirit will die and so will her body."

"And what about Alvaro?" Guillermo asked.

Diago looked away from him. *Stop acting guilty. I've done nothing wrong.* He forced himself to meet Guillermo's gaze. "What about Alvaro?"

"Moloch is using him as a hostage. How will that affect you?"

Diago shrugged. "Why should it?"

Guillermo's voice was gentle, but the truths he spoke were not. "In spite of everything, he is your father. You might not want to face it, but we often hold onto loyalties based on blood . . . and spirit . . . regardless of whether those allegiances are rational or not."

Diago's fingers tightened around his glass. A spiral of anger coiled in his gut. All of Guillermo's talk of trust was easy when they were safe at Santuari, but now, in the face of going below, he obviously had doubts.

"Let's be honest." Diago leaned across the table, unable to keep the hurt out of his voice. "What you want to know is where my loyalties lie. If I should have to pick between saving you or Alvaro, who will I choose?"

"No." Guillermo's ire rose like the color to his cheeks. "You're wrong." His palm smacked the table. "You've never betrayed me, Diago. Never. And you've had ample opportunities before now." He leaned back in his chair. "No. I'm worried about *Alvaro* deceiving *you*. Or worse, luring you onto the bridge."

He's telling the truth. Guillermo could be as transparent as a mortal when he chose. *He's concerned about me.* Diago's rage slipped away. "What cause have I given you for concern?"

"It's like Candela's rape," Guillermo said softly, digging at a wound Diago didn't know how to close. "You never talk about it."

"And we're not going to talk about Candela now," he snapped.

Guillermo raised his hand in a gesture for peace.

"And I'm not suggesting we do. It simply illustrates a pattern of your behavior." Diago opened his mouth to protest, but Guillermo talked over him. "Anytime something bothers you, you tuck it away in some quiet corner of your mind and simply ignore it. You need to learn to deal with your feelings, Diago. You've got to stop carrying all of your guilt and shame inside." Guillermo sighed and looked at the window for a moment before turning his gaze back to Diago. "Talk to me like we used to talk. Tell me what is in your heart, my friend."

Diago stared into his glass. "My heart . . . is a dark song best kept silent." He felt Guillermo's stare like a hand on his face. *Give him something or he won't let the subject go.* "I've talked with Miquel about Alvaro. A little. I remembered something. Last night. My father left me with my aunt. He promised to return. He never did. I didn't see him again until I met him in Moloch's lair. Once I may have loved him, but after he abandoned me, I forgot him. I deliberately forgot him." *Like Candela and how she raped me.* He lifted his head and met Guillermo's gaze. "Alvaro hasn't meant anything to me in this life."

"Yet you tried to hide him from Garcia." It wasn't a question.

"I wasn't worried about Alvaro. I was concerned Garcia would make it seem as if I was colluding with my father. I was worried what you would think of me." He drained his glass and set it on the table with a thump. Unsure how to untangle his conflicting emotions enough to articulate them, he murmured, "It baffles me."

"What is that?"

"I spent my whole life either hating Alvaro, or not thinking about him at all. Now, when I'm with Rafael, I wonder . . ." The thought drifted away like the sun behind clouds. Diago was ready to let it go until Guillermo snatched it back.

"Wonder what?"

"I wonder if he was a bad man, who followed his heart, or if he was a good man, who just made bad choices."

Guillermo shook his head. "I don't know. You may never know. Just promise me you will open your eyes until you're certain. Look for the truth of his motives, not what your heart wants to see."

It was wise advice. Outside the window, drops of rain spattered the balcony's railing. "All I know for sure is that the time has come for me to take a stand, even if it means standing against my kin."

Guillermo reached across the table and gripped Diago's forearm. "It's not an easy thing, but I've got your back."

Uncomfortable in the face of his friend's love, Diago attempted to lighten the mood. He teased gently. "You said Garcia had my back."

"Garcia is an asshole. I'm not." He gave Diago's arm a squeeze before he poured them another round. "This will be just like old times, routing daimons and fighting in the labyrinths."

"I'm getting too old for daimon routing and labyrinth fighting."

"You'll be fine." Guillermo raised his glass. "Salut."

"Salut." Diago tipped his glass against Guillermo's.

A rap at the door interrupted their drinking.

Diago raised an eyebrow. Could it be Amparo? So quickly?

Guillermo scowled at the entrance and rose. He padded to stand behind the door. Even without a weapon, he was a formidable opponent. One of his massive hands around an intruder's throat would stop all but the biggest of mortals.

He motioned for Diago to answer the door.

A woman stood in the hall. She was dainty with black wiry hair and dark slanted eyes. The subtle tones of her skin placed her mortal parentage somewhere between China and Africa. The light shining in her pupils marked her as an angel-born Nefil.

"What do you want?" Diago asked.

"I'm Amparo." Her voice was a deep contralto, rich as the newly-turned earth.

Guillermo nodded, and Diago stepped aside to let her in.

"Who are you?" she asked as she shimmied past him.

"Diago Alvarez."

"You're the new one." She gave him a good once-over. "Funny. I expected you to have horns."

"I take them off when I go among the mortals."

The riposte won him a wry smile, which vanished the moment Guillermo spoke. "You got here fast."

"I was supposed to meet Suero a couple of blocks away this afternoon with the fragment. I offered to walk here, but Suero brought me. He's upset. I can always tell. He drives like a madman."

"Sit down." Guillermo patted one of the chairs. "Sit right here, and tell me what the fuck happened last night."

She remained standing, and though small in stature, her self-confidence more than compensated for her lack of height. "It's a short story. I was arrested for being out after curfew. I spent the night in jail."

"Why didn't you call me, or Garcia?"

"Mieras wouldn't let me near a phone. There was an angel at his side."

Diago asked, "Did he look German?"

Amparo nodded. "He is visiting the Urban Guard in an advisory capacity. He goes by the name Anselm Engel and claims he is from Berlin. He has a message for you."

Guillermo's glare turned cold. "Does he now?"

"He said Los Nefilim were created to be soldiers, and soldiers obeyed their superiors. He said Los Nefilim have become arrogant."

Oddly enough, Engel's words echoed Prieto's concerns. As a matter of fact, the sentiment was *identical* to the one Prieto had voiced during Diago's very first meeting with him. The angels seemed to be very apprehensive about Guillermo's allegiances, and with good cause. Los Nefilim were their ground soldiers. Clearly, Diago wasn't the only one concerned with which side Guillermo would take if the angels engaged in civil war. *Or if he will take one at all.*

"Prieto said something similar in our first meeting," Diago said. "The angels are using your Nefilim to gauge your intentions. They want to know if you're going to follow orders, or if you're going to act on your own." He glanced at Guillermo, but his friend remained impassive and kept his gaze on Amparo.

She shrugged. "I can't find Prieto, so I don't know what he says. Engel wants to talk to Alvarez."

The revelation jump-started Diago's heart. *Does Engel think I'm working with Prieto?* If so, Diago suspected any "talks" with Engel wouldn't be pleasant. "What does he want with me?"

"He didn't say."

Guillermo's features could have been cut from stone, but Diago saw a spark of anger flash in his eyes. "Then he doesn't see Diago. He should have submitted his request through a Spanish angel, or directly to me. Kidnapping one of my Nefilim and using her as a messenger isn't how we conduct business in Spain. I don't know anything about this angel, so until I have evidence otherwise, I'll consider him a rogue." He produced his lighter and thumbed the lid open and shut. "Now you tell me, Amparo: who are you working for? Engel, or me?"

"You, my king." She knelt before him and kissed his ring. "But Garcia's fidelity wavers. He spoke at length with Engel."

"I know all about Garcia and Engel."

The remark was calculated to elicit a reaction from Amparo. It was a technique his friend had used in the past.

Surprise flitted across her features.

Got you, Diago thought. "Agents provocateurs," he said. "He's using your own Nefilim against you."

Amparo's eyes narrowed at him. "Are you suggesting my loyalty is suspect?"

He'd flustered her even more. "Just making an observation."

Guillermo took Amparo's hand in his and made her rise. He reached into his pocket. She tensed until she saw the wad of banknotes in his fist. "Take this." He separated several notes from the roll. "Go to Valencia. I have a safe house there. Ask for Rosalía Yglesias. I'll send for you when things quiet down here. Stop at Santuari tonight and pick up provisions. Rosalía will let me know when you've arrived."

The money disappeared into the folds of her coat. "My lord king." She bowed and when she rose, she shot Diago a scathing glare. Then she slipped out the door, shutting it with a soft click.

Diago asked, "Do you trust her?"

"No, but there isn't much I can do right now. I'll have Rosalía keep an eye on her. Lock the door." Guillermo went into the bedroom. He returned with a guitar case, which he put on the table. "Are you sure you want to do this?"

Diago was certain. To run from the daimons was to invite a chase. For Rafael's sake, he couldn't afford a long-drawn-out confrontation. He needed to stabilize his son's life, not bring more chaos to him. "I'm positive."

Guillermo nodded and opened the case's lid to reveal several blades, alongside brass knuckles, a revolver, and two speed loaders for the revolver. Diago chose a dagger. Although knives meant closer fighting, Diago preferred them over guns in the tunnels. Less chance of ricochet, and the blades also made excellent conduits for a spell, especially for one that needed the sharp edges necessary to cut a life-strand.

Guillermo chose a heavy knife with a wide blade. He took the case back into the bedroom and shoved it under the bed.

Instead of returning to the main room, Guillermo took off his tie and suit jacket and gestured for Diago to join him. "Save your good clothes. You should be able to find something to fit you." Opening the wardrobe, he tossed a heavy turtleneck to the bed's coverlet.

Diago joined him and selected a wool sweater for himself. They quickly changed clothes and shoes. When they were done, they looked more like two ruffians than a doctor and a landowner. The bulky clothes also gave them more freedom of movement and hid their weapons.

Diago's sweater was too large. He rolled up the sleeves. "Do you think Suero has had enough time to get back to Santuari?"

"We'll give him another hour." Guillermo rummaged through the various sizes and styles of shoes in the back of the wardrobe. "Ah. I thought I'd left it here." He emerged with a crowbar in his hand. "We'll be going under, I presume?"

"Yes." Diago returned to the kitchen and searched for some paper. Shoved in the back of a drawer were a dirty pad and a blunt pencil. He sat beside Guillermo and drew the sewer passages he recalled from his days of hiding from the Church. Within moments he had sketched a labyrinth of intersecting tunnels. He darkened the route he intended to use.

"Here is what we're going to do."

CHAPTER SEVEN

Outside the rain pissed cold hard drops into the alley. A stray dog licked an empty food tin against a wall, while a cat huddled on a stoop and watched with envious eyes.

The rain had almost stopped by the time Diago found the manhole cover they needed. He dragged the toe of his shoe across it as he surveyed the area. No one was around, nor did anyone appear to be lingering near their windows.

Guillermo jammed the crowbar into the cover and slid the metal aside.

Diago went first, shimmying down the slick ladder. When his foot touched the concrete walkway, he moved aside to give Guillermo room.

Within the darkness of the tunnel, the piercing fear he'd experienced with Garcia on the subway returned.

It never goes away, Garcia had said.

Maybe. Diago knuckled down on the emotion. *But I have to control it; otherwise, the daimons will smell my terror and use it against me.* He inhaled deeply, calming himself with thoughts of Miquel, Rafael, and the warmth of their love. From the back of his mind, he heard Rafael singing his lullaby.

Sleep, child, sleep.

Diago's crippling anxiety slowly reverted into a dull throb of uneasiness. The apprehension remained, but it was manageable now.

The grinding of metal against brick was loud in the shaft as Guillermo maneuvered the cover back into place. He descended the ladder more slowly.

Electric lights, spaced several metres apart, rendered just enough illumination to see. Great patches of darkness lay between the lights. Two narrow walkways flanked a canal containing black water. The stench was magnificent. Diago breathed through his mouth.

Guillermo reached the bottom of the ladder. He drew the crowbar from his belt and offered it to Diago. With a shake of his head, Diago declined the weapon. Instead, he drew his dagger with his left hand.

They followed the tunnel until they reached a junction of two passages. There, Diago motioned for Guillermo to go right.

The larger Nefil took a place in the darkness where he could watch for Diago's return.

Diago ventured into the left-hand tunnel. The floor sloped downward. He switched the dagger to his other hand and trailed his fingers along the damp concrete as he walked. At the next Y-junction, he felt both walls. To the right, a slight hum indicated the tentacles of Moloch's bridge were close. He followed the passage.

The tunnel narrowed until it became a crumbling stairwell, which led down to another level. At the bottom of the stairs, a small metal pipe jutted from a wall and leaked water into a canal. The new passage broadened until it was the same size as the one Diago had just left.

The bridge's hum was stronger here, almost audible. Diago sensed the vibrations on his skin like an electrical charge.

He should be close enough for his father to hear him. "Alvaro?" he whispered. He wanted them to find him, but he didn't want to be obvious. "Show yourself if you can. I've come to help you."

The only answer was the slow trickle of water through the canal at his feet. He edged farther down the passage. A circle of darkness in the wall caused him to slow. As he neared, he saw it was a large overflow drain, the top of which reached his hips.

He paused and hummed a light into existence. Squatting beside the drain, he sent the glowing song into the concrete pipe. Rats squealed and clambered over one another to run around a distant bend in the duct. His magic died and left the conduit in darkness once more.

Satisfied the drain was devoid of any supernatural threat, he stood and continued on his way.

He reached another curve and eased around the

corner, calling his father's name. Still nothing. Diago hesitated. Judging by the wall's vibrations, he was close to the bridge.

I'll go four more metres, and if nothing happens, then I'll return to Guillermo. He counted his steps as he moved forward, stopping twice to whisper his father's name, only to be greeted with silence.

It was no good. He wasn't going to trip whatever ambush the daimons planned for him. *Damn it.* There was nothing to do now but go back to Guillermo and devise a different strategy.

Just as he turned to retrace his steps, the light over his head dimmed, and then brightened again. The wall vibrated more strongly beneath his fingers.

Maybe I haven't failed, after all.

He wasn't sure whether to be glad or afraid. Fear won. Sweat crawled across his scalp as he looked over his shoulder. In the blackness between two electric lights, the bridge's purple tentacles oozed into the tunnel. On the other side of the bridge, the faint outline of a person wavered as someone approached the border.

Diago squinted and tried to detect whether the silhouette belonged to a male or female. It was impossible to tell. He tried again. "Father?"

The shape became clear. "Diago?" It was Alvaro.

Diago exhaled slowly.

The colors of Moloch's magic still encased Alvaro's soul. He touched the border of the bridge. The boundary's shadows flowed around him, bursting into vibrations of reds and deeper shades of sangria. The darkness momentarily obscured the sight of him.

Alvaro retreated until the explosion of color faded. "You came." His voice was weak, probably strained from fighting Moloch's chains. "Help me, son. Take my hand. Help me cross over."

The pain in Alvaro's voice was so real, Diago took a step toward him before he caught himself. *Careful. Look closely.* Guillermo was right. *I must see what is true, not what I wish.* "You crossed to the mortal side at the metro. Why can't you cross now?"

Alvaro appeared unruffled by the question, almost as if he expected it. "Moloch punished my transgression. He strengthened the chains holding me to his realm."

The beams of the electric light over Diago's head barely reached his father's face. Yet the word LIAR seemed fainter. *Could it be a trick of the light?* He examined the scars. Although the cuts still oozed black drops of blood, the wounds seemed to be healing.

Diago frowned. Blood. If he was a ghost, how did he bleed? *And his eyes. What has happened to his eyes?* No longer green like Diago's, red and umber sparks floated in place of Alvaro's irises and pupils.

Shocked, Diago forgot any pretense at deception. His disbelief was real. "What has happened to you?"

"Moloch has changed me. He holds me captive." Alvaro tried to push forward again, sending off another disturbance through the currents of the bridge's song. Defeated, he fell back until the colors dimmed. "I can't do this without you, Diago. You're my only hope. You have to save me."

Did he? Diago reexamined Moloch's vibrations, which surrounded Alvaro. The corrupted sound waves of puce and gray pumped Moloch's magic into Alvaro's ghost. The threads of the spell pulsed, not like chains, but like an umbilical cord. Another hot wave of fear washed over Diago.

This was a birthing song.

How did I miss it? He tried to reconcile the enchantment before his eyes with the image he had glimpsed from the subway car. Everything was the same, the colors, the song—all that had changed was his focus and his proximity to Alvaro. On the train he had been intent on the words Alvaro shaped from the smoke, a sleight of hand which had distracted Diago from the spell around his father. *But the words were unimportant. Alvaro tantalized me with a mystery so I would come to the bridge for answers.*

What he'd missed on the metro was obvious to him now. Moloch was changing Alvaro into something else—a creature never before encountered by either daimon or angel.

"You lie," Diago finally said. "You are being reborn." And his father was obviously at a critical point in the process. If he crossed into the mortal realm, and the link was accidentally severed, then they would have to begin again.

Alvaro didn't deny it. "Moloch is turning me into a new kind of soldier. An experiment. Like you." He couldn't hide the pride in his voice.

"You've sold your soul to them." Diago wasn't sure why he felt so betrayed. *Because I'd hoped—in spite of everything I knew about Alvaro, I'd hoped I was wrong—and Guillermo had seen my hope, and it made him afraid for me.*

"It's not what you think." Alvaro's voice was slick like oil and his words just as treacherous. "The blood I drank throughout the centuries bound my spirit to the mortal plane. I was dead. I was not. Every womb I tried to enter rejected my tarnished soul, and I could not be reborn. Moloch captured me. He and the other daimons branded me." He pointed to the word LIAR on his forehead, but the gashes were fainter, more like welts than cuts. "They hold me captive and force me to do their will. Please, I beg you, save me from this hell, Diago."

If the daimons had truly branded Alvaro, the wound would never close. Yet the cuts on his forehead were healing. Diago was certain of it now. *My eyes are opening, and I am beginning to see like a Nefil once more.*

Another thought jarred Diago. *He's distracting me with his chatter. Throwing me off guard so Lamashtu can attack.* He glanced over his shoulder. The ambush was in place. The others should come now. But the passage behind him remained empty.

Where was Lamashtu? On the other side of the bridge, closer to the subway tracks? If she remained within Elena's body, then she might take longer to arrive. And Moloch's other two 'aulaqs. Where were they? Did they guard the injured daimon? Or were they circling through the passages to cut him off from Guillermo?

Surely Moloch hadn't sent Alvaro alone.

Alvaro seemed to guess Diago's thoughts. "There are no others," he said. A drop of black blood seeped into his eye and sizzled in the fires burning within. "Help me, Diago, like I helped you deceive Moloch." He reached out his hand. "We cheated him of his deepest desire—to feed on a dual born child."

No. That wasn't right. Diago thought back to his initial encounter with Prieto. "Prieto said Moloch demanded the child of a Nefil in exchange for his idea. He said nothing about a dual born child."

Alvaro frowned. "Why do you think Candela chose you, my son?"

The memory of the angel's enchantment rose to haunt him. *She promised me a song and insisted no other Nefil would do.*

Now he knew why. The facts clicked together and formed a seamless tapestry of deceit. Both the angels and the daimons had spent centuries experimenting with genetics in order to create the perfect Nefil— the perfect soldier. The angels possessed the ability to give Moloch what he needed—the angelic spirit— the one thing the daimons couldn't replicate in their Nefilim.

That explained why Moloch worked so closely with the angels. He used his idea for the bomb as both incentive and bait to lure the angels into creating such a child. But why?

Because it wasn't Moloch's plan—it was Ba'al's. The thought struck Diago like a blow. The daimon king had unified his divided tribes. While the angels were distracted by the rivalries within their own ranks, Ba'al prepared his daimonic armies to take full advantage of the conflict with a new race of Nefilim.

"You son of a bitch." Diago's breath was tight in his throat. "You're using me to create a new breed of Nefilim."

Alvaro opened his mouth, but Diago cut him off before he could speak. "Moloch never had any intention of feeding on Rafael. He wanted to raise the child as a daimon. The only reason he allowed Prieto to dictate the terms of the meeting was because the daimons wanted to test *my* allegiance one last time. When you saw I'd substituted a golem for Rafael, you went along with my deception, knowing I would inadvertently lead Moloch to Rafael."

"Think about it, son." Alvaro narrowed his eyes. "Moloch murdered me. He murdered your father!"

Look closely at his lies. Think like a daimon. Prieto was right. Alvaro's allegiance had always been to the highest bidder. His father's pride about his new form was the second clue. The patterns fit together neatly.

Diago said, "You were tired of crawling through the night, sucking the blood out of drunks and addicts. The only way you could change was to die, but Moloch wasn't going to allow your death to be wasted. It was all merely a matter of timing for maximum effect. Yet another test for me." He glanced over his shoulder again. The tunnel remained empty. "Moloch simply underestimated Rafael's power, and my love for my son."

Alvaro's fingers curled like the legs of a dying spider. "Love? You don't know what love is. Love is giving up your child for a greater cause, like I gave you to the daimon-born Nefilim. I taught you betrayal. I taught you hate. I gave you to your aunt so she could train you."

Cold now, Diago watched his father the way he would observe a viper. "You told her to sell me, didn't you?"

"Of course I did. How else were you going to learn your true nature?" The fires in Alvaro's eyes flared.

"And I wanted to believe you had some good in you. But I know what you are now." Diago spat. *I know and I will never wonder again.* While the closure should have brought him some sense of relief, Diago felt nothing but sorrow. It was as if Alvaro had died.

Not Alvaro. *It's my hope that has died. I mourn any chance my father might have loved me.* Diago backed away.

Alvaro didn't follow him. *He doesn't because he can't. He's already stretched to the limit of Moloch's umbilical cord.*

Alvaro dropped the last of his illusions. He grinned around razor teeth, and Diago detected a glimmer of madness in his father's eyes. He wasn't sure if Alvaro's insanity was the by-product of his new condition, or if he had always been so. Nor did it matter. The lines were drawn. They were enemies now.

Diago risked a quick glance over his shoulder.

"Are you looking for Lamashtu? She's not here." Alvaro snarled. "By now, she has probably found and killed Guillermo."

"Liar." Diago paused. He resisted the urge to call out to Guillermo. This could be a trick to get him to reveal Guillermo's whereabouts. Lamashtu might not know where he was hiding.

"Did you think you could trick Moloch? This is his realm, Diago. He saw you descend into the sewers and guessed your plan." Alvaro hissed like the serpent in the garden.

Diago strained his ears for any sound of a fight, but the passages gave him only silence. No. Alvaro was trying to spook him. Guillermo was fine.

Alvaro leaned toward the mortal realm. The bridge exploded in hues of scarlet and sangria. "Lamashtu will possess you. She will force you to go to Santuari and murder Miquel. After it's all done, you will bring Rafael home to us. You *will* be a part of Ba'al's army, and so will Rafael. It doesn't matter to us if you enlist willingly, or if you're conscripted. Keep yourself whole, Diago. Save Miquel's life. Swear your allegiance to us, and we will send Lamashtu back to Samael."

Diago started moving again. This time, he didn't stop.

"Think of how Los Nefilim will interpret this excursion. You deceived Guillermo. Brought him to his death and betrayed your king once more. They will see nothing but a traitor when you return." Alvaro's shouts followed him. "You will never be fast enough to escape us! We are a part of you! Always!"

Diago shut out his father's taunts. He retraced his steps with as much speed as the narrow ledge allowed. Within moments he reached the overflow drain.

A woman's hand emerged from the concrete pipe. Diago never saw the syringe, but he felt the needle stab his thigh. The hot rush of morphine flowed into his leg.

Blind with panic, Diago plunged off the walkway and into the black water of the canal. He splashed forward eight more steps before he halted. With numb fingers, he ripped the needle from his leg. Over half of the morphine was gone. He dropped the syringe into the muck and crushed it beneath his heel.

The drug caused him to lose control of his magic, his awareness, but of course that was what she wanted. Under the morphine's influence, she would easily penetrate his mind as if he was mortal.

Diago whirled in time to see her crawl out of the drain. Elena's pale face floated over the collar of her soiled black dress, but it was Lamashtu who peered through the maid's eyes. She advanced cautiously, as leery of him as he was of her.

"Relax, Diago," said Lamashtu. "Let the drug work." Her words, brown as old blood, fell from her lips and dripped down her chin.

How long did he have before the morphine took him down? Five minutes, ten? He had to draw her away from the power of the bridge. He pointed his dagger at her chest and retreated.

Alvaro's laughter rolled down the passage. His distant voice sent the hair at the back of Diago's neck straight up.

"You were right, son! I lied. She never went after Guillermo. She was by the tracks. I hit the bridge so she would know where we were. I gave you a chance, Diago. You've brought this on yourself."

Diago slipped.

Lamashtu took two quick steps, but stopped when he caught his balance.

She used Elena's melodious voice to offer him quiet words. "Ignore him, Diago. Your father is wrong. It will be better this way. You won't have to think anymore. You can relax and let the world go by, watch it all from a distance. Feel nothing. Be nothing. We'll raise Rafael as he is meant to be raised, and you will be freed from these torturous conflicts of loyalty."

"I'm not conflicted." He assured her as he stepped back onto the walkway. "If I wanted to lose my mind to you, I would have taken Alvaro's hand." He kept moving, trailing his fingers along the wall.

His heel struck the first step of the crumbling stairs and, unprepared for the jolt, Diago fell backward. He landed in a sitting position.

Lamashtu lunged forward.

Diago rose and slashed at her with his dagger. The tip of his blade snagged the sleeve of her dress. A thin cut oozed blood on her wrist.

She licked the blood from the wound and retreated to a safe distance. "I hate mortals. They're so clumsy. Nefilim are faster."

"We are," he said as he carefully backed up the stairs. Numbness spread up his thigh and into his hip as the morphine found its way into his veins. His speech slurred. "Don't forget it."

Lamashtu cocked her head. "Morpheus has come for you. Fall into his arms. Sleep. And while you sleep, you will let me in."

He made no sign he heard. She wouldn't rush him on the stairs. Not with the prospect of taking over his body. Crippling him wasn't her goal. No. She simply had to be patient.

Diago climbed faster. She followed, staying far enough behind to prevent him from kicking her down the stairs.

The morphine eased into his mind, clouding his thoughts. How close was he to the junction where Guillermo awaited him? Diago tried to assess his surroundings.

Several metres away, the passages branched again. On the wall, a bulb shattered behind its wire cage and spewed sparks onto the walkway. The explosion of light momentarily blinded him. Panic rose from his chest and into his brain, strangling his thoughts.

He tried to warn his friend. "Guillermo! It's a trap." *It's a trap and I am caught.*

"Let him come," said Lamashtu from somewhere nearby.

Too close, she is too close. Still partially blinded by the flash, he stumbled into the canal. Holding out the dagger, he spun and slashed wildly, but the only resistance he found was the sewer's damp air.

His vision finally cleared. He turned quickly until he located Lamashtu. She remained on the walkway, a smile on her lips.

Diago pointed the dagger at her. He sang a low note and traced a sigil with the vibrations of his fear. Then he flung the ward at Elena's dead eyes.

Lamashtu used Elena's voice to sing a sigil of her own. The patterns of her magic slammed into his glyph and turned it back on him. The morphine slowed his reaction time. He tried to summon another sigil, but he sang off-key. His song died before it was truly born.

When Lamashtu's ward reached him, electric pain ruptured in his mind. He managed to stay on his feet, but the dagger flew from his hand.

From somewhere behind him, Guillermo's shout rolled through the tunnel. "Diago? Where are you?"

Diago gasped an answer. "Go back." He barely understood himself. The morphine swallowed his words and spit them out as gibberish. "Get out."

"He won't." Lamashtu wasn't perturbed by Guillermo's presence. "And by the time he finds us, I will be you." Thin spectral fingers protruded at the edges of Elena's lips as the daimon crawled up through the maid's throat. She readied herself. The moment Diago became unconscious, the daimon would jettison her spirit between his lips and into his mind.

Diago reeled away from her.

Guillermo shouted. "Answer me, Diago! I'm not leaving you."

Diago's heart hammered in his chest. "Guillermo?" He meant to yell, but all he was able to produce was a murmur. As much as he wanted his friend to flee, a cowardly part of him wished Guillermo would save him.

Don't let her take me. Don't let her wear my face and hurt my boy. He tripped and caught himself on the edge of the walkway.

Lamashtu vocalized again.

As Diago righted himself and backed away from her advance, the fluid in the canal grew thick and black. It was like trudging in deep mud. Shadows pearled along the walls, weeping down the mortar black as rain.

He could barely move his feet. The stream of darkness picked up speed. A frigid current washed over his calves.

"Diago!" Guillermo sounded closer.

But not close enough. Diago struggled to answer. The morphine dried his tongue. A burning desert filled his veins.

The muddy water turned into a river. The walls vanished beneath shadows.

Lamashtu's voice drifted through the haze. "Sleep, child, sleep."

"No," Diago whispered. He couldn't sleep. He couldn't give her what she wanted . . .

A faint buzzing noise nuzzled the temporal bone

behind his ear. He thought of flies swarming over a corpse. The pulsations grew stronger and bled into his skull, causing his jaw to tingle. Goose bumps rippled across his flesh.

Diago lifted his hand to ward off the sound. His wedding band flared and left a silver trail in the air. Half blind from the morphine, he took two sideways steps. His shoulder struck the wall. Webs of shadows twined in his hair and snatched at his wrists.

Lamashtu followed him. The thrumming sensation behind his ear returned. "Go down, Diago. It's time to sleep."

She stepped off the walkway. Before he could move, she darted in and kicked the back of his knee.

He went down. Blackness splashed his face and clouded his eyes. It filled his nose and his lungs. The water closed over his head, and he floated beneath the waves . . . without sound, or light, or guide.

Reaching out with his left hand, he searched for something to grab, anything to anchor his body so he could lift himself free of the void. His questing fingers touched nothing.

A single spot of radiance moved with his hand. His addled senses mistook the light for a star. *No. Not a star. My ring.* The silver wedding band pushed back the dark. He remembered Miquel's voice, soft in the night. *With this ring, I pledge my love* . . . They had stood in a garden hand in hand. Miquel placed the ring onto Diago's finger . . . *my love*. . .

Diago tried to call out his lover's name. "Miquel . . ."

But the black filled his mouth, bitter as hate on his tongue, and choked off his cry. He whipped his head and tried to rise. A hand pushed his face into the muck. The hum returned to the base of his skull.

Let me in. Lamashtu tried to shove him deeper into the dark.

In spite of the daimon's spell, Diago's ring blazed. His eyes seized the light.

Somewhere in the distance, a child cried out. *Papa! Papa! You come back right now! Now! Make him come home, Miquel!*

Diago saw his family as clearly as if he stood behind them in Guillermo's house. Rafael pointed at the picture he'd drawn of Diago, Miquel, and himself beneath an angel sun.

The figure representing Diago had begun to fade. The bright colors dulled until all that remained were the caricatures of Miquel and Rafael, holding onto a ghost's pale hands.

Save him, Miquel!

And his wise Miquel placed Rafael's palms on the picture of Diago so that they covered ghost-drawing with their hands. Juanita joined them, and when Miquel vocalized a song, she added her ethereal voice to his. She lent them the strength of an angel, and together, they guided Rafael's small fingers to fashion a sigil of protection over Diago's picture. Miquel's gold ring threw off amber sparks, showering the drawing with their love.

The patterns of their song reached out over time

and space. The warmth of their love touched him where he lay beneath Lamashtu's malice. His wedding band shone ever brighter as Miquel's voice pushed back the darkness.

. . . *come home, my bright star . . . stay with us . . . don't give in . . . come home. . .*

To fight for the ones he loved meant he had to fight for himself, too. Diago couldn't give up. *I will not be Alvaro. I will fight for them and myself.*

And this was war.

Diago struggled against Lamashtu's hold. Her body slid to the right. She hooked her leg over his hips and tried to regain her position.

He shoved himself upward. His head broke the surface of the black mud. Twisting hard to the right, he used Lamashtu's instability to throw her from his back.

The darkness receded and in the distance, he saw the soft glow of orange and red and gold. *Guillermo's song.* He was still searching, calling to Diago.

Because love, it takes so many forms.

Diago stumbled to his feet. Lamashtu's black notes swirled around his thighs. He dragged up his hand and coughed a hard note. The luminance of his wedding ring dimmed. No. Not hate. He heard Rafael's voice. *Love kills the dark, Papa. Love. . .*

Love. Drive her back with love.

Diago summoned the image of Miquel, his dark eyes luminous in the moonlight. He beckoned into his heart the tenderness he nourished for Rafael. His poor Rafael, who had barely begun his long road to healing—the daimons would destroy the good in the child and teach him to thrive on anger and fear and hate.

Just as they tried to do to me.

Diago drew on his memories—not the terrible things that had happened to him over his long life, but the good. He took the moments he wanted to keep close to his heart, and he shaped them into a song. He nurtured the patterns of devotion into a sigil and sent it flying like snow driven before the wind.

But the morphine crippled his magic. The sigil wavered, the edges blurred. No sooner had he set the spell in motion than he realized the poorly woven song was going to miss Elena's body. Lamashtu swayed to her feet and lifted her hands.

Then, from behind him, Guillermo's voice thundered a chord both bold and hard. The fiery sigil singed Diago's hair as it flew past him. Guillermo's ward caught Diago's, and redirected the spell toward Lamashtu.

The combined glyphs entered through Elena's eyes. Gold and silver light danced through her veins and burned her flesh. Lamashtu screamed as the maid's body burst into white fire. Just before she fell, Diago detected a glimpse of Elena. Her confusion lasted merely a moment before understanding turned to horror. She didn't even have time to scream before the flames engulfed her, and she was gone.

Without the shelter of a physical form, Lamashtu's

spirit swirled through Elena's lips. She became a mist that united all the colors of the night. Gauzy echoes of gray and white drifted around her.

Twin tethers branched away from her body, just as Diago had told Guillermo they would. The thicker of the two disappeared down the passage, leading back to her corporeal body somewhere in Sitra Akhra. The other flowed upward into the mortal realm.

Now. They had to attack now. Diago took a shaky step and skidded on the wet floor.

Guillermo caught him. The big Nefil supported Diago with one hand and didn't hesitate. Just as they had practiced in the apartment, Guillermo formed a note in D. He drew his blade and designed the glyph that would sever Lamashtu's thread to the fragment. As his hand slashed through the vibrations of his song, he called on the power of his signet ring. Fashioned by an angel, the stone within his ring flared like an aurora borealis. The multicolored beams ensnared Guillermo's sigil and turned it into a ring of fire.

Even as Guillermo threw the glyph at the daimon, Diago saw the edges were too dull. As strong as Guillermo's ward was, it wouldn't be enough to cut the thread.

Diago vocalized, but he was hoarse and unable to reach the proper pitch. He stopped. *Let me hit the note,* he prayed to whatever god might be listening. Then he closed his eyes and sang again. This time, he began softly. As his voice strengthened, he culled the note and channeled the sound waves forward to merge with Guillermo's glyph.

Their magic reached the tether, and for a moment it seemed to hang there, halted as if running against a wall.

Lamashtu's spirit shimmered. She laughed at their feeble attempt to harm her, not understanding their intent. She floated toward them, feeding on Diago's fear.

And then their sigil snapped the thread.

Guillermo inhaled and let loose a vocalization that shook the stones. He designed a second glyph of fire and targeted the broken tether. The flames grabbed hold of the damaged thread, glowing like the fuse to a bomb, and hurtled upward into the mortal realm. The odor of burning parchment filled the tunnel. Wherever it was, the sigil burned.

Lamashtu rushed forward, still determined to possess Diago.

All he had left in his soul was a lament, one last cry to mourn the fragile hope Alvaro had broken. Diago sang his grief and shaped a ward to cut Lamashtu's life-strand. It took all his strength, and even then he wasn't sure it would do the job.

But Guillermo lent his voice, and once more called on the power of his ring. Together, they directed the sigil, burning with Diago's sharp edges and channeled with Guillermo's skill. They directed it toward the tether.

Too late, she realized what they had done. There wasn't time for her to stop. As Lamashtu surged forward, the sigil met the life-strand, and sliced it neatly in two.

Lamashtu's spirit vanished.

Silence fell sudden and deep. Diago wondered if he'd gone deaf.

Without Lamashtu's magic, the black water receded. Diago went to his knees, control no longer wholly his own. A spasm of nausea rattled through his body. He leaned forward. Then Guillermo was beside him, holding him while he vomited.

"Fucking morphine." Diago spat. "Christ, I'm sick."

"It's okay," Guillermo whispered. "Are you done?"

Diago nodded weakly. "I think so."

"Can you walk?"

"Alvaro . . ." He wanted to tell Guillermo everything, but another round of dry heaves rattled his frame.

"What? Is he coming?" Guillermo looked down the passage.

"No." Diago gasped. "He is becoming something we've never encountered before. And we have to find a way to stop him. Permanently."

"What do you mean?"

"We have to destroy his soul. Give him the second death." The final death, the one from which no Nefil could ever reincarnate. *Otherwise, he will haunt me forever.*

Guillermo was silent for a moment, clearly disturbed. "That isn't easily done. We'll talk about it at Santuari. Not here."

Diago looked over his shoulder. "I will end him." It was a threat. It was a sacred vow. "I will."

Guillermo hoisted him onto the walkway. "Let's get out of here before Moloch sends us company."

"I lost the dagger."

"It's all right." Guillermo got his arm around Diago's waist. "Lean on me."

They wobbled along like a pair of drunks to the next junction. Guillermo guided them back the way they came. When they reached the ladder, he propped Diago beside the cold metal. "Can you stay awake?"

Diago nodded. "But I can't climb." His arms were like jelly.

Guillermo patted Diago's shoulder. "You let me worry about the climbing." He ascended the ladder.

While Diago waited, peace suddenly descended over him. The morphine. He had no idea how long the euphoria would last before it was followed by the next round of panic. He would cycle like this for several hours—his emotions rolling up and down with a velocity that terrified him. *Might as well enjoy the good while it lasts.* Diago's eyelids slipped shut and he fell into a light doze.

"Diago?"

He started awake. Disoriented, he tried to remember where he was. From the cold and damp, he wondered if he'd drunk too much and stumbled into an alley. He looked up at a disheveled handsome man staring down at him with concern.

The man spoke with a low rumble. "Put your arms around my neck."

Diago blinked at him drowsily. "I would, but I'm attached to someone else."

Guillermo's shock last for merely a second. He grinned. "That's good, because so am I."

Consciousness came forward in a rush. Horrified, Diago realized what he'd said. He noticed the gray light and the open manhole cover overhead. *Put your arms around my neck.* Guillermo intended to carry him up the ladder.

A blush set Diago's cheeks on fire. "I'm sorry. I was . . ."

Guillermo turned his back and simply stared over his shoulder.

Diago coughed. "I realize what you meant . . ." He put his arms over Guillermo's shoulders and closed his eyes. "It's the fucking morphine."

"Ya, ya, ya," Guillermo murmured as he used his belt to lash together Diago's wrists. "You're just trying to let me down easy."

"Can you please forget I said that?"

Guillermo chuckled. "Never."

Diago buried his burning face against Guillermo's sweater. He managed to hold on to consciousness until they were only four rungs from the top. When he

awakened again, he was lying on the ground with the
rain falling against his face.

A ragged girl not much older than Rafael stood near
the wall and assessed Diago with eyes far too cunning
for a child her age. "Did you kill him?"

"Don't be stupid," Guillermo's voice came from Diago's left. He moved the manhole cover back over the
hole. "If I'd killed him, I'd be putting him down there,
not bringing him up."

The girl asked, "Did he get drunk and fall down in
the sewer?"

"Yeah. That's what happened." He tossed a couple
of *pesetas* at her as he hummed a song of forgetfulness.
"You found some money on the ground. Buy yourself
some shoes."

She caught the coins and dashed off.

Guillermo pulled Diago to his feet. "Feel like walking, lover?"

Diago smoothed his rumbled sweater in an attempt
to regain his dignity. "Stop teasing me."

"Never." Guillermo took Diago's arm and steered
him in a more or less straight path.

"Where are we going?"

"Home. Where we belong."

"Are we going to walk?"

"I'm not calling Suero to bring the car. Not after
we've been wallowing in a sewer." Guillermo gave Diago's arm a gentle squeeze. "The walk will do us good.
It'll be like old times."

"Fuck old times." The edginess had returned. His nerves were on fire. "I hated walking everywhere. It was always cold. Or raining. I hated shitting in the woods. I want indoor plumbing and furnaces."

Guillermo laughed. "I'm taking you to those luxuries now."

Diago stared ahead. Black as a vulture, depression swooped down on him. He was suddenly weary, so very weary. "I'm scared. What if I'm not strong enough to be a member of Los Nefilim?" He leaned on Guillermo, who merely supported him just as he always had.

"You? Not strong enough?" Guillermo scoffed at the statement. "You've always eaten your fear and spit it back at them. You're strong enough, Diago. After all you've lived through, you are strong and wise, and I need you at my side."

The depression didn't immediately fade away, but it was made slightly more bearable by Guillermo's faith in him. They walked in silence through the winding streets and cut across empty lots. When they reached a construction site, they found an outside spigot and managed to wash the worst of the stink off themselves.

By the time they left Barcelona behind, the clouds had departed and night had fallen. Guillermo led Diago into a field. There, he called down an owl from the sky. He cooed to it in the language of birds and sent it off.

"What did you do?" Diago asked.

"I told it to fly ahead and tell Juanita we are safe, and that we're coming home."

Home. Tranquility finally chased away Diago's depression. Just the thought of their little house with its cramped rooms warmed his heart.

As they walked up the country road, Diago told Guillermo about his encounter with Alvaro and all the things he learned about his father. He left out nothing, especially not his pain. *Guillermo is right. I've carried too much alone for too long.*

And Guillermo, for his part, listened with his customary patience. He kept his hand on Diago's arm, not because Diago's step was unsteady, but as a friend. His touch lent Diago the strength he needed to get through his tale.

It was late by the time they reached the lane to Diago's house. He had sweated most of the morphine out of his system. Peace, which had nothing to do with the drug, settled over him.

Guillermo paused at Diago's door. "Come to the church tomorrow at nine. That will give me time to call a small council. I want you to tell them about Alvaro. I'll break the news about Garcia and Engel. Then we'll figure out what to do. Get some rest." Guillermo started to walk away but when he saw Diago lingering by the window, he paused. "Do you want me to go in with you?"

"No," Diago murmured. "I just want to look at them for a moment."

Inside, Miquel stretched out on the couch, his arms around Rafael. The child rested his head on Miquel's shoulder, his stuffed horse clenched under one arm, and his thumb in his mouth.

Rafael's body heaved with hiccups. A few tears leaked from the corners of his eyes. Miquel wiped the child's nose and murmured to him.

"Diago?" Guillermo whispered.

"Thank you."

"For what?"

"For believing in me when I didn't believe in myself." Diago opened the door and went inside.

Miquel sat up and smiled. "See? I wasn't worried." The dark circles under his eyes testified otherwise. He placed Rafael on his feet. "Look who is home."

Rafael blinked at Diago. His lower lip trembled, and he pointed at his drawing, which was on the table. The ghost-Diago was vibrant and brightly colored again. All three of the figures held hands beneath the angel sun and smiled.

"You started to disappear and you scared me, Papa." Rafael stumbled and bumped into the table. "You shouldn't scare me like that. I thought you were dying." Then he started to cry.

"Hey." Diago shut the door. "Don't cry, Rafael." He went to his son and picked him up. "Ya, ya, ya," he sang the soothing words. "Everything is all right. I'm home."

"You scared me." Rafael hiccupped his way through a sob, but his tears were slowing. He made a face. "And you smell bad."

"Ew, Jesus, yes." Miquel rose. "I'm going to run a bath. Get out of those clothes so I can burn them."

Rafael wrinkled his nose, then put his arms around Diago's neck and kissed his cheek anyway. "I don't care if you stink. I'm glad you're home."

"I am, too." He carried Rafael to his bed and tucked him under the covers. No crumbs surrounded his pillow this night. He'd been too worried to steal a slice of bread.

"Ysa said you were fighting daimons with her papa. She says I worry too much. She says we are Los Nefilim and we always win, but you weren't winning, because you started to disappear in the picture, and Miquel and Doña Juanita helped me bring you back, and then an owl came, and Doña Juanita said it was okay for us to come home. Did you fight a daimon, Papa? Is that why you stink?" Rafael paused for a bone-cracking yawn. "Do Los Nefilim always win?"

Diago found a handkerchief and wiped Rafael's nose. "Yes, I fought a daimon." He skirted the other questions for now. "And I will teach you how one day."

"Then I won't be afraid anymore, right?" Rafael's eyelids drooped.

The time to indoctrinate his son about life's realities would come soon enough. For now, he deserved to be a child. "You don't have to be afraid now. Miquel and I are here, and we won't let anything happen to you. Go to sleep, and when you wake up, we'll have breakfast together."

Rafael closed his eyes, and within moments, his breathing deepened.

Diago brushed back his son's curls. "And I will not let them hurt you. I will not let them take your sweetness away."

Miquel returned and touched his shoulder. "Come on. Let's get you cleaned up."

Diago rose and followed him into the bathroom. With Miquel's help, he peeled off his clothes and slipped beneath the warm water.

Miquel took off his own shirt and knelt beside the tub. He soaped the washcloth. "Lean forward." His words fell as white as almond blossoms into the water.

Drowsily, Diago touched the soft vibrations before they dissolved. Water trickled down the side of the tub in shades of silver and blue.

"What happened?" Miquel moved the washcloth in slow circular sweeps across Diago's back.

Haltingly at first, then with increasing confidence, he told Miquel about the day. By the time he reached his meeting with Alvaro, his eyes burned with the tears he'd dared not shed in front of either his father or Guillermo.

Miquel passed the wet cloth over Diago's forehead. "Let yourself weep, my star. It's all right to mourn." Concern tinged his words in shades of brown. "It's only when you hold your grief in your soul does it turn into poison."

"I've had enough poison for one lifetime." He drew his finger across the vibrations of Miquel's voice and allowed his tears to come. With his thumb, he caressed

Miquel's lower lip. "Stop frowning, my sweet Miquel. I'm all right. I am."

Miquel took Diago's wrist and kissed his palm. Their wedding bands touched—Miquel's gold against Diago's silver, and the tingle of his lover's magic wrapped Diago in warmth.

"Your colors are so beautiful. Sing to me."

"Quietly though," Miquel said. "So we don't wake Rafael."

"Quietly," Diago murmured.

Unlike his other attacks of chromesthesia, this one was almost languid. These were the gentle sounds. Shades of peace . . . and love. Miquel swirled the cloth in the water and hummed a soft song filled with saffron and gold. The sound spun over Diago's skin. Miquel's tenderness drove away the dark, one melodious note at a time, and wrapped Diago in the silken colors of home.

PART THREE:
THE SECOND DEATH

CHAPTER ONE

Barcelona
2 December 1931

Clouds the color of gunmetal obscured the morning sun and heralded another gray day. These last weeks seemed full of them. Pale shades of smoke and ash washed through the bathroom's narrow window. Diago flipped the switch by the door. Electric light flooded the room and touched the reflection of a man who'd taken the hard end of a fight.

He shut the door and dropped his bloodied napkin into the hamper.

"Jesus. What a mess."

A thin line of blood oozed from a deep cut on his cheek. He found a clean washcloth and pressed it against the gash.

Last night, the daimon Lamashtu had given no quarter in her battle to possess him. She had shoved him against the sewer's concrete floor as if he'd been a rag doll. Had she possessed the body of a Nefil rather than that of a mortal, she might have won.

She did enough damage as a mortal, he thought. His clothes concealed the black bruises on his chest and back, but the lacerations across his cheeks and forehead were impossible to hide. If the road map of cuts and bruises were any indication, his journey with Los Nefilim had taken a rough curve. "I've turned into a gangster."

A hard rap on the bathroom door caused him to start. Miquel didn't wait for an answer. He opened the door. "Are you talking to yourself?"

Diago's fingers tightened around the washcloth. "Did you come to help me or berate me?"

"Let me see," Miquel said, ignoring Diago's question and gently prying the cloth out of his hand. With a gentle movement, which was meant to soothe, he rubbed his thumb over the bandage that covered Diago's missing pinky.

Once more Diago felt the 'aulaq's hot breath as the vampire bit off his finger. He gave an involuntary twitch and Miquel released his hand.

As he focused on Diago's face, Miquel frowned. "You should have seen Juanita last night. This one could have used stitches like this other one." He caressed the scar on Diago's opposite cheek.

"At least I have a matching set." Diago's attempt at humor won him a scowl from Miquel. "You're right. I should have gone to see Juanita, but I wanted to be home." After his battle with the daimon, he had craved the sight of his family like a drug. Yesterday his pain had been distant, soothed by the presence of Rafael and Miquel. This morning, though, the aches crept over his body and pummeled him with thuggish glee. "I need some more aspirin."

"After lunch," Miquel murmured.

Diago placed his hand over Miquel's and increased the pressure. Deep or not, the cut would heal. Regardless of what Miquel thought, Diago knew he'd done the right thing by coming straight home. Getting through this morning might be another matter entirely. "Guillermo wants us at the church at nine."

"What does he need you to do?" Miquel asked.

"He wants me to tell the council about Alvaro." The council would then determine how best to proceed against Diago's father.

Alvaro, with his trickster ways, was becoming a creature unlike anything the Nefilim had ever seen. Just the memory of his burning eyes and razored smile twisted Diago's stomach. Worse was Alvaro's utter lack of remorse—he'd exulted in his transmogrification.

"What are you going to say?" Miquel's question jerked Diago's thoughts back to the present.

"That he should be given the second death," Diago said. The second death, the final death from which no Nefil could ever reincarnate, was reserved for only the most recalcitrant of Nefilim.

Miquel frowned. "That's extreme."

Guillermo had felt the same way last night, but his resistance to the idea would have to be overcome. "Alvaro deserves it."

A loud thump came from the kitchen. "Papa?"

"Everything is okay," Diago called to his son. "Finish your breakfast."

Miquel sighed. "Let me go check on him. I'll be right back. We need to talk about this proposal of yours before you mention it to Guillermo's council."

"Go. I'll be fine."

Miquel hurried back to the kitchen.

Diago turned to the mirror and whispered, "Patricide." The soft consonants drifted over the sink to touch his reflection. How could such a hateful word taste so sweet on the tongue? Surely if anyone merited such an end, it was Alvaro.

Or did he? If I had chosen to follow the daimons, wouldn't Alvaro's metamorphosis be justified, celebrated even? The question was moot. Diago was Los Nefilim. He'd chosen his side just as Alvaro had.

Why, then? Revenge? That was possible. Alvaro had done Diago no favors. He had plenty of reasons to loathe his father, more than enough to justify a desire for retaliation. *Is that why Guillermo resists the idea of the second death? Does he question my motives?*

Diago turned over the thought in his mind. It was possible. Guillermo's position meant neither he, nor any of his Nefilim, could openly oppose the daimons without cause. To do so might fracture the uneasy truce between the angels and the daimons.

But since I am neither, everything I say or do is suspect. I need an irrefutable reason that will convince Guillermo to validate such an extreme death sentence. Miquel had inadvertently given Diago a starting place when he'd explained how Los Nefilim moved as a unit. The question became, quite simply: how would Alvaro's death benefit Los Nefilim as a whole?

"I'll find a reason," Diago whispered to his reflection. The morning's meeting was the perfect opportunity for him to convince high-ranking members of Los Nefilim to act. "I am the deceiver. I know the art of persuasion."

Miquel's voice drifted down the corridor. "Put your dishes in the sink. We'll do them when we get home." He came back to Diago. "Here, let me see."

"Is it still bleeding?"

"I think it's stopped. Yes. It has." He cupped Diago's face and frowned as he examined him. "Look at you. What is this?" He wiped a tear from the corner of Diago's eye.

"The light is too bright." Diago tried to pull away, but Miquel held him.

"Uh-huh. Tell me what's wrong."

"It's nothing. It's just the hangover from the morphine." But that was also a lie. The morphine Lamashtu had injected into him last night was long gone from his system.

Of course, Miquel saw through the ruse and kissed his forehead. "You don't need morphine to make you morose."

Having a partner who read him so thoroughly could be a disadvantage at times. *Deceiving strangers is far easier than duping those who live within our shadows.*

"I'm just exhausted." Closer to the truth, hopefully close enough to deflect any further questions. "Juanita is right. I've been doing too much, too soon."

"You're healing faster." Miquel assured him. "The more you use your magic, the quicker your wounds will mend. You're going to be fine."

Looking into Miquel's eyes, Diago almost believed him.

"Papa?" Rafael squeezed past Miquel. "Are you all right?"

Diago looked down at his young son. Although he was dressed, his black hair had yet to meet a comb this morning. Dark shadows rested beneath his eyes, which were still puffy from last night's tears.

"I'm fine." Diago summoned a smile for the child.

"Good, because I have to use the bathroom. *Right now.*"

"I'm going to finish in the kitchen," Miquel said as he released Diago. "We need to get going soon."

From where he stood, Diago couldn't see the mantel clock in their bedroom, but he was sure it was after eight.

"Papa!"

"Okay, okay." Diago stepped into the hall. "Why does everything always start happening at once?"

The child tugged at his pants. "I can do it myself, Papa."

"*Ya, ya, ya.* If you miss the bowl, clean it up. Understand?"

"I will. I promise! Now go, please, before I do!"

Diago tried to hide his smile. He slipped out of the room and shut the door on his son's distress. Just like that, Rafael had dispelled Diago's gloomy mood. All of his morbid thoughts about Alvaro receded behind the normalcy of the household sounds.

Diago went to his son's room. Rafael's drawings were tacked to the walls in a profusion of colorful, childish interpretations of the scenes around Santuari. Horses were his favorite, but he had drawn Guillermo's bulls, too. Another picture showed Guillermo's daughter, Ysabel, and Miquel playing guitar together. In the drawing, Miquel positioned Ysa's fingers over the strings as he taught her a chord.

While Miquel rarely had the patience to teach the other children, he had a special fondness for Ysa, and she, in turn, worshipped him as only a seven year old could. Rafael had captured their tender moment with the stroke of his pencils.

He sees the world so differently from me, Diago thought as he brushed his knuckles over the drawing.

Miquel knocked on the doorframe as he passed. "Don't get lost, my star." He slipped into their bedroom and rummaged through the bedside table's drawer for his keys and change.

Diago blinked and realized Miquel was right—he didn't have time to lose himself in Rafael's world right now. He straightened the bed, and put the sketchbook and pencils in his son's satchel. Just as he finished, Rafael returned.

"I didn't dribble this time, Papa."

"Did you wash your hands?" Diago asked.

Rafael sighed and returned to the bathroom.

Diago followed him and picked up his comb.

"No! No!" Rafael ran his wet fingers over his unruly locks. "You don't need to comb it, Papa. I'm Gitano." He shook his head. "My hair is wild like my spirit."

"Wild spirits in this house comb their hair." Diago grabbed a towel and wiped his son's damp fingers. Stray hairs drifted into the sink's basin and joined those of Miquel and Diago. He wiped the strands off the porcelain. "It looks like a family of bears lives here."

Rafael giggled and raised his arms over his head, hands clenched like claws. He roared until the comb snagged a tangle. "Ow!"

Diago leaned forward and kissed his cheek. "Then stay still. Even bear cubs don't wiggle when their papas comb their hair."

"Bears don't comb their hair." The child's busy fingers found a chip in the sink's porcelain. "When I'm grown up, I'm never combing my hair."

"Don't you want to look nice for Ysa today?"

He picked at the sink's scar. "I want to stay home today."

"You can stay with Lucia and Ysa for a little while."

Rafael said nothing.

"Don't you like playing with Ysa?"

"Yes." Rafael rubbed his thumb around the chip.

"So?" Diago worked his fingers through a snarled lock and held his breath. Had he and Ysa fought? A generous girl, Ysa could sometimes be overbearing, but Diago had never known her to intentionally hurt another person. "Why don't you want to go?"

He shrugged.

Diago kept his tone even as a suspicion caught up with him. "Is it Lucia?"

A moment passed and Diago thought Rafael wasn't going to answer him. Finally, his son nodded.

"And what does she say?" Because it was Lucia, it had to be something out of her vicious mouth.

Another shrug. "Just things."

"What kind of things?"

"She said I should never go to Morocco, because I am small and dark like a monkey. She said someone would see that I am daimon and stuff me in a bottle and make me a jinni. Then she laughs like it's a joke, but her eyes are all hard and mean."

Jesus.

Lucia. Ysabel's governess made no secret of her hatred for Diago, which was fine with him, but taking out her pettiness on Rafael was a step too far.

Diago was careful to keep his anger out of his face and voice. He didn't want Rafael to think he was upset with him. Instead, he took his son's shoulders and gently turned the child so he could see his face. A river of tears would be preferable to the hurt he saw in Rafael's eyes. "You know what? You can come with us this morning. I'll bet Father Bernardo has someplace where you can sit and draw pictures while we talk, hmm?" He smoothed Rafael's hair and glanced into the hall to see that Miquel had joined them. How much had he heard?

Diago didn't have long to wonder.

Miquel came into the bathroom and stood behind Diago. "Pick him up."

Diago lifted Rafael so he could see himself in the mirror. Three faces, three shades of skin that passed from Rafael's light gold to Diago's tawny flesh, and finally Miquel's dusky brown.

Miquel made a great show of assessing their faces. "You know what, Rafael? I am darker than you."

"Miquel is Gitano, too," Diago whispered in Rafael's ear. "And everyone thinks he is very, very handsome." *Including me,* he thought as he examined his lover's reflection.

A ghost of a smile touched Rafael's mouth.

"And your papa is part daimon like you," Miquel said. "No one has stuffed him in a bottle and made him a jinni." He reached around Diago to touch Rafael's chin. "No one is going to mistake us for monkeys, or jinn."

"That's right," Diago said. "We're a family of bears."

Rafael gave a soft roar and the mischievousness returned to his eyes.

Diago gave him a fierce hug and set him on the floor. "Go get your satchel. We don't want to be late." Before Miquel could slip around him, Diago blocked the door and whispered, "He's not staying with Lucia again."

Miquel's eyes were hard as obsidian. "Agreed. But you say nothing. Let me handle it." Diago opened his mouth to protest, but Miquel touched his finger to Diago's lips as he spoke to Rafael. "Go get your coat and wait for us in the living room. We'll be right there." He waited until Rafael had gone before he continued. "I don't want Lucia speaking against you. She is a viper, and by the time you realize the damage she's done, it will be irreparable. She can't hurt my reputation with the others, but you're still in a vulnerable position."

Diago exhaled and nodded. He was stuck in a web of intrigue and until he formed a trusted network of his own, he needed to play a safe game, not simply for his sake, but for Rafael's as well. "All right, you handle her. But if she says one more thing to hurt Rafael—"

"I will hand her over to you myself. Let's get past this morning first."

"Fair enough." He turned off the light.

As they walked down the hall, Miquel said, "We had some promising prospects for governess. Maybe this afternoon we can look over the papers, and choose which ones to call back for a second interview."

"Did all of them like cats?" Diago asked, referring to the kitten he'd promised Rafael.

Miquel smiled and kissed the corner of Diago's mouth. "Yes."

In the living room, Rafael was busy unbuttoning his coat and mumbling to himself. Apparently, he'd missed a button the first time. Diago helped him while Miquel shut off the lights and closed the backdoor.

A loud knock at the front door jarred them. Diago frowned as he secured the last button on Rafael's coat. "Wait here."

Another round of pounding shook the door in its frame. Through the window, he glimpsed the sleeve of a uniform. *The Urban Guard. What the hell were they doing here?* And beyond that thought came another, which left Diago's mouth dry.

Were we near a window when Miquel kissed me just now?

Diago squelched the question. Within the safety of Santuari, he and Miquel didn't have to hide their love. Besides, there was nothing to fear. Santuari's wards shielded the town from mortal eyes, and the Urban Guard never entered without Guillermo's permission.

With his hand on the doorknob, he paused and looked out the window. It was Garcia, along with three other members of Los Nefilim dressed as Urban Guards.

Standing just behind Garcia was a slender and slightly bug-eyed Nefil named Jaso. He tugged at his scraggly beard and nudged the young pockmarked Nefil next to him, who kept looking over his shoulder in the direction of Guillermo's villa.

Moreno, Diago thought. Moreno was his name, and he was nervous as a rat.

The last Nefil, Acosta, towered behind the others. His small wicked eyes were pinned on the door. One meaty paw stroked the small battering ram he cradled in his arms.

Standing in the yard between two parked cars was the same angel Diago had seen Garcia speaking to yesterday. He was stout and muscular, with short blond hair and a reddish cast to his skin. His eyes were deep lavender shot through with streams of gold, and possessed all of the warmth of rime on water. He called himself Anselm Engel; Garcia probably thought his interactions with the angel were still a secret—and that's when it struck Diago:

Garcia wasn't here on Guillermo's orders. Engel's presence drove the point home as neatly as Acosta's battering ram.

Diago released the doorknob and backed away from the window. His and Miquel's guns were in the bedroom. He turned and almost tripped over Rafael. What the hell was he thinking? He couldn't have a shoot-out with his son in the room.

"Papa? Who is—?"

Diago snatched the boy off the floor and turned toward the kitchen. He needed to get Rafael out the back-door and to safety. Then they would deal with Garcia.

He almost ran into Miquel as his partner backed into the living room with his arms raised. Another Nefil was in front of Miquel. He kept his gun trained on Miquel's chest. Diago recognized him—Fierro was his surname. The youth was as thin as a stiletto, but nowhere near as sharp. Diago had only a passing acquaintance with him. The few words they'd shared weren't pleasant ones.

Fierro must have been waiting by the backdoor. Garcia had been smart enough to cover both exits.

"Slow and easy," Fierro commanded them until Miquel was in the living room. "Stop."

Miquel halted on one side of the couch, and Diago stopped on the other side. Rafael wisely remained silent. The child's arms and legs tightened around Diago's body.

The front door burst open. Acosta filled the doorway, the battering ram in his hand. The door hung from one hinge. Acosta stood aside so Garcia could enter. Moreno and Jaso waited on the stoop.

Garcia aimed his gun at Miquel. "Everyone stay quiet and no one gets hurt."

That remained to be seen. Even so, Diago didn't summon a ward. He had learned long ago to conserve his energy and watch for the right moment to attack.

Engel stepped onto the threshold and spoke to Garcia in heavily accented Spanish. "Which one is Alvarez?"

"Him." Garcia nodded at Diago. "Outside."

Diago started to put Rafael down.

"Take the boy with you."

The command sent Diago's heart racing. "No." When Garcia's eyes narrowed, Diago attempted a conciliatory tone. "I'll go with you. No fight, but we leave Rafael here."

"Take the boy with you," Garcia said again.

Miquel glanced at Diago and gave a minute shake

of his head. "Let's get Don Guillermo here, Garcia," he said. "If you've got something on Diago, he will take care of the situation."

Garcia shoved the barrel of his pistol against the center of Miquel's back. "Shut up." He jerked his head at the door. "Move, Alvarez."

Rafael's heart hammered against Diago's chest. "Don't leave me, Papa."

He pressed his lips against his son's ear. "If we get separated, don't panic. I will find you."

Garcia pointed his pistol at the base of Miquel's skull. "Go, or I'll blow his head off, Alvarez!" Garcia's voice carried a note of hysteria that spurred Diago into motion.

Engel stepped backward into the yard, an accommodating smile on his mouth. Jaso moved in tandem with the German angel. That left the pockmarked Moreno and the giant Acosta flanking the front door.

Diago would have to squeeze between them in order to get outside. He walked toward them and hoped one of them would drop his guard. *Just a moment. A split second of inattention. That's all I need.*

They remained infuriatingly alert. The Nefilim might be nervous, but they *were* professionals.

Diago held Rafael with both arms and stepped between them.

Moreno grabbed Rafael. At the same time, Acosta's arm went around Diago's throat, choking off his wind.

Rafael shouted. "Let go!" He grabbed handfuls of Diago's sweater.

Diago tightened his grip around his son's waist. He felt Rafael's heart pound against his, once, twice . . .

Miquel and Garcia argued with short clipped sentences, each barking orders at the other. Their furious words were lost in the darkness that fringed Diago's vision.

Their quarrel receded until Diago heard nothing but his pulse pounding in his ears. He had to shake Acosta. He twisted and elbowed Acosta's ribs. Acosta grunted but maintained his hold.

Moreno wrenched Rafael from Diago's grasp. Stumbling outside, Moreno barely kept his hold on the writhing child. "I got him!"

Rafael's scream went like a nail through Diago's head.

Without the boy in his arms, he was free to deal with Acosta. He gave a reverse head-butt. The back of his head struck Acosta's mouth. Diago barely felt the pain. The other Nefil loosened his grip on Diago's throat for just a second. It was all he needed. He snaked free and kicked Acosta's kneecap. The bigger Nefil went down with a howl.

Back inside the house, Diago became dimly aware of Miquel moving. A scuffle broke out. One of the guns fired. The shot came from Fierro's direction, and the bullet lodged itself in the doorframe.

Terrified he would find Miquel dead, Diago whirled.

Miquel was on his knees, holding the back of his head. Garcia had obviously pistol-whipped him. But he was alive.

Garcia brought down the butt of his gun on the back of Miquel's head a second time.

Knowing there was nothing he could do for his partner at the moment, Diago turned back toward the yard. He had to find Rafael.

The angel's fist caught the side of his face. Diago had moved right into the blow. He went down and tried to see through the haze of blurred vision. His son was still screaming.

Where are you?

His fingers sought a weapon. Two broken bricks near the foundation wavered, and then solidified into one. Diago grabbed the brick just as the toe of Engel's boot caught him in the stomach. The kick lifted him off the ground and drove the wind from his lungs.

Someone jerked him to his knees and pulled his arms behind his back. Cuffs snapped around his wrists. Engel grabbed a handful of Diago's hair, forcing him to look toward the two cars.

Moreno stood before the vehicle on the left. Rafael was in front of him, gripping the strap of his satchel and staring at Diago with glazed eyes. A bright red handprint covered his cheek. The barrel of Moreno's pistol was against the child's temple.

Moreno's pockmarked face turned splotchy and red. He looked away from the murder in Diago's glare.

Look at me, you fucker, look at me and see your death. He mouthed the words but couldn't gulp enough air into his lungs to say them. Spittle covered his chin, or maybe it was blood. He tasted blood.

Before he could speak, Engel jerked him to his feet. He purred in Diago's ear, speaking in broken Catalan. "No more fighting. Get in the car quiet. Or boom." He mimed shooting Rafael with his own pistol. "Understand?"

Diago gave a tight nod. *I understand we're enemies— oaths be damned.*

Engel aimed him toward the car and started walking.

Acosta popped his kneecap back into place with a curse, and hobbled to the passenger side of Moreno's car.

Diago looked over his shoulder in time to see Fierro step over Miquel's prone body.

Miquel appeared unconscious. *Please just let him be unconscious.*

"Should I shoot him?" The quaver in Fierro's voice indicated he didn't want to carry out the act.

Diago stumbled and were it not for Engel's iron hand around his arm, he would have fallen. *No. No, no, no. . .*

"Leave him," Garcia said as he walked away from the house. "He's sworn his oath to the angels. Once this is over, he will be forced to obey me."

Once what is over? What the hell is Garcia up to?

Garcia took Rafael from Moreno.

Moreno looked relieved. He got behind the wheel as Garcia got into the backseat with Rafael.

In the distance, the sound of a motorcycle shattered the sudden silence. Had someone from Guillermo's house heard the shot?

Diago pulled against Engel's grip, hoping to slow him. If Guillermo came with reinforcements, the angel might retreat.

Engel propelled Diago toward the second car. Fierro got behind the wheel, and Jaso took the front passenger seat. Engel opened the backdoor and shoved Diago inside. The angel got in beside him.

Diago hoped the two cars were going to the same place.

Down the lane, the motorcycle roared as the rider picked up speed.

Fierro turned the car around, and the other vehicle fell in behind them just as Guillermo arrived. Diago's heart sank. Guillermo was alone. Not even he could stand against so many, nor did Diago expect him to make the attempt.

Guillermo slowed the bike as he passed the cars and got a good look inside. He would mark them, though, mark them and remember them.

And they would pay.

Fierro and Jaso must have had the same thought. They tried to shield their faces from Guillermo's eye.

Idiots. Did they think he wouldn't find out? Diago met his friend's gaze for an instant before he glimpsed

Engel lifting his pistol. Diago stomped hard on the angel's ankle. Engel swore and punched Diago.

Diago curled himself against the door, waiting for the second blow that never came.

Jaso said something, but his words faded in and out like a bad radio signal behind the ringing in Diago's ears. Engel barked an order at him, but it, too, was lost in the haze.

Pain flooded his body, not in increments, but in hot heavy waves. It would be so easy to succumb, just let himself sleep.

The image of Rafael's frightened face suddenly rose behind his eyelids. Diago fought down his nausea. He opened his eyes and forced himself upright.

Fierro gunned the car as they hit the main road. A pothole jarred them all in their seats.

Jaso studied the passing countryside like his life depended on knowing the geography. Fierro risked a nervous glance in the rearview mirror.

Diago twisted in his seat to look out the rear window. He barely made out the figure behind the wheel of the other car, much less his small son, who was secured in the backseat with Garcia. Beyond Garcia's car, no one followed them.

Not yet, Diago thought as Santuari faded behind its wards. Guillermo would check on Miquel, and then gather his Nefilim.

Diago tested the cuffs by rotating his wrists. With his hands bound behind his back, he couldn't form a sigil. He could barely move.

Engel withdrew a handkerchief from his coat. "You speak Spanish, don't you, Herr Alvarez?"

Diago nodded.

"That is good. My Catalan is very bad. We will talk now in Spanish." He took Diago's arm and forced him to face the front of the car. "Guillermo has brought these troubles to you. Had he done as I asked, all this fighting would have been unnecessary. He is very lax with Los Nefilim. In Germany, Die Nephilim know their place and move accordingly."

That is a matter of opinion, but Diago didn't voice the thought. He tracked the movement of Garcia's car through the rearview mirror.

Engel spoke a word, and the mirror clouded. The car behind them disappeared. Diago tried to turn again, but Engel stopped him.

"Pay attention to me, Herr Alvarez." He dug his fingers into Diago's thigh and sent a bolt of angelic fire into Diago's leg.

The pain was sudden and vicious, like someone touching a live wire to his flesh. Diago cried out and tried to twist free of Engel's grip.

"Be still." The angel's command drifted through the agony.

Taking deep breaths, Diago stopped moving.

Engel relaxed his grip but didn't move his hand. "I have a job for you," said the angel.

Diago stared at the back of Fierro's head and made no response.

Undeterred by Diago's silence, Engel went on. "I need you to find your friend Prieto."

"We're not friends."

"Ah! You speak!" Engel laughed.

Jaso snorted and tugged at his beard.

Fierro's bony knuckles were white on the steering wheel.

"This heartens me," said Engel as he patted Diago's thigh.

Diago's skin crawled at the angel's touch.

Engel used his handkerchief to daub at the blood on Diago's face. "Maybe Prieto isn't your friend, but you know him. He shows himself to you, and Prieto has something that I need. I want you to convince him to turn the idea for the bomb over to me."

"Fuck you."

"I don't know that word." Engel tapped Jaso's shoulder. "What is that word?"

Jaso gave it to Engel in German. Now Diago understood why Jaso was involved. He was one of the few Nefilim fluent in German.

Engel frowned. His good humor evaporated. "Do you love your son?"

"Yes."

"And you want to keep him safe."

"Take him home. I'll take a binding sigil if that is what you want."

Fierro twitched behind the wheel, clearly disturbed. A binding sigil was the equivalent of becoming the angel's slave. Last night the thought of encountering Engel and taking a binding sigil had terrified Diago, but that was before he'd seen his son manhandled by the likes of Garcia. Now it seemed a small price to pay for Rafael's safety.

Engel shook his head. "No, we can't have that. Prieto would know I was involved if there was a binding sigil. We must use discretion in these circumstances. You see, I know Prieto is hiding at the lunatic asylum, Holy Cross."

Diago and Guillermo had been there yesterday to question Doña Rosa's son, José. While they were there, Prieto had revealed his presence to Diago. How much did Engel know about that meeting?

With a grin, Engel shifted his weight and leaned close. "Prieto thinks he is sly, hiding beneath the cries of the insane, but he is running out of time. His American counterpart is late, and he has yet to transfer the idea to her. You are going to convince him to give the idea to you so you can relay it to Guillermo."

"Why Guillermo?"

Engel shrugged. "Make something up. The important thing is that you acquire it and bring it to me."

"And if I can't?"

"What is this word, 'can't'?"

Jaso translated.

Engel scowled at Jaso. "It was a rhetorical question, you idiot."

Diago persisted. "If I can't?"

Engel smiled and oozed benevolence. "Then I will

let you kiss your son before I give him the second death."

And he will do it. Diago looked into those cold eyes and did not doubt for a moment that the angel would murder his son. "Why do you think Prieto will just hand it over to me?"

"Because you are half daimon. You are the deceiver." Engel released Diago and relaxed in his seat. *"Deceive."*

Diago clenched his jaw and tried to ignore the throbbing headache crawling behind his eyes. He rested his head against the window and let the cool glass absorb some of his pain. If he angled his head just so, he found he could see Garcia's car in the side view mirror.

The road behind Garcia's car remained empty. Surely Guillermo would send someone for them. He would take the abduction as a personal affront, because Diago was now a part of Los Nefilim. And Miquel . . . Miquel would come.

Wouldn't they?

A pebble of doubt nudged Diago's certainty. As much as he wanted to believe rescue was on the way, the evidence pointed in the opposite direction. The road behind them remained empty.

Miquel bragged that Los Nefilim watched out for their own, but Garcia wasn't watching out for Los Nefilim, and he had convinced four other members to desert with him. What if there were more? Santuari—the one safe place—had been breached. What if Guillermo had an insurrection on his hands?

His first priorities lay with Los Nefilim and securing Santuari. And no matter how strong Miquel's love, as Guillermo's second-in-command, he would be forced to remain at Guillermo's side until they stabilized the situation.

The pebble of doubt became an avalanche. The empty road stretched behind them as barren as Diago's hope. *We're on our own.*

CHAPTER TWO

Miquel awoke to find Guillermo's concerned gaze hovering inches over his face. He closed his eyes against the pounding in his skull. Rafael's scream still reverberated through his mind, and Diago . . . he remembered seeing Diago fall, just before the world went black.

"Look at me." Guillermo's voice was a low growl.

Miquel opened his eyes. "Did you see them?"

"I saw them." One large callused hand cradled Miquel's face. With the other, he held up two fingers. "How many?"

"Why are you so fucking calm?"

"Somebody has to keep his head. Today it is me. How many?"

"Two."

Guillermo patted his cheek. "You're okay."

Miquel allowed Guillermo to help him rise. He

wiped his bloodied nose and winced. "I'm going to fucking kill Garcia."

"Nobody touches Garcia until I'm done with him." Guillermo cautiously released Miquel. "Are you dizzy?"

Miquel shook his head and then wished he hadn't. Sharp pain hammered his skull and his face. He distracted himself by surveying the damage in the house. The couch sat askew and the coffee table was overturned. At some point during his scuffle with Garcia, he'd knocked over the bookcase. Books were scattered across the floor, their spines broken and their pages spread like the wings of dead birds.

He picked up a button that had come off Rafael's coat. "They were finally starting to feel safe," he whispered. Rafael had just begun to sleep through the night, and Diago . . . Miquel's heart twisted in his chest. Twice this morning he had kissed Diago without his lover glancing nervously at the windows. "He'll never believe me again."

"About what?" Guillermo asked.

"I promised to protect him. I told him if he stayed with me, then they couldn't take him." Every argument he'd used to bully Diago into moving north was rendered insubstantial by this attack. He kicked the couch. "What a fucking mess."

"You shouldn't make promises you can't keep." Guillermo put his hand on Miquel's shoulder. The tension in his fingers belied his calm façade. When they found Garcia, Guillermo was going to tear him apart. "Quit beating yourself up and get your gun."

Yes, his gun. He would definitely need his gun. Miquel pocketed the button and went into their bedroom. At the back of their wardrobe was the box that contained his and Diago's pistols. Miquel retrieved his weapon, along with two magazines filled with silver-tipped bullets.

He tucked his pistol in the waistband of his pants and returned to the living room, where he grabbed Diago's jacket off the floor. Someone, probably Garcia, had left a footprint on the back of the coat. Miquel slapped the mud from the fabric as he followed Guillermo to the old farm truck.

Guillermo said over his shoulder, "We're taking your truck and going back to my villa. I want to pick up more ammunition and see what Juanita found out from her conversation with Santiago. She was calling him as I left."

Miquel was certain he meant Carlos Santiago. Guillermo kept several Nefilim embedded in Barcelona's Urban Guard, and like Garcia, Carlos Santiago was an inspector, although Santiago covered the rougher La Ribera district near the docks. Santiago was wily enough to maneuver around Garcia's people, but whether he could do it quickly enough to find Diago and Rafael was another matter altogether.

As if reading the worry etched on Miquel's brow, Guillermo opened the truck's door and fished the keys from under the floor mat. "We're going to get them back."

Miquel nodded even though Guillermo's confidence did nothing to soothe the sick feeling lodged in his gut. He wouldn't have been as afraid if Diago was alone, but Rafael's abduction changed everything.

Diago could be reckless with his own well-being— the risk he'd taken by going after Lamashtu last night was a classic example. But with Rafael? *No. He will be careful with Rafael, maybe too careful.* If anything happened to that child, Diago would blame himself. *And if anything happens to either of them, it is on my head.*

Miquel jerked open the rusty passenger door and got inside. "Is Suero here?"

"He's at the villa." Guillermo cranked the truck and shifted it into gear. "Yesterday I told him to watch Garcia. He got as close as he dared. This morning, Engel and Garcia gathered the others and left the city before dawn. They picked their time well. There weren't many vehicles on the road. Suero was forced to trail them at a distance; otherwise, they would have seen him. Since they were coming to Santuari, he guessed that Engel and Garcia intended to talk to me. His miscalculation cost us time. This is my fault." He slammed the clutch to the floor and upshifted gears. "I never saw this coming and I should have. I want you to stay here and coordinate the others."

"I'm going with you."

"I have a rule."

Miquel knew the rule: Guillermo never paired two Nefilim who were romantically involved in an assignment. It was too easy for them to be used against one another, as this morning had unfortunately shown.

"Fuck your rule. *We're* not paired. Unless you're going to kiss me."

"You're not going."

"Suero can coordinate the Nefilim. Besides, if it were Juanita or Ysabel, would you stay behind?"

Guillermo didn't take long to think about the question. "Okay, you're coming." He wrenched the steering wheel to guide the truck around a rut in the road. "But no kissing."

"Don't worry. You're not my type." Miquel relaxed. It was better this way. He rarely disobeyed Guillermo and always felt like a deserter when he did. "Do we even know where to start looking for them?"

"My guess would be Holy Cross."

The lunatic asylum. "Didn't Garcia arrange for Diago to examine José Iniguez at Holy Cross?"

Guillermo nodded and pulled a cigar from his pocket. "Yes, and while Diago and I were waiting, Diago saw Garcia chatting with Engel."

Diago had told him some of the events over breakfast, but he had skimmed over quite a bit because of Rafael's presence. Miquel hadn't pressed him for details, because he had anticipated hearing the entire story at the council meeting this morning. *Unfortunately, it appears as if that meeting has been cancelled.*

Miquel asked, "Did Diago hear what Garcia and Engel said?"

"No, and Garcia made no mention of the meeting to me. Later on, Diago and I met with Amparo—I wanted to know why she hadn't stolen that fragment like I told her to. She said she was arrested. While she was in jail, Engel spoke with her. He told her to give me a message: he wanted to talk to Diago. The whole thing was unorthodox. I had no intention of sending Diago to Engel and said so. I thought that would force Engel to make arrangements through a Spanish angel, or directly with me. It never occurred to me that he would just show up on our doorstep and take Diago hostage."

"All of this is unprecedented," Miquel said.

"There's more. At the asylum, José died of a strychnine overdose before Diago could examine him. Garcia and Diago split up to look for the nun who might have given him the shot. Diago didn't find the nun, but he did find our friend Prieto."

"He is no friend of mine." Miquel unconsciously rubbed his chest where the angel had placed a binding sigil on him during their first meeting.

"Prieto is hiding from Engel, and the asylum is the perfect place." Guillermo leaned over the steering wheel and lit his cigar. A cloud of smoke momentarily obscured his face. "The mutterings of the insane conceal Prieto's presence from the German."

All of the random events fell into place. "And Engel thinks Diago and Prieto are connected."

"Exactly. So my guess is that they're heading to the asylum."

The lump of fear in Miquel's stomach grew heavier. The angels didn't mind leaving Nefilim casualties in their wake. "Engel will use Rafael as leverage."

Guillermo nodded. "And when Diago fails to perform . . ."

"You mean *if* Diago fails."

"I mean when." Guillermo downshifted the truck as his villa came into sight. "Engel is most likely after the idea for the bomb, and Prieto isn't going to give it up in exchange for a child. You know it, and I know it. That is not how the angels conduct their wars. *When* Diago fails, Engel won't hesitate to carry out whatever threats he's made against Rafael."

Miquel fingered the collar of Diago's coat. He looked down and found a black hair on the fabric. *We're a family of bears,* Diago had said to Rafael, but that was wrong. They were a family of wolves, because wolves watched out for their own. "Why didn't they shoot me?"

"My guess? This is about control. Shooting you would merely enrage Diago and provoke him into a rash act. Engel wants him compliant, not defiant." Guillermo clamped his cigar between his teeth. "There is more you need to know. Suero says that our friend Engel didn't come alone. He brought members of Die Nephilim with him."

Miquel frowned. Having the German Nefilim on Spanish soil was nothing new—the Nefilim from other countries traveled as mortals did and often passed through Spain. However, they never failed to notify Guillermo, or another high-ranking member of Los Nefilim, whenever they were in the area. It was a courtesy they all practiced whenever they passed through another country.

Miquel asked, "Is Engel coordinating them?"

"That is Suero's guess."

"That's practically an act of war."

"And then he abducts two members of Los Nefilim," Guillermo reminded him.

"Fuck him. That *is* an act of war." Miquel clenched the collar of Diago's coat in his hands. "Do we know how many members of Die Nephilim are with him?"

"Suero counted five. There may be more."

"How did Garcia get involved with this group?"

"He thinks I'm too lenient with the daimons, that I give them more rights than they deserve or need." They pulled into Guillermo's yard. "From what Suero has been able to piece together, Engel managed to convince Garcia that I am a traitor to the angels and their cause."

"He convinced him because Garcia already believed it in his heart. All he'd needed was validation from a higher authority. And you *are* too lenient with your own Nefilim."

"Everybody is a critic." Guillermo parked the truck beside his Mercedes and cut the engine. Quick as a viper, he reached over and grabbed Miquel's wrist. "Just remember, *Señor Crítico*, I'm the one that sanctioned your marriage to Diago over the other Nefilim's objections. You're also coming with me to find Diago. So as a beneficiary of that leniency, don't bite me in the ass."

Miquel felt his cheeks warm with shame. "I'm sorry. I just meant—"

"I know what you meant. I can't control every Nefil. I have to give them room to work, and that means trusting them." Guillermo released him. "I'm not omniscient."

No, he wasn't, but his sagacity and firm management of Los Nefilim often gave that impression. Miquel chided himself for his assumptions and his loose tongue. It was times like these—moments of failure—when Guillermo needed support, not a critique. "You know I've got your back."

Guillermo opened his door. "I'm counting on it."

Father Bernardo walked toward them, cradling a Mauser in his arms. Bernardo might wear the collar, but he was no priest. It was a ruse in case outsiders penetrated Santuari. With Bernardo, the town maintained the illusion of a village priest, and Guillermo had a Nefil embedded inside the Church, which still wielded too damn much control in Spain if anyone ever asked Miquel. Not that anyone did. Most of Santuari's inhabitants avoided the subject around him—Miquel wasn't even sure Diago listened to his tirades anymore.

Bernardo, on the other hand, still gave Miquel a sympathetic ear when he needed to voice his frustrations. The "priest's" heavy black brows and beard shadowed a pleasant face. Usually his light brown eyes were smiling, but not today. His anger seemed to suck the light out of the air. "Everything is quiet here, Don Guillermo. I've got a small force patrolling the fields."

"Good," Guillermo said as he walked to the villa. "Wait for Mariona. When she gets here, I want the two of you to strengthen the wards around Santuari. Juanita is going to help. Then you and Mariona assign some Nefilim for permanent patrols. Nobody gets in without us knowing it."

Bernardo nodded and held the door open for them. Then he resumed his guard duty on the porch.

They crossed the foyer and Miquel saw Ysa hesitate on the stairs.

"Papa?"

"It's all right, dove," Guillermo said. "Go upstairs."

Her demeanor possessed none of her usual liveliness. "Is Rafael okay? I heard a gunshot."

"Everybody is fine." Guillermo didn't wait to see if she obeyed him. He went to the kitchen.

Ysa remained on the landing, switching her questioning gaze to Miquel. "Is he, Miquel? Are Rafael and Uncle Diago okay?"

"The last time I saw them, they were fine. We're going to get them back." Painfully aware of the lies he'd told Rafael about Diago last night, Miquel wanted to bite his tongue in half. There had to be a better way to reassure children than to lie to them. He ducked his head and followed Guillermo, feeling like a coward.

In the kitchen, Lucia steadied the chair Juanita stood on in order to reach the highest cupboard.

Juanita removed a revolver from the back of the

cabinet and handed the gun to Guillermo. "Keep this one out of the sewers."

Guillermo smiled. "You are my angel."

"I *am* an angel and don't forget it," Juanita admonished him. "I spoke with Santiago. He wanted to make some phone calls. He will call back here in a few minutes."

"Good." Guillermo lifted her off the chair, and she kissed him.

"Come back to me," she whispered.

"If I don't, you will watch for me."

To watch for another was the Nefilim's death-hour vow to watch for their loved one in a different incarnation. It meant to seek the shadows of the soul in the face of every stranger until they were reunited.

Miquel refused to think about Diago dying. *He's going to be fine. He's been through much worse than this.* Even as the old mantra entered his brain, he heard Rafael's scream again, and his gut twisted with the same terror he'd felt earlier this morning. *Not like this. He's never been in a situation like this, and neither have I.* Nor could Miquel dwell on that fact. If he lingered too long on his fear, it would cripple him.

The phone rang, and Lucia hurried to the foyer to answer it. "Ramírez residence." She kept her head down as she murmured soft affirmations into the receiver.

She hung up and came back to the kitchen. "That was Santiago. Garcia has a meeting this morning at

Holy Cross with a German psychiatrist, Dr. Anselm Engel. That's all he could find out right now. He said he is going over to Garcia's precinct to see if he can uncover anything else."

"Anything about Diago or Rafael?" Miquel asked.

"No," she answered.

"It doesn't matter," Guillermo said. "They won't take them to the station. I've got too many people there, and Garcia knows it. My money is on the asylum, so that's where we're going." He went to the basement door. "Is Suero still downstairs?"

Juanita nodded. "He wanted to monitor the radio."

"Good. I'm going to have him contact the Nefilim in the city."

Lucia folded her arms across her chest and made a sour face. "Will they be listening for their radios?"

"They'd better be." Guillermo's voice took an ominous tone. "Anyone caught sleeping on the job will answer to me." He glared at Lucia until she dropped her gaze, and then he spoke to Juanita again. "We'll meet my people at the warehouse near La Sagrada Família. It's close enough to the asylum."

"Do you want me to come?" Juanita asked.

Guillermo shook his head. "I'd rather have you here in Santuari. Bernardo and Mariona will need your help. Use only the Nefilim you trust." He went to the basement door. "I'll be right back."

Juanita nodded. When he had shut the door behind him, she turned and seemed to notice Miquel for the first time. She glanced at the jacket in his arms.

Only then did he realize he still held Diago's coat. He smoothed the fabric. "He gets cold so easily."

"Are you all right?" Juanita came to him and touched his face.

He nodded and winced at her gentle probing. "I'm okay. I just want to go."

"I know." She stroked the back of her knuckles against his face and hummed a healing song. "We're all worried."

His headache dissolved and the throbbing agony in his face receded. "Thank you."

Juanita merely smiled as she guided him into the foyer.

Movement on the staircase caught Miquel's attention. He glimpsed a pair of golden eyes glowing in the stairwell's dimness. Ysa. She hadn't abandoned her vigil.

Miquel gave her a wan smile and tried to lighten his tone. "Go back to your room, Ysa. Everything is going to be fine."

Lucia followed them out of the kitchen and glanced up the steps. "Go on, Ysa. I'll be there in a moment."

"I'll take care of her, Lucia." Juanita started up the stairs. "Come with me, dove. I'll show you how to make a protective ward for Rafael like we did for Uncle Diago last night."

"Will it save him?" Ysa took her mother's hand.

"I don't know, but he will know you are thinking of him." Her voice faded as they moved out of sight. "And that will give him courage."

Miquel thought of last night and the song he and Rafael had used for Diago. Over space and distance, they could do little more than remind Diago he was loved. However, that small magic had been enough to center Diago so he could save himself from the daimon Lamashtu. *Sometimes a little courage is just enough.*

Lucia sidled up beside Miquel. "Are you hurt?" She reached up to touch his swollen nose.

Driven from his thoughts, he jerked his head clear of her fingers and blurted, "Are you happy they're gone?"

Miquel wasn't sure which of them was more taken aback by his outburst.

Lucia recovered quickly. "I'm not happy they're gone."

"Then why are you so horrible to Rafael? Diago, I understand, but not the child."

She blinked in surprise. "I'm not horrible to Rafael."

The insolence in her tone grated against his already jangled nerves. "You said something about turning him into a jinni. He said you made fun of him because he is dark."

"If I didn't like dark men, why would I be after you?" she shot back.

Her reply took the wind from his assault. He hadn't considered that at all.

She snorted at his confusion and folded her arms across her chest. "The truth is: Rafael is very sensitive. I didn't realize how much until after I made the joke, and that was all it was—a joke. I tried to tell him I was sorry, but he started crying and wouldn't speak to me again. I never meant to hurt him, Miquel." She glanced back toward the basement door. "He's moody, like his father."

"He's six years old. He doesn't know that you're joking. And Diago isn't moody. You just don't know him."

She pursed her lips as if she intended to spit. "I know he is daimon, and your excuses for him will never change that."

"And he is angel, too." Miquel retorted, suddenly tired of the argument. "He is Los Nefilim. He took the oath. You don't have to like him, but he is one of us now."

"He has you wrapped around his finger." Contempt dripped from her voice.

"And I wouldn't have it any other way. I've always loved him, Lucia."

"That kind of love isn't natural."

"Fuck you."

"Why don't you? Diago cheated on you." Her eyes narrowed until Miquel thought of weasels in the fields. She caressed his throat with her finger. "Who knows? Maybe he liked it. Maybe he's just trying to figure out how to let you down easy. You should make the first move." When he didn't resist her touch, she moved closer until her breast touched his arm. "Fuck me," she whispered. "Show him how it feels when he sleeps around on you."

She made Candela's rape sound like a dalliance.

Miquel resented the implication. "You are disgusting."

Lucia sighed as if dealing with a simpleton. "There was no rape, Miquel. A woman cannot rape a man. Diago had to have wanted her."

Christ, she was ignorant. Diago still refused to talk about the weeks he'd been held under Candela's spell. Miquel saw the torment in his lover's eyes as they sat together in the evenings. Twice over the last month, Diago had attempted to broach the subject, only to retreat behind silence before his hesitant words could become a conversation. Miquel didn't push him. Juanita had cautioned him to be patient with Diago.

Lucia seemed hell-bent on destroying him.

Miquel stared down into her dark eyes. "Garcia seems to hold your views about Diago being daimon, and he has defected to the Germans." He leaned down and put his lips against her ear. "Whose side are you on?"

Lucia jumped back as if scalded. "How dare you imply my loyalty lies anywhere but with Guillermo?"

"Then be careful of what you say, and who you accuse." He put his finger over her lips and smiled at her horror. "I'm watching you."

Her eyes narrowed to slits, but before she could respond, Guillermo emerged from the basement. He carried a small pack that no doubt contained more ammunition.

Miquel brushed past Lucia and followed Guillermo back to the truck. He'd caught her off guard, but this was merely the first feint in a potentially long war.

Lucia was more dangerous than Miquel had first surmised and needed to be reassigned somewhere far
from Diago. The problem was knotty, because she was
under Juanita's protection. Miquel didn't know the
details of their arrangement, but moving Lucia out of
Santuari would take diplomacy. He knew the game of
intrigue, too, and he had Guillermo's ear.

Guillermo tossed the bag onto the seat and got
behind the wheel. "Diago said that we have a traitor in our ranks. He implied that Garcia was feeding
information to the daimons. I disagreed with him.
I could see Garcia working with Engel, but not the
daimons."

Miquel covered the pack with Diago's coat and shut
his door. "You were right about Garcia."

"But we still don't know who is working with the
daimons." Guillermo cranked the truck and moved it
out of the yard.

Miquel frowned. This new development temporarily ejected Lucia from his thoughts. "It's not Diago."

"I know it's not," Guillermo said. "I'm worried the
others will think it is him if we don't find the individual
soon, though. I sent Amparo to Valencia last night. She
was supposed to come to Santuari for supplies before
she left. Bernardo told me this morning that she never
got here. Suero just confirmed through his sources
that she is no longer in the city."

"Are you saying Amparo is working with the
daimons?"

"I am saying that I don't know. I put Mariona on the

hunt for the informant." Guillermo turned the vehicle onto the main road and drove in silence.

Miquel took advantage of the lull. "We've got a problem with Lucia, too." While they rode, he relayed his conversation with her. "She should be reassigned," he concluded.

Guillermo withdrew a cigar from his breast pocket. "We need to integrate Diago into Los Nefilim. Give him a job."

"Did you hear what I just said?"

"I did. And that is my solution. Integrate Diago into Los Nefilim with a job." He snipped the tip off the cigar and tossed it out the window. "I'll take care of Lucia. Trust me to do that."

Reluctantly, Miquel nodded. "And Diago?"

"Needs to start pulling his weight. We've got to get them to accept him." He clamped the cigar between his teeth and lit it. "I want him to start working on compositions again. I need him to find the Key."

Miquel withdrew Rafael's button from his pocket and held it in his hand. The Key was the thing that made Diago so special to both the angels and the daimons. All angels possessed three sets of vocal chords that enabled them to form their sigils with the distinctive sounds they produced. Because Diago was dually born, his unique vocal range allowed him to harmonize with Guillermo and Miquel in order to form a melody no other group of Nefilim could reach. Those notes allowed them to mimic the sounds of an angel, and with that music, they commanded the ability to shift the realms.

Unfortunately, the Key was an arrangement that Diago had buried deep within his psyche and was unable to produce on a whim. Neither Guillermo nor Miquel had ever pressed him to remember the music, primarily for Diago's safety. If either the daimons or the angels believed Diago recalled the composition while remaining a neutral player in the war, they would have taken action. The daimons would have murdered him to keep the secret safe, or the angels would have forced a binding sigil on him. Now, as a member of Los Nefilim, he had some measure of protection from both sides.

Or did he? Miquel wondered. "I don't think it's a good idea. We can't protect him."

"Yes, we can." Guillermo insisted.

"We certainly fucked up this morning."

"The day is not over. I'm not worried . . . do I look worried?"

"You look pissed."

He sucked on his cigar and blew smoke through his nostrils. "Pissed is an understatement. I'm fucking furious. But I've dreamed the future and Diago is with us. Today is not his day to die."

"There are worse things than dying," Miquel whispered.

"Keep to the positive, or you'll go insane. We need to use this problem to our advantage."

"You're using him."

"I use all of you, and don't you ever forget it. That's the way the worlds work, Miquel . . . all of the worlds, the supernatural and the mundane . . . they are filled with the users and the used. At some point in our lives, we all get used. At other times, we're the users. No one is exempt. Not even the angels."

"That's depressing."

"Welcome to my world." Guillermo blew a cloud of smoke at the windshield. "Has Diago picked up an instrument?"

Miquel shook his head. "He says his arm hurts, or it's more important to help Rafael. He uses any excuse to avoid making music. I think he's depressed. The thing with Candela . . ." He leaned his aching head against the glass and let the coolness soothe his brow.

"He blames himself," Guillermo said. "And he's afraid, because the memory of those notes will resurrect the trauma he doesn't want to recall."

"He claims the maiming has ruined his music."

Guillermo grunted. "Bullshit. When he gets ready, he'll figure out a way to play. What about the violin? Have you tried getting him a new violin?"

"He hasn't played a violin since his Stradivarius was stolen." The truck hit a rut and Rafael's button bounced into the air. Miquel caught it and gripped it in his fist. "You know how obstinate he is."

"So am I. Keep working on him. His magic is coming back to him. You should have seen him last night." Guillermo guided the truck around a small herd of goats. "The power, Miquel. He was fucking magnificent."

"He's always been magnificent," Miquel said.

"Yes, yes. But last night—"

"Be careful with him."

"Why? You think he's going to break?" Guillermo scoffed. "You listen to me: Diago is a warrior. He'll be fine," Guillermo nodded to himself. "We'll get him back."

Miquel wasn't sure if Guillermo meant today's rescue or something deeper. He tightened his fist over Rafael's button, suddenly afraid for his lover. "Be careful with him," he repeated.

Guillermo reached over and squeezed Miquel's shoulder. "I will. I swear to you, I will. I love him like a brother. Besides, Rafael needs both of his fathers."

Miquel lifted his fist to his lips and kissed his wedding band. *Hold on, my star. We're coming.*

CHAPTER THREE

Blue-black clouds hovered over Holy Cross. The humid air was tinted in sallow shades of yellow and green. Tornados dropped from skies like this.

A song rose around the asylum. The sound waves had been sculpted into razored sigils, which were interlinked like chains of mercury and ash. The wards created a dome stretching from one end of the grounds to the other.

Diago's skin crawled with the foreign sounds. He glanced at Engel.

The angel smiled; his countenance simultaneously beatific and horrifying. "Die Nephilim," he answered Diago's unspoken question. "If Prieto tries to leave the asylum, we will catch him."

Maybe, Diago thought as he returned his attention to the side view mirror. Garcia's car still followed them. Diago wasn't sure whether to be relieved or worried.

He settled for relieved. *At least if Rafael is close, I can find him easier. If I manage to get away from Engel, that is.*

They skirted the main drive and followed a narrow lane that ran between the buildings. He gauged how close they were to their destination by Jaso's nervousness.

Jaso constantly picked at his facial hair, rubbing his chin. By the time they reached the back entrance of the hospital, he had switched to worrying the cuticle around his thumb until he bled. Diago couldn't help but think of an animal chewing off its leg to escape a trap.

Fierro twitched like a rat. He kept turning his head in a vain attempt to check the rearview mirror, but Engel had never reversed his spell. The glass remained clouded.

Engel, on the other hand, grew more and more relaxed, almost jovial as Fierro brought the car to a halt at the rear entrance. Diago looked up at the barred windows overhead. He knew the building. These were the wards for criminally insane. No one would question his handcuffs here, and any protests of innocence would be ignored.

Diago recalled the locked wards and the needles used to quiet the men. The smell of his own fear choked him.

Get it under control, he told himself. He didn't have time for hysterics. If Engel had no intention of using a binding sigil in order to secure Diago's assistance, he wouldn't resort to drugs. *Not when he has the perfect hostage to extort my compliance.*

Four orderlies emerged from the building along with a young doctor, who carried a clipboard. Diago recognized Dr. Vales. The mortal had been in charge of José Iniguez's care, at least until José's untimely death from an overdose of strychnine.

Vales had seemed to like Diago—had seen him as a colleague. With a little charm, he might be able to convince Vales to take charge of Rafael. If he could get his son away from the angel, he could buy time.

Just as the thought crossed Diago's mind, the rearview mirror cleared. At first he didn't recognize the disheveled person staring back at him, and then, with dawning unease, he realized the wild eyes in the mirror belonged to him. His hair was in disarray from his scuffle with Acosta and Engel, and his clothing torn. The cuts and bruises from his fight with the daimon Lamashtu paled behind the bruise Engel had left on Diago's face. Blood smeared his chin and throat. He looked as though the officers had beaten him into submission.

And that is precisely how Engel wants me to appear. Heart sinking with the futility of swaying Vales, Diago leaned forward and tried to glimpse his son in the other car. Engel blocked his view.

"Let me see him," Diago said.

"In time," Engel purred.

Fierro parked the car, and then got out to open Engel's door.

Engel called a greeting to Vales, who nodded tersely, his gaze on Diago. The angel apparently planned to claim Diago was insane. Fair enough. It was a tactic Diago himself might have employed.

Vales appeared to be miserable. Diago didn't feel much better. However, he knew that if his appearance was alarming, then his demeanor needed to be calm.

Most reasonable person in the room wins, Diago thought as Jaso left the vehicle and came to Diago's side. The trick would be not to struggle.

Jaso opened the door and yanked Diago from the car. Graceful as a cat, Diago got his feet under him and stood with as much dignity as he could muster.

He tried to catch Vales's eye, but the doctor studiously averted his gaze.

What the hell had Engel told him?

The four orderlies approached the car. Engel spoke to them in German, and the tallest one, a strikingly handsome man with short blond hair, nodded.

By the light in their eyes, Diago noted that all four of them were angel-born. Like chips cut from the same ice floe, they shared pale features. They were Die Nephilim.

Engel glanced over his shoulder and spoke to Jaso. "Adler will take charge from here. Get the child inside."

Jaso released Diago to the blue-eyed Nefil.

Adler's grip was a vise around Diago's left arm while another Nephil clamped a meaty hand around his right. Diago could barely move between the two of them. Even if he managed to break away, the third and fourth Nephilim had taken their places directly behind him. He was boxed between them.

Dr. Vales stepped closer.

"Careful, Doctor." Engel cautioned him. "As you can see, he gave us some trouble." He indicated Diago's face. "He dislocated poor Sergeant Acosta's knee. He's not the gentle doctor he portrayed himself to be. He's a criminal."

Diago didn't like the distrust in Vales's eyes.

"There has been a terrible mistake, Vales," Diago said.

Vales refused to look at him. "I'm sure it will be straightened out soon."

"He had us all fooled," Garcia said as he strolled up to follow the orderlies that surrounded Diago. "Even Don Guillermo thought he was a doctor, but I cracked this case. Alvarez is part of a crime syndicate."

"You should write novels." Diago twisted in the German's grip to face the inspector and then froze. Just beyond Garcia, Jaso grabbed Rafael's arm. The child's lip was swollen, and his eyes were glassy with tears.

Diago's heart turned black with rage. "Did you strike my son again?"

Rafael took a step forward. "Papa?"

Jaso jerked the child toward another door.

Vales looked from Diago to Rafael. "Is this your son?"

"Yes," Diago said. "He is! And you're right, Vales. We will get this straightened out. Please, just take care of my boy until we do. I'm begging you. Take care of him."

Before Vales could answer him, Engel went to the

mortal and liberated the clipboard from his hands. He quickly signed off on the paper. "Inspector Jaso and his officers will take care of the child until arrangements can be made with a local orphanage."

Moreno and Fierro waited with Acosta beside a different door. Jaso joined them, dragging Rafael along with him.

The child pried at Jaso's fingers. "Papa!"

Diago dug his heels into the gravel and resisted his captors. "Run if you can! I will find you!"

"Wait!" Vales's eyes widened in alarm. "Don't tell him to do that!"

Diago ignored Vales. "Do you hear me, Rafael?"

"Yes!" Rafael cried out as Jaso dragged him inside.

Adler's palm clamped the back of Diago's neck. "Shut up and walk," he growled in broken Spanish.

Garcia moved ahead of them and opened the door.

Vales turned to Engel. "I am concerned about the child."

Engel paused beside Vales and put his hand on the young mortal's shoulder. The angel's demeanor became pleasant, engaging. He captured Vales's gaze with his own and said, "There is nothing to be concerned about. The boy will be fine. The police are professionals."

Diago's hope withered with the glazing of Vales's eyes.

"Of course," the mortal said.

"Vales!" Diago yelled as the Germans hustled him into the building.

Engel smiled at Diago and led the doctor a few steps away. To anyone watching them, they were merely two doctors, consulting one another about a patient. Diago knew Engel was probably erasing any memories Vales might have of either Diago or Rafael.

Erased. That was a good word. *They will erase us if they can.*

Garcia led their little group away from the doctors. Other members of the hospital staff, nuns and orderlies alike, parted to either side of the wide hall, giving Diago and his captors room to pass.

"Garcia," Diago whispered in Catalan. "Engel will turn on you next."

Garcia's shoulders twitched; otherwise, he made no sign he'd heard.

Adler squeezed Diago's arm until he thought his bone would break.

"He's using you," Diago said. "And when he's done, he'll destroy you. You've turned traitor on Guillermo. You'll turn on him, too. Engel knows it. He'll kill you before you get the chance to betray him."

Garcia unlocked a door leading to a stairwell. He blocked the doorway and faced Diago. "You hiss like the serpent in the garden, but you won't talk your way out of this, Alvarez. I intend to take command of Los Nefilim. Guillermo cannot be trusted by either angel or daimon—not anymore. He has forgotten our true cause. The angel-born Los Nefilim were created to fight the daimons in the mortal realm. And your insidious whispers will not drive me from my holy path to do just that." He stepped aside and gestured for them to continue.

"You are a fucking lunatic," Diago spat at him as they passed.

Adler jerked Diago to a halt on the landing and pointed him toward a long flight of steep stairs. "You can walk, or fall. Your choice," he said in his heavily accented Spanish.

Diago felt someone's hand move between his shoulder blades. A mild push would send him flying.

"I'll walk."

"Good." Adler waved the others back, but kept his hand on Diago's arm. "How do you say it in Spanish? *Vamos*, huh?"

Vamos, pendejo. Diago clamped the words behind his teeth and let Adler set the pace. By the time they reached the next landing, Engel had joined Garcia. The other three orderlies remained on the first landing, probably to block Diago's escape, which was ludicrous.

Even if he managed to get free, Engel's presence alone guaranteed Diago wouldn't get far. He couldn't defeat an angel. Nor could he defend himself against the other Nephilim with his hands bound.

No, now wasn't the moment to fight. For the time being, compliance was his only recourse. He needed to keep his wits about him and wait for an opening.

They descended two more flights of stairs until they reached a basement. The corridor was lit by a single naked bulb.

Cells lined both sides of the hall. Each barred

window was as black as a priest's heart. A light burned under the threshold of the last door. The cell was silent, like a scream held behind closed lips.

Garcia unlocked the door and opened it. Adler shoved Diago inside. He fell to his knees.

"Wait in the hall, Adler." Engel stepped inside and motioned for Garcia to enter the cell. "Join us, Inspector. You might find this enlightening, as well."

Adler saluted Engel and shut the heavy metal door, but he didn't go far. Diago felt him hovering on the other side, peeking through the small observation window, as excited as a child.

They weren't alone in the room. In a single bed, which consisted of nothing but a bare mattress, was a woman. Wiry hair framed her face in a dark halo. Her features were the marriage of mixed mortal parentage somewhere between Africa and China. Diago recognized her. Guillermo had called her the best thief he had.

"Amparo?" Her name burned in Diago's throat.

She didn't answer. Her eyes were open, staring up at the ceiling without seeing. Her lips moved, but no syllables touched the air. She shivered uncontrollably. Open wounds marred her exposed flesh. They had cut her and beat her.

Diago remembered her voice. She had a beautiful contralto, sweet as honey and soft as summer. Guillermo had given her money and told her to go to Valencia. *Why hadn't she gone?*

Diago glared at Engel. "What did you do her?"

"I know you've studied neuropsychiatry," Engel

said. "I'm sure you're familiar with the mortal theory that inducing seizures can cure the insane."

Diago gaped at the angel as he struggled to shift his mental gears. The last thing he'd been prepared to hear from Engel was an analysis of medical treatments for the insane.

After a moment, his stunned brain extracted the information he needed. Doctors in mental institutions had been using high dosages of metrazol to induce convulsions in patients for years. The treatment didn't work, but that didn't stop mortal doctors from utilizing it, along with lobotomies, to make their patients more compliant.

"Well?" Engel prodded. The angel was enjoying himself immensely. "Have you?"

"I'm familiar with it," Diago whispered through dry lips.

"Excellent!" Engel went to the cot and placed his fingers on Amparo's temples where burn marks were visible.

Diago couldn't be sure, but he thought Amparo flinched and whimpered. *What had Engel done to her?*

"There is a professor in Italy." Engel continued. "Cerletti is his name. He is using electricity in small doses to simulate the effect of metrazol. Right now, he is experimenting on animals with his electric shock treatment." Engel straightened and evaluated Diago with a frown. "Ah, I know what you're thinking."

Cold and sick, Diago was certain Engel had no idea what he was thinking.

"This"—Engel gestured at Amparo's inert body— "is not an animal. Correct?" He raised his eyebrows and waited for an answer.

Diago gave a sharp nod. He wasn't sure if he was capable of more.

"No. You are wrong, Herr Alvarez. This is an animal. Do you know why?"

"Stop fucking with me and just say what you have to say."

Garcia backhanded him hard. Diago would have fallen if Garcia hadn't caught his arm right after and jerked him upright.

"Answer him," Garcia growled in his ear.

Diago licked the blood from his lip and glared at Engel. *Play the game. Amparo is gone. I can't help her now—not even Juanita can bring her back from this.* He closed his eyes and fixed Rafael's face in his mind. *Stay alive for Rafael's sake. Just play his game.* Diago opened his eyes and said, "No. I don't know why."

"Because she is a traitor, Herr Alvarez. She was giving information to the daimons. You were right. There was a spy." He gave Diago two heartbeats to absorb the information before he continued. "Who knew your final plans for yesterday? Suero and Amparo. Suero is no spy. He is loyal to Guillermo and Miquel, but Amparo was seen speaking to the Ferrers' maid, Elena, several times yesterday. Most importantly, after she left her meeting with you and Guillermo, she and Elena had coffee."

And by that evening, Elena was possessed by the

daimon Lamashtu, and Amparo had been ordered to depart for Valencia. If Engel could be believed, Amparo had no reason to meet with Elena.

"Fortunately, Garcia—who *is* still loyal to the angels and our cause—observed these interactions and took corrective measures."

That explained the bruises and cuts on Amparo's body. *Corrective measures.*

"Amparo's betrayal makes her an animal that must be destroyed." Engel looked down at her shuddering body. "But killing a Nefil is a tricky business. And of course, we don't want her to reincarnate. She will simply go over to the enemy again. Why should we keep fighting the same battles? Hmm, Herr Alvarez?"

Suddenly, he saw where Engel was going with his lecture. He intended to give Amparo the second death—the one from which no Nefil could be reborn. "Our incarnations change us," Diago said, hoping to change the angel's mind. "We're not the same as we were in our firstborn lives, or even subsequent ones. Our experiences change us—"

Engel applauded with slow claps.

Diago felt his cheeks redden. Now he understood why Guillermo had balked last night when Diago had said he wanted to give Alvaro the second death. The second death left no chance for redemption. "Sometimes all we need is a second chance," he persisted, selfishly thinking of his own second chance in Guillermo's service.

Engel shook his head. "No need to plead for her. The decision has been made."

"Who? Who made that decision?"

"Forces beyond us both," Engel said.

Diago clenched his fists. Engel could only mean the Principalities, those angels who were aligned with the various countries and provinces of the earthly realm. Messenger angels, such as Engel and Prieto, were of a lesser caste and merely followed the commands of their reigning Principalities.

When the Principalities warred with one another, their conflicts were echoed by the mortals in the earthly realms. Guillermo believed that Spain's conflicts mirrored a greater conflict within heaven's realms. Was he right? Were the angels at war and if so, whose side was Engel on?

And which Principality had ordered Amparo's death? Diago knew he wouldn't get an answer from Engel— the angel was too in love with his own plans. But even in his predicament, Diago couldn't help but wonder.

"Listen carefully, Herr Alvarez. In the name of science, we tried Professor Cerletti's electric shock treatment on this animal. We broke her mind. Then note by note, I learned her death song. That is how you render the second death. You must know another Nefil's death song and sing it against them."

Diago closed his eyes against the hot wave of nausea washing over him.

"Open your eyes, Herr Alvarez. There is a lesson

here for you." Engel put his hand over Amparo's face. "I want you to see what awaits your son if you fail."

"Stop. I told you I would summon Prieto. There is no need to do this." He tried to rise, but Garcia's hand landed on his shoulder. Diago's teeth clicked together and he bit his tongue. The sharp taste of his own blood stung his mouth.

Engel shook his head as if dealing with a stupid child. "Summoning Prieto and bringing me the idea for the bomb are two different things, Herr Alvarez. Daimons are slippery with their promises. Amparo took Don Guillermo's hard-earned money with every intention of serving the daimons. And you, during your days as Asaph, were deceitful, too." Diago winced at the use of his firstborn name. "Asaph promised to help Solomon, only to turn his back on his king. Do you see the message here, Asaph?"

"Asaph is dead. I am Diago."

Adler giggled from his place in the corridor. Garcia's fingers tightened on Diago's shoulder and sent a flash of pain down into his back.

"You are Asaph." Engel's mortal form shimmered. Spectral flames engulfed his arms. "Look upon my works and tremble."

He chanted a song in the angel's language while channeling his fire at Amparo's head. Small grunts passed through her lips as the flames consumed her. Her hands waved in the air, and her heels thumped against the mattress, like a blind woman running in a panic.

The smell of burning hair filled the cell. Amparo's face melted beneath Engel's hand. Her soul rose from her body. Colors of umber and gold shot upward, but the notes were broken. Her song scattered and ended before it truly began. She swirled in frayed chords. Unable to fight Engel's angelic fire, she tried to escape.

Amparo's soul swooped toward the door. Adler sang a harsh chant with guttural syllables. He carved a sigil filled with bars and threw it in her path.

Falling back into the cell, she sought a corner, a crevice, some place to hide.

Garcia clamped his hand over Diago's mouth to prevent him from singing.

Engel sent his flames around the umber colors of Amparo's soul. He sang her death song and tore the chords of her soul until she burned a second time. The force of her anguish rattled Diago's teeth and sent blood spurting from his nose to run across Garcia's knuckles.

And suddenly . . . silence. The deep quiet of the grave filled the room. Amparo was gone. Her song forever smothered. Traitor or not, the world seemed colder without her magic.

Engel panted heavily. He produced a handkerchief and wiped the sweat from his brow. He had paled significantly.

Diago's breakfast rolled heavily in his stomach. All that was left of Amparo were bones bleached white from the angel's fire.

Outside the door, Adler moaned and gibbered

prayers to Engel. Garcia released Diago's mouth and wiped his hand on Diago's sweater. The Nefil's face was as rapt as if he'd witnessed the Christ's second coming rather than a second death.

Diago bowed his head. A drop of sweat hit his thigh. Or maybe it was blood. *Or tears.* Rage seeped into his veins and he let it come. He clenched his jaw and said nothing. There was nothing left to say.

Engel approached him. "You say you are not Asaph. You say your incarnations have changed you. Prove it to me. An hour, Herr Alvarez." He unlocked the cuffs. "I free you to work whatever magic you need in order to summon Prieto. You can't escape, so don't waste time trying. One hour, and I will return. I expect you to hand over the idea."

He and Garcia left the cell.

"The clock is ticking," said the angel. Then he slammed the door shut. "Show me whose side you are on."

Diago was barely aware of them locking the door. The blood rushed back into his fingers and brought stinging agony in its wake. He hugged his hands to his chest, listening as their footsteps receded. Minutes passed before the pain slowed, then stopped.

Somewhere overhead a door slammed.

Another rush of nausea shuddered through Diago's body. The cell had no toilet, only a bucket in the corner. Diago barely reached it in time.

When he finished, he wiped his mouth and examined the cell. The bed, the bucket, and Amparo's bones were all that they'd left him. That, and the fear of whatever might happen to Rafael.

He went to the door. Adler had shut the little flap over the grill and bolted it from the other side.

Diago slid down until he was eye level with the lock. He sent a soft questing note into the mechanism. An angelic ward flashed, knocking him backward.

The ward on the lock wasn't a surprise, but the force of the glyph was extreme. Diago rubbed his eyes and looked up. No windows, no vents—not even a crack in the mortar.

"Rafael," he whispered his son's name. Where was he? Had he managed to free himself? Or was he, too, locked in a cell somewhere—alone and afraid, feeling as if his father had abandoned him? "Hold on. Hold on," he said, although he wasn't sure whether he chanted the assurances to calm Rafael or himself.

Diago paced the cell from the door to the back wall, then to the door again. He avoided the charred remains of Amparo's body.

There had to be a way to circumvent Engel's demands. Diago was no fool: Prieto wouldn't sacrifice the bomb for Rafael's life—no matter how important the child might be to the angels—but perhaps Diago didn't *need* Prieto. He looked toward the bed and Amparo's bones as he formed the outline of a plan.

The trick would be to form one song with two distinct melodies. Not normally difficult with other Nefilim, or with instruments to use in lieu of voices, but all Diago possessed for this song was the instrument in his throat. And while doing so, he needed to make Engel think he was trying to summon Prieto while he simultaneously sang down into the daimonic world.

Because it wasn't Prieto who would save Rafael.

If Diago expected to dupe Engel, he needed Moloch, for only the originator of the bomb could forge a convincing facsimile.

Diago went to the bed. "Of course, Moloch will be very happy to see me."

Amparo's bones made no comment on his sarcasm.

"No matter. We do what we have to do." He gently retrieved Amparo's skull from the pile. Some members of Los Nefilim would see what he was about to do as sacrilege. Then again, some members of Los Nefilim saw *him* as sacrilege, so what could he do? "Dark choices call for dark magic," he murmured to her empty eye sockets.

Running his fingers over the bone, he listened carefully. He soon detected the faintest hint of her contralto, sweet as honey and soft as summer. After death—even the second death—a Nefil's song remained in her bones; the stronger the Nefil, the clearer the notes.

Amparo's soul might be destroyed, but her bones still held traces of her magic and would for many thousands of years. Diago intended to tap those notes, and even though she was dead, she would live again in his composition. He brushed pieces of the charred mattress from her eye sockets and carried the skull to the center of the room. Carefully, reverently, he placed it on the cold concrete, facing the door.

Now what should he use for a sigil? He thought back to the advertisement Prieto had initially used to lure him to the Scorpion Club.

Was it only a month ago? It felt like years. Yet Diago clearly saw the scorpion drawn on the flyer, its tail wrapped around the logo. Prieto hadn't created that advertisement. The angels never used scorpions in their communiqués. *But the daimons do.*

Engel probably saw Prieto as a traitor, too. Prieto had negotiated with the daimons for the idea for this bomb. *But Prieto was working on instructions from a higher authority—possibly even Sariel, the Princess of Spain.*

The thought didn't cause Diago to hesitate. He answered to no higher authority than Guillermo. His friend had been careful to take that precaution when Diago had sworn his oath.

Swear your oath to me, no one else.

Now Diago understood why. To avow himself to one side or the other would have constrained his song to either the daimonic or the angelic side of his nature. Guillermo had wisely left him free to administer his music as he chose.

One by one, Diago gathered Amparo's bones and formed the crude outline of a scorpion with her skull serving as the head. Handful by handful, he placed her smaller bones and each vertebra to form the details of the scorpion's body.

When he had used every piece of Amparo's remains,

he examined the glyph from each angle. Twice he walked the perimeter, occasionally pausing to nudge a finger bone to the left or right, adjusting a vertebra until it was flawlessly aligned with its mate.

When he finally judged the sigil to be perfect, he looked down at his maimed right hand. This morning Miquel had rewrapped the bandage over Diago's missing finger, not that he needed the wrapping. The skin had healed. Yesterday and the day before, he'd worn the bandage as a disguise to better fit Guillermo's story that he'd lost the finger while trying to stop an anarchist's bomb.

But there was no further need for subterfuge. *No, I hide from myself like I've always done.* As the thought flitted across his mind, his fingers reached for the corner where Miquel had tucked the gauze to hold it in place. He unwrapped the bandage and forced himself to look at his hand.

The *'aulaq* had bitten Diago's pinky off at the knuckle. The puckered scar appeared to be healed. He rubbed the skin gently. *Then why does it still hurt?*

The pain was probably the result of the *'aulaq's* poison, which still roiled through his blood. Yet the venom hadn't interfered with his song last night. *Nor will it now.* But his gestures might be stiff, and that worried him.

Diago flexed his fingers. He needed dexterity for this spell, which depended as much on form as song. He held up his arm over his head and twisted his wrist, wincing at the pain, which shot into his shoulder.

Damn it. He stretched and concentrated on each muscle. Again he forced his arm high and rotated his wrist. The discomfort wasn't as bad this time. "Come on . . ." Time was slipping from him. Shaking out his hands, he extended his arms again. The movement was easier. The pain was still there, but it was manageable now.

Just as pain tends to be, given enough time.

Diago took two short steps, twice striking his heel against the concrete. He turned, raising his arms over his head, wrists touching back-to-back, hands open, fingers joined close together. Where he was supposed to extend his pinky, he extended the ring fingers of both hands so the gesture was uniform.

He held the pose and disregarded the ache in his right shoulder. His body had moved into the dance, muscles remembering what the brain had forgotten. On the third practice move, an electric smell entered the cell. Diago felt the charge snap from his heel on the second strike.

Almost there. How much longer did he have? How many minutes had passed?

"Too many," he murmured. *Don't think about it.*

Closing his eyes, he forced himself through the dance. His flesh warmed with the exercise. The next strike produced a spark.

Before he could doubt himself, Diago took his place in front of the skull. "And now, my beautiful Amparo, you will knock on Heaven's door while I break down the gates of Hell."

She grinned sweetly as he raised his arms over his head. He cupped his right hand and used the fingers of his left to strike his palm. His wedding band flashed streams of silver in the air. The beats grew faster as he closed his eyes. Reaching deep within himself, he thought of the stars and the endless void. He sent forth a cry, both wild and sweet, and as he did, he kicked his heel against the floor.

Green fire flew between the skull's teeth. Amparo's bones vibrated with the fury of Diago's song. As they clacked against the concrete, the last remnants of her magic flew free and took the form of a glyph. The music rose upward through the floors until it reached the upper levels of the asylum—high-pitched like whale song, the perfect tone for an angel's ear.

With the remnants of Amparo's voice entwined with his, Diago danced around her bones. His feet moved him without disturbing the arrangement. And as he leapt, he drew on his daimonic nature and sang a lament aimed at the caverns beneath the earth. His voice resonated through the vaults.

The power of his desperation blew out the naked bulb overhead. In the corridor, the other light exploded in a shower of sparks.

Other than the silver glow of Diago's wedding band, the basement cells were plunged into darkness. Diago didn't pause. He danced by the light of Miquel's love and sang for his son's soul.

CHAPTER FOUR

Rafael pulled against Jaso's grip, but the Nefil held him tight, dragging him down the corridor. Inspector Garcia and the bad angel had disappeared through another door with Papa. Jaso was going the wrong way.

"Where did they take Papa?"

"To a quiet place," Jaso said.

Moreno laughed like it was some kind of joke, but this wasn't funny.

Rafael knew about Holy Cross's quiet places. His mother had hidden him in the asylum. She had enchanted Sister Benita into taking Rafael into the children's ward. Likewise, he had learned how to charm his way into every nook and cranny of the hospital. During his first days in the asylum, he was sure Mamá hadn't gone far, so he had looked for her everywhere. As he'd grown older, and realized she wasn't coming back, he had wandered the grounds out of boredom.

Rafael knew about the quiet rooms where Papa's screams wouldn't be heard. This was the ward where they put the bad men who hurt people.

The farther they went, the longer it would take him to get back to Papa. *And I won't be able to find him.* Rafael dug his heels in and threw his weight backwards. "Let go!"

Jaso jerked Rafael forward and flung him at Acosta. "Here, you drag him for a while. I'm sick of the brat."

Acosta caught Rafael's arm. "Why me? Fucking Alvarez busted my knee. Look at me!" He gestured at his leg. "I can barely fucking walk."

"You were ugly and crippled before Alvarez ever touched you," said Fierro, who was nothing but bones and teeth.

Moreno picked at a scab under his chin and grinned. "You better watch him, Acosta. The little daimon might kick your other kneecap."

Fierro giggled and slapped the back of Rafael's head.

Rafael hated them and their mean laughter. He struck like a snake and sank his sharp teeth into the flesh just above Acosta's wrist. The Nefil tasted like bitterness and sweat, but Rafael didn't let go. He clamped his jaws and chewed.

Acosta stumbled into a row of chairs lining the hall, dragging Rafael along with him. "Christ! He's biting me! Get him off!"

The other Nefilim stopped laughing. Maybe it was the blood running past Rafael's mouth and onto the floor. Rafael worked his teeth into the Nefil's muscle. A blow to the side of his head sent bright lights spinning across his vision, but he didn't release his grip. Acosta howled.

Fierro grabbed Rafael's hands and growled at Acosta. "Stop jumping around!"

"Fucking Christ! He's eating my flesh, little fucking devil!"

Moreno edged between them. He pinched Rafael's nostrils. Unable to breathe, Rafael released Acosta so he could inhale.

Acosta jerked free and collapsed into a chair, mewling and cradling his injured hand.

Rafael took a deep breath. Then he bit Moreno's arm. Moreno was skinnier so Rafael had to bite harder.

Moreno shrieked.

Fierro flinched at the sound. "God damn it, Moreno! You sound like a toddler!"

Jaso entered the fray. He grabbed Rafael by the waist and tried to wrench him off Moreno.

Rafael snatched double handfuls of Moreno's sleeve and chewed on the Nefil's arm. Moreno was sweeter— his blood was wine and copper—and he kept making that interesting noise, somewhere between a squeal and scream. *But he isn't laughing. None of them are laughing now.*

Footsteps came from both directions. Men and women shouted in their flat mortal voices.

Someone ordered the officers to watch their language. Rafael's heart accelerated. He'd know that screech anywhere. It was Sister Benita, coming at them with God's righteous fury in her eyes. Her flesh hung loose on her sinewy limbs. Her lips, which always reminded Rafael of liver, were pulled back over her thick teeth. A curl of dark silver hair had worked free of her veil.

A new round of anxiety almost blinded him. Would Sister Benita recognize him with his fine clothes and his combed hair? Of course she would. Nothing escaped her piercing scrutiny.

The memory of his days in the children's ward and Sister Benita's sharp fingers were still all too fresh in Rafael's mind. If she caught him misbehaving, she might lock him in that dark room behind her office where she said she could keep an eye on him.

He never quite understood how she could see him behind the closed door in the dark.

Quick and supple as a mongoose, Rafael released Moreno's hand and kicked Jaso's knee like he'd seen his father kick Acosta.

Surprised by the sudden move, Jaso dropped Rafael.

Moreno flailed. "Mother-fucking-Christ! My fucking hand—look at my fucking hand!"

Sister Benita bellowed loud enough to rattle the windows. "God will strike you dead for that language!"

Moreno leapt backward, whether to get away from Rafael or Sister Benita, Rafael didn't know. Nor did he care. This was the time to go. He ran back the way they had come, keeping his head low just in case God decided to strike Moreno dead. He kind of hoped it would happen, and then felt a little guilty, but not too much. Moreno was a bad Nefil.

Rafael easily dodged the adults who were running toward the commotion. A man stepped into his path and tried to catch him, but Rafael threw himself flat and skidded between the man's legs. An orderly with mean eyes reached down, but Rafael regained his footing and took off again. He had always been the fastest boy in the children's ward.

Rounding a bend, he saw a stairwell door closing. He put on a burst of speed and barely slipped through in time. Something big hit the door. Rafael whirled to see Jaso's enraged face on the other side of the mesh window. He rattled the door in its frame. Rafael smiled. He knew the doctors locked the stairwell doors to prevent the inmates from accidentally falling down the stairs.

Turning his back on Jaso, Rafael ran. He clamored down two flights of steps and into the tunnels beneath the hospital. Here, the hospital's staff could move quickly from one wing to another without having to navigate locked wards.

Here he knew he could lose them.

Staying near the wall, he kept to the shadows and sang his quiet hiding song. The orderlies, nuns, and doctors who used the wide corridor didn't see him. Dodging from one shadow to the next, he soon found the mesh grill that led to a vent.

Working his small fingers behind the metal frame,

he quickly dislodged the grill and scooted into the opening. He had just replaced the grate when he heard Jaso shouting at the other Nefilim.

Rafael slid backward until the darkness enveloped him. The metal popped beneath his weight and he froze. Now was the time to become very still and quiet. *Like a mouse,* he thought. He would become a mouse, all brown and silent, not even twitching his whiskers.

He sat perfectly still and watched the legs of the various people as they moved toward Jaso's shouts.

A man wearing fine trousers stopped in front of Rafael's vent. "Inspector! What is all this noise?"

Rafael recognized his voice. It was the mortal doctor his papa had spoken to outside. *What had Papa called him? Vales. Yes, his name was Dr. Vales.*

Jaso was still out of sight but approaching fast. "We've lost Alvarez's son."

"Do you know which way he went?" Vales sounded alarmed. "This is no place for a child!"

"We understand," Jaso said. "We're looking for him."

"This low profile arrest of yours is getting out of control, Inspector."

"Everything is under control." Jaso's voice lost its edge and became soothing. He stopped in front of the doctor. Rafael was gratified to see blood spatters on Jaso's trousers. "As soon as Dr. Engel has evaluated Alvarez, we will remove him from your institution."

"I don't think you have the right man for the Ferrer

murders. I spoke with Alvarez yesterday. He is as sane as I am."

Rafael smiled and loved Dr. Vales. He was a nice mortal. Maybe he would help Papa.

"We've been through this, Doctor," Jaso said gently. "Alvarez was seen at the Casa Milà the day before the Ferrers were killed. Inspector Garcia has enough evidence to prove that Alvarez and the maid were seeing one another. His hypothesis is that they murdered the Ferrers in order to rob them."

Rafael glared at Jaso's legs. He wanted to tell Vales the truth. Papa wasn't seeing a woman. He was married to Miquel, but Rafael didn't say anything. Papa thought the mortals wouldn't understand his relationship with Miquel, and Rafael didn't want to make life hard for Papa. If he did, then Papa might send him away. Rafael worried that thought like a loose tooth while Jaso continued talking.

" . . . now the maid is missing, and Alvarez appears to have been in another fight. We're afraid he murdered her, too."

That wasn't true, either. Papa had fought a daimon, but Rafael knew from his experiences with Sister Benita that mortals didn't understand the angels and daimons.

"It's Alvarez's *modus operandi*," Jaso continued with a voice both smooth and soft as he lured the mortal into a trance.

Rafael didn't know what a *modus operandi* was, but he understood the kind of magic Jaso worked on Dr.

Vales—he'd sometimes used it on Sister Benita when she waved her ruler around. Rafael wondered if she used her ruler on Moreno for saying bad words. He was kind of sorry he'd missed it if she did.

Rafael's fantasy of Moreno holding out his hand for a smack from Sister Benita's ruler was interrupted by Jaso's explanation. "Alvarez secures a wealthy patron, ingratiates himself with them, and then cases their homes. When he knows where they hide their valuables, he murders the family, steals what he can, and moves on.

"He pulled off a similar crime in Berlin. That's how Dr. Engel got involved. Engel came to us, and we started putting the pieces together. Based on Alvarez's interactions with Doña Rosa Iniguez and her son, Don José, then with the Ferrers, we established a pattern. Now he has moved to Don Guillermo's household and is seeking protection there. It's possible we've saved the Ramírez family from a similar fate." Jaso moved closer to Vales and murmured, "You have to understand, Doctor. We went to question Alvarez. He attempted to flee. When we caught him, he started raving about angels and demons just as Engel said he would."

Your tongue is black with lies, Rafael thought. He hoped Jaso's black tongue fell out of his rotten head.

"Our concern," Jaso said and gave his words a sense of urgency. "Our concern is the boy. We must find him, Dr. Vales. I understand he used to live here. Perhaps one of the sisters might help."

Poor Dr. Vales. Mamá once told him that mortals

possessed their own magic, but they had neglected it for so long, they had forgotten how to use it. That made Rafael sad for the mortals.

"Of course, Inspector," said Vales. He sounded sleepy. "Sister Benita will know Rafael's hiding places."

She only thinks she does. Rafael hugged his satchel and held his breath, remembering to be small and quiet like a mouse. Sister Benita never found him unless he wanted to be found. Besides, Sister Benita didn't know everything. Miquel said so, and Miquel was a lot smarter than Sister Benita.

Jaso led the doctor away. "Let's keep our focus," he purred. "Look for Rafael."

Their voices faded beneath the sound of a rumbling cart. Rafael waited until the traffic in the corridor resumed its normal rhythm. Orderlies pushed food carts to various wards, joking about the patients and their strange ways. Nuns swished by, their rosaries dancing in their long black skirts. Every now and then, the sharp click of a secretary's heels clattered against the soft footsteps of the hospital staff.

Rafael slowly counted to one hundred. Then, just to be safe, he counted to two hundred. When all that time had passed and he still hadn't sensed another Nefil nearby, he opened his satchel. He withdrew his mother's carmine tear and the neatly folded picture he'd drawn of Papa and Miquel. Rafael had drawn himself standing between them in front of their little house. They were all smiling and holding hands. A white kitten with one blue eye and one green eye sat at Rafael's feet.

Ghost, Rafael thought with a smile. *Her name is Ghost, and Papa said she could live with us.*

Overhead, a bright yellow sun with angel's wings beamed down on them. At the bottom of the picture, Miquel had helped Rafael print "My Family" in block letters.

Rafael placed his mother's tear over the picture. He tapped the teardrop twice with his index finger before turning it clockwise and whispered, *"Gólpe, gólpe, vuelta . . ."*

Strike, strike, turn . . .

Golden light swirled up from the depths of the stone and became the veins of color within an angel's eye. The teardrop split neatly in half, like a pair of carmine eyes. Rafael hummed a mellow note. His aura passed through his lips in shades of green and amber. The breath of his magic swirled around the ruby eyes and became a small golden snake.

"Find my papa." Rafael used his index finger to guide the snake around the figure of Diago.

The snake curled through Papa's hair and whispered over his skin. The lines of the house squiggled free and changed shape until they took the form of a scorpion, drawn upon the ground. The caricature of Papa began to dance among the lines, his heel struck the paper, and sent miniature sparks into the scorpion's mouth. Then Papa disappeared.

Rafael blinked and bit his lip. He knuckled down on his fear and thought about what he'd just seen. This wasn't the same as last night when Papa had begun to fade away. Wherever Papa had gone just now, he had meant to go there. He had danced into the mouth of the scorpion, but no one had made him go. Maybe he had escaped Engel. Maybe he was looking for Rafael right now.

Because he promised. He promised not to go. He promised I could stay with him, and he said he would find me. Rafael chanted this mantra in his heart until his thoughts slowed. Recalling the fire in his father's eyes as they'd taken him away, Rafael grew certain that Papa hadn't left him. *We're a family of bears. He will find me, and then he will eat that bad angel up.*

Rafael took a deep breath and looked at the picture. The lines shifted and changed shape again. The caricature of Miquel walked to their truck and got inside. He held Papa's coat close to his chest and spoke to the driver. Rafael withdrew a pencil from his satchel, pressed the tip against the paper, and closed his eyes. His magic guided his hand. When he looked down, he saw he had drawn Don Guillermo.

Don Guillermo and Miquel were coming.

They haven't forgotten us.

The drawing blurred, and when Rafael blinked, two tears struck the page. Straight lines curled and became a tangled head of hair. Ysabel sat in front of a window and played her guitar. Her mouth moved in a song, and as Rafael's heart grew warm, he saw Doña

Juanita sitting behind Ysabel, singing along. He felt their love rise up from the paper and into his soul.

Los Nefilim were looking for them. They weren't alone. All he had to do was be quiet and wait. *And help Papa.* Yes.

Rafael wiped his eyes and went to work. He guided his snake over the picture of the kitten, Ghost. Diaphanous as her name, Ghost came to life and stepped off the page. She was little more than a white shadow with a silent cry, but Mamá had often said that small magic was better than no magic at all.

Ghost nudged his hand, and he felt the tickle of her spirit breath.

"Find my papa," he whispered. "Bring him to me."

Ghost opened and closed her mouth. Instead of going to the grill, she turned and scampered deeper into the vent. Rafael held the picture of his scattered family and listened to the hospital staff as they passed his hiding place. He made himself small and mouse-quiet and waited.

His mamá had left him in this horrible place, but his papa would come for him. He had promised. *He will come. I am not alone.*

CHAPTER FIVE

Guillermo stopped the truck at the intersection near La Sagrada Família's impressive eastern façade. An attractive woman wearing a fox stole sauntered toward a group of construction workers. She paused and spoke to one of the men. He pointed at the church's entrance as five of his coworkers came to offer their assistance as well. She gave them all a dazzling smile and left them gaping in her wake.

"Why are we sitting here?" Miquel asked.

"It's a stop sign," Guillermo said as he gave the woman's ass a lingering gaze. As Solomon, he would have found a way to justify the pursuit of a woman like that. Guillermo, on the other hand, might give her beauty an appreciative glance, but he wanted no one other than his Juanita. She filled his days and understood him better than any of his Nefilim. He would do nothing to jeopardize his life with her.

Diago is right. Our incarnations do change us, he mused as he eased the truck across the intersection. Now if he could just get the rest of his Nefilim to accept Diago the same way Guillermo did, he might have some peace within his ranks.

Miquel noticed the woman, too. "You were looking at her ass."

Guillermo drove past the church's western façade, which was nothing more than a construction site. "Are you jealous?"

Miquel snorted.

"You're not so innocent," Guillermo said as they reached the industrial district. "I've seen you giving other men that look. Diago notices, too."

"Diago doesn't get jealous."

"Diago doesn't say anything. He gets this"— Guillermo flicked his finger next to his temple—"spark in his eye when you do that."

Another snort.

"You watch him next time. I'm warning you. One of these days, he's going to say something when he catches you ogling another man."

"Do you think he'll ever be that comfortable with our relationship?"

Guillermo sighed at the note of hope in Miquel's voice. "Little steps, Miquel, little steps. He's wearing his ring." He slowed the truck in front of his warehouse. "For Diago, that's a leap."

The observation won him a wan smile. "You're right."

"Business, my friend. Focus on the business at

hand." Guillermo parked beside the curb. "What do you see?"

Miquel leaned forward and looked through the windshield. In the distance, the vibrations of a domed song encompassed the asylum.

"Was that here yesterday?" Miquel asked.

"No." Guillermo reached into his pocket and withdrew his lighter. He rubbed his thumb over the protective sigil Juanita had burned into the metal before she'd given it to him. "And it takes more than five Nephilim to make a web like that."

Before they could examine the song more closely, a woman emerged from the warehouse. She wore a white blouse beneath her jacket. Her trousers were loose, and her shoes were soft soled and made for stealth. Dark brown curls escaped her bun and clung to her pale forehead, framing a face that projected the cunning of a cat. When she recognized the truck, she withdrew her hand from her coat pocket—no doubt where she kept her gun.

Miquel was closest to the curb. He rolled down his window as she approached them.

"Sofia Corvo, my little angel of death." Guillermo grinned. Suero hadn't fooled around. Like the female angels, the female Nefilim possessed stronger magic than the males. They were also some of his most vicious killers. God, he loved them all, but Sofia Corvo was one of his favorites.

Sofia folded her arms on the door and looked inside.

"We saw them go in about ten minutes ago. Diago and Engel in one car, Rafael and Garcia in the other."

Guillermo tapped the steering wheel with his index finger. "How many do you have with you?"

"Twelve."

"Who?" Guillermo asked.

She named them—all female Nefilim. With a coy smile, she said, "We will make fetching nuns."

Miquel laughed, but there was no mirth in the sound. He was itching to move forward. Guillermo felt his need like goose bumps crawling on his flesh.

Or maybe it was the song that caused Guillermo's agitation. Die Nephilim's chant was all bass and baritone, not a female voice in the mix. The music was tightly constrained and performed in perfect unison, with no extemporaneous movements whatsoever.

It wasn't the first time Guillermo had witnessed their magic. Their techniques were the opposite of those employed by Los Nefilim, who sang their spells with wild abandon, often improvising, playing off one another's strengths and weaknesses. Male and female worked together to achieve melodies and pitches that only one gender could never achieve.

Sofia noticed the direction of his gaze. "See how tight the sigils are? In order to do that, Die Nephilim must all be gathered in one area, led by a conductor. Find one—find them all."

Guillermo trusted her judgment. "Put a stop to that song."

"You want them all dead?" She picked at a broken fingernail.

"Bring me one for questioning if you can. Don't jeopardize yourself or your sisters."

"What about the traitors?" She spat into the gutter.

A cold wave of rage rolled through his stomach. "I want as many of them alive as possible."

Sofia bared her teeth with a smile that made Guillermo think of sharks. "I'll take them to western *finca*."

The *finca* was an old stone house on a secluded section of his western fields, far from his house and his daughter. In that isolated field, the screams of the interrogated couldn't be heard in his home.

He flicked the lid of his lighter just once, like the sound of a gavel pronouncing judgment. "Do it. I'll meet you there once we've secured Diago and Rafael." With a quick nod at the bag, he said to Miquel, "Give it to her."

Miquel handed her the bag of ammunition.

In a rare display of affection, she patted Miquel's arm. "Hold tight. We'll get them back."

Miquel nodded and gave her a salute, which she returned with a gleam in her eye. She retreated into the warehouse. Guillermo couldn't be sure, but he thought he detected a bounce to her step. Nothing pleased Sofia Corvo more than a bloodbath.

He pulled away from the curb, and reminded himself to give Suero some time off as a reward. Sofia might not fully trust Diago yet, but she respected his oath to Los Nefilim, and Guillermo had no doubt that

Suero had summoned others with the same deference to oath over personalities.

Of course, like Diago, Suero had suffered from the Nefilim's distrust. Born of one of the minor spirits, his song was good, but not as strong as the higher-born members. Garcia and others had questioned the assignment, worried that a lesser Nefil coordinated their actions, but Guillermo had stood by his choice. A Nefil with a powerful song was invaluable, but a Nefil with a sharp mind was just as treasured. He assigned them according to their talents. So far, whether from gratitude or allegiance, Suero had yet to let him down.

Then where did I go wrong with Garcia? He chewed the thought like a cigar, but couldn't identify a specific clue for the inspector's betrayal. Not only why, but when? *Who else have I missed?*

"What are you thinking?" Miquel watched him with eyes blacker than the storm hovering over them.

"When did Garcia begin working with the Germans?"

Miquel shook his head. "I have no idea."

"Guess."

"When Diago took his oath?"

"You think all of this was set up within a month?" He nodded at the dome of sigils that encompassed the sky over the asylum. "Look at that song, Miquel. It's been rehearsed for longer than a month."

Miquel became as still and quiet as a pool of water. "This doesn't have to do with Diago, does it? It's Rafael. They're after Rafael."

Guillermo considered the theory. " 'The hand that rocks the cradle rules the world,' " he quoted. He wanted a smoke but didn't light one of his cigars. He needed that edginess now. "It's plausible Engel wants both of the bombs—the one that Prieto guards and the one that Diago guards."

"Greed is a deadly sin." Miquel kissed Rafael's button and pocketed it.

"You've gotten attached to that kid in a short amount of time."

"He's a sweet boy, and Diago loves him. They are trying so hard to be good to each other, and they are so afraid of loss, it breaks my heart to watch them."

"How are you holding up?"

Miquel shrugged. "I'm fine."

"Really?"

"Yeah, really. I'm trying to be patient with Diago while he works through what happened with Candela. I've talked with Suero some."

Suero would know. Like Diago, Suero had suffered a rape; although he had been abused by another man. Guillermo nodded. "I wish the others knew to rely on one another like you do. If you ever need to talk, you can come to me, too. Or Juanita. Anytime. You understand?"

"Yeah. I will." Miquel nodded. "Thanks."

They fell silent as they neared the back entrance to the asylum. The hair on Guillermo's arms rose. He downshifted the truck and leaned forward to look out the windshield.

Miquel evaluated the dome over the asylum. "How are we going to sneak past that?"

"It doesn't appear to be designed to keep anyone out. Besides, it may work in our favor." The vibrations were rigid and were dictated to a specific function. "What are the odds of us being heard in all that noise?"

"What are the odds of us finding Diago and Rafael in all that noise?" Miquel countered.

Guillermo was almost sorry he'd asked Juanita to remain at Santuari. They could have used an angel's help, but she was of more value to him at Santuari. If anything happened to him, Juanita would guide Los Nefilim until Ysa was old enough to step into her place as queen.

He pulled the truck beside the curb. A thin line of jade- and umber-colored sigils rose over the rooftops. Rather than become entangled with Die Nephilim's wards, the glyphs filtered outward and spread like fingers into the buildings.

"Look." Guillermo pointed.

Miquel frowned. "That's Diago's song, and it looks like the other glyphs belong to Amparo, like they're singing together. Maybe she hasn't turned traitor, after all."

"She gets the benefit of the doubt until proven otherwise."

They watched the song in silence. Amparo's colors were wrong, almost sickly in appearance. Then the umber tones strengthened. They overtook the jade vibrations until the green was but a pale reflection within the golden hues.

Miquel said, "I've never seen Diago create a song like that. It's almost like he's using her as a microphone for his own spell."

Guillermo nodded. That was a good summation. Diago's song was prominent. *It is and it isn't.*

Before he could grasp what made the vibrations feel so wrong, he was distracted by movement at the hospital's gate. He shifted his attention to the two guards. They were watching the truck and talking to one another. Guillermo couldn't immediately tell if they were mortal or Die Nephilim.

"We've got eyes on us," Guillermo muttered.

Miquel followed his gaze. He unbuttoned his coat and placed his hand on the butt of his Luger. "Whenever you're ready."

"If they are mortals, let me handle it." Guillermo put the truck into gear and eased it forward. "Remember, they break easily, and if we kill one, other mortals will come looking for us. Don't make more problems than we already have."

"Understood." Miquel caressed the grip of his pistol. "But if it's Die Nephilim, let's give them the righteousness of our silver."

"In abundance," Guillermo replied as he dropped his lighter into his pocket. He reached beneath Diago's coat and slid his revolver within easy reach.

When the truck reached the gate, Guillermo saw the guards were mortal. The one on the right had only one eye, his scarred visage a testament of artillery fire. He was apparently a veteran of either World War I, or the Rif War. The conflict didn't matter. He possessed an aura of bravado the younger guard lacked, and that might be trouble for them.

Guillermo lowered his window. "Which way to the kitchens?"

"What are you delivering?" One-eye appraised the empty bed.

"Sacks of almonds are in the bed." Guillermo crooned the words.

The other guard hung back, fingering the black baton he carried. He cast an uneasy glance from the one-eyed guard to the empty bed.

The one-eyed guard nodded and gestured to a lane. "Take the road to the left. You'll see the kitchens just before the wards." He stepped back and waved them forward.

Guillermo smiled and sent a small veil of illusion over the younger guard's vision, too. Then he put the truck into gear and drove them through the gate. He cranked up his window and growled, "That was too easy."

"You think Engel is overconfident?"

"Or he wants us here." Guillermo pulled in behind the kitchen and shut off the engine.

The truck didn't appear out of place among the other service vehicles. A mule, which was hitched to a worn wagon, turned a baleful eye on them. Overhead, unobserved by the mortals who went about their business, Die Nephilim's sigils rose and fell, vibrations entwining to form a pulsing net over the grounds.

"Do we have a plan?" Miquel asked as he assessed an open door where the kitchen's steam poured into the cool air.

"The plan is to find Diago and Rafael, and then get the hell out of here. Sofia and her group will take care of Die Nephilim." Guillermo retrieved his revolver and placed it in his pocket. "Could you tell which building Diago's song came from?"

Miquel pointed. "That one."

Guillermo recognized the barred windows. A muscle twitched in his cheek. "That's bad."

"Why, what's there?"

"The ward for the violent inmates. It's where we found José."

"We need a disguise to get in. Neither of us will make fetching nuns."

"I don't know." Guillermo assessed Miquel's dark lashed eyes and full lips. "You'd make a pretty nun."

Miquel rubbed the dark shadow of his beard. "I shaved this morning. Can you tell?"

"I've seen nuns with worse." He reached under the seat and withdrew a clipboard with a dirty pencil attached to the clip.

Strung tight as a guitar string, Miquel slammed the door hard enough to rattle the window. "Who do we try to find first, Diago or Rafael?"

"The vulnerable one here is Rafael. Once we find him, we eliminate Engel's hold on Diago. Likewise, we limit any chance that Diago might act against his own best interests. Understand?"

"Are you implying that Diago might go against his oath to Los Nefilim?"

"I am saying, were it me and my daughter, *I* would. No one wants a child to die early in their firstborn life." Such an experience subverted a clean transition to their next incarnation and stunted the Nefil's emotional growth. More than that, though, even knowing a child would have another life made the loss no easier for the parent to bear.

Miquel produced Rafael's button from his pocket. "Let's see if we can find him."

Guillermo put his hand over Miquel's fist. "No magic. Not yet. They might sense our presence and we're outnumbered. Give Sofia and her Nefilim time to work. Let's take a walk. If anyone challenges us, we're here to make a delivery." He raised the clipboard. "And we got lost."

Avoiding the busy kitchen, Guillermo walked deeper into the complex. The sigils overhead grew louder and more disorienting with every step. At times, the sound of Die Nephilim's thunderous song almost drowned the voices of mortals.

Guillermo found a door and turned the doorknob. It was locked. He pulled a thin wire from his pocket and quickly picked the flimsy mechanism. That one was easy. He doubted he'd find the inside locks as simple to navigate, but complex problems had never stopped him in the past.

He and Miquel slipped inside and found themselves in a storage room. Bedding and pillows rose from the

darkness—neatly folded rectangles of blankets and
sheets occupied every shelf. Inside, Die Nephilim's
song was muted, the chords dampened by the mortal
thoughts that whispered through the walls.

Guillermo wound his way past rows of shelving
until he found the door that led into the corridor. He
waited for two nuns to pass before he stepped into the
hall with Miquel right behind him. He turned left,
walking as if he knew exactly where he was going. No
one challenged them.

He and Miquel wandered the halls for over a half an
hour, pausing intermittingly to send out a questioning
song. No answer came, either from Diago, or Rafael.

Guillermo moved in the direction of the wards for
the criminally insane. Following his instincts for the
shortest route, he led Miquel through the geriatric
ward. A couple of patients shuffled along, holding onto
the wall. Others sat in wheelchairs, staring out the tall
windows onto a small courtyard.

Miquel touched Guillermo's arm.

"What?"

"There." Miquel pointed to an elderly man with
long silver hair and small sharp teeth. He sat in a
wheelchair. A heavy blanket covered his lap, and he
twisted the folds of the fabric in his long elegant hands.

Unlike the ten fingers of a mortal, this man had
eight. His thumbs were almost as long and dexterous
as his fingers. He wasn't mortal, he was angel.

Miquel leaned close and whispered, "Prieto."

Guillermo hadn't even realized he'd grasped his

lighter until he heard the first click of the lid. Prieto smiled at the sound, but otherwise made no sign he knew they were there. *But he knows.* Guillermo didn't kid himself. Prieto wanted to be found; otherwise, Miquel wouldn't have seen him.

Guillermo went to the angel's side and squatted beside the wheelchair. Miquel put his back to the wall so he could watch the corridor.

"A lot of people are looking for you, Prieto," Guillermo murmured.

Prieto gave Guillermo a feral grin. "The party never truly begins until I arrive."

"Are we going to dance now?" Guillermo saw the insanity in the angel's eyes wasn't entirely feigned.

"I'm afraid not. No time for subtleties. I'm late for a very important meeting." He kept his fingers moving over a section of the blanket. Strands of sound whispered over a silk bag.

Guillermo fixed his gaze on the small purse. *The* idea.

Prieto noted the direction of Guillermo's stare and said, "It seems that I can't leave the asylum. The chords"—he waved at a nearby window where the notes of Die Nephilim's sigils covered the metallic sky—"of Engel's song, seek me. It has taken all of my skill to remain invisible to Engel and his pack of Nephilim. If I try to move past their song, Engel will immediately know where I am. He was always stronger than me. Now, in my weakened state, he will easily take the idea from me."

There was more to it than that, Guillermo thought as he assessed Prieto's pale features. In his efforts to remain hidden, the angel had expended his own song to the point of depletion. He was dying.

Prieto must have seen the knowledge in Guillermo's eyes. "I am trapped, Guillermo, trapped well and good." A shaky laugh trembled through his lips.

Even coming from the half-mad angel, the laughter brightened the dim hall. Several mortals nodded and smiled as if their hearts were lightened in the wake of the angel's mirth.

Guillermo was reminded that the angels had once brought only joy in their wake, but some had remained in the mortal realm for too long. While the archangels rarely descended from their heavenly home, the Messengers were becoming tarnished by taking the flesh, which sullied their spirits until they, like the daimons and the mortals, grew more caught up in worldly concerns than those of the spirit. Guillermo sometimes wondered if he wasn't wrong. Perhaps it wasn't the affairs of angels that affected the mortals—perhaps it was the other way around.

Prieto's laughter trailed into silence. He glared at the window where the net of sigils turned the sky the color of mercury.

Guillermo's lighter clicked softly in the hush that had fallen over the hall. "What's going on, Prieto?"

The angel breathed heavily and tracked the vibrations of Die Nephilim's song with deep brown eyes.

"Yellowcloud was delayed. I was forced to linger here in the asylum longer than was wise."

Guillermo glimpsed the claw of a talon at the foot of the blanket. Certain that if he pulled the blanket away, he would find the feet of a raptor, Guillermo reached down and adjusted the blanket so that Prieto's talons were hidden. That would explain the wheelchair. Moving on these polished floors would be treacherous—not to mention conspicuous—especially with all his power focused on keeping Engel at bay.

"Talk to me, Prieto." Guillermo spoke quietly.

"Where do you want to begin?" Prieto asked.

"Start with Garcia, end with Yellowcloud."

Prieto nodded and fumbled with the silk bag. "Engel has been working on Garcia for years. They're friends. That is why Garcia flagrantly disobeyed your command to bring any angelic orders to you before obeying them. Engel swears he is not ordering Garcia to act. He merely makes suggestions—innuendos and intrigues. Garcia believes he is acting of his own volition. In truth, his motivations are provoked by his own prejudices. He has long believed that you are too lenient with the daimons. Engel tells Garcia what he wants to hear and strokes his intolerance—and ego—into hate."

"That makes Garcia stupid," Miquel said.

"No argument from me." Prieto picked at his blanket as if pulling fleas from the fabric. "But this goes higher than Engel and Garcia. The Principalities are involved."

Guillermo's stomach did a slow somersault. "Which ones?"

Prieto said, "Aker."

Miquel whispered, "The Prince of Germany."

"Who else?" Guillermo asked.

"Poyel."

The Prince of Italy. Guillermo and Miquel traded a guarded look.

"What does Aker want with Spain?" Guillermo asked, though he suspected he knew the answer.

Prieto toyed with the silk bag. "Aker believes that Sariel is unable to govern."

This was news to Guillermo. As far as he knew, Sariel, the Princess of Spain, was in firm command of her realm.

Miquel articulated Guillermo's thought. "That's a lie," he said.

Guillermo raised a finger and Miquel fell silent. "How do you fit into all of this?"

"I am a spy for Sariel." Prieto's eyes changed. They turned into identical orbs of crimson and silver as the angel's power slipped again. "Sariel has experienced . . . conflicts."

"Conflicts?"

"Ideological intrigues within her own court. She needed to know where Los Nefilim stood."

Which explained Prieto's questions to Diago each time he encountered the Nefil. Prieto probably thought that Diago was far enough outside Los Nefilim's circle of trust that he could observe them objectively. In the

angel's mind, Diago would have not̶⟶̶ ̶̶⟶̶
forming Prieto of Guillermo's allegianc̶̶⟶̶

Prieto turned his horrible eyes on̶ ̶̶⟶̶
"Well? Do we trust you?"

"My allegiance is where it has always been̶—̶ ̶̶ith
Sariel. She is taking us in a new and welcome direction. I've made no secret of my support for her."

"Good, because you are about to acquire an entire
cadre of enemies, some of whom—you know, but still
not fully comprehend—are within your own ranks."
Prieto allowed his warning to hang in the air for a
moment before he continued. "This new direction,
what the Spanish call their Second Republic, is what
Aker sees as weakness. He is sending members of his
own court to advise Sariel's enemies. He wants to wipe
out Los Nefilim so he can bring his Messengers and
Die Nephilim into Spain."

Miquel looked like he had tasted something bitter.
"There are angels within Sariel's court working with
Aker?"

That would explain the impunity of the Messenger,
Engel, and his Nephilim.

Prieto scowled and the mortals around them
frowned. "Three generals in her army have made no
secret of their contempt for her. She has banished them
from her realm."

The angels were preparing for another war—
ideological or not, the conflict would overtake the
mortal realm—but none of Prieto's comments answered Guillermo's biggest question. "Internal politics

erstand. But why are the daimons working with the angels?" he asked.

"They want to create a new race of Nefilim to stand against the angel-born. They lost Diago's allegiance, so Moloch wanted to begin again. He thought that if the angels turned the child directly over to the daimons, the boy's loyalty would be secured. Moloch approached Sariel. He promised to design a bomb that would end all wars, but his price was the child."

"Rafael." Miquel's eyes went hard.

Prieto confirmed their suspicions. "Rafael. Sariel knows that whoever holds this new bomb of Moloch's will control the eventual outcome of the war. She thought one child was a small price to pay for the lives of millions. She also suspected that Diago wasn't as easily manipulated as the daimons thought. As he so often says, he is angel, too.

"Candela didn't want to give Rafael to either Diago or Moloch. She fled and hid the child. When she died, we found Rafael, but I made Diago's involvement a part of the deal. I didn't believe Diago would simply hand Rafael to Moloch. I had hoped that he would take the child and raise it apart from the daimons. Not in my wildest dreams did I see him joining Los Nefilim."

Prieto turned to Guillermo, his countenance severe. All around them, the mortals assumed pensive expressions. The angel patted the silk pouch. "My American counterpart is Betty Yellowcloud. She was supposed to be here days ago, but she was delayed. Had she arrived on time, I never would have been ensnared by Engel. I must get this idea to her, and she will transfer the idea to the mortal who will create the bomb."

"Will it leave Spain?" Miquel asked.

Prieto nodded. "Yes, and once it's gone, we will be done with it." He held out the purse to Guillermo. "We had arranged to meet at La Sagrada Família today at one. She is wearing the skin of her spirit animal."

Guillermo remembered the woman in the fox stole. No wonder she had caught his eye—she was angel. "She is already there."

"As you can see, I am . . . otherwise engaged and cannot elude Engel's trap."

Dying. He had almost said dying, Guillermo thought. *Because that is what is happening. We thought it was something designed simply to imprison, but whatever this song is, it is also slowly killing him.*

Prieto leaned forward and grasped Guillermo's wrist. "If I don't get this idea to Yellowcloud, all of this has been for nothing. You've got to help me."

The mortals all mimicked the angel's posture, reaching out and grasping one another's wrists. Prieto had been on this ward too long. If one of the nuns saw their patients exhibiting this strange behavior, they would set about to determine the reason.

"Let's take a walk." Guillermo extracted himself from Prieto's grip and released the wheelchair's brakes. He debated telling Prieto about Sofia and the others, but he didn't. If the angel suspected that Sofia would help him get free, he would forget Rafael, and

Guillermo didn't intend to let that happen. "Help us find Rafael. Then we will get you out of here."

Prieto turned to Miquel, who walked beside the chair. "Tell him, Miquel. Make him understand."

"He understands. So do I. Rafael first."

A few of the mobile patients shuffled behind them.

Guillermo picked up his pace. "Come on, Prieto. You trust me, then I might trust you."

"I have a higher stake in this than you think," Prieto retorted. "Candela was . . ." He hesitated, groping for a way to give them a comparable experience. "We were created from the same spark."

Guillermo jerked the wheelchair to a stop. "What?"

Prieto regained his verve. "Diago is my—how would you say it?" He pursed his lips. "Brother-in-law." He beamed at Miquel. "That makes you and me—"

"Nothing," Miquel snapped. "We are nothing to one another."

Prieto clucked his tongue. "We didn't get off to a good start, Miquel." He readjusted his blanket, smoothing his palms over the bag. "But your relationship to Diago makes us . . . kin." He grinned wetly and displayed a row of sharp teeth.

Miquel backed away from him. "Jesus Christ."

Through the window behind Miquel, the sigils in the sky flashed. All three of them turned toward the sight. Die Nephilim's glyphs frayed. Mercury turned to pewter which turned blue. One ward flickered like a projectionist's lamp before it died.

"What's happening?" Prieto watched the song die note by note.

Guillermo smiled. "Sister Sofia Corvo prays for you, my friend. She is one of my strongest Nefilim. Her mother is known as *La Belle Sans Merci*."

Miquel crossed himself and grinned. "Sister Sofia Corvo, hear our prayer." He went to the window and opened the latch.

As the members of Die Nephilim died, their web of magic grayed to become a thin fog.

Prieto rose from his wheelchair. "Without their song to alert Engel, I can slip away. By the time he finds out that I have left the asylum, Yellowcloud will have the idea and be gone. You have saved us, Guillermo. I could kiss you."

"No kissing." Guillermo gripped his arm. "We gave you freedom. You give us Rafael."

The angel closed his eyes and sent out a questioning song. The notes trickled through the vents and into the courtyard.

Prieto listened intently before he finally nodded. "In the basement corridor that links the campus buildings. He is there. Beneath the ward for the criminally insane." He opened his eyes and looked to the sky. "Good luck, Guillermo."

"And to you." Guillermo turned and followed Miquel, who was already several paces ahead. When he glanced over his shoulder, the window was shut, and the angel was gone.

Miquel reached the stairs first. He pulled on the door. "Locked. Damn it!"

Guillermo nudged him aside. He had yet to encounter a lock he could not break. "Be still. We'll get to him."

With Die Nephilim's wards gone, Diago's dark green sigils twined through the air alone. The umber vibrations of Amparo's song faded.

Where are you, my friend? Guillermo turned his attention back to the lock. *And what are you doing?*

CHAPTER SIX

Amparo's bones turned to dust. Soft as silt, they covered Diago's feet and whitened his clothes, his hands, his hair. Sweat cleared trails of bone dust from his cheeks. When the bulbs blew out, the impregnable blackness came down and extinguished even the lights of his glyphs.

Diago slammed the ball of his foot on the floor and brought himself to a stop. The only sound was his breathing, harsh and loud in the gloom.

A faint breeze stirred, and with it came the scent of machinery oil and metal—old and toxic with cordite. The click-click-click of scorpion claws on concrete ticked across the floor.

Diago traced a sigil in the air and charged it with his voice. Bright silver light pushed back the darkness. The scorpions tumbled away from the glyph in a writhing mass of bodies.

He was no longer in his cell, but neither was he free. Beyond the edges of his glyph, the scorpions clustered at the foot of a set of narrow stairs, which led up to a catwalk over seven metres off the ground. The catwalk spanned the greater part of the room and ended at an iron stage.

Mounted in the center of the stage was a bronze statue with a bull's head and a man's torso. Twin tanks took the place of lions at either arm of the figure's throne. The wings of planes bearing red swastikas curved upward from the effigy's back. A string of hollowed bombs formed a necklace; machine-gun turrets fashioned the crown. In the center of the statue's chest was an open door. Once, flames had burned inside the cavity, but it was dark now. The arms were lowered, palms up, ready to accept the offering that had not come.

Through the latticework of the stairs and platform, Diago noted two 'aulaqs flanked the statue. He recognized the male that had bitten off his finger, and the one-armed female that had scarred his face.

"Full circle," Diago whispered. This was the same room where he had given Alvaro the golem, which Miquel had made to look like Rafael. Oh, he had thought he was cunning with his lies to Moloch. When Alvaro had accepted the golem in lieu of Rafael, Diago had nurtured the hope that his father regretted the past. *But that, too, had been a lie, and the only fool in this room that evening was me.*

Neither of the 'aulaqs acknowledged his presence.

Diago said, "I've come to see Moloch."

They didn't answer him. Instead, the scorpions took to the stairs and flowed like a jittering black wave toward the effigy. They gathered in front of the statue and climbed one another until they took the shape of a man.

The female 'aulaq cried out a single note and threw a sigil of fire into the effigy's belly. The furnace blazed to life, momentarily blinding Diago. When his vision cleared, he saw it wasn't Moloch who stood before the effigy, but Alvaro.

The strange fires that had burned in his father's gaze last night were gone. Alvaro's irises and pupils had changed again to become the color of smoke and nickel. White eyes, as if he had no eyes at all.

Moloch's eyes. Diago kept his sigil burning. He didn't move toward the stairs. That would be a deadly mistake.

Alvaro lifted one hand in benediction. Four long fingers, the palms wide and flat, the nails long and sharp.

Moloch's hands.

"Welcome, my son." Alvaro's razored grin sent a chill down the back of Diago's neck.

Patricide. That ugly word swam to the top of his thoughts. "I came for Moloch."

"I *am* Moloch," said Alvaro.

A flash of anger caused Diago's sigil to burn brighter. "Don't lie to me, Alvaro. Rafael's life depends on me talking to Moloch."

"Look at me, Diago." Alvaro's voice carried none of last night's antagonism. "You won last night. You deserve respect for that."

Careful, he'll tell you what you want to hear. "Then take me to Moloch."

"He is here. Look closely." A scorpion ran down Alvaro's cheek like a shiny black tear.

Moloch's features burned beneath Alvaro's visage. They were like one image superimposed over another. When Diago examined them too closely, his vision blurred. He glanced away, and then back again. Alvaro and Moloch's images coalesced.

Alvaro had indeed become Moloch. They were one.

Diago murmured, "I don't understand."

Alvaro walked along the catwalk. "Why do you think the mortals are so important to us, Diago?"

The question took Diago off guard. The answer was known to all of the Nefilim. "The daimons and angels feed on their emotions."

"Correct. We derive our power from the mortals' beliefs. The stronger their belief in us, the more power we wield over them and world events. Yet the mortals have power over us, too. We must be flexible enough to change with their perceptions of us so we can give them what they need—validation for their existence. It is a mutually agreeable situation for both species."

Alvaro's eyes flashed as he strolled toward Diago. "Times change. Mortals are changing. Even as we speak, they are realigning their world, adapting new belief systems and merging them with the old. Their religions are becoming more syncretic. What you are witnessing, with my transformation, is the birth of a new god for a new religion."

Diago stared at his father and waited for some emotion to touch him, but nothing surfaced. Neither surprise, nor fear, nor love came to the forefront of his soul. He was wrung dry by Alvaro and his revelations. This was merely a new game. *And I need to learn the rules fast.* "Will you take a new name?"

"We are Moloch. That is our name. We will simply appear to the mortals in our new form." Alvaro held out his arms as he reached the top of the stairs. "But we are also Alvaro. And that makes you the son of a god."

Diago turned his head and spat. "Jesus."

"Just like him!" Alvaro laughed and performed a slow turn that was a more dignified version of Moloch's capering dance. "So you've summoned us. Tell us what you need, son."

Diago had no idea how much time had passed. He didn't mince words. "I need a facsimile of the idea for the bomb you gave to Prieto."

"Explain what has happened."

"An angel who calls himself Engel is holding Rafael. He wants me to summon Prieto and take the idea from him. If I don't bring Engel the idea within the hour, he will give Rafael the second death." Diago watched Alvaro's face carefully.

His father's good humor was gone. Three scorpions ran down his cheek. He licked them off his face and scowled.

Good. He took the threat seriously. Or did he? Was this another lie?

It doesn't matter. I'm out of options. Diago continued. "You and I both know Prieto is not going to give me the idea, so I need a way to trick Engel. Moloch made the original idea. He . . . *you* can create a convincing replica."

"Become our priest."

Another flash of anger surged through Diago's sigil. "Are you even listening to me?"

"We are listening. But there is a price, Diago. Nothing is free." Alvaro gripped the handrails and leaned forward. "Every god needs a priest, and so do we. We need someone to carry our word to the mortals."

"I am Los Nefilim. I cannot serve two masters. I will not be your priest."

"Then what do you have to give in exchange for this . . . replica?"

"Your grandson's life. You certainly went to enough trouble to bring him into existence."

"You're still angry about Candela's rape, aren't you?"

"There was no rape." The denial came too fast and sharp, because there *was* a rape and he *was* furious. *Why do I allow him to do this me time and time again?* And just as quickly, the answer came to him: *because he knows how to upset me.*

Alvaro grinned. "Oh, stop it! Lie to yourself, but don't lie to us. She subverted your will and used your body without regard for your wishes. It was rape by an angel—the very monsters you have taken an oath to serve."

He glared at his father. Time to shift Alvaro's game back on him. "What righteous indignation from the creature that sent his five-year-old son to a whorehouse."

Alvaro opened his mouth, and then clamped it shut. He cocked his head as if listening to voices only he could hear.

"I need a replica of that idea," Diago said. "Or your new race of Nefilim will die before it ever begins."

Alvaro flicked a scorpion to the first step. The arachnid skittered across the floor toward Diago. He ground the creature beneath his heel.

"We will help you," said Alvaro. "For our grandson's sake."

"You're not that altruistic."

"You're right. If you won't serve as our priest, then we want our grandson. We want to raise him as daimon."

"No." Diago's heart tore, but he'd rather lose his son forever than see him suffer under Alvaro's tutelage.

Alvaro evaluated Diago carefully before he answered. "Give him to us for a year, then."

This was too easy. Like handing him the golem, this was all too easy. "A year," Diago repeated tonelessly. This was what Alvaro had wanted from the beginning. Ask for the impossible and pretend to settle for a lesser price.

Alvaro nodded. "A year of his life. We want him to spend a year with us."

"No."

"A mortal year, Diago. Will you have him die the second death because you cannot compromise? Promise him to us for one mortal year."

The next two years were critical. Rafael had already lost the security of his mother, and had been thrown to a father he barely knew. Any more disruptions in his life could threaten the small headway Diago and Miquel had made to make the child feel secure.

"No."

The scorpions belied Alvaro's frustration by seething beneath his skin. "Do you really believe that keeping the boy close to Santuari for a few years will help him grow? How can you give him stability, Diago? How can you give your son something you've never known?"

Because I have friends: Miquel, Guillermo, and Juanita. They were the stability Rafael needed. "Nothing matters other than the fact that I am his father. I did not ask for him, but that does not mean I do not want him." How could he explain? He'd known from the moment he'd seen his son that they belonged together. Besides, even if he could describe his feelings, Alvaro would never understand. *But he doesn't need to understand. He simply needs to accept that this is true.* "And as his father, I will determine what is best for my son. Just as you did for me."

It could have been the shadows or the scorpions, but Diago thought he saw Alvaro wince. Could it be?

Is he actually ashamed of his actions, or is that merely what I want to see?

The scorpions beneath Alvaro's skin shifted, distorting his face. This wasn't going the way his father had planned. The meeting wasn't progressing toward either of their goals. And Diago couldn't ignore the passage of time.

"I made a mistake," he admitted. "I never should have come to you for help."

"Why?" Alvaro asked. "Why did you come if you thought it was futile?"

"You were my last hope." Diago laughed, not liking the sound of grief that clung to the sound. "I thought that if I didn't matter to you, maybe your grandson would. I was wrong."

Alvaro's eyes gleamed like twin moons as he descended the staircase. "I watched over you in your firstborn life."

Diago noted Alvaro's switch to first person in his speech. *He wants to establish intimacy.*

Alvaro continued. "When you were Asaph, I tried to guide you as a father would."

Maybe that was true, but Diago no longer cared. Alvaro gave too little, too late. "The clock is against me. I must go." He raised his hand to reignite his sigil.

"Hear me out, and I will give you a replica that will fool an angel." Alvaro stopped at the edge of Diago's glyph. "Just listen."

Diago lowered his hand.

"I warned you not to trust Solomon—that his arrogance would be his downfall. You did not listen. Against my advice, you took Benaiah as your lover, and when Solomon asked you about your liaison with Benaiah, you lied. You said you were close friends. You lived your life as a lie, trying to please both Benaiah and Solomon. When Solomon found the truth, he destroyed you."

Was it that simple? No. Nothing was that black and white when it came to relationships, especially when one of the individuals was a king. Diago shook his head.

Alvaro went on, his voice growing louder and echoing through the cavernous room. "Solomon forced you to renounce your love for Ben and take a wife. You were right to avenge yourself on him. You were right, Asaph!"

Lies and revenge never made anything right. Diago knew that now. Ashamed, he recalled his morning thoughts about Alvaro. He remembered how willing he'd been to give his father the second death—how he had considered manipulating Guillermo and Los Nefilim to help him achieve that goal.

The same desire for vengeance had been his downfall in his firstborn life. How could he say his incarnations had changed him if he was, once again, willing to lie for the sake of revenge?

"No," Diago said. "When I was Asaph, I had a hand in my own destruction. I made a deal with a devil, and betrayed Solomon to the daimons. They took him from the mortal realm and tormented him for years. All the while, I lived in guilt until I brought him back from the daimonic realms, and restored him to his throne. He never forgave me for that betrayal in our first incarnation, and I . . . I never forgave myself." Even as he said it, he knew it was true, but the memory of Solomon's rage no longer frightened him. "Asaph and Solomon are dead. I am Diago, and Guillermo is my friend. He accepts me now. Our incarnations have changed us."

"I am your father. A part of you will always belong to me. Guillermo will betray you just as he did when he was Solomon. And when that happens, you come home to your father. I will welcome a priest of your caliber."

"Are you done?" Diago asked.

Alvaro smiled and withdrew a pouch from his pocket. Diago recognized it. The bag was the same one that had held the original idea—the bag Diago had used to fool Moloch's vampires.

"Remember, my son. The true art of deception isn't in the number of lies you tell, but in the believability of a single lie. I will make Engel believe." Alvaro tossed the pouch to Diago.

He caught it neatly and pulled open the drawstring. Inside was a brass medallion. Diago knew without removing it that the case would fit comfortably in his palm. The brass concealed a magnifying glass. It had been a gift from Miquel sometime in the late seventeenth century, and Diago had thought he'd never see it again. He had exchanged it for Moloch's coin, which contained the original idea for the bomb.

Diago pivoted the cracked glass free of the cover, closed it, and returned it to the bag. "This won't fool an angel."

"It will by the time you return to him. Go back to your cell and wait. Then hope he keeps his end of the bargain." Alvaro raised his arm.

"Wait! Nothing is free. What do you want in exchange?"

"Consider it a favor. And one day, we might ask you for a favor, and when we do, you will remember this day." Before Diago could object, Alvaro made a slashing motion with his hand. The female 'aulaq sang another note and extinguished the fire.

The darkness descended once more, dousing even the light of Diago's sigil. He closed his eyes and when he reopened them, the world was still black. The pouch was heavy and warm in his hand. He knelt and touched the chalky dust of Amparo's bones. He was back in his cell.

Overhead, a door slammed shut.

CHAPTER SEVEN

Patience ceased to be an ally and became the enemy. Diago had arrived at the moment when he had nothing left to lose. It was time to fight, but he needed to choose the exact moment to attack. He hummed a tune and formed a barbed sigil of light, and then he brightened the ward's glow until the sharp edges were blurred.

Tracking his captors by their footsteps on the concrete, he spun the glyph to life.

The click of a key and the turning of a bolt announced Engel's arrival. The angel stood in the hallway flanked by Garcia and Adler.

Engel sniffed the air. His gaze swept over Diago, and he didn't try to hide his contempt. "Well?"

Diago tossed the bag to him, hoping Alvaro hadn't betrayed him.

The angel loosened the string and looked inside. A

bright flash of white lit his features. He emptied the contents into his palm and closed his fist around the magnifying glass. Eyes shut, he tilted his head back. A tongue of spectral blue fire licked the air.

Adler aimed his flashlight at Diago's eyes, but not before Diago saw Adler's hand resting on the grip of his gun. Likewise, Garcia shifted his position, his pistol in hand.

Diago held no illusions as to how this game would play. As soon as Engel pronounced his satisfaction with the idea, Diago's execution was certain.

The only weapon left to his arsenal was surprise. Now was the time to act. With a feral cry, he sliced his ward in half and used both hands to shove the sharpened glyphs into Adler's and Garcia's eyes. Engel looked up in time to see Diago running toward him, but the German angel was too slow. Diago rammed the angel's chest with his shoulder.

Engel stumbled backward four steps before he caught his balance. He tried to push Diago back into the cell, but Amparo's bone dust had turned slick with Diago's sweat. He wiggled free and dodged to the right.

Garcia wiped Diago's magic from his eyes. Diago punched the inspector in the face. The crunch of Garcia's nose beneath his fist was the most satisfying thing he had felt in days.

As Garcia reeled from the blow, Diago grabbed his gun. He jerked Garcia's body in front of him and used the inspector like a shield.

Adler staggered to Engel's side, his pistol raised.

Diago fired around Garcia's head. Adler's skull exploded.

Engel flung himself inside Diago's cell.

Diago spun Garcia around and shoved him toward the stairs. Garcia raised his hands and ran in front of Diago.

They reached the first landing. Careful to keep his hands in the air, Garcia whirled. "You can't win, Diago. Stop now."

"Shut up before I forget why I'm keeping you alive."

Engel called out. "Diago, you're making this worse!"

The angel was stalling. Already, Diago detected the shifting vibrations that indicated Engel intended to shed his mortal form. He'd have no chance against the angel once that happened.

He didn't answer. Instead, he dragged Garcia up the stairs. The stairwell was silent. None of the angel's Nephilim responded to the gunshot. *Of course, they didn't. They expected at least one shot and now think I'm dead.*

At the second landing, he paused and shoved Garcia into the corner. "How many are waiting upstairs?"

Sweat beaded under Garcia's mustache. He lowered his gaze. "Two of Engel's Nephilim."

Liar. There are at least three. Adler had accompanied them downstairs while the other three had remained behind. "Face the wall. Hands behind your head."

Garcia did as he was told.

Diago rifled through Garcia's pockets until he

found two more magazines. "How many more are in the hospital?"

"Eight."

That might be the truth. Eight Nephilim singing, three watching, plus Guillermo's five traitors—he had to find Rafael and hope that Guillermo had a comparable force somewhere on the grounds by now. "Where is Rafael?"

"Jaso has him."

Jaso. Diago might kill Jaso without waiting for Guillermo. "Let's go." He propelled Garcia toward the stairs again. "Put your hands down and walk normally."

Garcia obeyed him.

Diago stayed behind the taller Nefil. When they reached the top step, he rammed Garcia aside and yanked open the door. As he'd suspected, Engel's two Nephilim flanked the exit. He shot the Nephil on the left first. The one on the right threw a punch. Diago ducked and rolled. The Nephil's fist struck the wall.

Diago rose to his knees and fired two rounds into the Nephil's body—chest and face. Blood sprayed the industrial green walls with a merry shade of red.

Through the closing stairwell door, Diago glimpsed Garcia running back down the stairs. *Going for Adler's gun.*

Ignoring the shouts around him, he scanned the hall for the third German, who was nowhere to be seen. Diago rose and pocketed the gun.

Mortal orderlies hurried in his direction.

He formed a sigil and blinded them to his appearance. "Quick! It's Inspector Garcia! He shot the orderlies. He's hiding on the stairwell!"

Their eyes went wide at the sight of the dead Germans.

"Go on," Diago sang to the mortals. "Garcia is out of bullets."

The fear left their eyes and they approached the stairwell more confidently.

Diago ran.

Shouts echoed ahead of him. More orderlies were coming.

Diago turned left at the next intersection and ducked into a bathroom as another group of nuns and orderlies ran past. The mirror reflected a madman covered in bone dust.

Damn it. He was a mess, and he couldn't enchant every person he saw. Without wasting a second, he washed his face and combed his fingers through his hair. With a towel, he brushed the worst of the dust from his clothes. By the time he was done, his eyes were still bloodshot and his face bruised, but his appearance was such that he could easily deflect a causal inspection by a mortal. That was better.

Time to move again. Finding Rafael was going to be a problem. Diago didn't have the first clue of where to look. Where the hell would Jaso have taken the child? An office? But whose? Vales's? Was there a children's ward in the hospital?

Diago's heart steadied. That was the answer. Find

Vales and charm him, undo Engel's damage on Vales's mind, and elicit the doctor's help. Vales might know where Jaso had taken Rafael.

Diago went to the door. A glance into the hall assured him that it was empty. Noise and confusion echoed from the direction of the stairwell. Diago thought he detected Engel's voice in the fray. The angel spoke in rapid German, and from the gruff nature of his speech, Diago was certain he wasn't speaking to the mortals. Twice he thought he caught the phrase, "Meine Nephilim . . . mord . . . mord."

Definitely time to move on. Diago set a fast pace in the opposite direction. He passed a row of offices. One of the doors was open. Diago peeked inside. The secretary stood in front of a filing cabinet. Her back was to the door. A doctor's white jacket hung on the rack by the door.

Diago lifted the coat and put it on as he walked away. The wide pockets held a stethoscope, but nothing else.

He passed a window and looked at the sky. The sight halted him in his tracks. Pressing his fingertips against the window sill, he leaned forward, checking the heavy clouds in disbelief.

Die Nephilim's sigils had disappeared. Their net of magic was gone, utterly gone. Diago glanced back the way he had come. Engel's voice was louder. He shouted commands.

Meine Nephilim.

My Nefilim . . . but what was the other word? Mord. It sounded a little like *muerte.* Dead? Murdered? Diago had no idea. All he knew for certain was that the bombastic glyphs, which had covered the asylum grounds, could have only been destroyed by Nefilim.

"Guillermo is here," Diago murmured. *He is here.*

As Diago turned to go, the whisper of a kitten's breath touched his fingers. He looked down to find a flicker of white emerging from the shadows along the window sill. The figure of a kitten took form.

But not a real one. No, that was impossible. One ear was taller than the other, the mouth was slightly off kilter—it was a cartoonish creature, almost as if a child had drawn it.

With a thrill, Diago recognized it. It possessed one blue eye and one green eye. *Rafael's kitten!* Diago had no trouble summoning the kitten's name, because Rafael told anyone who would listen about Ghost.

The kitten leapt from the windowsill and trotted to a metal door. Ghost gave a silent meow.

Diago almost wept with relief. Jaso and Moreno would never allow Rafael to use his magic. *He's escaped them. Dear Jesus, he'd somehow gotten away from them.* "Where are you?"

The kitten sat in front of the door.

Diago hurried over. Through the glass window, he saw a stairwell, but the door was locked. "Shit."

The heavy slap of feet indicated someone hurried toward him. It was a nun with a face like an ax. If her dour expression was any indication of her personality, she'd cut him, and be happy to do it.

Thinking quickly, he patted his pockets as if searching for the key to the door. He didn't have to feign his frustration. "I can't believe this."

"Is there a problem, Doctor?" The nun's voice grated like nails on tin.

"Oh, Sister, maybe you can help me. I'm new here, and I've left my keys in my office. Is there an elevator nearby?"

She frowned at him, and for a moment, he thought she would summon the orderlies. The commotion down the hall grew louder.

Sweat formed on Diago's upper lip. He forced himself to focus on the nun.

"You would need your key for the elevator on this floor." To his relief, she rooted through her keys and chose one. "You should be more careful. We have more important things to do than shepherd negligent young doctors around." She unlocked the door. "Make sure you shut it firmly. There is a madman on the loose. We want to keep him contained on this floor."

"Of course, Sister . . . ?"

"Benita." She snapped her name at him and sucked her teeth.

The shock of the information dropped Diago's jaw. *My son wasn't in an orphanage. He was in a madhouse.* He shut his mouth a moment too late.

Her eyes narrowed. "You look familiar. Something about your eyes. Do I know you?"

"No. We've never met." He grasped at a straw and asked, "Didn't you used to work on the children's ward?"

"Yes, yes, I did, but I was recently reassigned here."

Jesus, this was *the* Sister Benita. She was more terrifying than he had imagined.

She cocked her head and he half expected her to peck out his eyes. "Are you certain we haven't met?"

"No, we have not met, but they speak very highly of you in the children's ward."

She blinked at him, and he realized it was her turn to be stunned. "They do?"

"Yes," he assured her, relieved that his flattery had worked. "Thank you, Sister." He moved to the landing and shut the door before she could ask another question.

Through the window, he saw her wipe her eye. Then she lifted her head and strode grimly down the corridor.

Diago shuddered and turned to the staircase. The kitten, which appeared to be grinning, had already reached the first landing. Diago followed Ghost to the basement. The wide corridor, utilized by the staff to quickly access the wards, bustled along with its usual traffic, happily unaware of the chaos above.

A quick glance in both directions indicated nothing but mortals. Ghost moved to the right, along the baseboards. Diago hurried after the caricature, bowing his head as if deep in thought. He was so intent on the kitten, he didn't see Jaso coming from the opposite direction until it was almost too late to hide.

Fortunately, Jaso had spotted the kitten and was so focused on the animal dashing into a ventilation grill that he didn't see Diago either. Grinning like a hunter who had flushed out his prey, Jaso knelt in front of the grill.

Fucking son of a bitch. Diago didn't try to contain his rage.

Jaso laughed. "I've got you now, you little fucker."

Diago walked faster.

And just as it had that morning, everything began to happen fast and hard . . .

Diago put his hand on the grip of Garcia's gun, but he didn't draw the weapon. Instead, he walked right up to Jaso and kicked the other Nefil in the face.

Jaso grunted and fell backward, holding his nose. "What the fuck?"

"Are you all right?" Diago bent down. As he did, he caught a glimpse of his son, huddled in the filthy vent. He put his finger to his lips. Rafael's grin lightened Diago's heart just enough that he decided not to kick Jaso again. He grabbed Jaso's collar and jerked him upright. With a smooth move, Diago also liberated the other Nefil of his pistol. "That looked like it hurt."

Jaso's eyes went wide. "You fucking—"

Diago slammed his fist into Jaso's face. He felt the cartilage of Jaso's nose break.

Jaso screamed.

Diago hustled him across the corridor and against the opposite wall. If Jaso tried to sing a glyph, Diago didn't want the fight close to Rafael's hiding's place.

Diago put his lips against Jaso's ear and whispered, "Shut your mouth, or I'll kill you where you stand."

Jaso shut up.

Mortals were pausing to gawk at them. Diago gave them a reassuring smile. "Everything is fine," he crooned. "I'm a doctor."

A mortal doctor with a mustache as heavy as his paunch hesitated beside them. "What happened?"

"I don't know," Diago said. "He was walking along and just collapsed. I think his nose is broken."

"Can you fix it?" The mortal asked.

"I'm not that kind of doctor," Diago said.

"Neither am I." The mortal frowned.

Jaso whined behind his hand.

"Here now, Officer," said the mortal. "Let us help you."

No, no, no, Diago thought, but he saw no quick way to stop the doctor without drawing more attention.

The mortal gestured to a petite nun. "Sister! Do you have a moment?"

When she turned around, Diago noticed a blood spatter on her veil. She deftly folded her black robes over the blood and came forward. One look in her light cinnamon eyes told him she was Nefil.

Two other nuns, who were clearly twins, trailed in her wake like black ghosts. The twins bore a striking resemblance to the petite nun. *They are sisters in blood, not the cloth.* And all were angel-born Nefilim.

This might work after all.

"Sister Sofia at your service, Doctor."

Although her name was unfamiliar, the murderous look she gave Jaso eased Diago's mind. Jaso, on the other hand, tried to twist free of Diago's grip.

The twins halted behind Sister Sofia. They folded their hands primly and bowed their heads in unison. Their names suddenly came to Diago: the Corvo sisters. Sofia was the eldest and the strongest singer of the three. Maria and Eva were the twins; although, Diago had no idea which one was Maria or which one was Eva.

At the moment, it couldn't possibly matter.

The mortal didn't notice the blood on the nuns' habits, or their icy appraisal of Jaso. He asked, "Sister Sofia, would you have a moment to escort this officer to the infirmary?"

She crossed herself and considered Jaso with her cold shark's eyes. "I would be delighted to help the good officer find his way home." Her countenance suggested she would enthusiastically escort Jaso to Hell and shove him into the fires.

Jaso shook his head. "I don't need her help."

"Of course, you do," Diago said. "What if you fall down again?"

Sister Sofia grinned. "Yes." She didn't give Jaso a chance to pull away. "What if you fall harder next time?"

He winced and scanned the corridor for help. None of Engel's people were around. Neither were the other Nefilim who had joined Garcia's little rebellion. Jaso was all alone, and his courage abandoned him like his comrades.

The mortal doctor patted Jaso's arm. "Well, that's sorted." He nodded at them, and then blustered on his way.

"See? It's sorted," said Sister Sofia. She leaned close to Jaso. "Don't make me sing your death song."

Her threat was enough to subdue him. "I didn't want to do any of this," Jaso protested. "It was Garcia. He said he had Don Guillermo's approval."

"Shut up," Sofia said. She turned to Diago. "Get Rafael. Go to the next junction. Take a right. The elevator will be halfway down the hall on the left." As she passed him, he discretely handed Jaso's gun to her. She allowed her sleeve to fall over the weapon. "Sisters Maria and Eva will assist you, Dr. Alvarez."

"Thank you," he bowed his head to her as she led the protesting Jaso away. He doubted she would ever know the full extent of his gratitude.

Sisters Maria and Eva drifted over to stand beside the vent. Like Sofia, they possessed eyes the color of cinnamon, but unlike their sister, their smiles were sweet. They pretended to speak in a hushed conversation. Instead, they sang a song that masked their presence to the mortals.

Diago slipped behind them. They used their wide skirts to shield him as he lifted the grill.

Rafael crawled out and threw his arms around Diago's neck. He wore his little satchel and clutched his mother's tear. Aside from being dirty and a little bruised, he seemed fine. Diago hugged him so tight, Rafael squeaked.

He kissed his son's brow. "You are my brave, clever child."

"I knew you would come." Rafael buried his face against Diago's neck. "I knew you wouldn't leave me." He pulled back. "Did Ghost help?"

Diago nodded. "Where did she go?"

"Back into the picture where she belongs."

"Good. Now we're going home where we belong, my little bear." Diago rose with his son in his arms. Holding Rafael against his chest, he quickly got his bearings and set off in the direction Sofia had indicated. Maria and Eva walked with him. One twin remained two steps behind to guard their rear while the other sister increased her stride until she was two steps ahead.

Los Nefilim had come for them, just as Miquel had promised. Overwhelmed with gratitude, Diago's eyes burned. *But we aren't free, yet, not even close.* And he wouldn't feel safe until they were in Santuari again. Blinking rapidly, Diago picked up his pace.

Sisters Maria and Eva had no difficulty matching his stride. Their heels struck the concrete. The rhythm was a battle march.

They reached the corner.

Rafael whispered, "Papa, he's coming."

"Who?"

"Inspector Garcia."

Diago turned right. From the corner of his eye he glimpsed Garcia, along with the German orderly Diago hadn't killed. They were searching every face, stopping nuns and orderlies alike, only to release them again. Both Garcia and the German had murder in their eyes.

And Engel? Where the fuck was Engel?

Then the sister just in front of him—whether she was Maria or Eva, he didn't know—touched his arm and pointed. A few metres ahead, Miquel stood beside the elevator. Guillermo held open the door.

Diago's heart pounded. *So close. We are so close.*

"Papa?" Rafael tightened his hold on Diago's neck. "He's coming!"

From behind them, Garcia shouted. "Stop! Stop them!"

"Run," whispered Sister Maria.

"Run," murmured Sister Eva.

Diago didn't look back. He ran.

Mortals scattered from their path and ducked down adjacent passages, or into workrooms. The hall that had seemed so full only moments ago was now deserted but for the Nefilim.

"Don't shoot!" Garcia warned the German. "You might hit the boy! There are other ways . . ." His words ended in a low note that caused the air to shimmer.

The German harmonized, and Diago's pulse hammered in time with the song. The air became oppressive. Overhead lights crackled and buzzed, flickering with black shadows.

Maria and Eva whirled and chanted together. They twisted golden vibrations into a bright ward that flared into a miniature sun to drive back the dark.

From his place beside the elevator door, Guillermo sang out a note and traced a protective sigil in the air. He thrust the ward toward Diago and the Corvo twins.

Diago's mouth went dry. *Our luck is gone and now it will go bad for us.*

He didn't see Garcia's ward, but he felt the effect. A hot wind rushed down the corridor. Diago's feet left the ground. Rafael's body locked against his. This was how it felt to be swept out to sea. For one terrifying moment, he thought he and Rafael would be crushed by the vortex of sound. When he hit the floor again, he stumbled.

Miquel dashed out of the elevator and caught him before he fell. "Quick! Get inside!" He shoved Diago toward the car.

"Eva!" Maria cried out.

As Diago reached the elevator, he saw Eva on the ground, Maria standing behind her. Maria ran to her sister and pulled her to her feet. She supported Eva, who stumbled as if she was drunk. Blood poured from her nose and mouth. She must have taken the brunt of Garcia's spell.

Guillermo got between the twins and Garcia. He lifted his revolver.

Garcia and the German ducked around the corner.

Guillermo spun on his heel without shooting and joined the twins. He swept Eva into his arms and carried her to the car.

When they were inside, Miquel threw the gate shut

and jabbed the button as if he wanted to kill it. Gears churned to life and the elevator rose.

Guillermo eased Eva to the floor. "*Ya, ya, ya,*" he sang softly.

Diago put Rafael down. He took off his stolen coat and used the sleeve to gently wipe the blood from Eva's lips and chin.

Maria knelt beside her sister and cradled her head. "Can you save her?"

"She is not going to die," Guillermo said. It wasn't a diagnosis, but a vow. "Hear me, Eva Corvo. Take my song as your own." He hummed and twisted the fiery notes into the sigil for life. The ward whispered between her lips and down her throat.

Nothing happened. If she had slipped too far into death's realm, she might not answer his call.

Guillermo created two more sigils. He placed one over her heart and the other on her brow. As the wards penetrated her flesh, the elevator seemed to slow—time itself crawled as if they'd passed into another realm.

Death, thought Diago. *Guillermo is pulling her back from death's realm.*

Guillermo pressed his thumbs against her temples. Red-gold light bathed his hands and her face.

"Eva Corvo! I command you to return!" Guillermo's voice ruptured the strange silence.

Time snapped into motion again.

Eva gasped. Her body convulsed as if she'd been electrocuted.

The thought of electrocution revived the image of Amparo in Diago's mind, and he flinched just as Eva opened her eyes.

"Don't be afraid." Eva smiled at Diago as she took Guillermo's hand and kissed his ring. "This is why he is king."

The tension loosened in Diago's chest. He was wrong. Luck was still very much with them.

Guillermo rose and brushed the dirt from his knees. His freckles stood out against his pale skin and his hands trembled. The power he'd exerted to reverse Garcia's spell had taken a toll on him, but a lesser Nefil would have failed to bring her back.

Diago reassessed his old friend in a new light. Guillermo's power had grown immense over the centuries, yet his countenance lacked Solomon's old bravado. He remained humble in a way that Solomon could never imagine.

The opportunity to change was forever denied to Amparo. Diago felt her loss even more profoundly. *I will not be so quick to recommend the second death, not even to Alvaro—although if anyone deserves it. . .*

Rafael wiggled in beside Diago and touched Eva's forehead. "Will you be okay?"

"Oh, yes." She stroked the child's cheek. "I am old and full of magic. Don Guillermo guided me back, and now I will heal."

They helped her to her feet. Her skin was still ashen, but she could move on her own power. Maria took the coat from Diago and fussed over her twin, wiping the last vestiges of blood from her face.

Miquel leaned forward and gave Diago a light kiss.

Lips tingling from his lover's touch, Diago was barely aware of Rafael working his way between them.

"Eww, no kissing." Rafael scrunched his face in disapproval. "Ysa says kissing is gross."

"Not if you do it right," Guillermo said. He glanced at Diago. "Where's Engel?"

Maria said, "He didn't come to see his Nephilim die." She sounded disappointed.

"I don't know where he is," Diago admitted. "I heard him barking orders at Garcia, but I didn't see him after I left the cell. He may think he has the idea for the bomb."

Guillermo turned around. "Why would he think that?"

Diago met his friend's questioning stare. "I summoned Moloch to ask him to create a replica of the idea. I told him the truth: Engel intended to give Rafael the second death if I failed to obtain Prieto's idea for the bomb. Rather than see Rafael destroyed, Moloch gave me a facsimile."

"You negotiated with the daimons?" Guillermo raised his eyebrows.

Diago's heart stammered. "I had an hour to procure the idea. I didn't know what was happening at Santuari. For all I knew, you had a full scale insurrection on your hands. I did what I thought was right. I gave

Moloch nothing. I also discovered more about Alvaro. He and Moloch now inhabit the same body. They have become a new god."

"He *what?*"

"They've become—"

Guillermo cut Diago off with a gesture. "No, we'll talk more later. Don't worry, though—you did fine. You might have purchased us enough time to get back to Santuari before Engel discovers the deception."

"We'll make it," said Miquel. "We've been through far worse than this."

"So you always say," Diago muttered.

Rafael touched Diago's palm.

Diago knelt beside him. *I let him go once. It won't happen again.* "Do you want me to carry you?"

Rafael shook his head. "I can run very fast."

Diago kissed his cheek. "So can I."

Maria checked her gun and hummed the "Flight of the Valkyries" as the car climbed to the next floor. Eva joined in her sister's song.

"Okay, my Valkyries, our floor is next." Guillermo put his hand in his pocket where Diago detected the outline of his revolver. "Remember, no shooting unless it's life or death. Mortals might get caught in the cross fire. Dead mortals make questions and questions cost me money. Everyone understand?"

The chorus of affirmations died just as they reached their floor. Guillermo opened the gate. Maria and Eva exited first, one going left, the other going right. They checked both directions before they signaled all was clear.

Guillermo went next and motioned for Diago to leave the car. "Miquel—"

"I've got the rear," Miquel said.

They moved as a unit. Maria and Eva hummed a veiling song. In response, the mortals parted to let them pass, barely glancing at them.

This was what Miquel had described to him merely two nights ago. *Los Nefilim moves as a unit . . . stop thinking of yourself as being separate . . . you are a part of us now.*

Eva turned a slow circle as she walked, scanning the hallway behind them. She smiled at Diago as she traced a sigil of protection in the air. Already the color was returning to her cheeks.

He gave her a tentative smile of his own before she finished her spin and faced forward again. For the first time since his life as Asaph, he felt as if he belonged to something greater than himself, and Los Nefilim were slowly becoming a part of him.

Amid the soft soles of the mortals, Los Nefilim's footsteps created a sharp beat: one, two, and a hard stamp on three.

Rafael picked up the rhythm and ran in time to the adults. *"Bulerías,"* he chanted the name of the dance step under his breath, and then he counted out loud. "One, two"—he stamped on three—"four, five"— another stamp on six. A spark scorched the floor beneath his heel.

They marched to the double doors and went outside. Guillermo halted them on the porch. Arcades shielded them from the open courtyard. Only a few mortals moved around the yard.

Beneath the cloudy sky it was even more apparent to Diago that Die Nephilim's song was gone. Not a single note lingered in the air overhead.

"The kitchens," Guillermo said.

Eva pointed to the right. Then they were walking again, faster now, their movements still synchronized. A hot wind cut through the autumn chill and gusted down at them.

"It's too warm," Diago said.

Guillermo scanned the darkening sky.

Lavender light burned behind the clouds. Streaks of sangria and silver poured across the heavens, followed by streams of orange that left tails tipped in black. A burst of thunder crashed overhead. Blood-colored notes dripped into the yard.

Just like that, Diago's chromesthesia had returned.

The profusion of color and sound disoriented him. Dizziness smacked him like a club. He almost stepped on Rafael, but Maria snatched the boy from Diago's path. Miquel grabbed his sleeve and barely prevented him from colliding into one of the pillars. He was vaguely aware of Guillermo moving to his side.

Guillermo took Diago's arm and steadied him. "Can you keep walking?"

Diago nodded and forced himself forward. "Angels." He pointed at the sky. "I saw Engel and

Prieto. They are in the sky. A third one is there. They're fighting." That explained Engel's sudden departure. He must have realized Prieto was gone. *He also must have discovered my deception.* Diago swallowed hard and ignored the fear creeping into the pit of his stomach.

Guillermo hesitated by a column and looked up at the sky. "The third is probably the American, Yellowcloud. It's out of our hands now."

"Are we ever really out of it?" Diago asked.

Guillermo spat. "Never."

As suddenly as it began, the episode of chromesthesia passed. Diago rubbed his eyes. The occurrences were becoming less frequent and of shorter duration. "I'm okay," he announced. He picked up his pace.

Guillermo slapped his back and moved to the front of their small company again.

Miquel squeezed his arm before releasing him and dropping back to the rear.

Diago strode to Maria's side and placed Rafael between them.

His son looked up. "Are you okay now, Papa?"

"Yes. Are you tired?"

He shook his head and danced alongside Maria with a determined look on his face.

Eva scouted ahead, weaving in and out of the arcades. She moved with the grace of a great black butterfly with wings of crimson and white. Her elegant dance came to an abrupt halt at the edge of the porch. When they reached her, they all saw why.

Garcia stood in the courtyard. Fierro and Moreno were behind him, along with the German orderly.

Guillermo's group automatically formed a protective circle around Rafael. Eva and Maria flanked the child. Miquel held his place at the rear of their group. Diago stood beside Guillermo.

Overhead, the angels warred in a clash of thunder and lightning. A hot wind tore at the fronds of the palm trees.

The lid of Guillermo's lighter clicked twice.

"You're all under arrest," said Garcia. "The Princess, Sariel, has lost her ability to guide Spain. Her own angels are bartering with daimons. She has forgotten who we are."

Guillermo interrupted him. "Who are we, Garcia?"

"We are Los Nefilim. We were created to serve as the angels' warriors in the earthly realm."

"And I do," said Guillermo. "I serve Sariel's will. I swore my oath to her. If I usurp her rule, then I will be a traitor—like you."

Garcia's cheeks reddened. "You have polluted yourself and Los Nefilim!"

Sparks of rage flew from Guillermo's eyes. "I've done no such thing."

Garcia pointed a shaking finger at Guillermo. "You consort with daimons and have inducted them into your ranks." He spat in Diago's direction. "Sariel's negligence has allowed you to lead Los Nefilim amok." He lowered his hand. "Well, that is done. Prince Aker is taking over the principality of Spain, and he has designated me to lead Los Nefilim in his name. Hand over the child. We'll determine whether or not he's been contaminated by the daimons."

Diago asked, "And if he has?"

Guillermo shot him a sharp look, but Diago ignored him. In any other confrontation he would take a subservient role to Guillermo, but not when it concerned his son.

Garcia didn't hesitate with his answer. "If the boy is unclean, we'll give him the second death."

"Christ," Miquel whispered.

Guillermo said, "You're not getting the boy. And we're not handing ourselves over to you. I will not abdicate my rule to you or anyone else. Stand down."

A slow rain started to fall. Garcia seemed unperturbed by Guillermo's refusal. "You have allowed the abomination of daimons to infiltrate Los Nefilim."

From the corner of his eye, Diago saw his son flinch. He clenched his pistol's grip.

Guillermo touched his wrist. "No guns. We settle this like Nefilim."

Diago nodded and allowed his hand to fall away from the weapon.

Garcia shouted, "Bow before me! I am the new king of Los Nefilim."

Thunder crashed overhead.

Garcia reached up and grabbed the thunder's black vibrations in his fists. He sang a note and twisted the noise into a sigil. Behind him, the German joined his voice with Fierro and Moreno to create a concussive glyph.

If he hits us with that, it will be enough to stun us. Diago didn't need to know what would happen next. Garcia wanted them alive. Probably for the same reason Guillermo wanted Garcia—information.

The skies opened up and the rain poured from the heavens.

Garcia fired the glyph with his Nefilim's voices. He threw the ward upward.

A bolt of lavender lightning struck the sigil. Engel. Even while fighting Prieto and Yellowcloud, the angel assisted his Nephilim.

The lightning shattered the glyph into six bolts of sound. *One for each of us,* Diago had time to think before Guillermo's deep voice ruptured the air.

Eva and Maria joined their melody with Guillermo's song. Miquel picked up the thread of the music and added his voice to their choir. Diago listened for the music's weakness. There. Between the chords of Guillermo's bass and Eva's soprano, the register was thin.

Diago caught up with them on the refrain. He sharpened the song with his tenor. Behind him, Rafael added his boyish soprano to the chorus. Eva and Maria opened their hearts to Diago and Rafael. They saw Diago's darkness and did not flinch. They wrapped Rafael in acceptance and joy, and drew the child into their song. Rafael leapt into the air and executed a twirl, adding his amber vibrations to their sigil.

Guillermo took the combined vibrations of their voices and formed a shield designed to absorb Garcia's sound. When Garcia's thunderous noise struck Guillermo's buffer, Diago's head rocked. But he didn't falter in his song, nor did the others. Together they held the shield, and Garcia's bolts of sound died.

Diago didn't wait to recover. He stepped past Guillermo and into the torrent of rain. He skimmed the sole of his foot over a puddle. Water sprayed in his wake, leaving droplets of sound. Diago sang a note and formed a sigil. Miquel joined his song and they created a ward to catch the wind. Eva, Maria, and Rafael twirled like dervishes. The skirts of the twins' habits raised the wind and water, turning it into a miniature tornado. Rafael shaped the tempest between his palms. Guillermo charged the ward with his voice and sent it flying.

Garcia formed a quick song. Moreno and Fierro followed Garcia's lead. The German caught on a beat too late. The tornado grabbed him and flung him into a nearby building. The sound of bones crunching carried across the yard.

The wind picked up speed. Lightning flashed blue and white across the sky. Orange and crimson light ringed the clouds roiling across the heavens.

Before Garcia had time to recover, Guillermo summoned another sigil and charged it with his song. Miquel sang with Guillermo. The twins harmonized. Rafael let loose a cry as he leaped into the air.

Diago caught the notes together and cut a sharp

sigil, charging it with the vibrations of his song. The ward sliced the air as it hurtled toward Garcia, Moreno, and Fierro.

Overhead, a brilliant flash of silver lightning turned the darkness bright as day. The electric charge descended into the yard and fired Diago's sigil. Static electricity made their hair stand on end. The bolts of lightning engulfed Garcia and his Nefilim, leaving them flopping in the puddles, helpless against the rain.

As suddenly as it began, the storm ended. The sun rolled behind the clouds and sent crimson and orange rays to border the storm. The light burned brighter and brighter. Diago noticed the lavender was gone.

Prieto and Yellowcloud had won.

The rain came down softer, feathering away until it was merely patters against the roof tiles.

Diago panted in the sudden quiet. Without thinking of who might be watching, he reached out and took Miquel's hand. His lover smiled and touched his forehead to Diago's brow.

Miquel murmured, "Are you all right?"

Diago nodded and turned in time to catch Rafael in his trembling arms. He lifted his son, checking him for wounds. Rafael was fine.

"Let's move, people," Guillermo growled at them. "We're not safe yet."

A nun emerged from an alley and ran toward the downed Nefilim. Diago realized it was Sofia.

"Quick!" she called out to someone behind her. "Be

quick if you want them alive! They have cyanide cap-
sules in their mouths."

Her words broke through their joy, but even as she
reached Garcia, Diago saw that the Nefilim were dead.

Garcia grinned up at the sky. His eyes open to the
last of the falling rain.

Two uniformed Urban Guards suddenly appeared.
They were followed by a Nefil in a worn suit. He was
older, with oiled black hair and soft gray eyes. His face
appeared as rumpled as his suit.

Guillermo glared at him. "It took you long enough,
Santiago."

Santiago reddened at Guillermo's rebuff. "I'm sorry,
Don Guillermo. I had to circumvent Garcia's orders
and charm the Chief Inspector. The affair required finesse."

Sofia loosened her veil and shook free her long hair.
"We have Jaso and Acosta in custody. I've ordered my
people to take them in for questioning."

"Yes. Thank you, Corvo." Santiago turned to face
someone behind Diago. He made languid shooing motions with his hands. "Please, go back inside, everyone.
I am Inspector Carlos Santiago." He lifted his jacket so
they could see his badge. "Everything is under control
now."

Several mortals lingered on the porch for a few
seconds before they returned indoors, murmuring
amongst themselves.

Dr. Vales detached himself from the crowd. Pushing against those who were going back inside, the

young doctor came forward. With a sideways glance at Diago, Vales faced Santiago. "What the hell happened here? Garcia and his men said that Dr. Alvarez was under suspicion for the Ferrers' murders."

Santiago blinked lazily, as if noticing the mortal for the first time. "And you are?"

"Vales, Dr. Vales. I signed off on Alvarez's admission to the hospital."

"Ah," Santiago assessed the mortal. "I'm afraid it was Inspector Garcia who was trying to cover his own crimes. We've been investigating him for several weeks. It was an internal affair."

Diago admired Santiago's new spin on the story. Without telling a lie, he had just outlined the entire situation.

"Sergeant Corvo"—Santiago gestured at Sofia, who had shed her nun's habit and now waited beside Garcia's body—"was undercover here at your hospital. Her sisters, Señoras Eva and Maria Corvo, were assisting. Dr. Alvarez was brought in from Sevilla to help us flush Garcia into the open. Don Guillermo graciously volunteered to help. Everything was going according to plan until Garcia and his cohorts abducted Dr. Alvarez and his son."

Vales wasn't entirely appeased by the explanation. "*Dr.* Alvarez shot three people." He pointed back toward the hospital with a shaking hand. "Aren't you interested in that?"

Santiago matched Vales's tone. "*Dr.* Alvarez is a veteran. He's seen active duty, and his ability to handle himself under adverse conditions was the reason we wanted him involved in our investigation. If he shot them, they needed to die."

Rafael rested his cheek on Diago's shoulder. Santiago came to Diago's side and ruffled the child's hair. Rafael gave him a wan smile.

Santiago smiled back. "The little guy looks like he's had a rough day. Why don't we let the doctor take his son home?" He tilted his head at Sofia. "Sergeant Corvo, would you escort Don Guillermo and his people to their vehicles?"

"Of course, Inspector." Sofia gestured for them to follow her.

Diago followed Guillermo.

"Dr. Alvarez!" Vales called. "Will you please come to my office tomorrow?"

Diago hesitated. He should just keep walking. Instead, he turned back. "Not tomorrow." Maybe not next week. "But soon."

Vales accepted the answer with a nod, and turned to converse with Santiago. Just beyond the spot where Vales and Santiago talked, a scorpion scuttled along the sidewalk.

Diago tracked the arachnid with his gaze. The scorpion ran to a column where it joined its mates. The scorpions took the form of a man.

Alvaro. A pool of ice formed in Diago's stomach.

Alvaro smiled at Diago, but his predatory gaze was on Rafael.

Diago shielded his son's body with his own.

"Are you all right?" Miquel asked.

"What is it, Papa?" Rafael tried to look over Diago's shoulder, but he covered the boy's face with his hand.

"Let's get out of here," Diago whispered.

Miquel frowned and studied the arcades.

Diago looked back again.

Alvaro was gone.

CHAPTER EIGHT

Guillermo didn't ask any more questions about Diago's descent into the daimonic realm, and Diago offered no further explanations. Instead, Guillermo and Miquel spent the ride telling him what they'd learned from Prieto, and in return, Diago told them about Amparo.

By the time Guillermo parked the truck beside their house, Diago was numb. Rafael dozed with his head against Diago's chest. In spite of his coat, and the combined warmth of Guillermo, Rafael, and Miquel, Diago remained cold.

Miquel opened the passenger door and slid out. "Give him to me." He reached across the seat.

Diago shifted his weight until Miquel could reach Rafael. Once he was certain that his lover had a good grip on the boy, he joined Guillermo beside the truck.

Guillermo's hand landed on Diago's shoulder. "Listen," Guillermo said. "Take this week off and just rest. We'll talk about your studio next week."

"What studio?" Diago asked.

"I need you to start work."

"Work on what?"

"We need the Key, Diago. You have it." He touched Diago's chest with one blunt finger. "Locked inside of you."

Of course. Time to earn my keep. Alvaro is right, everything has a price. For Guillermo, it is the Key. And for the Key itself . . . To search for that chord meant remembering secrets long past. Diago wasn't sure he wanted to resurrect those days.

Miquel waited by the front door, holding Rafael, who was just beginning to wake. "We can talk about this later, can't we?"

"Sure." Guillermo gave Diago's shoulder a squeeze. "Come to my house on Monday. I've had some plans drawn up, and we can go over them together. We'll see which ones you like."

Diago nodded, afraid to speak. He didn't trust the words that might spill over his lips.

Mercifully, Guillermo said nothing else. He lit a cigar and started back down the road toward his villa.

Diago couldn't stand it anymore. "Don't you want to know?"

Guillermo stopped, but he didn't turn around. "Know what?"

"Don't you want to know what happened with Alvaro and Moloch?"

Guillermo smoked. Diago counted eight puffs before the big Nefil finally spoke. "No." He turned and fixed his fiery gaze on Diago. "You'll do what's right. Even if you don't believe in yourself, I do." Before Diago could say anything else, Guillermo walked away.

Small fingers brushed Diago's palm. He started and looked down to see Rafael blinking sleepily by his side.

"Come inside, Papa. Someone fixed our door and cleaned our house."

Diago turned around to find Miquel gone. He took Rafael's hand and led the child inside, where he found that order had been restored to their little home. Miquel had tossed his jacket over the back of the couch. Diago retrieved it and hung it by the door along with his own coat and Rafael's little jacket.

Miquel emerged from the kitchen with a bottle of *orujo* and a couple of glasses. He poured the brandy and gave a glass to Diago. "You look like you need a drink."

Diago downed the shot and felt the brandy's warmth spread across his chest. "Who was here?"

"Juanita left a note on the kitchen table. Along with dinner."

Diago followed his lover into the kitchen. Bowls and platters were spread on their small table. There was enough food to carry them through the next two days. Diago stood in the kitchen door, his glass forgotten in his hand.

Miquel smiled and came to him. He touched the corner of Diago's eye. "What is this?"

Diago wiped the tear away. "It's the light. It's too bright."

Rafael placed his satchel on the coffee table and joined them in the kitchen. "I could use a drink, too," he announced.

Miquel laughed. "How about some hot chocolate for you?" He kissed the side of Diago's mouth before he went to the stove.

Diago sat at the table and uncovered the still-warm dishes. A bulging envelope rested beside one bowl. He turned the thick paper over and saw his name written on one side. He'd seen this script on one other occasion.

"What's that?" Rafael climbed onto his chair and swung his leg. The now familiar thump of his heel striking the table leg provided their backbeat.

"Stop kicking the table," Diago murmured absently. The paper reminded him of the calling card Prieto had left in the mirrored box in what seemed like so long ago. *But it was only a month ago.* Yet it felt like years. Still, Diago couldn't dispute that the handwriting on this envelope was the same. "Prieto."

Rafael ceased to kick the table.

Miquel turned from the stove to see. "What?"

"Not what, who."

Miquel shut off the stove and came to stand behind Diago. Placing his hands on Diago's shoulders, he massaged him gently. "Open it."

Diago slid his thumb beneath the seal. Inside was

the magnifying glass he had thrown at Engel, nothing else. Diago pivoted the glass free of its brass case. The magnifying glass had been removed and in its place was a mirror.

Etched into the glass was the silhouette of a woman poised to dance, her arms raised over her head, her face turned upward as if looking at the sky. She was dressed in rags that rose behind her and gave her the illusion of wings. The ethereal figure seemed to twist and turn in the kitchen's light. Around her throat was a small serpent with ruby eyes and golden scales. Beneath her feet was a scroll with the dates 1895-1929 etched into the glass.

Crimson and silver light bled across the kitchen floor. The rays gathered together and took the shape of the tall thin angel that called himself Prieto. The colors of his song leaked from his wounds like multihued ribbons. The right side of his face was burned red and tight. His long silver hair was matted with blood and shadowed his eyes, great crimson orbs shot through with streams of silver. Pain rendered his gaze feral and bright.

Rafael left his chair and came to Diago's side. He pressed himself close against Diago and watched Prieto with wide eyes.

Diago put his arm around his son, wondering if this day would ever end.

Prieto straightened and snuffed a smoldering patch of fire on his coat. "Don't be frightened, child. This is what happens when angels war."

"You should stop fighting," Rafael whispered.

Prieto laughed, and the sound drove their fear from the room. "Such good advice." He came to the table and sat on Miquel's chair. Gesturing at the etching, he said, "Her earthly name was Candela Maria Cortés Prieto."

Diago felt Miquel's fingers tighten on his shoulders.

Prieto didn't notice Miquel's sudden tension, or if he did, he didn't remark on it. Instead, he winked at Rafael. "When you are older, I will sing you her angelic name. She loved you very much. Engel murdered her when she refused to tell Prince Aker where she had hidden you. Engel gave her the second death." Prieto's lower lip trembled. "I have avenged her."

Diago finally found his voice. "You gave Engel the second death?"

Prieto pursed his lips and nodded. "Sariel sanctioned the death sentence." He reached out to touch Diago's wrist, but Diago moved his hand out of the angel's reach. "I just wanted to see that my nephew is loved."

"Now you've seen." Diago gently pivoted the glass back into the brass case. "Get out."

Prieto swallowed hard before he continued. "Teach him how to love, Diago. Don't let him live in fear of gods or mortals or angels or daimons. And definitely do not let him fear death. I beg you. Teach him how to love."

From their bedroom, the mantel clock chimed the

half hour. As if on cue, Prieto rose and went to the backdoor. He hesitated but didn't turn around. "I am sorry, Diago. For what that's worth. I am sorry for how you were used and that you were hurt."

The words fell like shivers in the air, and Diago couldn't tell if Prieto meant it or not. Nor did he care. He said nothing to absolve the angel of his sister's act, let alone his own. Forgiveness was a destination far beyond him at the moment. He merely stared at the table and waited for the angel to leave.

Prieto's colors bled from their kitchen and disappeared. Outside, the sun crept from behind the clouds and splashed golden light across their kitchen floor.

When he was sure the angel was gone, Diago pressed the magnifying glass into his son's small hand. "This," he said before he paused and cleared his throat. "This is a very important gift. Miquel picked out the glass for me many years ago. And it has been touched by daimons and by angels, so like you and me, it is augmented with the magic of both. And here"—he pivoted the mirrored glass to reveal the etching of Candela—"is your mother, who must not be forgotten. I'm giving it to you, because it's been touched by all of us."

Rafael held the brass case between his palms. "It's cold."

"Most symbols are," Miquel said as he knelt beside the boy.

"But we're not a symbol," said Rafael. "We're a family."

"A family of bears," Miquel growled and lifted Rafael into the air.

The child squealed as Miquel tucked him under one arm. He grabbed the chair Prieto had vacated and placed it in front of the stove. "Trade me." He offered Rafael a wooden spoon and held out his hand for the magnifying glass.

Rafael considered Miquel for a moment, and then he placed the brass case in his pocket. Snatching the spoon from Miquel's hand, Rafael gave him a closed fist salute.

"Excellent!" Miquel turned on the burner. "Stir your milk while I find some chocolate."

Their voices faded into the background. On the tabletop, where Prieto had folded his hands, a damp circle stained the wood. *Like a teardrop,* Diago thought.

As he watched, a sphere rose from the table's surface. The bubble grew until it was the size of a marble filled with streaks of crimson and silver. Diago reached out and caught the angel's tear before it could roll to the floor.

Still warm with Prieto's love, the stone pulsed softly against Diago's palm. He wasn't sure why, but he felt that Prieto had left it for him. Maybe he was truly sorry for the way the angels had used Diago.

Maybe.

Miquel returned to Diago's side. Frowning at the

stone, his dark eyes troubled, he traced the vein in Diago's wrist until he touched his palm. "Will you keep it?"

"Maybe." Diago kissed Miquel's knuckles and watched his son.

Rafael turned and grinned, and Diago smiled back. Maybe the angels were sorry, but Diago wasn't. Not anymore. He had his family, his family of bears, and together, they would roar.

ACKNOWLEDGMENTS

Always and always to my family, first and foremost. For my husband, Dick Frohock, who has to share me with so many people, and for my beautiful daughter, Rhi, and her husband, Andrew Hopkins. I couldn't do this without their love and support.

Special thanks continues to go to Josep M. Oriol for reading each and every rough drafts and helping me with terminology and places in Barcelona. If there any mistakes regarding history, street names or metro stops, those mistakes are mine and mine alone. When in doubt, I made it up.

For the usual suspects who read the manuscripts, sometimes two and three times, and caught my many errors: Anne Lippin, Peter Cooper, Glinda Harrison, and Justin Landon for all of their outstanding comments and guidance.

Thanks to Mark Lawrence, ML Brennan, Courtney

Schafer, Mazarkis Williams, Alex Bledsoe, Michael R. Fletcher, and Helen Lowe for their support.

To the most marvelous Mia for your fabulous help with cover copy. Your clear insight and excellent advice made a seemingly insurmountable job fun!

To my dear friend Lisa Cantrell for all of our Friday afternoons.

I'd also like to thank the unsung hero of all three of these novellas: Jenny Klion, my copy editor. If you found grammatical error, it's because I didn't heed her advice.

Special thanks goes to David Pomerico for his excellent editorial direction on all of the stories in this series: I'm very lucky to have such an excellent editor.

Most special thanks to Marlene Stringer, my literary agent, who keeps telling me to write something new, and so I will.

And thanks goes to the most important people of all: you, the reader. Without you, all of this wouldn't be half as much fun as it is.

ABOUT THE AUTHOR

T. Frohock has turned her love of dark fantasy and horror into tales of deliciously creepy fiction. She currently lives in North Carolina where she has long been accused of telling stories, which is a southern colloquialism for lying.

THE PRICE OF PASSION

"What would it take to get you to turn me loose?"

He raised one eyebrow at her and said nothing.

She rushed on. "Suppose I . . . suppose I let you make love to me in exchange for freeing me?"

He threw back his head and laughed. "Have you ever had a man before?"

She felt her face flame. "You know I haven't!"

"Then you might not be skilled enough to make it enjoyable."

She was incensed. "You're turning me down?" She lunged at him, scratching and clawing. If she could sink her nails into those arrogant blue eyes . . . !

Cougar caught her wrists and they went down in a heap as they struggled. He came up on top. He lay there, both of them breathing hard as he pinned her hands above her head.

"You little vixen! I ought to . . ."

He bent his head suddenly and covered her mouth with his. He kissed her deeply, thoroughly. For a long moment, she surrendered to his seeking mouth, her body molding itself against his.

Oh, God, no man had ever touched her like this, and the way her eager body responded scared her. . . .

Books by Georgina Gentry

APACHE CARESS
BANDIT'S EMBRACE
CHEYENNE CAPTIVE
CHEYENNE CARESS
CHEYENNE PRINCESS
CHEYENNE SPLENDOR
CHEYENNE SONG
COMANCHE COWBOY
ETERNAL OUTLAW
HALF-BREED'S BRIDE
NEVADA DAWN
NEVADA NIGHTS
QUICKSILVER PASSION
SIOUX SLAVE
SONG OF THE WARRIOR
TIMELESS WARRIOR
WARRIOR'S PRIZE

Published by Zebra Books

APACHE TEARS

Georgina Gentry

Zebra Books
Kensington Publishing Corp.

http://www.zebrabooks.com

ZEBRA BOOKS are published by

Kensington Publishing Corp.
850 Third Avenue
New York, NY 10022

First Printing: December, 1999
10 9 8 7 6 5 4 3 2 1

Printed in the United States of America

For my Apache friend, Irma Kitcheyan, who took me out to all the historic Arizona sites I needed to see and shared with me so many authentic Apache stories;

for my writer friend, Janis Reams Hudson, who first gave me some Apache Tears and told me the tragic legend;

and finally, for the Indian scouts who served so bravely and were, for the most part, unappreciated and unsung.

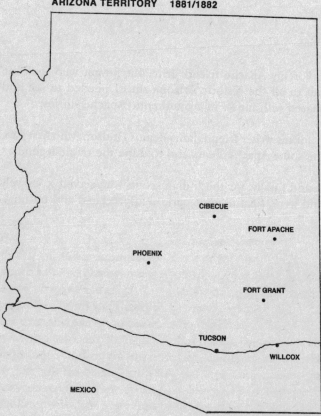

ARIZONA TERRITORY   1881/1882

CIBECUE

FORT APACHE

PHOENIX

FORT GRANT

TUCSON

WILLCOX

MEXICO

MEXICO

Prologue

Apache Tears. It is the name for the black, sometimes tear-shaped obsidian gemstones found in the sun-splashed wilderness of Arizona. An ancient Apache legend goes with the gem. Some of the tale varies, depending on who is telling it, but here is the basic story: A small band of courageous Apache warriors came up against a superior force of either soldiers or enemy braves. They fought valiantly, killing many of the enemy. However, eventually trapped on the top of a cliff, more than half the Apaches were killed as they held off the larger enemy group. Rather than surrender, the few brave survivors leaped off the cliff to their deaths. The grieving Apache women wept copious tears that fell to the ground and were turned into black stone. Today, Apache Tears still signify a great and undying love.

Indian scouts. The U.S. Cavalry of the Old West used a lot of them from many tribes. Among the best of these were the Apaches, who were brave in battle, relentless on

the trail and expert at tracking their quarry. Only once in
the entire history of the West did Indian scouts ever turn
against their white masters. When it happened in August
of 1881, those mutinous scouts were Apaches.

That much is recorded history. And maybe, just maybe,
there might also have been a romance between a red-
haired temptress and an Apache scout who desired her
with such passion, he would give her a necklace of Apache
Tears and risk everything to possess her. . . .

child's every wish, but they were gone now and her fortune seemed to have melted away. Since her mother's old friend had become her guardian, Libbie seemed to have a voice in almost nothing. Now even her heavily mortgaged California mansion had been sold to pay expenses. With increasing frustration, Libbie had reacted by becoming as difficult as possible.

Now she forced herself to smile as she peered out the window at the passing action on the parade grounds, soldiers coming and going, the orderly rows of adobe buildings shimmering in the early morning heat. "I must say I like what I've seen of Arizona Territory."

"Pah!" Mrs. Everett wiped dust and sweat from her beefy face with a dainty handkerchief. "It's a savage land, fit only for savages! Lieutenant Van Harrington must have been out of his mind to request an assignment like this. Thank the heavens we're on to Boston tomorrow!"

The sun was just rising over the hills to the east, painting the scene all red and gold and purple. Libbie caught her breath at the distant beauty of the untamed landscape surrounding the fort as the stagecoach pulled to a halt with a jangle of harness in the square of the parade grounds. Libbie brushed the dust from her green silk gown and felt the confining heat of her corset and long petticoats. Like it or not, it had already been decided that she would marry the wealthy young blue blood late next spring when Libbie graduated from Miss Priddy's Female Academy in Boston only two weeks before she turned eighteen.

At least, marriage would get her out from under Mrs. Everett's thumb. Although she'd only met him a couple of times, she remembered that Lieutenant Phillip Van Harrington was handsome and he did write lovely letters. Maybe she could make the lieutenant dance to her tune; men had always been smitten by her beauty.

The rangy old driver swung down from the seat and

came around to open the door, slapping his Western hat against his leg, dust billowing as he opened the stage door. "Here we are, ladies."

"My stars! What a godforsaken place!" Mrs. Everett snapped as he helped her down from the coach. Then she turned sternly to Libbie. "Don't forget your parasol! You mustn't take a chance on that sun ruining your skin."

"But I like the feel of the sun on my face," Libbie argued with a haughty shake of her fiery hair.

"Libbie, ladies do not have sun-tanned skin, and the Lieutenant expects to get a lady. Need I say more?"

Feeling both angry and helpless, Libbie sighed with frustration and snapped open the lace parasol. In the times she had seen the sun-drenched skies of this wild, fierce land as she passed through from California to Boston, she had come to love the desert and the vast landscape she had seen from the train window. But of course, her guardian was right; ladies were admired for their pale, delicate skin, and with her fair complexion, she tended to freckle anyway.

Damn! Someday, she thought, and gritted her teeth, *someday I'll be of age and then I'll defy Mrs. Everett and do as I wish. No you won't,* she thought as she stepped from the coach, *the wedding is planned for a few days before your eighteenth birthday. After you marry Phillip, he will make all your decisions for you. Well he might boss me, but he won't make me like it.*

Even as she thought that, there was the lieutenant striding toward her; mid-twenties, tall, handsome, and broad-shouldered with blue eyes under sandy hair and a square, mannish jaw. It was only his pale mustache, his thin, tight lips, and his manner that made him seem a little prissy, she thought.

"Ah, Mrs. Everett, and Elizabeth, my dear! Did you have a good trip?"

Mrs. Everett wiped her beefy face and grumbled about

the heat, but Libbie nodded as he bent to kiss her hand. "Yes, Phillip, actually, we did, although it is a long way from the train."

"Beastly country!" Phillip snorted. "Snakes and savages! I can hardly wait to return to Philadelphia and civilization." Now he turned his warmest smile on her pouty guardian. "Ah, so glad to see you again, dear lady! I'm sorry about the heat! Arizona is hell for civilized people."

Mrs. Everett simpered at him like a schoolgirl. "It was made agreeable only by the knowledge that you were waiting for us, dear boy. Isn't that right, Libbie?"

"What?" Libbie barely heard her. A man had caught her attention; a tall, big-shouldered, dark-skinned savage who leaned against the corner of a nearby adobe building and watched her with startling blue eyes in his dark, square-jawed face. More shocking was that he was bare-chested, wearing only a skimpy loincloth, knee-high buckskin moccasins, and an interesting necklace of silver and turquoise beads set off by tear-shaped black gemstones that hung against his massive, muscled chest. His black, straight hair reached almost to his shoulders and a red headband held it in place. She studied him carefully. He was perhaps three or four years younger than Phillip, but already much more of a man than the lieutenant would ever be.

The savage stared at her in a bold, impudent way that sent a chill of either fear or anticipation up her back; Libbie wasn't sure which.

Ndolkah leaned against the building and studied the haughty white girl who stared at him with such frank curiosity. So this was the future wife of the arrogant lieutenant. Everyone at the fort had been saying she would visit as she passed through from California on her return to school back East.

She was very beautiful and very young, Ndolkah forced himself to admit, noting the early morning sun glinting off the red hair that peeked from beneath her expensive hat with its sweeping plumes. The lace parasol partially shaded the pale complexion. Her green eyes matched her fashionable dress, and the bustle only accentuated her small waist and the creamy swell of her bosom. *Libbie*, the lieutenant had called her. A better name for the flame-haired beauty would be Blaze, Ndolkah thought. Yet she was more than beautiful; there was something about her that hinted that behind that ladylike manner, she was also as rebellious and headstrong as a wild mustang filly. One thing was certain—this beauty was too much woman for the prim tenderfoot lieutenant to tame. Ndolkah smiled ever so slightly at the thought.

"Elizabeth," Phillip scolded, "what are you looking at?"

She knew she shouldn't stare, but she couldn't take her eyes off the virile, half-naked man leaning against the adobe building. "Who is that?"

Phillip turned to look. "That half-breed savage?" he snorted. "Ndolkah, one of my Apache scouts; old Mac McGuire's son. Hey you, Cougar!" He shouted and made a gesture of dismissal, "haven't you got work to do?"

Ndolkah nodded to the English translation of his Apache name, gave the lieutenant a mocking half-salute, and looked boldly into Libbie's eyes before turning and sauntering away.

Libbie took a deep breath, unnerved from the frank appraisal of his gaze, but she watched him go, his long-legged stride accenting the hard muscles of his tanned, naked back. The nerve of that scout! His blue eyes had seemed to taunt her; almost seemed to undress her with his look as he left. "Ndolkah," she murmured, "what does it mean?"

Phillip made a gesture of annoyance. "Cougar, or so the Apache tell me."

Cougar. Yes, that name fitted him, Libbie thought, watching him saunter away with easy grace; tawny skin, muscular as a wild animal, moving with a powerful gait.

"He's an arrogant devil," Phillip snapped, "if he weren't so darned good as a scout, and old Mac's son, I'd let him go, and I may have to have him whipped yet."

"I wouldn't try that if I were you, Phillip," Libbie blurted without thinking, "he looks like he could take you in a fight."

"What did you say?" Phillip asked.

Mrs. Everett's fat face paled. "Libbie said she's really looking forward to tonight, didn't you, dear?"

Libbie sighed at her prompting. "Yes, of course."

Phillip beamed at the pair as he barked orders to some enlisted men about handling the ladies' luggage. "Oh, yes, I did write you that we'd planned a ball in your honor?" He took Libbie's elbow and they walked along the wooden sidewalk, her guardian puffing in their wake. "There's not much excitement out here at Fort Grant except trying to keep the savages from attacking settlers. I'm still hoping to get into a real battle and avenge my father's death." He smiled at Libbie and pulled at the sandy mustache above his thin, tight lips. "I'm sure you'd be pleased if I won a medal or two. If I'm lucky, I might get assigned to the President's staff."

"Isn't it tragic about the shooting?" Mrs. Everett asked, puffing along behind them.

"Yes," Phillip flung over his shoulder. "If Garfield doesn't survive his wounds, I guess I can kiss that promotion good-bye."

"Really, Phillip," Libbie said before she thought, "you might show a little compassion for the President! After

Lincoln, I'm sure the country thought we'd never have another assassination attempt."

Mrs. Everett poked her in the back again—hard. "We'd be thrilled if you won some medals, wouldn't we, Libbie?"

Libbie gritted her teeth and smiled prettily at him from under her parasol. "Of course, Phillip; every woman loves a hero."

Behind her, Mrs. Everett said, "And they'd look so good on your uniform in the wedding."

He threw a smile at the woman over his shoulder. "By then, I hope to be transferred back to Washington, whether the President survives or not."

"My stars! How exciting!" The dowager fanned herself as she puffed along. "Isn't that exciting, Libbie?"

"Hm? Oh, yes," Libbie said, stifling a yawn. "Somehow, I was hoping we'd stay out here. This is beautiful country; wild and untamed and savage." In her mind's eye, she saw the half-naked scout and the intimate way his blue eyes had assessed her. His bold gaze had said: *I want to possess you; to strip away all that civilization along with that green silk dress.*

"Ye gods, my dear, you must be joking!" Phillip snorted and patted the hand looped through his arm. "No civilized person would want to live out here; only the Apache feel at home in this wild country."

In her mind's eye, she saw the Apache scout galloping across this sun-splashed wilderness—uncivilized, untamed and free. In her imagination, he reached for her, swung her up on his pinto stallion, and galloped away with her.

"Elizabeth, are you all right?" Phillip peered anxiously at her as they paused on the sidewalk. "Your face is flushed."

Oh, dear God, if he should even guess at what she'd been thinking . . .

"It's this blasted heat," Mrs. Everett said behind them,

"and Libbie is such a delicate, high-strung lady. Thank goodness I brought some smelling salts!"

Smelling salts? What she needed was to get out of this corset and long petticoats. "I'm fine." She gave her escort a haughty shake of her head.

"Here we are." Phillip paused in front of an adobe building and opened the door. "I'm afraid this is the best we have to offer—not good enough for real ladies, but I'm afraid it will have to do." He stepped aside so they could enter.

Mrs. Everett beamed up at him, still fanning herself with a lace hankie. "You're such a dear boy! I knew I was making the right decision when I introduced you two at that Christmas ball!"

Phillip took her beefy hand and kissed it. "And let me assure you, sweet lady, that I will never forget the favor you did me in doing so! When I marry Elizabeth, there will always be room for her guardian at our home."

"Go along with you, Lieutenant." Mrs. Everett giggled like a schoolgirl as they entered and looked around.

It was much cooler inside the thick adobe walls. The room was primitive in its furnishing—a pair of beds, a chest, several chairs, and a Navaho rug spread on the wood floor. There was a big tin tub in the corner and Libbie looked toward it with longing.

The soldiers had followed and now put the luggage down. The lieutenant dismissed them curtly and they saluted and left. Libbie had a distinct feeling that the lowly soldiers didn't like the young aristocrat any better than Cougar did, but they weren't arrogant as he had been.

"Now, Elizabeth, dear," Phillip said as he bustled about opening the windows, "I'll have a girl sent over with food and bathwater. You two can rest until this evening."

"Oh, but I don't want to rest," Libbie protested as she

closed her parasol with a snap. "I want to see as much as possible; maybe go riding."

"But there's nothing to see!" Mrs. Everett looked aghast.

"Damn it. You don't have to go," Libbie said. Her patience with the woman was wearing thin.

"Libbie!" Her guardian gasped. "What on earth will Phillip think about a girl who swears? Can't you say 'darn it,' or 'drat,' or something?"

"I say what I mean," Libbie answered with a toss of her fiery curls.

"Never mind, dear Mrs. Everett," Phillip's thin lips forced a smile. "I'm sure when we're wed, I can tame the lady and teach her proper behavior."

Tame the lady. Damn it, she didn't want, didn't intend, to be tamed. Libbie looked at Mrs. Everett's stricken face and remembered their financial situation. With a sigh, she turned her most charming smile on the wealthy young officer. "I would love to go riding. I do ride very well, Phillip."

He took out his handkerchief and mopped his face. "Ye gods! Really, my dear, Mrs. Everett is right; there's nothing to see but desert and hills and savages."

She favored him with her most pretty pout. "I must warn you that I'm quite spoiled, Phillip; Daddy did that. I usually get what I want."

"I can indulge you a little now, my dear," Phillip frowned, "but of course, when we're married, I'll expect unquestioned obedience, as any husband would."

When we're married. Libbie sank down on a chair and took off her hat. She barely understood what it was a married couple did in bed, but she was certain it was awkward and embarrassing. The more she thought about Phillip taking off her nightdress and kissing her breasts with his thin, prim mouth and that wispy mustache, the more she was sure she wouldn't like it at all.

"My stars!" said Mrs. Everett, "Libbie looks faint."

Phillip came over to her chair. "My dear?" He took her hand and rubbed it anxiously. "Are you sure you'll be all right?"

His hands were as pale and delicate as her own, Libbie thought and imagined the Apache scout's dark, big hands. They would be strong and hard. She had a sudden vision of his full, sensual lips kissing her breasts. She felt an unexpected surge of excitement and took a deep breath. "Mrs. Everett is right, Phillip, I'm tired and need some rest."

"Fine." Phillip backed toward the door.

"However, I'd still like to go riding later this morning." Libbie stood up. "I wish I didn't have to use a sidesaddle."

"Libbie!" Mrs. Everett rolled her eyes. "You mustn't shock young Phillip with your jokes."

"I'm not joking," Libbie pouted.

The lieutenant paused at the door. "Of course you are, my dear." He used the smug tone of a condescending father to a not very bright child. "Very well, I'll bring horses over about ten and we'll go riding. However, we won't get too far out of sight of the fort. There's a lot of unrest among these savages right now, and you'd be a delicious prize to any of those bucks."

Mrs. Everett gasped at the image his words presented, but Libbie felt an unaccustomed thrill run through her. "Thank you, Phillip."

He smiled and bowed. "Ten o'clock it is then. I'll send a girl with food and bathwater."

Libbie watched him walk away from the door. He might be handsome, but even the way Phillip walked was prissy.

Mrs. Everett sighed with relief and closed the door. "My stars! What on earth were you thinking, young lady?" she snapped as she turned on Libbie. "The Van Harringtons have a high position in Philadelphia society; Phillip will marry a girl only if he thinks she is a real lady and as blue-blooded and proper as he himself."

"He's a prissy prig," Libbie frowned as she began to unbutton the green silk.

"But he's a *rich* prissy prig," Mrs. Everett said as she came over to help Libbie with her dress. "I went to a lot of trouble arranging to come by here on the way back to Boston so he could be reminded of how pretty you are. Phillip Van Harrington is quite a catch, my dear, and the only son of a prominent Philadelphia society leader."

"I don't care," Libbie sighed and stood up so her guardian could unhook the back of the green silk gown and begin to unlace her corset.

"You will care when you're out of money, Elizabeth Winters," the dumpy lady huffed as she struggled with the laces. "Now that we've sold your parents' home in California, that money should last less than a year, considering the fancy wedding we'll have to put on. But by then, we'll be into the Van Harrington wealth and won't have to worry anymore."

"I'm not worried," Libbie protested. "Money isn't important to me; freedom is."

"Easy to say when you've always lived in the lap of luxury," the other scolded, "but I haven't. As your mother's close friend, I'm trying to look after your best interests."

"My inheritance seems to have just melted away in the six years since their deaths in that railroad mishap," Libbie thought aloud. "I thought Daddy told me I would have plenty to keep me in the lap of luxury the rest of my days."

"Well, your father misfigured." She didn't look at Libbie as she began to unpack their luggage. "Expenses are higher than expected. Besides, it costs a fortune to keep you in that fancy Boston school." She sounded defensive and angry.

Why was the plump woman so upset?

"You didn't even ask me if I wanted to go to Miss Priddy's Academy. You just enrolled me." Libbie stepped out of her dress.

"You are not only spoiled, you are unappreciative!" Mrs. Everett took the gown, shook it, and hung it up without looking at Libbie. "Besides, it takes a lot to live the way we live; that's all."

"That's your choice, not mine," Libbie complained. "Except for horseback riding, my life is dull, dull, dull! And I don't care a fig about fine clothes and society balls—and I hate living back East!"

"You could at least think of me," her guardian complained as she fanned her damp face with a kerchief, "and if you weren't so silly and immature, you would care about all the good things money can buy. Don't let young Phillip see how spoiled and headstrong you are, or even your beauty might not be enough to cinch this deal. Remember, you might not get another chance at such a fine catch!"

Libbie whirled around. She started to answer that Mrs. Everett seemed more interested in her own comfort than Libbie's happiness, but decided she was wasting her time.

"Now what are you pouting about?" her guardian demanded.

"Nothing," Libbie said, and bit back a torrent of anger. At seventeen, she was underage and helpless; Mrs. Everett had complete control and would until she handed her ward over to Phillip on their wedding day. Libbie would never get to make any decisions on her own; she was powerless to do anything but sulk and make life difficult for those who commanded her life.

"That's more like it." Mrs. Everett brushed a wisp of gray hair back into her bun and began to shake out clothes and hang them up. "By the way, I saw the way you stared at that half-naked savage with such boldness. It's a wonder your fiancé didn't take offense."

"I wasn't staring."

"Yes, you were. Proper ladies keep their eyes downcast."

"Then it's a wonder more of them don't collide with walls and furniture," Libbie snapped.

"Don't get smart with me, young lady!" Her voice was as stern as her plain face as she returned to her unpacking. "We came by the fort just to dangle you like a carrot in front of the lieutenant's nose to remind him what a prize he's going to get next spring when you graduate."

"Damn it, I don't want to be a prize!" Libbie complained, flopping down on the bed, "I want to laugh every time I think of what it will feel like on our wedding night when he takes my nightgown off. His mustache will tickle."

Mrs. Everett paused and gasped, plump hand to her throat. "My stars! Such thoughts from an innocent girl! I'm frankly appalled! Remember that a woman is expected to do her duty in her husband's bed. Give him some heirs as quickly as possible and think of the money and prestige that goes with the union; that's the most a girl can expect."

"But I want more than that," Libbie insisted, "I expect him to make me want him to take off my nightdress, to thrill me with his kisses—"

"You must stop reading those trashy romance novels those naughty girls hide under their mattresses at Miss Priddy's," the lady scolded, shaking her finger in Libbie's face. "What's really important is making a secure match so we'll both have comfort the rest of our days."

"But I want love and excitement, and most of all, freedom!" Libbie's green eyes blazed.

"Then you expect too much"—the other shrugged—"especially for women of your social class—"

They were interrupted by a knock at the door, and Mrs. Everett turned and called out, "Yes?"

"Your breakfast, *señora*," a woman's voice called, "and some bathwater."

The plump matron opened the door and gestured. "Bring it in."

A pretty Indian girl entered with a tray. Libbie rolled over on the bed to stare at the girl and smiled. "Hello."

But the girl glared at her. "I am Shashké, your maid."

Libbie nodded and watched her. The Indian girl was about Libbie's own age—maybe seventeen or so, but dark, and her drab clothes hid a voluptuous body. A bright red flower was tucked in her black hair. *Now why would the girl frown at her?*

Libbie watched the girl set up a breakfast tray. "Is Shashké an Apache word?"

"Yes." The sultry girl did not smile. "I am named for the month I was born; whites call it January."

"You are very pretty." Libbie smiled.

The girl scowled. "My husband thinks so."

Mrs. Everett hissed at Libbie under her breath. "Don't be so democratic to the help; it isn't seemly for a lady. You," she addressed the Apache girl in a loud command, "get on with your work."

Libbie was embarrassed by her guardian's behavior, but she kept silent. She sat on the edge of the bed and Mrs. Everett drew up a chair. There was steaming strong coffee, fresh oranges, and warm tortillas with scrambled eggs and fried pork covered with spicy hot sauce. Libbie thought the food delicious and dug in with gusto, while her guardian complained about the peppery fare. The hostile Apache girl said nothing as she filled the tub with buckets of hot water carried in from a cart outside.

Libbie finished her food and pushed her plate away, curious about the Apache girl. "Have you worked at the fort long?"

The girl paused, eyeing her sullenly. "Not too long. My people are camped to the south of the fort."

"Libbie," Mrs. Everett reminded her, "you shouldn't

talk to the servants. You're interfering with the girl doing her job."

"No, I'm not," Libbie said.

The Indian girl finished filling the tub and frowned at Libbie. "You are as Ndolkah said, very beautiful," Shashké admitted grudgingly and her dark eyes shone with anger.

"Thank you," Libbie answered, still puzzled by the dark beauty's hostility. Why would the Apache girl be discussing Libbie with the scout? Was it only idle curiosity or was there more here than met the eye? Could the pair be a couple? A feeling passed over Libbie at the thought of the virile scout holding Shashké, touching her with the hot intimacy his gaze had hinted at as they swept over Libbie in such frank appraisal.

She had a sudden vision of the pair locked together in a torrid embrace and shook her head to chase the image away. To clear her thoughts, she asked, "Will you be at the dance tonight?"

The girl hesitated, then smiled, but there was no mirth in her face. "Of course. Someone has to serve the punch and clean up after the white people's dinner."

"You arrogant wench!" Mrs. Everett rose to snap at the Apache girl, "Get out of here before I report how uppity you are!"

Shashké turned and fled out the door.

Libbie frowned at the other. "There was no need to do that."

"That Injun wench was forgetting her place!" The guardian shrugged as she went over to the luggage and began to arrange Libbie's fancy soaps and delicate undergarments on a chair. "Almost as arrogant as that Injun buck this morning. How dare he stare at you that way!"

"I didn't notice," Libbie lied. "I'm sure you misread his intentions."

"Hah! An idiot could have seen what he was thinking

as he looked at you. Imagine the effrontery of that savage thinking about you with lust—"

"Oh, please, you exaggerate." Libbie took off her corset and lace pantalets, then slipped into the tub of steaming water with a satisfied sigh. She closed her eyes and leaned back in the tub, feeling the warmth against her skin and remembering the way Cougar's eyes had caressed her with heated emotion. If he truly belonged to Shashké, Libbie felt guilty about her strong attraction to the scout.

"Everybody knows Injuns can't be trusted," the other woman said as she bustled about, getting out fresh lace underthings for Libbie.

"Don't be silly, Mrs. Everett, these Indians work for the whites."

"That one scout looks like he wears no man's collar," the other predicted dourly.

That was what had been so fascinating about him, his arrogant independence and his rugged masculinity, Libbie thought, but of course she dared not say that. Instead, she began to take down her long, fiery hair so she could wash it and wondered idly what it would feel like to have a man tangle his fingers in her locks and pull her hard against him while his hot, demanding mouth dominated hers and his strong hands covered her breasts.

Libbie closed her eyes a long moment, trembling with excitement. Mrs. Everett was right; Cougar signified danger and forbidden excitement. Libbie wondered suddenly if he would be at the dance. Abruptly, she began to look forward to the night ahead.

Chapter Two

After her bath, Libbie put her hair up and slipped into a pale blue broadcloth riding outfit, complete with perky feathered hat and fine leather boots.

Mrs. Everett scowled at her charge. "Put some rosewater on your face and see if you can protect it from the sun."

"I will not!" Libbie flung up her head and strode to the door. "It's about time you stopped giving me orders!"

"You should learn not to be so sassy," the plump dowager warned. "Men don't like headstrong women."

"Would you believe I don't care?"

"You will care if you lose young Harrington and we're both out on the street begging!"

"I think you're more worried about your own future than mine!" Libbie snapped.

Before her irate guardian could reply, there was a knock at the door and Libbie rushed to open it, glad for the interruption.

Phillip stood there, looking dapper in his blue uniform

and holding the reins of two horses. "I'm here to take you riding, madam." He made a low, exaggerated bow.

She was almost glad to see him—any excuse to be away from the stern older woman and out into the fresh air. "Wonderful! I'm ready to go." She gave him a warm smile and went out, calling back over her shoulder, "We'll be back in a couple of hours."

Mrs. Everett followed them to the door. "Lieutenant, just the two of you? No chaperon?"

"Oh, for heaven's sake!" Libbie stormed.

Phillip seemed to force a smile, but he was plainly annoyed as he stroked his mustache. "Surely, dear lady, you aren't implying that I would take advantage of an innocent, respectable—"

"No, of course not," the woman backtracked, "it's just that with only the two of you, I thought the Indians might present some danger—"

"With me along?" Phillip gave her a self-assured look and patted the pistol at his side. "I'll protect her if some savage gets in our way. I'm an excellent shot you know; you should see my hunting trophies."

Reassured, Mrs. Everett closed the door.

Libbie turned from patting the dainty sorrel mare. "You know, Phillip, I'd almost swear you'd like a chance to shoot some Indians."

He shrugged. "That's what I came out to Arizona for— revenge. An Apache war party killed my father almost a quarter of a century ago when he was stationed in this miserable Territory."

"Oh?" Libbie mused, "I've read a lot of history, but I didn't realize there was any Indian trouble in this place about that time."

"It was one of those small, isolated incidents, the army said," Phillip answered. "Ironically, he was to have been sent back to Philadelphia the very next day."

No wonder Phillip hated Apaches. Her heart softened a little toward him. "I'm truly sorry," Libbie murmured. "It must have hurt you a great deal."

Phillip made a gesture of dismissal. "I was only four years old at the time. I don't even remember him. My dear mother and her unmarried sisters who live with us raised me."

A mama's boy. Libbie had suspected that.

"Here, my dear, let me help you." He put his hands out for her small, booted foot and lifted her up to the sidesaddle.

Libbie arranged her skirt and frowned. "I wish you'd brought me a regular saddle."

He paused as he was about to mount his own bay gelding. "I had thought you were joking. Ladies don't—"

"I know all about what ladies don't; it's been drilled into me enough. Just once, I'd like to grip a horse between my knees and gallop away with my hair flying in the wind."

Phillip grinned as he swung into the saddle. "Elizabeth, my dear, your exuberance is so refreshing!"

They turned and rode out at a walk, Phillip studying the outline of her ripe body in the fine blue riding habit as they started away from the post. *You sassy, spirited little bitch,* he vowed, *you need to be broken and trained into being a subservient and dutiful wife, and I'm just the man to do it. Once I control you and your fortune the only thing you'll ever get between your pretty thighs is me.*

Libbie adjusted her perky plumed hat and looked over at him. "A penny for your thoughts." She gave him her most winsome smile.

He grinned back at her. "I was just looking forward to our marriage, my dear. I think you are going to make me very happy and give me many sons."

Libbie flushed and looked away, as the image of his pale mustache on her breasts came to her mind again. Strange, he hadn't said anything about making her happy. "So where shall we ride?"

They were heading off the fort grounds at a lazy trot.

"We can't get too far away," Phillip cautioned, "there are bears in the area and some unrest among the Apache right now; some crazy medicine man is stirring them up, telling them the whites are going to disappear and they'll have their own land back again."

"Bears?"

"Don't worry, my dear." He patted the rifle hanging on his saddle. "I've killed dozens of them. The Apache don't like it, though."

"Why not?"

Phillip shrugged. "Who knows how a savage's mind works? Something about bad spirits or some such. Crazy people. If we don't kill all these Apaches, we ought to cage them."

"You can't blame them for wanting to be free," Libbie murmured, "that's a basic hunger of everyone."

"Ye gods! You sound almost sympathetic to the red devils," Phillip answered in a cold voice.

"Phillip, you can't hate all Indians because of something that happened so long ago."

"They're all alike," he snapped. "Because of savages, all my mother had to remember my father by was a couple of medals and a glowing letter from his commanding officer."

Libbie reached over and touched his hand. "It was a very long time ago, Phillip. For your own sake, you need to put it in the past."

"Never. Not until I have my vengeance," he murmured. However, he brightened at her touch and smiled. "Let's speak of happier things, shall we? Mother has been making grand plans for our wedding."

She didn't want to think about the wedding, even though

it seemed inevitable. "Where shall we ride to? Isn't there any friend of yours we can visit—maybe some ranches I can see?"

Phillip hesitated, looking over at her as they rode. "I suppose we might go out to Mac McGuire's ranch; I've only seen him a couple of times since I arrived six months ago. We don't really mingle, of course; different social class, you know."

He was as big a snob as his mother. Libbie had only met that remote, frosty socialite twice and hadn't liked her any better the second time. Well, if she must marry him, maybe she and Phillip would build their own home some distance from Henrietta Van Harrington.

The morning was warm, the breeze gentle. She didn't care where they rode as long as she could drink in these magnificent views of desert, buttes, and distant, shadowy hills. "Who's Mac McGuire?"

"Mac was my father's striker—you know, sort of an officer's Man Friday. He loved this wild country and after Father was killed, Mac retired out here and started ranching."

"Oh?"

Phillip's handsome face scowled. "Too sympathetic to the Indians, I'd say, for an old cavalry man. And I'm a little annoyed with Mac—he's got my father's ivory-handled Colt and won't give it to me."

"Did you ask him?" She was intrigued.

"Yes, and you know what he told me? Said it was bad medicine for the son to carry a dead man's gun. Old coot's been hanging around Injuns too long; beginning to think like them. Sometime, I think I'll just sneak in and steal it; he doesn't see or hear very well, so it would be easy."

"Why, Phillip, you wouldn't!"

He looked annoyed. "Well, why not? It's mine by rights anyway, and I surely don't want his half-breed son inheriting my father's pistol. Imagine a white man marrying an Apache girl!''

She shrugged. "So what?"

"Ye gods, Elizabeth, I hope you're joking! Lots of white men take up with pretty Indian girls, but they don't *marry* them; it's unthinkable."

"Why?" Libbie asked.

"Oh, Elizabeth," he scolded, "don't be so naive. A soldier doesn't have to do the honorable thing by a red-skinned squaw; just give her a few beads or trinkets and she'll believe anything."

Libbie winced. His comments didn't make her like Phillip any better. They rode a moment in silence, and a thought crossed her mind. "So Mac McGuire is Cougar's father?"

Phillip nodded and frowned. "Most arrogant scout I've got; speaks English and Mac's taught him to read and write. That half-breed thinks he's good as any white man. If it weren't for the friendship between Mac and my father, I would have booted Cougar from my outfit months ago."

Cougar. In her mind, she saw the big, wide-shouldered rogue and remembered the way he had looked at her with banked passion in those startling blue eyes. There was a subtle challenge there and in the way his muscles gleamed in his naked back as he'd turned and sauntered away, as arrogant as the mountain lion for which he was named.

"It certainly fits him," she thought aloud.

"What?" Phillip's head jerked up.

Damn it, she was going to have to be more discreet. In a few months, she wouldn't even be allowed to think freely. She didn't like to lie, but she didn't want to incur Phillip's wrath, either. "Nothing. I—I was thinking of the little ring bearer we'll have in the wedding—a close friend's younger brother. His satin suit is so cute on him."

"Hmm." Phillip yawned.

Libbie had noted before that unless the conversation centered on him or his family, the young aristocrat wasn't terribly interested.

They rode a number of miles in silence; Libbie enjoying the ride and the wild landscape, even though the heat was building in the late morning.

"Elizabeth, my dear, you're awfully quiet. What is that silly little head of yours thinking?"

She gritted her teeth. "Not much, Phillip, just silly little girl thoughts."

He smiled, missing the sarcasm in her tone. "Just as I thought! You're very much like my mother and sisters after all; nothing in your mind but fashion and parties. Philadelphia is already talking of the grand wedding your guardian is planning."

And it will take the last cent of my inheritance to do that, Libbie thought. She watched the rocky trail ahead of them, wondering how shocked Phillip would be if he knew that what she had really been thinking was how it would feel to be pulled into the half-breed's embrace and kissed with all the heat she'd seen in that sensual mouth?

The images set off such an unexpected storm of feelings in her soul that she succumbed to a wild urge to gallop across the desolate country, feeling the warm wind against her face.

"Let's race!" Libbie said abruptly and urged her mare into a lope across the rocky landscape, leaving the surprised Phillip behind in a cloud of alkaline dust as she galloped down an arroyo and through the silver sagebrush ahead.

"Watch out, my dear. You'll get hurt!" She heard his bay gelding clattering across the rocks behind her.

But instead of stopping, she threw back her head, laughed, and rode harder still. Libbie didn't stop until she had reached a plateau where she reined in, her mare hot and blowing. "I beat you!" She wheeled the mare around to shout with triumph.

He galloped up to her and she saw fury in the blue eyes and the set of the square jaw. "Really, Elizabeth, it's not seemly to try to compete with a man."

She raised her chin in defiance. "Why not?"

"It just isn't, that's all!"

"Not good enough!" she flung over her shoulder as she turned back up the trail. "I'd hoped you'd be pleased that I can be an equal partner."

He rode along beside her, his mouth under the wispy mustache drawn into a grim line. "Elizabeth, I don't want an equal partner; I want a wife."

"It could be the same thing." She had angered and embarrassed him by beating him and she knew it.

"You *are* frightfully spoiled, my dear," he said and he bit off his words, looking straight ahead. "However, I suppose that's to be expected, being an only child and then an orphan. But of course that will have to change."

He was really upset. Her first reaction was to tell him what a spoilsport he was, but then she remembered her financial situation. Libbie forced herself to duck her head and assume a humble tone. "I'm sorry, Phillip. I'll try to be more circumspect in my behavior."

He didn't look quite so annoyed. "It's all right. You're very young, Elizabeth, and I know you just need a firm hand and some discipline."

His smug tone rankled her. Libbie forced herself to laugh. "Daddy used to say I was untamed and untamable."

"We'll see about that," Phillip snapped under his breath.

"What did you say?"

"Nothing, my dear."

However, she had heard him and it rankled her. "Phillip,

I'm a modern woman; I don't expect to live in submission like a slave. Lincoln freed them, remember?"

He didn't answer, but his jaw was set. "Let's not fuss, shall we?" His thin smile looked forced. "It's a nice day, despite this horrid countryside. Mac will certainly offer us some lemonade."

"All right." She decided she would not pout or argue that this was wonderful, beautiful country. "Look," she pointed, "there's an adobe house in the distance and a horse tied up at the hitching rail."

Phillip cursed under his breath as they rode closer, staring at the big paint stallion. "Cougar's here; I've a good mind to ride on."

Cougar. She felt her hands tremble on the reins and was surprised at her own reaction. She wasn't certain whether she looked forward to or dreaded seeing him again. "Nonsense!" she pouted. "I—I'm feeling a bit faint and you promised me a glass of lemonade, remember?"

"I shouldn't have taken you out in this August heat. I hope you aren't about to swoon." He looked anxious.

"Perhaps if I got in out of the sun a moment . . ."

"Yes, let's ride on over to the house. Perhaps Mac will have some smelling salts, or at least some cold water." They rode into the ranch yard and three spotted mongrels came out of the barn, barking and wagging their tails. The big half-breed and a short white man with graying hair and beard came out on the covered porch as the pair rode up.

"Hello there! Good to see ye," the older man yelled in a Scottish accent as they reined in.

Phillip nodded in return as he dismounted and came around to help Libbie down. "I've brought my fiancée by to meet you, Sergeant."

"I'm no longer that, young man, but I'm never too old to entertain a pretty miss!"

Libbie smiled as they approached the porch, trying to ignore the bare-chested scout, who leaned against a porch post watching with a stony expression. She noted he still wore the unusual turquoise, silver, and ebony gem necklace. "Delighted to meet you, Mr. McGuire. I've heard so much about you."

"Hey? What's that?" He craned his head. "Ye'll have to speak up, lass, me hearing's gettin' as bad as me eyes."

"Nothing important." Libbie smiled at the old man.

Mac motioned for them to come up on the porch out of the sun and peered at her with age-dimmed dark eyes. "Ah, lass, 'tis good of you to come. The whole post's been abuzz with news of your arrival, but I wasn't expecting a personal visit from such a feisty girl!"

Libbie laughed. "What makes you say that?"

The other man filled his pipe, his dark eyes twinkling. "Cougar told me about the last half of that horse race he just witnessed from my window."

"You're a good rider," Cougar said to her with grudging admiration.

Phillip's face flushed. "It's not seemly for a woman to gallop madly like that, trying to beat a man. My mother would have been shocked if she'd seen Libbie's behavior."

"That so?" Cougar said coolly. "*My* mother would have liked it."

Damn it, Libbie thought, *they seem likely to start throwing punches right here on the porch.* She looked helplessly at the old man.

Even Mac McGuire must feel the tension between the two men, for he said, "It's hot, lass. Won't you sit down and I'll get us some lemonade? I've made it with water from the well; good and cold."

"That would be wonderful," Libbie answered, but she couldn't take her gaze off Mac's big, virile son and the way he stared at her. Looking up suddenly, she realized the old man must have seen it, but he said nothing as he went inside. Then she realized that Phillip was watching them both and she looked away.

Cougar motioned toward some chairs made of unpeeled branches. "Your face is flushed, miss. You'd better sit down."

"I'll look out for the lady's welfare." Phillip's voice was as cold as his azure eyes.

She was embarrassed about his bad manners. "I can look out for myself, thank you both."

Phillip said to the other, "I told her ladies didn't have any business out in this heat, but she insisted."

Cougar looked her up and down with a searching gaze as they took a chair while he continued to lean against a porch post. "Somehow, I suspect the lady will do as she pleases."

"Not after we're married!" Phillip declared.

Libbie started to make a remark, then remembered she must not push Phillip too far. She lowered her gaze in the awkward silence that followed.

Her fiancé cleared his throat. "Cougar, have you found some new scouts for our outfit?"

The Apache nodded, but Libbie was only too aware that he continued to watch her as he fingered his necklace. "A bunch of White Mountain Apaches. They're young and green, but eager to learn."

Phillip frowned. "You think they'll do?"

Cougar shrugged. "Like I said, Skippy, Deadshot, Dandy Jim, and the others are very young and new to the service."

"What funny names for them," Libbie smiled at the scout, but he didn't smile back.

"White men's names," Cougar explained. "They don't try to learn our Apache names. Anyway, it will take a while for them to get used to taking orders and build some loyalty to the army."

Phillip took off his hat and mopped his face and mustache. "Discipline's probably what they need; a few strokes across the back with a quirt would teach them."

The half-breed frowned. "A little kindness and some extra food for their families would do a lot more."

Libbie moved to defuse the tension. "Why does the army need more scouts?"

Phillip said, "Because a bunch of our regular Apache scouts are off in New Mexico Territory right now on the trail of Nana and his war party that crossed the Rio Grande a few days ago."

"Is the army expecting trouble here?" she asked.

"The army goes looking for trouble," Cougar retorted. "Haven't you heard the drums echoing through the hills? If the whites would just be fair to the Apache—"

"Judging from the letters he wrote home, my father tried to be fair with the Apache," the lieutenant snapped, "and they murdered him. An iron hand is the only way to deal with savages!"

Cougar started to say something, but seemed to reconsider. She watched that square jawline as he took a deep breath and gritted his teeth.

She had a sudden feeling he was about to pull back his fist and hit the officer. Both these men were tall and broad-shouldered, but the half-breed was younger by maybe three or four years and he had more muscle. She had no doubt which one would win the fight.

"Uh," she gulped, "Cougar, why don't you see how your father is doing with the lemonade?"

Instead, Cougar went down the steps, every line of his big body hostile. "I've got duties back at the fort; tell Mac I had to go." He swung up on the paint stallion and rode off.

"Ye gods!" Phillip cursed under his breath. "Damned

arrogant savage. He didn't even wait until I dismissed him."

Libbie watched the scout gallop away. He sat like he was part of the horse, a study in grace and speed. His back muscles rippled as he rode, and he gripped the stallion with strong thighs. There was something about the way he mastered the horse that excited something deep within her. She took out a handkerchief without thinking and fanned herself. "If that Apache's so hard to deal with, why don't you fire him?"

"Because he's the best scout we've got," Phillip admitted grudgingly. "He knows every redskin in the area and every rock and canyon for hundreds of miles. Funny though— he hadn't been so hard to deal with until today."

It had started with her arrival, Libbie realized with abrupt clarity.

Mac came out just then with a tray of tumblers and stood watching the dust disappearing over the horizon.

"Your son said he had business at the fort," Libbie said.

"Hey?"

Libbie repeated her words.

"Oh?" He looked at her a long moment, a question in his dark eyes. "Here"—he set down the tray—"a pretty lass like you deserves better than this poor place has to offer. Help yourself, Lieutenant."

"She'll get a lovely party tonight," Phillip said as he took a glass. "Are you coming, Mac?"

"Of course; biggest happening this year." The old Scotsman handed Libbie a glass and she gulped it gratefully, savoring the tart, cold taste.

"Delicious!" she declared with her warmest smile.

"So what do you think of the Territory?" Mac sat down in his chair and sipped his drink, then reached into his shirt pocket for a worn old pipe. "Do ye mind if I smoke, lass?"

"Not at all," Libbie answered. "I love this country; all wild and free like the mustangs and the Indians."

Mac leaned closer to catch her words, then sighed and lit his pipe. "But not for long, I'm afraid; settlers pouring in, the army trying to corral the Apaches. Eventually there'll be no refuge for either mustangs or Apaches except maybe in the mountains of Mexico across the border." He nodded toward the south.

"I can hardly wait to get back to Philadelphia," Phillip grumbled, "I came out here on a fool's errand, I guess."

Mac puffed his pipe and frowned. "Young man, I was your father's best friend, even if I was only his striker. Bill liked this country and these people."

"So they killed him for it!" Phillip's face flushed with anger.

There was a tense moment in which Libbie bit her lip, embarrassed for Phillip's bad manners.

The old man hesitated and sighed. "Forget the past, Lieutenant. My advice to you is to request a transfer far away from here and never come back."

Phillip stood up. "You were his best friend, and yet you tell me to forget it without attempting to take revenge? I don't even really know the details of how he died."

Mac combed his fingers through his beard and looked away. "I—I wasn't there when it happened. You got an official letter from his commander, didn't ye?"

Phillip nodded. "Yes, but it was pretty vague; he just told me what a hero Father was, dying in a skirmish with the savages. I always meant to ask him for more information, but he died several years ago, you know."

"I know." Mac didn't say anything else for a long moment. He smoked and stared into space. Or perhaps the old man hadn't heard all Phillip's words.

Mystified, Libbie enjoyed the rich scent of his pipe and waited.

"William Van Harrington was one of the finest men I ever knew," Mac said finally, looking up, "a man of principle with a great sense of honor; that should be enough for you. Be proud of him and let his spirit rest in peace."

"I will have my revenge," Phillip promised, "that's what I came out here for."

"Even if you start an Indian war?"

"Then I can kill even more of the red devils." The muscles in his square jaw clinched.

Damn Phillip for his rudeness to this nice old man. In the awkward silence, Libbie cleared her throat. "Well, now, Mr. McGuire, aren't you going to show me around the place?"

Mac nodded, seemingly relieved to change the subject. "Aye, lass, would ye like to see the house?"

"I certainly would." Libbie stood up.

Phillip took a deep breath and seemed to regain control. "Did I see some new horses out in the corral as we rode up?"

"Mustangs; broke 'em myself, me and Cougar," the old Scotsman said in his thick brogue. "The army looking to buy new mounts?"

"Yes. I'd like to see them. Maybe I could make recommendations."

Mac smiled. "Lieutenant, you head on down to the corral. I'll show the young lady the house."

Phillip started off the porch and Mac opened the screen door for Libbie. "I'm afraid it's pretty messy; I live alone, except for Cougar dropping by when he's not gone on a trip with the soldiers."

"Your wife has been dead a long time?" She followed the old man inside, speaking loudly so he'd hear.

"Aye, since Cougar's birth; died in my arms; didn't seem to want to live anymore. She's buried on a hill not far from here, where I can go up to put flowers on her grave."

Strange. For most women, a loving husband and a new son should have given her everything in the world to live for. Libbie wanted to ask questions, but decided it wasn't polite. Mac's sad expression spoke volumes. "You must have loved her very much."

"I did." He paused, his dark eyes wistful. "She was so spirited and so very beautiful; you remind me of her a little, young lady, except she had dark hair and eyes."

Libbie's gaze grew accustomed to the cool dimness of the room. It was a masculine place: leather chairs, a big stone fireplace, rifles hanging over the mantel and deer antlers on the wall, Navaho rugs on the wood floor. There was a big gun cabinet against one wall full of weapons, and shelves and shelves full of books, worn with wear. The room smelled of wood smoke, leather and tobacco. It looked comfortable, the kind of place rugged men called home. "I like it," she said.

"It's not fancy," Mac apologized. "I'm sure you're used to much finer and grander houses."

She shrugged. "Such things aren't very important to me. I'm getting awfully tired of civilization, too. That's why you stay out here, isn't it?"

He nodded. "Aye, lass. The West gets in some folks' blood. Some can't stand it; some of us can never leave it."

She picked up a small, faded daguerreotype off a table. In it, a much younger uniformed Mac McGuire smiled back at her standing next to a tall, broad-shouldered officer who was handsome, square-jawed and sported a fine mustache over a warm smile. "Major Van Harrington?"

Mac nodded.

"His son looks like him."

"What?" Mac looked startled.

She raised her voice. "I said Phillip looks like him."

"Oh, yes, of course." He took the photo from her hand,

staring at it a long moment, then sighed and put it down. "Such a tragedy."

"But you don't hate the Apache as Phillip does?"

The old Scotsman shook his head. "I understand them. Never expected young Van Harrington to show up out here; he belongs back East. This country is too hostile for him."

"He says he never really knew his father; maybe he's searching for answers."

Mac McGuire stared at the picture. "Sometimes a man should let well enough alone."

She waited for him to continue, but he only stared at the picture. Mystified, she studied the weathered old fellow. "You served with the major a long time?"

The other nodded and seemed lost in memories. "Aye, lass, why I remember a time . . ." Abruptly, he shrugged and smiled. "You're being polite, I know, listening to an old, deaf, half-blind soldier who rambles on and bores a young lady."

"I'm not bored," Libbie protested. "I'd like to hear more about Arizona and your experiences."

"Ah, no. Ye'd best be getting back so you can get ready for the ball."

They went out on the porch.

"I like you, Mac McGuire," Libbie said. "I'll save you a dance tonight."

He looked at her, a twinkle of admiration in his eyes. "I like you, too. You're frank and feisty—refreshingly different for a woman."

She felt herself blush to the roots of her red hair. "Will—will your son be coming to the dance?"

"Cougar?" Mac cleared his throat and looked embarrassed. "Miss, you don't understand how things work out here."

"Then enlighten me."

"The soldiers consider Cougar a savage; he won't be welcome at the party."

"But he's half white," Libbie protested.

"Actually, he's more than half white; his mother had a little French blood, courtesy of some passing trapper a couple of generations back. However, he's spent much of his life among his mother's people, so the army thinks of him as Apache."

"Oh." Libbie started down off the porch.

Behind her, Mac McGuire asked, "You're leaving tomorrow?"

"Yes, going back to school in Boston."

He came down the steps, and together they walked toward the corral. "And you'll be married back there?"

"Yes, next spring, as soon as I graduate. Phillip hopes to be promoted and transferred back East by then."

"In case we don't get another chance to talk, I want to wish you happiness and good luck, young lady."

She smiled at him. "Thank you."

"Hey, you two!" Phillip came out of the barn and waved. "Mac, you do have some fine horses; I'll talk to the quartermaster about them."

Mac nodded.

"Are you about ready to go, Elizabeth, dear? You look very tired."

She was tired; tired of Phillip's fussing over her. "All right."

They walked back to the house and mounted up.

"Good-bye, Mr. McGuire. See you tonight."

"Good-bye, miss." The old man nodded and said to Phillip, "She's a beauty, Lieutenant. Bill would have been pleased. May you have many children."

Phillip smirked. "I'll make sure of that!"

Libbie flushed at the mental image his words evoked.

She closed her eyes and bit her lip as they rode out. "Phillip, please. You embarrassed me."

"And that half-breed undressing you with his eyes didn't?" He sounded jealous.

"I don't know what you're talking about." She kept her gaze on the trail ahead.

"I don't know how you could have missed it; old Mac was certainly aware of it. Just looking at Cougar's face told me what he'd like to do to you. I had a good mind to thrash him soundly!"

"I don't think I'd try that if I were you," she murmured under her breath. The half-breed could probably kill the prissy officer with his bare hands.

"What?"

"Nothing," she snapped. "Damn it, I'm tired, Phillip. Let's go back to the fort so I can get a bath and some rest before the ball tonight."

"I'll overlook both your peevishness and your unladylike language," he said smugly. "After all, you're just a woman and it's dreadfully hot in this horrid place, not fit for civilized people at all."

Libbie gritted her teeth to hold back a rejoinder. She'd better learn to be as meek and mild as most women; Phillip expected it. On the other hand, she'd met Mrs. Van Harrington, and Phillip's mother seemed anything but meek and mild. A cold and stern dowager, Henrietta Van Harrington didn't seem like a match for the officer in the old daguerreotype at all. Well, maybe the lady had been a beauty in her day and maybe she'd been sweet and vulnerable before her husband was killed. Libbie looked about for some safe topic of conversation. "Tell me about Shashké."

"Who?"

"The Apache girl who brought our breakfast this morning. Did you know she's named for the month in which she was born, January?"

"Never was interested enough to inquire." Phillip snorted. "She's just an Injun wench who works as a maid around the fort. I've never given her a second thought; I don't know why you should."

"She seemed to take a special dislike to me."

"Oh?" He looked at Libbie a long moment. "What did she say?"

"Nothing much; it was her attitude, that's all."

"I suppose as far as an Injun wench is concerned, you've got everything and she resents it. Life is hard if you're not white in this country."

Libbie remembered the girl's faded dress. "I thought I'd give her a little gift or something when I leave."

Phillip yawned. "That would be a nice gesture; whatever you think, my dear, although the greedy little wench would probably rather have money to give her man for booze so he won't beat her."

"Beat her?"

"Don't be so shocked." He glanced sideways at her as they rode, evidently enjoying Libbie's dismay. "I hear it's commonplace among the savages."

She couldn't believe Cougar would beat anyone small and helpless, but what did she really know about him? She wanted to ask more, but decided it wasn't wise.

No, she couldn't imagine Cougar beating a woman, but she could imagine him making passionate love to one. With sudden clarity, in her mind, Libbie saw the big, virile savage wrapped in the sultry Shashké's arms while they made love together on the grass in the moonlight . . .

Abruptly, Libbie faced the truth; she wished for a love like that of her own, and she wasn't likely to find it with Phillip!

Chapter Three

Mac McGuire smoked his pipe and watched the pair ride away from his ranch. He stood there until they were out of sight; then, with a sigh, he started up the nearby hill to where his beloved was buried. He was sitting there on a rock by her grave pulling a stray weed from the flowers he so carefully tended, when he heard a step and turned.

Cougar came out from behind some scrubby trees, leading the paint stallion. "If I'd been an enemy, you'd be dead."

Mac nodded. "Aye, me hearing is gettin' as bad as me eyes, and that's a fact. Good thing I'm on good terms with all the tribes."

"They think of you as one of them."

Mac didn't look at him; his mind was busy with the conflict between the two younger men. "I thought ye had business at the fort?"

"I just wanted to get away from the lieutenant before I hit him."

"Cougar, listen to me," Mac ordered. "Grit your teeth and let him be. He'll be gone next spring."

"What did you think of the girl?"

Mac looked at him sharply. "Don't ye be thinkin' of her at all."

"She's leaving tomorrow." Cougar fingered his necklace absently, staring into the distance.

Mac sighed. He had once felt that same hopelessness over an unattainable woman. There was no way to make the younger man feel any better; he could only try to talk some sense into him. "Forget about that red-haired lass. She's high society, the same as him."

"You think I don't know that?" Cougar's voice was as anguished as his eyes.

"So don't be thinkin' about how her lips might taste or how soft her skin might feel under your hands."

"I can't help it; she was made to pleasure a man, give him sons."

Mac frowned and lit his pipe, shook out the match. He had never felt as much empathy for Cougar as he did now. "She was made to pleasure a wealthy *white* man."

"She's too much woman for the lieutenant; he'll never tame her."

"That's not your concern." Mac stood up and blew a cloud of fragrant smoke. "Stop what you're thinkin'. You know it's no good; red and white can never find happiness together." He looked down at the grave, remembering while his dark eyes misted.

Cougar reached out and put his hand on Mac's stooped shoulder very gently. "My head tells me you are right, but my heart—"

"Listen to your head, boy," Mac scolded. "There are some obstacles too great for love to overcome. Your own past should have taught you that."

"But not if it's a very great love," Cougar protested.

"You're dreaming, lad." Mac shrugged his hand off and turned to walk down the hill. "Just stay away from her; she'll bring you nothing but trouble."

"I've already got trouble," Cougar grumbled as he led his horse and fell in alongside Mac.

"That Shashké again?" Mac glanced sideways at him.

He nodded. "She's cheating."

"Damned silly little fool! Doesn't she know what the Apache do to unfaithful wives?"

"Sure she knows, but she's too vain and foolish to care."

"That's bad." Mac shook his head as they walked back to the house. "She's got such a pretty face."

Cougar shrugged. "If she doesn't stop, she won't have it long."

"Have you tried talking to her?"

"Yes, but she's like a bitch in heat; one man isn't enough for her."

Mac smiled as he remembered another, more delicate Apache beauty so many years ago. "Unlike Shashké your mother was a one-man woman. I'm sorry you never got to know her."

"You break Apache taboos in speaking of the dead," Cougar reminded him uneasily. "To do so calls them back from the Happy Place where the dead go."

"Sorry, sometimes I still think like a white man and as such, she's often on my mind. I wish she could have lived to see you grown up."

Almost absently, Cougar's hand went to the necklace he wore. "I wish it, too."

They walked the rest of the way in silence, Mac remembering the dark beauty he had loved so very much, but it hadn't been enough. He didn't want the same tragedy to happen to her son. "Maybe I won't go to the dance tonight. Maybe I'll stay here and we'll drink some *tiswin* and smoke and tell of hunts and battles; all the good old stories of the Apache. Bring along your friend, Cholla.''

"Cholla's scouting for the troops in New Mexico," Cougar reminded him. "Don't know when they'll be back. Old Nana and his warriors have crossed the border and are setting that Territory ablaze.''

"Then you and I will drink, and stare into the fire and listen to the drums.''

"No." Cougar shook his head and gently put his big hand on the other's stooped shoulder. "Go to the dance; you'll enjoy it. Maybe I'll ride along.''

Mac frowned. "You'd be better off if you didn't. The lieutenant was well aware of the way you were looking at his lady.''

"A woman like that is wasted on him," he said again.

"She must see something in him or she wouldn't be marrying him.''

"Funny, she doesn't look at him like she loves him.''

There was no reasoning with the boy. Mac turned and looked back up the hill, remembering that the heart never listened to reason. "That's not for you to decide. The lieutenant has wealth and a fine family.''

"You think I'm not aware of that?" Cougar snapped as he walked up on the porch, took out his makin's, and rolled a cigarette.

A long way off in the hills, a drum began a slow rhythm. The wind picked the sound up and carried it across many miles of hills and desert to all the Apache people.

Cougar listened a moment, then said, *"Noch-ay-del-Klinne* is telling the people that if they dance the dance and do the ceremonies, the white people will disappear.''

"I know. The Apaches tell me things they don't tell other whites.''

"That's because, in your heart, you are one of them. You loved an Apache girl; *really* loved her.''

Mac smiled, seemingly lost in a past memory. "And always will," he whispered.

They both turned to listen to the drums echoing faintly in the distance.

Mac said, "The drums have been talking all summer. If the soldiers will just be wise and patient and let that medicine man alone, the warriors will lose interest when nothing he predicts comes true."

Cougar took out a small metal match safe and struck a match, cupping his big hands around the flame as he lit the cigarette. "Have you ever known white soldiers to do the wise thing?"

"Mostly not." Mac frowned.

"The Holy Man says he will bring the dead chiefs I must not name back to life; the Apache need only believe that it is possible."

Mac watched him smoke, loving him more than any man could love a son. "Mangas Coloradas Victorio, and Cochise," he thought aloud, then peered at the younger man. "Do you believe that?"

Cougar smoked and slowly shook his head. "Some things Apache I believe; some things I am too white to believe. It is hell to be caught between two worlds."

"For that, I am truly sorry. When a man loves a woman, *really* loves her, nothing else matters. He doesn't think about how it will be for a mixed-blood son in a white world."

"Yet I'm beginning to see how a man could want a woman that badly." Cougar knocked the ash off his cigarette.

Mac winced. The sooner that flame-haired girl was away from the fort, the better. He didn't want Cougar to do something so rash, he would end up in trouble with the army.

"In the olden days," Cougar mused, "when a warrior

saw a woman he wanted, sometimes he just fought for her and took her.''

"These are not the olden days," Mac reminded him.

Cougar gave no sign that he had heard. He smoked and they both listened to the echoing drums carrying messages across many miles from the north.

"The soldiers may do something foolish," Mac said.

"They do that often." Cougar tossed his cigarette away.

"I meant I just hope they don't start a new Indian war."

"You'd be safe enough. The Apache like and respect you; you speak their language."

"I'm not thinking about myself, lad." Mac shook his head. "I was thinking of all the women and children, white and red, who'll suffer if there's an outbreak."

"Maybe you can talk to the colonel at the dance tonight; urge him not to do anything rash."

Mac nodded. "Aye, I'll at least try; my conscience won't let me do anything else."

"And I'll ride along." Cougar's rugged face was set and stubborn.

There was no use arguing with Cougar when he had made up his mind. "All right, but stay away from the lieutenant's woman."

"I know my place." His voice was as melancholy as his blue eyes.

"Good. I love you too much, lad, to let you repeat that tragedy."

Cougar didn't answer, staring out at the rough terrain while the drums echoed faintly through the hills.

He's too much like his mother to listen, Mac thought with frustration, *and Libbie Winters can only bring him trouble and heartache. Thank God she'll be gone tomorrow!*

* * *

That evening, Libbie dressed for the party with mounting excitement.

"My stars!" Mrs. Everett said with a smile, and mopped her wet brow. "You're certainly in a much better mood! You and the lieutenant had a lovely ride?"

"Ride? Oh, well, of course." Libbie looked through her jewelry case for her fine gold earrings. It unnerved her to realize she hadn't been thinking of Phillip at all.

"Wonderful!" Her guardian wheezed as she walked around the room, shaking the wrinkles from the pale pink sateen ball gown Libbie would wear tonight. "Thank goodness, then, you had the good sense to remember the wisdom of making a good marriage?"

Libbie merely murmured something noncommittal and tried to focus on Phillip, but her mind remembered instead the big half-breed scout and the way he had looked at her while they were all on Mac McGuire's porch. She could tell from his expression that he was mentally taking her clothes off very slowly and deliberately. She had been both shocked and fascinated by the virile maleness of him.

You're playing with fire, Libbie, she warned herself as she began to brush her hair until it shone. *Nobody knows what I'm thinking so what's the harm? And after all, I'll be leaving tomorrow and I'll never see him again.*

"Here, you need help putting your hair up." Mrs. Everett seemed in a rare good mood now that things were going according to her well-arranged plans. "Let me send for that sulky girl who was here this morning."

"I think we can manage," Libbie answered. "She probably has too many duties already." She didn't want to have to deal with the sullen Shashké. She dabbed a few drops of a faint lilac scent on her wrists and behind her ears. "Who all do you suppose will be there?"

"Well, everybody," Mrs. Everett gushed as she began to put up Libbie's hair.

"Everybody?"

"Yes, the officers and their ladies, and all the respectable white people," the other said as she put Libbie's hair up in elaborate curls on top of her head. "The Indians and the Mexicans won't be invited, of course."

Libbie's spirits fell a little. Damn. Well, what had she expected? Of course a half-breed Apache scout wouldn't be invited. Toying with Cougar was like playing with the wild animal he was named for—dangerous and forbidden. He couldn't be turned into a lady's obedient pet. She must keep her mind on Phillip and the fine marriage she would be making.

"You look beautiful!" Mrs. Everett put her hands on her plump hips and surveyed her handiwork. "Now all you need is for me to lace your corset a little tighter."

"My waist is small enough," Libbie protested with a pout.

"No, it isn't!" The other scolded as she reached for the laces. "A gentleman likes a woman to have a waist so small, he can touch his fingertips around it."

"He'd have to have awfully big hands," Libbie protested, but grabbed onto a bedpost so Mrs. Everett could lace her small waist even tighter. In her mind, she saw a pair of big, dark hands and imagined them encircling her bare waist.

"Lieutenant Van Harrington has a gentleman's hands; small and fine," the other woman remarked as she pulled the laces tighter still.

"Damn, stop it! I can hardly breathe!" Libbie protested.

"Tsk! Tsk! Will you never behave and talk like a lady? Now pinch your cheeks to put some color into them."

Libbie couldn't breathe and her tiny slippers hurt her feet. Mrs. Everett straightened Libbie's bustle and surveyed her handiwork with satisfaction. "You look beautiful; every man there tonight will want you."

But the man who interested Libbie would not even attend, Libbie thought with resignation and tried to focus her thoughts on the dapper young officer to whom she was engaged. It didn't work.

Finally they were ready—plump Mrs. Everett in no-nonsense dark gray faille, and Libbie in her pink sateen with ribbons and tiny flowers down the bodice and matching ones in her red hair. Libbie put on the fine gold earrings.

Mrs. Everett looked her over and nodded. "You'll turn a few heads tonight, I'll wager, and the lieutenant will want you more than ever. We can stop worrying about money."

"I never worry about it," Libbie snapped.

"I guess not!" her guardian scolded, "but I worry enough for both of us. Bargain with your beauty and youth, my dear, while you've got it to bargain with."

"I feel like a prize filly at an auction," Libbie complained.

"Now don't be acting spoiled and sulky on me," Mrs. Everett warned. "You be so charming, the young heir will be trying to move that wedding up to Christmas."

"With the kind of elaborate wedding you and Phillip's mother have planned, it'll take 'til next summer to make all the arrangements."

"What do you expect for the biggest society event Philadelphia has seen in years?" the other challenged. "It must be done right, with plenty of expensive pomp and ceremony. We don't dare let important people know you're almost penniless."

"Why not?" Libbie snapped. "You think it will matter to Phillip?"

"With your beauty, maybe not, but"—and the lady lowered her voice conspiratorially—"we wouldn't want him to suspect you might be marrying for money."

"Which I am. It isn't honest." The whole facade sickened Libbie.

"Honest!" Her guardian sneered and fanned herself. "Only the young think about honor and true love. Think instead about losing our present lifestyle, both of us working as shopgirls or governesses."

A loveless marriage terrified Libbie more than poverty, but there was no point in arguing with the older woman. "I'll leave all the details in your capable hands, Mrs. Everett; I've still got a whole year of school ahead of me."

Mollified, Mrs. Everett reached for her wrap, and about then there was a rap on the door. When Libbie opened it, Phillip was outside with a buggy.

"My!" he said, and his blue eyes widened with pleasure as he stared at Libbie, "don't you look splendid!"

"Doesn't she, though?" Mrs. Everett beamed at him. "I'll wager there'll be other young officers tonight who'll try to monopolize her time."

"Well, I don't intend to let them!" Phillip offered Libbie his arm and they went outside to the buggy, Mrs. Everett bringing up the rear. "It's not far, really, but I thought you wouldn't want to get dust on your dress."

They got in and drove the few hundred yards to the meeting hall. The Arizona night was hot with a thousand fireflies and the scent of flowering cactus. From the distant hills echoed a rhythmic beat.

Libbie cocked her head as they drove. "What is that sound?"

Phillip cursed under his breath. "Ye gods! They're at it again!" To Libbie, he said, "I thought I told you we're having a little trouble with some Injun medicine man over near Fort Apache. He's got this fool idea that he can bring dead warriors back to life and run all the whites out of his land with his magic. I'm one of those who've been urging the colonel to get tough and abide no nonsense. Might as well nip this in the bud."

Libbie's green eyes widened. "Is there liable to be trouble?"

He gave her his most charming smile and ran one finger over his pale mustache. "If there is, my dear, you can just wager I'll be in the thick of it and kill me a few savages!"

Mrs. Everett made a sound of approval. "Good for you, Lieutenant! Some medals across your chest would look mighty fine at the wedding."

Phillip reached over and put one of his delicate hands over Libbie's. "They would, wouldn't they?"

His hand felt moist and as dainty as a woman's, Libbie thought, but she couldn't pull away. "I don't think killing people should be treated so lightly."

"I'm a soldier, Elizabeth, that's what I do." Phillip's tone was condescending and lofty.

"Oh, really? How many battles have you seen so far, Phillip?"

She heard Mrs. Everett gasp. "Libbie! That wasn't polite! You must forgive her, Lieutenant; her parents spoiled her terribly."

Her parents. Their tragic deaths in that railroad incident had left her so lonely. But never had she felt so alone in the world as she did at this moment, riding along with these two people who now controlled her life.

However, Phillip shrugged and tightened his grip on Libbie's hand so hard it hurt, but she was determined not to cry out.

He said, "That's what I find so appealing about our Elizabeth—her youth and innocence. She simply needs a husband's strong guidance so she will behave like the proper lady she is."

Mrs. Everett breathed a sigh of relief. "I'm so glad you understand, young man."

Libbie jerked her hand from Phillip's and flexed it. It ached from his crushing her fingers together. She wanted to lash out at him, but remembered again how financially dependent she and her governess were on this union and bit back her words.

"I know your parents spoiled you, Elizabeth," Phillip said with an indulgent smile, "and they could afford to. Everyone back East knows the Winters were one of the wealthiest families in California before their unfortunate deaths."

But not anymore, Libbie thought, and then she wondered—would that make any difference to Phillip if he knew? Why should it? The Van Harringtons had plenty of money of their own.

The drums still echoed faintly through the hills as Phillip tied the buggy to the hitching post and came around to help the ladies out. Instead of offering Libbie his hand, he put both hands on her trim waist and lifted her down. His fingers felt hot and moist through the pale pink sateen and Libbie shuddered at the thought of them on her bare skin.

"Are you cold, my dear?"

"What?" She jerked up, disconcerted, her mind still on the distasteful images.

Mrs. Everett fluttered nervously, obviously upset by Libbie's inattention. "She's just so high-strung and delicate, like most ladies, you know."

"Of course." He was staring down at Libbie in the moonlight, puzzlement in his cold blue eyes. "Shall we go in, my dear?"

Libbie nodded, mentally scolding herself that she must remember to act like a ninny and giggle while hanging on Phillip's every word. Somehow, such silliness went against her nature.

They entered the crowded hall. It was hot inside, although all the windows were open. A large crowd of military men and their ladies milled about, the women fanning themselves delicately. There was a long table to one side with a punch bowl and refreshments, and at the front of the ribbon-festooned hall, a small band, composed of soldiers in blue, were tuning up their instruments. Now they broke into a lively, if slightly off-key rendition of "Camptown Races."

Phillip looked around. "I must introduce you to the commanding officer," he said above the music. Libbie let him lead her through the dancing crowd toward where the senior officers had formed a receiving line.

"Miss Winters, allow me to introduce the commander of Fort Grant."

The gray-bearded officer bowed deeply as Libbie extended her hand. "Charmed, Miss Winters. We've all heard so much about you."

Libbie smiled. "It was good of you to have a party in my honor. I'm very pleased."

"There's not much to entertain us out here," the senior officer said. "Any diversion is a welcome one, and a beauty like you is more than a diversion."

"You flatter me!" Libbie smiled, fluttered her eyelashes, and fanned herself daintily.

Phillip's chest puffed with pride and he took her down the line, introducing her to the other officers and their ladies. All commented on her beauty and the ladies were eager for news from the outside and what fashions the ships were bringing in to San Francisco.

However, most of the officers were unaccompanied. She commented on that as she and Phillip turned toward the dance floor.

Phillip shrugged. "Can't expect most white women to live in this hellish place. We'd all like to leave as soon as possible and give Arizona back to the Apaches and the rattlesnakes."

Mac McGuire joined them about that time. "Well, not all of us," he said by rejoinder, "some of us like it here."

"Mr. McGuire!" Libbie took his hand warmly. "I'm so glad you decided to come!"

He grinned and combed his fingers through his beard. "Well, as I remember, lass, you promised me a dance later."

"I certainly did." She looked around, not daring to ask. "Did—did you come alone?"

"Ah, lass, I did. I'm a widower, ye know."

The big half-breed hadn't accompanied his father. She tried to cover up her disappointment. "I—I thought you might have a lady friend."

Mac shook his head and his face saddened. "I only loved one woman, lass, and she'd not have been welcome in this fine company anyway."

Libbie's curiosity was piqued, but seeing Phillip's disapproving look, she kept silent. She liked the rough frontiersman, but she did not dare ask more about his personal life and his son without raising Phillip's ire.

The lively pace of the music changed as the band began a slow waltz.

"Ah," Phillip smiled, "if you'll excuse us, Mr. McGuire, I'd like to dance with my fiancée."

"Of course."

Phillip swept Libbie into his arms and they whirled out onto the floor. Phillip had a firm hand on her waist, his eyes trying to look directly into hers, but she looked away. "It's even better than I expected, Elizabeth," he said triumphantly. "Everyone here is looking at you and commenting on your beauty. You look like a vision in that pink dress and fiery hair. Those gold earrings must have cost a pretty penny."

She only nodded and smiled at the compliment, thinking that most rich men wouldn't be concerned with the value of a lady's jewelry. Libbie felt like a prize filly being trotted out for a horse show, but she tried to behave as was expected of her, nodding to ladies on the sidelines who were talking among themselves. They returned her nod with warm smiles. The officers looked at her wistfully as Phillip danced her around the floor.

They danced past the refreshment table about the time Shashké came through the kitchen door carrying a tray of dainty cakes. The Apache girl had an apron tied around her waist, and she scowled at Libbie as she carried her tray over to the table and began to place the tiny cakes on a platter.

Libbie saw the longing and the anger in the girl's dark eyes and felt sorry for her. "She'd give anything to be out here on this dance floor in a pretty dress rather than just working in the kitchen."

Phillip shrugged. "Ye gods, Elizabeth, whatever can you be thinking? It's a matter of birth, my dear; she's just an Apache wench. Everyone would be scandalized if someone like that actually attended the party."

Libbie watched, mystified at the girl's angry glare. Shashké put out her tray of cakes and went back into the kitchen.

As Phillip whirled her about, a movement outside an open window caught Libbie's eye. Cougar stood outside watching her. Libbie purposely looked away and whirled Phillip around so he wouldn't notice the scout.

"Elizabeth, dear." Phillip frowned. "I'm the man, remember? I'm supposed to lead."

She felt herself flush and she looked up at him with her most becoming pout. "I'm sorry, Phillip, I was just enjoying myself so much, I forgot."

He actually grinned at her. "It may take a little while for me to unspoil you, but I'm sure you are going to make me a wonderful, dutiful wife."

The thought of the meek, mild creature Phillip expected her to be almost made her groan aloud. Past Phillip's shoulder, she could see Cougar still standing outside the window staring at her. The frank, appraising way he looked at her made her feel warm and dizzy. If he didn't get away from that window and any of the soldiers noticed him, there might be trouble!

Cougar watched the white beauty as she danced with the prissy lieutenant. She had seen him, too. Her green eyes had widened and her expression had changed. Then she had whirled away so that Phillip did not see Cougar. Or maybe the move had been merely accidental.

He would be in trouble with the soldiers if they caught him out here spying on the dancers, but he couldn't bring himself to turn and walk away.

He was mesmerized by the red-haired vixen in a shiny dress the color of a new sunrise, with darker pink flowers and ribbons in that fiery hair. Golden earrings caught the lamplight as she whirled, but it was her hair that hypnotized him. If she belonged to him, he would give her a more suitable name: *Blaze*. Yes, that name fit her. Cougar gritted his teeth as the lieutenant pulled her even closer. It was mostly the possessive, smug way the lieutenant held the girl against his body that annoyed Cougar.

Even though he did not know how to dance the white man's dances, he closed his eyes and imagined himself out on the floor, whirling the girl about, holding her slender body close to his big one. He would dance her out a side door and into the darkness. Once outside, he would hold her so close, she could scarcely breathe while his mouth kissed her as he had yearned to do since the first moment he saw her stepping down from that stagecoach. From that moment on, he had known there could never be another woman for him.

He had a vision of carrying her out into the hills where he could make love to her the way she needed to be loved—totally, intently, and without interruption. He would take the pins from her hair so he could tangle his fingers in those fiery silken locks while he kissed her lips and eyes. Then, very slowly, he would unbutton that lacy pink dress so he could reach those full, creamy breasts and caress them the way she had never been caressed. And after he had made love to her, gently and completely, he would take her in a possessive embrace and hold her and protect her until the dawn. His manhood came up hard and insistent at the thought of holding the white girl in his arms.

He heard a step behind him and whirled to find Shashké standing there. "I saw you through the window," she purred. "Why do you look at her with such wanting when you have me here and now?"

Before he could protest, the sultry girl slipped her arms around his neck, pressed her full breasts against his naked chest, and kissed him. Oh, it was so tempting! Cougar needed a woman badly; he had not lain with one in a long time, and then it had been only a drunken Mexican whore in a border cantina.

For a moment, he weakened; then he took a deep breath and pulled away from Shashké's hot mouth. He glanced toward the window. Libbie Winters had seen it all!

Angry now, he pulled Shashké away from the window and into the darkness. "You little fool, anyone inside could have seen that if they'd been looking."

She threw her head back and laughed. "Who would care among the white people? You think that girl cares?"

"Keep her out of this!"

She looked up at him, beautiful and passionate, the scarlet cactus bloom in her dark hair scenting the night around them. "I want you; I've always wanted you; you know that." Her voice was low and husky with need as she slipped her arms around his neck again and rubbed herself against him.

He could feel every inch of her ripe body through the faded cotton dress even as her mouth sought his again, and she slipped her tongue between his lips.

Oh, it would be so easy to take what she offered. Shashké was hot and passionate; his for the taking with no obligations. Everything in him urged him to pick her up and carry her into the darkness where he could get his hands and his mouth on her eager, willing body.

"No, Shashké. I have a warrior's honor."

She ignored him, sliding enticingly down his body until she was on her knees, pressing her big breasts against his thighs. He could feel every tempting inch of her as her hands went to his breechcloth.

He wavered in his resolve and gasped aloud as her hot, wet mouth tasted him.

For a split second he trembled, fighting an overpowering urge to tangle his big hands in her hair and put his manhood deep in the sweetness of her lips, letting her please him until he was sated.

He wavered a long moment, wanting to let her take his seed in a long kiss, then steeled himself and caught her black hair in one big hand, pulling her away with a curse. "You slut! Have you no shame? You are a married woman, yet everyone at the fort knows you sleep with a white man."

She stood up, laughing easily, not at all offended. "So what? I can easily please more than one man."

Cougar leaned against a tree, trembling with anger and need. "Then you should go back to the village and please your husband."

"Him?" Her lips curled into a sneer. "Beaver Skin is

old; old enough to be my father, and there's no sap left in him for a young woman's lusts."

"He was once a great warrior who rode with Victorio," Cougar reminded her.

"So what?" She shrugged, her dark eyes defiant. "I got little say in choosing him, and I'm tired of living like a reservation squaw in a wickiup made of branches with me wearing a threadbare dress and no shoes. I'm pretty; I intend to use that to better my lot."

Cougar snorted in disgust. "You won't be pretty long if your husband catches you with another man. You know what the Apache custom is for cheating wives."

"I'm not worried." Shashké yawned. "My stupid husband trusts me. Besides, my white lover is going to buy me pretty dresses and take me far away from here."

Cougar shook his head. "You are the one who is stupid. The white man will not marry you; he will use you for his pleasure and then throw you away when he tires of you."

"I'm already tired of him," she admitted, playing with the scarlet cactus flower in her ebony hair. "He is not much of a lover and his manhood is small compared to yours. Pleasure me, Cougar; no one need ever know."

However, he drew himself up proudly and shook his head. "I respect the old warrior who is your husband and I value my own honor."

"But you do not mind lusting for the fire-haired girl who is promised to the lieutenant!" Her voice rose in anger. "Listen to me, Cougar! You will never lie between her thighs and put your son in her belly, so bring that hunger to me. Should you get me with child, I might convince my old husband it is his and he would be pleased."

"You play a dangerous game, Shashké," he warned with calm dignity, "take care and remember old Apache customs. You are vain about your pretty face; protect it with faithfulness.''

"Oh, you honorable fool!" She raged as she turned and ran back inside the kitchen.

With a sigh, Cougar returned to watching the dancers through the window, and this time he was careful to stand so that those inside could not see him. Libbie Winters still whirled about the dance floor, a vision in a cloud-pink dress of some filmy soft fabric, with her red hair catching the lamplight.

Absently, he fingered the necklace he wore that had been a token of love from his Apache mother to his white father. If it had belonged to his mother when she died, it would have had to be buried with her or destroyed, as was the custom of her people. However, now it was his. *Apache Tears*. What a tragic legend.

His mind returned to the fire-haired girl. Shashké was right. He was a fool because there was nothing Cougar wanted so much at this moment as to stride inside, pick up the arrogant white girl, throw her across his shoulder, and carry her off into the desert night, where he could possess her completely; body and soul. And pity the white man who tried to stop him!

Chapter Four

Libbie sneaked another glance at the window as she and Phillip waltzed. She had seen Shashké embrace Cougar, kiss him, and then Phillip whirled her away. When she turned her head again toward the window, she could no longer see the pair. Evidently they had faded into the night to make love.

Well, so what? That wasn't her business. Yet she found herself craning her neck, hoping to see something and absently stepped on Phillip's foot.

"Elizabeth, what is wrong?" he snapped and led her off the floor. "You seem totally distracted."

Oh, damn. "I—I'm just a little breathless," she answered, knowing she must not anger him, "shall we have some punch?"

They headed for the refreshment table, where officers and local ranchers and shopkeepers stood about sipping something stronger than punch and discussing the state of the country.

"They say the President is still alive after that assassination attempt," one said.

"Maybe he'll make it then," another replied. "I hope they hang that anarchist!"

"Speaking of hanging," a third remarked, "maybe it's time we hung a few redskins! Tiffany, you're the Indian agent, what do you make of it?"

Mr. Tiffany cleared his throat importantly and twirled his mustache, obviously pleased to be the center of attention. "I keep warning we need more troops. Can't expect much from savages."

A rancher put in, "Have you heard those drums?"

"They're driving us all loco," a stout civilian complained. "Just what the devil do you suppose those heathens are up to out there on Cibecue Creek?"

Mac McGuire had just walked up. He nodded to Libbie and then said, "It won't amount to much of anything if the army will just leave them alone. When *Noch-ay-del-Klinne* doesn't live up to his promises, the Apaches will lose faith in him and things will settle back down. I've told the colonel as much."

Phillip bristled as he handed Libbie a cup of punch. "Well, I for one am tired of doing nothing! I think we should go out there, bring that crazy medicine man in and lock him up! Force! That's the only thing these savages understand!"

There was a murmur of agreement around the circle of men.

Libbie blurted, "I think what Mr. McGuire says makes sense."

All the men turned and stared at her, evidently unused to women who spoke their minds. Phillip reddened and frowned. She had embarrassed him by speaking out, she could see; only Mac McGuire smiled at her.

Phillip cleared his throat in the sudden silence. "You

gentlemen must forgive Miss Winters. She's only a woman, after all, and doesn't understand about such things."

"Phillip, don't treat me like an idiot!" she snapped, setting her punch cup on the table with a bang. She'd done it now; most of the men were staring at her aghast, but she was too annoyed to care. Phillip's face had turned a dull, ugly scarlet.

"Anyway," one of the others said to cover the awkward silence, "Colonel Carr up at Fort Apache will probably be the one to go on that campaign; I'm glad it's not me."

"They may need help," another grumbled, "which means some of us might get transferred up there. In this August heat, it'll be a miserable trip."

Libbie asked, "How far is Cibecue from Fort Apache?"

Mac considered a moment. "Maybe forty or fifty miles to the northwest."

A bewhiskered settler chewed his lip and considered. "Will the army trust its Apache scouts in this fight?"

Phillip frowned again. "I suppose we'll have to. We've got a bunch of fairly new, young ones. Maybe they'll do all right; or at least as good as Injuns get."

The other men guffawed and Mac frowned, obviously straining to catch all the words. "That isn't fair; the scouts have always been loyal."

A thin, arrogant lieutenant looked down his nose at Mac. "Of course you would say that, with a half-breed son—"

"I hope ye're not about to insult him, Lieutenant Dudly," Mac warned; he seemed to be gritting his teeth.

"Here, here," said the minister, gesturing to everyone to lower their voices, "this is no place to start a fight, gentlemen; there's ladies present."

"Don't mind me," Libbie said before she thought, "it's just getting interesting."

She heard some gasps and knew she should have stifled her comment.

Mac took a deep breath, as if calming himself. "For myself, gentlemen, I'm going to discourage the army from attempting to arrest the Apache holy man. There's no point in deliberately starting an Indian war."

The music struck up again, the band playing a newly popular tune: "My bonnie lies over the ocean; my bonnie lies over the sea . . ."

Mac put his punch cup on the table and bowed gallantly to Libbie. "Miss Winters, may I have the honor?"

"Of course!"

They swung out onto the floor and Libbie breathed a sigh of relief. She remembered to raise her voice so he wouldn't have to strain to hear her. "I just couldn't keep quiet. Thank you for rescuing me!"

Mac smiled. "Thank you for giving me the excuse."

"My fiancé is furious; his eyes look like blue ice."

Mac glanced over at the simmering lieutenant and grinned. "Aye, Cougar was right about you."

She didn't want to ask, but she couldn't help herself. "What—what did he say?"

Mac laughed. "He said ye were too much woman for the lieutenant; he'd never be able to tame you. I'd say Cougar judged ye pretty well!"

She didn't know whether to feel complimented or insulted. "I'm not sure I want to be tamed! At any rate, Phillip is from a fine family and everyone says it will be a very good match."

"Yes, of course, lass." His tone was overly polite, but he didn't sound as if he meant it.

The doubts rose up deep within her all over again. She didn't seem to have any options, so she must not think about changing her mind. "So," she mused as they danced, "you seem to know the Apache better than anyone in the Territory. Is there going to be trouble?"

Mac frowned and blinked his faded old eyes in the lamplight. "Miss Winters, I'm afraid some of our young officers are bored and would like to win some medals."

She thought about Phillip. "Is there any real danger?"

"We're about to bring the Apache wars to a close here in the Territory, even though Jack Tiffany is as crooked an Indian agent as ever drew breath—he and his accomplices back east. But trouble could easily break out again if the army does something rash and foolish. The Apaches' loyalty is with their own people."

"Does that include Cougar?"

His dark eyes questioned her interest in his son, but he said only, "Cougar is a son of both worlds, but I think he would be loyal to the army, as long as his mother's people are treated fairly."

As they danced, she looked toward the window again, but there was no one there. She wanted to ask Mac McGuire a million questions about his half-breed son and Arizona Territory, but about that time the music ended.

"Thank you so much, lass." Mac smiled. "It's been a long time since I've held a pretty girl in my arms."

Libbie blushed, and in her mind she saw the image of a young Scotsman making love to an Apache girl and producing the big half-breed son.

They started back toward the refreshment table, where the young officers still gathered. Shashké came out of the kitchen just then and refilled the punch bowl, glaring all the time at Libbie.

"I just don't know," Libbie said, thinking aloud.

"What?" Mac asked, straining with one hand to his ear.

"That Apache girl." Libbie shook her head. "I haven't done anything to her, yet she acts like she hates me."

Mac seemed to be choosing his words carefully. "Envy," he said finally in his thick brogue. "You're white and have everything as far as she's concerned, and she doesn't have much to look forward to."

Libbie remembered the girl embracing Cougar. "I wouldn't say that."

"What?" Mac asked.

"Nothing."

As the pair reached Phillip's side, Mrs. Everett waddled over, fanning herself. She looked like a great, gray whale, Libbie thought.

Mrs. Everett said, "I'm tired. I think I'll leave early and go back to our room."

"Oh," Libbie said, "if we're to leave—"

"My stars! Not you, my dear." Her plump guardian held up a restraining hand. "You stay and have a good time. I'll just get someone to walk me back, and you two young people can come later."

In a flash, Libbie realized the older woman was deliberately plotting to get her ward alone with Phillip. Then it would be up to Libbie to enthrall the officer, make amends for her rash sassiness. Libbie realized all this, and yet she didn't want to be alone with the lieutenant.

"Madam," Mac said politely to Mrs. Everett, "I'll be happy to escort you back to your room before I join some of my old cronies for another drink."

"Come along then," the plump matron said with frowning disdain. Evidently, she felt herself a cut above the old man socially.

Everyone said their good-byes and Mrs. Everett left, accompanied by the rancher.

Libbie danced with several more young officers and then the band began to play, "Good Night, Ladies."

Phillip took her in his arms and held her close as they danced this final dance. "It's been a wonderful evening," he whispered against her ear.

Libbie stiffened at his touch, then remembered that, after all, he had the right to be affectionate toward her. "Yes, it has, hasn't it?"

The dance broke up. Libbie said her thanks to the ladies and senior officers, and then she and Phillip went outside into the hot night.

Phillip said, "Let's walk back. It isn't far and we can talk."

"All right." She looked around, wondering where Cougar was. Probably having a drink somewhere with Mac McGuire and his old cronies. No, more likely lying under a bush making love again to the sultry Apache beauty. Around them, couples were leaving in their buggies or walking back to their quarters. Now that the music had ended, she could hear the drums again, carried faintly on the summer breeze.

"Ye gods!" Phillip cursed under his breath. "Damned savages!" Then he apologized for swearing before a lady. "I can't help it, dear; I'm concerned about your safety tomorrow. I wonder if I should ask for a military escort for your stage?"

"Oh, Phillip, don't you think you're overreacting?"

"When you've heard as many tales as I have about how bloodthirsty these savages are in battle, you wouldn't think so. Remember, this is their country and they're as much at home in it as tarantulas and rattlesnakes and just as deadly. Even their name, *Apache*, given to them by the Zuni tribe, means 'enemy.' "

She was only interested in one Apache, but she must not mention his name. "Hmm," she said.

"Elizabeth, your behavior tonight was abominable." Phillip's tone was cold. "I thought young ladies from Miss Priddy's Academy had better manners."

She resisted the urge to slap him, but of course, she must make amends so this marriage would go through. She ducked her head as if abjectly chastened. "I didn't mean to upset you and embarrass you in front of your friends."

He took her hand as they walked, evidently mollified. "I know you've been terribly spoiled and are a little head-strong, but a wife must never contradict her husband."

"Even if he's wrong?" Libbie said under her breath.

"What?"

"Nothing. Of course you are right, Phillip. I must remember you are *always* right!"

"Of course." He sniffed with satisfaction, evidently missing the sarcasm of her tone. "It isn't wise in this Territory to come to the defense of Injuns; sneaky, untrustworthy devils that they are."

"Mac McGuire seemed more worried about what the army was liable to do than the Apache," Libbie said.

"Well, what do you expect from an old Injun-lover like Mac?" Phillip snorted in derision as they walked back toward her quarters. "He's still talking about what happened here ten years ago when this place was known as Camp Grant."

"So what did happen?" She glanced over at him as they walked through the moonlight.

He shrugged. "Nothing much. Some troops and settlers from Tucson lured a bunch of Apaches here with food and liquor, then slaughtered them."

"Women and children, too?"

"Yes, but so what? After all, they were Apaches."

"Why, Phillip, that's terrible!"

"I'd expect a woman to think that," Phillip said with arrogant amusement, "but not an old soldier like Mac. As close friends as he and my father were, I find it incredible Mac could be so forgiving of his killers!"

"It's been a long time, Phillip," Libbie suggested, "maybe it's time to forget the past."

"I made a vow to my mother," Phillip said, "that I would avenge my father's death."

Libbie didn't say anything. She had found Mrs. Van

Harrington difficult to like—a cold, proud, snowy-haired dowager who seemed overly possessive of her only son. Her house was a shrine to William Van Harrington's memory; portraits of him hung everywhere, and the widow still dressed in black after all these years. Libbie hoped she wouldn't be expected to move into the Van Harringtons' mansion where Phillip's mother ruled with an iron hand over her old-maid sisters and a timid group of servants.

Undesirable option that that would be, it still wasn't as bad as being out on the street, homeless and penniless. Mrs. Everett was right; Libbie had no alternatives. That didn't make Libbie any happier about the wedding.

She would not think of that now. It was a lovely night; the breeze carried the scent of blooming flowers, and night birds called. From a distant hill, a coyote wailed. In this exotic, sultry atmosphere, her thoughts inevitably turned to that most primitive of passions. In her mind, Libbie imagined Cougar and Shashké together under the stars. She took several deep breaths, attempting to stifle her rising passion as she pictured herself in his arms instead.

"Elizabeth, are you all right? The way you're breathing, perhaps I've overtired you walking from the dance."

"No, I—I'm fine." She was embarrassed at her forbidden thoughts.

The moon went behind drifting clouds and Phillip paused, almost to Libbie's door, and pulled her under a vine-covered arbor.

"Let's talk a moment here where no one can see us," he said.

"All right." She sighed and let him take both her hands in his. She knew she should flutter her eyelashes and flirt with him, but she just didn't care that much. Phillip bent his head and kissed the backs of her hands. His wispy mustache tickled as it brushed against her knuckles. "My dear."

She managed to stifle laughter at her thoughts about the mustache. "Yes, Phillip?"

He looked down at her, his blue eyes bright and earnest in his handsome face. "Mother was right; you are the perfect choice for me."

His mother again. "Oh?"

"Elizabeth, I'm crazy to possess you! I can hardly think of anything else but our wedding night!" He kissed her on the mouth then. Libbie stiffened in protest, then remembered and let him kiss her. It was as uninteresting as she feared it would be, his mouth prim and dry, his mustache tickling her skin.

She must think of the positive things, she thought as his lips moved feverishly across her face. Yet she instinctively tried to pull away from him. He was breathing hard and pressing his body against hers. She could feel his rigid maleness through her pink dress. "Phillip, please! This is highly improper—"

"I can't help myself. I want you, Elizabeth, even if you are spoiled and too headstrong! I think of nothing else but marrying you and the sons you will give me!" Phillip tightened his grip, molding her against his tall figure as he kissed her again. His passions became more heated and his hands roamed up and down her back while he breathed harder.

Libbie started to protest again, but Phillip's mouth covered hers as he tried to force his tongue between her lips. His hand came up and tore at her bodice.

She struggled to pull her face away. "Phillip! Please!"

"Let me, Elizabeth, please let me!" He was panting hard, trying to rip her bodice open, leaving a trail of wet kisses across her face. "We're engaged. It's only a matter of time before we do it anyway."

"Phillip, no—!" But he blocked her protests with his

mouth, tearing at her bosom while dragging her toward a grassy area in the secluded shadows beside the building.

She managed to get her mouth free. "Phillip, please, what will people think?" Libbie struggled with him, but he was a tall, big man. He was going to take her whether she consented or not.

"Ye gods, Elizabeth, we're engaged! In only a matter of months, I can take you any time I want!"

The thought horrified her. "But we should wait until we're wed—"

"You'll not put me off!" he whispered in a fever against her mouth while he pulled her toward the shadows. "By God, I'll have you now!"

She dared not scream for help; it would be too humiliating. Instead, she struggled with him, her common sense telling her she should submit. In only a few months, he'd have the legal right to her body anyway. Still she didn't want Phillip's kisses or his touch and she tried to push him away, but he panted out loud, his sweaty hands reaching inside her bodice to paw her breasts.

A full moon came out from behind a cloud, and a sudden shadow fell across them both.

They jerked apart, Phillip cursing. "What the—?"

"Excuse me, sir," Cougar said, "I was wondering if you had any orders for me before I go to my quarters?"

Phillip glared at the big scout, then seemed to gain control of himself as he straightened his uniform.

Libbie took a deep sigh of relief, rearranging her mussed bodice. "Good night," she said, then turned and fled the few yards to her quarters. Once inside, she shut the door and carefully locked it. Mrs. Everett was sound asleep; Libbie could hear her snoring. She leaned against the door and tried to hear the conversation outside, but to no avail. Thank God Cougar had happened along and interrupted Phillip's ardor. She frowned as she realized the scout had probably been lying in those nearby bushes with the eager Shashké and had heard the disagreement.

No doubt tomorrow Phillip would be contrite and apologize for his ungentlemanly conduct and want her even more. She would be wed by the time she was eighteen without ever having really tasted life or been in control of her own destiny. With a sigh of resignation, Libbie slipped into a lightweight cotton nightdress, crawled into bed, and lay there sleepless.

Outside, Phillip glared up at the big half-breed. "What the hell do you mean, sneaking up on us like that?"

The scout's face was as expressionless as stone. "I'm sorry, sir. I was in the neighborhood and thought I'd better check with you."

Phillip considered the possibility. Maybe it was an accident that Cougar had walked up just as Phillip was about to overwhelm the cold beauty. If the savage had waited just another ten minutes, Phillip would have taken her virginity, and the girl would have felt obligated to go through with this marriage. Phillip had a strong feeling that Elizabeth Winters was having second thoughts. Even though she was only seventeen, she was headstrong enough to change her mind.

After tonight, Phillip wanted Elizabeth with a lust he had never dreamed possible. Well, he would have her and he would break her spirit until she was a meek and obedient wife. He dared not let her change her mind or Mother would be terribly displeased with her only son. Henrietta Van Harrington desperately wanted this marriage to take place.

"Sir, did you hear me?" Cougar asked.

"Damn it, yes, I heard you!" Phillip came back to the present and how much he disliked the half-breed. It occurred to him suddenly that if there were an expedition out to capture that Apache medicine man at Cibecue Creek, maybe in the confusion, a stray shot might kill Cougar and no one need ever know. Phillip was an excellent shot. His plan made him smile. "Let's just both call it a night."

"All right, Lieutenant." The scout saluted and they both turned, walking in different directions.

Shashké put away the last of the dishes in the big kitchen and blew out the lamps with a sigh as she took off her apron. Such a lot of work for this party honoring the elegant Miss Winters!

Her lip curled with a jealous sneer as she left the hall and went out the back door. The post was deserted, everyone long gone to bed except some distant sentries. The night wind carried the rhythmic beat of drums. She paused and brushed back her ebony hair, fingering the red cactus blossom behind her ear and thinking about the men in her life. She dreaded going back to her wickiup and her old husband, but of course, she must. Perhaps he would be drunk on *tiswin* and asleep so that he wouldn't try to make love to her when she crawled between the blankets.

She grimaced at the thought as she started away from the building. Old Beaver Skin wanted a son, but most of the time, he couldn't perform the act, leaving his young, hot-blooded wife frustrated and needing a man. She smiled with longing as she thought of Cougar. If she could ever persuade him to make love to her, no doubt the virile half-breed would give her a son on the very first try, and the child would look enough Apache to fool her husband.

The problem with Cougar was that he had an old-fashioned warrior's sense of honor. She smiled to herself as she walked. Tonight she'd managed to touch him and rub against him. After he'd thought about that a couple of hours, maybe he'd need a woman badly enough that he'd come looking for her. The thought of mating with him made her take a deep breath, and a warmth spread through her ripe body.

A tall, broad-shouldered man stepped out of the bushes in front of her. *Cougar?* Her heart beat with anticipation.

The shadowy silhouette said, "I know I shouldn't, but I've been thinking about you."

Her spirits fell as she recognized the voice. "It took a while to clean up after the party. The way you looked at the white girl, I didn't think you would want me."

"She's just a girl; you're a woman," he murmured and began to unbutton her faded dress.

"And I know how to please a man." Shashké caught his hand and guided it to her full breast; then she reached up to kiss him.

He squeezed her breast. "You're trouble; nothing but trouble."

"But such pleasant trouble, no?" she whispered against his lips.

"Yes, you slut!" He jerked her hard against him, kissing her again, thrusting his tongue deep into her mouth, his hand ripping at her bodice. "I told myself I must not see you again, but I can't help myself!"

"You won't be sorry." Pleased with his confession of need, she led him to the shadow of the bushes and they lay down.

"Suppose your husband wakes and finds you not there?"

She threw back her head and laughed, exposing her throat to his feverish, seeking mouth. "Let me worry about him; he is old and stupid." She opened her bodice for his eager hands and let her thighs fall apart.

"I need you!" he whispered urgently again as he positioned her. "I'm going to take you more than once tonight!"

"I need you as many times as you can do it." She pulled him down on her and raised her hips to meet his thrusts as he came into her. She knew the white girl had aroused this need in him, but Shashké was the one who could fill that need.

"Tell me you love me," she pleaded as he thrust into her.

He didn't answer, his mouth on her breast, his breath hot against her dark skin as he rode her hard.

"You'll make me your woman so I can leave my old husband?"

"Shut up!" he ordered, breathing hard as he rode her. "Ye gods, shut up and let me finish!"

Maybe he might love her a little, Shashké thought, but she had a sinking feeling that she was only satisfying the lust that the beautiful white girl had created in Lieutenant Phillip Van Harrington.

Libbie lay sleepless and restive in her bed as the hours passed. Through the open window of the hot night, she could hear the faint beat of drums carried on the desert wind.

She was still shaky from her unexpected ordeal, knowing she had come very close to being raped. *Well, no, when it's done by your fiancé,* she thought ruefully, *it would probably only be considered compromising a young lady. Had Phillip sensed that she was having second thoughts and was trying to put her in a position where she would be obligated to marry him? The*

*raw lust in his blue eyes had scared her. If Cougar hadn't happened
to come along . . .*

Libbie twisted restlessly in her bed, listening to Mrs.
Everett snore. What had the half-breed been doing out
and in that area? Then she remembered the scene she'd
witnessed through the window. Of course he'd been out
in the nearby bushes coupling with Shashké and was on
his way back to his quarters. She remembered the way the
two had looked in their embrace and imagined what it
would feel like to go into the arms of a man who knew
how to please a woman.

She felt her face burn. Damn! What on earth was she
thinking about? She was having primitive, uncivilized
yearnings about a man who belonged to another woman.
How shameful! Libbie felt a sheen of perspiration on her
body. Good heavens, this room was hot!

Quietly she got up, slipped on a light wrap over her sheer
cotton nightdress, and opened the door. The breeze felt
cool and inviting. Libbie hesitated a moment. There was
no one around; not a soul stirred nor a dog barked. The
whole post must be asleep. Maybe she would just go stand
outside in the cool air a moment and then go back to bed;
no one need ever know. Mrs. Everett would be shocked,
but then, Mrs. Everett was snoring away like a beached
whale; oblivious to everything.

Libbie took a deep breath, surprised at her own daring,
and stepped outside, closing the door behind her. It was
quiet out here except for the distant beat of drums. The
primitive sound seemed to blend into her heartbeat.

Abruptly, a tall, wide-shouldered figure loomed up out
of the shadows. Startled, Libbie opened her mouth to
scream, but the figure clasped one big hand over her
mouth.

Oh, dear God! Phillip had come back to take her,
whether she liked it or not.

Libbie tried to break free, but he jerked her up against his powerful body, fighting to keep his hand over her mouth. "Stop it! I won't hurt you!"

She froze in surprise and blinked up at him. It was Cougar!

Chapter Five

Libbie looked up at Cougar, her heart pounding with shock.

"Will you please not scream?" he whispered.

She nodded, and very slowly he took his hand from her mouth.

"How dare you!" She slapped him hard.

His head snapped back and his expression turned as dark as thunder. He rubbed his jaw. "If you were a man, I'd kill you for that."

She realized suddenly that she was standing outdoors in a very flimsy nightdress and wrap. Her nipples must be visible to him, judging by the way he was staring at her. Self-consciously, she crossed her arms over her breasts. "What are you doing lurking out here?"

He smiled and leaned against a post. "I wasn't lurking; I was guarding your door."

"Guarding my door! You have to be the most arrogant man I've ever met. I've got hundreds of soldiers to guard me."

He smiled faintly. "That's who I was guarding you from; I half expected the lieutenant to come back in the middle of the night and sneak into your quarters."

She was almost speechless. "Lieutenant Van Harrington is a perfect gentleman."

"Uh-huh." In the moonlight, she could see the intense emotion of his blue eyes. "He looked like a perfect gentleman when he was about to rape you a couple of hours ago."

Libbie felt her face flame. "Phillip is my fiancé. He— he might have gotten a little carried away."

Cougar regarded her with thinly veiled amusement. "You're spirited, but you're naively innocent, Miss Winters. If I hadn't stepped out of those bushes, he'd have had you flat on your back like some two-bit whore."

"Damn you! I don't have to listen to this!" She whirled, grabbing for the doorknob, but Cougar reached out and put his hand on the doorjamb next to her, blocking her entry.

"I didn't mean to offend you," he said softly, "I just wanted to warn you about the lieutenant."

She should go in; everything in her told her that being here was highly improper and her reputation would be ruined should anyone see her. She should push his hand off the door and run inside. Yet the magnetism of this man was enough to hold her. In the moonlight, she could see the necklace gleaming around his brawny neck and the sinewy muscles in the brown arm that blocked her escape. Very slowly, she turned around to face him, but he didn't step back.

He was close enough that she could feel the masculine heat from his half-naked body. "You're wasted on the gutless lieutenant," he murmured.

"My choice is hardly your concern."

"I know that." His big hand reached out and brushed

a dainty tendril of red hair from her face. His fingertips brushed across her forehead, his touch was so gentle and so tender that it surprised her.

His bare chest was close enough that she could touch him if she reached out, but of course she did not. In the moonlight, she noted the scars here and there on his virile frame and the way the moonlight shone on the striking necklace he wore. The tension felt like lightning crackling across a hot desert sky.

Looking up at him, she studied the curve of his sensual mouth. She must not look at that mouth and think of it covering hers. "Where—where is your woman?"

He looked mystified. "I have no woman; I have not chosen yet."

"But isn't Shashké—?"

He threw back his head and laughed, exposing white teeth. "When I choose a woman, it will be one who is faithful, not one who exchanges her favors for money and gifts."

He still had her entry blocked with one big arm, standing so close that it made Libbie tremble. *He had no woman,* Libbie thought. *Why should she feel such relief?*

"Are you cold?" He seemed amused by her discomfort.

"No." What should she do? She could scream for help and bring everyone running—at the cost of her reputation.

"Are you afraid?" His voice lowered to a soft, soothing whisper.

"No!" she lied, looking up at him defiantly.

"Don't ever be afraid of me," he said, "I would kill the man who hurt you; this I promise."

She stared deep into his eyes and knew he meant it. "You arrogant rogue! What gives you the right to be my protector?"

"It is a decision I have made," he answered, his voice firm, "but of course, I can only protect you in my own country." He stepped back with a sigh. "You will leave tomorrow, Blaze?"

"My name is not Blaze; it's Libbie."

"What does that name mean?"

"I don't know," she snapped, thinking how ludicrous it was to be standing out here all but naked, discussing her name. "I was named for my grandmother."

He reached out to touch her fiery hair. "Blaze would be a more fitting name for you." She didn't pull away from his hand, and he ran his fingers through her tangled curls.

"Phillip would kill you for that," she said, jerking her head away from his hand.

"Are you going to tell him?"

"I might."

"I think not. A fire-haired hellion with a name like Blaze would not go whining to a cowardly lieutenant."

She must not admit even to herself that she had liked the way his fingers felt in her hair. She must not; she must not. She let her arms fall helplessly to her sides. "I—I must go in now. It's late and I leave in the morning."

"I'm not stopping you." He kept stroking her hair.

"Are you going to stay outside my door all night?"

He nodded. "I told you I was going to protect you." He frowned and reached up to finger the massive necklace he wore. "You may be in danger if the trouble with the Apache grows worse; a war party might attack stage routes."

The thought shook her. "Should I ask for an army escort? Phillip has offered—"

"The Apache are as silent as rattlesnakes when they strike, and like the rattler or the tarantula, this is their country. Many an army troop has been wiped out by warriors they never saw."

"Then what should I do?"

He looked down at her a long moment, his blue eyes troubled and uncertain in his dark face. Then slowly, his hands reached up and took the necklace from around his neck. "This necklace was given by my mother to my white father. Do you know the legend of the Apache Tears?"

She shook her head. "No, but I've admired your necklace."

"Once, a long time ago, a large number of enemies attacked my people."

"Were they soldiers or other Indians?" She didn't want to ask, but she was as fascinated by the mysterious black stones as she was the Apache.

"No one seems to know for sure. Our warriors were outnumbered, but they fought bravely until the enemy backed them to a top of a cliff. Our women watched from the valley. Finally, wounded and at a loss for weapons, our warriors leaped from the cliff to their deaths rather than surrender or give the enemy the satisfaction of killing them."

"And the women?" Libbie looked up at him, fascinated by the legend.

"The Apache women wept great tears for their fallen heroes and where the tears touched the ground, they were turned to black stones. They have been known ever since as Apache Tears."

"What a beautiful, tragic story," Libbie whispered.

For a long moment, Cougar did not answer, staring down at the magnificent silver, turquoise, and black gemstone necklace in his big hand. "My mother wept enough tears to fulfill the legend," he said. "In this country, white and red cannot love without causing tragedy, and no one knows that better than I." Very slowly, he reached out and put the necklace around Libbie's neck, but he didn't move his hands away. The silver was still warm from his body, as warm as his fingers on her throat.

"What are you doing? I can't accept this!" She couldn't retreat any farther. Libbie reached up to touch the black,

tear-shaped stones, and her fingertips touched his, causing
her to take a deep, ragged breath.

Now it was his hard hands that trembled as his fingers
moved to cup her bare shoulders. "I give this to you, Blaze,
for the same reason that my mother gave it to my father;
it will protect you."

She wondered when Mac had given it to their son, but
she didn't ask. Too aware of the feel of his hands on her
shoulders, she glanced down at the necklace. Its silver
gleamed in the moonlight against the curve of her breasts
above the sheer nightdress. "Protect me from what?"

She looked up at him and felt his big hands tighten on
her shoulders. For a second, she had the oddest sensation
that he was about to sweep her into his arms, hold her
against his scarred, naked chest, and kiss her with a passion
that she could only envision in her dreams.

"If your coach is waylaid by any Apache, Blaze, show
them this necklace. As long as you wear this, no Apache
will harm you."

"Why?"

He looked down at her, confident in his masculinity.
"All will recognize it, and none will dare to touch a woman
Cougar protects."

How very arrogant of him! He was looking down at her
possessively. If she gave him the slightest sign of surrender,
she had a feeling he was going to swing her up in his arms
and carry her away. His nearness was creating such a heady
sensation that she wondered if her legs might give way
under her. She took a deep breath and shook her head
defiantly to break the spell. "I—it's your dearest treasure,
I can't—"

"Yes, you can." He caught her hand as she reached up
to take the necklace off. "Trouble may break out at any
time, and it's a long way back to Willcox and your train.
Wear it, knowing I want you safe."

"You have a lot of nerve making yourself my protector. Phillip would be furious!" She must go in before he jerked her into his embrace and she couldn't stop him from doing what her heart hungered for him to do. With a confused and angry cry, she tore out of his grasp, turned blindly, groping for the doorknob, and went in. Slamming the door behind her, she shot the bolt. She leaned against the door, gulping for air and watching her guardian anxiously, but Mrs. Everett snored on.

Libbie was shaking as she climbed into her own bed and lay there looking at the ceiling. She reached up to touch the necklace and remembered the feel of Cougar's strong hands as he placed it around her throat, his fingertips touching the swell of her breasts. She had felt a terrible need for his hands to go lower still in the sheer nightdress and cup her breasts and caress them.

Was she out of her mind? She had a sudden impulse to jerk the necklace off and throw it against a wall. No, better yet, she would open the door and throw it in his face if he were still outside. Breathing hard, she sat up in bed and considered that. The necklace was as warm as his hands about her throat. *The thing was a mark of possession,* she thought, *like a dog collar . . . or a wedding ring.*

Phillip. Oh, God, what would Phillip think if he saw the necklace? How could she explain how she'd come by it? It would mean trouble for Cougar, she knew.

A shadow crossed the window, a shadow that she recognized from the long hair, the width of the powerful shoulders, and the square-jawed silhouette. Cougar was keeping his word about staying near her door all night. It both touched and infuriated her that he should take on the role of her protector when she had a fiancé. She ought to get up, open the door, and throw the necklace in his arrogant face.

However, as she started to rise, she reconsidered. Somehow, she was half-afraid that if she opened that door, neither of them would be in control of what might happen next. So she lay there, sleepless and angry, for a long time before she dropped off into a troubled sleep.

In her twisted dream, her name was Blaze and she wore nothing but the necklace, her long red hair blowing in the wind. She rode naked on a galloping mustang and a big, dark warrior came riding in pursuit. Just as he was about to pull her from her pinto, Libbie awakened, gasping for air.

Outside the window, a pale pink dawn kissed the distant hills while in the next bed, Mrs. Everett snored blissfully away. Libbie glanced down, remembering last night, and reaching up to touch the necklace, she took it off. It was a thing of beauty. *Apache Tears.* She remembered the legend of great love that time and death could not conquer.

What was she to do with the thing? She must not let anyone see it; it would be too difficult to explain how she had come by it. Quickly, she got up and hid it under some clothing in her valise. She would decide what to do with it once she got away from the fort. After all, in a couple of hours, she would be on her way back to the train and would never see the half-breed again. She was startled at how troubled that knowledge made her feel.

She poured some water in the bowl, washed, then dressed in a no-nonsense peacock-blue bouclé traveling costume. She buttoned the fitted jacket and put up her hair. Finally, she awakened Mrs. Everett so the two could breakfast and get ready.

Later, while they were packing, there was a knock at the door.

Mrs. Everett was out of sorts and grumpy. "Now who could that be?" she asked as she waddled to the door to open it.

Libbie held her breath. She half expected it to be Cougar, wanting his necklace returned.

"Oh, it's you; about time you got here," Mrs. Everett snapped.

Shashké entered, wearing an old cotton dress and a fresh scarlet cactus bloom in her dark hair. She looked at Libbie with cold eyes. "I was sent to help you pack."

Mrs. Everett frowned at her and motioned. "Well, don't just stand there, girl, get busy!"

The plump lady returned to her own luggage as Shashké picked up Libbie's valise and began to fold long lace petticoats and put them inside.

"I can do that," Libbie said and rushed to take it from her hand. "I think Mrs. Everett needs your help more than I do."

"I certainly do!" grumbled the stout lady. "You're not much of a maid; you'd never hold a job back East."

The Apache girl scowled and opened her mouth as if to reply, then shrugged and began to help Mrs. Everett.

Libbie held her breath, watching the girl. Had Shashké seen the necklace when she opened the valise? She had made no sign if she had. Libbie drew a great sigh of relief and continued packing the bag. Then she hesitated. As Cougar had said, it was a long way back to Willcox, where they would catch their train. The necklace would do her no good if she weren't wearing it should their stagecoach be attacked by a raiding party. Worse than that, suppose someone like Mrs. Everett or a maid found the necklace during their train trip? There'd be hell to pay. What to do?

"Here, girl," her guardian snapped at Shashké. "Help me get these trunks packed so the soldiers can load them."

"Yes, *señora.*" The girl sounded resentful, but she went to help. They were both bending over a trunk, trying to find room for an extra bustle and Libbie's riding boots.

Libbie took advantage of their diverted attention to slip the necklace out of her valise. She hesitated only a moment before placing it around her throat under the high collar of the peacock-blue jacket she had selected. Quickly, she buttoned the traveling outfit so the jewelry could not be seen. When Libbie reached a place where no one would notice, and she was safe from marauding Indians, she would toss the necklace away. *How dare that half-breed scout put his collar of ownership on her?*

Without thinking, she reached up to touch the hidden jewelry. Libbie was all too aware of the feel of it. If she closed her eyes, she was once again standing out there in the night with his big hands gently touching her throat.

Another rap at the door. "It's Phillip, my dear, here to see you off."

Was she crazy? There was no telling what would happen if Phillip saw the necklace. Libbie reached up to touch the neck of her jacket again, making certain it was buttoned so that it hid her throat. "Just a minute; we're almost ready."

She opened the door as Shashké closed Mrs. Everett's trunk. Phillip smiled, extending both hands as he entered. "Well, my dear, it's a lovely day for travel; not hot yet."

"Well, thank God for that!" Mrs. Everett puffed. "This place has the heat of Hades. I can hardly wait to go!"

"Nonsense!" Libbie protested, "I love Arizona! I wouldn't mind coming back someday."

Phillip laughed as he motioned the servant girl to leave and directed the two soldiers who were waiting outside to gather up the luggage. "Surely you jest! This country is as wild and untamed as the Apaches who inhabit it; no place for civilized people at all!"

"Libbie," Mrs. Everett scolded, snapping open a parasol with a flourish, "here you must remember to protect your delicate skin from that sun. As hot as it is, I don't know why you chose such a high-necked dress."

Phillip frowned. "She's right, my dear—you really should change."

In a panic, Libbie thought fast. "I—I was protecting my delicate skin from the sun, just as I've been told."

Phillip shrugged, but Mrs. Everett smiled at her suddenly obedient charge as she handed Libbie the parasol.

She took it with a sigh, wondering what the stern dowager would think of her erotic dream of galloping naked across the desert wearing nothing but a savage's necklace and with her bare bottom exposed to the relentless sun?

The travelers started out of the room, the soldiers burdened down with luggage. Phillip offered Libbie his arm, and she hesitated only a moment before she took it as they exited into the bright desert morning. She hardly heard him as he chatted about how much he would miss her until he saw her again next spring. "Hopefully, I'll be permanently transferred by then—unless a big Apache war breaks out."

She gave him her most appealing smile from under her parasol while looking past his shoulder, searching the area for Cougar. "Is that likely?"

"Not if we go up to Cibecue Creek and nip this thing in the bud. I have asked to be sent on the campaign— good chance for promotion and some medals."

She nodded at the appropriate places as he talked, but her mind was on the gemstones around her throat, as warm as a man's fingers. She imagined trying to explain to Phillip how she had come by the necklace, but of course, he would never know she had it. They strolled slowly toward the stage stop while the soldiers and Mrs. Everett hurried ahead with the luggage. As they reached the waiting stage, the regimental band was gathered there and began to play the old army tune, "The Girl I Left Behind Me."

The elite and the curious had gathered around to see the ladies off. The unkempt old driver frowned and spat tobacco juice from his perch on top of the stage as the soldiers loaded the luggage.

"Oh, dear," Libbie said.

"What's the matter, my love?"

"Phillip, I meant to give a small gift to that Apache girl." Libbie looked anxiously back toward her quarters.

Phillip stifled a yawn. "Don't worry about it; she's not used to having much. Apache women are treated like horses around here, kept for a man's convenience."

"That's terrible!" Libbie dug in her reticule. "Here, here's the pair of gold earrings I wore last night. I could tell she admired them." She put them in Phillip's hand. "Tell her I thank her for her help."

"Libbie," Mrs. Everett scolded, "that's too nice a gift for some little Injun squaw."

"Listen to your guardian, Libbie," Phillip said.

But Libbie shook her head. "I felt sorry for her; she doesn't seem to have much of a life. Promise me you'll give them to her, Phillip, and tell her I said thanks?"

"Oh, all right; I'll humor you in this. I suppose you can afford to give away gold earrings." He put them in his pocket.

Mrs. Everett opened her mouth, then seemed to think better of it. "Well, of course she can. She has lots of jewelry, don't you, Libbie?"

The necklace seemed to burn into her throat. "Uh, yes, I do."

"All aboard!" the driver yelled. "Or you ladies will miss your train."

There seemed to be no other passengers. Even with the music, the sound of distant drums echoed faintly on the early-morning air.

Mrs. Everett frowned. "Don't the savages ever stop?"

"I'm sorry they disturbed you," Phillip said smoothly as he helped the plump lady up the step and into the stage. "We'll kill a few Apaches and take care of that little problem."

The soldiers put the valise in the boot and the big trunk up on top of the stage. Now Phillip paused before Libbie. "Well, I guess this is good-bye, my dear." He took her by the arms and she realized he was going to kiss her.

"Phillip, please, people are watching."

"Oh, you're so proper! Let them watch; after all, we are engaged. We'll correspond, my darling, and spring will be here before you know it."

Mrs. Everett leaned out of the coach, fanning herself with her kerchief. "That's right, Lieutenant, and there's a million things to be seen to with a big society wedding."

"Right." He was looking into Libbie's eyes. "About last night . . ." He lowered his voice to a whisper.

Libbie looked past his shoulder, remembering the violent way he'd torn at her clothing and put his hands on her. "You needn't apologize, Phillip."

"Oh, but I do. It's just that I want you so much, Elizabeth. Men have earthy appetites and I got carried away."

"I said I understand, Phillip." She did not look at him, wondering what marriage to this man would be like, yet certain she had no alternative. Abruptly, in the shadow of the buildings, she saw Shashké watching, her mouth a hard line, her arms folded defiantly across her full breasts. What was upsetting the girl? Perhaps she had expected Libbie would leave her a coin or two. Shashké was in for a pleasant surprise when Phillip gave her the fine gold earrings.

Libbie looked in another direction. Under a lone cotton-wood tree, Cougar sat his paint stallion. When he caught her eye, he reached up slowly to touch his neck and nodded to her. Libbie pretended not to see either of them.

"All aboard!" The driver shouted again. "If we don't get a move on, you ladies will miss the train."

"Good-bye, my dear." Phillip kissed her. It was little more than a dry, passionless peck, but after all, a crowd was watching.

"Good-bye." She could hardly wait to get out of his embrace. "We'll write."

"By next spring, I hope to have a chest full of medals," he bragged as he helped her into the coach.

To cover the awkward moment, Libbie laughed, perhaps a little too heartily. "Of course, Phillip!"

Now she nodded and, lifting her full blue skirts, climbed in. She pulled out a handkerchief and leaned out the window to wave as the coach started with the crack of a whip and a jingle of a harness. They pulled away in a cloud of dust. Libbie tried not to look back at either Shashké or Cougar, but they both watched her stoically. Instead, she laughed and waved at Phillip, who blew kisses until the stage rounded a curve in the road and Fort Grant disappeared from view.

Libbie leaned back against the plush horsehair seat with a sigh and touched the neck of her dress. She could feel the silver against her throat like a reminder of Cougar's touch.

Phillip watched until the coach was out of sight, then smiled and felt the gold earrings in his pocket. What an extravagant gift for an Injun squaw! Well, the silly little heiress could well afford it. He intended to put these earrings to good use. Right now, he had a meeting with the fort commander to see what action he intended to take about the heightened tension up in the northern part of the Territory. He could hardly wait for the chance to kill a few Apaches. That wouldn't bring his father back, but it would feel damn good!

The drums beat all day. When Phillip ran into Cougar in the stables, he asked, "Don't those damned things ever stop? They're getting on everybody's nerves!"

The big half-breed didn't smile. "I think that's the purpose."

"How good are those new scouts if we need them?"

Cougar considered. "I wouldn't suggest the army use them against their own people yet. Some may still have old loyalties."

Phillip swore under his breath and wiped the sweat from his patrician face. "The devil wouldn't claim this country."

The Apache looked back at him impassively from blue eyes under the scarlet headband. "Lieutenant, this place is disturbing you; you ought to ask for a transfer out."

"Not yet! I came for revenge; my dear mother has talked of nothing else my whole life."

Cougar lowered his voice almost gently. "The major found only a grave in this country; that should be a warning to you."

Phillip laughed without mirth. "They're the ones you should be warning." He jerked his head in the direction of the distant drums. Then he took a sudden closer look at the big man before him. "What happened to that necklace you always wear?"

Cougar touched his own neck and shook his head. "I seem to have lost it somewhere since yesterday."

"You don't seem too upset," Phillip snapped. "I thought it was your finest possession. You lose it gambling?"

Cougar hesitated. "You might say that."

Phillip snorted with scorn. Who could understand how the minds of careless savages worked? Once again he marveled at how Mac McGuire could have loved and married an Apache girl. Lusted after, yes, keep one as a mistress, of course—but make her respectable by *marrying* her? Preposterous!

"Anything else, Lieutenant?"

Phillip shrugged. "The commander's calling a meeting tomorrow morning for all of us who are being transferred to Fort Apache."

"That include me?"

"He said the top scout, and your name was mentioned," Phillip said in a grudging tone.

"Fine. I'll be there." He turned to go.

"Aren't you forgetting something, Injun?"

Cougar paused, gave him a half-hearted salute, and sauntered away, leaving Phillip glaring after him. *If there is action,* he thought with a malicious grin, *I'm going to see that damned scout gets a bullet in the back and let the hostiles take the blame for it.* With a sigh, he returned to his duties.

That night, Phillip lay on his bunk, watching the deepening shadows and thinking about Elizabeth. In less than a year, she was going to belong to him, and he could do whatever he wanted with her fortune and her body. He licked his lips at the thought. Last night, he'd gotten impatient and almost ruined it all. Well, he probably wouldn't see her again until right before the wedding, so all he had to do was keep writing sweet letters and poetry to her.

Phillip smiled. Women were such stupid ninnies—all but his dear mother. It was Henrietta who had helped set up the introduction at the ball, which Phillip had attended to look over the available heiresses. Elizabeth's beauty had been an extra bonus, because even if Libbie hadn't been pretty, his mother would have insisted he court her and marry her because of the fabled Winters wealth.

He needed that wealth. The Van Harringtons had lost plenty in some bad investments Phillip had made a couple of years ago and some gambling debts he'd run up. Now they were all but penniless!

Chapter Six

The rattle of gravel against his window brought Phillip up off his bed. About time! He'd been expecting his visitor, so he was only partially dressed. He went to the door, opened it, and peered into the night. Shashké beckoned to him from the nearby shadows of a Joshua tree, the cactus blossom in her black locks scenting the air. He smiled with pleasure and looked in both directions to make sure no one was around before motioning her over to him in the doorway.

"Sweet, I've been thinking about you." He reached out and grabbed her breast. "Come on in."

Shashké brushed his hand away and shook her head. "Hah! You've been thinking about that red-haired white girl, and now that she's gone, you want me again."

Ye gods! Spare me from a stupid, jealous slut. "Now, sweet, you know you're really the one I love. However, my mother is going to insist I marry her because of her social position and because she's inherited lots of money."

"Has she? She didn't leave me even a small coin to show her appreciation as her maid."

He had the gold earrings Elizabeth had left for the Apache girl in his pocket. "Ah, but I have something nice for you, something I took from Elizabeth's purse when she wasn't looking."

The girl's greedy dark eyes brightened. "A gift for me? Give it to me!"

"Later. Come on in." He gestured. "It's more comfortable in my quarters than in that old barn."

Shashké shook her head. "I can't come in there. You have dead bears in there; it's a taboo place."

"Dead bears?" Phillip looked over his shoulder, then threw back his head and laughed. "It's a bearskin rug and a head mounted over the fireplace. I like to hunt."

She scowled at him, pretty with the exotic blossom in her hair. "You break Apache taboos in killing bears. We believe the spirits of our dead inhabit the animals' bodies."

Damn stupid Injuns. He caught her hand and tried to pull her inside, but she resisted.

Shashké shook her head. "I have to be most careful of offending the bear spirits because of the month I was born."

Phillip didn't want to hear about ignorant Injun beliefs and he didn't give a damn what month she'd been born in. All he wanted was to get her under him for a few minutes. "Aw, sweet, come on in and I'll give you that present."

She backed away, shaking her head. "Bring the present. I'll meet you in the usual place." Shashké disappeared into the night.

Oh, hell. The barn was clear across the parade grounds. Phillip scowled and stared after her a long moment before he shut the door and walked across the pine floor, wondering where he'd left his boots. His bare foot came in contact with the bearskin rug's head and he stubbed his toe, cursed, and kicked the head hard. "Apache superstitions, bah! I'll kill all the bears I want!"

This was probably the last time he'd enjoy the lusty Apache girl. Rumor was that his unit was being transferred up to Fort Apache to put down the unrest at Cibicue Creek. He was getting tired of Shashké anyway and maybe there'd be plenty more like her around the other fort. He made sure he had the gold earrings in his pocket and smiled to himself as he went out the door and sauntered through the darkness to the barn, humming to himself with satisfaction.

It was ironic, really, that Elizabeth's gold earrings were about to buy him an evening of lust. But on the other hand, it was going to be her money that paid for the pretty white mistress he would choose when he returned to the East. Even if his new wife did find out he was unfaithful, there wasn't much she could do after they were wed and Phillip had control of all her wealth.

Shashké was waiting in the hay of the cavalry barn. "Give me the present," she demanded.

Greedy little bitch. "Let's make love first," he bargained, sitting down on the hay.

"No, present first," she insisted.

"Okay." Phillip pulled the gold earrings from his pocket and held them out. The moonlight gleamed through a broken plank of the barn and reflected on them. "Here, do you like these?"

"Oh, the white girl's earrings! They are beautiful!" Shashké grabbed them from his hand. "I saw her wearing them at the ball."

He grinned. "They'll look better on you, sweet. You're much prettier."

"She gave them to me?" Shashké put them on.

Phillip considered. So what if his fiancé had asked him to give them to the girl? Shashké would never know, nor would Elizabeth. The Apache girl would be very free with her favors for the brief time left before he was transferred. "She doesn't know you have them," he lied. "Like I told you before, I stole them out of her purse to give them to you."

"You really love me after all." She was all smiles now, the gold earrings gleaming in the moonlight when she turned her head.

"Why, sweet, could you ever doubt it?" He took the cactus blossom from her hair and tossed it aside. "Now show me just how grateful you are." He pulled her to him and kissed her long and hard while she pressed her big breasts against his chest until his manhood came up rigid and throbbing.

She lay back, her ebony hair spread like smudged ink on the yellow hay, gold earrings reflecting the moonlight. He reached to pull her blouse to her waist, knowing she wore nothing beneath that would discourage his seeking hands. Nor pantalets either, he thought with a smile as he ran his fingertips up her bare, warm thigh.

"I've thought of nothing but you, sweet," he whispered, "my gift proves that, doesn't it?"

"I love you, Phillip. You'll take me back East with you when you go?" She reached up and began to open his shirt.

"Yeah, sure." He almost smiled at the ridiculous idea. What would Mother think if he showed up with an Injun slut in tow? Shashké was a stupid, trusting wench. His body ached with the thought of taking beautiful Elizabeth's virginity. Soon, she would belong to him and he would have her at his mercy in the marriage bed. Now he closed his eyes, pretending those were Elizabeth's fingers tracing circles on his bare chest.

"I run a terrible risk if my man ever catches me sleeping with you before we leave Arizona."

"You won't get caught; stop worrying about it," he breathed as he bent to her breast. He didn't care whether she was in any danger or what Apaches did to cheating wives. Passionate, pretty Shashké was only entertainment to while away the long, dull nights until he found another more interesting slut or got transferred out. He sucked her nipple into his mouth while he stroked her lush body, and she responded by running her hands inside his shirt, digging her nails into his shoulders, and pulling him down on her.

"No," he gasped and pulled away from her, "you know what I want." He reached to unbutton his trousers, and even as she protested, he grabbed her by the back of the neck, forcing her face down into him. "Do it!" he demanded. "You know what I want!"

She hesitated, but as he pressed her face against him, she opened that hot, sweet mouth and caressed him with her tongue. He made a sound of pleasure and relaxed, letting her play with him. When he was Elizabeth's husband, he could force her to do this to him whether she liked it or not. As his wife, she would be almost powerless legally. Phillip fully intended to humble that spoiled little bitch!

Now, as his passion built, he wanted more. "Take it!" he demanded. "Take it all!"

She struggled just a moment, but he had one hand on the back of her neck, forcing her. After a moment, she surrendered to his will until he reached a pinnacle of pleasure. Then he lay there a long time, breathing hard.

"What about me?" Shashké demanded.

"What about you?" Phillip yawned. Satisfied now, he was ready to return to his quarters. He sat up and began to button his shirt.

"I still need a man." She was sulky.

Phillip shrugged, bored now with the stupid, illiterate girl. "So go home to your husband."

"He's old and can almost never do it," she fumed, combing the straw out of her tumbled hair with one hand. "You could at least tell me you love me when we do this."

"I love you," he repeated automatically. "I need to be getting back now."

"I'll wager if you had that redhead here with you, you wouldn't be in such a hurry to return to your bunk."

He paused in pulling on his boots and thought about the elegant Miss Winters lying naked and defenseless on silken white sheets, her long red hair in complete disarray as she awaited his pleasure. When he thought about her, his passion began to build again. He intended to keep her on her back until he got her with child. Elizabeth's wealth and an heir would please his mother. By then, he'd probably be tired of the lady and could return to his wild, whoring ways. Mama wouldn't care, and his wife couldn't stop him.

Shashké put her hand on him, began to stroke him. "Make love to me," she demanded, "or I'll scream that you attacked me and bring everyone running."

"Is that a way to thank me for the nice present?" If he didn't satisfy the slut, she was just vengeful enough to do it. Shashké had become a real problem for him. With a sigh, he rolled over on top of her.

She took his full weight gladly, thinking the lieutenant wasn't very virile, or skilled at lovemaking, or nearly as big as she would have liked, but he would have to do. Her lusty appetite might have been satisfied by Cougar, but the big half-breed would not give in to her; he had too much respect for her old husband. Yet here in the moonlight, with his broad shoulders and square jaw, the lieutenant looked enough like Cougar that with a little imagination, she could pretend that at last she was mating with the man she really wanted.

"Can you do it?" She locked her thighs around him and offered him the feast of her breasts as she dug her nails into his hips and broad shoulders.

It took him a few minutes to build up enough rigidity to please her, and then he rode her hard while she tore at his chest and back with her nails, using him for her pleasure until she was satisfied.

With a tired sigh, he rolled off her and sat up. "Okay, now I've really got to be getting back."

"You never stay and hold me and tell me you love me," she complained.

He was truly sick of her. Phillip stood up and brushed the hay from his clothes. "Maybe next time."

"There is a rumor around the fort that some in your unit might be transferred up to Fort Apache."

He was counting on it to get away from the tiresome girl. "Maybe; I don't know."

She stood up and grabbed his arm. "Take me with you when you pull out."

"Now, sweet, you know I can't do that. I'll send for you later." He brushed her hand off his arm.

"But later might be too late!" she protested. "More and more of the Apaches know about us. My old husband might hear that I have been betraying him."

Phillip didn't care what happened to the girl now that he was going to be moving on. "I'll send for you later," he lied.

Shashké looked up at him, knowing he was lying, yet powerless to do anything about it. Her husband truly loved her, she ought to go home to him, but the young white officer could offer her dresses and more jewelry, all the things that fine white girls had. If she could only get Phillip to stay a little longer here with her, maybe she could convince him. Yet he was even now starting for the door. "Come back, Phillip; it's not late."

He scowled. "I told you I have to go."

How could she make him stay? Then she remembered and slowly smiled. "I know a secret you would like to know."

"I doubt that." He yawned as he turned to go.

"I know something about your white girl," Shashké whispered desperately, "something you would want to know."

It had the desired effect. He stopped and looked at her. "Elizabeth? What about her?"

Shashké shrugged and playfully poked with one bare toe at the straw. "Oh, just something."

He stared at her as if attempting to decide whether she was bluffing, then grabbed her arm and twisted it. "Tell me, you stupid slut!"

"Oww, Phillip, you're hurting me!" She had never seen this side of him before.

"I'll hurt you more," he promised between clenched teeth, "if you don't tell me!"

She was weeping now, but he only tightened his grip. "I—it wasn't anything."

"Tell me and I'll decide that." He twisted her arm harder.

"Stop, you're hurting me! I'll tell!"

He didn't turn her loose. "So tell."

"Jewelry," she sobbed. "It's about the necklace." She wished she hadn't mentioned it now. She didn't mind bringing trouble to the hated, stingy white girl, but she truly cared for Cougar. "Maybe she—she stole that, too."

"What necklace? Elizabeth wouldn't steal anything. Tell me!" He twisted her arm again.

If she screamed, would anyone come before he could really hurt her? Shashké struggled to pull her arm away, but he didn't let go. He seemed to be enjoying her pain. This was a side of the aristocratic officer she had never seen before. "The necklace; she has the necklace."

Phillip didn't let go. "What necklace? She's got lots of those, pearls, diamonds, gold lockets—"

"Cougar's Apache Tears necklace!" She almost screamed it.

To her relief, Phillip gasped and his blue eyes widened in surprise as he turned her loose. "What the hell—?"

She sobbed, favoring her injured arm, but Phillip didn't seem to notice. "I—I don't know how she got it, but I saw it in her luggage when I helped her pack this morning."

"Cougar's necklace?" Phillip scratched his head slowly, his handsome face puzzled. "How—? Does she know you saw it?"

Shashké looked up at him and shook her head. "I don't think so; I didn't say anything."

"How the hell did she—?" His voice trailed off and he seemed to be trying to figure it all out.

Shashké backed away, shaking her head. "I only know she has it."

The officer's face was a mask of fury. "I'm going to get to the bottom of this!"

She was afraid of his anger. "You don't want to challenge Cougar. He is a skilled warrior; he would kill you and then you would never take me away from here so I can live like a white girl!"

He didn't even seem to hear her. "Maybe it wasn't his necklace, maybe it was another like it that she bought at the trading post."

Shashké shook her head. "There is no other necklace in all Apache country like that one. They say Cougar's dead mother gave it to his white father as a sign of her love."

She didn't like the jealous fury she saw on the lieutenant's face.

"Why would that damned Injun buck give it to Elizabeth?"

"I don't know." She looked away, wishing she had never told him.

"What else do you know? Tell me, you dirty Injun bitch!" He grabbed her and slapped her hard.

She cried out and put her hands to her face, tasting the warm, coppery blood from her cut lip. All she had for her fortune was her pretty face. Without her beauty, she would never escape from her poor, dull life. "Maybe—maybe she liked it and bought it from Cougar."

"Don't be a fool! Everyone on the post has admired that necklace and tried to buy it, me included. Cougar said there wasn't enough gold in all Arizona to buy it, so why would he let Elizabeth have it?" He grabbed her by the shoulders, digging his fingers into her flesh, and repeated his question through clenched teeth. "Why would he let her have it?"

"Didn't you see how he looked at her?"

Phillip heard nothing more. A red rage began to blur his sight as he imagined anything, everything. He threw Shashké to the ground and strode away, oblivious to her sobbing entreaties behind him. Yes, he had seen the way that big breed looked at Elizabeth—as though he'd like to pick her up and carry her away someplace so that he could ravage her virginity.

The image of the big Apache lying between his fiancée's thighs angered him past all reason as he strode toward the barracks. Then he pulled up short and smiled. What was he thinking of? Prissy little Elizabeth was so frigid, she would hardly let Phillip kiss her; there was no passion in the society miss. He could not say the same for the virile scout. Phillip had seen the banked fire in the Apache's blue eyes as he looked at the lady. The gall of that breed! Phillip would teach that savage to lust after a white woman!

He aroused four of his biggest, meanest troopers, men who owed him favors for lending them money at cards or getting them out of the guardhouse when they'd run into trouble fighting or slacking off. He put his finger to his lips as he awakened each of them, motioning them to dress and come outside. They joined him, half-dressed and yawning.

"Don't ask any questions," he snapped. "I've got someone I need to get information from!"

"At this time of night, sir?" Jones scratched the tattoo on his massive arm.

"I said no questions!" Phillip barked and started walking. "We're going to pay a little visit to Cougar."

Behind him, the men faltered.

"Beg your pardon, sir," Hans, the big blacksmith volunteered, "he's not an easy man to—"

"There's four of you!" Phillip swore. "And this is important!"

"The lieutenant's right," Corrigan argued. "I don't like that big breed; he thinks he's as good as a white man!"

Rollins had been a teamster before he enlisted. Now he flexed his rippling muscles. "There's five of us. We can take him!"

The five of them began walking again toward where Phillip knew Cougar camped when he wasn't at his father's ranch. The scout liked to sleep under an open sky in a grove of trees at the edge of the fort. Phillip told the four rogues his plan, and they faded into the underbrush near Cougar's camp. Phillip himself walked boldly in.

Alert as the animal he was named for, Cougar heard just the slightest sound of a boot on gravel before he came up out of his blankets, grabbing for a rifle.

"Whoa." The lieutenant laughed, holding up his hands. "It's just me! Nobody could ever sneak up on you, could they?"

Cougar frowned and relaxed, throwing his weapon to

one side. "I'm an Apache, Lieutenant, we live on the edge of danger. What do you want at this time of night?"

Phillip shrugged. "I just wanted to know if you've heard any rumors from the Apaches. Every soldier I've talked to is jumpy."

The drums had begun beating again in the background.

"At this time of night? Can't you wait until morning to see what the commander has to say?"

Phillip shrugged. "Why don't you make some coffee and we'll talk? Maybe we've had our differences in the past, but we're maybe going into a difficult campaign up north, and I thought you might have heard some rumors."

"All right." Frankly puzzled and still a little sleepy, Cougar got up and knelt by the ashes of his fire to stir it to flames. "You'll be disappointed in how little I know. Most of the Apaches don't tell me much because I work for the army and am loyal to it. Believe me, though, there's no plotting going on. If everyone will keep their heads, this will all blow over, and—"

With his head down as he poked at the fire, he heard a sudden noise and came up fighting even as he felt a terrible blow to the back of his head. He went to his knees, struggling to stay conscious through a haze of pain. He heard running feet and then he was pinned to the ground.

"We got 'im, Lieutenant!"

Someone was holding his arms and legs.

Even with the blinding pain, Cougar fought to break free and almost succeeded, lashing out with one powerful arm.

"Hang on to him! He's a strong devil!"

The next few seconds were a blur of pain and confusion, but finally Cougar found himself tied up and propped against his saddle.

The lieutenant looked down at him, grinning, but there

was no humor in the cold blue eyes. "Thanks, boys," he said to the four men in the shadows. "You can leave now."

Cougar tried to bring his vision back into focus as his assailants fled. He never got a good look at those who'd attacked him. "What in the hell is this all about?"

"Call me sir," the lieutenant commanded and kicked him hard in the groin. "And I'll ask the questions, you dirty savage!"

Agony exploded through Cougar's lithe body and he doubled up, but he did not cry out, even though he was numb with pain. He would not give the other that satisfaction.

Phillip glared down at him. "What's happened to that necklace you always wear?"

A warning shiver went up Cougar's muscular back. "I— I lost it."

The officer sneered and kicked him again, sending agony through every nerve. "For something that meant so much to you, you don't seem very concerned that it's lost."

Surely the lieutenant couldn't know the truth. Cougar gritted his teeth against the red haze of pain. "What— what is this all about?"

Abruptly, the officer bent and struck him hard across the face. "You red heathen, you know what this is about!"

Cougar looked up at him through a murderous haze, his own scarlet blood coppery warm in his mouth and dripping down his chin. He said nothing, thinking instead how he would kill the officer, slowly, painfully, if he got a chance. No, of course he could not do that; he would be breaking an old Apache taboo.

Phillip squatted before him, caught Cougar by the hair, and raised his head, twisting Cougar's hair until the pain made him gasp.

The lieutenant smiled at his pain. "You arrogant son of a bitch! You gave the necklace to Miss Winters."

He must protect the white girl; she was fragile and innocent. "No, I—I lost it. If she's got it, maybe she found it. How—how did you know—?"

"Because she told me about it, you ignorant bastard!"

He couldn't imagine the flame-haired beauty doing that. "No." He shook his head. "No, I did not give it to her!"

"You lie!" The lieutenant struck him across the face again.

He fought against the blind rage building in him. No matter what Mac said, no matter the Apache taboo, he yearned to kill Phillip Van Harrington. Cougar pulled hard at his bounds until his strong muscles rippled and knotted, but he couldn't break the ropes.

The lieutenant grinned, seeming to enjoy his struggles. "Elizabeth told me you gave it to her and she laughed about it. You hear me? She threw back her head and laughed at the ignorant savage who'd taken a shine to her. She thought it was so amusing! We both had a good laugh about it before she got on the stage this morning."

Cougar winced. The lieutenant's words hurt him as the harsh blows never could. Could he have misjudged the spirited beauty so badly? Could the white girl have been so shallow and so cruel? Would she have made a joke about the sacred gift he had bestowed on her? He remembered watching from a distance as she got on the stage. Phillip had kissed her. Cougar remembered watching that, wanting to be in the lieutenant's place, imagining what it would feel like to hold her. He tried to remember every detail. Yes, she and Phillip had been laughing together. He couldn't believe Blaze would take his gift so lightly, and yet, there was no other answer, no other way that the officer could have known about the necklace. "What—what did she do with it?"

"She threw it away! What do you think she did with a worthless thing like that? She's a rich white girl with lots of jewelry, and she took it as a big joke!"

In his mind, Cougar imagined the fiery girl throwing back her head and laughing, tossing away his most precious possession. The image hurt him as no battle wound ever had. And in his heart began to burn a fierce anger for the arrogant Elizabeth Winters. At that moment, he had never hated anyone as much as he hated the red-haired white girl.

"I see by your face that you're a little upset!" Phillip sneered, striding up and down before him. "I just wanted you to know this is what you get for trying to cross the color line—ridicule and punishment. How dare you offer a gift to my fiancée!" The officer kicked him hard between the thighs and Cougar doubled over with a strangled moan. As he lay writhing in the dirt, Phillip kicked him in the face with his riding boots.

"Remember this every time you think of even approaching a white woman now, you lusty savage!" Harrington snarled through gritted teeth. "Stay in your place! You'd better learn that lesson, or by God, next time I'll figure out a way to hang you!" At this, he turned and strode into the darkness.

Cougar lay there half-conscious, his big muscles stiffening and aching from the blows and beatings. He tried to untie himself, but he'd been well bound. He lay there with the dew falling on his aching body and the hate in his soul growing stronger with each beat of his heart.

Libbie Winters. Blaze. He had given her the necklace in good faith, trying to protect her from any Apache attack on the stage and she had made a joke of it, shared the ridicule with the uppity lieutenant. Mac had been right; Cougar could not cross the invisible barrier. It brought only the heartbreak and tragedy it had brought his parents. He had thought a very great love would make color and social position unimportant, but he'd been wrong.

Strange, he would not have believed the white girl would

do this thing; she had seemed so touched by his gift. It showed that he had been mistaken in his judgment; she was as cruel and shallow and arrogant as her fiancé.

Cougar lay there in pain through most of the night, his anger at Elizabeth Winters growing as he planned his revenge should she ever return to the fort. Toward dawn, he heard a step and, still struggling to free himself, looked up with alarm. The lieutenant might be having second thoughts about Cougar filing a complaint with the commander and come back to silence the scout permanently.

Shashké came out from the shadows of some mesquite trees. "Cougar?"

He didn't want anyone to see him this way; bloody and injured. It was too humiliating for a warrior, but he needed help. "Over here."

Her dark eyes widened with shock as she ran to him and bent down. She said a curse in Apache. "Oh, Cougar, how bad are you hurt?"

"Bad enough, although I don't think any bones are broken. Untie me. How did you know I was here?"

She was busy untying him so he couldn't see her face, but he felt her start. "I—I let the lieutenant make love to me. He bragged about what he was going to do, but I didn't believe him. What was this about, anyway?"

He considered his answer as she untied his arms and he rubbed his raw wrists. Shashké would probably throw back her head, laugh, and ridicule him for being so naive as to give a gift to the high-born white girl. "Just a difference of opinion between me and the officer." He began to untie his legs.

She stepped back and winced as she surveyed his injuries. "It must have been a big difference of opinion."

"Forget it; it was something between men." He managed to stand up, but every sinewy muscle in his big body ached.

She seemed to be struggling with a decision, her pretty face troubled.

He paused and stared at her. "Where'd you get those earrings? Those belong to the white girl. Did you steal them?"

"No, she—he gave them to me. After all, she has plenty." Shashké seemed both angry and defensive, but he dismissed her attitude as petty and unimportant. After all, he had more important things on his mind right now. He picked up his rifle.

Shashké caught his arm. "Cougar, you won't kill him? The lieutenant is my only chance to get away from here."

He groaned aloud as he straightened up. "Little Bear Tracks, you're a fool; the lieutenant uses you for his pleasure until he leaves. He cares nothing about you. Go home to your husband and be a good wife."

She shook her head. "The lieutenant has made me promises. I want to live like a white girl."

Cougar sighed. There was no reasoning with her. "You know what will happen to that pretty face if you are caught cheating. The gossip already spreads among our people."

"It is worth the risk!" She glared back at him stubbornly, the gold earrings glinting under the late night stars. "You will not kill the lieutenant?"

He could not kill the lieutenant, even though he hungered for revenge. To do so would break an Apache taboo, and his soul was more Apache than white. All he could do was hate the man, yet he hated the arrogant Elizabeth Winters even more. If she ever dared to return to this country, Cougar would take his revenge; there was no taboo against killing her. No, humiliating her would be even more satisfying, if he ever had her at his mercy.

"Your lieutenant is safe, Shashké," he assured her, "the army would hang me if I killed him. And thank you for coming out here to see about me."

She did not meet his eyes. "It's all right. If you ever change your mind about us—"

"No." He shook his head. "I've got an Apache heart, Shashké. I cannot do that which is dishonorable to our people."

"And I have done much to dishonor our people, haven't I? I should tell you—"

She hesitated, then abruptly turned and fled. He stared after her in puzzlement. She acted as if she were guilty of something. Well, of course he had just shamed her for dishonoring her husband, but he had more important things on his mind right now than a foolish, ambitious girl.

It would be dawn soon. With a sigh, he reached for his saddle. He'd ride out to the ranch and let Mac patch him up. What he hated most was that the old man would scold him and say, "I told you so."

It was hopeless for Cougar to yearn for that which he could never possess, and his passion for the fire-haired girl could bring him nothing but trouble and pain. Only a very great love could withstand crossing that forbidden line between their two peoples, and she felt no love. Elizabeth Winters had betrayed him and laughed at him. So now Cougar's love had been replaced by a burning hatred!

Chapter Seven

Cougar rode out to the ranch. As he reined in, Mac came out on the porch. Cougar dismounted slowly and painfully. "Don't even ask!"

The dour little Scot stared in shock, then hurried down the steps to assist him. "All right then, I won't, but I can guess."

Cougar leaned on him as Mac helped him up onto the porch where he collapsed in a chair. Mac pursed his lips, combing his fingers through his gray beard and surveying him. "Can ye not avoid trouble?"

He had expected such a lecture, but Cougar only grunted and shrugged. "I've tried. The lieutenant's taken a special dislike to me."

"Do you think he suspects—?"

"No, it's not that," Cougar assured him with a tired sigh.

"Aye, and I knew he'd be trouble the first time I saw him here at the fort. He's already been here, you know, wanting the major's pistol." Mac's brow furrowed with worry.

"He wouldn't if he knew—"

"I hope he never finds out," Mac said. "Some things are better left alone."

Cougar rolled and lit a cigarette with an unsteady hand. "Among the Apache, everything a dead person owns is buried with him."

"Aye." Mac nodded. "But whites buried the major and they brought back those two things."

Cougar blew smoke and thought a long moment. "I hope they don't both bring bad luck."

"Enough of this uneasy talk," Mac said. "Wait here; I'll get some liniment." He went inside.

"Bring me a drink, too," Cougar yelled as he leaned back in the chair with a sigh. He knew he must look as bad as he felt; bruised and battered.

In moments, Mac returned with ointments, rags, and a bottle of good Scotch whiskey. "This ought to fix things." He poured the other a drink and then cleaned the cuts on Cougar's face with a gentle, gnarled hand. "Reminds me of when you were a lad; always gettin' banged up, you were. What started this?"

Cougar winced. "He brought some toughs and came looking for me."

Mac paused. "Why?"

"Same thing you used to ask me when I was a kid." There was a long silence as Cougar sipped his whiskey and looked away. He didn't want to bring trouble to Mac by getting him involved. "Nothing much; just a disagreement. Forget it."

"Ye have never been a good liar, lad." He put a comforting hand on Cougar's broad shoulder, "Are you sure he doesn't suspect—?"

"No." Cougar shook his head. "It wasn't that. It was about the girl."

"Ahh." The other nodded as if that explained everything.

"I hope you're not going to say 'I told you so.' " Cougar gulped the rest of his drink and wiped his mouth with the back of his hand.

" 'Tis tempting," Mac admitted. "She was a beauty, all right, but out of your reach."

Cougar scowled and stood up. "Don't you think I know that?"

"What happened to your necklace?"

Cougar didn't answer. His hand went automatically to his neck.

The older man peered up at him a long moment as if in disbelief. "You've never taken that off in all these years."

"I lost it."

The other looked troubled, shook his head, and filled his pipe. "I know ye too well, lad; don't lie to me. You gave it to that girl." It was a statement, not a question.

"And the spoiled little bitch threw it away and laughed about it with Phillip!" Cougar made an angry, dismissing gesture.

"Hmm." Mac scratched his gray beard. "Somehow, she didn't seem like that type."

"I was a fool!" Cougar started down off the porch, then paused. "I should have listened to you."

"A man listens to his heart," Mac said gently. "I did, even though it brought me heartache, as I knew it would."

Cougar paused by his big paint stallion and smiled at the other. "Thank you."

He shrugged. "For what?"

"For everything; you know."

Mac snorted and tried to make light of the words, but his brown eyes misted. "No more than any man would do

for a son." He looked toward the hill where Cougar's
mother slept forever. "Loving women causes most of the
world's troubles, I think."

"Then why don't we smarten up?"

"Ah, lad, because we can't live without them; and
because any man worth his salt listens to his heart, not his
head." Mac wiped his eyes. His mind seemed a long way
off, as if he were lost in memories.

"You miss her, don't you?" Cougar blurted, not caring
that he must not speak of the dead.

"Every hour of every day; but she left me you."

"I was not your obligation; the Apaches would have
raised me."

Mac shrugged. "Aye, and they helped. But I wed her so I
could protect her." He looked into Cougar's eyes. "You've
been the best son any man could want. Be careful, boy. I
promised her as she took her last breath, and you took
your first, that I'd always look out for you."

Cougar smiled gently at him as he stood up. "You've
kept that promise, but I'm a grown man now. You can't
protect me forever."

The other cleared his throat awkwardly. "I would if I
could."

"Sooner or later, all eagles must take to the air, even if
they take a chance on falling," Cougar said gravely as he
went down the steps and swung up on his horse. "I don't
want to worry you, so I'll try to stay out of the lieutenant's
way. It will be tough; he's got it in for me."

In the background, the drums began to beat again.

Mac turned and peered toward the distant hills, blinking
with his poor sight. "Looks like you both may soon be too
busy to carry on a personal feud."

"I know." Cougar, too, stared off into the distance and
frowned. "I think some of us may be transferred up to
Fort Apache, so I may not see you for a while."

"They nervous about a possible Apache outbreak?"

Cougar nodded.

Mac scowled. "Aye, and well they should be, the way that crooked Indian agent, Jack Tiffany, and his cohorts are cheating them. White men just never care enough to understand Indians." Mac's weathered face creased into worried lines.

"Only you." Cougar nodded affectionately. "You understand, and they trust you."

Mac acknowledged the praise with a nod. "I've tried to do right by them and keep my word; that's protected me all these years while ranches around me were burned and raided."

"The Apaches always remember their friends," Cougar promised, and as he turned his horse, he muttered to himself, "and their enemies." He nudged his paint stallion into a walk.

"Take care, boy!" Mac called after him.

Cougar waved acknowledgment as he rode away, heading back to the fort.

Behind him, Mac McGuire watched him leave. At that moment, the grizzled old Scot almost called out to him that he loved him, then hesitated and the moment was lost forever. Men did not say such things to each other, and yet the boy meant more to him than his own life. One woman Mac had loved in all his many years, but she had not loved him. Still, every time he looked into Cougar's face, he saw her dear face and remembered. In a way, he still had the mother through the son.

Cougar rode back to the fort and dismounted at the stable. A passing young private stared at him, seemed to be about to ask, then thought better of it. "They're in a meeting; rumor is it's important."

The meeting. He had forgotten about it after what had happened last night. Cougar cursed under his breath and nodded to the young Apache scout who came out of the stable.

Dandy Jim looked up at him earnestly and asked in their language, "You have had trouble?"

Cougar touched his bruised face absently. "Since the day I was born."

Dandy Jim turned and looked toward the distant hills, where the drums echoed. "We will not have to fight our own people? The others worry—"

"I will try to reason with the white man." Cougar put his hand on the young Apache's shoulder. "Maybe they will just send us up there to warn the Apaches. Take care of my horse."

Cougar handed over his reins and hurried toward headquarters. He dreaded facing those curious white men, but there was no help for it; he was a head scout and he had to be there. He came in late and stood near the door, ignoring the curious stares at his cut and swollen face. Phillip smiled ever so slightly and pulled at his mustache.

"Well," said the commander, pausing in mid-speech while pointing at a big map, "I'm so glad our head scout has finally graced us with his presence."

Quiet titters went around the room, but Cougar ignored them and snapped a salute. "My apologies, sir."

The officer took a good, long look at him. "You braves been guzzling *tiswin* and fighting over squaws again?"

More laughter. Cougar took a deep breath to control his temper and looked at the lieutenant. Phillip lounged in his chair, completely at ease. He knew the Apache brave wouldn't complain or tattle on him. "I suppose you could say it was over a woman, sir."

The colonel shrugged and turned to the map behind him. "So as I said, a few of you are headed up to Fort Apache. Lieutenant Van Harrington has volunteered, even though the mission may turn out to be dangerous." He beamed at Phillip.

Phillip colored modestly. "It's in the blood, sir; my father was much decorated."

Cougar stifled a groan, and the other men in the room frowned. Young Van Harrington was not too popular with the other soldiers.

The senior officer cleared his throat and tapped on the map with his pointer. "My guess is Colonel Carr will have orders from headquarters to go out to Cibecue and arrest that damned medicine man before he stirs up any more trouble."

"If you please, sir," Cougar blurted, and everyone turned to stare at a lowly Indian scout who would dare interrupt the colonel's briefing.

"Yes, what is it?" The colonel scowled blackly at him.

"I think the army's making a mistake," Cougar said without thinking, then realized he'd made a second blunder. "That is, sir, if they will just leave that Ancient One alone, soon his followers will realize that his omens are false and the trouble will fade away."

There was a silence that seemed to echo. It was so quiet, Cougar could hear the distant, faint commands of soldiers marching on the parade grounds and the buzz of a horsefly through the window in the simmering August heat.

The senior officer's face reddened with anger. "This meeting is adjourned!" he snapped. Men saluted and began to file out. "You, Cougar," he called, "you and Lieutenant Van Harrington stay here."

Now what?

Phillip looked worried, running a nervous finger around his collar. He needn't sweat, Cougar thought with contempt. It was beneath Cougar's dignity to report what had happened between them.

The room was empty now except for the three of them, and the old man was scowling at Cougar.

He had committed a great mistake, Cougar knew, blurting out opinions unasked before the cavalry officers. Cougar had no idea what the commander would do to him for being rash enough to comment, but at least his conscience was clear. Riding out to arrest *Noch-ay-del-Klinne* could only lead to a major rebellion and bloodshed across the Territory.

The commander gestured Cougar and Phillip forward. "At ease," he muttered, scowling darkly at Cougar but smiling warmly at Phillip. "Your father was a great man; he helped me when I was a green young pup, fresh from West Point. All the men who served with Bill loved him."

Phillip beamed. "Thank you, sir. I hope to follow in his footsteps. Perhaps you could put in a word for me in Washington about an assignment back East?"

The other nodded. "Well, yes, of course; least I can do. I intend to do good things for you, Phillip; I owe it to your father. You can win some medals on this Cibecue thing; look good on your uniform."

"Thank you, sir. I'll see you're invited to my wedding next spring."

"I met the young lady, remember?" The colonel smiled again. "My wife's already looking forward to it. She says it will be the social event that has all Philadelphia talking."

Blaze. In only a few months, she would belong to Cougar's hated enemy. The thought of Phillip making love to the fiery-haired beauty tore at Cougar's heart. Then he reminded himself again that the arrogant girl had ridiculed and laughed at him, then thrown away his most prized possession.

The colonel returned to poring over his maps. He seemed to have forgotten about Cougar. Cougar was used to that. White men often treated Indians as if they were invisible. Cougar cleared his throat. The officer looked up, frowned, and motioned him forward. "You're old Mc-Guire's boy, aren't you?"

He hoped there weren't going to be any snide comments on that. "Yes, sir."

"I remember him, too; good man. Mac's legendary for his fierce devotion to Major Van Harrington. That's why I'm cutting you some slack."

An alarm went off in Cougar's mind. "Were you—were you in this area when the major died, sir?"

The other shook his head. "No, I'd been transferred out. Real tragedy; ambushed way out in the hills by a war party, the troopers said. Don't know what Bill was doing out there without his striker; he hardly went anywhere without Mac riding along."

"Damned murdering savages!" Phillip said. "The commander wrote my mother that they buried him where he fell. I would have liked to put a fine stone on the grave, but that commander is dead now and the soldiers either dead or scattered, so I'll never be able to find it."

Cougar fidgeted, but he knew the others wouldn't notice. He wasn't of any importance to either of them.

"Yes, it's too bad we'll never know the details." The colonel sighed and went to the window, absently watching a cavalry squad riding past toward the barns. "But what matters is that Bill was well loved and well thought of by the men he served with."

"Yes, sir, my mother treasures the letter his commanding officer sent—and of course, the medals."

Cougar stirred uneasily and looked away. Yes, the major had been well loved. Cougar knew about the major's death—Mac had told him—but the secret was to be kept forever.

The commander continued to stare out the window. "I am in the devil's own country," he said softly, "not a place for civilized men. I don't know why we insist on trying to hang on to this blasted land. We ought to give it back to the Apaches.''

"Sir!" Phillip gasped, evidently shocked.

"Forget I said that," the senior officer snapped as he whirled around.

"The Apache think it's a very good idea," Cougar said.

Phillip glared at him. "No one asked you."

The senior officer ignored Cougar's comment.

Cougar frowned. "Permission to speak, sir."

"Yes, what is it?" The officer rubbed his jaw impatiently.

"Everyone knows the Indian agent is crooked and has partners back East. Between them, they are making big profits from selling off the supplies the government sends for the Apache."

"I'll pretend I didn't hear that, scout." The senior officer frowned and dismissed him with a curt nod. "I'm not responsible for the agents or the government program. I'm only responsible for keeping the peace."

"But, sir—"

"Dismissed!" the officer snapped. "Ready your scouts to accompany Lieutenant Van Harrington and his patrol up to Fort Apache."

"Yes, sir." Cougar saluted, ignoring Phillip's pleased grin. It was a long way to Fort Apache. He'd have to be careful and keep an eye on Phillip. He was certain the older man would not be above shooting Cougar in the back—or getting some of his bully boys to do it.

However, the long ride north to Fort Apache was uneventful, although there was Indian sign all along the hostile buttes and ridges, while the drums still echoed without ceasing across the lonely desert. Cougar stayed alert and saw more than one lookout watching the little group as it rode north in the late August heat. The scouts noticed, but Cougar shook his head at them to remain silent. The white men seemed to see little, but then white men missed much of nature and the things that happened around them. As the patrol traveled north, Cougar kept a keen eye on the Apache lookouts who came and went from one bluff to another, fading like ghosts in the shimmering lavender gray of dawns and crimson sunsets.

Cougar kept an eye on Phillip, too, certain that the officer intended to get the scout killed if he had half a chance. For his own part, Phillip ignored him.

They reached Fort Apache and were immediately called into Colonel Carr's office.

The senior officer greeted Phillip warmly, only nodded to Cougar. "At ease, men." To Phillip, he said, "How was the trip up?"

"No trouble," Phillip assured him, pulling at his wispy mustache. "Didn't see a single Indian. I think this whole thing's overblown."

Cougar started to speak, but thought better of it.

Colonel Carr stared at him. "You have something to say, scout?"

"Begging your pardon, sir. I hate to contradict the lieutenant, but the hills were full of lookouts and smoke signals. The soldiers just failed to see them."

Phillip turned an angry red. "Now, see here—"

"He's probably right, Lieutenant." Colonel Carr ran his hand through his graying hair. "That's why the army relies on Indian scouts. You know, about a dozen years ago, I was fighting Cheyenne Dog Soldiers. A bunch of Pawnee scouts led me right to Tall Bull's camp. Because of those scouts, we ambushed the Dog Soldiers and almost wiped them out completely."

Phillip brightened. "Killing Indians; yes, I'd like that! Where was that, sir?"

"Summit Springs, Colorado Territory. Buffalo Bill Cody was along."

"I've heard of him," Phillip said grudgingly. "But surely the army could have handled those Dog Soldiers without Indian scouts—"

"I don't think so." Colonel Carr shook his head. "I always respected my scouts' opinions, so pay attention to what your scouts tell you; they know this country better than you."

Phillip looked furious. "Begging your pardon, sir, I wouldn't put it past these murderous Apaches to lead us right into a trap!"

Cougar's first impulse was to hit Phillip; then he remembered where he was and let his doubled fists drop to his sides.

Colonel Carr stared at Cougar keenly, judging him, but when he spoke, it was to Phillip. "I've heard of your father, Lieutenant, a legend in his time. I hope you can someday fill his shoes."

"I hope so, too, sir, but I'm beginning to wonder if I'll ever be able to live up to everyone's expectations." Phillip frowned. Perhaps he was weary of living in his father's shadow.

"Oh, I'm sure you will; maybe with this next assignment."

"Sir?"

The senior officer smiled and brushed his gray hair back. "Unfortunately, Gatewood is on leave, so you'll be working with Lieutenant Cruse."

Cougar almost groaned aloud. The Apaches all knew and respected Lieutenant Gatewood, whom they called *Bay-chen-daysen*—Big Nose. He did not know this Lieutenant Cruse. He hoped Cruse wasn't as vain and inexperienced as Phillip.

"Lieutenant," Colonel Carr continued, "we are riding

up to Cibecue Creek tomorrow to arrest that old medicine man who's raising such a ruckus."

Phillip smiled. "Excellent!"

Cougar felt the hair rise on the back of his neck. "Sir, the army intends to enter *Noch-ay-del-Klinne's* stronghold?"

"What's the matter—scared?" Phillip sneered.

"Lieutenant, remember your dignity as an officer in dealing with underlings!" Carr chided. Then, in a patronizing tone, he said to Cougar, "I take it that you are questioning my orders?"

Cougar shook his head. "No, sir, I'm questioning the wisdom of whoever gave that order—"

"Of all the audacity—!"

"Silence, both of you!" the senior officer stormed. He looked at Cougar as if he couldn't quite believe Cougar's foolhardiness. "You may continue, scout. I'd like to know why you think West Point's best are such idiots."

Cougar took a deep breath. "Sir, attempting to arrest the holy man might set the whole Territory ablaze. If you could force that Indian agent to give the Apaches their supplies instead of stealing them, and just be patient, the Apache will settle back when none of *Noch-ay-del-Klinne's* visions come true."

"Hmm." Carr chewed his lip thoughtfully. "Then you don't think there's anything to this Ghost Dance thing?"

"Not unless the army tries to put a stop to it," Cougar said.

"Nonsense!" Phillip blurted. "We'll take some troops, ride out there and nip this uprising in the bud!"

The colonel took out a handkerchief and wiped the sweat from his gray mustache. He looked at Cougar. "Can I count on the Apache scouts' loyalty?"

Cougar considered. "Some of our men are brand new and idolize the holy man. It would be best if they weren't put to the test that soon."

"Ye gods," Phillip grumbled, "he's trying to keep from going into battle."

"I've survived more fights than you'll ever see," Cougar snapped, "and I don't ask others to do my fighting for me."

"Silence!" the senior officer thundered. He turned to stare out the window again, his shoulders slumped with the weight of decision. Outside, the soldiers still marched in the late August sun, and the scent of dust and horse sweat rose on the hot air. "I need the scouts," he said finally, "but I'm hesitant to have a troop with me that I'm not sure I can depend on."

"Some of the scouts are very young yet, sir," Cougar said by way of apology, "but they are brave and good fighters."

The colonel paced up and down, his face furrowed with indecision. "And maybe someday they'll get a chance to show that, but I think this is not that time. I've got to talk to Lieutenant Cruse about this, but my heart tells me not to take newly enlisted scouts."

"A man should always listen to his heart." Cougar remembered Mac's words aloud. "Now if I could convince you not to go out to Cibicue at all—"

"You are dismissed, Cougar!" the colonel roared. "The last time I checked, I was still commanding officer here!"

"Yes, sir." Cougar kept his face immobile as he snapped a salute and turned to go. Phillip smiled with pleasure as Cougar turned and strode from the building.

Phillip watched him go, more than a little pleased with himself. "If I may say so, sir, a civilized man should listen to his brain, not his heart. I know you will make the right decision."

The other frowned. "I wish I could be so sure, Lieutenant. Will you take a message to the telegraph for me?"

"Certainly, sir." Phillip reached for a pad and pencil.

The senior officer paced up and down as he considered. "It's to Major General Orlando Willcox, Whipple Barracks, town of Prescott. Stop. Going to Cibecue Creek tomorrow to arrest the medicine man known as *Noch-ay-del-Klinne*. Stop. Question some of my new Apache scouts' loyalties. Stop. Ask permission to leave most of them behind. Stop. Will await your approval. Stop. Best Regards, Eugene Carr." He paused and looked at Phillip. "You get all that?"

"Yes, sir."

"Good. Get it on the wire immediately. Unless I get orders to the contrary, I'll expect I'm supposed to take the scouts."

"Yes, sir." Phillip picked up the pad, saluted smartly, and left the building, snickering as he went. That damned Injun had looked like a fool and Phillip couldn't be in a better position with the colonel. Unlike the senior officer, Phillip had little regard for the fighting abilities of this bunch of scruffy savages, and he intended to win some medals on this campaign. He went immediately to the telegrapher and stood and watched as the soldier sent the message.

"It may take a while, sir, to get an answer back."

Phillip scowled. "It better not take too long," he grumbled, "we're riding out tomorrow, whether we get an answer or not."

"Yes, sir. I'll let you know as soon as I get a reply."

"Do that!" Phillip ordered and strode out of the office. He smiled as he thought of Cougar's bloody and bruised face. This campaign was a perfect time to rid himself of the savage who had dared to look at Phillip's future bride with lust. Indeed, if a battle broke out, who was to say from which direction a bullet came?

Thinking about Elizabeth made him want a woman, any woman. Tomorrow, maybe he would have a chance to kill that impudent Injun. Tonight, maybe he could find a

Mexican whore or an Injun girl working as a maid here at the fort.

He found one, not as pretty as Shashké or as desirable as the red-haired vixen, but available. He met the new slut behind the barracks to slake his lust. And while he took her fast and brutally, he imagined she was Elizabeth Winters and he was enjoying her while Cougar watched in helpless frustration.

At the army post near the town of Prescott, the telegraph key chattered, and the soldier at the desk grabbed a pencil and began to write, then yelled at the man in the outer office. "I've got an urgent message from the commander over at Fort Apache." He handed the young man the paper. "Get this to General Willcox at once and get me an answer."

General Willcox looked up from his meetings with his staff officers as a knock sounded at his door. "Yes?"

The soldier entered, saluted. "Message from Fort Apache, sir."

"At ease." The general took the note and read it. "Hmm. Let me give this some thought." He reread the message, tossed it across the desk to one of his officers. "What do you think?"

The other man read it and shrugged. "Well, Eugene Carr has worked with Indian scouts before; Pawnee, I think. If it's his gut feeling not to trust those green scouts, it just makes sense to leave them behind."

"That's what I thought, too." He turned to the waiting soldier. "Take a message and get it out right away."

The other whipped out a paper and pencil.

"To Colonel Eugene Carr, Fort Apache. Use your own

judgment about including the Apache scouts on your mission. Stop. Signed Major General Orlando Willcox."

"Yes, sir." The man finished writing, saluted, and left. The senior officer leaned back in his chair and sighed. "Damn, I hope we're not about to get into another Apache war."

"Oh, I don't think so; not once they go out there and arrest that crazy medicine man."

The other nodded and fanned himself with the telegram. "Damned worthless country! Fit only for Apaches and rattlesnakes. We ought to give it back to them and get out."

"I'll pretend I never heard you say that, Willcox." The other man laughed. They both stared out the window at the soldier striding across the parade ground to the telegraph office with the reply.

At that moment, somewhere deep in the wild country between the two locations, an Apache brave climbed a straggly pine tree. The drums had been speaking for days, saying that the white men were increasingly uneasy and afraid. All knew that when white men were unsure, they called to each other on the talking wires to send more troops. If the wire no longer talked, the bluecoats were helpless.

The Apache reached for the sharp skinning knife at his side, cut the humming line, and smiled to himself as it fell. Now the soldiers could not use its magic to send messages. If the white men took to the warpath, they could not call for more soldiers.

The warrior grunted with satisfaction as he climbed down the tree, quick as a bobcat, swung up on his swift spotted pony, and rode back to the Apache stronghold.

* * *

At Fort Apache, within the hour, the telegraph operator was back in Colonel Carr's office. "Pardon me, sir, but for some reason, the telegraph's down. I'm not sure whether our message got there, and I'm not getting anything from them."

The old officer swore under his breath and ran his hand through his gray hair. He wasn't prepared to take the responsibility of making that decision alone, not when he had doubts about the dependability of some of the younger, more inexperienced Apaches. On the other hand, the campaign needed those scouts. If his troop was undermanned and rode into an ambush, he'd catch hell from the big brass for not taking them along. Without an agreement from Willcox, he couldn't share the responsibility; he'd have to make the decision alone.

He clasped his hands behind his back and paced the floor. "I wish Gatewood was back from leave," he muttered. "Cruse and Van Harrington are so inexperienced with Indians."

"Sir?"

He paused. "Never mind. How long will it take to get the wire fixed?"

"We've got to find the damage first, sir."

Oh, hell. He'd have to send out a patrol to find and repair the break. Had it been an accident or a deliberate prelude to a major Apache offensive?

His common sense told him it would take days to repair the telegraph and get authorization. He didn't have that much time before events appeared to be headed for an all-out Indian war. If there was a major outbreak, there'd be hell to pay when the politicians and the newspaper started looking for someone to blame. "Well, keep trying, soldier. Maybe we'll get lucky."

"Yes, sir." The soldier saluted and left.

Colonel Carr paced up and down, staring out at the merciless sun pasted against a still, faded sky. "Damned hot, godforsaken country," he muttered. "Whether I take the scouts or not, I've got to ride out to that Apache stronghold tomorrow!"

Monday, August 29, 1881

It was the palest of lavender dawns, before the sun had even risen above the eastern rim of the hills, when Cougar stuck his head in Colonel Carr's office and saluted. "We're still riding out to Cibecue today?"

"Yes." The officer looked as if he hadn't gotten much sleep. "I haven't heard whether I'm supposed to take the new scouts or not; so I guess I'll take them."

Cougar frowned in disapproval, but it was not his decision to make. Some of the Apache scouts were under twenty years old and had only been with the army a few weeks. "I'm not sure how the green ones will react if there's a fight."

"I have no choice unless I get approval from General Willcox to leave them behind. Besides, not knowing what we're riding into, we may need the extra manpower." His expression said the old officer was troubled, but was weary of discussing it. "We'll be leaving as soon as we can get mounted. You're dismissed."

"Yes, sir." Cougar hesitated, but decided there was no point in arguing with the officer. All he might do was get himself thrown in the guardhouse and he needed to be along on this campaign to see if he could keep the peace and save lives on both sides.

In less than thirty minutes by the sun, Cougar had his

men gathered up and his big paint stallion ready to go. Now he wheeled his horse and cantered toward the white troops. He passed near where Lieutenant Van Harrington was assembling his cavalry and pretended not to see him. Cougar rode back to his troop of scouts and dismounted.

There were twenty-three Apache scouts, a few experienced ones like Sergeant Mose, many of the others new to army life.

"Cougar," the young one called "Skippy" by the whites asked softly, "where are we going?"

"Out to Cibecue Creek." He saw the men exchange doubtful looks and there were expressions of disapproval on some of the brown faces, but no one said anything.

Listen to his heart or his brain? Cougar wished Mac was there to advise him. Well, it was not his decision to make, and he had warned the colonel; he could do no more. It wasn't fair to put new scouts' loyalties to the test this soon, when they might be going up against their own blood kin.

He shrugged and reined in his dancing, restless stallion. Cougar still felt sore and stiff from the beating Phillip and his bullies had given him, and he wasn't at all certain that if Phillip got the chance, he wouldn't put a bullet in Cougar's back. In the meantime, they were facing a long ride, about forty-five miles to the northwest under a broiling August sun.

The sun was just beginning to rise as the troop rode out—Colonel Carr and his Sixth Cavalry, including five officers and seventy-nine enlisted men as well as the twenty-three Apache scouts.

From Cougar's viewpoint as a seasoned scout, this action had "disaster" and "danger" written all over it. He wasn't afraid of the fight—he had numerous battle scars over his muscular body—it was just that he had no confidence in the whites' judgment. He reached up out of long habit to touch his necklace for luck, then remembered. Cursing himself for a fool, he nudged his big horse forward and fell into the line of march over the hot and rocky terrain.

The sun beat down on them pitilessly as they rode, heat waves rising off the barren land. Cougar licked his dry lips and watched the horizon in all directions, wary of a trap, and more wary of Phillip Van Harrington. With all the broken promises the whites had made them, and the way the Indian agent had been cheating them, the Apaches were angry and suspicious.

The troop camped halfway, and the next day rode into the Apache camp on Cibecue Creek, to be greeted with cold and distrustful faces. The colonel signaled Cougar to ride up beside him. "Act as my interpreter. Tell them we have come to arrest *Noch-ay-del-Klinne.*"

"If you please, sir," Cougar cautioned, "it is not good manners to be so abrupt. You should bring out gifts and food, sit down for a long parlay."

At the colonel's other side, Lieutenant Van Harrington said, "If I may be so bold, Colonel, why should we go through all this ceremony? We're just dealing with ragged savages, not Queen Victoria."

"Watch your tone, Lieutenant," Cougar snapped. "They can sense scorn even if they don't understand English. There's respect involved here."

The colonel seemed to think it over even as he looked around the circle. Cougar could tell he had just realized the troop was in the middle of a sizable Apache force. "All right, we'll parlay with them."

Cougar breathed a sigh of relief. Maybe they would get back to the fort with their skins intact after all. Damned if the lieutenant didn't look disappointed. Cougar turned and began preparations for a long parlay.

The two sides talked all afternoon, with the Apache leaders and the frail medicine man protesting that he did not mean to start a fresh war. The soldiers insisted that they only wanted to take him back to the fort and discuss the problem with him. Cougar had second thoughts as he translated.

The old medicine man asked him in their language, "Can I trust the whites?"

Cougar hesitated, torn between loyalties. These were his mother's people, but the other half of him was white. "I am not sure," he said truthfully. "I do not know the one called Carr well, but he wants to avoid bloodshed and war."

Finally, *Noch-ay-del-Klinne* agreed to go back to the fort with the soldiers. Cougar breathed a sigh of relief, but he heard angry muttering among the distrustful Apache.

"What are they saying?" The colonel leaned over to Cougar.

"They don't like it, sir. They're afraid something bad will happen to their holy man once he's in custody."

Phillip snickered. "Now wouldn't that just be too bad."

"Watch your mouth, Lieutenant," the older officer snapped. "I remember when the army tried to take Crazy Horse into custody and killed him right there on the grounds of Fort Robinson. Then we had a Cheyenne war on our hands. I'd like to avoid that here, if possible."

"Yes, sir." Phillip glowered at Cougar; his wispy mustache trembled in rage.

The frail medicine man mounted up and rode out with the soldiers, the watching Apache grumbling louder.

"Whew!" Phillip said to the colonel. "I thought we were going to have to fight our way out of that."

"It isn't over yet," Cougar cautioned. "They might still send a war party after us."

"Oh, they won't do that," Phillip sneered. "They're cowards and they can see how well armed we are."

Cougar gave him a cold look as they rode out. "Lieutenant, believe me, if they come after us tonight, you won't know it until you feel that cold blade slicing through your throat.''

Phillip turned pale and swallowed hard.

Cougar's gut feeling hung over him that whole afternoon as the troop started back toward Fort Apache. Though most of the soldiers seemed oblivious to it, the scouts were aware that they were being trailed by warriors.

That night, as the soldiers made camp, as Cougar had feared, all hell broke loose.

Chapter Eight

Just as Cougar had feared, when the troops bedded down for the night on their way to Fort Apache, the warriors following them attacked, trying to free their medicine man.

Captain Hentig looked about wildly. "What's happening? I thought Apaches wouldn't fight at night?"

"Only in desperation!" Cougar yelled. "A rumor has spread that *Noch-ay-del-Klinne* will be murdered at the fort as Crazy Horse was up north!"

Then there was no more time to talk or reason as the Apaches began firing from the bushes and bluffs around the camp. Yelling confusing orders to the troops, the officers tried to rally the soldiers to make a stand and keep from being overrun, but in the darkness and the noise, no one could bring order to the chaos as they were attacked. Gunfire echoed from both sides, and horses whinnied and reared in terror, throwing their riders. Men ran helter-skelter in the noise and dusty darkness. All about Cougar, men fell bloodied and screaming.

He had to at least get his scouts into a defensive position! Cougar fought his way to his horse while yelling orders to the Apache scouts. Some didn't seem to hear him above the hellish din and echoing gunshots. Others, suddenly thrown into their very first fight, ran about, seemingly confused as to what to do, and loath to fire at their relatives and friends.

As he watched, Captain Hentig clutched his chest and fell with a shriek. Cursing under his breath, Cougar swung up on his paint stallion and galloped into the fray, trying to organize his men to provide cover for the soldiers as they retreated. In the flickering firelight and flashes of gunfire, alkali dust clung to bloody, sweating faces, both white and brown. An Indian scout shouted in pain and went down, caught in the deadly crossfire.

Dirt seemed to grit between his teeth from the clouds of dust, and he could smell the warm blood on the chilly desert night. As Cougar watched, a soldier screamed and fell with bright blood bathing his shiny brass buttons. On the other side, too, warriors chanted war songs that were cut off abruptly as bullets found their mark.

Terrified, Cougar's horse reared and whinnied at the strong scent of blood, gunpowder, and swirling dust. However, Cougar himself was cool and brave under fire, assessing the situation, noting that the troop was surrounded and outnumbered. Maybe if they would free *Noch-ay-del-Klinne* and make an orderly retreat, the Apache wouldn't follow them.

Even as he thought that, he saw Phillip raise his rifle and aim it at the bewildered medicine man. "Damn that Injun for causing all this trouble! I'll fix him!"

"No!" Cougar yelled in protest, knowing that to kill the holy man might seal all their fates, but his shout came seconds too late. *Noch-ay-del-Klinne* clutched his chest, stumbled, and fell in the sand.

Cougar swore loudly, but under the barrage of echoing rifles, he couldn't hear his own words, much less the commanding officer who was out there somewhere in the middle of this firelit hell. At least, maybe he could save a few lives. "Retreat!" he yelled. "Get back where there's more cover!"

However, the soldiers' lines had been breached. In the confusion, instead of a solid line of troops and scouts facing off the warriors, hand-to-hand fighting had broken out, and the young Apache scouts paused uncertainly, looking about. Their relatives and friends were fighting to save the medicine man, who lay on the ground, seemingly wounded but still alive, and they didn't seem to hear Cougar shouting orders.

He groaned aloud as he realized that as he had feared, some of the greenest scouts were now joining up with their kinsmen, enraged over the shooting of the holy man. He still might manage to bring them back to the army's side; the young scouts liked and trusted Cougar. Even as he spurred his horse to ride forward to rally his men, he saw the sudden glint of a rifle barrel and glanced over to see Phillip's grinning face as he looked directly at Cougar, aimed, and pulled the trigger.

For a split second, Cougar's brain denied the action, refused to believe that a cavalry officer would turn his weapon against one of his own men. Even as his brain denied it and he froze in horror, the bullet tore through his right shoulder and almost tumbled him from the saddle. Agony washed over him, causing his own rifle to drop from his nerveless fingers. Cougar managed to hang on to his horse as it reared and snorted. He saw the smile and the glint of triumph in the other's blue eyes and realized, as the lieutenant raised his rifle again, that this time Phillip would kill him!

"No!" Pain almost overpowered him as he clung to his

saddle and fought to stay conscious. In that heartbeat, Cougar realized how badly he'd underestimated both the officer and how much Phillip hated him. And now Phillip was aiming at him again and Cougar was without a weapon, unarmed and defenseless. In that second, he did the only thing he could do to save his life; he urged his horse forward, galloping straight toward Phillip.

His big paint stallion leapt over the lieutenant, and Cougar kicked his weapon aside as he passed him and galloped across the perimeter of the circle. Hostile Apaches were between him and the army lines now, and there was no way to get back through the gunfire to rally the scouts. Worse than that, Cougar was bleeding badly; he felt the warm blood running from his useless arm, dripping onto the saddle, and staining the stallion's spotted coat scarlet.

Now the soldiers were retreating, losing men at every step.

Amazingly, *Noch-ay-del-Klinne* still lived. He crawled forward on his belly, trying to reach safety.

"Ye gods, the bastard's still alive! I'll fix that!" Before anyone could stop him, Phillip grabbed a hatchet, ran forward, and killed the wounded man. Then Phillip stumbled to his feet, shouting and gesturing wildly. "Look, men, Cougar's gone over to the enemy! Get him! Somebody get him!"

Even as Cougar opened his mouth to shout a denial, he saw the glint of rifle barrels as terrified and confused bluecoats turned their weapons toward him. Reeling in the saddle, near fainting from pain and loss of blood, Cougar acted instinctively. Spurring his horse, he turned and galloped out of the melee, many of the confused younger scouts following him. He wasn't certain where he was going; he only knew he had to get out of rifle range!

He could barely sit his horse, and his eyes were almost blinded by a haze of pain and swirling dust churned up by galloping horses and running men. He had to return to his scouts, help save them, let the colonel know he was loyal, that he wasn't a traitor or a deserting coward. Dimly, he clung to his saddle as the paint carried him away from the confusion and bloody battle. Some of the scouts had followed him out of the fray; others were still back there in the fight, Apaches on both sides, some breaking that most ancient taboo, brother killing brother.

He was several hundred yards out into the darkness now, the firing growing dimmer as he struggled to stay conscious. Just what he had warned about had happened with his inexperienced scouts and their divided loyalties. The realization hit him as he fought to stay in the saddle; then darkness claimed him and he knew no more.

When he awakened, it was dark and one of the other scouts had put some herbs on his wound and tied it up to stop the bleeding. In the distance, he heard occasional gunfire. "What—what happened?"

"The army is retreating back to the fort under cover of darkness, with the warriors harrying them," the other said. "There are many dead on both sides."

Cougar groaned aloud. "What about *Noch-ay-del-Klinne*?"

The men around him scowled. "Did you not see the lieutenant finish him off with an axe as one would kill a wounded dog? It is only fitting now that the lieutenant die at the hands of an Apache!"

"Phillip!" Cougar gasped as he struggled to sit up. "He has tried to kill me."

One of the very young runaway scouts, Dead Shot, peered at him hopefully. "Would the colonel understand? Some of us lost our heads in the excitement."

Another asked, "What will the army do to us?"

Cougar didn't speak. He knew what the answer would

be, but yet he could hope. "Maybe the colonel would listen. None of us meant to desert the soldiers and become traitors."

It was ironic, he thought; he, who had tried to help, who had remained loyal, was now a deserter along with these young, green scouts. If only Mac were here to give counsel, Colonel Carr might listen to him.

A scout held a canteen to his lips, and Cougar drank long and deep, relishing the cold, clear water, trying to think of his men's welfare. "When word gets out, the army will send reinforcements. They will hunt us down like coyotes and kill us without mercy."

"You are gravely wounded," a man said. "Shall we take you to the ranch?"

Cougar shook his head. "No, that's the first place the bluecoats will look."

His friend, Turtle, agreed with a nod. "It would bring trouble to the man called McGuire, who is a friend of our people."

"I must ride to the fort and explain to the colonel," Cougar gasped.

Another caught his arm as he tried to stand, keeping him from falling. "You are too weak to ride. We all need time to rest; many are hurt."

There was nothing Cougar could do but agree as the men lowered him to the ground.

"It was the lieutenant who started this," said another, "I saw him shoot our holy man. I saw him try to kill Cougar."

"I doubt the whites will believe that," Cougar whispered with a growing anger.

"Why does the officer hate you so?" one asked.

"I made a gift to his woman and she told him," he admitted bitterly, automatically reaching up to touch the necklace that no longer hung around his massive neck. He had been betrayed by both the red-haired beauty and his own heart. A blind fury began to build in him, fueled by his own stupidity at giving his heart to a white seductress who had laughed and thrown his most precious possession away. Because of the haughty Elizabeth Winters, he could not go back to the bluecoats; no one would believe him. Even if he returned, Phillip would plot to kill him again; he would have to watch his back continually. At the moment, it was a moot point; he couldn't even stand, much less ride.

In the distance, the shots echoed across the barren land as the cool night deepened and the soldiers fought their way back to the fort. Cougar could do nothing but lie there and listen, gritting his teeth against the throbbing pain of his wound. After a while, he drifted into unconsciousness, and in his tortured dreams he saw her face and those bright green eyes. A hatred for the fiery-haired beauty crowded out the passion he had felt for her, and he imagined his big hands on her fragile throat. If he had her at his mercy, there was no end to the things he would do to her!

Days passed as Cougar drifted in and out of consciousness in the cave. Old Owl Woman, the wet nurse who had raised him, came to care for him and brought him news.

"Our warriors harried the soldiers all the way back to the fort, surrounded and attacked it, but the bluecoats sent for reinforcements."

Cougar groaned aloud. "I knew it! A new Apache war is starting!"

The old woman nodded. "Many of the Apaches are on the warpath or have fled the reservation and headed for the old stronghold deep in the mountains of Mexico, where they will be safe from soldier attacks."

"What about my scouts?" He tried to sit up, but she restrained him.

"Some of them went in and surrendered to the soldiers. They are sorry for their actions in the heat of the moment, but the soldiers would not listen and threw them in jail. It is said they will put them on trial."

"By Ussen, if I could only get to that trial to make the whites listen—"

"You think they would?" Her brown face furrowed as she shook her head. "You know the man called McGuire will try to help, but all say it will be useless. Besides, the soldiers are looking for you, too. They call you a traitor."

A traitor. For many years he had faithfully served the white man's soldiers—and now this! If only he could talk to Colonel Carr, if only . . . No, he was still too weak to ride. There was nothing he could do for now. Phillip. Phillip had had a large part in this, and it was all over that red-haired temptress. Cougar's life had been turned upside down and destroyed for love of the girl he called Blaze. As he lay helpless and recuperating, his hatred for the white beauty built until it glowed like a hot flame that consumed him.

Things were very dull in Boston, Libbie thought as she left French class at Miss Priddy's Academy and went to check her mail. It was chilly now that it was late September. President Garfield had died in mid-September after lingering for weeks from the assassin's bullet that felled him in July, and of course plans were under way for a big trial; there seemed to be little else in the newspapers.

Her thoughts went to Arizona, and she wondered what was happening out there. She had written Phillip a polite note when she got back to school, thanking him for a lovely visit. She tried to think of something to say about their coming marriage that was enthusiastic, failed, and finally didn't mention their wedding plans at all. On the other hand, she hadn't received a letter from Phillip since she'd left Fort Grant, and she was torn between relief and worry. *Had she said something to offend him? Did she care?* With Mrs. Everett reminding her often that her inheritance was almost gone, she supposed she should be concerned, but maintaining their present lifestyle seemed much more important to her guardian than to Libbie.

Now here at last was a letter from Phillip in her mailbox. Libbie sighed and stared at the envelope: then she took it up to her room to read.

My Dearest Elizabeth:
I'm sorry I haven't written sooner, but there has been a terrible outbreak with the Apache here. . . .

Libbie's interest picked up when she saw Cougar's name. By Phillip's account, there had been a mutiny while the army tried to arrest some evil medicine man. The troops had killed lots of savages. Eight soldiers, including a Captain Hentig, had been killed or died later from wounds. He himself had barely escaped with his life while, of course, saving the day for the army. There was some talk of a medal, and wouldn't it look splendid on his dress uniform for the wedding?

Damn Phillip for his shallow arrogance. Libbie sighed and scanned through the rest of the letter quickly. Cougar, that cunning half-breed, had helped lead the rebellion. The medicine man was dead, and some of the scouts who had mutinied had given themselves up or been captured. Of course there were going to be trials for the traitorous Apaches.

Traitors. Libbie reread the whole thing, but the last part was rather vague, and Phillip veered off the subject, talking about a hunting trip he was planning. He hoped to kill another bear and maybe a wolf to stuff for his library back home.

Libbie read the letter again. *Was Cougar one of those being held in jail for trial?* She couldn't be sure. The memory of the man came back to her as if they had met just last night—the touch of his hands on her skin as he placed the necklace around her throat, the torment she'd felt when he stood so close. *Was she out of her mind to be having such fantasies over a half-breed scout in a faraway place?*

Tears came to her eyes as she hurried to take the necklace from where she had hidden it in a box under her bed for safekeeping and away from the curious eyes of her schoolmates. For a long moment, she held it, remembering that night, that man. He had seemed so honorable and protective. *Could he possibly be guilty? What did they do to traitors? Did they hang them?*

Quickly she reached for pen and paper and began to write a note to Phillip, asking for more information about the mutiny. But then she paused and considered. What would Phillip think if she wrote and asked about Cougar? He might be suspicious and jealous. Very slowly, she crumpled the letter and began again in a very casual manner, commending him on the possible medal and asking for further details of the event.

After she mailed the letter, she began watching the newspapers, searching for every scrap of information on that faraway Territory. Arizona might as well be on the moon as far as civilized Boston was concerned, Libbie decided, or at least, it was all being pushed off the pages by earthshaking events such as the death of President Garfield and the coming trial of his assassin.

There was almost no mention of events in Arizona Territory, except that several days later, Henrietta Van Harrington did send her a friendly note telling her Phillip had been transferred back to Fort Grant, along with a clipping from the Philadelphia paper about Phillip's heroism, and how much young Van Harrington was like his father, who, the paper reminded its readers, had been slain in battle by that same tribe of savages almost a quarter of a century before.

Phillip lay back on the straw in the dimly lit barn and reread Elizabeth's letter, then laughed aloud. "Ye gods! She's trying to be so casual, but damn her, she doesn't fool me!"

"Doesn't fool you about what?" Shashké rolled over on him, rubbing her naked breasts against his bare body.

He reached up and caught one of her big breasts in his hand absently. "Nothing that concerns you, my pet."

Her pretty face turned into a pout. He did have to admit she was very arousing with her black hair in a tumble and the fine gold earrings gleaming in the light.

She put the scarlet cactus blossom between her white teeth, playing with it. "It is that red-haired lady again, isn't it? I thought you were going to tell her about us?"

"I am; I am," he lied. "This just isn't the right time yet, that's all." Damn, he was tired of this stupid Injun slut. She was getting too possessive and jealous, threatening to tell the commander and anyone who would listen of their relationship.

"When is the right time?" the slut insisted.

"I don't know. Maybe after the holidays—January, or maybe later."

She brightened. "January, the month of bear tracks. A good omen for me."

He hardly heard her. All he knew was that she was smiling again, which meant maybe she'd let him vent his lust on her nubile body. He pulled Shashké to where he could get his mouth on her breast, and his manhood began to build to hardness again. Yes, he was weary of the slut, but he hadn't figured out how to dump her yet. In the meantime, Elizabeth must think he was pretty stupid himself not to see through that letter. He could read between the lines; she wanted more information about that damned scout's fate. Phillip didn't have any intention of relieving her anxieties. After all, when the army did capture the elusive scout, they were going to hang him, along with those other scouts who had come to the fort after Cibecue to surrender. But first, there had to be the formality of a trial.

Hell, let Elizabeth stew a while and get over her attraction to the scout. After he married her next spring, he'd control her and her fortune. He was looking forward to the use of her beautiful body. He'd do what he damned well pleased with all her wealth, too, and if she complained about anything, he'd beat her senseless.

Shashké nuzzled his ear. "I shouldn't keep meeting you in broad daylight," she murmured. "It makes it easier for my old husband to find out."

What did he care? He rolled her over on her back and made ready to enter her ripe body.

"You don't ever tell me you love me," she complained, trying to wiggle out from under him.

He wasn't going to be stopped now, not when he felt ready to explode with lust. "I love you," he whispered, frantically forcing himself into her before she could change her mind. He had a rich fianceé, a lusty Injun mistress, a possible medal, and his bitter enemy, Cougar, was on the run, being hunted down like a hapless coyote.

"Life can't get any better than this!" he assured himself as he rode Shashké hard and brutally, pretending that it was the genteel Elizabeth Winters. Well, next spring, it would be!

* * *

In the bright moonlight, Cougar noted that the desert nights were turning colder with the coming of autumn. Soon, in the mountains to the north, there would be snow. Cautiously, he rode through the night and reined in, checking for an ambush. Now he whistled a bird song, waited for the answering call. He had to give the signal three times; the old man's hearing was getting worse. When the answering signal came, he nudged his horse through the dark night toward the secret meeting place—his mother's grave.

"Boy? Is that you?"

His heart warmed at the familiar voice. He dismounted and threw his arms around the old man's shoulders. "I've missed you!"

"And me you!" The other stepped back, wiping his eyes awkwardly in the moonlight. "Ever since Turtle came out here to bring me the message that ye were still alive, but wounded, I've been worried to death."

Cougar sat down on a rock. "Have the soldiers been here?"

"Aye, many times. That was why I was afraid to come to ye, afraid they would follow. My eyes and ears aren't what they used to be, I'm afraid."

"Thanks for sneaking us the supplies through Turtle. I knew the lieutenant would watch the ranch, and I did not want to bring you trouble by coming here too soon."

The other man smiled warmly as he lit his pipe. "Ye've been bringing me trouble since the day ye were born, but I wouldn't have traded a minute of all these past years."

Cougar felt his own eyes tear up, and he cleared his throat awkwardly. "What is the gossip at the fort? What has happened to those scouts who surrendered?"

Mac puffed his pipe and avoided Cougar's eyes. "There

was a quick trial, not much of a defense. The poor devils didn't even seem to know what was going on, since none of them speak English.''

"Did you speak in their defense?" Cougar asked.

"Ye know I did." Mac nodded and smoked. "But the army thinks of me as the father of the most traitorous half-breed scout, so no one listened."

Cougar swore under his breath. "You know I was no traitor! The lieutenant tried to kill me at Cibecue and my horse bolted, so I ended up outside the army's lines."

Mac shook his head. "I told ye you'd make a bitter enemy of him over that girl."

"Don't even mention that red-haired bitch to me!" He spat to one side with contempt. "So what of my scouts?"

Mac sighed. "Some are being sent away to prison—three of them, unless the new President, Arthur, commutes their sentences, which isn't likely. The army will hang Skippy, Dandy Jim, and Dead Shot at Fort Grant next March."

"Aiyeh!" Cougar agonized for a long moment. "Maybe if I went in, gave myself up, tried to explain—"

"No!" Mac said. "They'd hang you for sure! You dying won't help those poor devils. The whole territory's aflame now with a new Apache war. The only safe haven for any of you is Mexico."

"Those scouts are my men. I've got to try to save them."

"Cougar"—the old man laid his hand on the broad, scarred shoulder—"ye can do nothing more for them. I'll try to send messages by Turtle if anything changes. I'd advise ye to get yourself a woman, cross the border, and try to make a new life for yourself."

He thought of the flame-haired beauty who had scorned his humble gift. "There's only one woman I want."

Mac sighed. "Aye, and you're a fool to want what ye can never have! Don't waste your heart on a girl whose love belongs to someone else."

"You're a fine one to be giving advice," Cougar said pointedly. "I'm only doing what you did."

"Aye, and you see what it brought me." The old man smoked and peered with dimmed eyes at the grave.

"Would you do any differently if you had it to do over again?"

Mac smiled slowly and blinked back the sudden moisture in his eyes. "You know I wouldn't. The little time she was mine was worth the heartache." He stood up and handed Cougar a bundle. "Here, I've got a few supplies for you. Not much—a little meat, some matches, a blanket."

"Thanks." He took the bundle and they embraced one last time. "May Ussen look after you."

"I'm not the one in danger," Mac cautioned. "You be careful now. Phillip's at Fort Grant and there's talk of a big promotion for him next spring for his gallantry at Cibecue."

"Gallantry?" Cougar snorted. "He caused the trouble."

Mac shrugged. "You know how the army works; they're very good at covering up their mistakes."

Cougar stared at the grave. "So you've told me."

"Sometimes there's no harm in it if the truth would cause pain."

Cougar looked at him a long moment, loving him so much that for a moment he could not speak. "You have an Apache heart, you know that?"

Mac blinked rapidly and cleared his throat. "So your people tell me. Good-bye, boy. I'm not much on religion, but I'll pray for you."

"Pray for Phillip," Cougar said through clenched teeth, "he's going to need it!"

Mac shook his head. "You can't."

"I know." Cougar nodded as he swung up on his paint stallion. "But such evil cannot go unpunished."

"Then let Ussen punish him," Mac said.

Cougar nodded. "But if that arrogant white girl ever comes here again, I will have my revenge! There is nothing I wouldn't do to her for the way she has scorned and humiliated me!"

"Then I'll pray she never comes to Arizona again."

Cougar didn't answer as he wheeled his horse and galloped away.

Mac waved and watched Cougar ride out, wishing he could take the burden of a broken heart from him. He watched until the silhouette was swallowed up by the night shadows. Then Mac turned to the grave and remembered the past. "Ah, me gentle beauty, how I miss you! He's grown up now; you'd be so proud!"

Somewhere in the darkness, a night bird called as if answering his lonely voice. Mac swallowed the big lump that threatened to choke him as he recalled the terrible, terrible night she died. It hadn't been his name she had called out in her last moments.

Chapter Nine

As autumn deepened, the days and weeks seemed to crawl past for Libbie in Boston. As Christmas approached, her guardian and Mrs. Van Harrington corresponded frequently about wedding plans and met several times, although Libbie seemed so casual about it all to her guardian that Mrs. Everett reprimanded her privately when Libbie went to her town house for tea. "We must hook this young man! I'm going to be spending the last of your inheritance on this big wedding!"

"What would happen if I changed my mind?" Libbie said idly, looking out the window at the barren trees swaying in the icy wind and remembering the golden warmth of Arizona.

"My stars! Bite your tongue!" Her plump guardian paled and wheezed hard. "You'd have to go to work like some shopgirl, and then what would happen to poor me?"

"You might have to go to work, too," Libbie said.

The other drew herself up proudly. "I am a lady!" she

announced with a superior sniff, "I wasn't cut out to be some parlor maid or seamstress; that's for immigrants and the lower classes!"

Libbie bit her lip and didn't say anything. She looked out window at the cold, feeling very much alone as she remembered other holidays with her parents—and the warmth of Arizona and a big man's arms last summer.

Obviously taking silence for meekness, the older woman changed the subject. "Have you been writing Phillip regularly so he won't forget you?"

"Some," Libbie murmured. "I've been so busy with my studies."

"Hmm." The stout lady looked unimpressed. "And have you heard from young Phillip lately?"

"More than I've written him. He's terribly busy, I suppose. There's trouble with the Apache attacking outlying posts and ranches ever since that Cibecue thing. He's gotten a commendation for that and is hoping to be promoted to captain, as well as getting a medal."

"Well, I've got a surprise for you!" Her guardian fanned herself briskly. "We've been invited to spend the Christmas holidays at the Van Harrington mansion. You know, we've hardly seen their home; she's always come here to work on wedding plans."

"Oh." *Damn. She hoped Phillip wasn't coming in on leave.* On the other hand, if he were, she might hear details of a certain big half-breed.

"Well!" Mrs. Everett huffed, "you don't seem very excited about the prospect."

"It's just that Phillip surely won't be there." Libbie tried to cover her lack of interest. "With all that trouble with the Apaches, I'm sure he can't get leave right now."

"Arizona. Apaches. My stars! Do you realize how often you mention that horrid place and those half-naked savages?" Her guardian snapped.

"I was just thinking of Phillip," Libbie said, reaching for her coat. She hadn't realized until now just how often that faraway place was on her mind. And Phillip was her only link to that place. She wondered suddenly if she might have a letter in her box at school. "I must be getting back," she said, "to work on my needlework and knitting." Libbie hated doing fancy needlework, but all genteel young ladies were expected to be accomplished in it.

"Just make your plans for Philadelphia," the plump lady reminded her, "and for heaven's sake, be sweeter to Mrs. Van Harrington and more enthusiastic about the wedding."

"Yes, of course." Libbie straightened her hat and hurried out the door to the carriage. With any luck, there might be a letter from Phillip. His last letter had said the traitorous Apache scouts had been sentenced to hang, but there was a possibility of appeal. Mac McGuire would do something, she thought—surely he wouldn't let his half-breed son go to the gallows!

The holidays at the Van Harrington mansion turned out to be a disaster as far as Libbie was concerned. The weather turned especially cold and miserable, and as she and her guardian alighted from the carriage at the mansion, Libbie's heart sank. "It looks like a dreary old castle," she muttered, staring up at the gray stone turrets.

"Behave yourself, young lady!" her guardian snapped. "It's a fashionable mansion that has been in the Van Harrington family for several generations. They are old Philadelphia society, you know, and very, very respectable."

Libbie gathered up her skirts off the dirty snow as the coachman came around to help them with their luggage. Possibly she would become mistress of this dungeon upon her marriage to Phillip, but she wasn't looking forward to it.

The door opened and Mrs. Van Harrington came sweeping out, lean and grim, still dressed in widow's black, although Major Van Harrington had been dead a quarter of a century. "Ah, my dears! You're here earlier than I expected! Do come in!"

She bustled about, snapping orders to meek and trembling maids who came out the door to help with the luggage. Libbie tried to smile and let her future mother-in-law embrace her and plant a dry, cold kiss on her cheek. Mrs. Van Harrington's thin lips smiled, but her cold gray eyes did not. Again, Libbie was certain that she would be making a mistake to marry into this family.

She must stop thinking like that; of course she was going to marry Phillip. Her inheritance was almost gone and what would a genteel lady do without money? Somehow, the idea of going to work didn't frighten her as much as it did her plump guardian, but then, what kind of position could Libbie hold with a knowledge of French, playing the violin and not very good needlework? Perhaps a governess? With a sigh, she followed the two other women into the house and prepared her mind for a long, dull holiday.

She was not disappointed. Inside, the house was as grim and foreboding as Mrs. Van Harrington herself. The lady ruled the mansion with an iron hand, and Libbie had a feeling she wasn't about to give up control to a very young daughter-in-law. The assorted nieces, nephews, old-maid sisters, and cousins who came for the holiday were as hostile to her as possible, except they did seem to have an unusual interest in Libbie's financial holdings, which puzzled her. She brushed all questions aside with vague answers, hoping the women of that family didn't suspect Libbie was almost broke and marrying Phillip for the security of the Van Harrington fortune.

Even a Christmas tree didn't seem to cheer up the grim, dreary mansion as the holiday progressed. Looking about, the place seemed a trifle threadbare to her, but perhaps they were only old-fashioned and very conservative with their spending. Mrs. Everett was delighted with everything, already picturing herself ensconced in cozy large rooms of her own in the mansion, no doubt enjoying ordering the maids about and living a life of ease.

On the second afternoon she was there, Libbie discovered the library. On its wall were dozens of pictures of the late major at various stages of his life. Libbie studied the photos, wondering about the man. In the earlier ones, he looked fairly happy, but as the photos aged, there was something sad and haunting about those bright blue eyes.

Mrs. Van Harrington came into the library. "Wasn't William a handsome man?"

Libbie nodded, still looking at the photos. "He looks like Phillip with those wide shoulders and that strong jaw."

"Doesn't he, though?" she said proudly, picking up a small, silver-framed photo from the desk. "You'll have such handsome sons, my dear."

Sons sired by Phillip. She pictured herself naked in bed with Phillip . . . No, she didn't like that thought at all. She stared at the photos again, then blinked. *Was she out of her mind?* The thought that had just crossed her mind was simply too outrageous. To banish it, she turned and smiled at the lady. "You must have loved him very much."

"I did. Oh, we had some problems, as all young couples do, but we adored each other. Now I lavish all my love and attention on our son."

A mama's boy. Libbie had sensed that from the first.

Henrietta still stared at the old photo. "William died a hero, you know, killed by those terrible savages out there where Phillip is now. I've seen to it that my son doesn't forget he must avenge his father's death. He was only four when his father was murdered."

"Yes, I know," Libbie said softly, "Phillip told me." She looked around at the other pictures. In them all, Henrietta Van Harrington was smiling; William was not. There was something tragic about his expression. Maybe the marriage hadn't been as happy as Mrs. Van Harrington thought.

"Well, enough of these sad thoughts." The lady put the photo back on the desk. "I shan't wear black to the wedding, of course, but you know, I've spent my whole life mourning William. Now his son, my precious boy, is my whole life, my only reason for living."

A warning bell went off in Libbie's head. She was going to have to compete with her mother-in-law for Phillip's love and attention. She realized she didn't much care. "I think I hear guests arriving." She turned, relieved to be able to exit gratefully.

"Yes, we must join them." The other woman lifted her skirts and started for the door. "All my dear friends want to meet you. I've been in such deep mourning, my dear, I haven't redecorated in many years. Since you'll be living here, after the wedding, we must redecorate. I've already chosen the wallpaper and fabrics."

Libbie set her jaw. *Damn. So she wasn't to have a home of her own. Well, what had she expected from a mama's boy?* "As the future mistress of this house, shouldn't I do that?"

The other turned and smiled ever so slightly, but there was no warmth in the cold gray eyes. "I'm sure you will like what I've chosen."

Her tone was almost a challenge, and Libbie was about to rise to it when she remembered Mrs. Everett's dour warning about how close they were to being penniless. "Of course," Libbie managed, swallowing a protest, "I'm sure I shall."

With a sinking heart, Libbie realized what she'd always

suspected was true; Mrs. Van Harrington did not plan to give up control of either the money, the house, or the son. She expected—no, would demand—a pliant, meek daughter-in-law to produce heirs for the Van Harrington fortune. She felt like the proverbial lamb being led to the slaughter. But that was not a good comparison; Libbie was anything but meek!

Mrs. Everett dropped her powder keg in late February. First, Libbie received a hastily written note from her by messenger saying there was something very important to discuss. Mrs. Everett asked her to please come to tea that afternoon and make herself as beautiful as possible. Libbie stared at the note with a sigh.

Was Phillip in town? If so, wouldn't he have let her know? Maybe his mother was visiting to finalize all the nuptial plans. Libbie had a beautiful, extravagant wedding dress, bought with almost the last of the inheritance. If this wedding didn't go through, Mrs. Everett had warned her, they were both going to be selling apples on the street. That, Libbie thought as she began to dress, seemed more and more desirable rather than becoming mistress of that gray-stone dungeon.

Libbie put on a beautiful green-velvet walking suit that brought out the color of her eyes and added a wonderful matching hat with perky feathers as she made ready for the visit to her guardian's town house. She had been saving a little money here and there since before the Christmas holidays, but it wasn't much; certainly not enough to finance her escape from this straitlaced school and that very respectable marriage. All the other girls had been congratulating her on her nice catch.

Now she called for a carriage and arrived on a snowy, cold afternoon at her guardian's place. *I'll wager it's warm in Arizona, and I hate the cold,* she thought as she stood shivering on the doorstep and rang the bell.

"Do come in." Mrs. Everett, wearing an oppressive dark-olive dress, opened the door and caught her hand. "Something terrible has happened!"

"Phillip's changed his mind?" She tried to sound worried as she entered, but felt relief instead.

"My stars! No, worse than that!" She closed the door against the cold wind and motioned Libbie to a chair. "Sit down. Let me get you some tea." The plump woman waddled away and returned with a tray of dainty cups, steaming with the hot brew, and a plate of sugar cookies.

Libbie sipped the steaming tea gratefully, savoring the bracing warmth. "I am so tired of the cold weather; too bad the Van Harringtons don't live farther south."

"Are you not listening to me?" Mrs. Everett scolded. "I said something terrible has happened!"

"Are you ill? Has someone died—?" Libbie began.

"Worse than that! The Van Harringtons have no money!" The lady leaned back in her chair and reached for her smelling salts, fanning herself all the while.

"What?" Libbie paused with her tea cup halfway to her lips.

"That's what I said!" The lady warmed to her tale, evidently pleased at catching Libbie off guard. "When we were there at Christmas, I became suspicious because everything seemed so threadbare, so I began making inquiries. The Van Harringtons have gone through their fortune— bad investments and Phillip's wastrel ways before he went off to the army. That's why he went out of his way to get an introduction to you at that ball; he's a fortune hunter!"

Libbie paused and let the words sink in. Then she put down her cup, threw back her head, and began to laugh.

"Libbie, what is the matter with you? Have you taken leave of your senses?"

"Don't you see?" Libbie wiped her eyes and laughed some more. "The joke's on us; we were after money, too."

"This is not funny!" She fanned herself rapidly. "I can already see us both working as shopgirls. I've contacted Mrs. Van Harrington and broken the engagement in no uncertain terms."

"It might have been nice if someone had let Phillip and me make the decision," Libbie said sarcastically. "Do they know we're broke, too?"

"No, thank goodness, so we can start looking for a more suitable match right away."

Libbie began to laugh again, partly from sheer relief. "I don't have to marry Phillip Van Harrington?"

"Stop laughing! This is serious! We'll be out of money by this summer, and if you aren't engaged by then—"

"Suppose I say no?" Libbie snapped.

"Of course you can't say no." The other looked at Libbie as if she'd lost her mind. "What is a well-bred young lady to do except marry well?"

"I just might decide to go West; I really liked it there."

"Now I know you've lost your mind." Her guardian looked sympathetic. "Poor child, I know this is a great shock, but I've been thinking ahead."

"For just once, I'd like to make some of my own decisions."

"Don't get sassy with me, young lady!" Mrs. Everett shook her plump finger in Libbie's face. "I promised your dear mother I'd look after you—"

"Why have I always had the feeling that you were really looking after the Winters fortune?" Libbie was annoyed enough now to say what she'd been thinking for a long time. "And I'm sure Daddy left plenty of money; I can't imagine why we've run out."

Mrs. Everett's heavy jowls turned a mottled red. "How

dare you? Are you suggesting I've wasted or misappropriated your inheritance?"

"You tell me!" Libbie glared back at her.

Her guardian did not meet her eyes, hesitating uncertainly. "Why, you ungrateful, spoiled—!"

"So it's true!" Libbie fired back.

"So I played a little whist and tried to make a few investments; I was only trying to help," Mrs. Everett said self-righteously.

"So you've helped me right to the poor house!"

"This is no time to panic," the stout lady declared, fanning herself. "There are other fortunes to be had."

"What? Whatever are you talking about?"

About that time, the doorbell rang and Mrs. Everett looked relieved as she stood up.

Libbie blinked. "Are you expecting someone?"

"A possible suitor." Mrs. Everett smiled and waddled toward the door. "That's why I asked you to look beautiful."

"Damn! You've made all these arrangements without even asking?" Libbie was aghast.

Her guardian paused with her hand on the doorknob. "Well, we've got to do something drastic before the money runs out."

Libbie stood up. "I don't want to meet another suitor. I'll go out the back door."

The doorbell rang again.

"Sit still and behave yourself like a proper lady!" Mrs. Everett commanded even as she opened the door. "Well, Mr. Higginbottom, so nice of you to come!"

Higginbottom? She wasn't about to marry someone named Higginbottom, but it was too late to escape the introduction.

"My dear lady," she heard a quavering voice from the front porch say, "I was so pleased to be invited to meet your ward."

The two came into the room and Libbie stared, speechless.

"Libbie, my dear, may I present a dear old friend, Mr. Ebenezer Higginbottom."

Old was right. He was balding, very plump, and bandy-legged. He could easily have been Libbie's father. Or maybe even her grandfather. Suddenly, being penniless didn't seem like such a bad alternative after all.

"Charmed, my dear." He took her limp hand in his and kissed it. "Mrs. Everett didn't exaggerate your beauty."

Mrs. Everett glared at her. "Where are your manners, Libbie?"

"I'm pleased to make your acquaintance," Libbie said automatically, staring at him. His false teeth didn't fit well and they clicked when he opened and closed his mouth. However, there was no doubt he was prosperous; a big gold watch chain hung across his brocade vest, and his clothes were of the finest fabric.

"I am sorry to hear of your broken engagement," he said with great sympathy, but his nearsighted vision seemed to be focused on her breasts.

"That young cad misrepresented himself!" Mrs. Everett sniffed. "He was only a cheap fortune hunter, after my ward's inheritance."

Mr. Higginbottom leaned even closer to Libbie, absolutely leering at her. "You won't have that problem with me, my dear. I am one of the richest men in Boston; only the Shaws and the Van Schuylers are as substantial as I am."

Mrs. Everett beamed. "Yes, we met your partner in Arizona. You remember Mr. Tiffany, the Indian agent, don't you, Libbie?" she prompted.

Tiffany? Oh, yes, the crook who was getting rich cheating the Apaches with the help of dishonest partners back east. So this was one of the partners.

Her guardian took the caller's hat. "Do let me get you some tea, Ebenezer. Would you like something more substantial than a cookie? Perhaps a sandwich—?"

"Oh, dear me, no." He dismissed the offer with a shaky hand. "Too much meat is bad for my gout."

He was still staring at Libbie's bosom as Mrs. Everett poured his tea. "Yes, she is as lovely as you told me, Mrs. Everett."

Libbie crossed her arms over her chest and looked about as if to escape. She wasn't quite sure what she was expected to say.

"And she plays the violin and does needlework," Mrs. Everett volunteered.

"Good! A wife in my social position needs skills like that. Of course, I certainly would like some heirs." He grinned wickedly and Libbie stared back at him, imagining herself in bed naked with this old man. It was a worse image than sleeping with Phillip.

"I really need to be getting back to school," Libbie said and stood up.

Her guardian shot her a look like a dagger. "Must you, my dear? I'm sure Ebenezer would like to know more about you."

He was looking at her breasts again. "I think I know all I need to know," he lisped as his teeth clicked. "My dear, you're evidently a lovely young lady very soon to graduate from a good school, and I am a man in need of a wife. At my age, I don't see any reason to be coy about this."

Mrs. Everett smiled. "It might be a little unusual, but perhaps we could plan something for this summer."

"I must be getting back," Libbie said, a little desperately now.

Mr. Ebenezer Higginbottom stood and made a courtly bow. "I am at your service, my dear, and hoping to know you better soon."

"Perhaps you can take Libbie driving this weekend," Mrs. Everett suggested, "and show her your estate."

The old man's false teeth clicked as he nodded. "Splendid idea! I have a fine coach and the best matched set of carriage horses in town."

"I'll think about it." Libbie said and, grabbing her coat, hurried out the door.

Mrs. Everett called after her. "I'll send you a note, my dear."

Libbie didn't look back as she fled back to Miss Priddy's school.

What to do? She was out of the frying pan and into the proverbial fire. Or rather out of Phillip's bed and into Ebenezer's. Libbie shuddered at the thought. Phillip seemed almost appealing by comparison with the rich old geezer Mrs. Everett had found to replace him. She stopped to check her box for mail and found a letter from Phillip. She couldn't help but smile at the irony of it all; two penniless people trying to marry a fortune, and they had both been outfoxed.

She went to her room, sat on her bed, and read the letter. Evidently he hadn't heard that his duplicity had been discovered, because he opened with "Dearest Girl" and told her how much he and Mother were looking forward to the wedding this summer.

What caused Libbie to stop smiling was his last line:

. . . They'll be hanging three of the traitorous Apache scouts at Fort Grant the first week of March. Two others have been sent to prison. I'll be at Fort Grant as part of my duties to witness the executions, of course. The army is beefing up security, expecting that all these savages on the warpath might try to rescue the condemned men. I hear hanging's an awful death; you'll be fortunate not to have to watch. . . .

She paused and reread the letter, searching for the names of the condemned scouts. They hadn't seemed important enough for him to mention. Libbie dropped the letter from nerveless fingers.

Why did she have a terrible premonition that Cougar was thinking of her, as she was of him, at this very minute? Was it because their souls had seemed to speak to each other in that brief moment when he had bestowed his necklace on her? Was the army going to hang the scout who had put the beautiful Apache Tears on her throat and touched her so gently?

"Oh, please, no!" With a cry, she retrieved the necklace from its hiding place and sat holding it with tears dripping down her face. She touched each stone, remembering the warm caress of his fingers on her throat, and the sudden scary desire she had felt as he stood close to her. She had never felt that emotion before.

Now they were going to kill him and Phillip was going to watch; no doubt eager to give her the details later, even though gentlemen never told anything gory or shocking to a lady. She had a sudden feeling Phillip would relish telling her the details; he had seemed to dislike the scout so.

What could she do to help Cougar, especially thousands of miles away in this dreary frozen city? She rose and searched out the small purse she had hidden in her chest. After she counted the money in it, she sighed. There were only a few dollars, perhaps enough for a train ticket and a stagecoach one way. If she made this trip to Arizona, she couldn't get back.

Abruptly, she raised her chin and took a deep breath. She was tired of the life she was living and weary to death of her greedy guardian. Money had never mattered to Libbie. At that moment, she decided she wasn't coming back, not ever, no matter what happened. She'd rather take her chances in that exciting new Territory, taking charge of her own life rather than live a meek, safe existence as the rich Mrs. Ebenezer Higginbottom. Libbie shuddered at that thought.

She began to pack, making sure she included the necklace of Apache Tears. She wasn't taking much and she wasn't sure what she was going to do when she got to Fort Grant except try to save the Apache scout from the gallows. How she might accomplish that, Libbie hadn't the faintest idea; but she was desperate enough to try anything. She didn't look back as she grabbed her small valise, her reticule, and ran out the door. If nothing else, she wanted to see Cougar one last time before they hanged him!

Chapter Ten

February 28, 1882

Phillip felt happy as he crossed the parade grounds at Fort Grant. It was still chilly, but soon it would be spring. Because of his gallantry at Cibecue he had been offered a reassignment to an important post in Washington, D.C., where he might further his political ambitions. Then, with his bride's wealth, family prestige, and beauty, he was certain his future had nowhere to go but up!

However, he hadn't yet gotten his full measure of revenge against the damned Apaches, especially the one called Cougar, so he had delayed accepting the new post until late spring. Besides, he wanted to be present at the hangings. Phillip grinned with anticipation at the thought.

Yes, he was going to get to see that red-skinned trio dancing on air! His only regret was that Cougar wasn't among the condemned men. He scowled at the thought of the hated half-breed, who had gone on to leading war parties all over the Territory, raiding for food and supplies for those damned starving Apaches. He and his warriors struck like lightning, took horses and cattle, and then were swallowed up by the vast desert and buttes of this godforsaken land.

Well, with new reinforcements now combing all of northeastern Arizona Territory, it was only a matter of time before the red devil was captured, and Phillip hoped to be the one to pull the trap when they hanged Cougar, so it was worth it to delay his assignment to Washington.

Phillip's biggest problem now was Shashké who was making more and more demands on him, perhaps suspecting that he would soon be leaving and had no intention of taking her with him. He was tired of the sulky girl, and besides, he'd just noticed a sergeant's lusty daughter and was hoping to make a new conquest.

As he sauntered across the parade ground, a soldier ran up to him and saluted. "Telegram, sir, from your mother."

Phillip saluted carelessly and walked toward his barracks reading the wire.

Problem has arisen. Stop. Secret discovered. Stop. Engagement broken and Libbie has disappeared. Stop. Letter following. Stop. Love, Mother.

Ye gods! What could have happened? Maybe Elizabeth had found out about Shashké. Phillip crumpled the paper in his hand and considered. *Secret discovered.* Oh-oh. That high-and-mighty little society bitch had found out the Van Harringtons were penniless! Now he would never get his hands on the Winters fortune or get that temptress in his bed and at his mercy. He had planned all sorts of erotic pleasures once she was legally his.

Where could Libbie have gone? More important, could he find her and sweet-talk her out of breaking the engagement? To lose both her money and the pleasure of taking her virginity was unthinkable! However, with the hanging only days away, he couldn't get a furlough right now to deal with this. He wished he had more details, but with the Injuns harassing the mail and attacking supply caravans, it might be weeks before he got his mother's letter. He considered sending a telegram, then immediately shook his head. He certainly didn't want to wash the family laundry via the telegraph where all the fort would find out about it. *What to do?*

Phillip started walking again, thinking hard. Until he knew more, he couldn't plan a course of action. He paused and pulled at his skimpy mustache. Whatever it took, he was looking forward to bedding the beautiful redhead, and he wasn't about to lose all that dowry!

March 3, 1882, dawned cold and gray at Fort Grant. Phillip Van Harrington snapped to attention in front of his line of troops as the senior officers came out of the building and walked down the line of soldiers lined up on the parade ground. They paused before him and Phillip saluted.

"At ease, Lieutenant." The older man looked up and down at Phillip's troops. "Any sign of trouble?"

"No, sir, we've got plenty of reinforcements; the Apaches won't try to rescue them."

The other sighed and pulled out his pocket watch. "Damned sorry business."

"If you say so, sir." Phillip wasn't shedding any tears over three stupid Apaches. He looked toward the new gallows standing starkly against the coming chill dawn.

"I was hoping for a last-minute reprieve from the President," the senior officer muttered, following Phillip's gaze toward the gallows.

Phillip didn't say anything. He was delighted they were going to hang those three Injun scouts. He only regretted he could not witness hanging a lot more Apaches—particularly Cougar.

The senior officer looked around at the assembled troops and the civilians and dignitaries assembled on the parade ground in the cool morning wind. "Then we'll get on with it." The officer strode toward the jail behind the gallows.

Phillip yawned and wished this thing was over so he could go have another cup of coffee. He had already asked for a furlough to go help in the search for Elizabeth, but the senior officer had seemed preoccupied and waved Phillip out of his office.

He shifted his weight from one foot to the other as they all waited for the condemned men to be brought out. Damn the stubborn, spoiled little red-haired wench! He could only hope to find her and sweet-talk her into marriage. If so, once the knot was safely tied, he'd wear out his quirt on her little backside to turn her into a subservient and obedient wife. He listened to the flag on the parade ground flap in the cold wind and wished the officers would get it over with.

From the top of a distant hill, Cougar and his warriors sat their horses and watched the parade ground with its soldiers and crowds of curious white settlers. "We must attack the fort and save them."

"Are you mad?" asked Turtle. "Look at the number of extra bluecoats today. Not one of us would get out alive."

Cougar frowned. "What you say is true, but we must do something!"

"The three would not want our whole band wiped out in a rescue attempt," said the old warrior to his left.

In helpless frustration, Cougar clenched his fists and watched the scene below. The three scouts were being led from the jail in chains, armed soldiers surrounding them. Out on the parade ground, extra soldiers from other forts stood in formation with weapons at the ready. Cougar reached for his rifle.

Another warrior frowned. "What is it you do?"

"They would rather die by a friend's merciful bullet than be strangled like puppies with a string."

"The distance is too far."

Cougar brought his rifle up to his shoulder and sighted. The other brave was right; the condemned trio was out of rifle range. Dandy Jim, Skippy, and Dead Shot walked with dignity toward the gallows, heads high. Such silly names, soldier names, for three good warriors. Even Cougar couldn't remember their Apache names, he thought now as he watched with a heavy heart. He could see the heavy chains on the scouts' wrists and ankles, and the wind carried the faint clang of metal to his ears. *Did he only imagine he saw Phillip Van Harrington in that formation of soldiers standing at attention on one side of the parade grounds? He couldn't be sure.*

The trio of hapless Apaches stumbled as they walked, their heavy chains dragging as they were led toward their deaths. There seemed to be hundreds of bluecoats standing in the parade ground, their brass buttons and rifles catching the first faint light.

As Cougar and his men watched from their hilltop, the condemned men trudged up the steps to the gallows and the padre stepped forward. The three looked confused as they surveyed the huge crowd that had come to watch. One stared stoically straight ahead; one watched the ropes swing in the wind. One glanced up toward the hilltop, and his gaze seemed to lock on Cougar's.

That silent appeal wrenched at Cougar's heart. He

shoved his rifle back in the scabbard. "We must do something to stop this!" He spurred his horse forward.

However, even as he did so, old Beaver Skin reached out and hit him across the back of the head with the butt of his pistol.

With a groan, Cougar slid from his horse. The big paint snorted and reared, then settled down and nuzzled his fallen master.

The old warrior looked down at Cougar's prone form with a sigh. "You are a very brave man, Cougar," he said, "but we cannot save our three friends today. We must leave them to our god, Ussen. Our warriors will live to fight another day and woe be to the bluecoats!"

Phillip had the most uncomfortable feeling that he was being watched by silent eyes, but the parade ground was quiet except for the jangle of the leg chains on the condemned men and an occasional cavalry horse stamping its hooves. The priest had stepped forward to speak to the three Apaches. To Phillip, the three looked confused and bewildered, as if they weren't quite sure why they, who had scouted for the bluecoats, were now going to be killed in this most horrible manner.

Ye gods, why did they have to drag this out? Couldn't they just hurry up and get it over with so everyone could go have a nice breakfast? Phillip shifted his weight impatiently and stared at the scouts. He had forgotten how young the condemned Apaches were, not much more than boys. They looked pale but composed as the ropes were put over their heads and adjusted. Phillip imagined slipping one of those same nooses over Cougar's head and smiled at the thought. Now the black hoods were going over their heads and the minister was praying aloud.

Phillip glanced around in curiosity. Some of the soldiers

who had liked the three scouts looked grim and pale. He wondered for a moment if any of the three had wives and families. Injuns bred like animals with no more attachment to each other than coyotes; the wives would find other mates. Phillip wondered idly if any of the about-to-be-widowed Apache girls was pretty. Maybe he could fill in the void for the grieving widows.

The officer on the platform was reading the official verdict and sentence. He was reading in English, of course. No doubt the condemned men couldn't understand a word of it. The wind carried away the words, and they could hardly be heard anyway over the flag snapping in the early morning wind. Finally the officer stepped back.

Damn, that wind was cold for this part of the country! Phillip shivered and watched the gallows, willing this thing to be over so he could retreat inside for some coffee. There was a long pause, broken only by the cold March wind and a horse shaking its head, rattling the metal on its bridle.

Then an official stepped forward and sprang the trap. Around him, Phillip heard a collective gasp from some of the soldiers who were seeing men die for the first time. For less than a heartbeat, the bodies fell, then hit the end of the ropes with loud thumps.

Phillip smiled to himself as he watched the limp bodies swing at the ends of the ropes. Settlers were turning away, their faces pale and sick. Around him, he heard soldiers swallowing hard, as if they were nauseated. Phillip felt only a grim satisfaction. This would teach other Injuns not to revolt against their white masters. Three wasn't much of a payback for Major Van Harrington's death, but Phillip intended there would be more before he was finished. Next time, he vowed, it would be that damned Cougar. Who was it who said that the only good Indian was a dead Indian? Well, there were three mighty good Indians at Fort Grant this morning!

* * *

Cougar had stumbled to his feet even as the traps of the gallows were sprung.

"No!" he cried out, but the wind carried away his words. He tried to run forward, as if he would rush down to the parade ground and stop the execution, but Beaver Skin reached out and caught his arm.

"They go with Ussen to the Happy Place," the old warrior said.

The war party watched in sadness from the hilltop.

Young Turtle said, "Let us be gone from this cursed place."

But Cougar continued to stare at the bodies of his friends swinging from the gallows in the distance. They let them hang there a long, long time while the whites watched in silence.

Cougar's skull was throbbing with pain as he stumbled to his stallion and mounted up. He knew Beaver Skin had saved him from folly and did not hate him for it, but he hated the soldiers he had once served. "We will make them pay for this," he said solemnly as they turned their horses and rode out. "Sooner or later, we will make them pay!"

In the early dawn, Libbie got off the train at Willcox and smoothed the rumples from the soft-pink velvet dress she wore. Then, picking up her reticule and her small valise, she hurried to the connecting stage office. The door was locked. She rattled it and cursed under her breath.

Leaning on a post near the door was a rough-hewn, weathered man in faded jeans and shapeless western hat. "It's locked up."

"I can see that! I need to get the next stage out to Fort Grant," she said.

He looked her up and down and spat tobacco juice on the worn wooden porch. "Lady, the stage stopped running a week ago because they're expecting more trouble with the Apache."

Damn. She hadn't counted on this after she'd come all this way over the last several days. She was exhausted, almost out of funds, and now she was stranded in a strange town. However, Libbie wasn't one to give up easily. "Look, I must get to Fort Grant today."

"Wantin' to see the excitement, huh?" He grinned. "Half the folks in the Territory is headed over to watch the hangin'."

She didn't dare ask any details. "I—my fiancé is assigned there." Maybe she couldn't stop the army from executing Cougar and the others, but if she could save Cougar's life, she was bound to try. "Do you know where I could rent a buggy?"

"Maybe." He pushed the battered hat back and spat tobacco juice again. "What kind of man would let his sweetheart make that dangerous run across Apache country?"

"It's a matter of life or death." Libbie gave him her most winsome look while she calculated the last of her little hoard of funds. "I could pay very well."

"Lady, who can put a price on your life?"

She smiled at him. "You look like a mighty brave man to me."

He colored and kicked his boot toe against the floor. She could see by his expression that he was thinking it over. Finally he said, "I reckon since no stages have run for days, the Apaches wouldn't be expecting travelers; so maybe there'd be no ambushes."

She got her money out of her reticule so he could see

it. He appeared to be looking at her clothing, possibly judging whether she or her fiancé could possibly come up with more.

"My fiancé is Lieutenant Phillip Van Harrington," Libbie said, "of the Philadelphia Van Harringtons."

"Important galoot, is he?" He looked at the money in her hand with greedy eyes.

"Some would say so."

He spat again. "I might could get a horse and buggy, miss; but it'll cost you. If I'm gonna risk my life, I expect to be well paid."

She didn't even ask, just handed him what money she had left. "Just get me there. There'll be more if we make it." She wasn't sure where she'd get any more, but she was desperate to try to stop this hanging or at least see Cougar one more time. "Can we leave right away?"

"Soon's I can get the harness on." He disappeared out the back door. Libbie sat down on her suitcase and waited. What had she let herself in for? This man could be a robber or a killer, or he might take her money and run. On the other hand, he looked greedy enough that if he thought there'd be more at the end of the trip, he'd drive her.

In a few minutes, the man returned driving a worn and very creaky buggy pulled by an old chestnut horse. "Is that the best you could do?"

"It'll get us there. Get in, lady."

"All right." She threw her little valise up on the seat beside him and climbed up onto the back seat so she wouldn't have to sit next to him. Besides the fact that she didn't feel much like talking, she was also afraid that with all his spitting, he might get tobacco juice on her pale pink dress.

She reached up to touch the Apache Tears necklace she wore under the high collar of her dress. Would it indeed protect her from harm if they ran into Apaches along the way? Somehow, she had faith in Cougar's promise.

As they drove out of town, he took off his hat and scratched his tangled hair, looking back at her. "Lady, you must love that soldier a whole bunch to make this trip with the Apaches on the warpath."

"You're going, too," she pointed out.

"I'm doin' it for the money, and I'm thinkin' I must be loco. Them Apaches is all het up over that Cibecue thing. The army's hangin' some of them over it."

Her heart seemed to stop. "So you said. When?" She wanted to beg for more information, but she knew that if she acted too interested, the driver would wonder why.

"Don't know for sure; telegraph lines been down. Injuns keep cuttin' them. I thought today, but it might be tomorrow."

Today. Cougar might already be dead. No, she would not consider that possibility. "Can't you drive a little faster?"

In answer, he slapped the horse with the reins and it broke into a trot. He tried to keep up a conversation, but Libbie didn't encourage it. Her mind was too fraught with worry.

It was warmer now, the sun covering the landscape by mid-morning. The driver stopped the buggy once to water the horse. "We'll be there in a couple more hours."

"Can't we do any better than that?"

He grinned. "You must be awful eager to see that soldier boy."

Libbie made a noncommittal sound. She hadn't given Phillip a thought. If she ran into him, what was she going to do? It might be delightful to see his face when she told him she was as penniless as he was, but right now her mind was riveted on only one thing—Cougar. "Can we go on now?"

The driver got back up on the seat and whistled to the

horse. "No sign of Injuns yet," he threw back over his shoulder, "but I can almost smell 'em in the area. 'Pears to me that fancy lieutenant of yours should give me a nice bonus for gettin' you there safely."

"We'll see." Libbie frowned and wiped the alkali dust from her face, looking up at the sun moving relentlessly across the sky. If she couldn't stop the hanging, she wanted to at least tell Cougar good-bye. Where she would go or what she would do after that, she didn't know.

The driver spat off the side of the buggy as it clipped along the road, throwing up dust behind it. "I'd like to see that hangin.' Them scouts is guilty of treason. Onliest man who don't think we ought to hang the whole Apache nation is that rancher, Mac McGuire. He's been trying to save them redskins from the gallows."

Mac. Yes, maybe he'd give her shelter and help her figure out what to do. Libbie sank back against the seat and closed her eyes. In her mind, she saw Cougar walking tall and proud to the gallows even as she drove toward him. "Can't you drive a little faster?"

The driver snapped his little whip at the horse. "I tole you hit was gonna be a long ways, ma'am. You shoulda waited 'til the stage begins to run again."

That would have been too late, Libbie thought. Her heart sank as she thought, *Even now, I may be too late.*

The buggy moved down the road at a fast clip and into a little valley. Libbie reached up to touch her necklace and prayed that she wasn't too slow to intercede on the scout's behalf, even though she had no hope the commander would listen to her. Phillip would be furious if she tried to save Cougar, but what did she care? She could hardly wait to see his face when she told him she was as penniless as he was!

She was jolted out of her thoughts by the driver's startled cry as he glanced off toward the east. "Oh, my God!"

Libbie turned to look at what had caught his attention. In the distance, at the top of a butte, a large war party of Indians sat their horses and watched the moving buggy.

The driver swore and began to whip the horse. The startled chestnut set off at a gallop.

Libbie took a deep breath and grabbed onto the seat to save herself from tumbling off. "Maybe they haven't seen us," she said.

Even as she said that, the tiny, distant figures pointed toward the moving buggy and then began a slow, single-file descent of the butte.

The driver cursed and whipped the horse to run faster. The buggy moved now at breakneck speed, churning up dust. Libbie felt it clinging to her fair skin and tasted the grit of it as she gasped for breath. She coughed and hung on. "Can't you do something?"

"I've got a rifle, ma'am!" he flung back over his shoulder, "but you can't hit nothin' from a movin' buggy, and I ain't about to stop and take on a whole war party!"

The Indians were coming at them full speed now, although with the dust they were churning up, it was difficult to make out anything but bright war paint and running horses.

It was too terrifying to contemplate. Libbie closed her eyes in the choking dust, but from a distance, she could hear yelping cries as the Apaches hit the bottom of the butte and started after the buggy at full gallop. "We—we aren't going to be able to outrun them, are we?"

"Not with a buggy! We ain't got a chance!" There was terror in the driver's voice, and she could smell the fear sweat on him. Libbie reached up to touch the necklace under the collar of her dress. *Damn, why had she taken off on this foolhardy jaunt?*

Libbie glanced back over her shoulder, choking on the

swirling alkali dust. It was apparent their pursuers were gaining on them. All she could see was running horses and brown bodies. "What do we do?"

The buggy slammed to a halt as the driver pulled hard on the reins. She had to grab the seat to keep from falling out.

He grabbed his rifle and jumped down from the seat.

"You're going to make a stand?" Libbie asked.

He had his knife out, cutting the lathered horse loose from the rig. "Sorry, ma'am, I got no chance against that whole bunch! I—I'll go for help!"

Even as she watched in disbelief, the man swung up on the horse.

"You're leaving me here?"

He avoided her eyes, but she saw the ashen terror on his face. The man didn't answer as he whipped the lathered horse and galloped away toward the fort.

"Wait! Come back!" Libbie screamed in protest, but he was rapidly disappearing as the war party galloped toward her. *What to do?* She had no weapon and no horse. Well, she certainly wasn't going to sit here and wait for them to kill her! There were some brush and cactus a few hundred yards up the road—maybe she could hide there!

Libbie clambered down from the buggy, lifted her skirts, and began to run up the road. She didn't even know how far it was to the fort, but at least she would die trying to save herself.

They were gaining on her. She stumbled and fell, got to her feet, and ran on, cursing the tight corset that restrained her breathing. Libbie glanced back. In the swirling dust, most of the warriors had stopped to vandalize the buggy, but one was galloping toward her, bright paint across his dark face, his horse decorated for war. He was almost upon her, galloping as if to ride her down. She stumbled, got to her feet and ran on, heart pounding with terror.

When she glanced back again, the rider was almost upon her—and she could see that he had bright blue eyes, and those eyes were full of vengeance!

Chapter Eleven

She looked up at him in astonishment as he loomed over her on his galloping horse. "Cougar?"

He hesitated, pulling on the reins, causing the paint to rear and whinny. In the swirling alkali dust, she saw only his war-painted face and bright blue eyes. Those eyes widened now with surprise and hatred. "You!"

Hatred? His eyes were like glacier ice in that painted brown face. Instinctively, Libbie scrambled to her feet and took off running; she stumbled, fell, got up, and began to run again, breathing hard. Behind her, she heard the thunder of hooves. She glanced over her shoulder. The big stallion was coming at her in a dead gallop. He was going to ride her down!

Even as she screamed out a protest, he leaned from the saddle and swung her up before him on the saddle.

"Cougar!" she kicked and shrieked. "Don't you remember me? Put me down! How dare you run off my driver!" She beat her small fists against his bare chest.

He paid no more attention to her blows than if she were a child. Instead he threw back his head and laughed, but there was no warmth in that laughter. "Remember you? How could I forget? So we meet again, lieutenant's lady!"

So they hadn't hanged him after all—or maybe he had escaped. She was only too aware of the strength and the warmth of the arm gripping her through the pale pink dress. She had forgotten how big and male he was. Terrified by his tone and the fury in those cold blue eyes, she looked up into his face, but saw no warmth there. Past his broad shoulder, she saw the other warriors tearing into her luggage, throwing her things in the air. "Make them stop! They're destroying my things!"

"You're in the hands of savages, and yet you worry about fine clothes and jewelry," he sneered, but he didn't yell at his men to stop. Instead, he hung on to her, ignoring her struggles as he rode back to the buggy and spoke to his men in his own language. It was apparent to Libbie that he was urging them to hurry. Now he turned his own mount toward the south. "We will leave now," he informed her in English, "before your brave driver reaches the fort and brings a bluecoat rescue party."

"How dare you! I'm not going anywhere with you!" She struggled, but he held her against him firmly, paying not the slightest notice of her protest. Instead, he kicked his magnificent stallion into a gallop and pressed Libbie against his warm, naked chest.

And to think she had come to Arizona hoping to save this wretched half-breed from an army hanging. The ingrate! Now she wished he was on the scaffold and she was being given the privilege of pulling the trap.

"Listen to me!" she demanded, but he didn't even look down at her as he galloped south, surrounded by his warriors.

Soon Phillip will come to the rescue with a bunch of soldiers, she thought. Or maybe not. Phillip wasn't all that brave, and maybe he'd found out by now that Libbie was as penniless as he was. "Cougar, listen to me!" she screamed.

But his jaw was set, his mouth grim, and he looked ahead as he rode, paying no more attention to his captive than if she'd been a bundle of clothing he'd salvaged from the wrecked buggy.

What to do? There didn't seem to be anything she could do until they stopped and he was willing to listen to reason. Then she would show him the necklace she wore and demand that he respect his promise. Could she count on him remembering that promise, or was he only a heathen savage after all?

She didn't know how long they rode south. Her mouth was dry, and the sun scorched her delicate skin. Once the group stopped to rest in the shade of a mesquite tree and Cougar poured a little water in his hands and offered it to his horse, which drank gratefully.

She was scared, but she wasn't going to show it. She drew herself up haughtily. "If the horse can spare it, I would like a drink, too."

He glared at her darkly. "I need to keep the horse in shape so it can run. Perhaps if you do without until you are more humble, I will give you water, too."

If he thought she would beg for a drink, he was sadly mistaken. "What about the Apache Tears necklace?" she asked. "You told me—"

"Hush!" His face turned angrier still. "Don't remind me of my foolishness!"

The fury in his blue eyes silenced her. She wasn't certain why he was so angry, but now she was afraid to pursue it. Obviously, he regretted giving the necklace to her, or maybe it didn't mean anything after all. He had lied to her, perhaps in the hopes of seducing her. He was as bad as Phillip. And to think she had made this long trip hoping to save his neck from a noose! What a fool she had been!

The warriors mounted up again, the others paying no more attention to her than if she'd been a rifle or a saddle pack. Their expressions said she belonged to Cougar, and they were not interested in what he did with his possessions; that was his decision.

"You, get back up on the horse," he ordered with an arrogant gesture.

"I will not! I'm tired and sore," Libbie yelled back. "I demand that you return me to the fort."

"You are a captive, and as such will demand nothing." He picked her up unceremoniously and threw her up on the stallion in a swirl of white lace petticoats and pink velvet. For a split second, she wondered if she could urge the stallion into a gallop and escape, but at that moment, Cougar swung up behind her and slipped his arms around her waist. He pulled her back against his strong, half-naked body. The sensations that coursed through her at the feel of his flesh startled her.

"How dare you handle me so familiarly!"

"I dare because I own you," he snapped and pulled her closer still. "Now shut up before I throw you across a pack horse like a load of flour and tie your hands and feet under the horse's belly."

The others must speak a little English, or at least they understood the clash of wills, because the warriors broke into laughter.

She was furious. Cougar's hands were hot on her waist and she could feel his maleness as she sat in the vee of his thighs. "Perhaps you didn't understand me. I demand—"

"You will demand nothing," he said coldly and nudged his horse forward again. "You are my slave."

"Slave? But you don't understand—"

"No, it's you who doesn't understand," he snapped. "I

will decide what is to become of you. You are at my mercy, arrogant white girl!''

What was he so angry about? Whatever it was, this was no time to argue with him. When they finally got wherever they were going, maybe he would have controlled his temper and would listen to reason. And if not, surely that cowardly driver had made it to the fort and a cavalry troop was on its way to save her.

It was late afternoon and Libbie was so exhausted, she was reeling in the saddle. She tried to stay awake, but she kept falling asleep in Cougar's arms. She could feel his breath against her hair, the beat of his heart, and he was cradling her almost gently. She wanted to pull away from him, knowing this was not proper, but she was too weary to care.

Finally, the group reached a small camp of wickiups in some hills. Where were they? There was no way to know. Libbie had a sinking feeling that the Apaches had been careful to cover their trail so that army trackers would have a difficult time following the raiders.

Indians of all ages came running out to meet the group as they rode in. Libbie tried to ignore the hostile glares by sitting up as proudly as if she were a queen and these riders were her servants.

Cougar dismounted and held up his hands for her. She glared down at him and wondered if she could possibly turn the horse around and make a run for it.

"Get down!" he demanded in a voice that brooked no argument.

"I will not!" She put her chin up proudly. "You take me right back to the nearest white settlement and—"

He reached up, caught her arm, and jerked her out of the saddle. She fell in a heap at his feet while the surrounding Indians laughed. Her hair had come loose from its pins, and now it fell around her shoulders. "I am your owner now," he said, "you will do what you are told."

She looked up at him, defiance blazing in her green eyes. "How dare you treat me like this? How dare you—?"

He reached down without a word, picked her up, and tossed her across his shoulder like a sack of flour. She could feel the heat of his big hands across the back of her bare legs and her face pressed against his bare, muscular back. She had never met a man this strong. Even as she puzzled over what to do next, he turned and strode across the camp, followed by a curious crowd of Indians.

Cougar walked quickly, acutely aware of the warmth and softness of her body hanging over his broad shoulder and the silky feel of her legs under his hands. He had never felt such mixed emotions toward a woman—wanting to kiss her and kill her at the same time. Then he remembered how the lieutenant had said she'd laughed at Cougar, and his heart hardened. Now that he had taken her captive, he wasn't sure what he was going to do with her; let the rich lieutenant ransom her, probably. The Apaches could use the money for food and supplies. Cougar had stolen her on impulse because from the first moment Libbie Winters had walked into his life, he had wanted her as he'd never wanted another woman. A pity, since she was such a cold, arrogant bitch!

He strode toward his wickiup, ignoring her small fists beating on his bare back. Maybe he would use her to lure a soldier patrol into a trap. With his friends hanged just that morning, fury and grief still controlled his emotions. Or maybe he would use the girl for his pleasure before he let the hated lieutenant ransom his future bride. It would be a good joke on Phillip for Cougar to take her virginity and then toss her back to him as used goods. Probably Phillip wouldn't want her back if another man had touched her.

He could feel her small fists beat against his bare back as he walked with her. Her red hair had come loose from its pins and hung almost to the ground, brushing against his bare flesh like fiery silk.

"Stop that!" He slapped her hard across the rear.

"How dare you! How dare you touch my person!"

Libbie was suddenly afraid. Cougar didn't say anything, only kept walking. Damn! She was in a hostile camp many miles from any whites who might help her. Cougar had evidently forgotten his promise. Or worse yet, never intended to keep it.

Now he paused and carried her through the door of a thatched wickiup and dumped her unceremoniously on a pile of furs; then he stood glaring down at her.

Libbie shook her hair away from her face and glared back. "Return me to the fort at once!"

"So, Blaze, we meet again." He stood, hands on hips, frowning down at her.

"My name is not Blaze—it's Libbie."

"Blaze suits you better." He shrugged. "And since I own you at the moment, I choose what to call you."

"Like a pet dog?" She was livid.

"Exactly."

Oh, he was so arrogant!

He picked up a canteen from the floor. "Now, Blaze, would you like some water?"

She hesitated, watching him open the canteen and take a long drink. The water ran down both sides of his mouth and dripped onto his bare, muscular chest.

"Do you expect me to beg for it?"

He considered a long moment, then handed it to her. "That's not a bad idea. Slaves should be submissive."

"Submissive I am not!" Libbie grabbed the canteen and turned it upside down, letting the water run out on the ground.

He only smiled thinly. "Your arrogance is both challenging and annoying. But I will soon take that out of you. Very well, now do without!" He turned on his heel and started to leave.

"Wait, where are you going?" She was more afraid of the other warriors than she was of him. At least he spoke English; maybe she could reason with him.

"I have to report to the council." His blue eyes were cold as glacier ice. "Then I'll be back."

She glanced around furtively, wondering what the chances were of slipping away.

He must have read her mind because he said, "I wouldn't try it, Blaze. It's a long way through hostile country."

She didn't say anything as he turned and strode out.

Damn, why had she made that proud, silly gesture and poured out the water? She grabbed the canteen and turned it up to her lips, but there was only a drop or two in it. Maybe when he came back, she'd humble herself and ask for water. Or maybe not.

Mercy, she was smothering in this corset. She managed to unhook her dress, take the corset off, and put her dress back on. Now she had nothing on under the pink velvet except a long, lacy petticoat and the necklace, but who would know or care? She hesitated. He had grown so angry when she mentioned the necklace, maybe she should take it off and throw it away. Her hand went to her throat under the pink velvet. There was no place she could throw it or hide it that he might not find it.

Libbie amused herself for the next few minutes imagining the army coming to her rescue and capturing Cougar. Maybe they would hang him for kidnapping her. She took off her shoes and wiggled her toes, considering. Maybe they would offer to let her pull the trap that dropped him. That sounded very appealing right now.

After a few minutes, Cougar reentered the wickiup. "We're moving on after dark; less likely to be seen that way."

For the first time since her capture, she took a good long look at him. He wore nothing but the skimpiest of breechclothes and a pair of tall moccasins. She was both fascinated and shocked by his almost naked body. It was brown, muscular, and scarred. "Who is we? Surely you aren't planning on taking me—"

"I will take you wherever I want to take you, Blaze. You have no say in it. Eventually, we'll be crossing the border and into the Sierra Madre."

"Mexico?"

He nodded. "Out of the reach of pursuing soldiers. We can't go too far until we hook up with the gun runners who bring supplies."

She licked her dry lips, uneasy at the way his blue eyes were devouring her slim body. "Suppose I don't want to go?"

"Are you as deaf as old Mac? I told you, you are a pet with no choices in what I do with you. You are also a nuisance that will slow us down. Some of our people are not pleased that I brought you here."

"So why did you?" she challenged him.

He hesitated, not looking her in the eye. "Because you are worth a lot of cartridges and supplies to us in ransom money. I'm sure rich Phillip Van Harrington will pay well to get you back."

"Phillip isn't . . ." She paused. If the Apaches found out Phillip wasn't rich, then what? "Suppose he won't or can't ransom me?"

Cougar squatted and looked her over slowly with those hard eyes. "Any man who ever saw you would want you, Blaze. The lieutenant will come up with the money, believe me; I would."

She was unnerved by the frank passion in Cougar's eyes—passion and male need. She wasn't at all sure Phillip cared that much; but he might try to help her if he hadn't found out that she was penniless, too. She needed a plan.

Don't panic, Libbie, she told herself. That was what the average silly girl from Miss Priddy's Academy would do. *You're braver and more resourceful than that.*

What she had to do was stall for time and try to keep the Apaches from crossing the border until either the army could catch up to them or she could figure out a way to escape. Cougar was evidently a leader and gave orders. What would delay him? She saw the way he was looking at her, and she knew exactly what it would take. A shiver went up her back, and she wasn't sure whether it was fear or excitement. She had never believed she could be so daring, but then, she'd never been a prisoner of Indians before. "Suppose I—I offer my body as ransom?"

His eyebrows went up, and then he threw back his head and laughed sardonically. "You offer to bargain with what I can already take? Blaze, you disappoint me!"

She backed away from him, her trepidation growing. "You'd—you'd just—take me, even if I said no?"

"Does the thought of being loved by a savage terrify you so much then?" He seemed to be enjoying her discomfort hugely.

"No, I mean yes. I—I don't know what I mean."

"Then let's find out." He advanced on her, and she stumbled backward, knowing he was toying with her.

She was as angry as she was scared. "Damn it, stop that!"

"Stop what, Blaze? I haven't done anything." He wasn't smiling now as he advanced on her.

At this point, she tripped over a blanket roll and went sprawling backward. She lay there looking up at him, a confusion of red curls, pink velvet skirts, and a swirl of lacy white petticoats. "Don't you touch me!"

He threw back his head and laughed. "Spoken with all the ferocity of a cornered kitten. Do you bite and scratch too?"

"Try me!" She looked up at him towering over her. There was no way to get up and no place to retreat.

"Maybe I intend to, lieutenant's lady."

Libbie shrieked and crossed her hands over her breasts. "Don't you touch me! Phillip will shoot you—"

It had been the wrong thing to say, she realized that the minute she saw the added fury on the Apache's handsome face.

She could fight and scratch, but she didn't have a chance against this man. Still she intended to give as good as she got before she was raped. She lay there breathing hard and glaring up at him.

The big Apache stood staring down at her, an expression of aroused passion on his rugged face. She had never seen such desire in a man's eyes. "I am going to have you, Blaze, if it costs me my life. Taking your virginity is something I have dreamed of."

She desperately struggled to get to her feet. "It's just a woman you need; any woman, not me."

"I wouldn't be too sure. You underestimate your charms."

She shook her head. "No, it's just that you hate Phillip so much, you want his woman."

"And I will have her." With one big hand, he reached down and caught the front of her pink bodice and ripped it open even as she tried to strike his hand away. When the fabric tore, her full, pink-tipped breasts spilled out and he gasped and paused as his gaze took in the vision of her half-naked breasts. In that skimpy loincloth, his arousal was most evident and his eyes were afire with banked passion; and then they widened with surprise.

In that moment of silence, with both of them breathing

hard, he began to curse softly. "The necklace. You are wearing my Apache Tears necklace."

She scrambled to a sitting position, her hands going up to touch the necklace she had forgotten she was wearing. "You told me it would protect me."

Cougar was almost shaking with his need, standing looking down at her. With her hands at her throat, her beautiful, rose-tipped breasts were naked for him to see, her fiery hair in a tousled tumble over her shoulders. She was the most desirable woman he had ever seen, and he had never needed a woman as much as he needed one at this moment. No, not any woman—*this* woman.

The silver, turquoise, and Apache Tears stones lay against the swell of her creamy bosom. He reached out ever so slowly, tangled his fingers in the necklace, and pulled her closer to him. She dared not breathe, feeling the heat of his fingers against her naked breasts. No man had ever touched her so intimately before. The sensation was both exciting and scary. For a split second, she wondered if that strong hand was going to rip the necklace from her throat.

Instead, he gradually turned loose the necklace. "Take it off!" he commanded.

"I will not!" She straightened and glared back at him, fire in those green eyes, her bare breasts forgotten. "You said it would protect me!"

"You are a cold-blooded bitch to use that promise as a safe passage during an Indian war."

Her courage returned at his hesitation. "You didn't say there were limitations on it."

"What in the hell are you doing out here anyway?"

"I came because of the hangings," she blurted, "I thought you—"

"You thought I was being hanged?"

She was too annoyed to be truthful. "Of course. I wanted to see the army stretch your neck."

She saw the anger in his hard face. "Sorry to disappoint you."

"It isn't over yet," she reminded him, "and in the meantime, is your word good? Does the necklace protect me?"

"By Ussen, you know it does!" He had given her his oath, and he could not touch her or harm her as long as she wore that necklace of Apache Tears. Nor by custom could he forcibly remove it.

He gave her a black look, turned, and stalked out, leaving her trembling at her close call. Libbie realized suddenly that she was sitting here half naked and that he had seen her breasts.

He came back with a canteen and she crossed her arms over her breasts.

"I've already seen them," he said without expression as he handed her the water, "there's no need to hide them from me."

"All right then!" She was just scared enough to be defiant. She took her hands from her breasts, grabbed the canteen, and tipped back her head, drinking long and deep.

Cougar watched her, envied the droplets running down both sides of her mouth, dripping on her breasts. He had a terrible urge to sweep her up, kiss the cold water from her throat and nipples, but he did not move. If he touched her, he was not sure he could keep from throwing her down across those furs and taking her virginity, and rape was an Apache taboo. His people thought the raped woman's bad spirits would haunt a warrior. He had felt desire for women in the past, but never with this mindless, burning passion he was feeling now. "I'll get us some food."

She shook her hair back and tried to pull the torn edges of her bodice together, fastening them with a hairpin.

Cursing under his breath, Cougar went out. He couldn't bear to be within reach of Libbie Winters without wanting her lithe, creamy body. Damn her for keeping the necklace—not out of sentiment, but for safe passage to come see him hang. He walked to the big stew pot boiling in the center of the village. Someone had stolen a rancher's steer, and the tribe was eating well tonight. He got two gourds full, returned to the wickiup, and thrust one at her. "Eat and get some rest; we've got a long road ahead of us."

"All right." She ate slowly and watched him from under her lashes. She would delay this move as much as possible, she thought, so the army could catch up to them. Or maybe when Cougar dropped off to sleep, she could steal a horse and escape.

"Hurry up!" he ordered, "the camp is packing up to move out."

"I'll have you know I'm not used to gulping my food like some—like some—"

"Savage?" he suggested.

"I didn't say that."

"No, but you were thinking it. Let's go." He stood up.

"But I'm not finished."

"Yes, you are." He reached over, grabbed the gourd, and tossed it away. "I'm not so stupid, Blaze, that I don't know you're trying to delay us."

She was still hungry and furious. "So what if I am?"

He was gathering up weapons and canteens. "Apaches sometimes kill captives that can't keep up."

His words sent a chill up her back. He was bluffing. Wasn't he? "Why—would they do that?"

"Because trigger-happy soldiers are usually on our trail and we won't get our women and children killed over an enemy captive."

"I'm not going anywhere." She sat down in the middle of the wickiup.

"Yes, you are." He picked her up, flipped her over his shoulder again, and strode from the wickiup. "Don't try my patience, Blaze. I can't protect you if the council decides you're more trouble than you're worth."

That thought hadn't occurred to her. She didn't want to get herself killed trying to delay the march so that the soldiers could catch up. She hadn't realized how strong he was until he tossed her up on the horse. At that point, for the first time, she noticed the livid scar on his shoulder. He seemed to see her notice it.

"Compliments of your dear Phillip at Cibecue." His tone dripped sarcasm.

"Phillip? But you're on the same side."

"*Were* on the same side." Cougar swung up on the horse and pulled her against him familiarly. "He saw a chance to kill me and tried to take it."

"Phillip wouldn't do such a low-down—"

"Wouldn't he, though? You don't know your fiancé very well."

Something in his voice hinted there were many things about Phillip Van Harrington she did not know, but Cougar said no more, only spurred his horse to join the line of march to the south. A stretch of desert and low hills lay around them in a purple haze.

Mexico; they were going to Mexico, she thought in desperation. Once they were across the border, the army might never find her!

Chapter Twelve

Only an hour after the hanging, Phillip was in the colonel's office.

"What is it?" Colonel Carr snapped as he halfheartedly returned Phillip's salute.

"Sir, I'm requesting a furlough—"

"Are you out of your mind?" The other man slammed his fist down on his desk and stood up. "In case you've forgotten, Lieutenant, we hanged three Apaches this morning, and I feel rotten about it. Now I'm waiting to see if war parties attack the fort or set the whole Territory ablaze."

Damn the old man. Phillip cleared his throat. "Yes, sir, I realize that, but I've got important business back East—"

"We've got important business here!" The other paced irritably. "I don't understand you, Lieutenant. You were offered a chance to transfer and didn't take it. Now you come in wanting a furlough. Well, with all this Apache trouble, none of us are going anywhere. Your business can wait!"

"But—"

"Did you not hear me, Lieutenant? Now get out of my office!"

"Yes, sir." Phillip saluted and fled. When he looked back over his shoulder, the commander had poured himself a whiskey and was staring out the window at the gallows.

Ye gods! What was he to do? Because of those damned Apaches, Phillip was stuck out here, maybe for years—at least until the Apaches were all corralled. Or killed. He thought of his father. *Yes, killed would be better.*

In the meantime, Elizabeth would never warm his bed and he would lose all her beautiful money. Maybe Mama would have some ideas, but he hadn't gotten a letter from her yet, and the telegraph wire was down half the time because of those cursed savages.

At this point, getting drunk seemed like a pretty good idea. Phillip headed for his quarters. To hell with assignments. If anyone needed him, they'd have to search him out.

He'd had about three or four drinks when he heard a shower of gravel against his window. He peered out, then scowled. Shashké stood outside, looking about nervously as if afraid someone might see her. What a joke. Half the people at the fort had been gossiping about their year-long affair.

She gestured for him to come out. He needed a woman, and though he was tired of her, she was at least available. He went to the door. "Come in here before someone sees you."

She looked past him at the bearskin rug, frowned, and shook her head. *Ignorant savages.*

"All right then—meet you at the barn."

She nodded and fled. Had those been tears on her pretty face? He hoped she wasn't about to get emotional on him. He needed a woman, but he didn't have time to listen to some squaw cry. He was weaving only slightly as he walked to the barn.

Inside, out of the bright sun, it was cooler and the place smelled of horses and hay.

"Damn, you're pretty with that flower in your hair and those gold earrings." He lurched toward her and tried to take her in his arms.

"You're drunk," she said in disgust, pushing him away.

"Not as drunk as I'd like to be." He laughed.

She wiped away tears and sniffled. "You never think about my feelings."

"Okay, so what's the matter?" He didn't really care, but he had to make the gesture to get her clothes off.

"Dandy Jim's wife hanged herself a few minutes ago down in the scout's quarters."

"Who?" He wasn't quite sure who they were talking about or how it related to the well-being of Phillip Van Harrington.

"You know, one of the scouts they hanged this morning."

"Oh." Phillip blinked. "You mean she committed suicide? Why'd she do that? Probably another buck would have taken her—"

"Don't you understand?" Shashké screamed at him. "He's dead and she loved him and wanted to go with him."

"Okay, so she's dead, so what?" Phillip shrugged. He was beginning to get a bad headache.

"You don't care about anything," she stormed and slapped him. "Not me, not anything."

He slapped her back, hard. "You stupid squaw! Who do you think you are?"

She stumbled backward, weeping. "I thought you cared about me. I thought you were going to take me away from here. I have taken great risk in becoming your lover."

"I've got to go," Phillip said, yawning. In the mood she was in, she wasn't going to pleasure him.

"Is that all you've got to say?"

"I don't know what you expect from me." He was angry now as he shoved her aside and headed toward the barn door. "I'm going to marry Elizabeth Winters, not you."

"That terrible white girl? She won't even let you touch her—"

"Aw, she's not so bad," Phillip blurted before he thought. "She gave you those nice earrings . . ." His voice trailed off as he realized what he'd just revealed.

Shashké's hand came up slowly and touched one of the gold earrings as a light of understanding seemed to break across her face. "*She* gave them to me? You lied to me. You said *you*—"

"What difference does it make? Look, you stupid tart, don't bother me anymore. I'm sick of you!"

As he staggered away from the barn, there was a commotion out on the parade ground with men hurrying and shouting. *Ye gods. What now?*

For a moment, his blood froze in his veins and he wondered if the fort were indeed under attack. Then he realized it was a lone rider on a lathered old chestnut horse that still wore the remnants of a buggy harness.

Soldiers were running from every direction, and the bugle blew an alarm.

Phillip held back a moment, not wanting to take the responsibility of being the senior officer at the scene. Then curiosity got the better of him, and he strode over to the crowd. "What's going on here?"

The rough frontiersman had slid from the horse, breathing hard. He smelled as if he might have wet his pants, and his eyes were wide with terror. "Apaches!" he gasped, "took after me a few miles outta Willcox!"

Phillip recognized him now as a sometime stage driver.

"They follow you here?" He looked toward the distance in a panic.

"No, I came for help. When I looked back, they was coming hard toward the lady—"

"Lady?" another soldier asked. "You left a woman out there?"

"Well, there was only one horse, so I come for help."

Phillip was cold sober now. "What kind of a lady would make a trip on such a dangerous route on the day of the hanging?"

The other shook his head and leaned against the horse. "Dunno. Real looker, red hair. Said she was comin' to see her fiancé, a lieutenant. Said he'd give me somethin' for bringin' her."

"Red hair?" Phillip had a sudden premonition.

The other looked at the insignia on Phillip's uniform. "You Phillip Van Harrington?"

Elizabeth. Phillip grabbed the man by the front of his dirty shirt. "You left my fiancée to the mercy of a bunch of savages?"

"Like I said, there was only one horse and I come for help."

Elizabeth had been on her way to see him. Maybe she had planned to tell Phillip that his being penniless didn't matter, that she still wanted to marry him. He would have both her money and her virginity after all. But now the Apaches had her. "Someone get the colonel!" he barked. A private took off at a run toward the colonel's quarters.

Phillip confronted the shaking rider. "How many Apaches were there?"

"Could I have a little whiskey?" the man asked, "I'm a mite thirsty—"

"The devil'll give you a drink in hell!" Phillip shoved the man back against the lathered horse. "How many were there?"

"I dunno, a war party. Who stops to count in a spot like that? They was led by a big Injun on a fine paint stallion, though."

Cougar. Phillip didn't hear anything else in all the shouts and confusion around him. The damned scout hadn't died from his wounds after all, and he wanted revenge. Elizabeth had been on her way to Phillip and had been abandoned to Cougar. She might be dead, or at least raped and tortured by now. If anyone was going to rape Elizabeth Winters, he wanted to be the man to do it. Besides, if she was dead, Phillip could kiss her rich dowry good-bye.

The colonel strode to the scene just then. "Lieutenant, what is going on?"

Phillip gestured toward the rider and the lathered horse. "Apache raiders, sir."

"Damn!" The colonel took off his hat and ran his hand through his gray hair in frustration. "I just knew hanging those scouts was going to set this Territory ablaze! What happened?"

The rider filled him in.

"You abandoned a woman to the Apache?" The colonel was aghast.

"Like I told the lieutenant," the man whined, "there was only one horse, and I come for help."

"Anyone know who the woman is?"

Phillip sighed. "I think it might be my fiancée, sir, on her way to visit me."

"On the day of the hanging?" The older man looked incredulous.

Phillip shrugged helplessly. "I think there was an emergency."

The rider nodded. "Yeah, I think that's what she said, all right. Kept askin' me if I couldn't drive faster."

The colonel scowled at the rider. "Throw this cowardly bastard in jail until I see if there's something the sheriff

can charge him with." Then he turned to Phillip as soldiers
led the protesting man away. "Lieutenant, get a patrol
together."

"Yes, sir." He snapped a salute and took off running
toward the stable for his horse. Phillip was as furious with
Cougar as he was worried about Elizabeth. How dared that
half-breed take Phillip's woman? He'd make the Injun pay
for that!

Phillip picked some of his best men, and in thirty minutes the patrol was riding out of the fort in the midday
sun. He was cold sober now, his head aching, but he was
eager for revenge. *Cougar.* Phillip recalled now the way the
arrogant scout had looked at Elizabeth that time she came
to the fort last August, as if he wanted her as no man
should ever need a woman.

It was still cool for March, he thought grimly as he led
the patrol away from Fort Grant, headed south. Along the
road to the fort, they found the wrecked buggy and a
woman's clothes scattered everywhere. Phillip dismounted
and picked up a lacy corset cover. It smelled faintly of lilac
perfume, the scent that Elizabeth favored. Except for her
scattered things, there was no sign of her.

They had a white tracker with them, and Phillip noticed
the man walking around the wreckage and then walking
farther out. The tracker knelt and studied some tracks,
then yelled to Phillip. "Hey, Lieutenant, come here."

Phillip strode to the tracker's side. "What did you find?
I don't see anything."

The other pointed. "Here's a woman's footprints; I can
just make them out in the rocks. Looks like she tried to
run and then got ridden down. See? The footprints end
where a horse galloped up beside them. I'd say the rider
swung her up on his horse."

Cougar. Phillip seethed with the knowledge. Only Cougar
would be strong enough to lift a running woman to a horse

from a mounted position. In his mind, he saw Elizabeth fighting and Cougar holding her close, maybe putting his hands on her, maybe . . . No, the Apache raiders wouldn't stop for that right now. They'd be too afraid the escaping driver would bring help from the fort. "Which way are they going?"

The tracker walked in a circle, staring at the churned-up ground. "They're headed south, sir; probably runnin' for the border."

"South? Into Mexico?"

The other man nodded, and Phillip saw him exchange glances with some of the soldiers. They figured she was as good as dead by now. "How much of a head start have they got?"

The soldiers looked at him and each other uneasily.

The tracker spat in the dust. "Lieutenant, you ain't planning on riding off down toward Mexico with just this small patrol?"

"Oh, hell, I don't know." Phillip swore in frustration, then pulled at his wispy mustache and looked south. All his life, his mother had told him what to do, but Henrietta Van Harrington wasn't here right now. Phillip ground his teeth with rage. *Cougar.* This was just the kind of arrogant gesture the half-breed bastard would make, stealing Phillip's woman. Hanging was too good for him. In the silence, a buzzard glided on air currents overhead, throwing shadows across the men below.

The tracker said, "Lieutenant, there's no tellin' how many Apaches are up ahead of us, joinin' up as this group crosses the country. We might wanta report back to the colonel and get more men and supplies if you're going after them."

"Yes, of course." Phillip swung into the saddle and wheeled his horse back toward the fort. "When we catch up to them, I've got a personal grudge to settle with the leader.''

The others fell into formation and rode along behind him. The buzzard threw a shadow across Phillip, and he glanced up. *Oh, he'd feed Cougar to the buzzards all right, preferably alive.* They said a buzzard always tore a man's eyes out first and then started on his belly. Phillip grinned. *That might be even better than hanging that Injun bastard.* ''How far can they get before sundown?''

The tracker, riding alongside him, thought a minute. ''Ridin' hard, Apaches can cover a hundred miles a day, but that's a war party. Their women and young'uns'll slow them down a little, but Apache women are tough, used to hardship. A white woman isn't up to that.''

He didn't say anything else; he didn't need to. If Elizabeth became a liability, they might kill her. Otherwise, when they camped tonight, they would probably amuse themselves with her. In his mind, Phillip saw her in a circle of warriors, her clothes torn away as Cougar dragged her into the firelit circle and took her. He could imagine the tumble of red hair and the creamy skin as the dark, muscular savage spread her out and enjoyed her. Then he'd share her with the others.

Phillip swore and spurred his horse into a gallop, heading back to the fort. The army would catch up to those Apaches, all right. If anyone was going to take Elizabeth Winter's virginity, it was going to be Phillip!

It had been both a torment and a pleasure to ride holding Libbie Winters in his arms, Cougar thought as the shadows lengthened and the day passed and the little band headed south.

Libbie had been so warm and soft against him, and he was keenly aware that her torn bodice was barely held together by her makeshift fastenings. Holding onto her trim waist, her bosom kept brushing against the backs of his hands. It took all his willpower not to cup those fine breasts with his hands and stroke them. No, he must not touch her as long as she wore his necklace. He had given her his word, as she had reminded him, and he was a warrior of honor. He glanced down now at the necklace lying against her throat and the torn pink velvet, resisting the urge to take it off her.

He had been loco to kidnap her, but his passion had overcome his reason the moment he had seen her in that buggy. What was she doing in Arizona? But he knew why. She had come for the hanging and maybe to marry Phillip while she was here. She was his enemy's woman—and now she was at Cougar's mercy.

The Apache raiders reined in near a creek, and a warrior rode back to him, looking over the tousled girl with interest until Cougar frowned at him. "What say you? Shall we camp for the night?"

Cougar nodded. "We must have food and rest. Our old ones cannot take this very long." In truth, there weren't very many old ones along; Cougar had asked Beaver Skin and many of the others to stay in their village near the fort. The army wouldn't bother them, and they would pick up much information.

The warrior frowned at the girl in his arms. "The soldiers will come after us because of her and she slows us down. Better you should kill her."

"I will kill the man who even thinks that!" Cougar snapped in their language, and his tone brooked no argument.

The warrior acted as if he might argue the point, seemed to see the anger in Cougar's eyes, wheeled his horse, and rode off.

Libbie stirred in his arms and moaned softly. She was

spoiled and soft, he thought, not used to this kind of pace. And then he remembered her laughing at him and her cold-blooded design in wearing the necklace for protection, and he hardened his heart against his pity. Why had Phillip told him she had thrown it away? But they had laughed at him; Cougar had seen them at the stagecoach's departure. Now he was torn between desire and hatred for the lieutenant's woman.

"What's happening?" she asked.

He swung down off the horse and held his arms up for her. "We're camping for the night."

She ignored his outstretched arms and slid from the horse. However, she had been on the horse too long and her legs buckled. Instantly, Cougar caught her to keep her from falling, but she jerked away from him. "Don't you touch me, you—you—"

"Savage?" he suggested with a thin smile.

She must not show fear, she thought, and leaned against the horse to keep from falling. Sooner or later, the cavalry would be coming to her rescue. "I would like a bath and some food and water," she said, drawing herself up proudly. "The lieutenant will reward you handsomely for taking good care of me."

Cougar threw back his head and laughed. "We're counting on it! His money will buy a lot of ammunition and supplies for us." He caught her arm and propelled her along, leading his stallion with his free hand.

"You're holding me for ransom?"

"Of course. Can you think of any other reason for me to drag you along?" He sounded angry, which mystified Libbie.

Oh, God, suppose he found out Phillip is penniless? With no ransom forthcoming, what would they do with her? She didn't even want to think about it.

Women were hurrying about, building fires, unpacking

blankets and food. Several of the pretty young women smiled at Cougar invitingly. He didn't even seem to notice. "So, Blaze, can you do anything useful like build a fire or cook?"

She decided she would not answer. She was Elizabeth Winters, lately of Boston, and she would not answer to a savage's name for her.

"Are you hard of hearing?" he snapped.

"No."

"All right, be stubborn. Here"—he gestured—"you can help Owl Woman put up a wickiup."

"I will not!" Libbie was enraged. "You kidnap me and then expect me to work?"

"All right. Sit there then and watch the old woman do it all." He dismissed her with a curt nod and walked away.

Libbie tossed her hair and sat down on a rock, watching the wrinkled Apache woman put up the temporary shelter of sticks covered with brush. She felt guilty because the gray-haired woman looked weary, but she only smiled at Libbie as she worked. In less than a hour, the camp was settled in around a big campfire, horses staked out and women nursing babies while others cooked.

Libbie took a deep breath and smelled cooking meat. She was hungry and thirsty, too, but she would die before she asked for a drink of water. She licked her cracked lips.

Cougar walked up just then. He must have noticed her licking her lips because he pulled out a canteen. "I'm not stupid enough to hand it to you this time," he said. "Water in these parts is too precious to waste."

She didn't want to pour it out, she wanted to drink it, but she wasn't going to beg.

"Here," Cougar said. He poured some of the water into his cupped hand and held it out to her.

Libbie hesitated. *Damn him for his arrogance!* He was determined to break her, but she was too thirsty to argue the point now. She caught his big hand to steady it and drank the water from his palm. It was cold and good.

Then he turned his wet hand and wiped it across her hot, dusty face. It felt so soothing, she closed her eyes and let him stroke her face.

"You're becoming a very obedient little pet," he said as his hand slipped around the back of her neck.

"I'm nobody's pet." Before he realized what she was up to, she turned her head and sank her sharp little teeth into his wrist.

He jerked back, rubbing his arm and swearing Apache curses. "Damn you, Blaze, I ought to strip you down and take a quirt to you for that."

"You wouldn't dare!" She was scared but defiant.

He didn't answer, favoring his injured wrist as she glowered at him. He'd kill the man who tried to put one mark on that soft skin of hers. He took a deep breath to control his temper. "If I scar you up, the lieutenant might not pay a big ransom to get you back."

"Besides that," she said, and tangled her fingers in the necklace she wore, "I am under your protection, remember?"

"So you keep reminding me!" He glared down at her, favoring his bitten wrist. He had the most overwhelming urge to tangle his fingers in that necklace and tear it from her pretty throat, even if to do so would sully his honor as a warrior. "Blaze, don't push me!" he warned. He turned on his heel and strode away.

Libbie heard smothered laughter and looked up. The old woman had seen it all, and now she laughed and nodded as if pleased to see a woman give the big warrior as good as he got. Then the old woman returned to her work.

Libbie glanced around. There were no Apaches close to her now, everyone being preoccupied with their tasks.

Cougar had tied his stallion to a tree branch as he left. This was the best horse in the camp. No doubt it could outrun anything else in the Apaches' herd. Libbie was an expert rider, even though she had always used a sidesaddle. Did she have a chance at mounting up and getting away, taking them all by surprise? They wouldn't be expecting such a bold move. Well, nothing ventured . . .

She looked around again. No one was paying her the slightest heed. In a heartbeat, Libbie jerked the reins free, swung up on the stallion, and turned to ride out.

The old woman shouted the alarm as Libbie took off. Behind her, people were shouting and gesturing. Libbie looked back over her shoulder and saw the black thunder on Cougar's face as she started away at a gallop. She was going to make it!

Abruptly, behind her, she heard Cougar's sudden sharp whistle. The big paint slid to a halt, and she fought to keep her balance, but she managed to stay mounted. Oh, damn! Libbie could hear Cougar's moccasins coming at a run as she kicked the horse in the sides, urging it forward. It didn't budge, obeying its master's command.

Cougar reached out and caught her trim ankle. "You conniving little bitch! Get off that horse!" He pulled and she came off in a tumble into his arms. Her torn bodice had come open and there she was, fighting and kicking to get out of his arms with her naked breasts pressed against his massive bare body.

"Let go of me, damn you!" She pounded on his chest, but he ignored her as he turned and strode back to the wickiup that the old woman had almost completed.

"Blaze, I guess I will just have to stake you out like a pet dog."

Libbie bit and scratched, but he knelt and held her down while he tied a length of rawhide around one of her ankles. Then he tied the other end to a stake he drove in the ground before the new wickiup. "You can't treat me like this!" She shrieked and yanked hard on the stake, "I am Elizabeth Winters, not some stray dog—"

"You are my slave," he returned coldly, "and you will stay where you are tied."

She eyed the stake. Maybe when he left, she could pull the stake up and . . .

"Don't try it," he said. "You haven't got a chance of escaping, so save your energy."

"You bastard!" She came to the end of the tether and lunged at him, but he stepped backward and the stake held her just out of reach.

"I am that." He didn't smile. "And you are a spoiled, uppity, and annoying girl. Now shut up and sit down. Maybe if you're good, I'll feed you."

"I don't want your damned food!"

"Think twice about that, Spoiled One. It may be a long time before we eat again. We'll be riding hard tomorrow. The army's probably hot on our trail." Cougar turned and sauntered away.

Phillip. Yes, if that cowardly driver made it to the fort, Phillip would come to her rescue and bring soldiers. That thought gave her some comfort. But would he come because he loved her or because he might still think she was rich or simply because he hated Cougar? There was no way to know. What difference did it make anyway? And to think she'd come all the way to Arizona with some fool notion of saving Cougar from the hangman. Of course, if she told him that, he'd never believe her.

Twilight fell on the camp. Libbie retreated the length of her tether inside the wickiup to escape the curious stares of the passing women and children. She noted that they looked thin and weary. Through the opening of the wickiup, Libbie could see the men gathered around the fire.

Occasionally, one of them glanced toward the wickiup. Cougar was frowning. *Were they discussing her?*

Out by the fire, Cougar listened patiently to the others.

"The army will come after us because of the white girl," one said. "Better we should kill her and hide the body."

"She is too valuable to kill," Cougar argued. "The whites will pay ransom to get her back unharmed. We can use the gold to buy rifles and supplies."

Geronimo frowned. "All Apaches know gold is sacred to Ussen and we are forbidden to dig in Mother Earth's body and violate her to get it. The whites care little for our sacred ways."

"True," Cougar agreed, "but we have violated no taboos in taking what the whites have dug. We can trade it to the Mexican traders and some of the white gunrunners for supplies."

"Will they pay so much for one small woman?" an elder asked.

Another laughed. "Have you seen the woman? They will pay."

"Who is her man?" Geronimo asked.

"The lieutenant who kills bears," Cougar said.

A murmur of disapproval went around the circle that anyone would do such a forbidden thing.

An elder shook his head. "Does he not know bears carry the spirits of our Apache dead?"

Cougar shrugged. "He does not care; he hates the Apache because of his father."

The warriors exchanged glances. Many of the old ones had known the major.

"Does the lieutenant know—?" Geronimo asked.

Cougar shook his head. "I doubt it. He would not believe it anyway."

A rider came into camp, dismounted, and hurried to the fire. Geronimo looked up. "You come from the fort?"

The other nodded and sat down cross-legged before the fire. "It was hard to sneak away. Dandy Jim's woman has killed herself from grief."

A murmur went around the circle, and Cougar gritted his teeth. It had been a sad day. "What will become of Dandy Jim's sons?"

The new man shook his head. "No one knows. One of the soldiers says he might take them to raise."

Geronimo rolled a smoke in a corn husk, lit it with a burning twig from the campfire, took a long puff, then passed it around the circle. "The Apache have lost three good men to a terrible, shameful death today."

The others nodded.

"There will be no peace for us until the white men are driven out," said one.

Cougar shook his head. "I have lived among the whites. We cannot win a war against them. They are as many as the needles on the cactus. But if they force us into it, we will have no choice."

"We will reach decisions later," Geronimo said. "We ride out before dawn. Maybe the soldiers will lose our trail, give up, and not follow."

"Won't they come after the woman?" another asked.

"Will the lieutenant pay gold to get her back?" another queried Cougar.

Cougar looked toward the wickiup. From here, he could see the occasional shine of her fiery hair when she moved, and he blurted out his thoughts. "If you owned a woman like that, would you not ransom her, no matter what it cost?"

The others nodded in agreement. She was indeed a very beautiful woman who would give a man fine, strong sons.

Gray Sky poked up the fire. "If the Long Knife does not

ransom her, she could be sold to Coyote Johnson. He could get a good price for her from a Mexican whorehouse.''

Cougar winced at the thought of turning her over to the white gunrunner, but he said nothing. He hated her, he thought, and he should be pleased to think that the spoiled, arrogant white girl might end up servicing any man who wanted her. But he was not pleased. The thought made him set his teeth. ''She is mine,'' he reminded them, ''I captured her.''

The others nodded. Geronimo said, ''So she is. Very well, Cougar, you may do with her as you will—as long as she does not slow us down.''

''She will not slow us down,'' Cougar said. He stood up.

''Will you pleasure yourself with her tonight?'' Gray Sky said thoughtfully as he smoked.

''She wears my necklace. I promised her its protection.'' *By Ussen, why had he done that?*

Another warrior laughed and rubbed his groin. ''For a woman like that, a warrior might forget his honor.''

Cougar shook his head, even though he felt the hardening of his own manhood. It had been a long time since he lay with a woman. ''My honor means much to me. I will not sully it for the pleasure of her body.''

Geronimo frowned. ''You made your promise to a white. Perhaps you need not—''

''I will think on it.'' Cougar's voice was gruff, mirroring his annoyance with both himself for making the promise and the arrogant white woman for expecting him to keep it. He had an urge to stride into that wickiup and rip the Apache Tears from her neck. No, of course he could not do that. But if she took it off of her own free will . . .

Cougar only half listened to the final discussions, his attention on the wickiup. It was dark now and it was going

Chapter Thirteen

Libbie sat hunched inside the wickiup, watching the proceedings at the fireside with a mixture of fear and fascination. Every once in a while, one of the braves would look her way. *Was her fate being decided out there?* She reached up to touch the Apache Tears necklace for reassurance. Cougar had promised her his protection, but what if the council decided otherwise? In the meantime, she was tired, hungry, and cold and staked out like a naughty puppy inside this brush shelter. How dared that savage do this to her!

As she watched, Cougar stood up, walked over to the fire, and filled two gourds from a kettle hanging over the flames. Then he strode toward the wickiup, stooped, and came inside. "You hungry?"

"I might be." She wasn't going to beg if she starved to death.

He snorted. "Your pride gets in your way, my pet. Here."

He thrust one gourd at her and knelt, putting the other one next to his knee as he began to build a small fire.

She resisted the urge to throw the food back at him. It smelled good, and who knew when he would offer her food again? "You didn't give me any silverware. How do you expect me to eat this?"

He looked up from the fire he was building. "I'm not loco enough to give you a knife."

"If I had a knife, I would stick it between your ribs."

He turned his head, smiling ever so slightly. "You think I don't know that?" He returned to piling twigs on the tiny flame.

Libbie watched him. Maybe she could slam the gourd across the back of his arrogant head. No, it wasn't heavy enough to do any damage; she'd just make him mad. She had a feeling that when Cougar was angry, his mood could turn as black and dangerous as a thunderstorm. "I'm not sure I want to eat this—"

"Hush and eat it!" he ordered.

Hurriedly, she picked up the gourd. No wonder he was a leader, Libbie thought; no one would dare argue with him.

He had the fire going now. He sat down across from her cross-legged, picked up his food, and began to eat with his fingers.

Anyway, she decided there was nothing to be gained by fussing with him now. She hesitated, then began to eat with her fingers. It was a steaming hot and tasty stew. "What is this?"

He shrugged and finished his. "Ground maize and some beef we took from a rich rancher. I don't suppose you can cook?"

She looked down her nose at him. "Ladies have servants to do their work."

He scowled at her. "Then what do ladies do besides sit

about on pillows like small dogs, waiting for a rich husband to snap his fingers?''

A lap dog. She hadn't thought of it before, but yes, that was what she would be for some wealthy man. "You wouldn't understand. Ladies do watercolors and embroidery. They host club meetings and play the violin."

"Sounds dull. *Our* women will teach you something useful, like cooking and weaving baskets."

"Ha! I don't expect to be here that long." She finished her food and tossed the gourd to one side, passing up the temptation to throw it at him. She suspected he could be a dangerous man if pushed too far. "If you think you're going to turn me into a slave—"

"You are already my slave," he answered coldly. "The Apache life is a hard one. Each must work and help or we can't survive."

"You think that bothers me?" she sniffed. "I don't intend to learn to do lowly work—"

"It is not your fault you are useless except to amuse a rich man," he said calmly. "You will soon adjust."

"Adjust!" she screamed at him. "You don't understand, you—you savage! I will be returning to civilization, and Lieutenant Van Harrington will hunt all of you down and kill you."

Cougar grinned. "He'll have to catch us first and the lieutenant is a greenhorn. We aren't worried."

"You can't treat me like a common servant!" Libbie fumed, forgetting that only moments ago, she had feared him. Obviously he didn't intend to kill her, or he would already have done so.

"There is much work in an Apache camp," he said as he rolled a cigarette and lit it with a burning twig from the fire. "All share the work and the food."

"Do you know who I am?" she announced loftily. "I am

Elizabeth Winters, lately of Miss Priddy's Female Academy
and a debutante—''

"And were you happy, Blaze?"

Libbie hesitated, caught off guard. She'd never given
that much thought. It was the only life she had ever
known—the spoiled rich girl. And now that she had no
money, what would her life be like?

"You do not answer, so you are not sure." He shook his
head and smoked, frowning at her. "Think on this; you
came out here to see the army hang the scouts. My friends
are dead, and your fiancé's testimony helped hang them."

She saw the anger and the pain in his blue eyes and was
angry herself that she had been accused so unjustly when
she had come to try to save him from the gallows. He
wouldn't believe that if she told him, and after all, she had
her pride. "I wish you *had* been one of those they hanged!"

He scowled at her and blew smoke into the air. "Maybe
you'll get your wish, but in the meantime, the army will
think twice about attacking us because we've got you."

She was a hostage and when they didn't need her anymore . . . Libbie trembled at the thought.

Cougar looked over at her a long moment. "Are you
cold?"

Was she shivering that badly? "No, I—I'm fine."

He tossed his cigarette into the fire. "You're not much
of a liar and a little too delicate for this life." He stood
up and came toward her.

She glared up at him. "What—what do you plan to do?"

He reached behind her, got a fur robe, and put it around
her shoulders. He held on to the edges of the fur so that
his hands were close to her face. He looked down into her
eyes for a long moment as if deciding whether to cover
her lips with his own; then the muscles in his jaw tightened.
"Don't worry; your honor is safe . . . for now." His fingers
trailed across the fur and touched the necklace at her

throat. "In a couple of days, we'll meet some white gunrunners at a rendezvous. We're desperate for weapons and supplies."

She was only too aware of the touch of his fingers on the necklace and tracing along the swell of her breasts beneath it. If she pulled away, he would think she was afraid and she would not give him that satisfaction. She glared at him and gritted her teeth as his big hand trailed along her throat. "What is that to me?"

He did not move his fingers. "Do you know what gunrunners would give for a beautiful woman they can use for their pleasure or sell in Mexico City?"

She felt herself blanche at the thought. "I will hold you to your promise."

"Ahh!" He nodded. "One minute I am a savage, the next you expect me to behave like a knight in shining armor."

She didn't answer, surprised herself at how much she had come to depend on him for protection.

Cougar let go of her and reached out and caught her trim ankle.

"What are you doing?" His hand was big enough that it encircled her small ankle.

"Checking to make sure your leash is secure, my little dog. She tried to pull out of his grip, but he held on to her ankle while he checked the rope that tethered her. Then he sat down across the fire from her. "You underestimate your value on the open market, Blaze. A beautiful, desirable white girl is worth much in guns and supplies."

The thought of being handed over to a bunch of cutthroats and renegades made her swallow hard.

"So that thought gives you pause?" He looked deep into her eyes. "As well it should. I can assure you, renegade gunrunners will not treat you like a high-born lady."

"I thought I had the protection of your necklace?" She reached up to touch it.

"From me and other Apaches." He smiled wryly. "But I am not responsible for how your next owners treat you."

"You're trying to get around your oath." She licked her lips nervously. "Anyway, the question is moot. Phillip will pay much ransom to get me back."

Cougar only grinned ever so slightly. "I'm sure he will. I would if your body was promised to me and I had the gold."

Oh, God. Phillip had no money; what was going to happen if the Indians found out?

"You don't dare do anything to harm me," she shot back, "the army will destroy you for that."

He nodded. "Maybe, but right now, we know this country better than they do, and they've got to find us to destroy us." He stretched and yawned. "I'm tired."

Maybe she could escape while he slept.

"Come here," he commanded.

"What are you going to do?"

"I'm going to make sure you don't stab me or do some other mischief as I sleep." He stood up, reached out and caught her, then twisted her arms behind her.

Libbie struggled as he put her wrists together and began to tie them. "I promise I won't try to escape."

"You're not Apache," he said, "your promises are no good."

She fought to get away, but with his great strength, he held her, tying her hands behind her back, then whirled her around, pulling the fur closer around her. "Be a good slave, Blaze, and lie close and warm your master."

"I will not! If you think you're going to—"

"No, tonight I'm just going to use you for warmth." He pulled her toward him, then jerked her down on a pile of furs near the fire.

"Phillip will be furious."

"Phillip isn't here," he said and pulled her close against him, "so he won't know if you don't tell him. Besides, it will keep you warm, too."

"I'm not cold! Besides, you promised!"

"Blaze," he said patiently, "I haven't killed you, raped you, or hurt you. You strain my patience. Now shut up and go to sleep. We've got a long day ahead of us tomorrow."

He pulled her into his embrace, and with her hands tied behind her, there wasn't much Libbie could do except let him mold her slight body against his big, muscular one. Her head was on his shoulder, his face in her tousled hair, his arm thrown across her slim waist.

She hadn't realized how cold she was or how much heat his big body gave off. She tried to keep her body stiff and unyielding as he dropped off to sleep. The warmth of him was a temptation and besides, he was asleep; he wouldn't know. Libbie curled into the protective curve of him and stopped shivering as he drew her even closer. The curve of his muscular body almost seemed to have been made for her small one to fit into.

Libbie relaxed and watched him sleep. The small fire gave off enough light to see his face. If he weren't a savage and her captor, she would think him handsome. Yet how dared he lie with his arm across her so possessively? She looked down at the black gemstones lying against the creamy swell of her breasts. Cougar's honor was the only thing holding his tumultuous passions in check; she could sense that. If he changed his mind, he could use her for something more than just a bed warmer. He could . . . No, she must not think of that.

Finally, she curled up against his warmth and slept, dreaming of getting her hands free and stabbing him with his own knife.

Libbie awakened just before dawn and wondered for a

long moment where she was. The glowing coals of a small fire illuminated the area, and when she tried to move, she realized her hands were tied behind her and she was tethered by one ankle. Then abruptly, she became aware of something else. A dark, half-naked man lay with her, his head against the swell of her breasts. She took a deep breath to scream, then remembered. She must not bring the other Apaches down on her. As it was, Cougar's face was pillowed on her almost naked breasts. She could feel his warm breath on her skin as he breathed. One of his arms held her to him; the other hand was hot and possessive on her bare thigh, since the torn pink dress had worked its way up her body. She lay there a long moment, gathering her wits, then slowly wiggled until she was out from under him.

At that point, he awakened, looked puzzled, then sat up and smiled. "Did you sleep well? I did."

"Damn you! Phillip will kill you for this." She sat up, too, and shook back her tangled hair.

"Maybe it was worth it. Here, let me untie your hands." He reached around her, his bare chest brushing against her breasts as he untied her.

Libbie held her breath as he worked on the ropes, only too aware of his massive chest pressed against her.

"There," he said, "I hope today you'll behave a little better."

Her arms were asleep, and she moaned when she tried to move them forward.

Sympathy crossed his rugged face, only to be replaced with a look as hard as blue glass. He caught first one of her arms and then the other, rubbing them. "If I could trust you, I wouldn't tie you up."

"Some night," she said coldly, "you'll forget and I'll cut your throat with your own blade, steal your horse, and escape."

"Don't count on it, Blaze." He stood up, hauling her to her feet. "I had thought you would become more reasonable and obedient."

"Never!" She screamed it at him.

"Then today I shall teach you that you must obey me." He untied her ankle, too, his hands lingering too long on her slim calf and she saw the need in his eyes. It would be so easy to push her over on her back, mount her, and enjoy her. Instead, he stood up, pulled her to her feet, and pushed her out of the wickiup ahead of him. "Perhaps today you shall walk beside my horse instead of riding."

She spat at him like a ruffled kitten, but he paid her no heed. The old woman came out of a nearby wickiup.

"Here," Cougar said, "this is Owl Woman who wet-nursed me and raised me when my mother died."

He said something to the woman in her own language, and she nodded and led Libbie into the brush to relieve herself, then gave her a bit of gruel in a small bowl. It tasted like ground acorns, Libbie decided. She started to complain that this wasn't nearly enough food, then noted the other women and children didn't have as much in their bowls as she did, but no one was complaining. Perhaps she was a tiny bit spoiled, Libbie conceded.

Now as the sun rose over the rim of the hill to the east, the Apaches finished tearing down the camp, and mounted up. She stood and waited, hoping Cougar had forgotten about her, but he came, caught her arm, and started to swing her up in his arms, but she resisted.

"I will not ride with you!" she taunted as she fought him.

"As you wish." His voice was as cold as his blue eyes as he dumped her on the ground beside the big paint. "Today you will walk until you are a more obedient slave."

"Damn you, I'm not used to walking."

"I know that, Blaze." He looked down at her as he

looped a rope around her trim waist and tied it to his saddle. "You give me no choice but to teach you who is master here. I am going to break you as I would a wild filly."

"I will not be broken, and I will not walk." She sat down in the middle of the path as the Apaches fell into line and began to ride out.

"Very well, then I shall drag you."

"You wouldn't dare!"

"Try me!" His blue eyes flashed glacier fire and that square chin was set.

This was not a man who could be pushed around by any woman.

"You dirty rogue!" She scrambled to her feet and began to walk.

He rode alongside her. "When you decide you are going to behave yourself, I will let you ride."

"You'll wait a helluva long time!" She struck him on the leg, making the horse snort and dance about.

"Such language for a lady," Cougar chided, "you may have more starch to you than I give you credit for, Blaze."

"My name is not Blaze!" Libbie screamed at him.

He looked down at her. "No, maybe you don't deserve that name. It is a good name for an Apache woman, not a spoiled, weak white girl." He nudged his horse on and didn't look back at her.

What to do? Libbie wavered. If she sat down, she had no doubt that she had challenged him to the point that he would indeed drag her. On the other hand, if she behaved herself, he was going to put her on the saddle before him so he could put his big hands on her waist again and pull her up against his virile body. *What to do?*

She would show him she was not a mare to be broken obediently to a man's will.

"Okay, I'll show you! I will walk!" She put her nose in the air and lifted her skirts, striding along.

He looked back over his shoulder and nodded. "That's a good slave. Remember, all you have to do is ask politely and I'll let you ride."

"I'll crawl first."

He smiled thinly and clucked to his horse. "Suit yourself, stubborn one."

Libbie took a deep breath and began to stride after his horse, tied by the leash around her waist like a disobedient puppy. She who had been willful and full of pride was now being treated like this man's pet, and he had full control over her destiny. She could not bear it!

All around her, quiet Apache women rode along, looking back at her. Why had she never noticed how thin and tired these women and children were? Phillip had said Indian agent Tiffany was taking good care of his wards, but they certainly didn't look like it. No wonder he and his partner, elderly Ebenezer Higginbottom, were getting rich; they must be cheating the Indians out of most of their government supplies.

Don't be an idiot, Libbie, she scolded herself. *Why should you worry about the welfare of a bunch of savages that have kidnapped you?*

Her little handmade shoes were going to be worn through by these rocks and cockleburs, but there was no help for it. She gritted her teeth, stared straight ahead, and walked. She knew that Cougar glanced back at her frequently, his face troubled, but she ignored him and kept moving.

The sun was beginning to climb in the March sky, and the day got warmer as the little group headed south. At least she was holding the tribe up with her slow walk. Maybe she could delay them until the army caught them.

After a while, the Indians stopped to rest by a small

creek. She waited for Cougar to offer her a drink, but he only nodded toward the water as he filled his canteen. She knelt next to his horse and drank her fill, trying not to think what the girls back at Miss Priddy's would think if they could see her on her knees. In the meantime, he had remounted. She could feel his gaze on her back. Libbie whirled and glared at him. "I can hardly wait to see you hang!"

He grinned. "Phillip is probably having to use a white or a Zuni tracker, and he'll find they aren't as good as Apache scouts. He'll never catch us. Let me know when you're tired enough to ride."

Libbie hesitated. Her feet were sore and aching. "And beg for it? I think not!"

He shifted his weight in his saddle. "Suit yourself, spoiled white girl."

Damn him. She was so very, very tired, but she wasn't going to admit it if she laid down on the trail and died right there. "I'm feeling very refreshed, thank you."

He chewed his lip as if fighting a battle with himself. "All right, then. Everyone else has already pulled out. Get moving!"

With her head high in the air, Libbie followed after him and his big stallion. Her feet were getting blisters on them and her legs were so weary, she wasn't sure she could keep moving. He glanced back over his shoulder and tugged on the line around her waist. "Hurry it up. You're slowing the march down."

Which was precisely the idea, Libbie reminded herself. In the distance, she could see low-lying purple hills. If she could slow the Apaches, maybe the army could catch up to them.

It was past midday and warm. She felt perspiration running down her breasts as she walked, and she wondered if she were getting sunburned. The thought made her

smile. Mrs. Everett had been so concerned about her ruining her pale skin. She wondered where her plump guardian was right now. That thief! Without Libbie as a meal
ticket, the woman was going to have to go to work in a shop
or as a maid. The thought cheered Libbie considerably.
Having stolen Libbie's inheritance and wasted it, it was all
the snooty dowager deserved.

Cougar looked over his shoulder again and tugged on
the line. "You'll have to walk faster than that. We can't
get left behind the line of march."

"So drag me." She stumbled, righted herself, and kept
walking.

"Libbie—Blaze—if you'd beg me, I might give you a
ride."

"Not if my life depended on it." She took a deep breath
and kept walking toward him.

"We've got a long way to go," he warned. "You can't
possibly walk that far."

She shrugged and kept moving, stumbled, went to one
knee.

In a flash, he was off his horse, catching her. "You little
fool! Will you let your pride kill you?"

"I will not beg," she said and struggled to get out of
his arms.

"You're the damndest woman I ever met." He gathered
her into his arms and carried her to his horse. "I always
said you were too much woman for the lieutenant."

"Let me be the judge of that, you savage."

He reached and pulled the canteen off his saddle horn,
then held it to her lips. She hesitated.

"Libbie, don't tell me you'll turn down water?"

She thought about it a minute. "I suppose not."

He looked relieved as she drank; then he poured a little
in his hand and wiped it on her face. "Now you're going
to ride."

"I don't think so." She struggled to stand up, but he caught her, hoisted her up on the stallion, and remounted behind her.

"We'll have to hurry to catch up to the others." He nudged his stallion into a lope.

Libbie took a deep breath and leaned back against his massive chest, ignoring the arm that went around her waist even though her breasts rested against the heat of that muscular arm. The truth was, she could not have walked much farther.

Cougar was both ashamed of himself for what he'd put her through and angry with her for not giving in.

"Stubborn woman," he grumbled and held her close as he rode. He was both exasperated and proud of her. She was made of better stuff than he had imagined. He was only too aware of the soft heat of her in his embrace, the weight of her breasts against his arm, and the tangle of red curls falling against his bare chest. He had never wanted a woman as much as he wanted this one—both wanted and hated her.

He vowed then that he would have Libbie Winters in his blankets, even with Lieutenant Van Harrington coming hard on his trail. The only problem now was how to get that necklace off her without force and what to do with her once he'd had his fill of her charms!

Libbie said, "Since I'm slowing you down, you might as well turn me loose. The army is bound to be gaining on us."

He resisted an urge to tangle his fingers in those fiery locks and see if they were as soft as they looked. "We've sent back a little welcoming party for the lieutenant."

Libbie sat up stiff and straight and tried to look past his wide shoulder. "An ambush! You've set up an ambush!"

Cougar nodded and hung on to her. "The lieutenant

doesn't know much about Apaches or this country. He'll lead his men right into our trap."

She must warn them. Libbie opened her mouth and screamed.

"Damn you, Blaze!" He clapped his big hand over her mouth, and they struggled as she tried to break free and get off the horse. The stallion snorted and reared as she sank her teeth into Cougar's hand and tried to scratch his face. He began to swear and she could taste his blood, but she didn't stop fighting. She managed to fall from the horse, biting and clawing. Her ripped dress came open, and he grabbed a handful of the soft lace of her bodice and tore it away, then stuffed it in her mouth while she gagged and fought him. "You fiery bitch, let's see you warn the soldiers now!"

She was both angry and terrified as she fought him, but he was much stronger than she was and he had both her small wrists in one big hand. Abruptly, he stopped, staring. She followed his gaze downward. Her breasts were completely bare, with the black gemstones resting against them. He reached out very slowly and paused uncertainly, his big hand only inches from her bare breast.

She froze and stopped fighting, looking up at him with wide green eyes, then down at his poised hand. She couldn't get the gag out of her mouth to scream or curse or protest.

He pulled back, his voice was a hushed whisper of awe. "No man has ever touched these, have they, Blaze?"

Oh, if she could get loose, she would sink her teeth in his arm so deep, he would bleed to death! She glanced down, frozen by the image of his big dark hand so near her naked breast. Her nipple went taut and swollen.

"Just what I thought," he whispered, and his eyes were hot with need. "You could be a passionate woman, Blaze. You just need the right man to teach you how."

She tried to twist out of his grasp, tried to tell him through the gag how much she hated him and how she could hardly wait to see Phillip shoot him or hang him, but her words were unintelligible. With his big hand holding both her small wrists, she couldn't do much of anything, but she made sure her eyes flashed green sparks of warning.

Now he cupped her chin in that free hand and turned her face up to look into her eyes. "Sooner or later, I intend to have you, Blaze," he promised softly. "You were meant to warm a man's blankets and give him sons, and I intend to be that man, necklace or no necklace."

She glared up at him, struggled to get away from his hand, and tried to tell him through the gag how much she hated him and what would happen if she ever got loose and got her hands on a knife or gun.

Cougar smiled. "Well, we'll see, Blaze. It may be a long time before the army ever tracks us down. In the meantime, we'll be camping in another hour or so, and we still have tonight to finish this conversation." He reached into his saddlebags for a scrap of rawhide to tie her wrists together, then threw her up on his stallion and mounted behind her. He nudged his horse into a lope to catch up to the others.

If she could only get this gag out of her mouth! She tried to rub it against his bare chest, hoping to dislodge it, but he only laughed, a touch of anger in his tone. "Behave yourself, Blaze. I promise I'll give you the attention you deserve once we get camped."

His words struck fear in her heart. Tonight, when he felt safe from pursuit, would he use her for his pleasure?

Behind them, in the distance, she heard the sudden echo of rifle fire. Cougar glanced over his shoulder. "Looks like our green lieutenant and his men have ridden into our trap. I'll secure you and then I'll go back and help."

With that, Cougar nudged his horse into a lope and rode along a narrow trail to a stronghold high in the rocks. Behind them in the distance, she heard the rattle of gunfire.

He was off the stallion before it was even stopped, lifting her effortlessly and carrying her to a place in the rocks. Her bare breasts were against his naked chest, but Cougar seemed to pay no attention. He made sure she was tied securely, said something to the old woman, then checked his rifle and remounted. He took off back up the trail toward the sounds of battle.

Libbie struggled with her bonds, but they held firm. It was only a couple of hours until dusk, and she could only guess where she might be in the wild, rugged countryside. *Mexico?*

No one paid any attention to her, not even Owl Woman. Libbie was a prize that belonged to Cougar, she realized. If he didn't come back, what would happen to her? And if he did come back, had he decided to use her for his pleasure and his vengeance and forget the promise he had made her?

Chapter Fourteen

Libbie watched Cougar ride out with most of the other warriors to fight the soldiers who had been hot on their trail. Everyone seemed busy; no one was paying any attention to her. Maybe now was the time to escape. She rubbed her gag against a rock until she freed her mouth; then she began to work on the ropes that bound her with her teeth. Minutes seemed to race by as fast as the beat of her heart as she struggled with the ropes. Finally, she had them loose enough to slip her hands free.

She glanced around furtively. The children were running and playing, the women busy setting up camp. In the distance, she could see the horses grazing on the sparse desert vegetation. From over the rise, the firing still echoed through the canyons. She looked for old Owl Woman, but she was busy setting up a wickiup. Libbie made her plans. Maybe if she made her escape and worked her way back toward the soldiers, they might find her before it got dark.

Very quietly, she sneaked through the chaparral toward

the horses, her heart pumping with danger and excitement. If anyone spotted her trying to escape, there was no telling what they would do to her. She hesitated, then decided she had to take that chance before Cougar returned to claim his prize. From the way he had looked at her and everything he'd said, she had a feeling that tonight he might ignore the promise of the necklace and take her. The thought scared her, but it was also oddly exciting. He was big and powerful and primitive, with only a razor-thin veneer of civilization. She had a feeling that what he laid claim to, he took.

Of one thing she was certain—the snooty lieutenant would no longer be interested in her if another man had her first. And if Phillip weren't interested in her, he wouldn't be so eager to rescue her.

A dark gray mare grazed at the edge of the herd. Libbie looked around again to make sure no one noticed her movement. Everyone was too busy with children or setting up camp. She didn't even have a saddle. Could she ride bareback? Of course she could, but what would she do for a bridle?

Taking two long hair ribbons from her fiery locks, she tied them together and moved closer to the mare. Very slowly, Libbie approached, thinking that if it bolted and fled, the others might stampede. "Hey, girl, whoa there; don't move," she crooned, moving closer.

Then she felt silly, thinking the horse only understood Apache. The mare raised her head and snorted, but allowed Libbie to walk up to her and pat the dark velvet nose. Quickly, Libbie looped the pink hair ribbons around the mare's lower jaw in a makeshift bridle. It wasn't the best, but it would have to do. Taking a deep breath for courage, Libbie stepped up on a rock and climbed up bareback. For a long moment, she waited for some Apache to shout a warning, but there was no sound save the distant gunfire. It took all Libbie's self-control not to panic and do something rash, but she nudged the mare into a slow walk away from the camp and through the chaparral.

She didn't dare breathe or look back as she walked the mare away from the herd, expecting to hear a shout of alarm or worse yet, feel a bullet's sting as she rode out. Unconsciously, she reached up to touch the string of Apache Tears, thinking how angry Cougar would be when he returned to discover she had escaped.

What to do now? She wasn't sure from the confusing echoes of gunfire in just which direction the army patrol was holed up. If she weren't careful, she would ride right into the fighting. She decided she would just ride north until she ran onto some white civilization.

The sun had disappeared behind heavy banks of clouds, and the wind had picked up and changed direction. Libbie paused, no longer certain which direction to ride. The shifting pattern of the wind had muffled the gunfire so that she was no longer sure exactly where the soldiers were, and she dared not ride right into the Apache warriors. Perhaps if she swung in a wide circle, she could miss the Apaches and still find the soldiers. That decided, she rode cautiously, stopping now and then to listen, but the echoes through the canyons were blurred and confusing. *Suppose she didn't find the soldiers and ended up out in the night alone?*

The thought made her shiver. There were bears, bobcats, and rattlesnakes out here in this rugged country, and it was only a few hours until dark. No, she must not think of that, she must think about how nice it would be to return to civilization and . . . what? There wasn't anything waiting back there for her except a greedy young officer who was after her money or a cranky old geezer who wanted to trade his gold for her body. *Well, maybe she could find a job. Doing what?* Speaking French and playing the piano hardly qualified Libbie to make her own way in the world.

That wasn't the problem of the moment, she thought as she rode on. Getting back to white civilization was what mattered now.

Cougar was going to be so angry! Libbie smiled with satisfaction at the thought. He was the most arrogant, insolent male she had ever encountered, and he hated her with a passion that mystified her. For a moment, her memory lingered on the way he had held her against him, the heat of his big body cradling her as they slept, the hunger in his eyes when he looked at her. No man had ever looked at Libbie that way before, as if possessing her meant more than anything in the world to him.

"Are you crazy?" she scolded herself as she rode through the yucca and cactus. "He didn't care about you. He only saw you as a commodity to be traded for rifles and supplies."

And yet, the way he had looked at her lingered in her mind still. Why, tonight he had probably planned to . . . Her pulse quickened at the images that came unbidden to her mind when she thought about Cougar and the way his big hand had trembled as it hovered close to her breast. She didn't know whether she feared or anticipated his caress. *You were meant to pleasure a man and give him sons.*

"You arrogant bastard!" she said under her breath, "you won't be the man I'll pleasure. I'll teach you to kidnap me! I'll see you hang!"

If she'd been paying more attention to the trail ahead rather than thinking about Cougar, she might have seen the rattlesnake lying coiled up on a rock near the trail sooner than she did, but she barely got a glimpse of it before her mare whinnied and reared.

"Whoa, girl!" Libbie fought to hang onto the mare's neck, but with no more than a ribbon for a bridle and no saddle, Libbie flew off in a tumble of torn pink velvet and tousled red hair before the mare took off at a gallop. The snake promptly scurried away into the rocks.

"Damn it, now what do I do?" Libbie stood up and brushed herself off. She was sore and limping from her tumble, her ankle possibly sprained. She paused and looked around, realizing with sudden clarity that she was a long way from either white civilization or the Apache camp. This was rough country, with little water and no food. With the sun behind heavy clouds, she wasn't even sure which direction to begin to walk. She paused and listened.

From a distant hilltop, a wolf howled. That and the beating of her own heart were the only sounds she heard. The gunfire had ceased. *Was the battle over or were both sides taking a rest while they reloaded their weapons?* There was no way to know.

Libbie licked her dry lips and wished she had grabbed a canteen as she left. She could do without food for a day or two, but she had to have water. Well, she would just have to walk until she found some. She squared her small shoulders and set off with a determined step, limping in the direction that might take her toward the army patrol. Damn. Her ankle was beginning to swell and she wondered just how far she could go. The wolf howled again; it sounded closer now.

She might be spoiled and sheltered, but she could be resourceful, too. She picked up a stick to use as a weapon and kept limping along. It would soon be dark, and who knew then what wild animals, snakes, tarantulas, and Apaches would be out there in her path? No, she would not think about any of that. Libbie stuck her chin out with stubborn determination and kept walking, using the stick as a cane.

* * *

"Retreat! Sound retreat!" Phillip shouted as he waved frantically at his men scattered through the rocks. All around him, soldiers were pinned down by deadly Apache gunfire, the shots ricocheting off the boulders.

Damn those Injuns! Phillip stumbled backward, running for his horse. In the confusion of retreat, men shouted and screamed as they fell wounded. So this was what war was really like; not parades and medals, but men dying, all sweaty and bloody. Was this the way his father had died, terrified and sweating, screaming as Phillip was screaming deep inside?

Ye gods! He must get hold of himself! Phillip struggled to mount his rearing, snorting horse. He felt cold sweat running down his back, although the day was not that warm.

"Lieutenant!" Phillip turned in his saddle as a grizzled old sergeant rose up out of nearby rocks. "What's your orders, sir?"

"Orders?" Phillip was intent on saving himself, he wasn't thinking of command.

"Shall I sound recall, sir? Try to get the wounded out?"

"Yes, of course. I—I'm headed back to the fort for reinforcements!" And with that, Phillip spurred his horse into a gallop and headed away from the battleground.

Damn those Apaches! He'd sworn he'd seen Cougar in the midst of the fighting. Too bad he hadn't managed to get that half-breed in his gunsights. Phillip was miles away from the fighting when it dawned on him that in his panic, he hadn't given much thought to Elizabeth Winters. Phillip shrugged. She might be dead anyway, or even worse, raped by those savages, so she might as well be dead. He didn't want a wife who'd been had by Injuns, no matter how rich and beautiful she was.

Once safely away from the battle site, he slowed his lathered horse to a walk and glanced back over his shoulder. Behind him, the men had regrouped. Wounded and weary, they slumped on exhausted horses as they followed him toward the fort. Phillip wheeled his horse to ride back to the grizzled old sergeant. "We rode into an ambush, bad business."

The old sergeant wiped blood from a cut on his forehead. "Yes, sir." He didn't say anything else; he didn't need to. The sergeant had warned him they were riding into a canyon that would make a great place for an ambush, but Phillip, eager to catch up with the Apache and slaughter them, hadn't listened.

Now that he realized he was in no immediate danger, Phillip calmed down. He might still figure out a way to get a medal out of this and make Mama proud. "Sergeant, we'll report in, muster a larger force, and go after them again."

"Begging your pardon, sir, but my men have been hit pretty hard."

Phillip shrugged and tried to look concerned. "Anybody killed?"

"No, sir, but some of them hurt bad and we've lost a horse or two as well as a pack mule loaded with ammunition."

"Damn!" Phillip wiped sweat from his mustache with the back of his blue-clad arm. "Now they'll be shooting at us with our own bullets."

"Apaches are pretty good at that, sir—that is, if we find them again. We're not too far from the border. Once they're across that and reach the Sierra Madre we can forget about chasing them."

Elizabeth. That half-breed bastard, Cougar, had Elizabeth. Tonight, he would be using her for his pleasure, something Phillip had never gotten to do. The thought made him so angry, he clenched his teeth until his jaw hurt. "Sergeant, we've got to go after them again. They've got a white woman with them, and we all know what that means."

"Yes, sir." The old sergeant looked sympathetic. Everyone in the outfit knew by now that the abducted girl was Phillip Van Harrington's fiancée.

It was dark before the remnants of the patrol stumbled into the fort. Phillip was more than a little aware of the soldiers gathering silently as his defeated men rode toward the barn.

He might as well get it over with. With a sigh, Phillip turned his horse toward the colonel's office and dismounted, then went inside. "Lieutenant Van Harrington reporting in."

The pimply-faced young private at the front desk hopped up and gave him a quick salute and a curious stare before retreating into the inner office to announce him. Then he held the door open. "The colonel will see you now, sir."

The colonel's expression grew as black as a thunderstorm as Phillip limped in and saluted. "At ease, Lieutenant. You look like you could use a drink."

"Yes, sir." He sank gratefully into a chair. "We ran into an ambush."

The colonel handed him a whiskey and frowned. "Ambush? You had some experienced men with you—didn't they warn you?"

Of course they had, and Phillip had ignored them. He was, after all, a major's son and part of the aristocracy of Philadelphia which made him too superior to listen to common scouts and soldiers. "Perhaps I was too intent on rescuing Miss Winters."

"Oh, yes, I had forgotten your fiancée." The officer

hesitated, running his hand through his gray hair. "I don't know how to broach this delicately, Lieutenant, but you must realize that by the time you get her back, the warriors may, well . . . have had their way with her."

Rape. He meant rape.

"They wouldn't dare!" Phillip was seething as he threw the drink down the back of his throat. But he knew Cougar. Cougar would do anything he damn well pleased. "What I meant to say, sir, is that I expect they will hold her for ransom and won't harm her; she's an heiress, you know."

"I doubt the Apache know that—"

"Excuse me, sir, but Cougar's leading them; I think he knows."

"Hmm. Ransom." The colonel didn't look too certain. "Army policy wouldn't allow us to give them weapons, no matter how much danger the girl is in."

"But we could give them money, couldn't we, sir, for food and supplies? Of course, I intend to attack the camp and wipe them out before they could ever spend a dime of it."

"Excuse me for pointing this out, Lieutenant, but from what I saw from my window as your outfit rode in, I'd say the Apache are the ones who are doing the wiping out."

Phillip felt his face burn with humiliation and anger. Damn the old man for that observation. "I—I may not be as good a soldier as my father, sir, but—"

"Oh, yes, Bill Van Harrington." The colonel nodded. "Good man. Even the Apache respected him."

"Sir? The Apaches murdered him."

"Oh, yes, I'm sure that rumor . . ." The older man cleared his throat. "Of course. So what are your observations, Lieutenant?"

Phillip leaned forward. "If I can have more troopers, sir, and start tomorrow—"

"Unless you get a good scout, you're wasting your time,

Lieutenant." The colonel's voice was curt. "Washington won't stand for another ambush like this one. I'll have to give this some thought."

"Thought?" Phillip's voice rose in disbelief. "Ye gods, sir! Miss Winters——"

"I know, and I'm sorry if something happens to the young lady, but we need someone who knows both the country and the Apaches before I send out more troops. You're dismissed, Lieutenant."

"Yes, sir." Phillip came to his feet and saluted smartly. There went his newest medal. He wasn't going to get to be a hero and have his picture in the Philadelphia newspapers. Mama would have been so proud that he was following in Father's footsteps, killing Apaches. By the stern set of the colonel's face, there obviously wasn't much use in arguing with his commander. Phillip started to say something else, but the colonel was already digging through the papers on the desk.

Phillip turned and went out. *Damn the old man and damn those Injuns.* He smiled, imagining how it would feel to get Cougar in his rifle sights. It would be more satisfying than killing big game. By fair or foul means, he intended to see that half-breed dead!

What he needed now was another drink! Phillip limped back to his quarters and opened a fresh bottle of whiskey. It was late afternoon and would soon be dark. After dark, would Cougar use Libbie for his pleasure? Maybe he had already done so? He gritted his teeth in frustration and gulped another drink. Obviously it was going to be a day or two before the colonel authorized another patrol. Phillip knew he should go down to the base infirmary and check on the welfare of his men, but it was comfortable here in his room and he was tired and annoyed.

The bear's head over the fireplace seemed to glare down at him in a way that made him uneasy, as if it were still alive. "Damned Apache superstitions!" He threw the whiskey bottle at the mounted head and caught it across the snout before the glass crashed into the stone fireplace and shattered in a tinkle of shards.

A knock sounded at the door. Phillip reached to open another bottle. Maybe if he ignored the knock, whoever it was would go away. He didn't feel like talking to anyone right now; he only wanted to plan his revenge and drink.

Again the knock, more insistent this time.

"Go away! Damn it!"

"Lieutenant, it's me!" Shashké's plaintive voice called.

Phillip grinned. He'd sworn he was not going to bother with the sultry Apache bitch again, but he needed a woman and if she was willing . . . or even if she weren't . . .

"Just a minute, I'm coming!" He staggered to the door and threw it open. She stood on the step, her face buried in her hands, her shoulders shaking with sobs. Libbie's gold earrings flashed in the dim light and a pathetic, wilted flower drooped in her hair. "Come on in, you pretty little—"

Very slowly, she moved her hands, and he noticed the red on them and wondered about it even as she raised her head.

"My God!" Phillip stumbled backward in horrified shock as he got a good look at her face. It was slashed and bloody, and part of her nose was gone. "What the hell—?"

She burst into sobs, holding bloody, entreating hands out to him. "My old husband found out about us! But you still care about me, don't you? Remember how much pleasure I've—"

He retreated in horror from her bloody, outstretched hands, shaking his head at her. "Get away from me! You look like a monster! Get the hell out of my sight, you ugly—"

"But Phillip, I have no one, no place to turn—"

"You think I give a damn? You knew what you were

doing when you took that chance." He shook off her bloody hand that grasped his arm as she begged and pleaded.

"My beauty was all I had to offer. Where shall I go now? What shall I do?"

"Honey, that's not my problem." He shoved her off the doorstep, slammed the door, and locked it, then stood there a moment shaking as she pounded against the door and cried. After a moment, there was only silence outside.

"God, I need another drink!" He staggered over to wash her blood from his hands and open another bottle. When he looked up, all the dead bears in his room seemed to be glaring at him.

Shashké slumped in the dirt in front of the lieutenant's quarters, staring at the door that had just been slammed in her face. She was in pain and distraught and now her last hope had vanished. The penalty among Apaches for an unfaithful wife was disfigurement, and her beauty had been all she had to offer.

Very slowly, she rose and walked away from his door, weeping with anguish. The area was deserted as she walked across the parade ground and faded into the desert beyond. She had held the slightest hope that the lieutenant had actually cared a little about her and would take her in or at least give her a little money. She had nowhere to turn now. No Apache would befriend her, with her scarred face betraying her guilt at breaking the old taboo. In her heart began to burn a fierce hatred for the white soldier who had used her and tossed her aside.

What to do now? She was in pain, distraught, and homeless. Surely there must be someone who would help her. Shashké stopped weeping and thought about it. The desert chill had descended on the area when darkness fell, and she shivered with the cold. Shashké thought a moment, then smiled. Yes, there was someone who cared about the Apaches. Hadn't he once taken in another Apache girl who was suddenly alone? Yes, she knew who might help her without judging, without asking any questions; a kind, gentle man.

Shashké began to walk, and as she walked, she planned her revenge.

Cougar had aimed his rifle at Lieutenant Van Harrington as that officer began his pell-mell retreat from the battle site. Just as he started to squeeze the trigger, he remembered. He must not, could not, spill Phillip's blood. Regretfully, he lowered his rifle. Too bad the lieutenant had no such qualms about shooting at Cougar!

He watched with satisfaction as the lieutenant and his patrol retreated in confusion and disarray. It would be a long time before the army got on their trail again. Once they reached the stronghold high in the mountains of Mexico, the Apache could live happily again.

Blaze. What was he to do about her? He frowned as he thought about that vexing problem. Cougar mounted up and signaled his warriors to ride out and rejoin the camp a few miles to the south. No doubt tonight the council would insist he send a messenger to the fort with their terms of ransom. Yes, they needed the food and supplies, all right, but the trouble was, Cougar did not want to give up the girl.

Damn her. He told himself she was his enemy's woman and that he hated her, but yet she drew him to her in a way that no other woman ever had, a way that made him weak and willing to do anything if she would only send a smile his way. After the way she had humiliated and spurned him, he had not meant to grow attached to the fiesty white girl, and yet his attachment grew with each passing hour.

He glanced down at his bitten hand as he headed back to camp. He had to admire her spunk, even though she had journeyed to Arizona to see him hang. Maybe if he enjoyed her once, he would lose interest and realize that she was just a woman like a hundred others, even with that fiery mane of hair that she tossed like a wild mustang filly. He both desired and hated her—hated her because she made him want her so badly when a dozen pretty Apache girls would be happy to warm his blankets. But for him, there was only Blaze, and he was certain there would never be another he wanted so badly.

And she hated him with a passion that made it certain she'd kill him with his own weapon if she ever got the chance. He'd be smart to let the lieutenant ransom her and get the redhead out of the Apache camp. She was born to be in Phillip's bed, not Cougar's. Still, the thought of the other man holding her close, kissing her, stroking her, and finally mating with her, drove him into an anguished rage. He could not use her for his pleasure because of his honor, and yet he decided at that moment that he would not give her up without a fight, no matter how much gold the proud lieutenant offered.

Cougar rode into camp, dismounted, and tossed his paint's reins over a bush.

The Apache women began a chant to welcome their triumphant warriors' return. Someone had started a big fire for the dancing. Cougar smiled. He was looking forward to the feasting and the repartee with the fiery white girl. He strode toward his wickiup.

At that moment, Owl Woman ran toward him, wringing her weathered hands. "She is gone! Your captive has escaped!"

Chapter Fifteen

Cougar dismounted and gently comforted the hysterical Owl Woman. "It is not your fault. How did this happen?"

Quickly, she filled him in, wringing her hands. "I hardly took my eyes off her."

"I know." Cougar nodded. He couldn't help admiring Libbie's resourcefulness and daring. "She's not your average, whimpering white girl."

"I should have watched her better. I know the council has great need of the ransom she would bring."

"No one could have done better," he assured her, laying a gentle hand on her stooped shoulder. "The girl is as ornery and slippery as any Apache."

"What will you do?"

Cougar glanced toward the dark sky. "There are many dangers out there for a woman alone in this rough country. I'd better find her fast or ..." He didn't even want to think of the things that could happen to the red-haired vixen.

Cougar swung back up on his horse, his worry making him increasingly annoyed with Blaze. He had counted on taking his ease by the fire all evening, feasting his eyes on the flame-haired beauty. But now, like the unpredictable little wench she was, she had taken off, trying to find her way back to civilization. Damn her for her foolishness! She had a better chance of crossing the trail of wild animals or dying of hunger or thirst, and it would be his fault. He had to find her.

Leaving the others dancing and smoking around the big fire, he rode around the camp, asking if any horses were missing. A woman complained that she had checked the herd and her sleek gray mare was gone. Cougar rode out to inspect the herd, knowing he couldn't tell much in the dark. As he looked, his keen vision spotted a lathered gray mare standing quietly, and when she moved, she limped. Then Cougar noticed the length of pink ribbon tied as a makeshift bridle and now dragging along the grass.

Cougar took a deep breath of relief and dismounted to inspect the mare. He took the hair ribbon and held it a long moment, remembering how it had tied back Blaze's long locks. What could have happened? Evidently she had taken the mare and something terrible had happened. Perhaps she had been thrown. He felt sudden alarm as he pictured her lying dead or injured somewhere in the wilderness at night.

Why couldn't Blaze behave herself and do as she was told? And yet, he knew she wouldn't have been half so intriguing if she'd been a conventional, obedient woman. She was a challenge for any man, and the one who finally tamed her would have a superior mate. Mate? She hated the sight of him, and right now, if he had her in his grasp, he would shake her until her teeth rattled and she yelled for mercy.

He grinned at the thought in spite of himself. Libbie Winters wouldn't beg for mercy if he spanked her little bottom until she was so sore, she couldn't sit down. At this point, that was a very tempting thought.

The moon came out then, round and full. Cougar rode away from the herd, following the limping tracks of the gray mare. However, the ground was rocky, and sometimes it took all his tracking skills to follow the trail. Now and then, he dismounted to take a closer look at the faint prints in the moonlight. The desert night had turned chill. He was a hardened warrior, used to the worst of elements, but Blaze was inexperienced. She probably had no food or water, and if she were hurt and afoot . . . He must not think about that, and yet he worried, knowing he could never forgive himself if something had happened to her.

Patiently, he followed the faint tracks, stopping now and then to listen. Somewhere in the distance, a wolf howled and Cougar automatically reached for his rifle, making sure it was loaded. Besides wild animals, there could be other enemies in the open country, Mexican troops or renegade whites, or tribes that were enemies of the Apache.

He dismounted again, peering at the ground in the moonlight, reading the sign. Here was where she had been thrown from the horse and it had gotten away from her. At least Blaze could walk, although she now appeared to be limping. Cougar followed her small footprints across rocky soil, saw a place where she had fallen, gotten up, and walked on. Here she had lost a shoe. He picked it up, noted how small it was, and tucked it in his saddlebag.

Up ahead, a movement caught his eye and his heart quickened. But when he investigated, it was only a torn bit of pink fabric caught in a cholla cactus. He picked it up, running his fingers over it, thinking it was not half so soft as her skin. He had a sudden image of her, all silken and soft and yielding in his arms, and the terrible need made him angry with her all over again. No man should feel such a hunger for one woman; it put him at her mercy.

Cougar gritted his teeth and refused to acknowledge that need. He was angry, he told himself, because Blaze was so disobedient and had caused him so much trouble. If he were going to keep her, he needed to teach her obedience. No; he shook his head. Of course he could not keep her. He must trade her for guns and supplies. Rich young Lieutenant Van Harrington was going to pay a fortune to get her returned to his bed. That thought made him even angrier. She was too much woman for the prissy officer.

He began to walk again, leading his horse and watching for Blaze's tracks. Then he saw a faint print that made his heart almost stop, and his horse snorted and stamped uneasily. Cougar knelt and examined it, hoping it was an old track, but his keen senses told him it was fresh. A bear, a big bear by the look of the footprint, was on Blaze's trail, too. Bears were coming out of hibernation at this time of the year and they would be hungry and cantankerous.

Did Blaze know she was being followed by a bear? Probably not. Her tracks were moving at a limping walk, not a run, and bears could move silently if need be. The bear would have the advantage over both the humans. Every one of Cougar's sharp senses was heightened as he followed the trail, pausing to smell the wind and listen for the slightest sound.

Was that the scent of her perfume? Of course he must be imagining that. For a moment, he remembered the clean scent of her hair against his chest as he had held her. She had been so warm and soft in his embrace, and he had yearned to cup her naked breasts in his hands, kiss and caress them. If he had touched those, he would not have been able to stop himself from giving in to his passion. He had fought a terrible need to hold her close, to kiss and protect her. Now she was out here with no protection. If anything happened to her because he had carried her off, Cougar would never forgive himself.

Yet to care too much was a weakness he couldn't allow himself. Cougar shook his head. It wasn't that he cared about the girl, he told himself stubbornly, it was that she was such a valuable hostage for the Apaches—too valuable to lose.

Cougar took the scrap of pink fabric and tied it around his paint's muzzle so it would not whinny and alert the bear, although the scent was blowing toward the horse and rider. Then he paused, listening. Nothing but the wind and, somewhere, a coyote yipping at the coming night. Impulsively, he called out, "Blaze? Blaze, are you out here?"

No answer. Of course it had been stupid for him to yell her name. Even if she were within range of his voice, Blaze was too ornery to answer and make it easy to find her. In some spots now, the brush was so thick that he might walk right past her without seeing her if she hunkered down and kept quiet.

Where was the bear? He wasn't sure, and he dared not call out a warning about her danger. The knowledge that a bear was also on her trail might cause her to panic and go running blindly through the brush and over a cliff in these rough hills. On the other hand, he thought with grudging admiration, Blaze was not the typical white woman. She'd probably be as brave and resourceful as any Apache girl. He paused and considered. She couldn't be that far ahead of him. Maybe if he swung in a wide circle, he could come up on her other side and get between her and the bear.

Quiet as a shadow, Cougar moved off the trail, trying to judge just how far ahead of him she might be. If that bear caught up with her before he got there, Blaze didn't stand a chance. At that moment, his stallion got a scent of the bear and bolted, tearing the reins from Cougar's hands and galloping away, his rifle hanging on his saddle. Well, damn, now he was without a weapon except for a knife in his belt; not much use against a bear.

Libbie had paused and listened to Cougar's voice calling, "Blaze? Blaze, are you out here?"

Oh, damn! He was somewhere behind her, but she didn't intend to be recaptured. She quickened her step, not about to answer and lead him to her. She'd lost one shoe, and her ankle was swollen from the fall. Her dress was also badly torn from catching on passing cactus. Maybe the chances of walking until she found the soldiers was slim, but she had to try. Libbie kept moving, trying to be very quiet. Behind her, she heard a crashing sound through the brush and looked back, breathing hard. Cougar was usually as silent as a ghost, but maybe his big horse was making the noise. Yes, it did sound like a horse galloping away. Maybe he was afoot, too.

Could she outrun him? She shook her head as she considered. Not a chance, but she might outsmart him and still get away. It would be dark soon; maybe she could lose him in the darkness. She realized that was a small chance, too; Cougar was one of the army's best scouts and trackers. Still, what other option did she have? Even if she eluded him, it meant spending the night out here alone in this rough country with no food or water. Yet tomorrow she might run into an army patrol; all she had to do was be brave and resourceful tonight.

Libbie moved on, limping even more. Behind her, the crashing sounds through the brush sounded even closer. It couldn't be the horse again. Then the thought came to her: *What or who had made the stallion panic?* Cougar wouldn't

make that much noise. She took a deep breath for courage
and picked a small limb off a stunted tree. She wasn't even
certain whether what she heard was real or a figment of
her vivid imagination, but right now she was scared. She
braced herself against a tree stump with her club raised
and watched a clearing a few hundred feet away as the
crashing sound grew louder and another sound was carried
on the breeze, a sound that was half snarl, half roar.

Abruptly, something big and black loomed up out of
the brush. Libbie bit her lip to hold back a scream and
gripped her club tighter as a giant bear reared up out of
the shadows, roaring and raking the air with powerful
claws.

Now she did scream long and loud. The bear was close
enough that she could feel the heat of its big body, smell
the fetid scent of it, see the gleam of its teeth. Libbie
screamed again, stumbled backward, and went down, the
bear lumbering toward her.

At that moment, a form stepped out of the woods behind
her and stood straddling her prone body as he faced the
beast, unarmed but holding up his hands toward the bear.
Cougar. She could only lie there watching, too terrified
to even scream as he faced the giant animal unarmed.

The bear hesitated even as Cougar said something to it
in his native language. At that, the bear reared up again,
hesitating uncertainly. Again Cougar spoke to it in Apache,
his tone soothing.

The big bear paused, swaying on its hind legs, looked
at him a long moment, then went to all fours and ambled
away through the brush.

"Blaze, are you all right?" He turned and held out his
hand.

Libbie was crying and shaking so badly, she could barely
grasp his hand, and as he pulled her to her feet, she went
impulsively into the safety of his big arms.

He held her very close, stroking her hair. "It's all right. I won't let anything hurt you."

She couldn't stop crying, and now he was kissing the tears from her face. "Shh, Blaze, dear one, you're all right."

She realized suddenly that she was in his embrace, her arms around his neck, trembling and seeking the shelter of his muscular arms. *Was she out of her mind?*

Libbie pulled away from him awkwardly, embarrassed. He was her captor, yet she had gone unthinking into his embrace. "What—what did you say to it?"

He let her move away from him. "I simply said, 'it is me, Grandfather,' and the bear, knowing who I am, did not attack."

"That's crazy." She shook her head.

"So the whites tell me, but you saw what happened. It is forbidden to kill bears; Apaches think our ancestors' spirits reside in them until they go to the Happy Place."

"But Phillip killed bears," she blurted, remembering how he had bragged about his hunting trophies. She was still staring after the disappearing bear, thunderstruck with awe.

Cougar shrugged. "He who kills the bear will feel the bear's wrath. Can you walk?"

Libbie took a step and winced. "Damn you, I thought I was about to get away."

"You were about to become my ancestor's dinner," he snapped. "Now Grandfather's spirit has spooked my horse and we're stranded out here until daylight. I don't want to risk running into that bear again in the dark. Next time, I might not have time to speak to him."

"I'm not returning to the Apaches."

"But of course you are."

She was tired, her ankle hurt, and she was discouraged at being recaptured. "I can't walk."

He looked around at the growing darkness. "I think we'll camp here until sunup. Maybe by then my horse will have come back."

"Fine. Have you got any food?" Maybe by morning, the soldiers would show up or she could outfox Cougar and lose him in this rough country.

"I've got my knife and maybe a match or two hidden in its sheath. If I can find a barrel cactus, that gives us water and we can peel and eat some prickly pear fruit. In the meantime, you could be at least a little grateful for my saving you."

"Grateful!" she snorted. "I wouldn't be in this fix if it weren't for you."

He looked annoyed as he began to build a small fire. "We'll make out all right until morning, and the fire will keep the animals away."

There went her idea for sneaking away into the darkness while he slept. There was nothing she could do but settle down by the small fire and wait while he went off into the darkness and came back in moments with part of a barrel cactus and some red prickly-pear fruit. It tasted good and she noticed he gave her his share. She started to say something, then decided he deserved to go hungry for getting her into this mess.

Now he took her other shoe off and examined her feet. "I'll have to get you some soft deerskin moccasins."

His big hands felt good massaging her instep. "I don't intend to be here that long."

"We'll see how fast the lieutenant comes up with the ransom." He rubbed each of her feet gently. "If the horse doesn't come back, I'll have to carry you."

"Don't you dare touch me!"

He glared at her, sighed heavily, and settled down before the fire. "Blaze, I'll touch you anytime I feel like it. As your captor, it's my privilege."

There was no point in arguing that. "So we're just going to sit here all night?"

He fumbled in his belt and came up with a small pouch of tobacco and papers. "Unless you want to take a chance on running into Grandfather bear."

"What—what would it take to get you to turn me loose?"

He raised one eyebrow at her, then returned to rolling a smoke.

She rushed on. "Suppose I—suppose I let you make love to me in exchange for freeing me?"

He threw back his head and laughed. "Have you ever had a man before?"

She felt her face flame. "You know I haven't!"

"Then you might not be skilled enough to make it enjoyable."

She was incensed. "You're turning me down?"

He seemed to be enjoying her confusion. "Let's just say the pleasure might not be worth the amount of ransom I'd have to forego. Besides, this isn't a very comfortable place for that, although I will admit your body would make a soft mattress."

"Oh, you half-breed bastard!" Libbie lunged at him, scratching and clawing. If she could sink her nails into those arrogant blue eyes . . . !

Cougar dropped the cigarette, threw up his hands to protect his face, then caught her wrists. They went down in a heap while they struggled. "You little wildcat! Stop that!"

"I am going to claw you to death!" Libbie fought to reach his face as they tumbled and rolled near the fire.

He came up on top. He lay there on her, both of them breathing hard as he pinned her hands above her head. "You little vixen! I ought to—"

He bent his head suddenly before she realized his intent, covering her mouth with his. He was too heavy for her to move as he pinned her down and kissed her deeply, thoroughly. His tongue invaded her mouth, ravaging it as he explored her lips, tasting and teasing, probing deeply with his tongue. No man had ever kissed her like this before. For a long moment, she surrendered to his seeking mouth, her body molding itself against the hard planes of his. She could feel his throbbing maleness through her torn dress and his skimpy loincloth. He was breathing hard, kissing her lips, her eyes, her throat as he murmured soft words she did not understand even as his mouth claimed hers again and his free hand moved down past the Apache Tears necklace to stroke her naked breasts.

Oh, God, no man had ever touched her like this, and the way her eager body responded scared her, arching up against his seeking fingers as the kiss deepened. At this point, she came to her senses and bit him.

Cougar pulled away from her with an oath, wiping one hand across his bloody mouth. "You are like embracing a viper!"

She sat up, pulling away from him, breathing hard, angry with him that she had momentarily surrendered with eagerness to the touch and taste of him. "Must I remind you that I am under the protection of your necklace?"

He paused and glared at her blackly, still wiping blood from his sensual mouth. "Don't push me, Blaze. It's already all I can do to keep from ripping it off your neck and taking you like you ought to be taken."

"Don't you touch me!" She knew her voice rose shakily as she backed away, knowing this was a big, virile stallion of a man. If he decided to throw her down and take her, she wouldn't be able to stop him, and from the look in his eyes, that was what he was thinking of at this very moment.

He took a deep breath and moved away from her. His hands were shaking as he rolled a cigarette. "The faster your lieutenant comes up with the money, the better it will be for all of us. You've been nothing but trouble from the first moment I laid eyes on you."

She realized that she was not in any immediate danger and pulled her knees up before her, resting her chin on them. Her dress was so torn, her bare legs were visible and he was staring at them, but she couldn't do anything about that. She wondered what it would be like to have the big savage make love to her. Would it be violent and exciting? Tender and gentle? "Have you made love to Shashké?"

He laughed without humor and continued to smoke. "What brought that on?"

"I saw you two outside the window the night of the dance."

Cougar shrugged. "Shashké's too ambitious to pick an Apache as her lover. She wants . . . anyway, she is a married woman. It would not be honorable for a warrior to take her." Even though he had told her once before that Shashké was not his woman, she was surprised to realize she was relieved that Cougar had never been the greedy girl's lover. *Who* would *an ambitious girl choose*? "Are you telling me she's got a white lover?"

He started to speak, then shrugged. "You wouldn't believe me if I told you. Now settle down and let's get some sleep."

Did he know something he wasn't telling? No matter. Libbie looked around at the darkness uncertainly. "You think the bear will come back?"

He shrugged again, obviously enjoying her uneasiness. "Who knows?"

A coyote howled in the distance, and the sound echoed across the hills.

"Can you build the fire bigger?" She hunched closer to it, shivering a little. The desert night was growing chill.

"Not without either setting the whole desert afire or

alerting every enemy for miles. Settle down and get some sleep, Blaze.''

If the army were near, that wouldn't be a bad idea, she thought, but he was too smart for that. "I will never answer to Blaze," she said as she rolled up before the fire.

He shrugged, his face immobile. "You're right. It is not a proper name for a white girl; it is too fiery and free for anyone less than an Apache."

"Aren't you going to sleep?"

He didn't look at her, but stared into the fire and smoked. "Someone has to keep watch; you're under my protection."

Libbie settled down and closed her eyes. Somehow, she took comfort in the fact that he was watching over her. Libbie drifted off to sleep.

Just before dawn, Libbie awakened to a gentle touch on her shoulder. She opened her eyes and looked up into Cougar's blue ones. For a moment, she was puzzled, and then she remembered. She was still a captive; she hadn't escaped.

"My horse came back," Cougar said. "Are you ready?"

She sat up and groaned. Her body was stiff and sore from yesterday's adventure. "I'm not sure I can move."

"Then I'll carry you." Before she could protest, he swung her up in his big arms easily.

She started to struggle, but decided it was a waste of time. Cougar was the most stubborn, determined male she had ever met, and he would have his way. She let her face rest against his wide chest as he put her up on the paint stallion and swung up behind her. He held her against him and nudged the horse into a walk back toward the Apache camp. "The Apaches should have moved out before dawn. You have held us up," he scolded. "I hope you've given up trying to escape."

She couldn't help but smile up at him. "You know me better than that."

And now he actually grinned. She had forgotten how handsome he was when he smiled. "Blaze, I'd be disappointed in you if you gave up."

They rode back to the Apache camp. There were heavily ladened packhorses tied in the middle of the camp, and Libbie almost shouted with relief at the sight of white men sitting around the fire. She was saved!

Cougar frowned and helped her to dismount, then held up his hand by way of greeting. "I thought we would meet you on the other side of the border."

"Hello, Cougar." The men smiled and nodded. They were a scruffy-looking bunch, Libbie thought with sudden alarm, and she pulled her torn bodice closed. The lustful way the five white renegades looked her over made her very nervous. She found herself moving closer to Cougar, and he put an arm around her. This time, she welcomed the feel of that protective embrace. She almost shuddered as she looked over the leader. He was dirty and bearded with tangled hair. One of his eye sockets was empty.

The one-eyed one stepped forward and offered his hand to Cougar. Cougar hesitated a long moment before he shook it. "Hello, Coyote Johnson."

As close as he stood, she could smell him now and drew back from the rank scent of dried blood and whiskey. Johnson's good eye roamed over Libbie freely and he leered at her, showing broken yellow teeth.

"Cougar, the council did not lie when they told me of your captive. The woman is beautiful and worth much, and I know where I can sell her. Whatever ransom her man offers, I will pay more to own this white captive!"

Chapter Sixteen

Libbie shuddered and instinctively crept closer to Cougar's protective arm.

Johnson turned his empty eye socket toward her and grinned with jagged yellow teeth. "What's the matter, girlie? Scare you? Sheriff shot my eye out while I was escapin', and now I shoot every lawman I see."

She didn't say anything, horrified by the filthy, tangled beard and the smell of him.

Johnson laughed. "I hate women like you—dainty, high-class bitches who wouldn't spit on me." He looked at Cougar. "They tell me she's yours. What do you say, Cougar? We got a deal?"

"No!" Libbie shouted, her anger overcoming her horror. "I'm not his woman and I won't be yours, either!"

Johnson winked at her with his one good eye. "Spirited! I like that. Where'd you get her?"

Libbie interrupted. "I've been stolen from near Fort Grant. My fiancé is an officer there." She started to say more, but Cougar gave her a warning look and she lapsed into silence.

"An officer's woman?" Johnson rubbed his dirty, calloused hands together. "That makes it even better."

Cougar frowned. "The girl is a captive, that's all. I expect the rich lieutenant to pay plenty for her safe return."

Johnson looked over his shoulder at the grave Apache warriors sitting around the campfire. "Why don't we sit and smoke and talk a deal?"

"Why doesn't anyone ask me?" Libbie fumed.

"Hush up, girl," Johnson said. "You got no say in this."

"That's right," Cougar said, "but I don't want to sell her."

Johnson rubbed his mouth. Libbie noted that his rawhide vest was as filthy as his beard. "I got a good bottle of liquor and a wagonload of food and supplies to trade. Let's parlay."

Cougar hesitated, looking toward the supplies and then back toward the hungry, silent women and children standing in the shadows. "Maybe we might trade you a few good horses for flour and blankets."

Johnson grinned. "That ain't the filly I had in mind." He gestured toward Cougar's wickiup. "We'll drink and talk. Maybe we can work something out."

Cougar took Libbie's arm, pulling her with him as he led Johnson into the wickiup past the four other gunrunners who were eyeing her with lust as they sat around the campfire.

She started to say something, but Cougar motioned for her to sit by the fire and be silent. Then the two men sat down cross-legged by the fire and Johnson pulled out a bottle, took a long swig, and handed it to Cougar. Cougar barely took a sip, but Johnson didn't seem to notice. His evil gaze was on Libbie as he took out a small sack and began to roll a smoke. "I've got some prime weapons, blankets, and plenty of dried beef and flour."

"No doubt our own supplies stolen from the shipment by the Indian agent." Cougar frowned.

Johnson laughed. "I didn't ask him where he got the stuff; I just bought it."

"Look," Cougar said, "we need those supplies. We've got a few good horses to trade, and if you'll trust us for the rest—"

"Trust you? I wouldn't trust my own mother," Johnson snorted as he lit his smoke.

Cougar watched him thoughtfully. "Later, when the girl is ransomed, we'll have gold. We could pay you then."

Johnson looked at Libbie again with his one good eye, bright with lust. "I don't do business on credit, you know that."

"But those are our own supplies, stolen from us, and we need them."

Johnson spat to one side and grinned at Libbie. "You can't prove that, Injun. You know the kind of trade I want."

Libbie realized in growing horror that he was talking about her as he ran his tongue along his lower lip.

Cougar shook his head, watching the fear on her lovely face. He didn't want her to hear this discussion, so he spoke now in border Spanish. "Don't even think it, *hombre.* Her rich officer is going to give us plenty of gold and then we can buy supplies."

She looked at him curiously, but he ignored her.

Johnson laughed and said in Spanish, "Don't want her to know, huh? *Bueno.* We'll discuss the terms so she won't understand. Women have a tendency to get hysterical about such things."

"I told you no, *hombre,*" Cougar said. "I'll wait for the gold from the officer."

"*Sí,* but that may take weeks," Johnson said, "and in

the meantime, you've got hungry children in this camp. I would buy the girl from you, for—oh, let's say, one thousand dollars worth of flour and blankets?''

Cougar could see by Libbie's face that she was about to demand an explanation, so he silenced her with a stern shake of his head and replied in Spanish. "You could buy a dozen Indian or Mexican girls for that much."

Johnson nodded in agreement. "*Sí,* but they don't have red hair and green eyes. There's a whorehouse in a port on the Mexican coast that caters to rich travelers. They would give twice that for a girl like this one, provided she could please at least a dozen men a night."

Cougar closed his eyes for a long moment as if he were thinking. In his mind, he saw dozens of men lining up to take their turn rutting on the delicate body of the girl sitting by the fire. An anger began to grow in him.

Johnson took another gulp of the liquor. "Think about it, *compadre.* There's a ship I know sailing in a couple of weeks. Some Oriental potentate or Arab sheik would pay plenty for a beauty like this for his harem."

Cougar frowned. "I told you, I don't want to sell her. She's too fiery for most men; no one could ever tame her."

"I could have a helluva good time myself tryin'," Johnson said good-naturedly. "I tell you what, *hombre.* If you don't want to sell her, maybe I could pay you just to enjoy her the rest of the day until we pull out."

The fury in Cougar's heart became almost uncontrollable. "I told you no. The white officer won't pay if she's returned dishonored."

"She's a virgin?" The trader rubbed his groin and licked his lips. "I'll up the ante then. I ain't never had me no virgin. What do you say, Injun? Her man will never know the difference if she don't tell him. You'll get my gold and what he's willin' to pay, too." He gestured toward Libbie and said in English, "Stand up and let me get a look at you, honey. I wanta see what I'm buyin'."

She turned horrified green eyes on Cougar. "You've sold me? You rotten bastard—"

Before Cougar could answer, Johnson reached out and caught her arm. "Stand up, honey. I want to see if you're worth the money—"

"Enough!" Cougar thundered, and his big hand shot out, caught Johnson's arm, and twisted it, freeing Libbie, who backed away.

The ugly gunrunner shrieked in pain as Cougar twisted so that the man was on his face in the dirt. "You're breakin' it off! My God! you're breakin' my arm!"

Libbie shrank against the side of the wickiup, terrified of the look on Cougar's face. She had heard of murderous rage, but this was the first time she had ever seen it in a man's eyes. Cougar kept the other man pinned, groveling and twisting with pain. "I'm going to let you up, Johnson. If you know what's good for you, you'll get out of here and take your men with you!"

He let go of the man's arm and Johnson stumbled to his feet, favoring his arm and sobbing. "I'll get you for this! I'll see your people never get another side of beef or even a measly blanket!"

Cougar grabbed the man and pitched him headlong out of the wickiup. "Get out of here, you carrion! Your money's no good here!"

Libbie ran to the door and looked out. Johnson was rounding up his men, swearing and still favoring his injured arm.

Cougar looked at her. "Are you all right?"

"You were going to sell me?" She glared up at him, shaking with the realization.

"You know better than that," he answered softly.

She didn't mean to cry; she intended to put up a hard

facade, but she couldn't keep the tears from beginning to overflow.

"You're all right; he won't get you." He pulled her into his arms and she let him. It felt so safe and reassuring in the circle of his powerful embrace. "Shush, Blaze, everything's all right now." He held her tightly against him, stroking her hair, while she clung to him, sobbing.

He didn't mean to, but he leaned over and kissed the top of her head, wanting to reassure her, wanting to protect her. If she noticed, she gave no sign, only clung to him, all soft and yielding and trembling. He wanted to tell her at that moment that he had tried to hate her for who she was, but he knew now that he had loved her from the first moment he saw her step off that stagecoach wearing a green dress with the sunlight reflecting off that fiery hair. No one would ever harm her as long as he had breath enough to lift a hand in her defense. He kissed the top of her head again. "Blaze," he murmured. "Oh, Blaze . . ."

She managed to get control of herself. *What was she doing, going into the arms of her kidnapper?* She wouldn't even be facing danger from men like Johnson if it weren't for Cougar. "Yes," she remarked suddenly, pulling away from him, "of course I'm safe. After all, I had forgotten you expect to get a big ransom for my return."

He turned away with a resigned sigh. "That's right. If I let Johnson take your virginity, you would be of much less value—even to our prissy lieutenant!"

"Why didn't I realize that you were thinking of the money, you—you savage!" She lashed out at him with both small fists, angry and confused, unsure of her own emotions.

Cougar threw up his hands to protect his face from her ridiculous attack as she pummeled him. She was so small, he was capable of breaking her back across his knee, but he could not hurt her. He only waited until she exhausted herself hitting against his massive chest; then she turned away, sobbing.

He watched silently, feasting his gaze upon her beauty. Each time she moved near him, he came closer to losing control of his passions. Just now, with her so warm and trembling in his arms, he had been torn between two emotions; he wanted to comfort and protect her, yet he yearned to pull her down on that pile of furs by the fire and take her with the need that had been building in him ever since the first moment he saw her. In his heart, he knew now that there would never, never be another woman for him.

And in that moment, he knew something else, something he had realized just now as he held her. No matter what he had told her, he couldn't give her up, not for any amount of gold. He could not bear the thought that the white man would be the first to take her, that Phillip's lips would be the first to taste those breasts. At this moment, as he watched her, he knew that no man would ever touch her but Cougar. He would kill the man who even looked at her with lust as he had just come close to killing Coyote Johnson.

Yes, he was going to keep her for his own if he had to keep her against her will. There was not money enough in all the world to free Cougar's slave. To hell with Lieutenant Van Harrington's gold!

He made his decision in that split second as he watched the firelight play on her fiery hair. And at that moment, he knew that eventually he would have her body, if not her love. It was only a matter of time. His obsession with her would not be denied. Once Cougar had put his son in her belly, no doubt the lieutenant would not want her returned. Not that it mattered, because Cougar was not ever going to let her go.

Now she seemed to gain control of herself and cleared her throat. "You've sent the ransom message to the army?"

"Yes." He didn't look at her. "Yesterday. We're waiting for a reply. Maybe tomorrow or the next day." His friend Turtle had left with the message, all right, but no matter how much the lieutenant offered, Cougar would not accept it. Maybe if he hurried the tribe, the Apache could be safely in a hideaway near the border before Phillip's troops could find them again. No white man save trusted Mac McGuire knew the location of that place. From there, it was only a couple of miles across the border and to their old stronghold in the mountains. Once there, the Apaches were safe from pursuit.

He wanted to reach out and gather her into his arms again, tell her how much he cared about her, but of course, he could not do that. She was awaiting rescue and escape from him, the uncivilized half-breed. He would have to lie to her, impugn his honor, but all he could think of now as he watched the firelight play on that fiery hair was how she had felt in his arms and how it would feel to make love to her. Maybe after he had put a fine, strong son at her breast, she would forget about escaping and resign herself to being Cougar's woman. His passion and need for the flame-haired temptress overruled everything else.

She looked up at him, wondering about the emotion on his rugged face. "What are you thinking?"

"Nothing," he snapped, avoiding her gaze. "Let's go outside and make sure the gunrunners are out of the camp."

"All right." *There was something wrong.* She had gotten to know him too well over the past several days, better than she had ever known anyone in her whole life. They went outside.

The dirty renegades were just riding out of the camp.

The one called Johnson looked back at her with a gaze that made her shiver.

When Cougar saw the way Coyote Johnson looked at her, he put a protective arm around her. She stiffened for a long moment, then let him pull her close against him. She trusted him, he realized, and here he was planning how to foil Phillip's rescue efforts. Cougar felt guilty, but he could not help his hunger for this woman.

Geronimo came over and said to him in Apache, "You did not sell her?"

Cougar shook his head. "I have decided I want to keep her for my own."

Geronimo scowled. "She will bring you much trouble."

Cougar sighed. "She already has, and yet I would do it a thousand times and count it worth it."

The other shook his head. "No man should be such a fool for a woman."

"I admit I am a fool," Cougar said. He wanted his green-eyed beauty in his blankets where he could make love to her night after night, teaching her about passion.

The other considered. "Warriors tell me there is a white officer who will stop at nothing to get her returned."

"That is true," Cougar admitted with a shrug, "but if we pull out in the morning and hurry our pace, we can be safely away from here and the army will never find her."

"Does she understand?" Geronimo asked.

Cougar glanced down into her trusting green eyes, then looked away and shook his head. "No, she thinks she is to be ransomed and returned to white civilization. But once her belly is heavy with my son, what other choice will she have? The rich white man won't want her then, and I'll make sure she'll never have a chance to escape."

"She will hate you for it."

Cougar sighed. "My need for her is so great, I am past caring about that."

"Women!" Geronimo made a sound of disgust and walked away.

Libbie looked after the other man, then up at Cougar. "What is being said? Are you discussing me?"

"Yes." He didn't look at her. "We will ride on to a secret hiding place just this side of the border. There we will wait for Turtle to bring us information to arrange your return."

"But why don't we just wait here?"

Cougar shook his head. "The army knows this place; they might plan an ambush. Trust me, Blaze. You are going to end up where you belong."

She looked relieved and smiled. "I was beginning to fear . . . but of course I know I am safe because of the necklace and the promise you made me."

He didn't answer, only nodded and avoided her gaze, which puzzled her. No matter. What was really worrying her was whether Phillip might be able to come up with the ransom money. If he were penniless and she was, too, where could the gold possibly come from?

Cougar seemed to sigh with relief as the renegades rode out. "There goes supplies that are rightfully ours. We need to get them back." They returned to the wickiup.

"Tell me what is bothering you," she said.

He shrugged. "Nothing. Tell me again why you returned to Arizona. Did you come to see me hang?"

He probably wasn't going to believe her, but she would tell him anyway. "I wasn't sure you were one of the condemned. I hoped to be able to talk the commander into delaying the sentence, or at the very least giving me a chance to say good-bye to you."

She wasn't certain he believed her, but what did it matter? She was only now admitting to herself that she had been attracted to the big scout the moment she saw him leaning against the corner of that adobe building as she got off that stage.

"Let us not talk of this," he said briskly, "or your ransom." He looked her over critically. "That pink dress is ragged. Maybe old Owl Woman can come up with something better."

"I'd also like a bath if I had any soap," Libbie agreed. "I don't want to look too terrible in front of all those troops at the exchange."

"Of course." He avoided her gaze. "I'll be leaving on a hunt later this morning with the other warriors, since we failed to get supplies from Coyote Johnson and his gunrunners."

They went outside, where he spoke to the old woman in Apache and she smiled, nodded, and disappeared into her wickiup. When she returned, she held up a soft doeskin dress, a pair of moccasins, and some yucca root.

Libbie looked at Cougar, a question in her eyes.

He said, "Yucca root makes good soap; you'll like it."

She had a sudden suspicion. "You aren't going to watch?"

"Are you inviting me?" He smiled and she realized again how handsome he was.

"You know I'm not!"

"Good thing," he said. "I might not be able to stop myself from joining you in the water—and I wouldn't want to bathe."

"You're terrible!" She found herself bantering with him; not really afraid anymore.

"No, I just want you, Blaze." The need for her burned in those startling blue eyes for all to see.

She reached up and touched the necklace automatically.

"You don't need to remind me; I know," he said.

"I trust your honor," Libbie said and turned to Owl Woman. The two women started for the nearby creek. While Owl Woman stood guard, Libbie scrubbed herself thoroughly with the yucca soap and washed her tangled mop of hair. Soon all her problems would be behind her if Phillip could find the money to ransom her. If he contacted her old governess, maybe she would be smart enough to borrow the money from crooked old Mr. Higginbottom. Mrs. Everett would probably lie to the old geezer and tell him Libbie had changed her mind about marrying him.

Libbie returned to her wickiup and was sitting inside before the fire in the doeskin dress, moccasins, and his necklace, drying her hair on a scrap of her old petticoat, when Cougar entered suddenly.

"You look beautiful," he blurted and she saw the passion for her in his eyes. "Here, let me help you put your hair up."

"That's not necessary," she said.

"But I insist." He sat down cross-legged, reached for a porcupine-tail brush, and pulled her between his thighs. "You have beautiful hair." He began to brush her long locks.

She started to protest that she could do it herself, but his stroking felt good and she closed her eyes and enjoyed it.

Behind her, Cougar brushed her hair slowly, breathing in the clean scent of it and feeling the softness. So much taller than she was, he could look down over her shoulder and saw she wore nothing under the doeskin dress. He could see the naked swell of her breasts, and he yearned to reach under her arms and cup those breasts, pull her against him so he could kiss the back of her damp neck, but he dared not do that. He did not want her to know how much he cared. The white girl would exploit his weakness. He wasn't sure he believed her explanation of why she had returned to Arizona, but he wanted to believe it.

One of the men yelled at him from outside.

Cougar stood up and began to gather his weapons and

canteen. "We'll return after dark from our hunt," he said. "Am I going to have to tie you up to make sure you don't run away?"

Libbie laughed, feeling lighthearted as she looked up at him. "Why should I go to all that trouble when I'll be ransomed any day now?"

He only nodded, not meeting her eyes as he turned and strode outside. Libbie followed him and stood with Owl Woman, watching the warriors mount up. She had forgotten how graceful he looked on a horse, big and masculine. She noted several pretty young Apache girls smiling at him as he rode out. Somehow that annoyed her, although she wasn't sure why. Sooner or later, he would take a wife and she'd be back in white civilization, so what did it matter? Still, for some reason, it bothered her.

Now that the warriors had left, Libbie found herself helping around the camp under Owl Woman's guidance. Some of the women smiled at her with encouragement as she used the one or two Apache words she had learned. Small brown children ran about the camp, and she found herself laughing at their antics and playing with them. Libbie loved children and had always regretted that she was an only child.

The old woman showed her how to cook over a campfire, how to grind corn with a pestle, and how to stretch and cure a deerskin. For the first time in her life, Libbie felt useful, and she realized that people were pretty much the same everywhere, whether they be brown or white. Life in an Apache camp was not so bad after all, and the Apache clothing was much more comfortable than the tight stays and bustle she'd been used to wearing.

The camp settled down quickly after sunset. The landscape was alive with the coming spring. Libbie helped Owl Woman with chores such as carrying water and banking the campfire so that the coals would make it through the night. There were few men left in the camp, mostly old warriors. Soon she would be returning to civilization. And to what? Now Libbie faced cold reality. She didn't want to marry Phillip, and he had no money anyway. Life could be hard and lonely for a penniless spinster.

She loved the West. Maybe she could stay and open a little shop of some kind. *How could she do that with no money?* Maybe she could get a job teaching on the reservation. She'd grown to respect and understand the Apache people the last few days and she'd learned a few words in their language. Well, what she would do with the rest of her life wasn't today's problem, she thought with a sleepy yawn as she settled down in her wickiup. In another day or two, she would have seen the last of Cougar. Funny, she should be glad, but she felt a little empty at the thought; she'd grown to depend on him so much. Gradually, she dropped off to sleep, still thinking about him.

She awakened with a start. What was it? She rose on one elbow, straining to hear, but the camp was quiet. *There was someone in the wickiup with her.* For a moment, she thought it was her imagination; then she heard a slight sound and smiled, wondering if the warriors had returned early. "Cougar?"

She smelled the rank scent as she drew a breath and abruptly she knew! As she opened her mouth to scream, a hand reached out and clapped over her mouth. "Be quiet, bitch! He won't sell you, so I'll have to steal you!"

Coyote Johnson. For a split second, Libbie was frozen with horror. Then she came to life and began to fight him.

Chapter Seventeen

She fought her assailant in the dark wickiup, but she was a petite woman and Coyote Johnson was strong. The small campfire flared abruptly, and she could see the gleam of triumph on his bearded, dirty face as he stuffed a scrap of blanket in her mouth, tied her hands, and threw her across his shoulder. Now he put his hand up and patted her bottom familiarly. "You just behave yourself, girlie, till we get out of this camp. You ought to be glad I'm rescuin' you from these Injuns."

He chuckled and carried her out of the wickiup and across the sleeping camp.

Was there any chance he was really taking her back to civilization? Maybe Mrs. Everett had come up with the ransom after all. Libbie was paralyzed with fear and indecision, but there was nothing she could do to stop him at the moment anyway.

He carried her out beyond the edge of the camp and threw her up on his horse. "Yesirree." He grinned at her.

"And maybe when I get tired of you, I might even let your fancy officer ransom you."

Oh, damn, she was in more trouble now than she had been as a captive in the Indian camp. If she could just get the gag out of her mouth and scream, Apaches would come running from everywhere to help her. It surprised her that she was now thinking of the Indians as friends and allies against renegades like Coyote. She tried to break free, but he had tied her securely. He mounted up behind her. "Just riding with you, girlie, is gonna be fun."

He put his arms around her, pawing her breasts and thighs as he clucked to his horse and they rode away from the camp at a walk. She tried to jerk away from his hot, grimy hands, but he only laughed, his mouth close to her ear. "You uppity little bitch! As soon as I get you back at my place, I'm gonna do more than just handle you!"

Oh, God. Libbie almost retched at the thought. Of course that was what he intended to do to her—probably share her with the other gunrunners once he'd satisfied his own lust.

Cougar, where are you? She hadn't realized until this moment how much she depended on the big half-breed and how much she trusted him to always be there for her.

Johnson rode slowly away from the Indian camp. "Don't want to wake anyone by hearin' a horse gallop." He ran his hands up and down her body as they rode and laughed close to her ear. "Honey, by the time those Injuns find out you're gone, I'll have you under me a long ways from here, and are we gonna have some fun!"

She shuddered at the images that came to her mind.

"Now, honey, don't be like that! I'm gonna teach you how to please a man, and if you please me enough, maybe you can just please me and my buddies, not get yourself sold to that Mexican whorehouse on the coast."

She didn't know which sounded worse—ending up in

an untraceable bordello or having to be the whore for the slimy renegades.

She stopped fighting her bonds, realizing she must not waste her strength, but must think of a plan. Libbie decided to stay calm and wait for her opportunity to escape . . . if there was one. Maybe once he took the gag out of her mouth, she could talk Coyote Johnson into letting down his guard. Yes, that was what she would do. She stopped struggling and didn't react when he squeezed her breasts and ran his dirty hands down her thighs.

"Honey, you learn fast. Now, that's more like it! And if'en you think that Injun cares enough about you to ride into my camp, you don't know Injuns very well. One woman is as good as another to them. I reckon Cougar will just go out and steal another girl."

She shook her head violently, and Johnson snickered again as they rode through the night. "Don't believe that, huh? You ain't gettin' sweet on that brave, are you now, girl?"

She shook her head again. Of course it wasn't that, it was just that every time she'd run into trouble lately, Cougar had been there for her, rescuing her, comforting her. The thought surprised her.

Or was Johnson right? Maybe Cougar wouldn't care enough to come; or maybe he wouldn't be able to track them.

Well, she'd deal with that when she got to it. Libbie took a deep breath and began to think of ways to escape or get her hands on a weapon. She listened in vain for the sound of horses' hooves, hoping rescue was on the way. Once she even imagined she heard a horse, but decided it was only her wistful imagination.

Several hours passed as they rode. The night was cloudy, hiding the moon, and she had no idea which way they were going. Even if she did escape, would she be able to find her way back to the fort or even to the Apache camp?

Finally, Johnson reined in near a brushy canyon. "Hello the camp!"

"Coyote, that you?"

"Damn right, and if I'd of been an Apache, I'd have cut your throat by now! Bif, you ain't keepin' much of a watch."

"Against what?" grumbled the other, walking out to meet him. "You ain't seen anyone, have you?"

Johnson shook his head and rode into the circle of tents. "Look, Bif, I brought us a play-pretty."

She could see the other man in the firelight. She remembered him now from the circle around the fire at the Apache camp, one of the gunrunners. He was short and stocky and looked like he needed a good bath. "Oh, Holy Christ, Coyote! You went back and stole that girl that belongs to that Apache brave?"

"He's not there. He don't know the difference." Johnson dismounted by the small fire and pulled Libbie from the horse.

The other man squatted down and spat tobacco into the fire, peering at Libbie with lust. "That's a fancy necklace she's wearin.' Worth anything?"

Coyote laughed. "Shows she's owned by that big Apache. We'll try to sell it down in Mexico."

Bif stared at her. "We all gonna get a chance at her?"

"Sure." Johnson nodded. "Share and share alike, remember? Now, you go on to bed. I'm gonna enjoy this sassy little bitch a while, and when it's your turn, I'll wake you up."

The other rubbed his groin. "Okay. Just make sure I'm next. I don't want to wait until the rest of them get through with her."

Johnson guffawed as he threw Libbie across his shoulder. "Don't worry. I'll wake you first."

Libbie's heart was pounding so hard, she was sure Coyote Johnson could feel it through her doeskin dress. The other man yawned and disappeared into his tent. Johnson carried her into another tent and dumped her, still bound, on a pile of blankets next to a small fire.

She looked up at him, asking for mercy with her eyes, but he only appraised her as if she were a toy he'd just purchased. "Yes sir, honey, I'm gonna find out if that big buck knew what he was talkin' about when he told me you was a virgin." He reached out, ripped open the doeskin dress with his dirty hand, and licked his lips as he looked at her exposed breasts. "I can hardly wait to get my mouth on these."

She closed her eyes against the lust in his one good eye and tried to keep her wits about her.

Coyote reached out and pulled the gag from her mouth. "Now, honey, it won't do you any good to scream. All that will do is wake the others. Since I stole you, I want to be first."

Libbie licked her dry lips, trying to think of ways to stall him or outwit him. "I—I won't be of much worth if you take my virginity."

He laughed, reached out, and squeezed her left breast hard. "Would you believe I don't care? To top a gal like you is worth whatever gold you lose in value. Now you behave yourself, since you can't get away nohow." He reached down and untied her hands.

Instead, Libbie suddenly came alive, scratching and biting. If she could get out of this tent and into the darkness, he and his friends might have to spend hours searching for her while she slipped away.

"Why, you ornery little bitch!" He was angry as he tried to corner her, but Libbie's desperation made her strong. If she could just get her hands on a knife or gun, she'd make him wish he'd never stolen her.

However, Johnson must have read her mind, because
he jumped in front of his stash of weapons. "No, you don't,
you little slut!"

The tent opening was off to his left. If she could get
through that ... Libbie tried to run past him, but he
reached out and caught her dress, ripping it almost off as
they fell to the ground. He was half on top of her as she
struggled to get out from under him, but he was a big
man, and he jerked her arms up above her head and
paused, leering down at her bare breasts.

"Honey, I'm gonna give you a pokin' you'll never
forget!"

"I'll die first!" Libbie was fighting him with sheer desperation. She might not be able to escape from his slimy
hands, but she wasn't going to be raped quietly and without
a struggle.

"Gal, stop this! I'm gonna have you, and you might as
well let me before I knock you senseless and take you
anyways!"

In answer, she jerked one hand free, reached up, and
stuck her finger in his one good eye. He cried out, cursed,
and struck her across the face.

She lay there, temporarily stunned, tasting the blood
from her cut lip. "No!" she protested. "No!" She began
to fight again as he struggled to get between her thighs.

A shadow loomed over them suddenly, and Johnson
jerked up. "What the hell—?"

One of the other renegades, Libbie thought in terror, and
then she saw the sudden glint of the firelight on the steel
blade coming down as a big hand clapped over Johnson's
mouth. The renegade made a strange gurgling sound,
jerked, and went limp. Libbie opened her mouth to
scream, but a terse voice ordered, "Blaze, keep quiet!"

"Cougar! Oh, Cougar!" Even as she began to sob, he
dragged the dead renegade off her and tossed him to one

side. She went into Cougar's arms, weeping. "Oh, I knew you'd come. He said you wouldn't, but I knew you'd come!"

He held her against him and kissed her hair again and again. "It's okay, Blaze. Are you all right?"

She managed to nod. "The others," she gulped, "the others—"

There was a sound and a muffled scream from somewhere outside.

"My warriors are taking care of them right now. Did he hurt you?"

"Just a little. I'm all right now that you're here."

He swore under his breath. "If I'd known that, I'd have kept him alive and tortured him."

She shuddered, thinking sometimes he was more Apache than white. She clung to him, still shaking, her doeskin dress torn to pieces as Cougar lifted her and carried her easily across the camp to his horse.

"Blaze, dearest, can you stand up?"

She nodded, but when he tried to stand her on her feet, her legs collapsed under her and she had to grab the paint's saddle to keep from falling. Cougar caught her in his arms, kissing her face, her eyes, her lips. "Take it easy. You're all right, Blaze—you'll always be all right as long as you're with me!"

She began to cry with sheer relief, comforted by his feverish kisses. "Oh, Cougar, I knew you'd come!"

He was still kissing her cheeks and eyes as he dragged her to him and held her tightly, his mouth covering hers in a possessive hunger. His lips teased hers apart, and he thrust his tongue inside. She surrendered, letting him taste and explore her mouth. She made a little whimpering sound and threw back her head as his lips moved down her throat.

"My Blaze, how I've yearned for you to let me touch

you!" He bent his head, his mouth seeking her breast, and she arched her back, offering up her nipples for his eager lips. He held her close, his hands caressing her.

"Yes," she whispered. "Yes!"

"Not here," he murmured against her throat. "Not here." He swung her up on his horse and mounted behind her, his big hands reaching out to protect her, to hold her close against him.

She was safe now, she knew that. She would always be safe from anything and anyone who would harm her as long as she was within the circle of Cougar's powerful arms. She leaned back against him, feeling the hardness of his rigid maleness. She knew she should stop him, but the sensations his skillful fingers evoked as he stroked and caressed her skin were making her tremble all over.

Apache warriors came running out of the shadows of the camp. Turtle came to Cougar. "We have killed the others. Now we will take back the supplies and the guns."

Cougar nodded. "I will meet you back at the camp."

At that, he wheeled his horse and cantered away, holding Libbie close, one hand cupping her breast in a gesture of ownership, the other on her bare thigh where her dress had pushed up. The touch of his fingers on her bare flesh sent a thrill up her body that she had never felt before.

"No man but me is ever going to touch you again!" he murmured under his breath.

Had he forgotten his vow? Surely he would not break it. She reached up to touch her necklace. As long as she wore this, her life and her virtue were safe.

The camp was still dark when they rode in, everyone sleeping except a few sentries. Libbie clung to Cougar as he dismounted and took her from the stallion. He carried her across the camp and into his wickiup, where he sat her down gently on a pile of furs and looked into her face. In the faint firelight, she could see the concern in his blue eyes. "Are you sure you're all right? I couldn't stand it if he'd—"

"No, you got there in time." She had to swallow hard to keep from sobbing, but she was shaking.

He took her in his arms. "Blaze, don't be afraid. I'll always look out for you; you know that."

"I know that, Cougar." She turned her face up to him, tears on her cheeks, and he kissed them off. She didn't pull away as his lips moved to her mouth.

He was kissing her feverishly now, as if he couldn't get enough of the taste of her lips. She threw back her head, and he tangled his fingers in her hair, kissing his way down her neck. She went slowly to the blankets and let him kiss her throat and the hollows above her collarbones. She had never felt this way before and she wanted him to continue. She arched her back and offered him her bare breasts.

Cougar groaned aloud as his mouth went to the hollow between her breasts. "If you only knew how I've dreamed of this, how I've hungered to taste these." And then his warm mouth covered her breast.

For a moment, she could only gasp at the sensation; then she caught his head between her two small hands, guiding him to her nipple. He caught it gently between his teeth, and she forgot that she was saving her virginity, that no white man would want to marry her if a half-breed Apache had been with her. Nothing else mattered but that she wanted him, too.

He pulled her to him, kissing her lips, her eyes, her breasts. "I'm going to love you the way no other man ever could, Blaze, my dearest one," he whispered as he reached out and threw open her torn dress. She lay there looking up at him, wearing nothing but the black and silver necklace that nestled against her breasts. He began to kiss his way down her belly.

Her pulse seemed to be beating in her head like a drum. Libbie closed her eyes and lay back, letting his hot mouth tease its way down her belly. Then he moved to her thighs. Libbie stiffened. Surely he wasn't going to . . . ?

"Relax, my darling," he whispered against her bare thigh. "Relax . . ." And with those words, his mouth found the bud of her womanhood, tasting and teasing there, thrusting into her with his tongue until she was wild with desire.

She gave a little cry and let her thighs fall apart, holding his face against her, pleading—no, demanding—that he satisfy her own hungers.

His skillful mouth obliged until she was crazy with her need, pressing him against her, wanting him to drive her to new heights of excitement. She reached out and touched his throbbing manhood.

"Yes, Blaze, I want to give you that," he promised, moving back up her body to kiss her mouth. "I want to join with you and turn you into a woman! Tell me you want me! Tell me!"

She hesitated. Her emotions were thrilling and new, but now that she had a moment to think, she hesitated. A woman could only give her virginity once. Her heart and soul cried out that this was that special man, worthy of that gift, but her head warned her what an impossible union this was. Only the greatest of loves could transcend the differences between two cultures, two races.

In that split second that she hesitated, he pulled away from her and sat up. "I am a fool to think you cared! Worse yet, I dishonor my vow!"

What on earth had she been thinking? She had been about to give away her most precious asset to this penniless half-breed on a blanket in an Indian camp, and yet . . .

Libbie wasn't sure whether she was relieved or saddened by his reluctance to continue. "You could take me anyway."

"Take you? You stupid little fool!" He reached out and caught the necklace, pulling her to him as he twisted his fingers in it. "What I wanted was to share this ecstasy with you, not use you like a whore!"

With a terrible oath, he stood up and stalked out of the wickiup, leaving her puzzled and trembling, struggling with emotions that she didn't understand herself. She hadn't wanted him to stop until he'd brought her down from the emotional peak she'd just ascended. She felt angry and frustrated as she pulled the furs over her naked body and waited for the coming dawn. Maybe she was a stupid little fool, to almost give herself to her half-breed kidnapper out of sheer . . . gratitude? *Was it nothing more than that?* Libbie didn't want to think about it. Instead, she would concentrate on being rescued.

Yes, that was what she would think about—her future life. Maybe today or tomorrow, the soldiers would meet with the Apaches and ransom her if Phillip could get the money together. Now that she was cool-headed and logical, she realized she'd almost done something very, very foolish. No high-born white girl would waste her virginity on a half-breed scout who had nothing in the world to offer her. Nothing but his love and a way of making her feel that if he would only take her and make her his own in the universal way a man possesses a woman, she could count herself the luckiest woman in the world.

Phillip hadn't been able to sleep all night. He had paced his quarters, throwing things at the mounted bear head's baleful eyes and thinking about what might be happening in the Apache camp. He wondered if Cougar had enjoyed Elizabeth yet. Every time Phillip closed his eyes, he could see them together. Sometimes he even imagined that she made love to the warrior eagerly, welcoming his touch.

Ye gods! No, of course the frosty Miss Elizabeth Winters wouldn't enjoy passion. Like most women of her class, she would only endure it as her duty. Still, the thought that Cougar had probably already taken her virginity drove Phillip nearly crazy with jealous rage. He paused in his pacing and considered. No, Cougar was a reasonable man. He'd know that no white man would pay ransom to get Libbie back if the breed had been using her for his pleasure. And the Apache did want ransom. A young warrior named Turtle had come with Cougar's demands and conditions yesterday.

Phillip had promised to meet the demands and sent the messenger on his way, when what Phillip really yearned to do was hang the man. He had telegraphed Mama, who was trying to connect with Mrs. Everett. The plump guardian had indicated she would send the ransom. Of course, Phillip had no intention of paying it.

He paused and grinned, pulling at his mustache. Somehow, he intended to come out of this with the girl and the money, too—and Cougar's neck in a noose. He hoped he got the privilege of putting the rope around Cougar's thick neck himself.

It was almost dawn. Phillip went to the window and peered out. *How was he going to make all this happen?* Cougar would be too smart to walk into a trap. The Apache held all the cards. He'd make the arrangements to meet someplace where he couldn't be ambushed.

Phillip walked across his room and kicked the bearskin rug. "Taboo, ha! I'll show these stupid Injuns what I think of their ignorant beliefs! I'll take my revenge for my father's murder yet!"

To get to Cougar, he was either going to have to outsmart him or trick him. Either would be hard to do because

Cougar was such a cunning rascal. No, the only way to get to Cougar was through someone the Injun trusted.

Mac McGuire. Phillip paused and smiled to himself. Mac surely knew where the Apaches were; they all trusted the old man. Maybe Phillip could trick Mac into leading him and a troop to the Apache stronghold. He'd have to lie to Mac to do that, but what the hell? Lies didn't count if you were dealing with an Injun lover, even if the old man had been his father's best friend.

At dawn, Phillip saddled up and rode out to the ranch. The barking dogs brought Mac onto the porch as Phillip reined in. The old man was yawning and his hair was mussed as if he hadn't been awake long.

"Hello, Lieutenant. I'm just barely out of bed." He did not smile.

"Well, you might at least ask me in for a cup of coffee." Phillip dismounted.

Mac nodded. "Out of respect for your father, I'll do that." He led the way inside the cabin and back to the kitchen.

Phillip looked around. "Honestly, Mac, I don't know how you stand it out here alone in this solitary place; it would drive me crazy."

Mac indicated a chair at the rough table and checked the fire under the coffee pot in the old stove. "I'm not alone; I've got a lot of critters and my memories. Sometimes friends drop by."

"Speaking of which"—Phillip pulled at his wispy mustache—"I don't suppose you've heard anything from your son?"

"Cougar?" Mac paused in getting two mugs out of the cabinet. "You wouldn't expect me to tell you that if I had."

Phillip scowled and took a deep sniff of the aroma of coffee drifting through the small kitchen. "Now and then, you might remember you're on *our* side."

"I'm on humanity's side," Mac snapped and poured the coffee. "By the way, it wasn't right, the way you treated Shashké."

"That's hardly any of your business." Phillip shrugged and accepted the steaming cup. "She was just an Injun slut; that's all."

Mac looked as if he were having a hard time holding his temper. His jaw worked a long moment before he spoke. "I took her in because she had noplace else to go. She's horrible to look at, and she'll never be accepted back into her tribe."

"She knew what chance she was taking." Phillip sipped the strong brew gratefully and warmed his hands around the mug. Then he paused and looked around uneasily. "Is she here?"

"I checked the spare room as I walked to the door; she's gone, along with her things. Don't know where the poor thing thinks she can go."

"Who cares?" Phillip shrugged. "Maybe her husband will take her back."

"What?"

"I said, who cares?" Phillip raised his voice. "Let her go home to her husband."

Mac's hand tightened around his coffee cup so hard, his gnarled knuckles turned white. "Ye haven't heard then. Old Beaver Skin has died—the Apache say of a broken heart, for hurting her. He loved her, but she had dishonored him."

"Too bad; but that's not my problem." Phillip sipped his coffee, savoring the strong, hot flavor.

"You're at the bottom of this tragedy, and we all know it."

Phillip shrugged. "I was like most soldiers, just looking for amusement to pass the time. Shashké shouldn't have been so greedy and naive."

"Your father would turn over in his grave because of this." Mac glared at him. "Bill was very sympathetic to the Apache."

"And look what it got him!" Phillip snapped. "The savages killed him for it."

The old man looked as if he would say something more, then paused and took a deep breath, as if reconsidering. Then he leaned against the cabinet and pulled out his pipe. "So what is it you want, Phillip?"

Phillip finished his coffee; wondering how to bring up the question he really wanted answered. "You knew Cougar kidnapped Miss Winters?"

"Aye, I've heard; bad business." He filled his pipe and lit it.

Phillip leaned closer. "I thought you might help get her back."

Mac frowned and puffed his pipe, scenting the rough-hewn room with the sweet smell. "It's a bad business, him taking her, but he's wanted the girl from the first moment he saw her."

"You know this is crazy." Phillip frowned. "He can't just pick out a woman, steal her like he'd steal a mare, and keep her."

Mac smiled ever so slightly. "Looks like he's done just that."

"Yes, and got the whole United States Army on him. We'll hunt him down if we have to chase him clear across Mexico."

Mac blew a cloud of fragrant smoke. "Maybe the girl's with him because she wants to be."

"That's impossible!" Phillip sneered. "Miss Winters is an elegant aristocrat from the finest family. She couldn't possibly be happy out there in the wilderness with that— that savage."

"Sometimes love can bridge anything."

Phillip stood up, scowling. "Just because you took up with an Apache doesn't mean other whites could do it."

"No, you're right," Mac said. "It takes a very great love to bridge a chasm like that, but it can be done." He turned and looked out the window toward a distant hill.

What in the world was the old fool looking at? Phillip took a deep breath and decided to try a different tactic. "Mr. McGuire, you were my father's dearest friend. For that reason, I came to you."

Mac turned and looked at him. "Yes?"

"You know that the army will hunt those Apaches ruthlessly until we get Miss Winters returned?"

"You'll have to find them first, and the army will never find them."

"But you know where they are?" Phillip waited, but Mac only stood and smoked. "Look, in the name of my father, I'm asking for your help."

"You're asking me to turn in Cougar—?"

"No, I'm asking you to lead me out to talk to him, to reason with him," Phillip said earnestly. "Maybe you could convince your son to let her go."

"And suppose she's happy with him and doesn't want to leave the Apaches?" Mac looked at him intently.

Phillip sighed. "Well, I guess I'd just have to accept that, but I want to know."

Mac smoked, thinking. "Are you saying just you and me would ride out and meet with the Apaches?"

Phillip nodded. "I give you my word as an officer and a gentleman." He held up his hand as if he were taking a solemn oath. "If she wants to stay with him, that's one thing. But if she's being held against her will, I'm duty bound to try to rescue her."

"Your father was a great one for honor and duty," Mac said.

There was no sound for a long moment. Then abruptly, up in the nearby hills, a coyote began howling.

Mac jerked around at the sudden sound and peered out the window. "Lieutenant, I—I've got to go."

Damned old Injun lover. Probably an Apache out there bringing him a message from his renegade son. "If I give you my word, would you take me out to meet with Cougar and Miss Winters, see what the situation is?"

Mac hesitated. "It would take an awfully brave man to ride out and face up to all those Apaches."

"My father would have done it." Phillip drew himself up proudly. "I am, after all, William Van Harrington's son."

"Aye."

The coyote howled again.

Mac fidgeted, then seemed to come to a decision. "All right, Lieutenant. I'll lead you out to meet with Cougar and find out what the young lady wants to do. You swear it's going to be just you and me, no tricks?"

Phillip held up his hand solemnly again. "My only concern is Miss Winters' welfare."

The coyote howled, louder and more insistent.

Mac went to the back door and peered out. "All right, Lieutenant, I'll send you word where to meet me—tomorrow, maybe, or the next day. Now I've got to go. I—I think maybe my horses have gotten out of the corral."

"That's all right, I can let myself out," Phillip said, standing up. "I'll be awaiting word then."

Mac nodded as if he hardly heard him before heading out the back door and up the hill.

Damned old Injun lover! Mac wasn't fooling Phillip. He was meeting some messenger out there by the corral. Well, Phillip couldn't do anything about that right now. His biggest problem now was setting up a meeting with Cougar face-to-face. Phillip turned and strode back through the house toward the front porch.

Mac met with the young Apache messenger, Turtle, and told him to pass the word to Cougar that Mac would be coming for a meeting and bringing the lieutenant with him.

"Is this wise?" asked the Apache in his own language.

Mac sighed. "That girl doesn't belong with Cougar, no matter how much he wants her. If he doesn't give her up, the lieutenant will never quit until one of them is dead. Tell Cougar I'll be careful. The lieutenant has promised me on his father's honor that this is no trick, and surely even the worst of villains would not sully such a fine man's memory."

Turtle looked dubious.

"Tell Cougar I will bring the lieutenant to the secret place just this side of the border. If he is indeed holding the girl against her will, he needs to consider what ends the army will go to to rescue her."

The young Apache nodded, swung up on his bay pony, and disappeared into the brush.

Mac stood looking after him a long moment, then returned to the house. *Was he doing the right thing?* There was no way to know, but if the girl were being held against her will, it was only right that she be returned to her fiancé, no matter how dislikable Phillip was.

And poor little Bear Tracks; what would become of the disfigured Shashké? Ostracized by other Apaches and too ugly now to be a soldier's whore, she was a walking dead person running out of time and alternatives.

Still deep in thought, Mac walked into the living room, puffing on his pipe. The lieutenant had left the front door open. Out of habit, Mac shuffled over to close it. As he turned away, his straining old eyes focused on the gun cabinet. One of its doors hung open. Now why—?

He limped over to close it. Something was different. For a long moment, it did not register, and then he realized that the major's pistol was missing from the cabinet.

Mac ran out the door onto the porch. "Lieutenant?"

His voice was getting as weak as the rest of his senses, Mac thought, peering into the distance. Phillip was only a moving dot on the horizon, headed back to the fort. Would Phillip have taken that Colt? Surely Bill's boy wouldn't stoop to thievery. *But if not Phillip, who?* Then Mac remembered how annoyed the young officer had been when Mac refused to give him his father's pistol. Mac couldn't tell him the Colt's history or that he'd felt it would bring Phillip bad medicine. Good Lord, he was thinking more and more like an Indian.

Mac closed the gun cabinet and went back to the kitchen for more coffee as he considered his dilemma. He would ask Phillip about the pistol tomorrow when he saw him again. Despite all his misgivings, Mac felt he had no alternative but to take Phillip out to meet with Cougar. It was ironic that the two were such enemies, considering . . . ah, well.

He wasn't at all sure he could trust Phillip, even with the snooty officer swearing on his father's honor. Yet Mac must bring about the meeting to protect the Apaches. Phillip Van Harrington bore them, and particularly Cougar, such hatred that they would never be safe as long as he was alive to pursue them. Mac could only hope that the lieutenant would be transferred back east before he found out things he would not want to know.

And what had happened to Shashké? Poor thing, she would have been welcome to stay, but she had been terribly distraught. He hoped she hadn't killed herself the way Dandy Jim's wife had done.

Well, it would all come to a finale tomorrow or the next day. Mac wasn't looking forward to it; he sensed events were headed for a terrible tragedy!

Chapter Eighteen

Once Cougar stalked from their wickiup after he had rescued her from Coyote Johnson and returned her to the Apache camp, Libbie was so weary that she dropped off into a heavy sleep. In the middle of the night, she awakened, chilled from the desert air. As she lay there, she heard a noise and tensed. However, she couldn't stop shivering. With eyes half closed, she saw Cougar looming over her.

Had he returned to take that which she had so foolishly almost given him only hours ago—her innocence? Even as she wondered and tried to plan a course of action, he leaned to pull a blanket over her and tucked it in. Then he brushed a lock of hair from her forehead and sighed. As she watched, he returned to his place on the other side of the small fire and lay down. Libbie was touched by his tender gesture, only one of many over the last few days. Then she remembered that she must not let her heart soften toward her half-breed kidnapper. Sooner or later, the army would be coming to rescue her and probably kill him. Somehow, that thought didn't bring her the pleasure it once had.

Dawn came. When Libbie awakened, Cougar's blankets were empty. Across the foot of her blankets lay a magnificent beaded doeskin dress and fancy moccasins to replace the torn clothes she wore. It was so beautiful, she realized it must be very fine and expensive. It was also very soft and comfortable. Thrilled, she put the dress on and went outside, thinking she had never realized how beautiful sunrise could be when she lived in a house and hardly ever saw the dawn.

The Apache were up and taking care of simple tasks, getting ready to move the camp to another, safer location nearer the border. The women smiled and nodded to Libbie as she walked among them. Funny, she no longer saw them as red-skinned monsters; they were just people, after all. The Apache lived such simple, peaceful lives . . . as long as the soldiers weren't chasing them. With a start, Libbie realized how relaxed and carefree she felt. It was exhilarating not to have to wear a corset, worry about attending dull social events, or wonder if there was going to be enough money for carriages and fancy teas. Of course, when she returned to civilization, she'd have to deal with all that again. She found the prospect depressed her.

The camp was alive with women preparing food and children running between the wickiups. Libbie found herself smiling when she spotted Cougar's tall, lithe form walking through the camp toward her.

"Ah, Blaze! So you are finally up."

"Where did you get this lovely outfit you left me?" She indicated the fancy dress and moccasins she wore.

He shrugged. "You needed something to put on; it's not important. Look"—he dug in the pouch hanging over his shoulder—"I've shot a rabbit. If you can get some coffee going, we'll have a nice breakfast."

She started to tell him that she was a society girl and had never cooked in her life and wasn't about to for him, but then she looked around and realized that everyone else was sharing the work. "All right. I'll have to get some water."

She took a big copper pot and walked down to the stream to fill it. Returning, she was struggling to carry it when Cougar hurried toward her. "Here, let me. That's too heavy for you."

He took it from her hand and they walked back to the camp, others greeting them cheerily as they passed.

Libbie nodded to them. To Cougar, she said, "I'm surprised they seem to accept me."

Cougar laughed. "They think you have shown great heart."

"Oh?" She didn't want to ask, but her curiosity got the better of her. "What else do they say?"

"They think Blaze would be a good name for a red-haired woman of the Apache."

"I'm not Apache," she reminded him.

"They say you have enough courage to be one. You surprise them; they expect white women to be weak and whining."

She couldn't help but laugh. "Even you said I was spoiled."

He nodded as they approached the wickiup. "Spoiled, yes, but you couldn't help the way you were raised. You're a strong woman, Blaze. The lieutenant is no match for you."

She agreed silently, but she said nothing. Whatever happened, she didn't intend to marry Phillip, even if he took her back to civilization. However, the thought of being her own woman, making her own choices and decisions didn't scare her as it once had.

They came to the wickiup and he set the kettle down. "Blaze, you make the coffee, and I'll skin the rabbit."

She started to remind him again that her name was not Blaze as he walked away, decided he was as stubborn as she was, and shrugged. Old Owl Woman came into the wickiup, smiling and nodding. She gestured, showing Libbie how to put the water on to boil and make the coffee.

Libbie went to the wickiup door, wondering what was keeping Cougar. He stood in the center of the camp circle, the rabbit hanging from his hand, talking to a very pretty Apache girl. The girl was flirting shamelessly with him, and he was nodding and smiling. An unfamiliar emotion rose in Libbie's heart. "Hey," she called, "I have the coffee ready."

Cougar nodded to the girl and came over, handing Libbie the skinned rabbit.

"Who was that?" Libbie demanded.

Cougar shrugged. "Little Fawn. I had once thought of asking for her in marriage. Pretty, isn't she?"

"Some might think so." Libbie bristled. "She's also a shameless flirt!"

"What do you care? You're engaged to the lieutenant, remember?"

Libbie felt her face go hot. "I—I don't care. She's just very bold, if you ask me."

"I didn't ask you," Cougar said. He turned and looked after the girl's shapely form as she walked through the camp. "A man needs sons and a woman. After you're gone, maybe I'll think about her again."

Libbie didn't like the emotions she felt at the way his frank appraisal took in the disappearing Apache girl. Libbie jerked the skinned rabbit from his hand, took it back inside, and the old woman helped her cut it up and cook it. "Little Fawn," she muttered through clenched teeth, "thinks she can have Cougar any time she wants him!"

Owl Woman said in English, "If you don't want him, why should you care?"

Libbie gasped. "You speak English! Why have you never told me?"

The other shrugged. "To what purpose? You would have bothered me with questions I might not want to answer."

"Where did this dress I'm wearing come from?" Libbie indicated the fine doeskin outfit.

"He paid much for it, five horses, but he was determined to give it to you. It is the finest dress in the whole tribe."

Libbie felt flattered. "Why would he do that?"

"You do not look into his heart and see why?" Owl Woman left the wickiup abruptly before Libbie could ask more.

Libbie puzzled over the answer while she finished cooking the rabbit. Later, Libbie served it to Cougar as he sat cross-legged before the fire. He took a bite. "Very good. You do have some talents besides your beauty, it seems."

"I suppose it's edible," Libbie admitted, trying not to blush at his praise. Then she was annoyed with herself that his compliments had pleased her. *What was wrong with her?* This half-breed savage was holding her hostage, and soon she would be leaving here. Yet she was beginning to admire Cougar for his bravery and the decisions he was making in leading this little band. This was a man in every sense of the word—brave, strong, yet gentle when need be. "Thank you for this fine dress," she said. "Owl Woman told me."

He scowled. "She talks too much; it was nothing."

"No one woman among all the Apaches has anything so fine; I know this."

"I would not have any say I do not dress my woman in

a manner which shows my status as a warrior." He made a gesture of dismissal and returned to his food.

His woman? The nerve of him! She must remember that she hated him, she reminded herself as she got herself a tin cup of coffee and a portion of roasted rabbit. It was more delicious than any pheasant or squab in cream sauce that she had ever eaten at fancy parties.

Before the dew was off the stubby grass, the Apache were mounted, moving south. *We must be moving closer to the border,* Libbie thought, but she asked no questions as she unpacked her travois and, with Owl Woman's help, began to build a new wickiup.

About midday, a young Apache she recognized as the one called Turtle came galloping into the camp and dismounted. Libbie watched Cougar stride out to meet the young man. They engaged in very animated conversation, both occasionally turning to look toward the wickiup. They must be talking about her, Libbie decided.

Cougar finally dismissed the messenger and strode over to the wickiup.

Libbie said, "Well?"

"Well, what?" He poured himself some coffee.

"Don't evade the question," Libbie said. "That was about me, wasn't it?"

"White women are very spoiled and think the whole world revolves around them," he said coldly, not looking at her.

"Is Phillip bringing the ransom?"

He frowned. "Do you really intend to marry that prissy officer if I free you?"

"That's hardly your concern, now is it?" She had already decided she wouldn't marry Phillip even if he were rich, but she didn't want to give Cougar the satisfaction of knowing that. Maybe Mrs. Everett had talked crooked old Ebenezer Higginbottom into providing the ransom.

"I don't want to talk about this now," Cougar said finally. "I have some thinking to do."

"If he's not offering enough money—"

"It's not about the money!" he snapped at her and strode away.

What was eating him? This was what he wanted, wasn't it? Trading her for a lot of gold so the Apaches could buy supplies? The black expression on his face as Cougar walked away warned her not to bring the subject up again.

The day passed slowly, with the women cleaning up the camp and settling in. Libbie helped Owl Woman arrange her few belongings in her wickiup, but the old woman stubbornly refused to speak English to her again.

To pass the time, Libbie played with some of the Apache children. She loved children and had always hoped, as a lonely only child, to have a large brood of her own someday. She realized now that her attitude toward the Apache had changed over the last several days. After living with them, she really didn't hate them anymore, and she didn't want the army to hurt them. They were just people, after all, even though they spoke a different language.

She was picking up a few of the words herself from the children. *At this rate,* she thought, *in a few weeks, I could speak to them in their own language.* Of course, she wouldn't be here in a few weeks; she'd be somewhere among the whites, dealing with all the problems and complications that went with that civilization. The thought depressed her.

And when she was gone, Cougar would pick a mate, someone like Little Fawn, and sire children by her. The thought of him in the arms of that dark beauty made Libbie swallow hard. He deserved better than that. *Was she out of her mind?* What he deserved was to be strung up by his thumbs and whipped for kidnapping, that's what he deserved!

Evening came. Cougar sat in the wickiup, staring into the fire. Why was he so preoccupied? *What decision was he struggling with?* Libbie had let the smiling Owl Woman teach her how to grind maize and put together a stew from the leftover rabbit. Cougar nodded appreciatively as she handed him a bowl.

Outside, dust painted the sky with hues of purple and pale pink. Cougar ate and stared at the sinking sun. "Soon we will be moving across the border and into Mexico."

"How soon?"

"A day, or maybe two. There we'll be safe from the soldiers."

A day or two. The thought sent a chill up her back. If he didn't free her before then, she would be many miles away in the mountains, where the soldiers would never find the Apache. Well, of course Cougar had sent a message back to Phillip concerning the ransom; she had seen Turtle ride out. Any time now, she would be free. She was startled to find that she wasn't terribly excited about the prospect of leaving these people.

As darkness fell, the people had built up the campfire and were dancing.

Cougar looked at her a long moment. "Would you like to go out by the fire?"

She wanted to ask him about the messenger, about her future, about what was worrying him, but noting his moody expression, decided now was not the time. "Sure, why not?"

They went out by the firelit circle. The old mother brought them each a gourd.

Libbie sipped it. "What is that?"

"*Tiswin*—Apache beer," Cougar said. "Drink up or you'll insult her."

Libbie drank. It warmed her and she felt more relaxed standing here by the fire, watching the dancers. The drum rhythm seemed to move through her and she swayed to it.

"Here"—Cougar motioned—"dance with me."

"Oh, I couldn't!" Libbie protested.

He shrugged. "I could ask Little Fawn."

Libbie looked over at the Apache girl, who was smiling invitingly at Cougar from across the circle.

"On second thought, I've changed my mind." Libbie let Cougar lead her out into the circle. "I—I don't know the steps."

"Just do what everyone else is doing," Cougar said. "Let the drum tell you."

Libbie closed her eyes and began to move to the hypnotic beat. When she opened them, Cougar was dancing, watching her as they stepped rhythmically around the big fire. She caught her breath at the lithe sensuality of his muscular, half-naked body swaying to the drumbeat. When his blue eyes looked deep into hers, they seemed to be asking a question.

She found herself looking back at him, her heart beating faster, her mind a little foggy from the beer. She shook her hair loose so that it fell around her shoulders as she swayed to the music. *Blaze.* Yes, she was beginning to feel that maybe the name did fit her. His eyes were hot with desire as he looked deep into hers, and then she realized that it wasn't the money Cougar wanted for ransom. He wanted her body; every heated glance he sent her way betrayed that. Could she trade her virginity for her freedom? Did he want her badly enough that he would free her if she went into his arms willingly tonight? She was torn between two emotions and two civilizations.

Libbie danced, swaying close to him so that their bodies brushed against each other. Around them, more *tiswin* was passed around and people laughed and men pulled women into the shadows. Cougar's blue eyes were even more intense as he stared down into hers. Libbie made her decision then. Even if she returned to white civilization, she wanted to spend one night in this man's arms and see if it was as wonderful as his passionate gaze promised. With her eyes, she told him so.

He hesitated, as if wondering if the unspoken message might be a mistake. Libbie smiled at him again.

Hesitantly, he reached out and pulled her to him.

"Yes," she whispered, "yes!"

He gave a low sigh and swung her up into his strong arms. "Are you—are you sure?"

In answer, she put her arms around his neck as she hung there. "I am very, very sure!" she whispered and reached up to kiss him.

He was tense against her as he turned and strode away from the fire, carrying her against his bare chest. "You don't know how long I've waited for this."

She ought to be terrified, or at least dreading it, but she wasn't; she was as tense as he was, her heart pounding with anticipation. "If I leave here, never having experienced this, I know I will regret it the rest of my life!"

He carried her in and laid her very gently on the furs, as if afraid she might break. "Making love to you has meant everything to me from the first moment I saw you stepping off that stagecoach," he confessed.

"And I have wondered what it would be like ever since the night you put your necklace on me and touched me with your hands." Very slowly, Libbie reached up and unhooked the silver chain, laying the Apache Tears necklace to one side.

"Blaze, are you sure?"

In answer, she took off the soft doeskin dress and threw it to one side so that she lay naked in the glow of the firelight.

His look swept over her, hot with desire. "Just let me look at you a moment; I have waited for this a long, long time."

"And I am only just now admitting to myself how much I have wanted you," she sighed.

No man could have wanted her so much, she thought as his fingers traced a path down the valley between her breasts. Even Phillip or Mr. Higginbottom had never looked at her with such intense passion. In answer to Cougar's caress, she arched her back, offering him the feast of her breasts.

With a heated sigh, Cougar bent to nuzzle them, playing with her nipples with his hot mouth, sending unexpected spasms of pleasure through her body as his big hands stroked her thighs. She caught his head between her two hands, directing his face against her breasts, urging him to suckle harder still as his hand crept up her thigh and touched her most sacred place.

Instinctively, Libbie let her thighs fall apart so that he could stroke and tease her with his fingers.

"You're wet," he murmured, "eager for me to take you."

She knew this night could only lead to sorrow, yet her body was responding to his mouth and skillful hands in ways that both thrilled and frightened her.

"I—I didn't know women could want this," she confessed, and then his mouth cut off her words as his lips covered hers, tasting the velvet depths of her mouth, sucking her tongue into his. Her pulse pounded even harder as she responded to his kisses and his stroking. She tried to think rationally, but her pulse was beating in her ears like the loud drums outside the wickiup, and there was no time for clear thinking; there was only the emotion of desire so long denied.

He caught her hand and brought it to clasp his rigid maleness.

He was so big, Libbie thought with awe as she stroked and explored him. She wasn't certain how she could take all that great length, but then he kissed her again, caressing her breasts with his skillful hands, and none of that seemed to matter anymore.

Cougar stood up suddenly and stripped off his skimpy loincloth and moccasins. "Look at me," he whispered.

She studied his magnificent body in the glow of the fire. He was scarred and well muscled, every bit a stallion of a man, and he was rigid and ready to mate with her. Libbie's heart pounded harder at the thought, and she felt her body thrill with anticipation as old as time itself. She lay there, slowly holding out her arms to him.

He lay down on the furs, pulling her so that she was lying half on top of him. "Now, my beautiful one, you make love to me," he whispered.

She nodded, breathing hard. Her heart seemed to be pounding louder than the drums outside. "I—I don't know how."

"Listen to your heart, Blaze, my love, and follow it."

Tentatively, she closed her eyes and slowly lowered her face to brush her lips across his. Her heart was pounding so hard, she no longer heard the drums outside. There was nothing else in the universe but this man and this moment. She kissed him; awkwardly at first; then he opened his lips and she forgot everything except that his lips were so warm and hungry for her own. Very slowly, she probed his lips with her tongue as she pressed her naked breasts against his hard chest and his hands came up to caress her hair as it fell around her face.

At that moment, he opened his mouth to accept her

tongue and she became the aggressor, plunging her tongue inside, tasting and caressing his mouth. His hand caught the back of her neck, pulling her mouth down on his, still deeper, as his other hand played up and down her bare back. His hand was big and rough; possessive yet protective. And she felt goosebumps on her naked skin as his fingers seemed to touch every nerve, as his hand moved up and down her back, then settled on her bottom.

She moaned aloud against his mouth and moved restlessly, but he only lay there, letting her lead the way, although she could feel his manhood, hard and insistent against her body. "I—I don't know what to do," she whispered.

"Yes, you do, my Blaze," he said against her mouth, "yes, you do."

Libbie gasped and half moved on top of him, supporting her weight with her elbows so that her breasts were above his face. He reached out and caught her breast with one hand, moving her so that she was more convenient for his mouth to reach and suck her nipples, playing with her breasts.

Libbie threw back her head, breathing hard. *Blaze*. Yes, she felt as if she were on fire when this man touched and caressed her. She felt his turgid manhood against her body and she wanted him, wanted him with an urgent need that surprised her. *This is crazy*, she thought, *tomorrow or the next day, you'll be leaving this man forever, yet you're giving yourself to him freely*. Then she knew that there was no man in this universe that she wanted to share this with more, and her own need could not be denied.

Then he raked his teeth gently across her swollen nipple, and she forgot everything but cooling this fever that seemed to be about to burst into an uncontrolled fire.

"Make love to me, Blaze," he commanded. "Make love to me."

This wasn't the way she had pictured this seduction at all. She had imagined he would throw her down across the blankets and take her hard and fast. When he satisfied himself, it would be over in only a few seconds. Yet this gentle teasing and touching seemed to go on and on and was driving her wild with a desire she hadn't realized she was capable of. Parting her thighs, she sat atop his thighs and surveyed his manhood. "I—I can't. You're too big for me."

"No, your body wants me; it will be all right. Make love to me, Blaze, mount me and ride me."

And, abruptly, she wanted that more than she wanted anything else in the world—the feeling of being one with this magnificent stallion of a man. Hesitantly, she came up on her knees over him, then came down very slowly on the hard dagger of his manhood. She didn't take it all, but paused while he breathed hard and seemed to be fighting to control himself. "Take it, Blaze, take every inch of it!"

She could feel him throbbing hot and hard inside her as she tried to come down on him, but the thin silk of her virginity held her back. "I—I can't. You'll have to help me. . . ."

His big hands reached out and caught her small waist, almost encircling it with his strong fingers. He was trembling, his sinewy muscles shiny with perspiration. "This may hurt."

She threw back her head, her fiery hair going everywhere, her eyes half closed, wanting the completion, hungering for the sensation of him totally buried in her depths. "It doesn't matter. Do it. Do it!"

In answer, he arched his muscular hips while holding onto her trim waist and ground her down on his body hard. Libbie felt his turgid maleness tear through the silk of her virginity and then he plunged deep inside her. She bit her lip to keep from crying out as he ground her down on him, impaling her on his throbbing manhood.

He reached up and caught both her breasts in his two big hands, running his thumbs across her nipples as she began to grow accustomed to the sensation of having him inside her. Slowly she began to move in a timeless, erotic rhythm. She had never imagined that mating could create this kind of pulse-pounding need.

"I love you," he whispered. "I've loved you since the first moment I saw you!"

And she loved him, she realized; it was crazy, it could never be, but she loved this man as she could never hope to love another. She could not think; she could only feel, reveling in the sensation of his body inside hers as he throbbed and stroked her breasts into a mounting excitement that she could not control. She leaned over and kissed him, touching his tongue with her own as she rode him hard. She had not expected it to be like this, and now nothing else mattered but this man and this moment.

"Blaze, I don't know how much longer I can hold back," he gasped against her mouth. "I'm waiting for you. . . ."

She didn't know what he was talking about, but she didn't stop riding him harder and faster, driven by her own wild need. It felt as if she had climbed to the top of a summit and was about to fall over the edge of the precipice. "Cougar, I—I don't know how—"

"Relax and let it happen," he whispered fiercely as he reached for her. "Trust me, Blaze, trust me to love you."

And at that moment, she stopped fighting her desires and let them sweep her along as she moved on his body. She felt his hand catch her waist again, grinding her down on him so that she could feel every inch of him throbbing deep within her and she was swept up in an unfamiliar emotion that she had never known before. She gasped aloud.

"That's it!" he murmured. "Come with me. Come with me, Blaze, my dear one."

At that moment, his virile body began to convulse under her. It seemed she could almost feel the heat of his seed surging deep within her. Then she thought no more because her own body began to tremble and she wanted nothing more than to fall into the rhythm of giving and taking as they meshed and strained together.

For a long moment, she seemed to be floating in the most delicious blackness. When she opened her eyes, her head was on his wide chest as she still lay on him and he was tenderly stroking her hair. "Did I—did I do it right?"

He laughed gently and kissed her forehead. "It was more wonderful even than in my dreams over these past few months."

He sounded relaxed and sleepy. Funny, she felt the same way. She lifted her body from his, noting the smear of her virginity on her thighs, and settled down into his embrace, her head on his shoulder. He reached to pull a blanket up over them both. She felt safe here in the circle of his strong arms.

I have just sacrificed my virginity, she thought, but she didn't regret it. Cougar reached to cover her breast with one big hand, and his touch made her gasp with new need. She turned her face and kissed him.

The kiss lengthened and deepened until he took a deep breath and rose on one elbow, looking down at her. "You want me again as much as I want you." It wasn't a question; it was a simple fact.

And now, looking up into his honest blue eyes, she had to be truthful even with herself. "Yes, I want you," she admitted. "I didn't know it could be like this."

In answer, he rolled over on top of her, tangling his fingers in her fiery hair as he pushed between her thighs. "I'm going to love you all night; I've waited so very long for this." He bent his head to her breasts and her own urgent desire surprised her.

"I will never get enough of you, never! Not if I loved you a dozen times a night, my darling," he whispered as he stroked her face. "You are mine in a way you can never belong to anyone else because you gave me your virginity."

A dozen times a night. With his hot mouth on her breast and his virile manhood hot and hard deep inside her, she thought a dozen times might not be enough for her newly discovered desire. She forgot about white civilization and the consequences of what she'd just done; at this moment, she forgot everything except tilting up her body so she could take him even deeper. She dug her nails into his hard hips, locking her long slim legs around him, holding him to her so that he couldn't escape until her hungry body was satisfied. She panted aloud and clawed his muscular back, pulling him down into her, meeting him thrust for thrust until they both reached that pinnacle of pleasure and plunged over the edge.

They lay there breathing hard only a few minutes before Cougar began to ride her again, teasing her nipples into two swollen points of desire with his demanding mouth, and she climaxed under him even harder, clawing at his back while he smothered her face with kisses.

It was nearly dawn when they finished their night of frenzied mating. Then they dropped off to sleep, wrapped in each other's arms. Libbie had never slept so soundly or so dreamlessly. *Tomorrow could take care of itself,* she thought. This love might be forbidden, but she had never known such passion and pleasure as she had found in this man's arms!

Chapter Nineteen

Libbie awakened, smiling at her memories of last night's lovemaking. In the early dawn light, she found herself snuggled down in Cougar's protective embrace. Then reality struck. *What in God's name had she done?*

Libbie sat up, thunderstruck. She had surrendered her virginity like some wanton woman. No, not surrendered—*given* him her innocence and enjoyed doing so. Even now, her face burned at the pleasure he had given her.

"It wasn't my fault," she whispered, "I didn't know it could be like that."

Her whisper apparently awakened Cougar, and he smiled and pulled her down to him. "I didn't know it could be like that, either."

He kissed her and snuggled her against him for warmth, stroking her hair. "I love you, Blaze."

Love? No, this hadn't been love. It had been—what had it been? She had never unleashed her emotions like that before. Last night, she had felt wild and alive and free.

Now in the cold light of dawn's reality, she had second thoughts and misgivings. She was a captive in a savage's camp and today or tomorrow at the latest, she would be returning to her own people.

And yet, when he began to stroke her body with one big hand, she shivered at his touch and the anticipation of what might come. The touch of his fingers ever so gently on her skin wiped out all her guilty feelings.

In turn, her fingers reached up and traced his high cheekbone. "You're very, very good at that," she admitted softly. "I had no idea it could be so—"

"And will be again." He cut off her words with his kiss and began to make love to her all over again.

Libbie tried to remember that this was crazy, that such a love could never surmount all the obstacles that lay between their two peoples, but the way his hands were cupping her breasts, the way his lips were tracing a path down her belly, made her lose her reason. She forgot everything except how pleasurable it was to lie in this man's arms and let him touch and tease and thrill her into whimpering submission so that she wanted nothing so much as she wanted him between her thighs, putting his hard maleness within her, making her gasp and pull him to her, urging him deeper still.

"I love you, Blaze," he said again as he began to make love to her.

Love? No, this could not be love. Yet at this moment, there was no place in the world she would rather be than in this man's arms as his lips moved gently down her throat, and no one she would rather be with.

He had taught her something last night—taught her to want him, to burn for him with an overwhelming need that seemed to sweep through her very core like a forest fire. She must not let him do this to her again; it made her feel defenseless. Libbie tried to think, but all that mattered was the way his hot mouth caressed her breast, making her arch up and hold his face against her.

She must not let him stroke down her thighs with his skilled fingers, touching her deeply where no man save he had ever touched. And when his mouth went to kiss her there, she forgot what she must not want because she was swept up in an overwhelming need to be one with this man.

Then he meshed with her, and all she could think of was the sensation of him taking her, the emotion of taking and giving of her deepest self as she surrendered to that need. "Cougar. Cougar!"

"Yes, my love, yes, my Blaze, go with me," he urged. "Trust me enough to go with me."

He was holding back, waiting for her. She could feel his great effort as he thrust deeper still. She clawed his back, pulling him even closer as they went into a frenzied rhythm of love, bare flesh slamming hard against bare flesh as she rose up to meet each thrust, wanting him, urging him to go deeper still.

At the precise moment when she had reached a pinnacle of need, he wrapped his arms around her and they were only one person as he carried her far away into a place where there was no time and nothing save being together in a half-conscious world of mutual need and desire.

Afterwards, he lay holding her, kissing her face. "And to think I ever considered letting you go."

Libbie stiffened. "I thought that was the bargain; I would let you pleasure yourself with me, and you would let me go free."

He sat up suddenly, his dark, handsome face turned ugly with anger. "You bargain with your body like a whore? I thought you wanted me, too."

She had needed him so badly, she had lost all sense of shame or reason. Her face burned with the knowledge, but she would not admit to that. "You—you had been wanting my body. I thought if I submitted, you would lose your obsession with me and—"

"Submitted?" His blue eyes were so full of fury, she was afraid. "If I had known that—"

"Would you have turned the offer down?" she challenged. "I think not!"

With an oath, he stood up. "You plot to take advantage of my love for you."

She didn't want to think about love, or about last night, about how it had felt to lie in his arms. She felt angry with herself that it had meant so much to her that she had thrown reason to the wind. "Why are you so angry? I thought it a fair trade."

His features turned as dark as thunder. "Your little trick of playing the whore has done you no good, Blaze. I don't intend to let you go!"

With that, he dressed and stalked out.

He had enjoyed her body, so why did he care whether it had meant anything to her or not? And yet she was ashamed as she remembered the deep hurt in his eyes. He was not only hurt, he was furious, and he did not intend to let her go. She rolled that thought over in her mind and was not as devastated as she expected. After all, what did she have waiting for her in white civilization? Only everything she had ever known. And yet, those moments in Cougar's strong arms had made her forget her own heritage, forget everything and yearn to go with him, wherever that journey might lead.

Was she out of her mind? The canyon between their two civilizations was too wide to bridge; their union could never work. However, soon the Apache would be pulling out, headed deep into Mexico, and once there, her chance of returning to the whites was gone forever.

Apache Tears. Libbie picked up the necklace, touching each stone, remembering the legend of the warriors and the women who loved them. He had given her the necklace as a symbol of his love and protection. Very slowly, she fastened it around her throat. It was like feeling his fingers touching her neck, gentle and strong.

What he had given was more than mere sex, and he wanted the same from her. Well, he wanted too much, she thought with a determined shake of her head. She wasn't Blaze of the Apache, she was Elizabeth Winters, a refined debutante lately of Boston, and after Cougar cooled off and thought it over, she would be turning her back on this wild and dangerous life to return to the more sedate and safe life she had always had. *Safe? Dull was more like it.*

Her emotions in confusion, Libbie went to the door of the wickiup and looked out. Cougar was sitting by the fire with several other men, making arrows. When she looked at him, she wasn't sure about the emotion that coursed through her. This was the man to whom she had given her virginity, and she was surprised to find herself smiling when she thought of last night. She didn't regret it at all, which shocked her into scolding herself silently: *Libbie Winters, you shameless hussy!*

Of course Cougar would change his mind, once he thought it over, and free her. After all, the Apaches did need the food and supplies the ransom would bring. If Phillip were going to meet with Cougar, he had come up with the money somehow. As she watched, Cougar gathered up his weapons and swung up on his big paint stallion, obviously going off to hunt. She had no doubt he would bring in enough meat for his lodge and many of the others.

She went outside and began to grind maize to make bread, smiling and nodding to the women who passed.

When Little Fawn walked past on her way to the creek, Libbie gave her a satisfied, contented smile that told the girl how pleased she had been with Cougar's lovemaking last night. The girl looked resigned to defeat and shrugged as she passed.

Several hours later, Libbie and Owl Woman baked some flat bread in the primitive stone oven. It tasted better than the most delicious white rolls Libbie had ever eaten at fine dinners.

"Owl Woman, why won't you talk to me?" she demanded.

The other shrugged and gave her a stony stare. "You break his heart," she answered, "and even now, he struggles with his choices."

No more than she, Libbie thought in surprise, but did not answer.

She was playing with one of the toddlers when Cougar rode back in. Sure enough, he had a fat deer slung across the back of his horse. He rode up to her and dismounted. "There will be plenty to go around," he said. "I'll skin it and cut it up. The woman and children of Cougar need never go hungry."

But she was not going to be that woman. She found herself feeling empty at that thought. Little Fawn hurried up, smiling and making much of the deer he had brought in. Libbie found herself bristling at the girl. *Yet why should she care?*

She deliberately looked away. When Libbie glanced up, Cougar watched her and frowned. Then he strung the deer carcass up in a tree and began to skin it. After a while, he brought her some of the meat. "Cook it!" he ordered.

She had a million things to say to him, and yet nothing seemed adequate, so she kept silent. After she cooked the venison, she handed him a gourd full of the corn tortillas and roasted meat and their hands brushed and he looked away. She felt troubled by the way he looked at her, and by the touch of his hand, remembering last night and this morning. She knew deep in her heart that no other man would ever be able to arouse such a frenzy of passion in her very soul.

Finally, he said to her, "The arrangements have been made; the exchange will take place about sundown tonight."

"How—?"

"Hush!" he thundered. "Isn't it enough that you are returning to your lieutenant?"

"Oh, yes, the gold." She felt a slight disappointment that his desire for the ransom was winning out after all.

He swore under his breath. "You look but you do not see!" he thundered. "It is not the money I want; it was you, from the first moment I saw you stepping off that stage. I remember every small detail. You wore a green dress and carried a parasol, but the sunlight reflected off that fiery hair and from that moment on, I wanted no other woman but you!"

"But after last night, wasn't that enough?"

Cougar shook his head, reached out, and touched the necklace at her throat. "No, last night only made me want you by my side forever."

"But this could never work out," she protested and reached up to unclasp the necklace, but he caught her hand.

"No," he said, "don't take it off. I want you to have it as my mother gave it to my father—as a symbol of my undying love."

Why was her throat choking up? She should be thrilled and relieved that she was going to be ransomed at last. She could only nod at him. "I—I'll never forget you, Cougar."

He swallowed hard, turned, and strode away.

She watched him a long moment, remembering last

night, then turned and went back in the wickiup. It was about midday. At dusk, unless Cougar changed his mind, she would be rescued and returned to white civilization. From the tortured expression on his dark face, she wondered if he might not change his mind again and hurry the little band across the border to safety. She knew that should worry her, but it didn't.

Phillip looked at the sun, high in the midday sky. By sunset, he hoped to see Cougar dead and Elizabeth Winters riding beside him, on her way back to the fort. The more he thought of her, the more desirable she became. He had been sent the money for the ransom, but he didn't intend that the damned savages should get one penny of it. And Elizabeth would marry him, all right, if he had to rape her to get her. Once dishonored, she wouldn't have much choice in the matter, and Phillip would not only have her ripe body for his pleasure, but her wealth as well. All he had to do was rescue her from that damned half-breed.

Now he remembered how he had plotted with the other officers about how this campaign would be conducted. He glanced sideways at old Mac McGuire as they rode, remembering. The others had not been in favor of tricking the trusting old man, but Phillip had insisted.

"He's getting old," Phillip had said, dismissing their doubts, "and his hearing and eyesight aren't all that good anymore. If we're careful, he'll never know until it's too late."

Sergeant Tribby had rubbed his hands together nervously. "Sir, beggin' your pardon, but this plan of yours is putting people in danger. Why don't you just go out there under a flag of truce, give them the money, and get Miss Winters released?"

"You expect to deal with a bunch of savages with honor?" Phillip had scoffed. "No, I've okayed it with the colonel; he told me to do whatever I deemed necessary, so I'll handle this my way," Phillip said coldly.

"Beggin' your pardon, sir," the sergeant had said again, "don't you suppose by now she's already been ... well, you know, outraged?"

Outraged. Phillip ground his teeth together now at the thought as he and old McGuire rode along across the rough desert. In his mind, he saw that big, virile half-breed lying between Libbie's shapely thighs, his hot mouth on her fine breasts. His groin went hard just thinking about it. Even with her lying there, frigid and ladylike, she'd be enjoyable. He could hardly wait to outrage her himself. But he only shook his head. *That damned Injun wouldn't dare touch her! If nothing else, he'd be afraid he wouldn't get paid the ransom.*

Old Mac peered at him. "Carryin' on a dialogue with yourself now, are ye, Lieutenant?"

He felt like a fool. "Just thinking. I've got ten thousand dollars in gold in my saddlebags that was just brought by train from a Mr. Higginbottom—Miss Winters's lawyer, no doubt. You don't think Cougar would try to double-cross us and steal the money—?"

"Cougar is a man of honor," Mac said coldly, "and he knows the Apaches need that money to buy food and supplies. They're starving, since that crooked Indian agent steals most of their supplies."

Phillip made a gesture of dismissal. He didn't want to hear all that. Right now, as the pair rode, he amused himself with thoughts of the trap he was setting up to kill as many Apaches as possible. His father was finally going to be avenged after all. Better than that, with any luck, Phillip could keep the ransom money and have Elizabeth Winters, too. So what if he'd given trusting old Mac

McGuire his word of honor? Honor didn't count when dealing with savages. Tonight he hoped to be the one to put a bullet in Cougar's brain. He reached out and patted the rifle hanging from his saddle. No, not in the brain— in the gut, so the half-breed would die a slow, agonizing death. Phillip grinned at the thought.

It had been a long, troubled day for Cougar. Every time he looked up, the white girl was looking at him. He both loved and hated her at the same moment. Damn her for letting him make love to her! Now she was a fever raging in his blood that he never wanted to recover from. Yet she did not share his affection; she had cold-bloodedly bartered her innocence for her freedom and was now looking forward to being free of him. Well, it couldn't come soon enough for him.

Young Turtle had brought him word late last night about how the exchange would work. The trusted old white man would be bringing Phillip with the gold. Yet Cougar did not want to let her go; he loved her too much. It would be a simple choice if she loved him, too, but she had made it very clear that all she wanted was to be returned to the whites. *Why was he even puzzling over this?* She was his captive; he needn't meet with Phillip at all. Cougar could just throw her across his horse and take her up into the mountains of Mexico, where he could sleep with her in his arms every night and never, never let her return to her old life. She would produce fine, strong sons for him, and after a while, maybe she would stop yearning to return across the border.

When he glanced at Blaze as he went about his chores, she was looking at him. He couldn't read her expression. No doubt she was regretting giving herself to him. Truly, making love to the fire-haired girl had brought him more ecstasy than he had ever thought possible, and now he was

going to lose her forever to a man who was his own . . .
no, he must not think about that; it was too ironic.

Libbie watched Cougar, wondering what he was thinking. Her own thoughts were troubled and confusing. After
last night in his arms, she was no longer certain what she
wanted to do. But of course there was only one choice for
her.

She reached up and touched the Apache Tears necklace
she wore, remembering last night, remembering Cougar.
It reminded her of him, all right, his strength and his
honor and the way he had held her close and made love
to her. She did not ever want to lose that memory. She
knew then that she was no longer a spoiled, whining girl;
she was a woman. And like an Apache woman, she could
be strong and independent, make her own choices, chart
her own path. Being with these people, and most of all,
last night in Cougar's arms had changed her in many ways.
She was not afraid of what the future might bring; she
could handle whatever Fate threw at her.

She had had one night of ecstasy, and she never expected
to find such passion and fulfillment in another man's arms.
Yet tonight she would be leaving this man and returning
to her own civilization. It was the sensible thing to do; the
only thing to do. *Then why did she feel so empty inside?*

As the sun crept closer to the western horizon and the
Apaches began to pack up their camp to cross the border,
Libbie made ready for the exchange and would not allow
herself to think of anything else. By tomorrow, she would
once again be the very civilized Miss Elizabeth Winters!

Chapter Twenty

It would soon be dusk. Young Turtle had ridden in at a gallop and was now jabbering excitedly to Cougar. Libbie watched them, feeling almost detached as she fixed food, while around her the small band was gathering up the last of their things and making ready to leave this place.

Cougar came over to her. "Phillip and old Mac have been seen several miles away. This will all be over for you soon." He started to say something else, hesitated, but looked troubled.

What was bothering him? He would get a lot of gold for her and now the starving Apaches would have supplies, probably bought with Mr. Higginbottom's dishonest loot.

"I have food ready," she said softly and held out a gourd.

"Did you not hear me?" He was testy, knocking the gourd from her hand. "In an hour or so, you can ride away with Phillip and never see me again!"

"I heard." She nodded.

"I expected you to dance with joy at that news."

Damn, she had expected that also! "Cougar"—she put her small hand on his arm—"I want you to know that even if I do go back with Phillip, I'm not going to marry him. You've taught me I can be a self-sufficent, independent woman."

He shook her hand off. "So what will you do?"

She shrugged. "I don't know for sure; maybe get a job out West someplace."

He looked at her for a long moment, his gaze softening. "The white civilization is a scary place for a lone woman."

"I know that; but I've grown up quite a bit lately. I can make my own decisions."

"I've half a mind to throw you across my horse and take you across the border with me."

"You wouldn't want me under those circumstances," she said calmly.

He chuckled, a forced laugh because his eyes were grim. "You know me too well. Besides, it would be asking too much of a white girl, asking her to turn her back on everything she knows when I have nothing to offer but danger, hardship, and sometimes hunger."

And love, she thought, but she said nothing, watching the people gathering their few possessions, loading them on horses and making ready to ride out the minute the exchange was finished. They depended on their leader to keep them safe and see that they were led into good hunting areas. Cougar's responsibilities were great. *He can handle it,* she thought to herself and was surprised at how confident she was in his abilities.

When she looked at him, he was watching her, a slight smile on his sensual lips.

"What is it?" she asked.

Cougar shrugged. "I just like to watch the sunlight reflect on your hair. It is the first thing I ever noticed about you; that day I decided I must have you for my own."

His own. The gentle tone sent a shiver up her back. She had reveled in the ecstasy of him possessing her body and soul last night.

"What are you thinking, Blaze?"

Blaze. She liked the image now, it brought to mind her time with the Apache band—wild, free, and defiant. "I am not an Apache woman," she reminded him. "I am Miss Elizabeth Winters, a very ordinary and compliant white girl."

He shook his head. "Nothing about you is ordinary. That's why I desired you as I never wanted another."

She must not let him talk like this; this all must end in an hour, and then she would put these moments with him behind her forever. Except for the necklace.

He stood up, staring at the sun moving closer to the Western horizon. "I will make ready. By sunset, my people will be safely across the border; it's only a couple of miles and then we're headed up into the Sierra Madre."

Before she could say anything else, he strode away.

She watched his broad shoulders as he walked toward his horse and tried to get excited about being freed. Just before sunset, she would no longer be a prisoner. She would be headed back to civilization to join her own people.

Very slowly, she finished packing up the few things from Cougar's wickiup. Penniless, she thought; he owned nothing more than some weapons and a few horses, and he had traded five of them for a pretty dress for her.

Libbie nodded to old Owl Woman as she gathered up the last of the stuff and placed it on Owl Woman's travois.

"He will never forget you," the old woman said in English, frowning at her.

"Nor I him," Libbie whispered, "but he'll find another woman."

The other shook her gray-streaked head. "Cougar is like

his father. He gave his heart completely, and he could not live without her."

"What are you talking about?" Libbie asked, "Mac—"

"Not Mac McGuire." Owl Woman shook her gray head.

"What?"

Ignoring Libbie's questions, the Apache woman walked away to finish her packing.

Mac McGuire reined in his horse and peered at the sun now low on the horizon. It had been a long day, and he was weary and eager for this to be over. He glanced over at the young officer who rode with him. "Lieutenant, I reckon we ought to meet up with the Apache in less than an hour."

Phillip grinned. "Good. I had begun to despair of ever getting Miss Winters returned."

Mac sighed. "Aye. I reckon Cougar's good sense has prevailed, from what Turtle said. The Apaches really need the supplies that gold can buy. You bring it?"

The lieutenant reached back and patted his saddlebags. "Right here. I'll hand it over at the same time Miss Winters is freed."

Mac stood up in his stirrups and looked around. "You hear anything?"

Phillip shook his head. "No. You're imagining things, old man."

"Aye, that's probably true; my hearing and sight aren't what they used to be." Yes, he must be imagining things; there were only the two of them riding through these rugged canyons toward the secret camping place near the border. Phillip had agreed to that condition. Certainly Bill Van Harrington's son might be dislikable and snooty, but he was a gentleman and wouldn't go back on his word.

Mac nudged his horse into a walk again, and he and the

young officer rode across the rough terrain. "I've got to hand it to ye, Phillip, you're braver than I thought ye were, coming alone out here with me, just the two of us to meet all those Apaches."

Phillip nodded. "I'm my father's son after all."

Which reminded Mac. He couldn't think of a polite way to ask. "Lieutenant, when you came out to my ranch—"

"Yes?"

"It wasn't good manners to help yourself to my belongings."

Phillip looked blank. "What?"

Was he going to lie about the pistol? Well, maybe Phillip thought he had a right to take it from the gun cabinet, since it had belonged to his father. "You know what I mean."

The lieutenant shrugged. "I don't think I do."

Mac stuck his pipe between his teeth, considering. This was not the time to get into a fuss with the lieutenant; not when they were on their way to ransom Miss Winters. *Should Mac tell him the terrible secret behind that Colt?* No, of course not. Mac had helped Bill's commanding officer hide that truth for more than a quarter of a century; it would serve no purpose to tell the son now. In fact, if the young officer returned to Philadelphia soon with his rescued fiancée, there was no need for him to ever learn how his father had died. "So Phillip, as soon as you retrieve Miss Winters, you'll be returning East?"

Phillip ceased puzzling over the old man's queries and nodded. "My mother has pulled some strings in Washington; we'll be returning almost immediately." Funny old codger looked positively relieved. *Ye gods, what did the old man think Phillip had taken from his house?* Mac was not only getting a little blind and deaf, his mind must be going.

"Good. This is no place for ye." The old rancher looked relieved.

Doesn't want me killing his half-breed son, Phillip thought with annoyance, wondering when he would get a chance to double-cross and kill Cougar, as well as any other Apaches. He owed it to his murdered father.

As far as the gold . . . Phillip glanced back over his shoulder at the saddlebags. He had no intention of letting the Apaches get away with that money, although he might tell Mr. Higginbottom they had. If he could manage it, Phillip planned to end up with Elizabeth Winters, her inheritance, and all this ransom, too. He smiled at his own cleverness and kept riding, thinking how easy it had been to fool old Mac merely by giving his word of honor. Lying to the crazy old Injun lover didn't count.

Phillip glanced at the sun. In less than an hour, it would be sundown, and he and Mac would be meeting with the Apaches in a secret canyon that could never be found without the old man's help. Mac was too naive to realize Phillip planned to turn this canyon into a trap. Phillip smiled, thinking that, with any luck, not a single Apache would escape. Thank God the old man's sight and hearing were bad, so he couldn't know soldiers were riding just out of sight behind them. Certainly Phillip wasn't crazy or brave enough to ride into a meeting with Cougar all alone. He hummed to himself as he rode. A canyon was a great place for an ambush. After Libbie was safely out of the Apache's hands, he'd instructed the soldiers to turn their guns on the little band from their superior positions along the canyon rim. Phillip didn't intend that Cougar should escape alive!

The Apache camp was packed up and ready to move out. Libbie went into the wickiup one last time and stood there, loath to let go of last night's memories.

Before she could go outside, Cougar came into the wickiup. "Are you ready to go? Mac and Phillip have been sighted."

She turned to him. There was so much to say, yet nothing to say. "Once you hand me over and get the gold, you'll cross the border?"

He nodded. "In a couple of hours, the Apache will be safe in the Sierra Madre, where bluecoats cannot find us."

"I—I see." She had expected to be thrilled at the thought of returning to white civilization. Instead, she remembered the love she had shared in this man's arms. "Cougar, thank you."

He swallowed hard and shrugged. "I want you to be happy, Blaze. No, I guess you were never Blaze; you are Miss Elizabeth Winters after all."

She reached out and put her hand on his arm. "I will never forget you."

"Don't do that!" He scowled and shook her hand off. "It's going to be hard enough to give you up."

"That's it, then? After all we've been through together, we're just supposed to shake hands and walk away?"

With a strangled sound, he enveloped her in his strong arms, kissing her in a way she could only have imagined, as if he were putting a lifetime of love in that kiss. She was lost in his powerful embrace, the passionate domination of his lips. She didn't intend to, but she was so shaken by his ardor, by the strength of his big body, that she clung to him, returning his kiss with all the feelings that were in her. When she finally pulled away, she was not sure she could speak. It was relief, she told herself, relief at finally being rescued, returning to civilization. "I'll never forget you," she said again.

He blinked rapidly, his voice unusually gruff. "Forget me, Miss Winters, forget you were ever stolen and loved by a savage! Return to your safe, ordinary existence, marry

Phillip or someone just like him, and spend your life as you were supposed to do."

Her safe, ordinary life seemed to stretch ahead of her like a prison sentence. She had gotten used to the free, roaming life of the Apache, but most of all, she had been introduced to love by this man, and she knew she would never find ecstasy like that again.

Outside, a warrior shouted something.

Cougar took a deep breath. "It's time to go now; they're waiting out in the canyon."

"Yes, of course." Libbie swallowed hard. She would do the safe, sensible thing. To do otherwise was unthinkable. She followed him out of the wickiup. Outside, the Apache were mounted up, some horses hooked to travoises. Libbie nodded and smiled at the Owl Woman who looked sad, but nodded in return.

She followed Cougar to the paint stallion. Her throat had grown so thick, it seemed to be choking off her breath. She looked up at Cougar a long moment, thinking how handsome and magnificent he was, wearing only a breechcloth on his muscled body. A thought occurred to her and she reached up and touched the necklace of Apache Tears she wore. "Oh, I can't keep this; it's your most precious possession."

"*You* were my most precious possession." He made a gesture to stop her. "Keep it and wear it until you are out of Apache country; it will protect you. After that, you can throw it away or keep it as a souvenir. Maybe your friends back East will be amused by it."

The bitterness in his eyes told her there was no point in telling him she would treasure the necklace forever. It would be a souvenir, all right, the only remembrance she had of the greatest moments of ecstasy she would ever experience. She fought to keep her eyes from tearing up. "I guess I'm ready."

His strong, square jaw worked a long moment. "All right; let's not drag this out. Will you ride with me one last time?"

She nodded. "One last time."

He swung up on the big stallion and held out his hand to her. Libbie hesitated only a moment before she took it. His hand was as big and strong as she remembered as he lifted her up behind him. She had meant to sit stiff and remote, but she couldn't stop herself from putting her arms around his lean waist, laying her face against his muscular brown back. She was weeping, but she wasn't sure why. Today should be the happiest day of her life; she was being rescued. Rescued from a people she had grown to love, a savage she had come to trust and depend on.

"Miss Winters, are you sure you're all right?"

"Y—yes, of course." She realized then that she was trembling against him.

She felt him sigh, and then he signaled to the others and the small band rode out of the old camp, headed for the big clearing in the canyon.

She was about to be freed and returned to civilization. By this time tomorrow, she would be back in stiff corsets and many petticoats with everyone supervising her life for her. She was Miss Elizabeth Winters, soon to be sent back east and putting all that had happened in the last several weeks behind her. But one thing she would never forget— the way Cougar had held her, the way he had taught her passion. Without meaning to, she tightened her hold on his waist. In turn, his big hand reached down and gently covered her small one, patting it as if offering reassurance. He was right; it was all for the best; to think otherwise was foolish.

Silently, the little band of Apaches rode toward the meadow. She craned her neck to see around Cougar's big body. From this angle, she could see two men on horseback out in the clearing. There was Phillip, all right—Phillip and old Mac sitting their horses all alone out in that vast meadow, the red walls of the steep canyon rising about them. The late rays of the sun reflected off Phillip's brass buttons. He looked very stiff and ill at ease; so very, very civilized.

He was braver than she had realized, Libbie would have to give him that. She would not have believed Phillip would have the courage to ride out and face Apaches alone, with no one but old Mac as an interpreter. Perhaps she had underestimated him; perhaps she should reconsider. Given half a chance, he might make a good husband after all. She thought about letting him make love to her and winced, remembering the passion she had shared in Cougar's arms. Well, Phillip need never know about that.

Around them, the Apaches reined in their horses. Cougar kept riding, moving toward the pair. They reined in a few hundred feet apart. Cougar swung down off the stallion, as graceful as the big cat whose name he bore. He reached up for her. She had never seen such pain in a man's eyes.

She went into his arms, let him lift her down. He was so very strong, and she always felt so safe and protected with him. He was looking down into her eyes with those startling blue ones and she noted with alarm that there were tears in those eyes; Apache tears. "Good-bye, Miss Winters."

"Good-bye, Cougar."

Now he turned toward the pair of white men, took a deep breath, and shouted, "Did you bring the ransom?"

Phillip nodded and shouted back. "A Mr. Higginbottom sent it. Libbie, are you all right?"

She nodded, thinking. Crooked old Mr. Higginbottom, the cheater of Indians. Well, it was only right that his ill-gotten gains should be given to these hungry Apaches. She wondered if Phillip had found out yet that she was broke.

"All right," Phillip yelled, "then we'll get off our horses and make this trade in the middle."

He was so much braver than she had given him credit for, Libbie thought, with this little band of armed warriors watching this exchange.

Cougar nodded, but he said nothing. She looked over at him. One look into his eyes told her everything she needed to know. This man was dying inside, his agony at losing her apparent in his face. "Always remember I love you," he whispered.

She nodded, her throat too thick to speak. "If—if you care so much, why are you letting me go?"

"I want you to be happy," he said under his breath. Now he took her arm. "Are you ready to return to civilization, Miss Winters?"

She didn't answer, her eyes suddenly blinded by tears as she let him guide her. Phillip would think they were tears of relief, and he need never know the difference. "Let's go."

Behind them, the little band of Apaches watched silently. Libbie and Cougar began to walk toward the pair standing alone out in the meadow, Phillip with his saddlebags thrown across his arm. It seemed a million miles across that grass with the late afternoon sun throwing long shadows. She could see Phillip closely now, his handsome face triumphant, satisfied. She felt Cougar's strong arm tremble as he held hers.

The four were only a few feet apart now. In only a couple of minutes, Cougar would be just a memory, and she would be watching him ride away into Mexico with the other Apaches, riding away from her forever.

Abruptly, she made her decision, hesitated, and stopped.

"Phillip, I think you should know I don't have any money. I'm as penniless as you are."

"What kind of joke is this?" Phillip shook his head. "You're hysterical from terror."

"I have never been more decided in my whole life. I'm penniless, do you hear me? Mr. Higginbottom probably sent the money because he hopes to marry me."

Phillip looked stricken. "But you've got all that wealth—"

"No, I don't, Phillip." Now it was her turn to shake her head. "We're two of a kind!"

"That's not true. I still want you. We've got the ransom— we'll still be rich!"

So he had never intended to give the gold to the Apaches. "You don't understand, Phillip. I—I've made my decision. I'm not returning with you. I'm going with the Apaches!"

"What?"

All three of the men looked at her, thunderstruck.

Cougar appeared confused, startled. "Think hard, dear one—don't make a choice that you'll regret later."

"Miss Winters," Mac began.

"I am no longer Elizabeth Winters." She said it with conviction now, her chin coming up. Yes, this was right, she could feel it in her heart. "I am Blaze of the Apache, and I am now and forever Cougar's woman!"

Phillip swore a murderous oath and threw the saddlebags aside. "You dirty Injun! What have you done to make her say that!"

"Nothing, Phillip, he hasn't done anything!" she protested.

However, Phillip was staring into her eyes, screaming. "He's had you! I can tell by your face! The dirty bastard has had you!"

She threw up her hands in an appealing gesture. "He didn't force me. I wanted him. I—"

"You dirty Injun! I'll kill you for this! I'll kill you!" With a maddened shriek, Phillip charged at Cougar, and they went down, meshed into a fight, tumbling over and over.

"Stop them!" Blaze screamed. "Oh, for God's sake, someone stop them!"

But there was no one to stop them. Old Mac stood by helplessly while Libbie wrung her hands. The Apaches did not move, stoically watching the two men battle.

Cougar came out on top, his rage uncontrollable as he slugged Phillip. "You rotten no-good! I've ached to do this since the first time I saw you!"

Phillip reached up abruptly and hit Cougar at the base of the nose with the heel of his hand.

Cougar gasped at the pain, temporarily helpless. Phillip pushed him away and scrambled to his feet. He grabbed up a rock and ran at Cougar.

"Cougar, look out!" Blaze screamed.

As fast as his namesake, Cougar dodged to one side. Phillip, still charging, could not stop his momentum and went down, rolled over, and came to his feet as Cougar attacked again. The two went down in a jumble of flying fists, their shadows long and grotesque in the last rays of the sun.

What could she do to help? Nothing. The two men were in a life and death battle while everyone else watched silently. They rolled over and over, each trying to gain the momentum, tumbling under the hooves of Phillip's horse, which whinnied and reared, its hooves narrowly missing the fighting pair as they struggled in the dirt beneath it.

Phillip had his hands on Cougar's throat. "I've hated you since the first minute I saw you! Now you've dishonored my fiancée and I will kill you for that!"

The saddlebags. Phillip had dropped them when he

charged Cougar. Blaze ran for them, struggled to lift them. They were full of gold, all right. She charged, swinging them at Phillip, and caught him across the shoulder, knocking him off Cougar.

With a curse, Phillip stumbled to his feet. "You slut!" He slapped her hard. Blaze stumbled backward, tasting blood from her cut lip as she fell.

Cougar's eyes turned as cold as blue ice as he came to his feet in a crouch. "For hurting my woman, I will kill you!"

Mac shouted, "No, Cougar! Remember the taboo!"

But Cougar already had his hands on Phillip's throat, throttling his breath away. Arms flaying wildly, Phillip's hands went to his uniform and pulled out a hidden knife.

"Cougar, look out!" Libbie screamed, but Cougar, as quick as a mountain cat, caught Phillip's knife hand, twisting his wrist until the officer screamed in pain and dropped the blade.

It fell with a clatter onto rocks, and now Cougar reached for the gleaming dagger, murder in his eyes as he brought it up for the death blow.

"Cougar!" Mac implored, "remember the taboo! You can't kill your own brother!"

His words seem to bring the half-breed back to reality. With a shuddering sigh as he seemed to fight for self-control, he stood up and tossed away the knife. "He's right," he said. "It's taboo to kill my own brother."

"No!" Phillip stumbled to his feet. "You're crazy! What does he mean?"

And then Libbie looked from one to the other and she could only wonder why she had never noticed it before—the same wide shoulders, strong jaw, and startling blue eyes. And in that moment, she understood what Owl Woman had hinted at. "Oh, my God, Phillip, he's right. You two look alike!"

"No!" Phillip shook his head violently, turning to old Mac. "Tell her she doesn't know what she's talking about! Tell her—!"

"It's true." Mac nodded. "Your father fell in love with an Apache girl and she was expecting his child. But he was being transferred back East."

"No!" Phillip shouted violently as if shouting could change that. "No, my father was murdered by Apaches—"

"Lieutenant," Mac said, "Bill killed himself because he could not bear to leave her, but his honor was sending him back to a loveless marriage. Your father put his own Colt in his mouth and pulled the trigger!"

"No!" Phillip shouted in denial, but even in his desperate eyes, Libbie could see he knew it was true.

"I'm sorry if I've hurt you, Phillip," she said gently and, picking up the saddlebags, started walking back toward the Apache lines.

"No, Libbie, you can't go," Phillip yelled after her. "Don't you see? This is madness! You can't give up everything the civilized world has to offer and run away with some penniless, half-breed scout. You are Miss Elizabeth Winters—you can't do this!"

She paused only once and looked back at him. "I am no longer Elizabeth Winters," she said. "I am Blaze of the Apache and I am Cougar's woman! Are you ready, my love?"

Cougar looked at her as if he could not believe her words. "I am ready."

Then he swung her up in his big arms and walked back toward the Apache with powerful strides.

Her heart was so full that she could hardly stop herself from weeping as Cougar set her on the ground, mounted, and held out his hand. She handed him the saddlebags full of gold, Ebenezer Higginbottom's crooked gains stolen from the Apaches. He tossed the saddlebags across the cantle of his saddle and reached for her. Everything in this world that meant anything was there in his eyes to read. This man would die for her. A love like that was worth whatever it took to keep it.

"I love you," she said and swung up behind him, slipping her arms around his lean waist and laying her face against his back.

"No," Phillip protested again. "No, I can't let you do this!"

Blaze looked back as old Mac shouted a warning. Phillip had run to his horse and grabbed his rifle from the scabbard. "I'll kill you!" he screamed, aiming at them. "I won't let you take her!"

It happened in a split second, Phillip aiming the rifle and Blaze throwing herself against Cougar's back, intending to take the bullet meant for him.

And in that split second, from the cliff, a woman's voice called. "Phillip! Phillip, beware of the bear!"

They all turned to look, Blaze straining against the setting sun to see who was calling. She saw the glint of sun on a pistol, and a pair of gold earrings. Shashké, Blaze thought in horror—Shashké with her torn, ruined face up there in the rocks. And in that split second, Blaze knew with a terrible certainty who had been the Apache girl's white lover.

Phillip had turned at the shout, swinging his rifle around. "Who—?"

Shashké. For a moment, he saw a flash of a scarlet cactus flower, the glint of earrings, and the reflection of the setting sun on a pistol.

"Look out!" he heard Mac shout. "She's got the major's old Colt!"

And then Phillip didn't see a girl anymore; instead, there was a shadowy apparition that slowly took form—the spirit of a bear. *Beware the bear spirit when you break an Apache taboo*. Phillip screamed once in terror and denial as the pistol fired.

Blaze gasped and put her hand over her lips to hold back her cry as Phillip crumpled to the ground. When she glanced up toward the rocks again, she saw nothing at all. Had it only been an illusion, a trick of the setting sun?

Mac ran to Phillip and took him in his arms. He looked up at Cougar and Blaze. "She's had her revenge," he said. "She took the gun from my house."

Abruptly, a line of soldiers appeared around the canyon rim, the last dying rays of the sun reflecting off their brass buttons and rifles.

With horror, Blaze looked at the many soldiers. The outnumbered Apaches had no chance to escape now. Phillip had had no honor after all.

A sergeant called from the troops on the hillside. "Mr. McGuire, I don't know what to do—"

"Let them go," Mac said. "They've done nothing wrong, and she's leaving with him of her own free will."

"That's right." Blaze reached up to touch her necklace, then put her arms around Cougar's waist and laid her face against his back.

His hand reached down and covered hers. "Blaze, my love, are you sure?"

"I'm very, very sure. Everything important to me I hold within the circle of my arms. Let's go to Mexico!"

The setting sun threw blue and purple shadows across the canyon as old Mac waved farewell. While he and the soldiers watched, the little band of Apaches turned and rode out, Cougar and Blaze in the lead. The old man blinked away tears as the little group grew smaller and smaller against the setting sun. "Good luck to ye!" Mac shouted and waved again.

The pair paused once on the rim of the horizon, silhouetted against the orange sun. *Love that's great enough can overcome any obstacle.* Mac looked after the pair of lovers, his old eyes blinded by tears. "Ah, Bill," he whispered, "I did the best I could to keep your secrets and look out for your two sons. I hope you know that."

The sun made one final burst of light, as if in answer to his words, before it slid behind the horizon. The pair in the distance waved one more time, then turned and galloped south toward the safety of the Mexican border. Mac smiled through his tears and watched until they disappeared from view. Cougar and Blaze had their freedom and each other's love. No one could ask for more!

Epilogue

Immediately after Cougar, Blaze, and the warriors galloped away toward the safety of the Sierra Madre, the soldiers, accompanied by a few Apache scouts, rode up to the rocks to arrest Shashké. However, the girl had disappeared as though she had been swallowed up by the lengthening shadows and lavender twilight. They found nothing but an old ivory-handled Colt pistol, a pair of gold earrings, and a wilted scarlet cactus bloom lying in the dust. There was no trace of a woman's moccasin tracks—only the print of a bear's paws.

The soldiers scratched their heads in puzzlement and wondered how this could be. A pistol couldn't possibly shoot such a great distance. The Apaches watched and said nothing, but they looked at each other and nodded silently and knowingly. All knew the bear spirit had returned to take its revenge on the hated lieutenant. One did not kill the bear and escape unpunished in Apache country!

One more thing: many years later, sometime around the turn of the century, whites and Indians alike began to report a young and unusual warrior leading an occasional Apache war party riding out of Mexico to bedevil outlying army posts and steal livestock from rich ranchers along the border.

They say he was a magnificent, broad-shouldered specimen, riding half-naked on a great paint stallion as he came charging down out of the Sierra Madre, leading his men to hit and harry and then disappear back across the border. However, what was most unusual about this young chieftain was that while his skin was darkly tan with Apache features, his long hair was the color of fire. The few who saw him up close and lived to tell about it swore that he had green eyes, a strong, square jaw, and that around his sinewy neck he wore an ancient silver necklace of turquoise and Apache Tears.

TO MY READERS

The tragic events at Cibecue Creek, on August 30, 1881, happened almost exactly as I told it, except that the actual officer in charge of scouts was Second Lieutenant Thomas Cruse, not the fictional Phillip Van Harrington. Lieutenant Cruse would later write a classic book called *Apache Days and After*.

As ironic as it may seem, Major General Willcox had sent Colonel Carr a telegraph message to use his own discretion and not take the Apache scouts if he questioned their loyalty. As I told you in my story, unfortunately, the wires were cut so the message never got through to Carr. If it had, no doubt the Cibecue incident need never have happened.

For those who ask if there ever actually was a half-breed Apache who rode as an army scout, the answer is yes. His real name was Mickey Free.

You might also be amazed to know that among the Apache, there is an old legend of a red-haired warrior who led the warriors sometime around the turn of the century. No one has ever given a plausible explanation of who he was or where he came from. I like to think he might have been the son of Blaze and Cougar.

At Cibecue, only one Apache scout, Sergeant Mose, fought on the cavalry's side. All the others, because of tribal loyalties or confusion, turned and fought the army. Unfortunately, eight white soldiers were killed or mortally wounded, including Captain Edmund Hentig.

Immediately after the Cibecue battle, the Apache put Fort Apache under siege, and the garrison had to send for help. The first rider didn't make it; the second, Sergeant Will C. Barnes, outrode the Apache war parties to reach Fort Thomas for help. Barnes, for his heroism, was awarded the Congressional Medal of Honor and later wrote a popular book called *Arizona Place Names*.

The Cibecue incident reignited the Apache wars that burned across the Territory for another five years until Geronimo and most of his followers were exiled to Florida in 1886.

While eleven of the sixteen Congressional Medals of Honor awarded to Native American scouts during the Indian Wars were given to Apaches, that group is better known as the only Indian scouts to ever mutiny against the army. However, after Cibecue, they served honorably for the many years of their remaining service, as did the other Indian scouts.

Dandy Jim, Skippy, and Dead Shot were hanged at Fort Grant on March 3, 1882, as I told you, while others were sent to Alcatraz. Dead Shot's wife then committed suicide, leaving two orphaned little boys. Dead Shot's sons were raised by Will Barnes, who became a rancher in the area after he left the army. Those sons became army scouts themselves, as did Dandy Jim's son. The final detachments of Indian scouts were disbanded in 1943, the remnants transferred to Fort Huachuca, and the last three sergeants were retired in 1948.

One more thing: in 1890 the Indian scouts had been given their own special insignia, "U.S.S." over crossed arrows. In 1942, when the army was looking for an image for their tough, elite combat unit, the Special Forces, someone remembered the bravery and the heritage of the Indian scouts and paid homage in an unusual way. America's best, the Special Forces, were given as their insignia the old Indian scout emblem, crossed arrows. Perhaps it is as fitting and just a tribute as the Indian scouts will ever get.

I made two trips to Arizona to walk the historic ground where this story takes place. I spent two days with my San Carlos Apache friend, Irma Kitcheyan, who owns Moccasin Track Tours in Phoenix. She took me to places few white people ever see and shared much of the authentic tribal lore that is found in this story.

Fort Grant is now inactive and used as a correctional facility. However, the Apache tribe now controls Fort Apache and is restoring it for visitors with a wonderful museum and General Crook's headquarters. Also, at Fort Huachuca which is still an active fort, there is a good museum with displays of the Apache scouts and the Tenth Cavalry, the black regiment known as the Buffalo Soldiers, who served out of that post. Both groups are also honored with large statues. Fort Huachuca is located southwest of Tombstone.

Near the town of Superior, Arizona, are found deposits of the obsidian stone known as Apache Tears. In this area, at a cliff called Apache Leap, legend says the warriors jumped to their deaths rather than surrender, and their women's tears turned into the jet-black stones.

As always, I'm providing a list of research books that you might find at your local bookstore or library for further reading: *The Red-Bluecoats,* by Fairfax Downey & J.N. Jacobsen, published by the Old Army Press; *Wolves for the Blue Soldiers,* by Thomas W. Dunlay, University of Nebraska Press; *Apache Days and After,* by Thomas Cruse, the Caxton Press; *The Conquest of Apacheria,* by Dan L. Thrapp, University of Oklahoma Press; *Once They Moved Like the Wind:*

Cochise, Geronimo, and the Apache Wars, by David Roberts, a Touchstone Book (Simon & Schuster); *Indeh: An Apache Odyssey*, by Eve Ball, University of Oklahoma Press; *The Great Escape: The Apache Outbreak of 1881*, by Charles Collins, Westernlore Press; and *Western Apache Raiding and Warfare*, from the notes of Grenville Goodwin, edited by Keith Basso, the University of Arizona Press.

I will close this story with a quote on display in the Fort Huachuca museum:

> *We were recruited from the warriors of many famous nations; we are the last of the army's Indian scouts. In a few years, we shall go to join our comrades in the Great Hunting Grounds beyond the sunset, for our need here is no more. There we shall always remain very proud of our Indian people and the United States army, for we were truly the First Americans, and you in the army are now our warriors.*
>
> *—Sinew Riley*
> *Apache Scout*
> *Fort Huachuca*

The display says Sinew Riley was Dandy Jim's son.

* * *

Apache Tears is the eighteenth novel in my ongoing Panorama of the Old West series in which I am gradually telling you many of the historic events of America's Western heritage. All my stories connect in some manner, so my regular readers should remember Cougar's friend and fellow scout, Cholla, as the hero of his own book, *Apache Caress.*

My series is written in such a way that you do not have to read the stories in order. In fact, that would be almost impossible since some are written out of sequence and many are out of print. Ask your local bookstore which ones they can still order or check Zebra's ordering service. However, those of you who have been searching for my most scarce and beloved book, *Comanche Cowboy,* will be delighted to know it was reprinted in May, 1999.

If you would like a newsletter and an autographed book-mark explaining how all the stories fit together, please send a letter-size, stamped, self-addressed envelope to: Georgina Gentry, P.O. Box 162, Edmond, OK 73083-0162. Also, if you have a computer you may read my Internet Web Page at: http://www.nettrends.com/georginagentry.

My next romance, *Warrior's Honor,* is presently scheduled for December, 2000, but remember that publishing dates are always subject to change. Check with your favorite bookstore as the date draws closer.

Wishing you much love
and few tears,
Georgina Gentry

Enter The APACHE TEARS
SWEEPSTAKES

WIN THE STUNNING NECKLACE FEATURED ON THE COVER OF APACHE TEARS. THIS UNIQUE PIECE, WITH ITS UNUSUAL DESIGN, WAS CREATED ESPECIALLY BY
GEORGINA GENTRY
FOR ONE LUCKY READER. THE NECKLACE, VALUED AT $150.00, IS MADE OF TURQUOISE, SILVER AND BLACK APACHE TEARS STONES, NATIVE TO ARIZONA.

OFFICIAL ENTRY FORM
Please enter me in the "APACHE TEARS" Sweepstakes.

Name_____

Address_____

City_____State_____Zip_____

Tel. # (optional)_____E-Mail (optional)_____

Where book was purchased_____

Mail to: "APACHE TEARS" Sweepstakes
c/o Kensington Publishing Corp.
850 Third Ave., NYC 10022-6222

Sweepstakes ends 3/31/00

OFFICIAL RULES — "APACHE" TEARS SWEEPSTAKES

1. To enter, complete the official entry form. No purchase necessary. You may enter by hand printing on a 3" x 5" piece of paper, your name, address and the words "APACHE TEARS." Mail to: "APACHE TEARS" Sweepstakes, c/o Kensington Publishing Corp., 850 Third Ave., NYC 10022-622.

2. Enter as often as you like, but each entry must be mailed separately. Mechanically reproduced entries not accepted. Entries must be received by 3/31/00.

3. Winner selected in a random drawing on or about April 30, 2000 from among all eligible entries received. Winner may be required to sign an affidavit and release which must be returned within 14 days or alternate winner will be selected. Winner permits the use of his/her name/photograph for publicity/advertising purposes without further compensation. No transfer of prizes permitted. Taxes are solely the responsibility of the prize winner. Only one prize per family or household.

4. Winner agrees that the sponsor, its affiliates and their agencies and employees shall not be liable for injury, loss or damage of any kind resulting from participation in this promotion or from the acceptance or use of the prize awarded.

5. Sweepstakes open to residents of the U.S. except employees of Kensington Publishing Corp., their affiliates, advertising and promotion agencies. Void where taxed, prohibited or restricted by law. All Federal, state and local laws and regulations apply. Odds of winning depend upon the total number of eligible entries received. All prizes will be awarded. Not responsible for lost, misdirected mail or printing errors.

6. For the name of the prize winner, send a self-addressed, stamped envelope to "APACHE TEARS" winner, c/o Kensington Publishing Corp., 850 Third Ave., NYC 10022-6222.

<u>BOOK YOUR PLACE ON OUR WEBSITE</u> <u>AND MAKE THE</u> <u>READING CONNECTION!</u>

We've created a customized website just for our very special readers, where you can get the inside scoop on everything that's going on with Zebra, Pinnacle and Kensington books.

When you come online, you'll have the exciting opportunity to:

- View covers of upcoming books
- Read sample chapters
- Learn about our future publishing schedule (listed by publication month *and author*)
- Find out when your favorite authors will be visiting a city near you
- Search for and order backlist books from our online catalog
- Check out author bios and background information
- Send e-mail to your favorite authors
- Meet the Kensington staff online
- Join us in weekly chats with authors, readers and other guests
- Get writing guidelines
- AND MUCH MORE!